Of

LIGHT

AND

FREEDOM

by

RACHEL FALLON

OF LIGHT AND FREEDOM

RACHEL FALLON

ISBN: 979-8-9894637-3-2 Digital Online)
ISBN: 979-8-9894637-3-2 (Paperback)
ISBN: 979-8-9894637-4-9 (Hardcover)

Any references to historical events, real people, or real places are used fictitiously. Names, characters, and places are products of the author's imagination.

Cover design, map illustrations, and book design by Rena Violet @violet.book.design.

Editing by Heather Creeden @creedreads.

Printed in the United States of America.
First printing edition 2025.
Rachel Fallon
Billerica, MA 01821

For all those who sought a way out of hell, but didn't know what to make of heaven.

"Take courage my heart, you have been through worse than this."
– Homer, The Odyssey

CELESTERRA
ARGYRE
SVARG
PANCHAIA
EDEN
TRIDAS
SUNRISE
SONMATHION
PIRIAWIS
KOLOR
AARU
SLIEVENAMON
DAWN
TITHONUS
EMIAN
MANU
CHRYSE
AFFARAON
NYSA
DAMACULOUS OCEAN
GWAELOD
MAGH MEALL
BALTIA
AVALON
ETHERALTA
DUN
AILINNE
DAY
CANTREF
CAERSIDI
ABUZOLEAN SEA

TRITONIAN SEA
ZERZURA
DIYU
ARGADIA
SUNSET
BIARMA
BEREZAITI
SINIAWIS
IRKALLA
MOUNTAINS
MURIAS
GJOLL
EVENFALL
ASPHODEL
DUSK
FALIAS
ALFHEIM
EVENTIDE
NEUTRAL LANDS
NAMMIANIAN OCEAN
SEGIAS
LYONESSE
RANGE
EIRNE
MAEL DUIN
CORNBENIC
TAIRNGIRE
KERIS
NIGHT

STARSHINE
MOONGLOW
SHADOWGLEAM
BARRACKS
CITY HALL
COSMIC DUST STABLES
MENAGERIE
TRAINING GROUNDS
DRAGON CLIFFS

FAIRNGIRE
CRESCENT PARK
MOONDOME THEATHER
OTHERWORLD BAR
NEBULA HALL
ALTER
DARKELM FOREST
NOVA FALLS

Contents

Trigger Warnings

- Slavery
- Torture
- Torture/Death Camps
- Physical Violence
- Explicit Sex
- Use of a drink that lowers inhibitions during a sex party
- Classism
- Arranged Marriages
- Bipolar, Anxiety, and Post-Traumatic Stress Disorder in Main Characters
- Trauma and Grief Explorations
- Past Attempted Sexual Assault
- War
- Battles

Guide

Night Kingdom:

Capital: Tairngire (Tear-en-gear-ah)
Ruled by: House Erebus
Shift Animal: Dragon
Colors: Black and Purple

Members:

King Calix Orpheus Atarah Erebus
(Kay-liks Or-fee-us Ah-tar-ah Ah-ree-bus)

Indirect:

Princess Ndrita Luna Nuit
(N-dree-ta Loo-na New-eet)

Princess Liviana Chandra Atarah Erebus
(Liv-ee-ah-na Chan-druh Ah-tar-ah Ah-ree-bus)

Deceased:

King Orion Dreki Ancalagon Erebus
(Oh-rye-on Dr-ek-ee Uhn-ka-luh-gaan Ah-ree-bus)

Queen Jemisha Adalina Atarah Erebus (Atarah is her maiden name - Cousin branch
of House Erebus)
(Jem-ee-sh-ah Add-ah-lin-ah Ah-tar-ah Ah-ree-bus)

Lady Kaida Azlin Atarah (Jemisha's sister)
(Kai-duh Az-lin Ah-tar-ah)

Inner Circle:

Baach Dion (Ba-ch Dy-on)
Delia Galath (De-luh Gal-ah-th)
Eryx Rownan (Air-iks Row-nan)
Harpina Anand (Har-pi-na Ah-Naan-d)
Ilta Ledanos (Il-ta Lay-duh-nos)
Lilith Karærin (Li-luhth Kar-er-in)
Titan (Tai-tn)

Other Cities:

City: Segais (See-gas)
Ruled by: Lord Rhidian and Lady Alora Asman
(Rid-ee-an) and (Uh-lore-uh) (As-man)

City Lyonesse (Lie-uh-ness)
Ruled by: Lord Kyler and Lady Aisling Daram
(Ky-lur) (Ash-ling) (Deer-um)

City: Mael Duin (Mall Dew-in)

Ruled by: Lady Jasira Hanwi
(Juh-seer-ah Hen-why)

City: Corbenic (Core-Ben-ic)
Ruled by: Lord Ciaran Tolze
(Kier-ren Toel-ze)

City: Eirne (Ear-en)
Ruled by: Lord Polaris and Lady Zillah Nyx
Khors
(Poe-lar-is) (Zi-luh Nyx) (Kh-oars)

City: Keris (Keh-ruhs)
Ruled by: Lord Sterling and Princess Ndrita Luna Nuit
(Stur-luhng) (N-Dree-ta Loo-na) (New-eet)

Day Kingdom:

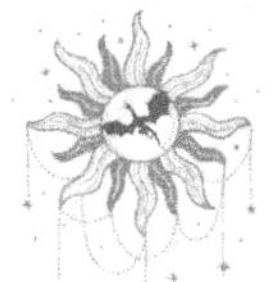

CAPITAL: AVALON (AV-AH-LON)
RULED BY: HOUSE EARENDEL
SHIFT ANIMAL: DRAGON
COLORS: GOLD AND PURPLE

MEMBERS:

King Aelius Earendel
(Ee-li-us Eh-ar-en-del)

Queen Aurelia Hemera Earendel
(Ah-real-ia Heh-mr-uh Eh-ar-en-del)

Princess Asteria Faelynn Earendel
(Uh-stair-ee-ah Fae-lynn Eh-ar-en-del)

Prince Arien Finn Earendel
(Eh-ree-uhn Fin Eh-ar-en-del)

OTHER CITIES:

City: Magh Meall (Mah Mell)
Ruled by: Lord Ayden and Lady Elvi Perendi
(Ay-den) and (El-vi) (Per-en-di)

City Cantref (Can-trev)
Ruled by: Lord Freyr and Lady Eliana Dievs
(Frey-er) and (El-ee-ah-nuh) (Dee-us)

City: Gwaelod (Guh-way-lod)
Ruled by: Lord Beltane and Lady Misae Zojz
(Bel-tayn) and (Miss-ee) (Zoe-ss)

City: Caersidi (Kai-sid-ee)
Ruled by: Lord Ergun and Lady Nia Sulis
(Er-gun) and (Nee-ah) (Sue-lis)

City: Dun Ailinne (A-lin-ae)
Ruled by: Lord Kem and Lady Mererid Latobius
(Kuh-em) and (Mare-uh-rid) (Lah-toe-be-us)
City: Baltia (Bal-tea-uh)

Ruled by: Lord Dritan and Lady Clara Owilo
(Dr-it-uhn) and (Klair-uh) (Oh-we-lo)

Dawn Kingdom:

CAPITAL: AFFARAON (AFF-FAR-ON)
RULED BY: HOUSE BATHALA
SHIFT ANIMAL: PEGASUS
COLORS: DARK GRAY AND RED

MEMBERS:

King Tariq Bathala
(Tar-ick Buh-thaa-luh)

Queen Oriana Bathala
(Or-ee-ana Buh-thaa-luh)

Princess Zerlina Bathala
(Zer-lean-uh Buh-thaa-luh)

Princess Sybella Bathala
(Sy-bell-a Buh-thaa-luh)

Prince Sulien Bathala
(Sul-lee-en Buh-thaa-luh)

Princess Danique Bathala
(Dan-eek Buh-thaa-luh)

OTHER CITIES:

City: Emain (Ee-main)
Ruled by: Lord Agim and Lady Willka Kisecaw
(Ah-gim) and (Will-kah) (Kiss-eh-caw)

City Manu (Man-ew)
Ruled by: Lord Taner and Lady Aruna Lindita
(Tan-er) and (Ah-roo-na) (Lyn-deet-ah)

City: Tithonus (Tuh-thow-nuhs)
Ruled by: Lord Eos and Lady Aurora Minenhle
(Ee-os) and (Uh-rawr-uh) (Min-in-hull)

City: Chryse (Ch-rye-sis)
Ruled by: Lord Dali and Lady Elaner Paiva
(Daa-lee) and (El-ah-ner) (Pai-va)

City: Nysa (Nye-saa)
Ruled by: Lord Kiran and Lady Zorya Rusudan
(Kir-an) and (Zor-ya) (Rusu-dan)

City: Aaru (Ah-roo)
Ruled by: Lord Vihan and Lady Tala Zoreial
(Vi-han) and (Taa-luh) (Zor-ee-uhl)

Dusk Kingdom:

CAPITAL: EVENFALL (EVE-EN-FALL)
RULED BY: HOUSE TYNAN
SHIFT ANIMAL: PEGASUS
COLORS: DARK GRAY AND DARK PINK

MEMBERS:

King Astraeus Tynan
(Uh-stray-us Ty-nan)

Queen Stelara Tynan
(Steh-lar-uh Ty-nan)

Prince Cyrus Jabez Tynan
(Sai-ruhs Jaa-buhz Ty-nan)

Prince Weylin Tynan
(Way-linn Ty-nan)

Prince Kian Tynan
(Kee-ahn Ty-nan)

Princess Daneiris Tynan
(Dan-eye-ris Ty-nan)

Princess Twyla Tynan
(Tuh-why-luh Ty-nan)

Prince Vikal Tynan
(V-ih-kuhl Ty-nan)

OTHER CITIES:

City: Asphodel (Az-fuh-del)
Ruled by: Lord Darcel and Lady Yvaine Ceirin
(Dar-cel) and (Ee-vayn) (Ker-ean)

City: Alfheim (Alf-hame)
Ruled by: Lord Aibek and Lady Siria Acheron
(Ay-beh-kh) and (Syr-ia) (A-kr-aan)

City: Gjoll (Guh-joll)
Ruled by: Lord Arrats and Lady Luna Itzal
(Auh-ratts) and (Lu-na) (I-t-zal)

City: Murias
Ruled by: Lord Oditi and Lady Asra Otieno
(Oh-dih-ti) and (Ahs-ruh) (O-ti-e-no)

City: Falias (Fah-lis)
Ruled by: Lord Visita and Lady Nisha Umbra
(Viz-ee-tah) and (Nee-sha) (Um-brah)

City: Eventide (Even-tide)
Ruled by: Lord Udaya and Lady Shirma Abital
(Uu-duh-yah) and (Sh-ir-mah) (Ah-bee-tahl)

Sunrise Kingdom:

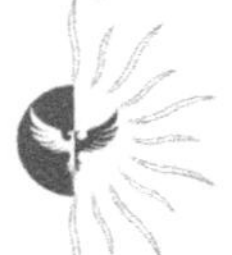

CAPITAL: PANCHAIA (PAN-CHAI-A)
RULED BY: HOUSE ARDIT
SHIFT ANIMAL: PHOENIX
COLORS: YELLOW AND TEAL

MEMBERS:

King Gravadain Ardit
(Gr-av-ah-dain Ar-dit)

Queen Idalia Ardit
(Ay-dahl-ya Ar-dit)

Prince Dagur Ardit
(D-uh-g-uu-r Ar-dit)

Princess Sunneva Ardit
(Sun-ee-vah Ar-dit)

Princess Isleen Ardit
(Is-leen Ar-dit)

Prince Altan Ardit
(Al-tn Ar-dit)

OTHER CITIES:

City: Svarga (Svar-ga)
Ruled by: Lord Baer and Lady Aditya Aferdita
(Bay-r) and (Uh-dih-tee-yuh) (Af-erd-ita)

City: Tridasa (Tri-dah-sah)
Ruled by: Lord Castor and Lady Dashinima Behrouz
(Ka-str) and (Dash-in-ee-ma) (Beh-ru-z)

City: Eden (Ee-den)
Ruled by: Lord Enver and Lady Tesni Dagfinn
(En-vaer) and (Te-z-ni) (Dag-finn)

City: Kolob (Koh-lob)
Ruled by: Lord Lairus and Lady Eadaoin Evseeva
(Lair-us) and (Aid-deen) (Ev-see-vah)

City: Piriawis (Piri-ah-wis)
Ruled by: Lord Tyr and Lady Aine Gwyndyd
(Teer) and (An-yah) (Gwinn-uth)

City: Argyre (Air-jir)
Ruled by: Lord Gunay and Lady Eostre Hina
(Gu-nye) and (Yow-str) (H-in)

Sunset Kingdom:

Capital: Biarma (Bee-arm-ah)
Ruled by: House Daanan
Shift Animal: Phoenix
Colors: Orange and Teal

Members:

King Tieran Daanan
(Teer-ehn Duh-non)

Queen Eveleen Daanan
(Eve-leen Duh-non)

Princess Dysis Daanan
(Dh-ee-s-ee-s Duh-non)

Prince Vesper Daanan
(Veh-spr Duh-non)

Prince Zakat Daanan
(Zuh-kat Duh-non)

Other Cities:

City: Arcadia (Ar-kay-dee-uh)
Ruled by: Lord Dimas and Lady Hesperia Nadirlo
(Di-mas) and (Heh-speh-ree-uh) (Nay-deer-lo)

City Diyu (D-ih-y-uu)
Ruled by: Lord Lycoris and Lady Amaya Morova
(Luh-kaw-ruhs) and (Ah-mah-yah) (Mor-oh-vah)

City: Siniawis (Sin-ee-ah-wis)
Ruled by: Lord Yureni and Lady Cyra Targaris
(Your-en-e) and (See-ra) (Tar-gare-is)

City: Zerzura (Zer-zur-uh)
Ruled by: Lord Sayanth and Lady Helia Kennez
(Say-an-th) and (He-lia) (Ken-nay)

City: Berezaiti (Ber-ah-zait)
Ruled by: Lord Lalil and Lady Fara Velairna
(Luh-lil) and (Far-ah) (Vel-air-na)

City: Irkalla (Eer-kal-la)
Ruled by: Lord Riluo and Lady Malina Cazriel
(Ril-uoh) and (Mah-lena) (Caz-re-el)

Pantheon of the Gods

EREBUS: God of Darkness; one of the two kings of the gods

EARENDEL: God of Light; one of the two kings of the gods

NOX: God of Night and the Moon; Patron God of Night Kingdom

HYPERION: God of Day and the Sun; Patron God of Day Kingdom

ASTERIA: Goddess of the Stars and Oracles; worshiped with Nox and Erebus as part of the Blessed Trinity in Night Kingdom; worshiped with Hyperion and Earendel as part of the Blessed Trinity in Day Kingdom

TALA: Goddess of Dawn; Patron Goddess of Dawn Kingdom

SHALIM: God of Dusk; Patron God of Dusk Kingdom

VAKARE: Goddess of Sunset; Patron Goddess of Sunset Kingdom

AUSRINE: Goddess of Sunrise; Patron Goddess of Sunrise Kingdom

ZIVA: Goddess of Love; Goddess of Soulmates

ANANN: God of War

FAUNUS: God of Beasts; twin brother of Florus

FLORUS: Goddess of Nature; twin sister of Faunus

HEDONE: God of Sex and Fertility

NAMMU: God of the Sea

ARAWN: God of Death and the Otherworld

OTHER PLACES:

THE OTHERWORLD: The afterlife where all beings go when they die; split into Elysium (paradise) and Tartarus (hell); there is a separate section inaccessible to Fae and humans where the gods live but is ruled by the two kings instead of Arawn, who rules over Elysium and Tartarus.

ADAMAH: The world in which Celesterra, Gemaria, Weathrian, and Chromatos are continents on.

CELESTERRA: Continent ruled by the Fae and blessed by the higher gods with celestial magic; kingdoms are balanced amongst each other.

GEMARIA: Continent ruled by the Elves and lesser gods are prayed to; magic is accessed via the use of crystals.

WEATHRIAN: Continent ruled by nature spirits who command magic related to their seasons.

CHROMATOS: Continent ruled by pixies whose magic is based on color.

Part One

CHAPTER 1

Asteria

THE world ceased to exist.

Everything around me seemed to fade away as I crumbled inside myself. My life had exploded in rather spectacular fashion. The very core of my being—the thing I should have been able to rely on above all, was hiding a secret so vast that I had no idea how I had managed to remain ignorant until now. *Only… I hadn't, had I?*

I'd known it was there all along. I just had never recognized, *couldn't have begun to guess*, what it was I was truly feeling.

I wasn't human.

I was *Fae*.

Everything was a lie.

Everything.

I couldn't begin to focus on Calix's declaration. I could *feel* the truth of it in my bones, in my *soul*, where the two of us had been connected from the moment I was born. The gods gifting each of us a soulmark to show the world we belonged together. One I knew had to be somewhere on my body now.

The horrible irony of the pain I experienced trying to stay away from him, of him trying to keep his distance from me—all to be loyal *to me…*

I couldn't deal with any of it right now.

Not when my entire being had been altered. Not when magic now sparked at my fingertips. Not when my body felt alien and strange, but somehow, more *right* than it ever had before.

That feeling I struggled with all my life, like my skin was too tight for my body, *well,* it had finally proven true, hadn't it? My Fae nature and its accompanying magic had been locked away behind a magical cage. Suppressing everything I truly was beneath it.

Ensuring I grew up human. As a slave.

How? How did this *happen?*

And why? This couldn't have happened on its own. Someone *did* this to me. Forcing me to grow up a slave, when I could have grown up free. The harsh truth of that felt like it ripped me open anew. Only now, my soul felt torn open instead of my neck.

"Asteria." Calix's whisper struck me like a bell. My very soul that was currently bleeding out onto the floor… it belonged to him too. He could surely feel the mess I'd become through the bond connecting our mated souls.

I forced my eyes up into those purple orbs I'd been dying to see since Cyrus had torn me from his side. But now… now, I was left adrift.

Lost.

Nothing made sense anymore.

"I—" Was all I could choke out. My heart was beating like the pounding of dragon wings cutting through the skies. I couldn't breathe, couldn't think.

"Asteria." I felt an arm slide across my shoulders, comforting and warm. "You need to calm down. I know this is overwhelming, but just breathe, okay? Follow me. In. Out." Eryx motioned with his hand as he breathed, and I followed his example. My breathing steadied with each inhale and exhale.

As I calmed, I closed my eyes and let my head drop. Unable to stop the sobs that were ripped out of me against my will. Calix grabbed my hand and squeezed, while Eryx kept his arm around my shoulders.

"It's going to be okay. I promise, my réalta. I know this is frightening, but we're going to be okay," Calix soothed as he caught my eyes, and I desperately tried to get my tears under control.

This was so embarrassing. I never cried. Only after Calix had freed me had I allowed myself that particular weakness. But now, I was a hiccupping mess.

"Fae feel things more intensely than humans do," Calix informed me quietly, his face lined with the agony of powerlessness. "I'm not sure what was done to you, but it may have suppressed some of that as well. It's all hitting you now, and you're struggling to control it. Fae spend many of our younger years adjusting to our emotions and learning to control them. Trust me, you wouldn't have wanted to see a young me in a rage. Don't be embarrassed. It's just us here."

His soft words were reassuring, and the knowledge that this wasn't just me overreacting settled that fear inside me. But my emotions were still like a tidal wave about to sweep me away in their current, leaving me gasping for breath as I struggled to surface.

But—wait…

"You—" I started, my words failing me for a moment. "You can feel my emotions, right?" I looked up at Calix, whose head was bowing down toward me already. He winced at my tone, which admittedly came out more accusatory than I intended. I'd already guessed it was the case, but I needed confirmation as my brain began working properly again.

For the most part, anyway.

"It's—it's part of the mate bond," he admitted, his eyes lowered. I took another deep breath. I couldn't deal with that now. I had to shut it all down. Get out of this Tartarus damned kingdom, and then sort out what in the Otherworld had happened to me, and why.

I could see the instant Calix felt me shutting my emotions away.

"Asteria…" Calix pleaded, a plaintive note in his voice. I just couldn't deal with a soulmate bond on top of trying to reconcile my own soul right now. I met the pain in his eyes with my own as I locked away the bond.

Internalizing his pain and knowing I'd carry it with me, right alongside my own.

"I need time," I whispered, pleading for his understanding.

He nodded, silvery-white hair flowing behind his shoulders as he pulled back, letting go of my hand and moving to stand. Even now, he was willing to give me the choice. He knew how important choice was to me and didn't even hesitate to give it to me.

It made me wish I could swallow my words back down and reverse the pain I'd just caused him. But that would only hurt us both in the long run.

"Of course." Calix nodded, face blanked of all the emotion that had just been swimming in his eyes. I nearly winced, seeing my dorchadas replaced with this grim king once more. His face was so locked down I couldn't get any insight into his feelings, and I'd locked the mate bond down before I got a whiff of his through it.

His posture was intimidating, his broad shoulders set back and power emanating from him like a second skin. I knew he was struggling to control his emotions, but it made him seem even more dangerous. Men with power being on edge didn't usually end well.

I couldn't blame him, though. I knew this hurt him, that *I'd* hurt him.

He'd been waiting over four hundred years for his soulmate, and it was just our luck the entire situation had gone to Tartarus.

He deserved a better soulmate than me.

Eryx squeezed my shoulders, helping me stand up when my legs were too shaky to do it myself. I grasped his arm, my first steps wobbly like a newborn rozeaffery.

"What—" I shook my head in confusion.

"Your body is different now." Like I needed the reminder, that was all I was thinking about. "You're going to need to adjust to the changes." Eryx's voice was apologetic, but he quickly let me go when he noticed Calix staring at where his hand rested on my arm.

I wanted to sigh in frustration. I couldn't deal with a jealous mate at the moment. I didn't even know enough about the bond between us to know how this would affect us now that it had been… triggered? Unsuppressed? Let loose?

I would need to find that out in addition to what happened to me.

"Can we please get out of this place?" I begged Eryx. He looked at me sadly, but he nodded, looking to Calix. Our king gave a sharp nod, and we followed him out of Cyrus's rooms.

I paused at the doorway, causing Eryx to look over at me in confusion.

"What's wrong?" He looked around, clearly worried. His posture was stiffer than I'd ever seen it. The boyish charm absent as he tried to serve as an intermediary between Calix and me after experiencing an intensely traumatizing moment.

I could recognize that even through the fog I was currently swimming in. I'd been bleeding out in his arms, and Eryx, the brother I never had, would certainly be affected by that. And Calix—I couldn't think of that now. I didn't have the strength yet to worry about other traumas on top of my own. *Not yet.*

I was still adjusting to caring about others in this way. I'd worried about myself all my life because the only other people who even remotely gave a shit were my par—*my parents.*

My parents who weren't my parents. *Couldn't be.*

I sucked in a sharp breath that felt like glass going down, cutting me apart from the inside as the realization hit me.

They were human, through and through. What did that mean? I could feel hysteria rising as I thought about them. About that last hug from my mom, my dad slipping me that iron dagger. I nearly choked on a laugh. I hadn't wanted to keep it on me. Hiding it away where I couldn't even access it when I needed it. Whatever had been done to me, it had somehow stopped iron from affecting me—a trade-off for losing my magic, maybe. But I still hadn't wanted that thing on me.

I suppose there was something to be said for instinct. I remembered flinching away from the iron door in Dusk...

"Asteria?" Eryx's voice cut through my rapidly spiraling thoughts. I startled, coming back to myself. Clearing my throat, I tried to rebuild my composure.

"Can I leave?" I finally asked, hesitantly. "Cyrus had a spell around the room, keeping me trapped inside."

"We removed it," Calix answered gruffly from a few steps away. My head swung to where he stood, currently checking the halls for any enemies that may try to prevent us from leaving. When his eyes finally found me, they drilled into me with their stare, straight down to my soul. "We were tipped off about it and how to remove it. You're free to leave."

His voice softened slightly, his throat bobbing as he swallowed and quickly looked away. I watched his hands tighten on his weapons. The urge to reach for him was strong, and I was sure it was even stronger for him after so long. But we'd both have to deal with that later.

I raised my foot, wincing as I put it through the doorway, expecting to hit the equivalent of a wall—but it sailed right through as I sighed in relief. Eryx tightened his fingers around mine, urging me from the room. I swallowed hard and let the rest of my body pass through the doorway.

My hands caught onto the frame against my will. My body shuddered. Once. Twice. I tried to control the emotions rioting through me, but tears leaked from my eyes, nonetheless. I had feared that I'd never leave that room.

I hadn't wanted to admit it to myself. Nor to Cyrus. But I truly was terrified, thinking I might die here. That even should Calix come, I wouldn't be able to leave with the spell in place. Leaving me trapped forever.

Broad hands fell upon me, one on my back, the other brushing back my hair. I squeezed my eyes closed as Calix's cheek brushed against mine, his body caging me in. But unlike that Tartarus damned room, this made me feel safe, instead of stifled.

"I know," Calix murmured reassuringly. "Just let it out."

I couldn't control the shaking of my body, and I barely heard Eryx's worried tone, the words he whispered to his king. "We need to get her out of here, Calix."

A low growl was his only answer, but Calix reached down and picked me up like I weighed nothing. I was braced against his chest, curling into it as silent sobs wracked my frame. I couldn't pay attention to anything beyond the general knowledge that Calix was hurrying us through the palace and to the secret exit we'd taken once before.

He left me to my tears, focused on our escape as he was. On *my* escape. But as we reached the gate, his silvery-white hair brushed my face as he leaned down, his fast gate making it sway back and forth. "We're leaving Dusk now. And I promise you, Asteria, you will not return here again unless it's to help burn it to the fucking ground."

A choked laugh left my throat, relief flooding through me. My eyes rose to see the gates straight ahead. A path to freedom.

Night's soldiers had Dusk's down for the count, and the gates were wide open for us to leave. I noticed there was a charred trail leading from those gates straight back to the palace. My eyes lingered on Calix for a moment, knowing he was responsible for the roasted corpses littering the ground and feeling only intense thankfulness that he'd done all he could to rescue me.

Maybe that made me a bad person. I couldn't find it in myself to give a fuck.

The guards bowed their heads as we passed, and I thought it was for Calix, until I saw their wide eyes focused on me.

"Why are they looking at me like that?" I whispered, my hearing still adjusting to the increased volume of the noises around me. Fae ears were obviously no joke.

A smirk tilted Calix's lips up, and it was the most he'd truly looked like himself since we'd left that horrible room. "They can feel the magic in you."

My head whipped over, my cheek nearly smashing into his armored chest. My eyes widened as my mouth dropped open, "They can *feel* it? What do you mean?"

Calix's eyes stopped scanning our surroundings for a moment and met mine. The shock of his intense, bright, lilac eyes nearly made me gasp. "You can surely feel the magic surrounding us, in us, now that you're able to access your powers. All Fae can sense the magic that resides in the land as well as in each of us. Like a… resonance, I suppose. You'd be able to feel my power, and it would feel greater than those around us."

But I'd always been able to feel that magic. I had thought everyone could, but was it possible that part of my true nature just couldn't be buried? I'd been so sure that all humans felt it, too. Though thinking back, Soren had always rolled his eyes at me when I mentioned the magic around us. I had never mentioned it to anyone else. There had never been anyone else to talk to.

"Your power—" I nearly jolted when Calix continued, my mind spinning too fast and leaving me distracted. "Your power is immense, Asteria. They can all feel it. That, combined with Liviana's visions…" I could feel my whole body shift as he trailed off and shrugged almost too casually. I tried to ignore the fact that he could lift me with so little effort that he could even shrug while doing so.

I was not thinking about Calix that way right now. I wasn't thinking about the Festival of Faunus. I wasn't thinking of the after-party. I wasn't thinking of the mate bond. I needed to focus on what had happened to me first. Thoughts of Calix and his… *abilities*—those needed to wait.

Watching him clench his jaw, the muscles moving as he ground his teeth back and forth, only made me think of him digging those same teeth into me that night. Before everything went completely sideways. Thinking of everything that had happened made my head hurt.

And my heart.

But I was distracted entirely by a flash of red hair ahead. I gasped, flailing upward, causing Calix to have to jerk his head back to avoid being hit in the face.

"Sorry!" I winced as I apologized frantically but still slapped his arms to get him to put me down. His slightly mulish look quickly transformed into a smile when he saw why I was acting like a crazy person.

He gently dropped me to my feet, and I barreled into Harpina like a tsunami. She fell backward, Baach having to steady us both so we didn't tip over, but all I could focus on was her loud laughter as she hugged me back.

"You weren't worried about *me*, were you?" She chuckled. I gasped a wet laugh, trying to hold back tears. Cyrus hadn't told me anything about what had happened after I was taken. Seeing that they'd all made it out okay overwhelmed me with relief.

"Of course not," I rasped, squeezing her tightly. "What a silly thing to say." We pulled back as she laughed loudly, then looked to the obviously brooding king behind me. Her eyebrows spiked up. "I thought he'd be in a better mood. Having rescued the damsel and all."

I narrowed my eyes at her, then sniffed. "I'm no damsel, first of all."

Her lips twitched, "Okay, but you did require rescuing. Twice." Her twitching lips broadened into a full smile as I shoved her over. Harpina chuckled as she regained her soldier's stance.

"Seriously though, what did you do to him?" she murmured out of the side of her mouth, like that would stop Calix from hearing.

His glare spoke volumes on the ineffectiveness of that plan. Harpina looked between the two of us before she stiffened. "Wait…"

Her eyebrows scrunched together and Baach meandered over as she looked at us like a particularly complex puzzle. He took the opportunity to drag me into him and engulf me in a hug, making me laugh as my feet left the floor. He twisted me back and forth, swinging me around like a child. But as a rumbling growl echoed behind us, Baach froze in his exuberant greeting.

He set me on my feet quickly, before his hazel eyes joined Harpina in looking between us both, searchingly. She seemed to finally land on something as she gasped dramatically, while Baach tilted his head to the side like a confused puppy.

"By the Otherworld." Harpina's words were breathed out more than spoken. "How? How is this possible?" Her eyes were wide and shining. In their depths, I could identify shock and certainly, but it was *wonder* that truly filled them.

"It appears that when Asteria was born, someone went to great lengths to hide her as a human." My head snapped over to Calix so fast I swore I heard my bones snap as well. His gaze was already on me. A complex mishmash of emotions hidden beneath the facade of an oh-so-serious king. It sort of made me want to shake him until his emotions came loose, but I knew that was a terrible idea for a number of reasons.

Completely different than the ones from just a few hours ago.

"You were always Fae?" Baach's questioning tone broke me out of my concentration on Calix.

I turned to him, my mouth somewhat trembling as I forced it into a smile. "Apparently."

He shook his head, some of his red hair coming loose from the tie he wore it in for battle. His eyes widened as his gaze shot to Calix.

"Wait, is she—?" He cut himself off, and the unspoken question hung in the air.

They'd all seen how Calix and I were drawn together. Half of them seemed to be rooting for us, while the others worried over his soulmate. The mate bond between two Fae was sacred, after all. Not to mention rare. It was considered a blessing for soulmates to even exist, let alone for them to find one another.

Calix's purple eyes burned intensely. His silvery-white hair getting mussed out of place as he ran his hand through it. He looked to Baach, who was watching him with his mouth hanging open, "Yes, Asteria is my mate."

Harpina let out a sound I could only describe as a squeak. She'd been the most insistent on Calix honoring his soulmate. Honoring *me*. The irony that she warned me away to ensure Calix was loyal *to me*... I could tell she was just as thrown by it as I was.

"A queen of stars..." Harpina mumbled, her eyes shooting to Calix, a wrinkle forming between her brows. His slight nod made her eyes widen. I knew starlight had burst out of me, but I had no idea what she meant. I was certainly no queen. Not to mention, I wasn't sure how she even knew I had starlight, since it wasn't a power I'd heard of before.

Fuck.

My emotions were a Tartarus damned disaster at the moment. I couldn't delve into this whole mess until I figured out the rest. It was too large a—a— not a problem. No. A... *thing*, to tackle.

Baach went to open his mouth, a smile already growing, when I prevented him from speaking by doing so myself.

"I need to know who did this. And why. I've spent my entire life enslaved because of this." My voice cracked, and my eyes fluttered closed for a moment. "It doesn't make any sense. Why would someone do this to me?"

"I mean," Harpina cleared her throat, "The kind of magic this would have required? Hiding you among humans? That says only one thing to me." Baach's nod backing her up made my stomach tighten with nerves.

"And what's that?" I strangled out through my dry throat. Harpina gave me a look filled with a kind of sympathetic compassion that was near enough to break me right now, and I turned my face from her to Calix, hoping to escape it, even as her next words rattled through my head.

"That you must have been in incredible danger. Anyone who would go to such lengths to hide you, well, I can't think of another reason for it." I didn't think it was possible to feel worse about this situation, but look at that! Apparently, anything was possible.

"It's likely." Calix agreed, nodding slightly. "We need to get home and check a few things, but I'm fairly sure I know where we can get you answers." He was looking at me intently enough that I was sure he saw the hope that lit up inside me, like the stars within sat up and took notice alongside me.

"You do?" I nearly cringed at how desperate I sounded, and Calix softened, his face taking on a look I'd only ever seen trained on me. One full of many emotions mixed together. A connection between us that no one could deny anymore. Not even me.

"Let's get back first. We'll have time for explanations, but we need to get out of enemy territory." I deflated a bit at having to wait for answers. Every part of me was screaming to demand he tell me now.

But I was already on the knife's edge of another breakdown. So many things swirled in my mind. My state of being, my parents, Calix, and—and what I'd heard as I lay dying. All of it struggled for prominence in my mind and threatened to send me over the edge again.

And Calix was right. I wanted to be far, far away from Dusk. There couldn't be enough distance between Cyrus and me.

But I could certainly try.

CHAPTER 2

Calix

Taking flight, I left my armies behind for the shivering woman in my arms.

My mate.

My mate.

That truth pulsed inside me. A beacon leading from my soul straight to hers.

The soul-shattering relief I felt when the bond connected was like nothing I'd ever felt before. The rush of power, emotion, connection—love. It fired through me and scorched everything in its path, replacing it all with *her*.

I'd struggled since the day I'd met her. The pull to her was so strong that staying away felt like the worst kind of torture. It all made complete sense now, but how could I have known she was my mate?

All mates could recognize one another on site, and despite being drawn to her, I didn't, *couldn't,* recognize that bond. She'd been human, and everyone knew a human and a Fae couldn't be soulmates.

I never could have imagined that she was actually Fae. That our bond had been buried beneath layers of magic like I'd never seen before. How was it even possible? I'd never heard of a spell to make a Fae appear wholly human. Rounding their ears, burying their magic, and dulling their shine.

Asteria wanted answers, but so did I, in truth. I'd spent the time since she'd come to my kingdom fighting the pull to her, all to be loyal to my mate. Thinking they were out there, also looking for me. Some Fae girl, possibly

13

far to the North, who couldn't make their way to my kingdom, not with me shutting the borders.

Asteria, however… she'd been an obsession I couldn't quit. After the Festival of Faunus, I couldn't imagine going back to a life without her.

Why would I ever want to stay in the darkness when she brought me such light?

I hadn't been able to decide what to do. Stay loyal to my mate, not knowing when I might meet them—possibly years after a human's lifespan, or give into the draw I felt to Asteria.

But then she was taken. And a black hole opened up inside of me. Sucking everything good into a void of nothingness. Without her, none of it was worth it. She had thoroughly consumed me, inside and out.

I'd recognized then that there was no going back for me. She may not have been my mate, but I couldn't imagine a connection more profound than the one between us.

I'd made my choice.

Only to realize there was no choice to be made.

Somehow, Asteria was Fae. Miraculously, she was my mate. I'd felt her starlight shine down on me, bathing me in the light she had always radiated. Nothing had ever felt more right, more true.

At least until she blocked me out. I knew she was overwhelmed, and I couldn't imagine what she was going through. Not when she wouldn't let me feel it with her.

And oh, did I want to feel her. I wanted every single bit of her—body, heart, and soul.

I was certain she hadn't yet realized how deeply the need ran in me to consume her fully. I'd told her before that I was not a good man, that I was a *dragon*. And dragons guarded our hoards jealously.

My kingdom. My people. My *mate*.

The trail of scorched bodies paving the way through Evenfall attested to that.

My wings flapped through the air as I held Asteria tightly to my chest. Her shaking didn't stop, but it did slow the longer we flew on. I had the presence of mind to try to calm her despite the tumultuous thoughts swirling through my mind.

"Look to the stars. Let them comfort you," I whispered, knowing her connection to them would bring her more comfort than anything else right now. I'd certainly found respite in the darkness when my own back bowed under the pressures I faced.

And the sky was certainly sprinkled with plenty of stars as we flew on. We passed over the villages and cities of my kingdom as we made our way to Tairngire. Where she would finally be safe.

I didn't know what Cyrus had done to my mate in the days he had her. Rage rose quickly at the very thought, and I had to bury it before fire erupted out of my mouth. My dragon reacted too strongly to the thought of Asteria at Cyrus's mercy. It had taken me over completely when he'd taken her.

That part of me had been all too anxious to have my mate back by my side. My soul was able to recognize her on instinct, even if the mind did not.

Thankfully, her shuddering came to a stop as her head unburied itself from my chest and hooked onto my shoulder, staring up at the stars I knew she loved to watch and lose herself in.

Her affinity for the sky made complete sense now. She was a Celestial Fae. I had my suspicions about which kingdom she came from, but her magic didn't match. It was the most curious thing. I had never seen magic like hers before. Pure starlight had erupted from her body.

But no Fae had the power of starlight. Asteria, her namesake and the goddess of stars, wasn't one of the gods with dominion over a kingdom. Not directly, anyway. Though, she did oversee both Night and Day Kingdoms, and was worshipped in both as a secondary goddess.

Something was amiss. Or, if not amiss, then something was certainly stirring. First, Liviana's visions. The gods had directed us to Asteria. They made sure Liviana knew she was of vital importance. And if what I suspected was true… then she certainly was. Only in more ways than I'd anticipated.

And she was my mate on top of all that.

I would *not* let her go. I didn't care what the future may hold. She was *mine*. We would find a way through whatever came. *Together.*

I just had to get her to open back up to me. This wall between us felt like Tartarus. Since we'd met, she'd been all I could think of. Even dealing with a looming war, the threat of chaos, and the challenge of freeing human slaves, my mind would not leave her.

I refused to let distance grow between us now. I tightened my hold on her, and whether she realized it or not, she snuggled deeper into me in response. It settled something in my chest that had rioted from the moment she blocked me off. Soothing my soul when it wanted nothing more than to connect with hers.

But her whole world had been turned on its head. A good mate should think of their mate's needs first. And she needed time and space to come to terms with this. She had spent years hating the Fae, only to find out she was one of us all along. That she'd been enslaved as a result of what was done to her… it enraged me beyond belief.

She deserved the world. And instead, someone had buried her brilliance and let her suffer under the yoke of slavery.

It could not stand. I would find out who did this to her. And most importantly, *why*.

I LANDED GENTLY, not wanting to jostle Asteria. She quickly jumped out of my arms, and before I could pull her back, a blonde hurricane barreled into her. Asteria's laugh was like music to my ears, and a smile came to my face just watching one grace hers.

Ilta and Priscilla had both launched themselves at her, and Asteria laughingly struggled to wrap her arms around them in return. I desperately wanted to keep her to myself, the mate bond driving me, but I shut down my impulse to hoard her like the treasure she is. She deserved this.

The two blondes held Asteria tightly, swaying back and forth. Eryx, Baach, Titan, and Harpina would be back with the army soon enough, and I knew they would equally want time with her. And, of course, Delia and Lilith would also demand some of Asteria's attention. I would need to readjust to sharing her with everyone else now that the bond was screaming at me.

My head tipped to the side as Ndrita slinked up to me, my eyes still focused on Asteria. Making sure she didn't somehow disappear, but giving my sister enough attention to know I was listening.

"You found her." Her relieved sigh was loud, and my eyes found hers momentarily before skirting back to Asteria.

"I did." I nodded back in confirmation. I could feel her eyes drilling into the side of my head, but I couldn't bear to tear mine off Asteria. My feet slowly followed as the girls herded her through the giant black double doors of the glittering palace.

But as Asteria walked through those doors, the silver runes that lined the edges in the ancient language of the gods, that had supposedly been inscribed into the doors when the palace was first created, began to glow. The silver glow lasted only as long as she was in their presence, and I paused, taking in the phenomenon with awe.

"Did you see that?" I questioned, looking to Ndrita as my brow furrowed. Only to find my sister's jaw slack in shock. She nodded slowly, dragging her blue eyes away from the runes along the door, and back to me. She swallowed hard.

"She's not the same. I was going to ask about that, but this…" She trailed off, looking at me. The look in her eyes was one I was familiar with. I raised a hand before the doors, letting my fingers connect to the silver runes. My fingertips trailed over them, the silver smooth and yet… strangely *warm*.

I looked at Ndrita, who still had that look in her blue eyes. The same one she gave me when she was growing up, after our parents had both died, when it was just Liviana and us.

She believed I had the answers to everything. Still looking to her big brother to set everything right in the world. I closed my eyes, my forehead hitting the doors. I breathed deeply, trying to get my spiraling thoughts under control.

My mind was going in a million directions at once.

"Calix, those runes, they've never lit up like that—" I cut Ndrita off before she could continue.

"I know, sister." My voice was weary as I lifted my head and turned to her. "She's Fae." I breathed out.

Her eyes grew wider than I'd ever seen. "What? But—" She cut herself off this time, seemingly at a loss for words.

I noticed the crowd we were beginning to draw. *Of course.* Their king returned from battle, having rescued our only hope, and now he was leaning wearily against the door. I could only imagine my guards' thoughts as they stood a few feet away, lined up and ready to move the moment I did.

"Come, sister." I sighed heavily. "I'll explain on the way." I ushered her into the palace. I'd lost sight of my mate, but I knew I would find her shortly. She was home, and that was what mattered.

She was home.

The shining walls of the rotunda greeted me upon our entrance. The elegant decor was meant to make those entering awed and yet comfortable. My mother had redesigned this room for explicitly that purpose. She'd been an amazing queen, dedicated to her people and her kingdom. They'd deserved to have her for far longer than they had.

We all did.

Thinking back to the prophecy, I couldn't shake the thought of a new queen, even as I mourned the last.

Ndrita followed alongside me as I walked down the carpeted halls. Passing tapestries and portraits of our ancestors and ignoring them all. My destination was the only thing I cared for as I explained to my sister what had happened in Dusk.

Her hand landed heavily on my arm when I finished, stopping me in my tracks. I looked down at her hand, then back up to her face. I so often saw the young girl I was left to help raise in the absence of our parents when I looked at her. It hadn't been fair. Not for any of us. A new babe and a little girl, all to be raised by a young brother, newly made king. I'd had no idea what I was doing and had been buried under all the responsibility heaped upon me after our parents' deaths. I'd done my best, but I knew they deserved better.

I still struggled to see the woman Ndrita had become sometimes. Seeing only the tears that tracked down her face as she asked when Father would be home, and knowing he would never be returning. Sometimes, I hated him for putting that look on her face.

Other times, I loved him for the legacy he left me, for the father he'd been to me while it lasted. My mother's death had hit us all hard, but none so hard as him. I'd been forced to watch him fade away slowly in the aftermath.

Chasing death like it owed him a debt.

Maybe in his mind, it had.

Having now felt the mate bond myself, I understood in an entirely new way. I breathed out, letting some of that old resentment go with it, and sent my apologies to my father in the Otherworld for ever holding it at all.

He'd done the best he could. Just as I had. Just as I would.

But I refused to lose my mate the way he lost his. A growl rose in my throat at the very thought.

"Brother, you must give her time," Ndrita pleaded, pulling on my arm as her eyes met mine. The guards around us shifted uneasily, their armor thankfully silent as night, per my specification. But I could see them out of the corner of my eye. Thankfully, their loyalty was assured. I knew they would never speak a word they heard.

Regardless, this was not the place for this conversation.

"Ndrita—"

"No!" she snapped, and my eyes widened at her response. "Do you understand what has happened to her? Her entire life has unraveled before her eyes. Her parents? They can't be her real parents. Not if she's Fae. The very Fae who *enslaved* her, and now, she's one of them. I can't imagine what she's going through. On top of that, the power coursing through her…"

I growled, frustration rising rapidly, "That is why I need to see her. That power will—"

"Do nothing over the next day. Give her that, at least. I know you want an excuse to go to your mate, Calix. Truly, I understand." Her eyes widened, urgency underlining her tone. "But if you force her to talk before she's ready, you'll have more of a battle ahead of you than needed." She sighed, blue eyes looking up at me and beseeching me to listen. "Just, give her time. Let her emotions calm a bit."

"I should be there for her," I whispered, defeat lacing my words. Fae hearing allowed Ndrita to pick up the words with no issue, which was another thing Asteria would need to adjust to. All her senses would have amplified, her very body altering. I sighed, my head dropping as I gave in.

I hated it, but Ndrita was right. Asteria needed time and space to come to terms with what had happened. She had requested it even. I needed to push down that instinct from the mate bond that was screaming at me to go to her.

Ndrita smiled in relief, hooking her arm through mine as she began to lead me to the war room. "Now, we need a debrief. Maybe, as king, you could handle such a thing, big brother?" She raised a brow teasingly, and I scowled back at her.

She giggled, pulling me along down the hall. I gave in, walking with her to the war room, where I found the lords and ladies who'd stayed behind when we left to attack Dusk Kingdom.

I considered myself a lucky king. My lords and ladies were loyal. Truly loyal, in a way that was rare among courtiers. But I'd established friendships with all of them, and they went farther than most would expect. I'd worked hard to extend what my parents had started, making our kingdom the very best it could be. Loyal and respectful. Prosperous and magical. My people wanted for nothing. Their urges for violence were curbed with our attacks. We had plenty of money and trade to go around. There was nothing we lacked.

And yet still… the prophecy the Oracle gave at my birth had been in everyone's minds for years. Until Liviana's visions of Asteria, at least, which shifted everyone's focus. I'd been relieved of the break from it, in truth. The waiting and anticipation everyone held for a queen. One who was foretold to stand with me, who'd see the entirety of Celesterra changed forever, to our benefit.

A queen of stars to light up the night.

I nearly snorted at the thought now. I supposed the Oracle had that right. If I could ever convince Asteria...

CHAPTER 3

"ASTERIA." Priscilla's eyes cut to me once again as we walked back to my rooms. She and Ilta had been sneaking looks at me on and off the entire way, and now, finally nearing my door, one of them was finally daring to speak for the first time since the moment they had caught sight of my ears.

I snorted, unable to help myself.

"I look a bit different, I know." A hysterical laugh crept up my throat, a mad giggle escaping my lips before I swallowed it back down. I didn't miss the worried glance they shared over my head. "Is Eris here, by the way?" I asked, looking between them. The silence that met my question had me turning to Priscilla. "Pris?" "She…" Priscilla trailed off for a moment, sighing deeply. "She needed some time alone to think about everything that happened. Once she learned what Emmie had done, she kind of lost it. Harpina helped find her a place in the resistance where she could work out some of her aggression."

I couldn't say I blamed her, but I mourned her presence. Maybe she would have understood the fundamental shift I faced; one little moment changing everything you thought you knew. Ilta and Priscilla ushered me into the room and took up sentinel positions on either side of me on the sofa. I looked around my star-themed room with a new appreciation. I'd always loved the stars, and this room had immediately spoken to me.

Now, I finally knew why.

"Asteria, what in the Otherworld happened?" Priscilla whispered, a fierceness in her eyes she often banked. I knew she had it within her to have survived Dusk as she had, but to see it in her eyes on my behalf left me a bit choked up.

After all we'd experienced together, a tight bond had grown between Priscilla and me. To see her worried about me now, even with the new points of my ears, soothed a fear I didn't even realize I'd had. That she might reject me now that I was Fae.

Silly, maybe, as she'd grown close with the Fae here in Night just as I had. She'd been taken into the little family we'd joined here and accepted them in turn, but fear didn't understand logic.

I tried to open my mouth and tell her everything, but the words caught in my throat. I tried once more, before pressing my lips together, frustrated tears rising in my eyes. Arms came around me from both sides, the two blondes holding me through the storm as I let all the pain out.

The fear I'd felt being back in Cyrus's clutches. The worry over the unknown fates of those I loved. Fear of the unknown, now that I was something else entirely. Resentment for all I'd suffered needlessly. And the suffocating feeling of loss for a humanity that was never mine to begin with was a grief I couldn't shake. So many feelings that had nowhere to go except spilling out of my eyes in tears and ripping from my throat in horrid gasps.

That grief was the most overwhelming. The loss of who I thought I was. The person I'd built myself to be was so largely based on my being human that I had no idea who I was now. Even my parents weren't real, had never been truly mine at all. How did I move on from such a crushing blow to my very *self*?

Grief was a wretched beast. It had me within its jaws, gnawing on my bones and spilling my blood as it tore into my marrow.

When I finally cried myself out, I lifted my head and met Priscilla's warm brown eyes, then shifted to meet the sweet blue of Ilta's. Both worried, but here for me, no matter what. Human, Fae, it didn't matter. And I soaked in that acceptance greedily. It was a ballast in a storm after the pain of Emmie's betrayal.

"I'm sure Calix told you what happened in Sunset?" I asked quietly, and both nodded in confirmation.

"He only came back here because Titan forced him to. They had to come up with a good plan to get into Dusk and ensure they could get you out. Kian came through, thankfully, and I demanded Calix bring you back to us." Priscilla sniffed, and I gave her an amused smile, wishing I had seen that. Ilta managed a quiet giggle beside me.

"When he got there, Cyrus wasn't willing to let me go without a fight. He—" I gulped, and soft hands landed on my back, rubbing as I tried to summon the words. "He didn't want anyone else to have me if he couldn't, so he took measures to ensure it. He slit my throat."

The gasps that reached my ears were expected, but I'd closed my eyes against the words, remembering the feeling of my blood leaking out, my body going cold, of death welcoming me into its embrace—until the magic broke through.

"While I was bleeding out, the cage holding my magic in finally broke. I've apparently always been Fae, but had somehow been hidden as a human all my life." I admitted softly. "I have no idea how, though Calix claims to have some idea."

"Who would do that?" Ilta shook her head, confusion in every word. "*How* would someone do that?"

"I have no idea." I sank back into the sofa, the soft cushions greeting me and letting me sink into them pleasantly.

We tossed ideas back and forth for the better part of an hour before tiredness overcame me, the exhaustive experience and travel home finally catching up to me now that I was safe and comfortable.

It was only through their urging that I found myself guided to my bed and not falling asleep on the sofa. They helped me change, promising to update Delia and Lilith for me, but admitted it was likely the two would just be ambushing me first thing in the morning. I let out a light laugh, nodding in agreement. No one would be able to hold them at bay long.

I fell to sleep, my worries forgotten for the moment, as Ilta sang softly and Priscilla brushed my hair back, the warm glow of friendship surrounding me in a way I'd never have expected for myself. Despite Emmie's betrayal, I couldn't help but be thankful that she'd broken down my walls a bit, nonetheless. I wouldn't have experienced this without it.

My dreams found Luna waiting for me, and I let myself breathe in the deep, dark night as I spun around her. I let my skin light up—all the worries of my waking world so far away when I was here, I could merely enjoy the starlight beneath my skin as it came forth—lighting the skies around me.

Luna, usually so quiet, let out a roar of joy. I laughed, letting her joy at my power feed my own as I danced. Until the darkness grew deeper, and I gasped as I turned toward it.

It wasn't mere darkness that greeted me tonight. Now, within my very dreams, the darkness hovered for a moment, reaching toward me, and slipped right past where the barrier usually kept us apart. As the fingers of darkness passed through, they slowly revealed actual flesh and blood fingers, then a hand, an arm, until finally… Calix stood before me, sheathed in shadows that writhed and danced around him like a halo.

"Asteria," he breathed, just as shocked as I was in that moment.

Of course. The darkness, it had been him all along. Somehow, the mate bond, buried and suppressed by the magic as it was, had still found a way to connect us across the ether. Our bond stronger than even the strongest of magic.

But I was by no means ready, and as he took a single step toward me, I gasped, my eyes shooting open.

I was disoriented, unsure of where I was when the stars on my ceiling looked so like those in my dreams. But a glance around my room confirmed I had somehow woken myself up.

I sighed loudly, covering my eyes with my hands as I breathed in and out, trying to calm my racing heart. Just one look at Calix had the damn thing beating out of control.

I fought my blankets and wormed my way out of my bed. I stretched out my muscles, only to find, to my great surprise, that they didn't hurt the way they usually did. I bent over, stretching to touch my toes, and found my back didn't scream in protest.

I blinked in surprise. The pain had been with me my whole life. The life that had been spent hidden in a mortal shell. Another thing whoever did this to me had to answer for.

I MADE MY way out to the training ring, determined to get an early start. My rage had taken a back seat to my grief and confusion, but it was an ever-steady hum in the background. I wanted to tear Cyrus to pieces for what he did to me. For what he was doing to everyone.

But for now, I let myself admire the sunrise cresting over the palace as I entered the yard, rarely awake enough to appreciate it first thing. I'd slept from mid-afternoon to morning, so after fourteen hours of sleep, I was awake and ready to go.

I went to the swords, only to pause as I found Lilith sharpening a blade. Her long brown hair was tied in a braid down her back, and she wore the same armor I'd donned this morning. She looked up as my shadow reached her, and a smile took over her face as she jumped up and pulled me into a hug.

I breathed out and hugged her back. There had been moments I wasn't certain I'd ever see any of them again. I'd hoped, but hope was such a new thing for me, that I often still didn't trust it.

"I couldn't believe it when they told me." Lilith pulled back and took me in, from the tips of my pointed ears to my feet.

"I still can't really believe it." I smiled wryly, and, ever empathetic, Lilith could see my desperate need for distraction.

"Come on, let's spar. You look like you could use it." She smiled softly, head tilting toward the training ring.

"Please." I nodded in relief, needing to get out of my head for a bit, only to be completely taken aback when we got going.

"There you go! Look at you!" Lilith beamed as I surged under her arm and came up behind her, my sword at her throat. I blinked quickly in surprise.

"Fae speed, I guess. I'd forgotten." I chuckled at myself. This huge change that rocked my life had occurred, and I hadn't even considered the abilities I would now have beyond my magic.

Lilith smiled softly, "You need to focus on the positives. Your speed, your strength, those are only a couple of the things you now have."

I nodded in agreement, but couldn't force myself to verbalize it. I merely lifted my sword arm in invitation, and our blades crashed against each other once more. Parrying and blocking until Lilith managed to knock the blade out of my hand with a combination of movements so fast, I could only see them thanks to my newly improved eyesight.

Her blade was leveled at my neck, and my own sword fell from my hand as I froze in horror, unable to breathe as my blood gushed from my neck, my life draining away. I collapsed to the ground and grappled for my throat, my hands clumsy with fear and shaking from the terror of my neck splitting open once more.

"Breathe, Asteria." Lilith's worried voice sounded far away, as if I was hearing her from underwater. "You're okay. You're okay." She repeated over and over as she rubbed my back.

It took several minutes for me to gain a solid breath in and realize I wasn't bleeding out. My throat wasn't gushing my lifeblood onto the floor; it was just a memory coming back to haunt me. I'd never reacted so strongly to something so simple before. I couldn't help wondering if what had happened had completely warped my mind.

"I'm sorry, I don't know what..." I trailed off, clearing my throat in embarrassment. What a pathetic Fae I made.

"There's nothing to apologize for," Lilith swore softly. "I can't imagine how frightening that was for you. And knowing you," she gave me a knowing look, "You've been trying to bury it and move on."

I flinched. It felt like her words tore off the invisible armor I kept around my emotions to protect myself. When your emotions are erratic, sometimes burying them is the only thing that helps you make it from day to day.

"You'll have to deal with what happened, Asteria." At the frantic shake of my head, she soothed me, running her hand down my back. "It doesn't need to be now. It can be on your own time. But we all understand and know how it is, I promise you that. It may not seem it, but we all have our issues." She smiled softly, despite her next words.

"Trauma is like a ghost that haunts you, and you can't decide when it will pop up to frighten you again. But if you face down your ghost, oftentimes, you can also take control of it."

THE NEXT TWO days were taken up with the girls trying to keep me from wallowing or freaking out and, alternatively, chasing Calix away so I had time to come to terms with the changes in my life.

But staring at myself in the mirror, taking in the now pointed tips of my ears and the way my eyes now truly looked like a bright blue sky, I knew I had to get myself together. I couldn't continue trying to run from what had happened to me.

It was time to get on with my life. Too much was left to do, and I knew I needed to get back to dealing with what we all knew was coming.

War.

With what happened in Sunset and Dusk Kingdoms, we all knew that the time had come. Soon, we would need to take the fight to Cyrus. The humans of Celesterra were depending on us and the balance of the entire world was at stake. If we failed to fix it, the magic would soon fade entirely from Celesterra.

A throb kicked inside me, strange and alien almost, but I somehow recognized my magic responding. Despite the turbulence in my mind, my body decidedly wasn't a fan of losing what it had only just unlocked.

I didn't know what I was now capable of. Where on a scale from zero to Calix, my power was. But I knew, despite all the hesitations I felt about it, all the pain associated with learning the truth… that I felt more myself than I ever had before.

My body was finally settled. No longer screaming and aching, trying to fit a mold it was never meant for.

I squared my shoulders, taking a deep breath in, and resolved myself to what had to happen next.

It was time to face my mate.

I turned to get dressed, only to catch a glimpse of a shimmer on my back. Frowning, I turned my head and gasped.

There on my upper back was a sparkling black tattoo in the exact configuration of my necklace. In the exact same spot as Calix's.

My soulmark.

My eyes softened. Despite the confusion over the situation with Calix, tears rose in my eyes. Soulmates were such a rare thing, and to be blessed with one was supposed to be the most extraordinary gift a Fae could have.

I'd wanted Calix so badly, but when faced with all that truly meant when the concept of another woman disappeared from the equation, I was left feeling… unsettled.

I barely knew who *I* was right now. I didn't know what I could do or how to control what I now had. Was it really the best time to start a relationship of any sort?

On the other hand, did I even have the ability to stay away?

Did Calix want to? He'd tried to stay away from me for the sake of his soulmate. And while we both knew now that it was me, that didn't mean it hadn't hurt. And it didn't mean that the knowledge just disappeared that— that Calix wouldn't have *chosen* me.

He would have chosen someone else.

If it was so easy to walk away from me, how could I trust that I was truly the one he wanted?

I didn't want him to be with me just because I was his soulmate. If I was going to entertain the idea of a relationship, I wanted someone who would choose me no matter what.

And Calix hadn't.

CHAPTER 4

Arien

"WE'LL begin moving forces along the border." My father moved his figures along the map as his lords leaned closer around it, half of them desperate for the opportunity to please him in some way. I nearly snorted. They should have realized by now what an impossible task that was.

"Lord Ergun, with Caersidi closest to Tairngire, you'll have the hardest job. You'll need to protect the borders along the south from direct assault." King Aelius instructed with a hard look at Ergun, who nodded once in confirmation, his blue eyes clouding like a stormy sea. My father expected the lords to fall in line, never expecting anything different could possibly happen. Not when, as king, his word was law.

I was almost perversely excited to prove him wrong.

"Lord Ayden." His stony gaze shifted to the lord of Magh Meall. "You'll protect the northern border we share with Night. Everything north of the Etheralta Mountains. Thankfully, Segais is the closest city, and it's so close to Dusk that I don't expect much movement from the north, but I'd rather be prepared."

"Of course, my King." Ayden's burnished short curls barely shifted as he nodded deeply, wax keeping them in place. Ayden had always been a slimy bastard in my mind. Something only proven when my mother failed in her quest to sway him. He was too obsessed with his own self-importance to give a shit about anything else.

"What about the coasts? Should Calix's armies take a ship from Tairngire around our border defenses, we'll be sitting ducks." Lord Beltane raised an eyebrow, tilting his head to the side as he studied my father, causing his dark shoulder-length locks to fall to one side. One wouldn't guess by looking at him and my father that there was any relation between our families, but then again, one wouldn't guess my father and I were related by looking at us.

I was proud we'd taken mostly after our mother, with the dark hair more common in Dawn and Dusk Kingdoms. My father's golden skin and light blonde hair were trademarks of the kings of Day, and just another reason of many why I was a failure to him. Only my sky-blue eyes matched his, and the only reason I didn't resent that comparison was because my twin also shared them. I would cherish anything that connected us, but we'd both undoubtedly gotten our looks from our mother for the most part.

If Asteria's skin was anything like mine, she fluctuated between our mother's pale skin and our father's golden, depending on the season.

A cousin of King Tariq of Dawn Kingdom, Lord Beltane shared the dark hair and pale skin that ran in Dawn's royal line, only changed with this most recent generation thanks to Queen Oriana's influence. Yet, Beltane was also a cousin of Aelius through marriage.

Not that it made Beltane or my father agree on anything. No, there wasn't any love lost there.

My father's eyes, a replica of my own, met mine, and it was hard to miss the expectation in them. I sighed internally, counting down the days until he was gone. Only a little longer, and I would never have to deal with him again.

I loved my job; I just hated him. Being General to the rightful queen sounded much better, in my opinion.

Still, I didn't keep him waiting and stepped forward slightly, my hand resting on the pommel of my sword, securely strapped to my side. My golden armor shifted with me and creaked slightly. Bulky and impractical compared to the armor of the foe my father would have us face. I'd raised the concern time and again over the years, but he cared more for the appearance of fine, golden knights than ensuring those men made it off the battlefield.

A golden massacre waiting to happen.

Or maybe not. If what the boy claimed was true, Asteria might be enough of a deterrent to see the lives of our men, good and bad, saved from the wrath of Calix.

Fighting fire with fire wouldn't work unless my father got his ass off his throne and into the sky, but that was unlikely to happen. Not when he preferred the comfort of his palace to battle these days. He'd rather leave it to me to handle, despite not believing me capable of it.

"Calix hasn't attacked that way thus far, Lord Beltane." I nodded to him, and his dark eyes were filled with a light of amusement. He never tired of the push and pull between my father and me. "He's much more likely to move his armies over land, or fly."

"And will you meet him in the skies if he does fly?" Lord Kem asked, shoulders back and eyes as green as the grass during the first blush of Pranvera, glaring at me with contempt. A little clone of Aelius, my father tended to treat him like the prince instead of me. His golden hair surely played a part, but more so the way he kowtowed to everything my father said. Kem enjoyed lording my father's superior opinion of him over me, as if I cared.

His stupid square jaw was set as his eyes trailed up from my boots to the top of my head, the pure disrespect of his perusal of a prince only bringing a smile to Aelius's face as he clapped him on the back.

"I'm much younger than Calix. My dragon won't have near as much fire-power." I reminded him needlessly. We all knew what this was. Just another power play to try to make me feel inadequate.

I'd grown used to it over the years.

Since others believed me to be an only child and the prophecy my parents received from the Oracle clearly indicated an important heir had been in her belly, it looked to most like the gods had forsaken me upon my birth.

Of course, I was never the heir at all. That honor belonged to my twin sister, Asteria.

Even if they knew the truth, these men would think me weak for not being chosen over a female. They were fools.

It pained me that I didn't know my sister enough to say who she truly was, but I did know this: she was no weak thing. She was worthy of the honor the gods had bestowed upon her.

"Of course." My father sneered at me before turning to Lord Kem, who snickered. I rolled my eyes subtly, Lord Ergun doing the same as he shot me a commiserating look. "We will have warriors ready with ballista's for Calix if he dares to fly over the border, but I highly doubt he'd leave his armies behind."

The other lords nodded, and the meeting continued in the same vein, with my father's snide comments about my leadership and planning how to head off any attack by Night. My father didn't know it, but I was increasingly confident we had nothing to worry about regarding Night. With Asteria now aware of who she is, she wouldn't attack her own people. I had to believe that.

Why my father was so sure Calix would turn his sights on Day, however, made me wholly uneasy. Calix hadn't dared risk the balance between our kingdoms thus far. Just because things were escalating with Dusk and Night, didn't mean Calix would attack *us*.

Unless my father knew something I didn't, and considering his opinion of me, I couldn't discount it.

After being dismissed with my final orders from the king, I made my way through the shining halls. The palace was largely gold, replicating the sun itself, as well as being one of our royal colors. It was broken up with splashes of white and blue for the sky, and purple as our other royal color, which at least kept things interesting. My eyes followed the filigree that ran along the top of the walls until I passed through the golden arch leading to the north wing where my mother stayed. My father slept in the south wing. Despite being mates, both preferred to be separated.

I felt a pang of sorrow for my mother. Finding our mates is something every Fae wishes for. My mother found hers, only to end up in a battle for the throne that would surely see him dead by the end if she got her way. A horror for any mate to consider, I knew.

But it was a sacrifice she was willing to make for her child.

Even through the sorrow and loss I felt for her—even for myself a bit, for what might have been had my father not despised me for what I represented—I felt incredible pride in her.

That she would sacrifice the love she was destined for, all for the sake of her child, was commendable. It wasn't something many would do. Not when mates were the be-all, end-all when it came to love.

Her situation was sometimes a comfort to me. I may have never gotten a soulmark, but who would want one if this was what it led to?

Asteria was the other half of me as far as I was concerned. I didn't need a mate to take that spot. But even my twin had been ripped away from me, and the blame for that lay squarely on Aelius.

I nodded to the guards posted outside my mother's rooms, and they knocked, announcing my presence. I entered, not surprised to find the boy already here.

Soren had my eye, and not in a good way. He was obsessed with Asteria, even if he wouldn't admit it. It went beyond whatever they'd once had. Something impermanent and shaky at best, but Asteria's Fae allure had surely drawn the boy in without either of them realizing it. And now, he had deluded himself that putting her on the throne would bring her back to him.

Based on what Mother reported about their last interaction, about the things Soren hadn't wanted to admit but eventually did, he had no chance of getting her back. Even if Calix wasn't in the picture, a human was no fit consort for a Fae queen.

But my mother found him useful, with his dedication to Asteria assuring his loyalty. In this court, that was worth its weight in gold. The battle between my parents had torn the court down the middle, and vigilance was needed to ensure loyalties didn't sway.

"Arien, my love." My mother smiled brightly, her mood much more upbeat since the news of Asteria's transformation.

"Mother." I greeted, giving her a smile before my eyes narrowed back on Soren, who'd drifted closer to her.

"How was the council session?" she asked, her lips pursing in aggravation. She'd tried for years, unsuccessfully, to get father to let her join the council, but he was convinced women had no place in such matters.

Precisely why he couldn't know about Asteria.

I sighed, slumping into the oversized stuffed chair across from her as I ran my hand through my long, black hair, so unlike the shoulder-length golden locks my father prided himself on. Her sitting area had the two navy blue chairs we were sitting in, with a matching sofa currently left unoccupied. They were perfectly situated in the funnel of sunlight from the arched balcony doors on the far wall. The white walls kept the room feeling bright, but the gold columns lent it a stately air I knew my mother prided herself on. "Father is convinced Night will attack," I told her, still turning the situation over in my mind.

Mother frowned, leaning forward slightly. "That makes no sense, Calix has never dared upset the balance in such a way. What has brought him to such a conclusion?"

"Why don't you ask him?" I snorted, and Soren glared at me. I turned to face him, staring him down until he lowered his eyes. Yes, he'd gotten much too bold since he began working with us. I had no issue with humans, just the ones who believed they had some sort of claim on my sister.

He obviously hadn't taken finding out about Calix well.

By Hyperion, neither had I, but for much different reasons. I suppressed a shudder. Some things a brother just didn't need to know.

"Very funny." My mother's lips twisted, like she wanted to smile and frown at once. "You know Aelius wouldn't tell me anything. I'm forced to rely on others for information." She gave me a pointed look, letting me know in no uncertain terms that I was one such other, and she expected me to tell her now.

"Truthfully, I have no idea," I admitted. "But I get the feeling he's hiding something." That made her sit up straight in her chair, worry clouding her eyes. I was just as uncomfortable knowing there was something we were missing here.

"That can't be good." Mother stressed, picking up her drink from the wooden end table beside her and taking a sip of wine as she thought on the news. "We should hopefully hear back from your sister soon. I sent the letter off, so now all we must do is wait. If your father has plans of his own, we must get ours in order."

The gleam in her eyes was familiar, one I'd seen often over the years as she raised me nearly single-handedly, my father rarely wanting to bother with his failure of a son. She'd spent years turning members of the court around to her side, getting them to abandon my father, all without him knowing. Preparing for the day Asteria was ready. That gleam told me she was plotting, and once she got going, she was a force to be reckoned with.

I let a smirk lift my lips as I asked her, "Should we not wait for the future queen to help decide how to move forward? There is much we're still unaware of. And we don't know how she will react to the revelation of who she truly is."

"Exactly." My mother sat back, satisfied as if I'd just proven her point. I raised a quizzical eyebrow at her, and she smiled back at me. "She will be inexperienced in these matters, Arien. We must guide her on the correct course."

An uneasy feeling slithered through me. Based on every report we'd heard about Asteria, she was not one who would take well to Mother's manipulations. The very idea of manipulating my sister was disgusting to me, but Mother had long been playing this game, and I was unsure whether she knew any other way now.

"Mother—" I tried to protest.

"Son." She cut me off, eyeing me sternly. "Prepare a battle plan to present to her. We must be ready. Aelius is making moves we're unaware of, and Asteria is now ready to take her crown."

She stood up, draining the last of her wine. "The time is now, Arien. We no longer have the luxury of waiting."

With that, she swept out of the room, her little pet following along behind her like the train of a gown as I narrowed my eyes at them both.

Something told me that when my mother and my sister finally met, it would be no less than two opposing forces of nature colliding.

CHAPTER 5

Calix

WITH my army finally arriving back in Tairngire, I was anxious to get an update from Titan and Eryx. I'd been doing my best to give Asteria the space she'd requested, but it was taking its toll on me.

Twenty-one years since my mark came in of waiting to meet my soulmate, plus the Nox-damned agony of trying to keep away from Asteria these past months… I could hardly be held accountable for my foul mood. I'd done my fair share of waiting already, and having her so close, yet so far, was what I imagined others felt when I inflicted the pain of Tartarus on them.

But I refused to give in. I wouldn't destroy my relationship with Asteria before it even began. She needed space. Needed time.

And I needed to kill something.

Anything to get some of this—this *feeling*, out.

It was like everything I felt for her was being stuffed down and pent up, and I wanted nothing more than to let it explode.

But not now. Not yet. I had to do this right if I was going to have any hope of keeping her.

I waited for Titan, Eryx, and Harpina to arrive, and they briefed me on the fairly standard exit from Dusk after we'd left. Thankfully, Cyrus and Astraeus were caught off guard enough that no real recourse had been made.

Not yet, at least.

We all knew it *would* come. Cyrus wouldn't let this stand. His deranged obsession with *my mate*, was another factor adding to my feral mood. I grit my teeth as a growl slowly escaped at the thought. I looked up to find the three of them watching me: Eryx with wide, surprised eyes, Titan looking more resigned than anything, and Harpina biting her lip to stop her laughter.

I rolled my eyes at her, but she merely snickered in return.

"What is so funny?" I ground out, my voice a heavy rasp as the fire I rarely called in my human form rumbled at the base of my throat. The dragon within me felt restless and aggravated.

"Nothing," Harpina replied innocently, her wide eyes not fooling anyone for a moment. She sighed dramatically, giving up and admitting, "I've just never seen you like this. I've heard the stories, of course, of how mates react around one another. But seeing it is something else."

Eryx laughed joyfully. "Oh great, so we have more of this to look forward to?"

I glared at him, but as usual, he was completely unaffected. Until Titan gruffly responded, "The bond between soulmates is sacred. To be blessed in such a way—"

He cut himself off, but the other two quieted instantly. Titan refused to talk much about his own past before he came to Night Kingdom during the reign of my great-grandfather. But what we had managed to get out of him over the years was that he'd loved and lost his own mate. To Titan, the bond was something to be revered, not made fun of. The reminder brought a lick of shame over their faces, and I couldn't help feeling badly myself.

Titan had been like a second father to me all my life. Especially after my father passed and I was left to take over ruling a kingdom and raising my two young sisters. I couldn't imagine how he must feel now, watching me find my soulmate, knowing his own was gone forever.

The very thought of such a thing felt like my heart being torn from my chest. A shudder ran through me, imagining having to live with half your soul torn from you forever. And to then have it shoved in your face that someone close to you now had what you lost.

"Titan," I began, but he merely shook his head.

"We need to assume the war will soon begin in earnest." He changed the topic, and I allowed it, nodding slightly.

"Yes, I know Cyrus will do all he can to get Asteria back," I growled, eyes flashing with color as rage overcame me. "We need to begin getting everything into place. Including allies."

"What allies?" Harpina questioned incredulously, cocking her head to the side. "We cut off all the other kingdoms."

"Yes, but circumstances have changed." I turned to my spymaster. "Eryx, I need eyes on Dusk. We need to know what their next move is going to be, and when they plan to make it."

Eryx nodded, his eyes hardening. "Of course. I'll get Nithe on it."

"In the meantime, I need to verify where Asteria came from and possibly reach out." I watched Eryx's brows furrow as he realized Asteria's origins weren't a mystery to me. But I continued before he could do much more than part his lips to begin his inevitable questions. I didn't want to discuss it with anyone until after I'd told Asteria. She should be the first to know that information. It was the very *least* of what she deserved.

"We also need to figure out what to do with Sunrise and Sunset. See if there's any fallout from our mission to Sunset, and whether it's as a result of our actions or the information we left them. Can you touch base with your spies in each? I need to know their thoughts on what's happening, and if any of the royals, or even the nobility, can be brought to our side." I instructed him while simultaneously thinking through our next steps.

We wouldn't be able to win this war if Cyrus aligned himself with all of the other kingdoms. It would simply be a numbers game, and he would have far too many. So, the groundwork had to be laid now, before Cyrus shored up his alliances.

"On it. I'll have a report for you by week's end." Eryx nodded, his entire bearing firm and serious as he took his orders. I'd always envied the way he could flip between work and play so easily.

As we discussed the next steps, Baach breezed into the room, shaking out his long red hair from the ponytail he'd had it up in. "Ah, home sweet home! How's the whole mate thing going?"

Eryx groaned while I rolled my eyes, getting on with the rest of what we had to cover. The remainder of the meeting was fairly standard, checking in on the kingdom in my absence, but there was a feeling of unsettled frenetic energy that everyone seemed to feel but not address.

The war for Celesterra was always an idea on the horizon, one without a sure timetable. But now, events seemed to be moving quicker than they had in years, all starting with Asteria. And now that they realized she was my mate, that meant the prophecy would be coming to a head. Just in time to meet Cyrus's own moves.

The thought of the prophecy that had haunted my every waking moment since birth was a complicated one. But thinking of the words, it made rather a lot of sense now.

Cyrus and his plans, the threat of chaos, all of that must be the darkness sweeping across the land. Meaning that Cyrus was planning a new order for Celesterra. The thought of it sent chills down my spine. With the threat of blood magic, we'd be at a disadvantage, and he would surely not allow that advantage to lapse. He'd be killing humans at a rate never seen before.

But that's where we'd come in.

A light to brighten my darkness. *Asteria.* Blood certainly did seep, her own lifeblood draining her enough to snap the cage on her magic and allow it to heal her, unveiling my mate.

An eclipsed star lost. Her power was starlight. And if I was right about who she was, then she was indeed "lost" to those who loved her. An eclipsed star, however… an eclipsed moon meant one hidden in darkness. I suppose that was one way to view what had happened to her. Who she really was, was hidden away.

The power of two will be her crown. That one alluded me, but I was sure it would make sense eventually.

Together, we would usher in a new age. That was the line that had my people so eager for so long. The promise of a new, better world in the aftermath. But aftermath was the keyword there.

Not without a war to wage. The war was now here, after all these years of biding my time and fretting about the balance. Cyrus seemed bound and determined to throw this world into chaos and drag the rest of us down with him. Bitter and angry, obsessive and paranoid, I couldn't think of a worse ruler for the people of Dusk. Even his father, despite being a dick, wasn't as bad as his heir.

The last lines of the prophecy, a queen of stars and a king of night, are the only hope to see the world made right… they deeply concerned me. They always had. The implication of the world being made right was that, of course, it would first be *wrong.* And somehow, only Asteria and I together could fix it.

Was the world doomed to fall to chaos?

Knowing what we were up against, I knew I had to get Asteria to talk to me sooner than later. Besides the pull I felt to her as my mate, we had to be aligned to face the coming war.

It was with that thought that I was determined to get through to her. I couldn't let Asteria be at risk just because I failed to reach out to her when it was needed most.

But I knew everyone in this damn palace would try to ensure she was left in peace to adjust. Blocking me at every angle. In any other circumstance, I'd be grateful to them for it. But now, it was a serious bother.

Thankfully, no one could avoid sleep forever. And I knew without a doubt that Asteria would be there in the darkness of my dreams.

I was probably more excited than I'd ever been to sleep. The drive to see my mate was riding me particularly hard as I tossed and turned in my sheets, wishing I could just reach out a hand and find her within them as well.

One day, if I got this right, she'd be there.

Darkness greeted me as an old friend. I sighed in relief to find myself in the dream space Asteria and I somehow seemed to share.

Details I was never able to fully capture with the barrier in place between us became immediately obvious now. Asteria was floating among the darkness, shining as brightly as a star. And to my surprise, she was petting an equally luminescent dragon.

My breath caught in my throat. I knew the myth of the moon and sun dragons from the time I was old enough to remember the stories my father told me. Always about our ancestors in some way, but spun in a more fanciful way for a child. As I grew older, he began to tell me the true versions, and he'd always insisted the moon dragon was real. The child of Erebus. A many times over great-aunt, I suppose.

And there she was. Just as real as my father had wholeheartedly claimed. I blinked away the sudden moisture in my eyes. I hadn't cried over my father since I'd learned of his death, and I refused to do so now, especially in front of Asteria.

I nearly chuckled as I realized she was *petting* the moon dragon. It was just such an Asteria thing to do. And surprisingly, the dragon trilled in pleasure at her attentions. At least until she seemed to start nudging Asteria toward… me.

Our eyes locked, and the darkness around me was taken up by pure *light*.

CHAPTER 6

Asteria

DREAMS held me in their grip.

Flashes of Cyrus, Calix, Emmie, Harpina, Eryx… on and on. I couldn't escape their hold.

My breathing grew frantic as I tried to free myself, but Cyrus was always there, holding me down and keeping me captive in his arms.

Until finally, a burst of darkness rolled in, and the flashes dissipated like morning mist. Leaving me in the comforting hold of the night sky, cradling me and reassuring me that what had haunted me were mere memories, ones that fled at the first touch of shadow.

Luna's shining scales caught my eye, and I let out a deep breath of relief as she unfurled from her curled-up position, darting over to me and nudging me with her snout in worry.

"I'm okay, Luna," I reassured her breathlessly. "Merely bad memories, but thankfully, you've come to my rescue." I tried to smile brightly at her, but by her worried rumble, it clearly didn't fool her.

"Well, I will be okay, anyway." I sighed, petting down her glowing silver scales, the cool and rough texture taking my attention.

At least until I felt the darkness begin to stir.

I could physically feel the presence in my midst, like a pull on my soul that spun me around toward him without my permission, encouraged by Luna's nudging snout. A gasp slipped past my lips unconsciously.

Calix stood before me, shadows writhing from him like spilled ink. We both stood, staring at one another. Neither one of us sure if the slightest

39

movement might break the magic of the moment and see the dream dissolve before our eyes.

At least until Luna's snout nudged me abruptly forward once more, and I yelped as I tripped over air. Calix's chuckle had me glaring slightly at him before I turned my glare on Luna. She looked much too smug somehow, and merely gave a flick of her tail before she flew off and curled back into a ball. The moonlight that was emanating from her fell over us, outlining Calix's shadows even as it blended into my starlight.

"Asteria." Calix finally spoke, his voice softer than I'd ever heard it. The agony he tried to hide in his eyes was enough to have me stepping forward, wanting desperately to reach out to him. Yet still unsure how.

I was so mixed up, emotionally, mentally, physically. And my feelings for Calix were just as much of a mess as everything else in my life was. Still, that desire for him beat ever steady within my heart.

My step forward seemed to relieve him, his shoulders slumping slightly, before he stepped toward me himself. "I know everything is… *a lot*, right now. And I promise you I'm not going to make you do or say anything. I'm hoping I can just… explain a few things."

I was shocked by how uncertain he sounded. I'd never heard him sound less than certain, about anything. And I somehow found myself nodding, my voice caught in my throat.

Calix sighed, his hand raking through his long, silvery-white hair. The shadows writhed around him, pulsing like his anxiety had seeped into them. "I should start with an apology."

I raised a brow at that, waiting to hear what exactly he planned to apologize for. My own anxiety fought against my curiosity. I was dying to hear his explanation as much as I dreaded it.

"You know I've spent many years waiting for my mate, for you." Lilac eyes met mine, a shock running through me at hearing the words once more. It still didn't feel real, somehow, while simultaneously feeling like the truest thing in my life.

I nodded slightly, Calix mimicking the small movement in turn before he continued. "I promised myself I would always be loyal to my mate. From the day my soulmark came in. But when we met, I was drawn to you immediately, and it fucking hurt trying to resist the pull to you."

I scoffed, rolling my eyes. His narrowed in turn, and he stepped closer to me, causing me to back up a step. It brought me right back to our first meeting, where he backed me into the wall of the alley in Dusk while I did my best to contain my emotions and keep him at a distance. Something quivered within my chest, and I swallowed hard, trying to brace myself.

"I know I hurt you." His words brought my feet to a stop, and he stepped close enough I could feel the heat of his body radiating into mine. "I *hate* that I hurt you." The pure despair in his tone had me balling my hands up into fists so I wouldn't reach out for him. "I never wanted that to happen. I was torn between what I thought was loyalty to my mate, and to you."

It was my turn to narrow my eyes. "But we both know you chose an imaginary mate over me." He opened his mouth to argue, a mulish look on his face, but I was determined to say my piece here. The pain of every time he pulled away was too fresh to forget.

"Time and again, you ran from me. Choosing the idea of your mate over me as a person. Had your mate turned out to be someone else, you would have dropped me in a second."

"That's not true." He snarled, the colors of the Aurora overtaking his eyes, but unlike the usual dancing colors, these exploded in a chaotic eruption. I blinked rapidly, having never seen that before. His hands came down on my arms, grabbing me and pulling me into him, my body crashing into his chest.

I growled, surprising myself with the sound. But the fire of my anger sparked, and I just rolled with it. Another item to add to the many already on my *To Worry About Later* list. "Yes, it is! You didn't *choose* me. Sure, you may not mind I turned out to be your mate, but you would have chosen whoever that turned out to be! My feelings be damned." It was easiest to focus on my anger. It was familiar ground for me. I knew deep down that this wasn't really the issue. The issue was me, and the chaos my life had been upended into. I'd never felt so insecure in myself as a person as I did now. This was the only thing I could latch onto in a sea of hurt. The only emotion that I understood.

"You see this place?" His question was just as snarled as before, except this time, it was a low, almost slurred one. His fangs had lengthened, growing long and sexy and getting in the way of his tongue as he spoke.

But the completely random question in response to my emotional words threw me completely. This man sent my head spinning every which way. I could never tell where up or down was as he threw me for loop after loop.

"I've spent years trying to reach you here. Reaching and reaching, but never able to get close. Feeling your emotions, but able to do fucking *nothing* about it." He spat, but the agony in his eyes was surely mirrored in mine at the reminder. All those dreams had torn me up inside, wanting beyond anything to reach the darkness that reached back for me.

And now here he stood, here *we* stood, touching at last.

The desperation to connect wasn't gone, it still rang through me like a bell. But too many things kept me from jumping into that bond that tied us together. We were somehow closer than ever before, and yet equally as distant as we'd ever been.

"After you were taken, I was a mess. And in my dreams, I found myself here. Knowing my mate was here, but *you* were somewhere out there in the waking world, needing me. I knew I couldn't keep you at arm's length anymore. Your capture tore me open inside, and I knew without a doubt I'd never be able to walk away from you, my réalta. Bond be damned."

The passion in his voice left me breathless. A part of me was dying to hear what he had to say, and I forcibly pushed my anger aside so I wouldn't open my big mouth and ruin it. I could feel my limbs tremble, that desperate desire for him just beneath the surface the moment I let the anger fade.

His shaking hand came up to cup my cheek, eyes boring into mine. "I walked away from the dream, didn't even bother trying to reach out, because I needed to find *you*, Asteria, not anyone else. Not even the mate I thought I hadn't met yet."

I remembered that dream. Remembered him pulling away. The confusing mix of feelings I felt from him within it, and the resolve that suddenly sharpened before he disappeared from the dream. He didn't return here until after he rescued me. *After he knew it was me.* My heart kicked almost violently in my chest.

"*I chose you.* I will always choose you," Calix declared passionately, as he nearly hypnotized me with the colors dancing in his gaze. "In this life and any other. There will never be another for me. No one with the fire, the passion, the rage. No one with the beauty, kindness, and drive. There is only you. The only star in my sky. The light in my darkness."

A ragged gasp left me, and I felt the moisture of a tear running down my cheek. It was everything I had secretly hoped for in the months I spent around Calix, trying to convince myself unsuccessfully that I didn't care.

The bond I'd buried, to both deal with my own emotions and prevent his from interfering, pulsed inside me. Like searing a brand on my heart, Calix's words successfully claimed the organ for his own.

Tears slowly fell down my face, and Calix brought his other hand up, so both palms now cupped my cheeks, wiping my tears away with his thumbs. His fangs had retracted, but his eyes betrayed his anxiety about my reaction.

"I'm a mess, Calix," I whispered, my hands reaching up to squeeze his. The mess of emotions inside me squeezing my heart and soul in their grip. "I spent my life desperately clawing for control over my fate. These past months, here with you, I finally seemed to be making progress. But now, it feels like everything has crashed down in flames around me."

I sniffed, trying to tame my tears. "I have no idea what to do. Everything I knew about myself is a lie, Calix."

I nearly winced at the desperation in my tone, but forced myself to continue. "Before, I would have literally jumped you and wouldn't have stopped until we were both sweaty and sated and unable to move. But I don't know how to be with you when I don't even know who *I* am. For Nox's sake, we've spent so much time trying to avoid the chemistry between us; we still have so much to learn about each other! To see if the feelings we both instinctually feel can actually be backed up in real life. We haven't known each other long enough to just jump into a lifetime commitment. Especially an immortal lifetime!"

My words got increasingly frantic until I was near hyperventilating, grappling for any kind of understanding, any way to move forward, but I was completely adrift. Calix shushed me, bringing his forehead to mine and breathing in deeply, until I instinctively followed his example. My breathing slowly calmed, and Calix pulled back to gaze into my eyes, the Aurora within his calming to a slow mingle of colors that managed to entrance me into calming even more.

Calix breathed out, an amazed sound that had me tilting my head in confusion. "Your eyes," he murmured. "My réalta, they're like nothing I've seen before. Like the night sky full of stars, but painted against the bright sky-blue of a cloudless day. When you panicked, the stars churned like a cyclone, and when you calmed, they did, too. Now the stars are just slowly spinning."

My breath caught in surprise, "My eyes? You mean like yours with the Aurora?"

He nodded in confirmation. "Your power and—well, that's part of the explanation I need to go over with you. But for now, I want you to know I don't expect anything from you, Asteria. I know you're going through a lot right now. I can be patient. I've already waited over four hundred years. I can wait a little longer."

I couldn't help the sigh I let out, my forehead crashing into his chest. His hands gripped my biceps before one slowly made its way to my hair. He began brushing a hand through the mass of dark hair down my back, and I tried to ignore how it immediately soothed me.

"I must be the worst mate in the history of Celesterra. You've already waited four hundred years, and now I'm making you wait even longer. I'm sorry you got mated to such a mess."

A disbelieving laugh left Calix's mouth. "Asteria, not only do you owe me nothing, but *I* need to prove myself to *you*. Because we didn't know you were Fae, I've done nothing to show you I'm worth your time, let alone someone you may even want to be mated to."

I jerked my head back, eyebrows scrunched together as I opened my mouth to argue, but a large hand came up and covered my mouth. My eyebrows now flew upward as he shook his head. "Nope. Don't argue with me. You deserve much more. I plan on proving it to you, my réalta."

I searched his eyes, and I could see he was absolutely serious about this. He thought he had to somehow prove himself to me. It was ridiculous. I was the mess here, not him.

Like he could sense my argument, and who knew, maybe he could, he continued, "You may think you're a mess, but you're handling this much better than many would. And those emotions you feel so strongly? That's part of what I want to explain to you."

"What do you mean?" I asked, my head tilting toward him.

"I promised you an explanation of your powers. I'd like to do so while I can test some things, so I'm afraid we'll both need to be awake for this." He smirked as I huffed.

He leaned in close, until his lips brushed my ear, causing a shiver to run through me. I could feel his lips tilt up into a smirk, but his whisper rattled through me, "It's time to wake up, my réalta."

CHAPTER 7

Cyrus

"PERFECT." I smirked, looking out on the new operations I'd instructed be set up while I was in Day, solidifying my alliance with Aelius.

Humans were already strapped to boards, or hung with ropes from their wrists or ankles, draining them of their lifeblood. When the final blow was dealt, that blood could then be used to increase my magic and make iron weapons. Already, Kesshuu, one of the lesser nobles who agreed wholeheartedly with my plans, was hard at work turning the useless sacks of blood and meat into something useful.

Kesshuu followed me as I walked the rows of humans, inspecting his work in my absence. He'd done very well. I knew he was angling for advancement, and his work here proved he could certainly handle more responsibility.

"I'd ask you to help with setting up sites like this across Dusk." I turned to the Fae, seeing a gleam of excitement in his eyes.

"I'd be honored, my Prince." He bowed, and I allowed a smirk to creep up my lips.

"As you should be." I nodded as he lifted his head. "Now, we have much to do. I want you to begin with Falias. Vissy won't argue with me, and he has plenty of slaves. I don't want to deprive any Fae of their workers, but we must get adequate sacrifices from each city."

"Of course, my Prince." Kesshuu nodded, writing down plans as he went. "Should we also target the smaller towns? Maybe bring in humans from each to a larger city hub?"

I considered the idea. I needed as many humans as possible, but not enough that we'd be depriving ourselves of slaves to help us, or sate us. With that thought, I clarified, "Yes, but make sure you are leaving families mostly intact, so we have more slaves incoming. And leave any particularly good-looking humans alone. Or better yet, bring them here."

The noble smirked back at me. "Good idea, your Highness. We wouldn't want to lose out."

"No, we most certainly wouldn't." I smirked back before thinking of the little human I was losing out on currently. The thought of her, now Fae, only served to sour my good mood.

Asteria would be back where she belonged soon enough. I would leash her to my side if I had to. In fact, that thought was enticing enough to bring a smile back to my face. Asteria could be collared and tied to the base of my throne. Kneeling before me as I ruled all of Celesterra.

My dreams of the future had only increased. The more blood magic I used, the more I saw glimpses in my dreams. Of me, ruling the entire continent. A new order. One where the gods had no bearing on who ruled or used magic.

They were the ones at fault. I only had to resort to blood magic because they had taken our magic. My lightning had even begun to wane, only coming back with the boost from the blood magic.

I nearly snarled at the thought. The gods and their *balance*. What a fucking joke.

I would bring a new type of balance to this world.

And those who opposed me? They would join the humans in chains.

Frustrated, I made my way back to the palace, only to find Zerlina await-ing me in my chamber. I groaned, rolling my eyes before turning to face her.

"What do you want now?" I raised a brow, watching her sipping her wine slowly as she relaxed back into one of my black velvet chairs. She was beautiful, I couldn't deny that—but she wasn't Asteria. And that only drove my rage on the nights she came to my bed. Until only the ring of bruises in the shape of my fingerprints around her neck brought me any satisfaction.

"Is it true?" she asked evenly. Her eyes met mine, and the tornado whipping through them belied her calm tone.

"Is what true?" I countered, bored already with this conversation. I had more important things to do than constantly reassure the insecure princess of her place. As long as I could dangle a crown in front of her, she'd at least play along, but I wished she'd be quieter about it.

Her lips pursed in annoyance. "Is Asteria truly Fae?"

Her question brought me pause. "Where did you hear that?"

Frustration rose immediately, almost violently.

"Oh, the gossip is all over the palace, Cyrus. About how your little pet was truly Fae all along. How you couldn't keep hold of her, and Calix came to steal her away *again*." Zerlina smirked, clearly enjoying herself.

Every single piece of gossip I'd hoped to prevent had, of course, made its way around the entire palace. My hands crackled with lightning.

Before I knew it, I'd launched myself at Zerlina. She squealed as the chair toppled backward, and my hands found her throat as I kneeled over her, snarling. "You will keep your mouth shut. And if you hear anyone speaking of such things, you will do well to report them to me. If I hear Asteria's name out of anyone else's mouths, they will soon find themselves without a head to speak. Do I make myself clear?"

"Aww." She pouted dramatically. "Are we feeling a bit insecure, *my Prince?*" she purred, running her leg up mine even as I tightened my hands around her throat. "Don't worry, I'm sure those outside the palace still have no idea you couldn't even keep a single human in li—"

Her words choked off in the most satisfying way. Finally sparking the arousal her purposely tantalizing actions couldn't.

"You'd do well to remember your place here is only by my will, Zerlina. You'll want to watch that pesky mouth of yours. By the time I'm done, there will only be one king. *And* one queen." Her eyes went wide in surprise, having kept most of my plans to myself until now.

"If you want that queen to be you, I'd advise you to get in line, yourself. Do you understand, my betrothed?" I purred back at her, happy to see the fight melt out of her as she nodded submissively. The appropriate amount of fear now in her eyes.

"Good," I growled as I pushed her dress up, releasing myself from my trousers before entering her in a swift thrust. I covered her mouth as she whined, not wanting to listen to her when I could imagine darker hair and brighter sky-blue eyes when I closed mine.

"WHAT DO YOU mean they haven't answered?" I leaned forward, facing Garridan, one of my Fae spies. He'd been loyal for years, and his lack of desire for more than he had was surprisingly helpful. Unlike Kesshuu, whose want for advancement could be manipulated, Garridan instead just loved the game. Spying was his forte, and he made no apologies for it. Working for me gave him the thrill and fulfillment he needed.

It was a mutually beneficial arrangement.

Still, his comfort with me after years of working together grated lately. He was currently leaning back casually in his chair, blond hair tumbling back. His green eyes sparkled with intrigue, and I found myself wanting to punch the answers out of him.

I took a deep breath, and he let his chair fall forward with a bang.

"It's as I said. Sunrise Kingdom hasn't answered your request." His flippant smirk had me grinding my teeth.

"Have you impressed upon them the importance of a swift answer?" I ground out, knowing the lightning in my eyes gave away my short temper when Garridan raised a brow at me.

"I can certainly remind them again." He nodded his head toward me, and his inquisitive nature proved it could definitely be a negative when he pressed, "Is there a reason you can't wait?"

I leaned forward, putting my elbows on the small table between us. Meeting in the brothel meant meeting in conditions below me, but it was a necessary condition to ensure those in the palace never looked too closely at certain people.

"Is there a reason you need to know?" I asked, malice sneaking into my tone. The blood magic made my temper a bit harder to repress of late, and I found myself having to stay my hand more than usual. "Maybe you should do what I tell you and not ask stupid questions."

Garridan scoffed. "One of the reasons I'm good at my job is I know why I'm doing things. It allows me to improvise. You always said that was one of the things you liked best about me." He raised his brows, widening his eyes as if to underline his point. "Has that changed?"

"My Prince." He added pointedly after a moment, causing me to deflate a bit.

Garridan wasn't my enemy. He wasn't one of the many looking to undermine me. Or seeking to usurp me from my rightful place. I needed to remember that. I couldn't let my anger over what happened with Asteria destroy everything I'd worked for all these years.

"You're right," I sighed, my shoulders slumping. "Things have been moving swiftly lately; it's made me a bit more on edge."

Garridan nodded once, acknowledging it before moving on quickly. Another reason to appreciate him.

"I need to ensure none ally with Calix," I told him sternly. "With Day and Dawn, we currently box Night in. But if he gains allies in Sunset or Sunrise, they can box us in. It's simple geography. I must ensure nothing gets in the way of my plans, and those two kingdoms have proven…" I searched for the correct phrasing for a moment. "*Reticent* to get involved."

"Understood. I'll ensure they understand the importance of their response." Garridan promised with a nod.

The silence of both kingdoms until now was hardly reassuring. At least, if anything, they seemed more inclined to stay out of affairs to the south of them than to help any other kingdom in particular.

With Day and Dawn with me, we had a good chance against Night. Should they increase their numbers, though, we could potentially face trouble. And I refused to allow Calix to win.

There was no reality where that was an acceptable endgame.

No. *I* would win. And then, I'd see Day and Dawn's kings and heirs stricken from the board. Sunrise and Sunset would follow swiftly. Having them close only made it easier to take them out swiftly when the time came.

My father would ultimately prove the biggest issue. What to do about him was a constant question nagging in my mind.

All my life, I wanted nothing more than his approval. But I was moving past that now. My plans were bigger than he or I.

I had a destiny to fulfill now.

And no one would stand in my way of fulfilling it.

CHAPTER 8

Calix

UPON waking up, I immediately started making plans. I knew if things went as I expected, Asteria was going to have an emotional day. So I went straight to Delia and Ilta, who were having breakfast together out on one of the patios overlooking the gardens. The bright and colorful backdrop was always one of their favorites on the grounds.

I sank down into one of the white wicker chairs beside them, grabbing one of the rolls from their breadbasket and getting my hand slapped for my trouble. I stuffed it in my mouth, raising a brow at Delia, but her scowl didn't lessen.

One of the many reasons I loved my friends. They didn't care about my station and treated me the same as everyone else. Slapping me for my poor table manners included.

"I need your help," I confessed, looking to them both, and while Delia watched with knowing eyes, Ilta bounced out of her relaxed slump, her wide eyes gleaming with excitement.

"What's going on, Calix?" Ilta demanded, leaning toward me like she might shake me for answers.

I huffed a laugh. "Today is going to be emotional for Asteria. I was thinking that it might be a good idea to go out tonight. Let her blow off some steam, you know?"

Ilta clapped her hands together, "Oh, yes! That sounds like a perfect idea. I'll plan it out!"

"Why, exactly, is today going to be emotional for Asteria?" Delia raised a brow at me, leaning forward and grabbing my hand suddenly. "Please tell me you aren't going to force a confrontation, Calix?"

I shook my head, "It's not like that. I spoke with her last night." Delia cocked her head, her eyebrows furrowing, and I continued before she could ask any follow-up questions. "She agreed to meet today so I could explain some things to her. It's important we figure out her magic. And if she is who I think she is."

"What does *that* mean?" Ilta asked, mystified, and I looked between the two.

Before I could answer, I heard another voice interrupt, "Calix knows who Asteria really is. Only he isn't telling."

I glared at Eryx as he plopped down next to Delia, giving her a soft smile that she was too shocked to return.

"What do you mean?" she asked, flustered by Eryx's sudden appearance.

I sighed, tilting my head back, as Eryx continued, "I mean, he knows who her parents are."

I felt something hit my chest and tilted my head back up to find Delia had thrown a piece of bread at me. I raised a brow incredulously as she glared back at me.

"How could you keep that information a secret?" she ground out, and I blinked, surprised to see Delia angry. She was usually more even-tempered, but apparently, she let her claws loose when it came to defending her friends.

Surprisingly, Ilta smiled at me until Delia kicked her foot, and Ilta kicked back, starting a foot war between the two that had me rolling my eyes. Eryx snickered, getting the two of them to turn their attention to him. I smirked as he raised his hands in surrender at their dual glares.

"What are you smiling about?" Delia finally demanded of Ilta.

She sighed, rolling her eyes, "Think about it, Dee. He hasn't told any of us, and he's arranged to talk to Asteria about it. I've worked as Calix's secretary for years, I know how he thinks. And he very obviously thinks Asteria deserves to find out that information first." She turned to smile at me. "Which is absolutely correct, by the way."

Delia deflated a bit, her cheeks turning a rosy hue as she blushed. Eryx watched her, his eyes going a bit out of focus as she colored. I'd been fairly distracted by Asteria during the Festival of Faunus, but I distinctly remembered the two of them together that night. It had been years since the last time they'd gotten together, but I knew Eryx still watched her whenever he thought he could get away with it.

"She's right, you know." Baach dropped in from out of nowhere, landing in the chair at Ilta's other side. She gave him a charming smile that he returned. Eryx watched them enviously, looking back at Delia with moon eyes.

If at least one pairing could get their heads out of their asses, I'd consider it a miracle.

"I thought you were right behind me?" Eryx raised a brow at Baach, who nodded.

"I was. I just figured I'd see if what you were talking about was interesting enough to stick around." He winked, and Eryx rolled his eyes.

"But as I was saying, that's definitely information Asteria should hear first. Especially from her mate," Baach continued, and I nodded in agreement.

Ilta sighed happily, "It's so amazing that you two are mates. I was rooting for you both, you know."

"You were?" I couldn't help asking. Harpina and Titan had made their own feelings clear. Both thought that I had to honor my mate and stay clear of any distractions. Eryx just didn't want me to hurt Asteria. I hadn't realized any of them had actually been in favor of Asteria and me.

"Of course!" She giggled, her eyes cutting to Baach, before looking back at me. "I could see the chemistry between you right away. I knew you'd be good together. It was just a matter of *you* realizing. Dummy." She pushed my shoulder playfully, and I rolled my eyes.

"I always knew that," I admitted quietly, and the others seemed to fall silent in turn.

"Good." Ilta finally nodded decisively. "Now, how are you going to show her that?"

The others leaned in as I tilted my head in thought. Trying to think of ways to show Asteria, to prove to her as I claimed I would, that she was it for me, and that I was a worthy mate for her in turn.

A slow smile came to my face. I knew how to start, if nothing else. What she really needed now, was to come to terms with the changes in her life.

And I could certainly help with that.

WATCHING ASTERIA SHIFT from foot to foot, clearly anxious to be face to face after our shared dream, felt like someone stabbing me with my own sword. The magic blade digging deep before being twisted. I sighed, shaking my head almost imperceptibly, reminding myself I needed to go at her pace. Unleashing all of my wants on her wasn't fair.

I knew this. *I did.*

But it didn't stop my body from rebelling against me. I could feel my heart rate pick up at the sweet scent of raspberries and vanilla that always drove me to distraction, now underlined more heavily with the scent of starlight. It didn't stop my hands from twitching, wanting to reach out and pull her against me.

It certainly didn't stop my cock from twitching at just the sight of her.

I took a step closer to her, and she stilled momentarily before shaking her head and squaring her shoulders. Her head snapped up to look at me straight on. I had to smother the smile that automatically came to my face at her defiance.

Her rage was like a siren song, no matter how it manifested. And it so matched the rage I felt. That I'd long since seized control of. That I now used to fuel my darkness and my fire.

Her rage called to mine and reminded me of all the things that enraged me.

My parent's deaths. Being left to control an entire kingdom before I was ready. Having to raise my sisters alone. The pressure of the prophecy given at my birth. The people who tried to get close to me for all the wrong reasons. The precarious balance tipping toward chaos, threatening our realm and our magic. The corrupt leaders dragging the realm toward it. Humans being enslaved and tortured.

Which, thinking about it in retrospect, I now realized a few things about *why* I became so obsessed with freeing humans.

But as I looked at my soulmate, my rising rage over the things I couldn't control was instantly soothed. I had learned to funnel my rage into control and action long ago. But it seemed I had another method now. One I hoped would work similarly for her.

I looked into Asteria's eyes, blue skies stretching out far and wide as she looked at me, the stars shining in a swirling tempest. The magic in her gaze so like mine in reverse it was uncanny.

"I need to see your magic again, along with your shift animal. What I saw from you was confusing," I admitted. "It's only a matter of time before things come to a head, so it's best if we figure this out now and help you gain control of it."

I watched as her eyes narrowed, a heartbreaking uncertainty swimming in their depths.

"Confusing?" She echoed, her tone indicating how unimpressed she was at the lack of any true information. I managed to catch my lips before they turned into a smirk, but barely.

"Yes, confusing." I let myself smirk truly then, just to see her reaction.

Any reaction was better than nothing. I'd rather have any bit I could than the cold nothingness she'd been attempting to give me. "Which is why I need to see your power."

Watching her bite her lip as she stared at me, wide, innocent eyes drilling into mine as I struggled to stop myself from launching at her and taking that lip for myself.

The mate bond called to me. It desired nothing more than for me to solidify the bond between us. The mark on my back seemed to burn with it. But I forced the feeling down, knowing this had to be handled carefully.

"I'm fairly sure I know who your parents are." My words landed harder than I meant them to, if her flinch was anything to go by.

"You—you do?" The shake in her words had me softening immediately. I could see the nervous anticipation clashing with her rage and fear.

I nodded slowly, "I believe so. But I would like to prove it true before giving you information that may be incorrect. It's a theory. A solid one, maybe, but still a theory."

I walked closer until she had to tilt her neck back to look up at me, even from her elevated spot on the Dragon Cliff's incline. Taking her hands, and thanking the gods she allowed me this outside our shared dream space, I squeezed them and brought them up to cradle against my heart. "Call to your magic."

She looked at me, jaw working back and forth. Her eyes skittered back to where her hands were held against my chest.

"I don't know how," she murmured, shoulders slumping. The frustration in her tone was telling, but I knew she was capable of much more than she was giving herself credit for.

"Look inside yourself. The magic is a part of you, my réalta. You just need to bring it to the fore, and then push it outward. Your intention, your *will*, that is what we use to control our magic." I let shadows coalesce around where our fingers were entwined, and made them snake up her arms. Her breathy gasp turned my mind in another direction. Remembering how she gasped so prettily while my cock split her open.

I shook my head— it was definitely not the time for that. No matter how she shivered at the touch of my magic.

I let my shadows gently slither around her arms and up her shoulders, brushing her skin in a light tease as I brought them back down to her wrist before letting them dissipate. She looked at me in absolute wonder, and I wanted to capture that look in my mind forever. Silver stars flecked over the blue skies in her eyes, seeming to go on forever.

Infinite.

"Your turn." I nodded somewhat gruffly before I got lost in her eyes and forgot what we were supposed to be doing here.

Asteria cleared her throat, her breathing still heavy, like maybe she had been just as affected as I was. She let go of my hands, and I stepped back, giving her space to try summoning her magic.

She raised her hands and closed her eyes, calling to the magic that had always lived inside of her.

CHAPTER 9

WITH my eyes closed, I didn't have to look into the swirling Aurora taking up Calix's eyes. I couldn't take it right now.

Magic. I needed to focus on calling my magic. If Calix truly knew who my parents were, I needed that information. I wanted to shake him until the information shook out from him, but I could understand his reasoning, as much as I hated it. I wouldn't want him to tell me only for it to turn out to be wrong.

That would be even worse.

So I tried to do as he said. I tried to look inside myself and find the place I felt before when my magic erupted out of me in that great burst of light. But I couldn't find it.

I squeezed my eyes shut, trying to force myself to connect to… something. I could still feel the magic all around me. I could sense it emanating from Calix. I could perceive the night magic in the very ground itself, floating through the air on invisible currents of energy. But inside of me… nothing responded.

I let out a screech of impotent frustration as I opened my eyes. "I can't find it." I ground out.

Calix's brow rose at my tone, or possibly my screeching, but he urged me on nonetheless, "Try again."

I glared at him as I tried, again and again. But I just… couldn't. I watched Calix as his brow furrowed, and he began pacing in a circle around me. "Why don't you try shifting? See if that gets us anywhere?"

I rolled my eyes, "Yes, because that sounds so much easier."

A soft laugh hit my ears, and I whipped around to see Calix was smiling. I glared back at him. "Is this funny to you?" I demanded, my hands going to my hips. "You're adorable when you're frustrated." He smiled wider, and I tilted my head, giving him a look that certainly conveyed how unimpressed I was with his response.

He just shook his head at me. "Try to shift."

"This is ridiculous!" I threw my hands up in the air. "I can't even find the magic inside me, let alone figure out how to shift. What exactly do you expect me to do? Just magically know how?!" My rage rose inside me, fast and consuming, more intense than it had been since the magical cage I'd been kept in was unlocked. It felt familiar and comfortable, and I let myself sink into it.

"I don't know how to do this!" I practically screeched at him. But the bastard of a mate I apparently now had just kept smiling, making my rage rise higher and hotter, as he stepped forward.

"Are you sure you aren't, maybe not consciously, but perhaps *subconsciously*, avoiding connecting to your magic because you don't want to?" he asked softly, staring down at me intensely.

I rocked back on my heels, staring down those gorgeous purple eyes that I currently wanted to gouge out. I ground my teeth before I opened my mouth to spit venom back at him, "You think *I'm* doing this?! I want to know who my parents are! I want to be whole!"

I raised my hands and pushed as hard as I could against those stupidly broad shoulders.

Only, I'd forgotten my new Fae strength. He went skidding backward, catching himself before he could fall completely.

Fucking Nox.

But he just righted himself with a smirk, meeting my wide and furious eyes. "I think it's easy to live with the knowledge that being Fae was something done to you, and harder to live with the knowledge that this is what you've always been. You hated the Fae for most of your life. And now here you are, Fae yourself. You have always been Fae, Asteria. You were never human. And embracing your magic, or your animal? That means accepting that truth. That this isn't just something that happened, it's *who you are.*"

His words felt like a dash of cold water, despite the way they heated my bloodstream. The truth slapping me in the face.

He was right.

I didn't want to face what I was. What I always had been. I knew it. I'd even said it, but I hadn't truly *accepted* it.

I wasn't human. I was *never* human.

All those years I spent living as one were nothing but an illusion. Magic cast for some reason I couldn't even fathom. Only that I was probably in danger then, and likely in danger *now* with the spell broken. But I would never learn the truth if I couldn't figure out who to ask, and considering I was a baby at the time, my birth parents were the best bet for answers. And I couldn't confirm who they were without my magic.

I used to fantasize about living a better life all the time. I'd look at the stars and dream of being a noble lady or a princess. Of handsome princes and kings fighting for my hand. Of a life where I wasn't a slave. The knowledge that it could have been my life had things been different stung in ways I couldn't explain.

Especially since I hated most of those who *had* lived that life. I always thought humans were better because they lived more truly. But now... now I didn't know anything. I was so confused. So lost. Like I'd been scattered to the winds.

I closed my eyes as I fought with myself, but I opened them as my rage grew hotter, that burning in my bloodstream, fighting to be let out. I coughed, blinking as a trail of smoke escaped my lips. I looked wildly at Calix, who only smiled widely. I coughed again, and again, until...

A stream of fire exploded from my mouth, while all my bones seemed to... *shift*. Starlight exploded out around me as my body changed. As the world grew farther and farther from me. My back ached with pure release as something unfurled and lifted me from the ground.

Wings beat as I rose higher.

Wait... Wings?

Confused, I looked down to see my body.

Silver scales highlighted with purple shone under the light of the sun. I paused, looking at myself in shock, only to feel my much heavier body begin to fall.

"Flap your wings!" Calix called from below, and I instinctively listened as my new wings, finally freed, beat against the air.

Calix watched me with awe written all over his face. I let out a roar, fire blasting out of my maw.

I was… a *dragon?*

How was this possible? Only royals from Day and Night Kingdoms had dragon forms.

So many things began clicking into place. I let my body soar on autopilot as I worked it out in my own mind. Remembering…

Emmie gossiping about Day not having an heir.

The prince and queen of Day Kingdom staring at me on Placement Day.

Soren being sent by Queen Aurelia to rescue me.

Was this really happening?

I let myself land, my massive body taking up more space than I could phantom as my tail hit a tree, accidentally knocking it over. I winced and willed my body to shift back, taking in a long breath as my body actually listened.

I blinked rapidly. Trying to sort out my thoughts.

"You're so beautiful, my réalta," Calix murmured, awe and wonder still all over his face as he walked closer. "Your dragon form… it's like none I've ever seen. All our dragons here in Night have black scales, matching the inherited power of darkness. Day's are gold, matching their sunlight. But you…"

"I'm silver," I rasped out, still feeling the effects of fire blasting from my throat.

"You are." He agreed with a nod. "It's gorgeous." His hand came up and moved a bit of hair behind my ear, his finger trailing down my cheek to my jaw. "Your magic is like nothing we've ever seen before, Asteria. You wield starlight, and your dragon's scales are silver. You're the one my birth prophecy foretold of. A queen of stars…" He trailed off, and I could see too much in his eyes.

His hopes. His dreams. His… whatever he may be feeling for me. Something I refused to guess at.

"What does this mean?" I asked, swallowing hard. Ignoring that bit about the prophecy for now, though we would certainly be returning to *that* later, I focused on what needed to be dealt with at this moment. "My parents… am I…?"

I struggled to get the words out. Calix seemed to understand, taking pity on me, "I believe you to be the heir of Day Kingdom."

I was already thinking it, but… the words still hit me like a fist to the gut.

"How?" I breathed, "How is that possible? They don't wield starlight, or have silver dragons! They…" I began moving, unable to stay still. Calix's hand fell from my face where he'd been cupping it as I began to pace back and forth. "There's never been a woman heir! And how do you even know I'm the heir? I could just be a child of some Day noble, right? I mean, or maybe of the queen, but *not* the heir? The queen definitely wanted me to go to Day; it's why she sent Soren, but—"

"What?!" Calix growled, shocking me out of my rant. I paused, sensing a predator about to emerge in a way I hadn't been able to before. I looked at him, seeing what I could explain as a dragon seething. I swallowed hard, suddenly very turned on despite myself.

He stepped toward me, nostrils flaring like he could scent exactly that. Thankfully, he didn't mention it, but I nearly wished he had when he instead asked, "Soren? The boy you were with in your village? When did you see him? What does Queen Aurelia have to do with it?"

Oh… this was a mate thing, wasn't it? I looked up at him, his sharp cheekbones looked especially cutting as his lips rose in a snarl. Despite how menacing he looked, he was still the most beautiful thing I'd ever seen.

I risked lifting a hand to his cheek, tracing the defined line of his cheekbones. He nuzzled into my hand in a way that seemed more animal than Fae. "I saw him briefly."

His snarl returned once more, and I let my thumb trail over his lips, soothing him. Letting instinct guide me, letting the desire I'd been trying to suppress guide me. "He showed up at Cyrus's. He was instructed to take me back to the queen of Day. I couldn't leave, obviously, but I told him I was going back to Night the second I got free anyway."

Calix seemed to calm some, and after a moment where he digested my explanation, he asked with a rough voice, like his animal still rode him, "And he just left you there? This *boy*," he spat the word out like a curse, "who claimed to love you?"

I nearly laughed at how offended he was on my behalf. "He showed back up, but he clearly got out of there as fast as possible once you and Cyrus got into it. I don't know what he was planning, but either way, it's always been clear to me that he doesn't truly love me."

Calix froze, looking up at me, "He would be a fool not to." I stilled, taking in the meaning of his words. *Did he…?*

I shook my head; I couldn't think of that now. "He loved an ideal of me that doesn't really exist. That's not love."

"No." His eyes glowed with green and blue, wrapping around the purple and shining bright. "No, true love accepts people as they are. It sees them for every aspect that makes them who they are, and loves that person because of them. Sometimes, even despite them. Love is gritty and real; it's not an ideal to live up to."

Water filled my eyes, and I desperately tried to blink it away.

Calix watched me, concern written all over his face. When I finally managed to get my emotions under control, he sighed, "I know you're the heir, Asteria, because I saw the glow surround you when your magic broke free."

I cocked my head to the side, looking up at him. "The glow?"

He nodded in confirmation, "It surrounds any chosen heir. Usually, it happens when they are born. However, what happened to you, when your magic was released… I don't know what you'd call that except for a rebirth. It makes sense it would appear again."

I took that in, along with a deep breath, but he continued, "Unfortunately, I wasn't the only one to see it. Cyrus saw it, too."

My head whipped back up to his, and he nodded grimly. "We know he was already making moves to align with Day—"

"And there's only one kingdom missing an heir. An heir he promised to find for Aelius." I concluded, a shiver running through me.

Calix growled, the rumble vibrating through me. "He will never touch you again. Ever."

I nodded slowly. "Then I better figure all of this out quickly."

Calix calmed some, clearly agreeing. "I did promise you some explanations. You told me before about the rage you always felt. Your emotions unable to be controlled at times?"

"Yeah?" My brows rose, unsure what that had to do with anything.

He smiled slightly. "That's the dragon within you. All dragon shifters struggle with similar issues. When I was younger, I had to learn to control my rage and other emotions to prevent them from controlling me. I can help you learn to do the same."

My mouth hung open in surprise. "You're telling me all the emotional upheaval I've always dealt with has been, what? Normal?!"

Calix nodded calmly, a reassuring smile forming on his lips, "Basically, yes. For dragons, anyway. Our emotions are always up and down, swinging hard one way or another. But rage? That rage fuels our fire. I can only imagine having your dragon side forcibly repressed for so long meant it often bubbled up in other ways."

It made too much sense, thinking back to the ways it felt like my blood would heat in my veins. I groaned out loud, "And you can help with this? Getting my emotions under control?"

Hope sparked in my chest, bright and loud.

"Of course. You'll learn to harness them and let them fuel your power." Calix lifted my chin up with his finger. "Those emotions are perfectly normal to feel. *You* are perfectly normal for feeling them." I didn't want to admit the way my eyes teared up at his reassurance. "It's all about figuring out how you are letting them affect you and your life. How you can prevent them from taking over and letting them control your actions. It's all about control."

Calix slowly smirked. "And you've always wanted more control over your life, haven't you?"

CHAPTER 10

Asteria

"Lesson one: fueling your fire and redirecting your rage." Calix began, standing in front of me on the cliffside. He said it would be easiest to release my fire and fly here, and I couldn't say I wasn't looking forward to it. Just that brief shift I'd experienced was amazing, and I couldn't wait to try it again.

"Find the rage inside you. Think of things that usually enrage you." He instructed, and I thought back to Cyrus. To the rage I felt when he had me captive.

"Once you've felt that rage, I want you to shift into your dragon form. Take all that rage and spit it back out as flame," Calix continued, and I let the rage build and build inside me.

When I finally felt that spark in my blood, like it was heating inside my veins, I let my dragon form take over once more. The shift from Fae to dragon was just as surreal as the first time, even being more aware of what was happening now.

Still, I focused on Calix's instructions, and I let the rage flow out of me, fire spitting from my maw over the cliffside and out into the sky.

"Good! That's a good first step!" Calix yelled up to me.

We spent the next few hours this way, until I was a bit more confident in my shifting abilities and beginning to understand how to release my rage in a healthier way. Though, I feared I still had a long way to go. This was all stuff Calix learned as a kid, and here I was, twenty-one and unable to handle my own emotions.

Or my magic.

I'd tried several more times to summon it, but it still wasn't answering me. It left me frustrated and feeling decidedly useless, but Calix promised I'd get there.

But I wanted to get there *now*. I hated feeling like I was failing at being Fae. I may not have wanted to be Fae, but I *was*, and I didn't want to be this bad at it.

"Come on." Calix swung his arm around my shoulders, leading me back to the palace. "We've got places to be."

"Where are we going?" I asked, eyebrows furrowing.

"Out for the night." Calix smiled wickedly, with just a hint of fang, "I had Ilta plan it out for us, but I figured you could use the night to blow off some steam after this afternoon."

A part of me melted. Knowing he'd thought ahead and arranged this for me, anticipating the truth I'd learned and everything after would be difficult for me... I had to choke back tears, but I let myself fling my arms around him in a hug.

He froze for only a moment, before his gigantic arms swallowed me up and hugged me back.

"Thank you, my dorchadas," I mumbled into his chest, feeling overwhelmed by the strength of my emotions in this moment.

His breath hitched, and I realized I hadn't called him that since I'd learned the truth about our bond.

"Of course, my réalta," he murmured into my hair, some of the stiffness leaking out of his limbs as he hugged me to him.

We both stood there, suspended in this moment, until the sound of someone clearing their throat had me jumping back.

Priscilla stood there with a smile on her face, looking slyly between Calix and me. "Sorry to interrupt, but we've got to get you ready if you want to be on time to go out."

I raised a brow in disbelief. "We're on a timetable?"

Priscilla rolled her eyes, shaking her head slightly. "You know Ilta."

I couldn't help the laugh I let out, and I turned to Calix with a shrug. "I guess I'll see you soon."

Priscilla grabbed my hand to pull me with her, but Calix caught my other before she could. "Of course. I'll be looking forward to it."

The words were so innocent, but his tone sent shivers down my spine. The sultry promise within made me suddenly glad we'd talked out some of our issues.

But I had to remind myself we weren't there yet. *I* wasn't there yet. I had so much to figure out and not much time to do it. Not with a war on the horizon.

Priscilla giggled as she dragged me back to my room, "So…" She dragged the word out, waggling her eyebrows at me.

I rolled my eyes at her, pushing her shoulder playfully. "So, what?"

It was her turn to roll her eyes. "Don't you *so what* me! You two obviously talked. Are you going to make me drag information out of you kicking and screaming?"

I laughed as she put her hands on her hips, looking entirely willing to do just that.

"I'll tell you if you tell me about you and Callisto," I countered, raising a brow. Priscilla blushed, and I couldn't help but laugh as she pushed me into the door to my room.

Delia was waiting, and she also had an expectant look on her face. "How'd it go?"

"Asteria was *just* about to tell me." Priscilla teased, flipping her blonde hair over her shoulder. I noticed it had grown out a bit. It had been shoulder length when we'd first met, but it was now past her shoulders, and I realized I'd actually managed to keep a female friend for long enough to see such changes. It was novel and exciting all at once.

The two pushed me into the chair at my vanity to begin getting me ready. While Priscilla wasn't technically my lady-in-waiting as Delia was, she enjoyed helping me get ready when she could. It was a familiarity we both enjoyed.

"Well, as it turns out, I'm the lost princess and heir of Day Kingdom." I tossed out as casually as I could, just waiting to see their reactions. Keeping my smirk contained was a herculean effort.

Both paused, Delia with her hands already in my hair and Priscilla with a brush halfway to my face. Delia leaned over to see my face as Priscilla sat back against the vanity top.

"What the fuck?" Priscilla screeched, and I couldn't help the laugh that burst out.

"Yeah, that's about how I felt." I agreed, nodding.

"Wait, are you serious?" Delia asked, mouth gaping open as she rocked back on her heels.

"Unfortunately," I grunted.

"Unfortunately?" Priscilla asked incredulously, her eyebrows flying upwards. "Asteria! Don't you realize what this means?"

"You mean aside from the fact that my biological father is apparently hunting me down? That he and Cyrus are already working together, and who the fuck knows what will happen now?" I asked seriously, but she shook her head at me.

"We'll get to all that in a minute," Priscilla said sternly, grabbing my shoulders and meeting my eyes. "Asteria, you've been wanting to help all the humans. If you have power in Day Kingdom, like Calix does here in Night, the two of you will be able to make *real* changes to Celesterra."

I sighed, rubbing a hand over my eyes before Priscilla swatted my hand away with a glare for nearly messing up her work.

"It's dangerous, for sure, but Priscilla is right," Delia added hesitantly, her warm brown eyes lighting up. "You and Calix will surely be able to use this. Two rulers are better than one when it comes to making changes like this."

"But I'm not the ruler!" I argued, throwing my hands up. "I'm only the heir. King Aelius—" I paused, having just connected in my brain that the king I picked apart at Placement Day was my actual *father*. I took a deep breath. "King Aelius wants to find whoever the power of the heir went to, right? Meaning, he'll be hunting me down. And Cyrus *knows* it's me. His alliance with Day hinges on turning me over."

"But he's your father. Won't he be happy it's someone in his bloodline?" Priscilla asked hesitantly, shaking her head in confusion.

"Well," Delia began, before biting her lip. "Aelius is very old school. He was enraged when his son wasn't chosen as heir. If the reason Arien wasn't chosen was because…"

She trailed off, her eyes meeting mine in the mirror, and I picked up her thread. "Because I was."

She nodded, "Exactly. He won't be happy to see a woman chosen as heir, blood or not. I would recommend waiting to see what happens first. I'm sure the others can advise you better as to tactics and politics, but be careful, either way."

I nodded, agreeing easily. I wondered how Arien felt about being skipped over. I thought back to Placement Day, when we had met one another's eyes.

He must have known. Just as the queen did. But he was… By the Otherworld, he was my *twin* brother.

This was absolutely *wild.*

We talked ourselves in circles as they got me ready. Thankfully, the revelation of me being an actual princess had waylaid any interrogation about Calix. But as we walked down to meet everyone, I couldn't help looking myself over in any mirror we passed by.

The short silver dress had called to me from my overflowing wardrobe. The memory of my scales still fresh in my mind, along with the knowledge they matched the starlight I couldn't figure out how to call.

The dress had an almost corset-style top with purple boning and glittering silver fabric, but it had a deep V in the middle that went to just under my breasts. The silver fabric extended to the skirt, slinking down over my hips and ending right at mid-thigh. Delia and Priscilla had helped me pick out matching jewelry, and the silver necklace dipped down much like the necklace I'd worn to the party in the Hedone room, reaching halfway down the open expanse of skin.

Calix was waiting in the rotunda with Baach, Eryx, Ilta, Lilith, and Titan. His eyes blew wide as he spotted me and left the others behind as he made his way over to me.

I looked up as he came to a stop right in front of me. His hand came up to my face, fingers lightly trailing down my cheek. "You're trying to torture me, aren't you, my réalta?"

His voice was roughened with an arousal that immediately had me reaching back for him. I let my fingers land on his lips, trailing over them lightly as he groaned. I smirked, my fingers trailing from his lips to his neck, until I could wrap my hand behind it and into his hair. I leaned up on my tiptoes, pressing my body into his.

"Hmm… maybe," I whispered into his ear. "I guess you'll just have to wait and see what happens next."

With that, I walked away, over to the others who were watching us in amusement. Eryx laughed and put an arm over my shoulder, steering me out the front doors of the palace and onto the walkway.

Ilta grabbed my free hand, pulling us along. "Come on! Tonight is going to be great!"

As it turned out, our first stop was dinner. Ilta led the way into a cute little restaurant. Its entrance was outlined by a line of Nymph trees with branches draping down onto the walkway. Moonlilies and starbells were planted between them, and the scent reached me easily. My enhanced senses as a Fae were something I was still trying to adjust to, but the smell of the flowers being so much more intense was definitely a benefit. They were lovely, and it felt like I got to experience them on a whole new level now.

But it was Calix's scent that was going to truly do me in. It was all too easy to ignore the scent of the others. Titan's scent struck me as somewhat familiar, but it was hard to concentrate on when Calix's night and fire scent overpowered them all. Whether it was because his magic was that much stronger, or because he was my mate, I couldn't be sure.

Ilta bounced up the engraved wooden door and led me in, and I realized the door's engravings represented all the elements. Inside was similar, with each corner of the restaurant representing a different element. The mishmash of decor actually blended perfectly together, with the very center of the restaurant where each elemental theme met, being where the bar stood.

"Oh, King Calix!" The woman at the hostess stand bowed her head. "I'll get a table together for your party right away." She quickly assured him before bouncing away to do so.

Calix sighed, shaking his head. I smirked back at him. His people wanted to make him happy, despite his wish to be treated like everyone else when he was out. I wasn't surprised to see some still jumping to assist when he showed up.

The hostess came back swiftly and led us to a table in the fire section, fittingly. She knew at least one dragon sat here, but I could only imagine her shock if she knew another sat with him.

CHAPTER 11

Calix

WATCHING Asteria as she sat among our friends, *our family*, and laughed along with the others as we ate dinner, something settled deep inside my soul.

Since the moment she was taken, I was on edge and volatile. It was only seeing her here now, safe and happy, that truly soothed me.

She never laughed enough. She had never felt safe enough to let her guard down enough to be happy, not to mention having to deal with tumultuous emotions she didn't understand because her mother had suppressed her magic. It had left her feeling like she didn't belong in her own skin.

Oh, I was sure Aurelia had a good reason. There had to be something I was unaware of that was dire enough for her to carry out such an extreme act. I was at a loss for how she even learned to accomplish such a powerful feat of magic.

I was thinking of this as we walked out of the restaurant and headed over to the bar. I watched Asteria with a smile as she had fun with the others, happy she was able to at least let her guard down with us. Even if Baach bumped my shoulder, wiggling his brows at me as he tilted his head toward her.

I shook my head at him, opening my mouth to tease him back about Ilta, when I stopped short.

My sister was standing outside The Otherworld Bar. That wouldn't be so strange if she hadn't told me she couldn't come tonight.

"Liv, I thought you weren't able to make it?!" Ilta bounced up to her, but Liviana just looked past her, at Asteria, and then at me. I recognized the look in her silver eyes then, and the sudden hush told me the others had as well.

I moved forward, putting my hand on the small of Asteria's back as I came up beside her. Worry about what might be coming rushed through me.

"Once you have gained control of the stars, you must follow Arawn's instructions," Liviana intoned, her voice layered with many others. It sent a chill down my spine, as it always did when she spoke prophecy or delivered a message from the gods.

I wasn't sure what she meant, but the way Asteria's back went ramrod straight, and her breath caught in her throat told me that she might.

"You *both* must journey through the Otherworld," Liviana spoke again in that strange multi-layered voice, silver eyes swirling as she looked between Asteria and me. "Find your way through Tartarus and Elysium, until you reach the city of the gods."

I drew in a sharp breath, unable to believe what I was hearing. No one was allowed into the Otherworld, and certainly not the city of the gods.

"Only the stars can lead you home. You will know when the time is right." Liviana finished, before her silver irises stopped spinning, and as she collapsed, Titan was already there to catch her.

Asteria's breathing was all I could hear as she let out a harsh breath, like she'd been holding it in too long. I rubbed my hand along her back but kept an eye on my sister as she stood up, with Titan's help, and made her way to us.

"I'm sorry." She gently grabbed one of my hands and one of Asteria's, her entire bearing apologetic. "The gods were quite insistent on the message being delivered."

"I suppose Arawn is a bit impatient," Asteria grumbled. "It hasn't been *that* long."

Liviana laughed, to my confusion, having no idea what Asteria meant. "No, it hasn't been. But the gods aren't exactly known for their patience."

"I suppose I better try to get my magic under control a little harder." Asteria gulped but the worry in her eyes quickly shifted into annoyance. "How in the Otherworld are we supposed to actually traverse the damn Otherworld?!"

I couldn't help the small laugh in my throat. "Why don't we start with what you're even talking about? Arawn's message?"

Asteria looked up at me, surprised, like she expected me to know what she meant. She shook her head, closing her eyes for a moment, leaving me waiting in anticipation. "When I was dying, before my magic kicked in, Arawn came to me."

I blinked in surprise for a moment. "*What?*"

It wasn't every day the gods made their presence known. I couldn't remember a time since they'd closed the portals and left us in charge of their protection that'd appeared so directly to anyone. "What did he say?"

"He told me that I must make my way to the Otherworld, but not by dying. That the gods needed to speak to me. He said that the fate of the world depended on the information they must give us. I honestly kind of thought I might have hallucinated that bit." She admitted sheepishly.

I blew out a heavy breath, running a hand through my silvery-white hair. This was unheard of. As was the number of visions Liviana had of Asteria. I was becoming increasingly sure that whatever was coming, Asteria was the key to it. Liviana had said before that she would not only be the catalyst, but the reason and the answer.

I couldn't help feeling like we were getting closer to figuring out what this all meant. What our roles in this coming war would be.

"We'll figure this out. For now, let's go get drunk. We can worry about gods, prophecies, and wars tomorrow." Ilta popped up, laying a hand on both of our shoulders.

Asteria laughed, her head falling forward before she looked up at me. I couldn't help the smile that crept up my face just seeing the one on hers. She reached for my hand, lacing our fingers together as hope lit my heart in turn.

"Come on. You heard Ilta." She teased, pulling me along.

"Of course. Nox forbid we don't listen to Ilta." I agreed sarcastically. Asteria's laugh was worth the slap to the head Ilta delivered on her way by.

Walking into The Otherworld Bar, right after the message about our necessary journey into the Otherworld itself, had me looking around the bar in a more serious light.

Tartarus was filled with all sorts of horrors by every account. The deepest pits of despair and the most deranged tortures imaginable. My own power could recreate that pain and turn it on others, something I always tried to avoid using. Unless those I loved were at stake.

But the thought of walking into Tartarus, of *Asteria* walking into Tartarus…

By Nox, I was sure the gods had a good reason for this, they'd never steered me wrong before. But *fuck*.

Asteria seemed to have easily blown off the news just dropped on us, already downing a shot at Ilta's urging. I noticed Callisto and Priscilla were already here, having chosen to have dinner together instead of with the group. I was happy to see they'd joined us. Priscilla was Asteria's best friend, and she'd need her support in the midst of all the changes in her life.

"Stop brooding," Baach complained, his arm landing around my shoulder.

I snorted. "I'm not brooding, you ass."

"Then let's drink!" Baach declared as he steered me to the bar, grabbing two shots off the tray Ilta had ordered. I grabbed one and shot it back immediately. Feeling the alcohol burn pleasantly down my throat. From the way Asteria was moaning at her next shot, she'd discovered the joys of drinking alcohol as a dragon.

I let a smirk cross my face as I watched her wide-eyed reaction. I leaned down to whisper in her ear, "It's the dragon in you. We burn our throats all the time, if it didn't feel good, it would be miserable. You're meant to spit *fire*, my réalta."

A sly smile rose on her face as she tilted her head to me. "Then maybe it's time to enjoy the burn."

With that, she tossed another shot back, and I joined her, grabbing a double shot for myself to catch up to her before she dragged me out to the dance floor.

I relished the feel of her body as she pressed against me. A part of me feared I'd never feel it again after everything that had happened. The way she'd pulled away from me.

I knew she wasn't ready for everything a mate bond encompassed, but I would take whatever she was willing to give.

My hands found her hips, while her own snaked around my neck and into my hair, earning a small growl as she tugged on it. Her giggle was entirely worth it. It was adorable, frankly, and something she should be doing way more often.

I was determined to make that happen.

Dancing with her proved as dangerous as always. Her hips and ass swaying against me to the beat quickly drove me to distraction, and I buried my face in her neck to try to gain some control over myself. But my cock refused to listen to reason.

Knowing this was my *mate* in my arms was overwhelming enough, but that it was *Asteria…*

It was almost too good to be true.

Her body had to have been crafted by the gods themselves. My hands roamed over her sides, the hourglass shape leading to her hips and an ass I wanted to sink my teeth into. I trailed them back up and skimmed the sides of her breasts, which brought me right back to the Festival of Faunus and watching them bounce as she rode me wildly. The memory of getting to explore all of her as she laid underneath me. Nox, I was fucking wrecked just from *dancing* with her.

That adorable little giggle returned as she ground that ass I was salivating over against my cock. Her all-too-brief dress was just too inviting, and I retaliated by running my fingers up her thighs, her dress riding up as I teased her in turn.

I could just make out the sound of her breath catching over the music, attuned to everything Asteria as I was now.

She spun around to the music before plastering herself against me. She hitched a leg up my thigh, and I couldn't stop myself from grinding into her. Her moan, as my covered cock hit her at just the right angle, was absolute torture.

I knew what she was wearing under that dress had to be nothing more than a tiny bit of lace, easily torn away. By the smell of her, she'd be soaking through them in minutes. A growl left my throat at the thought, and I grabbed her ass, palming both cheeks before pushing her solidly against me.

But my Asteria was a dragon, and she retaliated by biting my throat. I moaned, running my teeth down her neck before sucking and nipping along the slender column. Her panting breaths in my ear surely matched my own, but I was too lost in her to hear.

We kept up the dance, moving back and forth as we grinded into each other, my cock twitching and begging to be released.

I'd found Elysium inside Asteria, and I would do anything to return to it.

Anything but push her.

I knew, somewhere in the back of my mind, that she wasn't ready for this yet. Her body might be, but her mind wasn't. Pushing things too far now would only result in her pushing me away later.

But even knowing this, I couldn't help myself from leaning into every movement. Cherishing every moment.

The heavy scent of starlight, vanilla, and raspberry where my nose was buried in her neck, covered in the curtain of her hair.

The soft feel of her skin as my fingers ran over every exposed bit of it my hands could reach.

The stars swirled in her eyes when we pulled back to look at one another. It reminded me of Nova Falls, with all the falling stars spiraling down. One of my favorite places was reflected in her eyes.

Her arousal crept up my nose, and I inhaled it like a drug. My fingers tightened on her hips as I pulled her roughly into me once more. Her breathy gasp was like music to my ears. Her own hands explored my chest, letting them fall into the gap where my black shirt was unbuttoned and scattering across the iridescent black and purple scales decorating my chest.

With soft fingertips, she trailed from my chest to my neck, where she traced the tattoo on my neck.

"What does it mean?" She breathed into my ear, tracing the rune in the middle. "I've seen a lot of you with this same tattoo. Eryx, Baach, and Titan, even Harpina."

I groaned, the sweet torture she was subjecting me to making it hard to think. "It's the symbol for warrior in the old language of the gods. We get them when we complete our training as fully fledged warriors."

Her mouth closed over my neck, and I moaned as she let out a hum. "Hmm. And the scales?"

Her fingers trailed from my neck back to my chest. I grunted, leaning down and nipping at her shoulder, getting a sultry laugh in return.

"Represent my dragon form." I finally forced out. But her hands were already sliding down my arms, to where my forearms were exposed. Since my hands were still on her hips, she leaned back, hands clasping my forearms as she looked me in the eye. A dancing Aurora meeting a storm of stars.

"And these?" she questioned, raising a brow at me.

I smirked down at her, leaning a bit closer until we were nearly nose to nose. So close it would barely take any movement to close the distance between our lips.

"That, I'll tell you later," I promised, my voice rough with arousal.

Her eyes flared, and she leaned closer as if she might either kiss me or tell me off for not answering when starlight blasted out of her, momentarily blinding me.

Screams and shouts rang around the bar as Asteria's magic brought everything to a standstill. The music cut out, and the concerned murmurs of those around us took over.

Asteria's mouth was hanging open, her eyes wide and scared. I blinked at her, a little stunned by the force of her power that just exploded in the bar, and admittedly still a bit lost to arousal. Her show of power didn't help that in the least, increasing it, if anything.

But I could see how skittish she became immediately. Pulling back from me, she opened her mouth several times, as if she might say something. But no words came, and I watched helplessly as Asteria turned and ran with all her new Fae speed. A blast of wind rushed through the bar as she escaped.

I heard nothing but my own voice calling her name as she disappeared, echoing around me.

CHAPRER 12

I COULDN'T believe I had lost control of my power in such a way last night. My emotions had been rioting through me. My confusion over the mate bond and everything that brought with it, to the uncertainty over my very life. The escape I'd found for a moment in Calix's arms just made it worse by adding my arousal to the storm. Of course, it just had to all bubble up and escape in a blast of power that brought the entire bar to a standstill.

I ran before I could do any more damage, but I feared it might have already been done.

I could fully admit I had no idea what I was doing. Not with the knowledge of who I was. Not with my magic. Not with Calix.

I knew getting control of my magic had to be a priority. The gods were waiting on it, after all, and that seemed like a fairly pressing reason to figure out how the fuck to do it.

But my mind kept coming back to Calix anyway, like my love life was the most important issue as a war pressed down on us.

And yet, I couldn't ignore the pull between us. I just didn't know how much of that was the mate bond, and how much was actually *us*.

Did he actually want *me* with the passion that filled his eyes when his gaze devoured me? Or was the mate bond merely manifesting it?

Today wasn't the best day to examine that question, and I'd take any excuse to avoid examining my insecurities. After giving me several days to try to adjust to the change of my entire *being*, it was time to finally address the war to come.

Cyrus wasn't going to wait around, so we had to get moving and get our plans in place. I could worry about the state of my relationship with Calix later. My magic, on the other hand, didn't have that kind of time. I stood in front of my mirror once Delia finished getting me ready for the day, clad in my dragon-scale armored corset, cloud leather pants, tall boots, and my armbands. I felt ready for war physically, if perhaps not mentally.

The thought of Cyrus and what he may be doing even now caused the stars in my eyes to churn violently. The fire in my blood lit like a fuse, and I rocked back as starlight exploded out of me. The loud crash had me ducking and protecting my head on instinct.

I looked up to find my mirror had cracked in two. I raised my hand, trailing my fingertips along the crack, before letting my head fall onto it, my forehead clanging off the mirror. I could feel my forehead scrape along the ragged crack in the glass and the resulting blood that dripped from the wound. But by the time I lifted my head, it had healed completely.

Only a red drop of blood showed any proof the cut had even happened.

I raised my hand to wipe it away, looking at the blood on my finger. I wasn't sure I'd ever adjust to being Fae.

Maybe Calix was right, and that was why my magic didn't answer my call. It still responded to my emotions, at least intense ones, but it was like a dog that didn't listen to commands. It showed up, yet refused to do what I wanted.

I sighed miserably. How exactly did one accept their entire world shifting?

I supposed I'd have to figure that out.

Quickly.

I MADE MY way down to the training yard, determined to at least improve my fighting skills if my magic ones were going to keep failing me.

Titan was already there, watching me with a raised brow as I made my way out.

"You're overdue for training." He smirked, but it didn't reach his eyes.

I scoffed, making my way to the array of weapons. "Excuse me for getting kidnapped."

"You're not excused," he replied as I grabbed my sword. My head whipped over to him incredulously. "Our job is to make sure you won't be overpowered and kidnapped." His brow rose, and I ground my teeth, taking a deep breath so I didn't lash out.

"Well, I'm sure we don't have to worry about that anymore, right?" I swung my sword out dramatically, indicating my new Fae body.

But Titan shook his head, tutting. "That kind of thinking will see you back in chains."

My head reared back in surprise. "What?"

He advanced on me, and an uncomfortable shiver went down my spine. "You think because you're immortal, you cannot die?"

"Isn't that what immortal means?" I snapped back, raising my sword to block his sudden strike. I flinched as the clang of blades clashing rang out. His got much too close to my face for comfort.

"It means you won't age. Not that you can't be killed." He grunted, glaring at me. "It doesn't mean that something worse than death can't befall you. Do you want to end up back in Cyrus's clutches?"

I snarled, fangs appearing where before only sharper than usual canines had been. I stepped forward, thrusting my blade. Titan blocked it, and I swung the sword harder and harder. Titan blocked every swing, which only made me more furious.

"I will *never* be caged again," I growled, spinning around quickly and coming up behind Titan, his own fast turn to meet my blade, taking me back for a moment.

"Good," he growled back, blue eyes flashing. "Now, we need to ensure that. You need to work harder, train harder, than all of them. We won't stop until you can best *me*. And then, we'll keep going."

My jaw dropped. "You're ancient! How am I supposed to beat you?!"

That seemed entirely unfair. Titan smirked in response, "Until you can, there will always be someone out there who can beat you, Asteria. My goal is to see you *live*. A long, long life, if I have any say in the matter."

I paused, looking up at the man my mate considered a second father. I wondered if this was some strange version of bonding with a pseudo-in-law like the new wives in my village had done with their husband's parents.

Titan's hand landed on my shoulder. "You have many fights in front of you, Asteria. Gaining control of your magic will help, but I want you prepared for everything. You won't ever again be weak under my watch, do you understand?"

I nodded, silenced. He was right. Just because I was Fae now, didn't mean I suddenly knew what I was doing. I desperately needed more training. I didn't know what the war ahead looked like, but I knew I would face Cyrus before the end. I refused to accept any different. And I needed to ensure I could best him when that time came.

In the meantime, I was still vulnerable. Rage rose at the very thought. I could feel it building, but I thought back to Calix's lessons. I took a deep breath, simmering in that rage, letting myself accept it as part of myself, and then redirected it.

But not to fire this time—or perhaps, just a different kind of fire.

I let that rage fuel every swing of my sword. Every block, every parry. Being much smaller than the behemoth that was Titan, I moved around him like the wind. I darted in and out, bending back to avoid strikes, letting myself come up behind him, or jumping over to gain a flurry of hits on him.

Titan's smile was slow but sincere. I focused all my rage on the match, letting everything else fall away.

"Good." Titan declared as he finally swatted my sword out of my hand.

I watched it fall mournfully, knowing it was unrealistic to expect to win, but wishing I could, nonetheless. Titan had leagues of experience on me, and I knew he had slowed himself down and was hardly giving the fight his all. The point was to train me, not demolish me.

"Good?" I looked up at him hopefully, and he smiled warmly at me, clasping a heavy hand on my shoulder.

"Great." He corrected with an approving look. "The difference was distinct. Not only from the advantages of being Fae, though that certainly helped, but your focus and drive, your technique, all of it was improved in addition to your strength and speed."

A glowing smile lit my face at his assessment.

"But don't get cocky. We still have a lot of work to do." He smirked, and I slapped his shoulder as he laughed.

"You can't give a compliment without dragging it down, can you?" I sighed dramatically, shaking my head.

He rolled his eyes, "Come on, let's go again. We have time for more before the meeting."

The mention of the meeting had me straightening up.

The reminder of *why* I was doing this.

Not only of who I'd have to fight, who we'd all have to fight, but of the humans who were still unable to.

The humans relying on us, even if they didn't know it, to free them from a would-be tyrant.

I lifted my sword, letting the resolve and rage flowing through me blend together, and trained for every single one of them who was still enslaved.

ENTERING THE WAR room with Titan, I greeted everyone with a smile. Pretending like I hadn't fled the bar last night after losing control of my magic in front of half of them.

Thankfully, everyone seemed to be fine with that, and I was greeted with smiles around the table. Calix nodded, directing me to the spot to his right, while Titan came around to take the spot on Calix's other side.

"As things stand right now, we have feelers out to Sunrise and Sunset Kingdoms. Eryx is working on gathering information and seeing if alliances can be made. With Dusk, Dawn, and Day allying, we need more numbers and the strategic advantage of their location for this fight." Calix announced, looking out around the room.

My heart sank hearing it spelled out like that. That all three kingdoms surrounding Night were allied against us was a definite blow. I could see on the faces surrounding the table that they all knew it as well, and ruminating over what I knew of the complicated politics of those kingdoms and Cyrus himself, I forced myself to speak up.

"They may be allied now, but those alliances are shaky." I leaned over, looking at Dawn's sigil on the map laid out in front of us. "Cyrus and Zerlina are constantly at each other's throats, and he treats her horribly. She's only putting up with it because she wants to be queen. But if that betrothal fell apart…"

"Astraeus and Tariq are too close of friends." Eryx shook his head. "They'll remain allied regardless."

"Only if they're the ones in power," Calix spoke up. Eryx looked back at him with his eyebrow raised. "Cyrus's plans seem increasingly unhinged. It's only a matter of time until Astraeus realizes his heir is going behind his back, using blood magic and making plans he hasn't approved of."

"We hope, anyway." Eryx shook his head again, looking over the map with a critical eye. "Do we have a better chance of swaying Day Kingdom?" His eyes landed on me.

I breathed in, still unable to truly fathom any connection between myself and Day Kingdom. I shrugged my shoulders, "Your guess is better than mine, honestly. I've never interacted with them at all."

Everyone went quiet for a moment. The truth that everyone in this room knew my birth family better than I did was disquieting. The fact I knew *nothing* about them, even more so.

I felt the table rumble under my hands and realized with wide eyes my magic was causing it. I looked up to Calix, who grabbed my hands, bringing them to his lips. He pressed small kisses to my fingers, and I bowed my head, hiding my face with the curtain of my hair, taking deep breaths so the magic wouldn't burst out again.

When I calmed down, I lifted my eyes to meet Calix's. He was smiling softly at me, and I could swear I felt a foreign sense of pride fill me before it was gone as quickly as it came.

"Asteria." Eryx's solemn tone grabbed my attention, tearing my eyes from Calix to land on him. He approached me slowly, raising his hand which I noticed was now holding something out to me.

A letter.

Who in Tartarus would send *me* a letter?

The thought that Cyrus sent his taunts to me quickened my heart, but Calix's hand landed on my back, and the feeling of calm that spread through my entire body chased away all traces of anxiety. I sighed at the feeling, hating myself for it. I knew that wasn't me. Calix must somehow still be able to send me his feelings, even with the bond locked down.

I knew I couldn't give him what he needed, not now. It wasn't fair for me to take his comfort and leave him in the cold.

Dragons were beasts of heat and fire, after all.

"It's from Day Kingdom," Eryx explained hesitantly, his blue eyes meeting mine. If mine were the blue of a clear sky, his were the blue of a clear sea. Crystalline waters that lapped calmly at the shore, grounding in their reliability. "It arrived just before the meeting. I was going to wait until after to give it to you, but—"

He cut himself off with a small shrug, a reassuring smile tilting his lips. He looked like he wanted to reach out, but a glance at Calix's hand on my lower back had him just handing it over.

My hand shook as I reached out for the letter. Since hearing Calix's theory, I hadn't been able to stop thinking about it. A million questions became a swirling tornado that spun through my mind at all hours of the day and night. *Why* remained the loudest question at the center.

My trembling fingers latched onto the envelope, only for a large hand to envelop mine.

"What do they want?" Calix demanded, staring down his spymaster, his brother in all but blood, like he was an enemy. Over a letter. It was enough to snap me out of my own anxiety, which was clearly affecting Calix as well. I rolled my eyes before snatching the letter from both of them, ripping the wax seal containing the Day Kingdom's sigil to reach the letter inside.

"Asteria—" Calix attempted, but I lifted a hand to quiet him. This was beyond kingdoms and battles, and the king had no business being involved in this. Even as I told myself this, I tasted the lie like rancid meat on my tongue. He had *every* reason, but I was stubborn, and I needed to know what words lay inside *now*.

As I unfolded the parchment, Calix's hovering shadow encompassed me, and I bit my lip to contain my smile. Trying to protect me from a damn letter of all things. I nearly laughed, until I saw my name scrawled at the top in a feminine looping scrawl. Everything came to a halt. My busy mind, the calamitous room, everything came to a complete standstill.

My Dear Asteria,

I have waited twenty-one years to write this letter, and yet now that the time has come, I find my words are failing me. I am sure you have many questions, and now that your true nature has been revealed, there is probably much confusion over what has transpired. And perhaps most importantly, why.

I have answers to all of your questions, but as much as I am distressed at the thought of making you wait for your answers, I find I must tell you this tale face to face. I beg of you, let me look upon the daughter lost to me for all these years. The mere glimpse of you on Placement Day was not enough to soothe the heart that has ached terribly since I was forced to hand your shining little body into my lady-in-waiting's hands.

Your brother wishes as desperately as I do to meet you. Have you ever felt the phantom ache he complains about? I do wonder. Twins are a special circumstance, with a magic all their own. A bond that connects them across distance and magic and the fate of the gods. He wishes to reunite with his elder sister, though he insists the couple of minutes between you is hardly enough to call you elder at all.

But those minutes were enough to change our world, even if no one else realized it.

Please, allow Arien and me to meet you somewhere. Day is too dangerous for you, another thing we must discuss. And I do not trust Night, despite Soren's assurances you are happy there. Perhaps we could meet in the middle?

I eagerly await word from you, my darling daughter. I beg of you to not leave me rattling in nerves too long. Day Kingdom has been without its princess, but more importantly, I have been without half of my heart while you've been separated from us. I pray to the gods, much as I plead to you, that our time of separation is finally at an end.

Love eternally,
Mother

Aurelia Hemera Earendel

Queen of Day Kingdom

My muscles felt weak, but I leaned into the stalwart pillar of strength behind me. Calix's arms came around me, holding my waist as I let my eyes close. Starlight roared behind my lids that I couldn't hope to control. I opened them against my will, and in a flash of light, my power burst from me.

Screams filled the room as everyone ducked, dodging the rogue blast from the incompetent Fae in the room. The mate of their king, the heir to Day Kingdom… and I couldn't master my damned starlight.

A power I didn't even understand, let alone control.

I hung my head forward as tears filled my eyes. The loss of control, the letter, I couldn't be sure. But Calix merely squeezed me to him, running his hands over my back.

"Emotion brings out our powers. There's nothing to be ashamed of. We all had the same thing happen as young ones." Calix chuckled wryly, nudging at my temple sweetly. "You should have seen me when I was learning how to control the darkness. They were true shadows in every sense of the word, following me around whenever I was angry or anxious."

He shifted me in his arms until I faced him and lifted my chin with his knuckle. "Your mother clearly is behind whatever was done to you, and she is wholly responsible for you learning this later in life. But it's completely normal, I promise, my réalta."

I let my head crash into his chest and allowed myself a moment to enjoy being surrounded by his brilliant heat as I fought back my tears.

When I finally gained some semblance of composure, I pulled back and looked up to meet his lilac eyes. "What should we do?"

I caught the surprised smile before he could hide it and cursed myself internally. I was supposed to be maintaining my distance, not hugging him and using words like "we." I pulled back, and the frown that appeared on his face as a result had me closing my eyes briefly. I couldn't win.

Calix cleared his throat, stepping back as well and looking briefly at the others in the room, who all pretended to be busy with something other than staring at us. "The Etheralta Mountains sit on the border of our lands. It's a good, neutral point between us. We have a fort there that the miners use year-round. Write her back if you like, and tell her we can meet there in a week."

"And if I don't want to write her back?" I winced, feeling like a coward. But what did one say to the woman—to the *mother*, they didn't know? The one who'd abandoned them only to introduce themselves via letter and give no explanation.

The sympathy on Calix's face wasn't helping. I didn't want sympathy, I wanted to… I wanted to go shift and blow off some literal steam.

"Then don't." Calix shrugged casually. "I'll take care of it."

"Really?" I asked, my eyes lighting up. He chuckled warmly, and I was very proud of myself for holding back my response to the sound.

"Really. I'll let her know when and where to meet us and that you're looking forward to an actual explanation," he growled, his eyes narrowing.

A smile twitched on my face. *So protective.*

Chapter 13

FRUSTRATED with my father, as always, and now with my mother in a totally new way, with both sets of frustrations centered totally around Asteria, I couldn't stand to be in the palace any longer.

I quickly made my way to my rooms to change out of my armor. My rooms were one of the few places that had no gold in the palace. After a particularly bad fight with my father as a kid, I demanded that everything gold be covered up or replaced.

I couldn't say I regretted it. It was a nice break from the constant gold my father insisted be on everything.

"We must show others our superiority. Our blood is that of Earendel himself, king of all gods. The sun runs through our veins."

I scoffed, remembering my father's words now. Those very same gods he thanked for his powers now chose a woman, and he'd be all too willing to ignore *that*, according to the Oracle.

Though, he also seemed to ignore that Erebus was just as much king of the gods as Earendel was. It must chafe that Calix was equal to him in that way.

Either way, I was glad these rooms were *mine*. No gold, just a comforting cream and brown color scheme. Old leather and wood making the space feel warm and comforting, as opposed to the ostentatious displays of wealth my father preferred. Even the other buildings in Sunglint District used gold as a nod to the royal family. Sometimes, I just ached to escape to CloudBlur

District, where I could lose myself in the human slums. There was definitely no gold to be found there, despite being part of Avalon.

I was changing into my regular courtly attire when a breeze caught my attention. My windows were shut, so I grabbed the knife strapped to my side and turned quickly to the secret door in the corner of my rooms.

My shoulders dropped in relief as Lord Ergun casually strolled in, flicking a coin back and forth between his fingers.

"Sorry for just dropping in," he joked as he relaxed back into my brown leather sofa and made himself at home.

I rolled my eyes. Ergun had made a good show of following my father dutifully, to everyone except me. He didn't even want my mother to know the truth. He insisted that he wasn't going to follow *her*, but that his allegiance would be to the *next* queen, only.

I knew how much my mother would hate that, but we also needed every ally we could get. She'd just have to deal with it and forgive me once my deception came to light. Which would probably be sooner rather than later at this point.

"I'll ignore it just this once," I joked back. He dropped in like this every time he was in the city, passing along any information my father didn't want me knowing or that he'd found out from his own contacts.

His face quickly grew solemn, which roused a sinking feeling in my gut.

"Something is going on." He shook his head, leaning forward out of his casual sprawl. "Your father has been keeping secrets, even from us. Not even Kem seems to know what's going on for a change."

He scoffed at the idea, but it brought me pause. If my father was being paranoid enough to not even tell his closest advisors, something was surely afoot.

"What makes you think he's keeping secrets, specifically?" I asked as I finished lacing up my top, tilting my head so I could take in any nuances in his expression. I may be a General, not a spymaster, but I'd been raised playing this game.

"He's allied us with Dusk Kingdom, against Night Kingdom, but he seemed to slip as I was asking him questions after the meeting earlier," he explained, a skeptical sneer growing more prominent. "Apparently, we're allied with Prince Cyrus, not King Astraeus."

That brought me up short.

"What the fuck?" I spat out, blinking in shock. Ergun laughed wryly at my response, but this truly made no sense. "Why go around King Astraeus?"

"I don't know. Aelius didn't say why, he just quickly changed the subject. But as I was leaving, he was muttering to himself," Ergun explained, propping his chin up with his hand.

I sat across from him, letting myself fall into my favorite cream lambswool chair, before pressing him to continue. "And what was he muttering about?"

He flipped that damn coin around his fingers again. I hated to admit I was beginning to see why it drove my father so crazy when he did that.

"He said, and I quote, *'she will not have it'* before he cut himself off." Ergun elucidated, his expression growing grave. "I'm concerned what Cyrus may have told him, Arien."

I sighed, running a hand through my long, dark hair as that sinking feeling built in my stomach. "How would Cyrus even know? Her identity is only truly known by a few of us."

"We have no idea what he may or may not know. What we *do* know, is that Cyrus had her, Calix rescued her, and somewhere in between, the spell broke, and she was revealed as Fae." Ergun leaned forward, elbows resting on his upper legs. While he had the same coloring as my father, they couldn't have looked more different. Ergun had clearly inherited some traits from his mother, who'd originally hailed from Night Kingdom.

His sharp features reminded me of Calix, but his eyes were the blue of the sea, and his blonde hair was cut short, with only a single curl coming over his forehead. His own son had inherited his blue eyes instead of his mother's dark amber, but his blonde hair was beaten out by her vivid red hair. My own father resented that I inherited my mother's dark hair instead of his light, but every time I'd seen Ergun with his little boy, he'd been the kind of father I'd always wished I had.

I knew he, too, fought for a better world. He feared the chaos that it was clear Celesterra was slipping towards. He wanted his son to grow up with magic, in a city filled with all the wonders it offered.

Not in a land leached of all magic, forced to fight in other men's wars.

I could understand his concern, and it was appreciated. He knew Asteria was a better bet than the leadership we had now. His words from the day he'd sworn himself to our cause still lingered in my mind.

"Your sister can be taught how to rule. Your father cannot be taught how to unrot his soul."

"I'll check it out," I promised him. "I was about to go for a flight, but I'll work on figuring out what he's up to. Maybe some of our spies have seen something they didn't realize was important."

Ergun slumped back into his seat, a small smirk that looked only a little forced, tilting his lips as he flipped that damn coin.

"Good. I'll see myself out." He got up and made his way to the hidden door, but paused halfway through it, looking back at me with a contemplative look on his face. "I know whatever happens, it will be soon. When you finally see her, tell our future queen that Caersidi is with her."

I bowed my head in acknowledgment and thanks, and he nodded back before slipping through and shutting the door behind him, the seams blending back into the wall. I slumped back in my seat, running a hand down my face before I forced myself back up.

There was much to do, and I swore I could hear every piece of sand in the hourglass dropping as we made our way toward this conflict.

A conflict I was increasingly sure most of us already expected. How it would play out was anyone's guess at this point. Too many moving pieces were on the board, and too many unknowns lingered.

Either way, there was certainly no time to waste.

MAKING MY WAY out of the palace, I entered the large, open courtyard, the sparkling white stones laid over its grounds glinting under the sun. Golden arches that bulged in the middle stood at each end, and bright blue, gold, and white flowers were planted along the winding paths that led through the various seating arrangements set up for people to mingle. The courtiers always lingered here, so I was forced to increase my speed to get past them without being stopped for something trivial.

Exiting the palace, I prepared myself for the long walk ahead of me. The city of Avalon had been created to mimic the sun by forming a gigantic circle, so the infrastructure had been set up in a ring formation. The first ring outside the palace was the gardens, which separate the palace from the rest of the city's inhabitants. Each ring went all the way around the palace in a true circle, ensuring that the wealthy were kept far from the poor.

I entered the next ring, where the mansions and estates of the nobles had been built, before moving out of SunGlint District and into the StarFlare District, starting with the ring containing the higher-class shops and businesses, along with the artisans and business owners. Each ring progressed slightly lower in class, until the very last ring, circling the city in a wide orbit, so far from where the palace crested high in the center of Avalon that it was hardly visible. It may have been the widest ring, but it was also the narrowest, with the smallest amount of land despite the high concentration of people. It was, of course, where the poorest of the poor lived.

Humans.

My father didn't wish for humans to live among us. Oh, a few were approved to live in the city, but my father insisted that having all our slaves live and sleep near us would be ridiculous. They were instead forced to travel the distance of the entire city each morning and night. As if that wasn't ridiculous at all.

My mother's fight to get Soren approved to reside in the palace was just that—a fight. But she got her way in the end, my father wanting her to shut up and go away more than he cared about the slave himself being granted permission to live within the palace walls.

Looking around, I was struck by how quiet the ring was. Usually, CloudBlur District was filled with humans bustling about and going about their days and duties.

Instead, it was eerily quiet. Only one or two humans were walking around, and their slumped, defeated posture was hardly encouraging. It was like the life had been sucked out of them. The sound of someone loudly sobbing in the distance reached me. A mourning wail that sent a shiver through my bones.

I forced myself to move faster. Something was *very* wrong here.

I preferred to fly off from this end of the city instead of from the spot my father had designated near the palace simply because no one who mattered would see which direction I flew from here. If I kept to the clouds, I could pass entirely undetected, avoiding the gleam of the sun hitting my golden scales and giving me away.

I let myself shift into my dragon form, flapping my wings and soaring up high above the city. As I gained altitude, I caught a glimpse of my army on the horizon.

My soldiers were all following orders. A contingent was heading to Dusk Kingdom while another went to the border with Night, all according to plan. What wasn't to plan was the contingent of soldiers forcing along a long train of humans.

They walked a distance behind the soldiers who were heading to Dusk, so they hadn't been spotted yet, but they were clearly following them. The humans were all bound, with rope tied around their hands as they were led in a chain through the countryside.

What the fuck were they doing? I recognized a couple of the humans, even. Several loyal to Mother, a couple loyal to me. None of my father's favorites were here, and my gut feeling told me that it was no coincidence.

The soldiers leading the train conferred with one another as they gained on the unit ahead of them. As they reached them, the soldiers I'd sent to Dusk paused to meet them. I didn't know what was happening, but something was very off about this. I stopped flapping my wings to drop down enough that I could interfere if necessary.

But apparently not fast enough, as the soldiers who were leading the humans drew their swords without warning, magic beginning to be flung around as they fought the men they were meant to be fighting *with*.

I watched my men fall as I darted through the air, barreling toward soldiers who should have been following *my* orders as General of Day Kingdom's army. I snarled, giant fangs barred as I opened my maw with a roar of rage, letting it fuel me as their heads snapped up in surprise.

Some tried to run, and those I burned to a crisp with the flame that was all too ready to be let loose. The others, still fighting my loyal men, I couldn't risk using my flames on. Not when I could catch my own soldiers with it. So, instead, I used my claws to reach down and pick one up, throwing him into a tree with a satisfying crack. I watched his body slump as I used my long golden tail, glinting with purple scales on top, to whack several others away.

I roared once more as my men cheered and drove a talon through the chest of one of the Fae closest to me. Another had started to lift himself up from his slumped sprawl on the ground. I extended my neck out and opened my mouth, letting him witness the fire at the back of my throat, the saliva coating my fangs.

He began whimpering as I let my mouth close around his torso, biting him in half with a rough snap of teeth.

The few men left threw down their swords, surrendering. A collective cheer arose, and I quickly shifted back into my Fae form, landing back on my feet and straightening my jacket. At least the fight was over, so I didn't have to worry about not having my armor on.

"Prince Arien." Bellin bowed his head as he approached. I'd assigned him to be the commander of the force going to Dusk, so I was very glad to see he was one of the ones who'd made it. "Thank you for coming to our aid. We didn't expect our own men to turn on us in such a way."

His statement carried with it an unspoken question, and I shook my head. "Neither did I. But this has my father's fingerprints all over it."

A gleam appeared in his eyes as he nodded slowly. He'd been loyal to me for many years, and I knew he didn't agree with many of my father's choices. He'd worked his way up from one of the lower rings in the city. He participated in underground fights to win cash to put on the table, until his talent was noticed, and he was chosen to begin training under a proper warrior. His huge size was equal to his street smarts, and he'd proven himself time and again since he joined the army under my command.

I'd been tipped off about him by one of Beltane's people originally. My mother's cousin was just as anxious to be rid of my father as I was. My Aunt Giselle was all but a hostage at this point. Aelius had forced her into a marriage with one of his loyal lesser nobles. He'd let my mother invite her sister to court to ostensibly keep her company and have family with her, until my mother had dared to speak out in opposition to him.

That was when he had Giselle married off. He'd sent them away from court after the wedding, and though her husband appeared from time to time, Giselle wasn't allowed to join him. Keeping her sister all but captive ensured my mother wouldn't oppose him publicly. Aelius controlled her fate now, and Mother wouldn't risk her sister for anything.

Beltane was furious over the entire situation. He hated Aelius to begin with, but he would do anything to keep his family safe and get all of us out from under my father's yoke. He kept his ear to the ground, finding people we could trust when the time came to act.

Bellin was an excellent find on his part. He wasn't just one of my commanders, he'd become something of a friend in recent years. It was why I'd assigned him to this squad. He knew our true purpose and wouldn't act against Asteria no matter what Cyrus may try to demand.

I made my way over to one of the surrendered soldiers with Bellin at my back, his sword at the ready, dripping wet with the blood of our own.

Such a waste, and all thanks to my father. By Hyperion, how many of our men would fall before he finally did?

I grabbed the man by the jaw, forcing his head up to look at me. "What were your orders?"

The man just smiled widely, blood smeared over his teeth. I punched my fist into those teeth, ignoring the scrape as they cut my fingers open, knocking one of his teeth loose as the man howled in pain.

"We can do this the hard way if you insist. I could string you up and play with you like a piñata." I let my finger shift into a sharp talon, running it down his cheek and leaving a trail of blood in its wake as the sharp point broke the thin skin easily.

"Batting you back and forth until your guts spill out over the forest floor." I watched his throat bob as he swallowed hard. I hated having to make these threats, but this was war, and I knew worse would undoubtedly be required of me at some point. I forced my dragon side to the fore, letting its bloodlust take the reins. "Or I could burn you slowly," I rasped, fire licking every word. "Bit by bit." I dug my talon further into his skin, dragging it down his cheek to his jaw. "From foot to head, so you're forced to watch as every part of your body is torched slowly."

The man's eyes widened, and he tried to take a surreptitious look down at where his cock was hidden by his armor. Unfortunately for him, I caught it, and like a cat catching a mouse, I let a smirk take over my face. "Ah, I see. Maybe we'll start with your cock then."

He shook his head frantically, horror plastered all over his face. "No, please! Fucking Hyperion, *anything* but that!"

"Oh, yes," I purred, leaning in close. "I'll start with your balls, I think. Bring the sac to a nice, crisp roast, before moving on to the head of your cock." I let a burst of flame leave my lips, aiming just past his head, but close enough to singe the hair on the side of his head.

"King Aelius told us to round up the humans and bring them to Dusk!" He finally admitted, blurting the words out in a rush. The soldier's taunting smile was long gone, and he cringed away from me, fear and panic wafting off him as he spilled his guts. Thankfully, that didn't have to be literally.

"Why?" I drew the word out, my claw inching down to his neck as the solider began to practically shake, trying to maintain his composure and stop himself from crying out.

"We were to deliver them to Dusk." He repeated unhelpfully, looking at me with a plea in his eyes. But I was starting to get aggravated by the lack of information.

I grabbed him by the golden breastplate brandished with house Earendel's sigil and shook him, "Why does he want them? Why did you attack your own men? Answers!" I demanded, a growl caught in my throat. "Now."

"Cyrus needs them!" The man shouted, tears forming in his eyes as I began to unfasten his armor, leaving him, and more importantly, his cock, exposed. "Aelius made a deal with him. Something about a trade for his heir."

I went completely still.

"He told us to kill the soldiers you sent and take over the mission to Dusk. I don't know why he wanted them dead, I swear to you!" The man begged, looking up at me from his knees.

I sneered down at the coward before me. "Of course you don't. And did he tell you what Cyrus promised him regarding his heir? This trade you spoke of?"

He shook his head hastily, "Only that he would make things right once Cyrus delivered on his end of the deal. That's all I know! I swear to you, my Prince!"

I turned away from him, trying to hide the slight tremor in my hand. I nodded to Bellin, who raised his sword, and the man's screams were cut off with one quick slice.

I stepped away for a moment to get myself under control. Bellin came up beside me, eyeing me with concern.

"Free the humans. Have a couple men bring them to the border with Night. Ensure they know they'll find refuge there." I instructed, taking a deep breath. "They can't return to Day, not while my father lives. We can play this like I wasn't involved and don't know anything about what happened here easily enough."

I shook my head, looking back toward where Avalon Palace stood, its golden glory surrounded by the decimation of our human population.

But I couldn't spare them more thought than what was necessary to prevent my father from realizing I was here. He couldn't find out I'd had anything to do with preventing him from delivering the humans to Dusk.

"Arien." Bellin's worried tone reached me, and I only realized I was still shaking when he put a steadying hand on my shoulder.

But all I could do was gasp out a breath in horror.

"*He knows.*"

CHAPTER 14

Cyrus

CUTTING the throat of the human in front of me, I let the blood drip down to the bucket underneath him, not wanting to waste a drop of the liquid. It was much more precious than this mongrel's actual life.

"One down." I mused, looking up at the crowd of humans, ones not strapped down or hung up for their blood, but who'd instead been caught rallying others to try to free their brethren.

"Come now, don't be shy," I called, spreading my arms wide. "Someone here had the idea of trying to go against your king and prince. Of trying to go against the very laws of Celesterra itself." I moved forward, and the small crowd of riffraff before me scuttled backward, hitting the line of nickel-plated soldiers boxing them in from behind.

I had hoped when I took the humans for my project, it would be largely overlooked. None knew where the camps they were being kept in were located, after all. But it seemed that the humans cared more about their family members being taken than I'd originally considered.

If only my own family was so caring.

Now, I would be forced to put this group down. After getting answers, of course. But a point had to be made. Humans could not get away with going against us. It would set a dangerous precedent and ultimately lead to anarchy.

"One of you or all of you. I suppose that is the question." I announced, looking around the group of frightened sheep before me. Asteria had always stood out among the rabble. I could have kicked myself for not realizing the truth of her earlier. Though, I supposed even Calix hadn't. I tried to suppress the growl that instinctually wanted to arise. The very thought of my old friend with *my* Asteria caused my blood to boil.

A rough-looking human man stepped forward, defiance shining in his green eyes. His muddy brown hair was cut short, and a strong chin jutted out at me. What was so stunning on Asteria was decidedly less so on this human.

"It was me. Let these people go." I raised an incredulous brow at his demanding tone.

"Let them go?" I tutted, shaking my head. "You admit to treason, and still you stand here and make demands of me?" I prowled closer to the human who dared to challenge me.

I had to give it to the man. He tried to stay strong, but as I approached, his limbs shook, and his throat bobbed as he swallowed. Still, he forced his mouth open once more. "They did nothing."

"Nothing?" I laughed derisively. "What do you call this little act of defiance then?" I looked out at the humans herded together, wide, terrified eyes watching as I decided their fates. They were so confident until the repercussions of their actions caught up to them.

The man dared to raise his eyes and glare at me, snapping back, "What you have coming."

My head reared back as I blinked in shock. He would actually dare—I fumed at his defiance, wishing scornfully that I had the power to release breaths of flame to incinerate him where he stood. I reached out and grabbed him by the neck, snarling in his face, "Just for that, every single one of you will die. *Terribly.* As painfully as I can make it."

The man struggled to speak through my hold on his throat, and I loosened my fingers a bit to hear his response. "They now see you…" He struggled to get his words out. "For what… you are. We will… not… be the… last."

His words seemingly emboldened the other humans, as they began yelling and fighting to get free of my soldiers. I glared as I looked over the melee before me. They had no chance, and yet they were willing to fight and die for *nothing.*

I was completely mystified as to why they would waste their time. They lost their family members every Placement Day and always handed them over with no issue. They'd never fought back before. Not like this.

I growled, letting my hands rest on either side of this miserable human's head. With a quick move, I snapped his neck, and his dead body slumped to the ground. The other humans paused for a moment, looking at me with shock and horror.

"Bleed him dry," I instructed my soldiers, and they nodded in confirmation.

The other humans renewed their fight, but it was over quickly. Once subdued, I had my men take them to the closest camp to make themselves useful. Seeing them off, I let my wings unfurl and flew back to the palace.

I needed to wash the smell of unwashed human filth off of me.

"You need to be more careful." My mother glared as she watched me turn ordinary human blood into precious blood magic. The ancient words turning the sacrifice into something much more sacred than what it began as.

"The humans were easily put down." I countered, rolling my eyes at her caution. Humans were no threat to us. A few rebellions quickly done away with would mean nothing in the long run.

"Your father is getting suspicious of you, Cyrus. You cannot put plans of this scale in place without being found out!" she argued, pacing the room I had set aside for my work. It was deep within the bowels of the palace, where no one ever ventured. Meaning my father and siblings would never stumble upon it.

"I'm not worried about Father." I scoffed at her.

"You should be, " she insisted, her black eyes watching me with concern. She shook her head in exasperation before she tossed her wavy wine-red hair over her shoulder and stormed out of the room.

I shook my own head at her departure. She wanted me to remain heir, but wasn't willing to follow through on the tasks that had to occur for me to maintain my position. With the power I was taking for myself, my siblings would have no recourse against me. Even my father would be forced to admit who was the superior amongst us.

And Asteria… well, she wouldn't allude me for long.

Aelius might want her dead, but I wouldn't let that happen. Once I had everything in place, I would do away with Aelius and take Asteria as my concubine.

Had she not gone against me, she could have been Queen of Celesterra. Instead, she would be forced to watch Zerlina take the crown from her place at my feet.

I smiled at the very thought.

Calix, on the other hand, I had more elaborate plans for. Maybe I could find a way to separate Fae and dragon. Keep him chained like an animal to burn my enemies at my command. Or maybe I'd keep him mounted to the wall, making Asteria stare at his bleeding and broken body.

So many options!

Lightning crackled around my hands, but it quickly fizzled out. I glared down at the increasingly common occurrence.

"Fucking gods," I snarled. My magic fading on me was unfortunately becoming a more common occurrence the more chaos took over. Like the lack of balance was leeching the world of every drop of its magic, prepared to leave a bland grey wasteland in its wake.

But that was what blood magic was for.

I finished bottling this batch and quickly downed a vial, signing in relief at the feel of my magic sparking alive within me once more. The thought of living a life without magic was unacceptable. We were *owed* our powers, The very idea that they could be taken away was preposterous.

I made my way through the palace, thinking through the next stage of my plan. All of my spies were hard at work helping to bring different phases of the plan to fruition, all while monitoring my siblings and their own plots.

Speaking of my siblings, I walked into my solar to find Daneiris sitting and talking with Zerlina. The two quieted as I shut the door, and I paused as I took them in. They sat at a small wooden table by one of the large windows that helped light up the dark space, a tea service set out before them.

"What's going on here?" I asked, eyeing them both as I made my way across the room. My sister smiled up at me innocently, while Zerlina just rolled her eyes, snarking, "Tea, obviously."

Daneiris snickered a bit, her eyes going to my betrothed before shifting back to me. "I should be going, anyway."

She stood after one last sip from her teacup, wiping her mouth primly with a napkin before dropping it on her plate.

Zerlina stood with her, smiling, "Thank you for coming. I'm looking forward to later."

I considered them both with suspicion, not liking the idea of the two getting together and making plans.

"Of course!" Daneiris chirped, "I can't wait to go shopping with you! I need a fresh perspective." She was out the door with a wink and a "Later, big brother."

Silence reigned for a moment as Zerlina and I watched one another.

"What?" She finally huffed, putting a hand on her hips. The red dress she was wearing had a corset top that complimented her hourglass figure and her long, shiny brown hair that was streaked with blonde highlights from the sun. Her blue eyes were alight with something I couldn't place, and absolutely did not trust.

My hands curled, and I could feel the lightning shooting through my veins. But I leashed my anger for now.

Daneiris certainly bared watching more closely. After her attempted manipulations with Asteria, I was already suspicious of her motives. Now, with her and Zerlina bonding...

"What were you doing with her?" I demanded, stalking forward toward my betrothed.

"Enjoying some female company, Cyrus. Since my sister went back to Dawn, I'm all alone here." She sighed, sitting back down before looking up at me. "I just want a life here. Friends."

Zerlina could complain about not having any other female company all she wanted, but I still didn't like the two of them getting together to gossip.

I knew how to pick my battles, however. I already had people watching them both; I would ensure they paid close attention whenever they were together.

"Fine," I grunted, making a show of giving in, and Zerlina smiled in a strange way, getting up and giving me a kiss on the cheek.

"Thank you, Cyrus," she purred, her hands going to the collar of my dark violet and charcoal doublet, pulling slightly. "Now, let me show you my appreciation."

I smiled slowly, much preferring this side of her, and let her pull me into her, kissing her fiercely. I began to back her up when a knock at the door cut us short. I pulled back from Zerlina's lush lips with a snarl, "This better be good."

Zerlina writhed against me, and I squeezed her hips to get her to stop moving so I could pull myself away and open the door, despite her pouting.

"What?" I demanded, but blinked in surprise to see the Fae who opened the door.

"Your father has summoned you." Jeremi was responsible for my father's schedule and was only ever sent when it was especially important. "I'm to take you to his rooms."

I growled, running a hand through my wavy brown hair. This was the very last thing I needed right now. "Fine, let's go."

I followed him through the halls, up to my parent's wing, where my father's door was decorated obscenely. Too many golden statues for my liking. I was of the belief we could show our superiority in other ways. Gaudy decor didn't really do it for me.

Jeremi knocked, and my father's voice called for me to enter. Stepping in, I found my father sitting in his chair. It was overly large, with a tufted velvet for the seat in a bright pink color that matched our wings, and edges encrusted with jewels. It sat before two grey sofas, making the chair look more like a throne, especially as he sat there gripping the arms and staring at me furiously.

I sighed, moving to stand before him reluctantly. "Yes, Father?"

"What, *exactly*, do you think you're doing, Cyrus?" He ground out, rage lining his features as blue lightning shot through his eyes. The arms of the chair squeaked in protest as he gripped them mercilessly.

I stood at attention, hands behind my back so he couldn't see the way I dug my nails into my palm in response.

"Could you elaborate?" I asked blithely.

In a whirlwind of motion, my father was out of his chair, the expensive piece falling backward as he stormed toward me in a rage. I tried not to flinch back as he was suddenly in my face.

"Do you think me stupid?" He spat, voice increasing in volume as he went on. "That I wouldn't notice the humans disappearing? Or the soldiers in *my* army, suddenly going off on missions I haven't approved? You think to undermine me at every turn!"

My lip curled as I shook my head. "I'm doing what's best for our kingdom."

My father scoffed, his shoulder-length brown hair like a mirror of mine, flying as he shook his head furiously. "You do what's best for *you*, Cyrus. You always have."

I scoffed in turn, my hands flying out to the side, "Someone has to! You certainly never bothered."

His brows rose, "Is that what you think? I pushed you, yes, because I knew you could be better. I wanted my heir to be ready for the machinations of court. But you have lost yourself along the way, son."

His voice had dropped, sounding almost mournful, but I snarled back at him, "All you ever did was undermine *me*! You wanted Weylin to be your heir, admit it!"

"I wanted you to not take your position for granted, but it seems you've done the opposite." His eyes locked with mine, and I fisted my hands, lightning crackling along them even as I tried to force it back. "What have you done with the humans, Cyrus? What plans have you made behind my back?"

I ground my teeth, and at my silence his frown became even more severe. "Treason then?"

"No!" I denied, shaking my head. "I'm only doing what is necessary for us! We lose more of our magic by the day. I am ensuring we don't lose our power and positions so easily as the gods would wish."

His head reared back as he looked me over in shock. For so many years, I'd wanted nothing more than his approval. For him to be happy with anything I did as his heir. But it was only when I was doing as *he* wished that he didn't cut me down—that he didn't turn to my brother as a more attractive alternative.

"Is everything okay?" Emmie's head popped in from the other room, hiding her body behind the doorframe, and I rolled my eyes. Father had finally caved and taken her back, but not full-time as she was before. Her spot had been taken, so he now only called her when he needed her. Which was apparently right before meeting with me.

The fact that this slave girl ranked higher on his to-do list than I did made me want to scream. Only my father could make me feel this insignificant and small. Like I was a child once more, begging for attention. I forced myself to stand straighter. I refused to keep allowing him this power over me.

Emmie now reported back to me, and it was supposed to ensure I had eyes on him. I would absolutely be having words with her after this. She hadn't mentioned anything that hinted toward my father being suspicious of me.

If she had decided to be loyal to him instead of me, I would throw her in with the other humans currently serving a higher purpose.

"It's fine, Emmie. Leave us to this matter." My father insisted, shooing her away. She nodded meekly, returning to his bed. Surely, she should be happy with that, after all she'd done to earn her place there back. Throwing away friendships and a girl who was practically a sister to her...

I hoped it lived up to her expectations, I thought sarcastically.

"Tell me you have not ventured into what is rightfully *forbidden*, son," he pleaded, his voice cracking over the word.

My eyes widened, shocked and a little appalled, by the show of emotion from him.

"I won't let our magic disappear. The gods have seen fit to tear it away, all because we didn't play by their ridiculous rules!" I spat back at him. "The gods don't deserve their place anymore, Father. We can do better, be better, without them."

"How dare you speak of the gods in such a way!" he thundered, lightning crackling off him and hitting the wall. I let my own lightning play around my hands, glaring at him as he sneered at me.

"I dare, because they dared to take our magic!" I yelled back, trying to make him understand. "But when we stop playing by their rules, we can access even greater magic, Father!"

His look of disgust felt like a blade to the stomach.

"You're using blood magic," he whispered, aghast. "That's what you're doing with all the humans, sacrificing them to power tainted magic."

I laughed disdainfully. "Tainted? It allows us more power than the damn gods ever offered us!"

"There's a reason for that, son!" My father pleaded, his voice cracking as his face creased, his stormy blue eyes filled with incredulity and something that resembled fear. He tried stepping toward me, his arm out beseechingly, but I refused to move an inch to meet him. "Each use of blood magic will only drive us further into chaos. It will turn this very world on its head, Cyrus! You must see reason!"

"All I see is a king who won't step up to do what must be done. Who fears the power I now wield." I laughed again, but the mocking I intended quickly subsided in favor of the remembered pain. "I always failed to meet your high expectations. You worked *so hard* to ensure my position was challenged at every turn."

I stepped forward then, letting the blood magic he wrote off so quickly flow through me, my lightning encasing my limbs as my father stepped back, eyeing me warily. The power I felt at finally seeing the man I had always failed to impress now so uneasy before me was greater than any I'd ever known.

My father shook his head, but I continued, lowering my voice, "Now, *none* can challenge me."

My father's face changed, something new coming over him. The worry left him, and he gave me a mournful look. "You will not be swayed from this path?"

"No," I confirmed, raising my brow at him and letting the lightning play off my hands. A few stray bolts escaped me, hitting the ceiling, but I ignored them.

"I am still your king, not just your father, Cyrus." He countered, straightening, scrambling for the tattered remains of the royal air he so loved to maintain.

I smirked, feeling the confidence blood magic always infused me with rise to the surface. "And yet I'm the one able to wield true power, while you wield the sad scraps of what the gods left you with. What will you do, father?"

A sad look crossed his face, but the strength in his voice was clear. "I will do what is best for my kingdom. You cannot be allowed to destroy us all. Chaos would be the end of us."

His impassioned words made me snarl, my canines lengthening in rage, as I demanded, "And how will you stop me?"

"You are already committing treason. I could have you imprisoned." He countered, raising a brow at me, but I laughed his words off. "But you've made it clear that won't be enough."

My lightning writhed around me, striking out at random as my rage grew brighter.

"Look at you, Cyrus! You can't even fully control this power!" My father argued, his own lightning now rising, but with the waning of our gods-granted power, it was a fraction of what he once had. And so much less than what I now wielded.

"You don't know what you're talking about." I snarled, my body growing tight with tension as I waited for any movement from him.

He lifted his hand, and a bolt of lightning came shooting straight at me. I lifted my own hand on instinct, and my lightning met his in a bright blue clash. My bolt was so much stronger than his, demolishing it in midair.

We both paused, looking at one another with wide eyes. He'd actually tried to attack me. His *son*. His *heir*. He'd always been a dick, but this was a betrayal beyond anything he'd ever attempted before with petty court politics. My heart seemed to contract, the pain of the internal hit much greater than the physical one he attempted.

"And now you try to kill me?!" My words were more a tortured shout as my lightning grew around me, the buzz of it ringing in my ears.

"You are out of control, Cyrus! I can help you. Just let me—" he pleaded, hands stretching out toward me, but I let out a scream, cutting him short.

Every ounce of resentment I'd ever felt for him. Every moment he'd dismissed me or wrote me off. Turned to Weylin over me, or undermined me in front of the court. All played on my mind as blinding rage took me over.

My power responded in kind, and without even directing it, a storm of lightning bolts arced off of me and shot toward him.

My eyes went wide as I watched them slam into my father. His entire body shook from the force of the bolts, his eyes rolling back in his head as he collapsed to the floor. His body continued to spasm over and over.

I ran to him, kneeling beside his body, grabbing onto his arms in some futile effort to stop the spasms. Desperate shock and confusion made my own hands tremor lightly.

"Father?!" I screamed. "Father?!"

His body went still. The spasms stopped, leaving cold, still blue eyes looking up at the ceiling. His tanned skin looked paler than I'd ever seen it.

"Father?" I whispered, unnoticed tears building in my eyes as I shook him, trying to wake him up.

"No," I mumbled, unable to believe what had just happened. "*No.*"

"What did you do?!" A female screeched, and I heard running footsteps before blonde curls entered my vision.

Emmie fell beside my father, her dress billowing around her as she grabbed his face, "Astra?! Astraeus?! Please!!"

She began sobbing as I sat beside her numbly, still holding onto my father's limp hand.

I would never get his approval now. The thought popped into my head randomly, and I hated myself for it. I was supposed to be above that now.

And yet…

"What did you do?!" Emmie demanded, her tear-stained face scowling at me with red bloodshot eyes.

A bit of the haze around me lifted, and I scowled back at her. The implications of what just happened rushed through my mind as I reviewed and discarded contingency after contingency.

"Watch your tone, human," I told her coldly, but my voice came out more shaken than I'd prefer. I straightened slightly, letting the blood magic give me strength for what must happen now. "You're speaking to your king."

Emmie curled back into herself, looking appropriately afraid for the first time as the truth of what I now was settled over us both.

"You killed him," she whispered, defeat in every syllable.

"I did." I nodded, unable to deny the truth, even as my heart ached a bit at it. But a king couldn't let petty sentiment drive him. I turned to face her, letting go of my father's hand to grip her face, mushing her cheeks together.

"But you will not tell a soul," I murmured threateningly. "As far as anyone knows, he died a natural death. His heart gave out."

"Fae hearts don't just *give out*," she argued, glaring slightly despite the fear in her eyes.

"Maybe not, but no one will argue with the king." I gave her the ghost of a smirk. It felt like I was somehow outside my own body. I struggled to push aside my feelings as I knew I must. But staring at my father's body, I was barely capable of accepting what had happened.

Being king was everything I'd ever wanted, but I'd never wanted it like *this*.

"If you tell anyone, I will kill you. And I know how much you value your own life, Emmie." I taunted, knowing this girl and her kind too well. Graspers who would do anything to rise higher and secure their own place.

Emmie looked me over with narrowed eyes, considering. As much as I hated it, this girl knew enough to make things difficult for me. But killing her would be a waste when she could provide more valuable services elsewhere.

"As long as you take care of me." She countered predictably, and I rolled my eyes. Even holding the hand of her dead lover, she was already considering the next horse to bet on.

"Whatever. You'll be well taken care of." I promised dismissively. "Now, your role is to help me as I rise to be king of this damn continent."

There was no need to hide my plans now, not in front of her. She would be loyal to me; I would ensure it. Some could know bits and pieces, but none the full picture. Zerlina was aware of some, but I knew she had little care for her father's position as king as long as she was queen by my side. Emmie, similarly, didn't care about much besides her own position.

And I could work with that.

"Very well, my King." She smiled slightly, bowing her head, but I could still feel her body shaking with grief and fear. A cocktail of emotions I had unfortunately shared with her in this moment, if for different reasons.

I stood slowly, looking down at my father's body.

Leaning down, I grabbed the crown off his head and walked away, needing to escape the sight of his dead eyes.

CHAPTER 15

Asteria

WE managed to get ourselves back on track with the meeting, discussing our plans for how to sway Sunrise and Sunset, as well as how to handle the upcoming meeting with my—with Queen Aurelia.

As much as I hated it, whatever insane Fae royal family drama I was about to step into would also impact the coming war.

"I'm waiting for word back from one of my contacts," Eryx began, looking between Calix and me. "But I'm fairly sure that after your meeting with Day, everything will be set for you to take a trip to Sunrise Kingdom. They seem willing to meet, at least. They apparently aren't overly thrilled about the way Cyrus is handling things."

Calix nodded, satisfied. "Good. I'll have Ilta and Delia make the necessary preparations for Asteria and I. Titan, if you could choose a guard to come with us?"

Titan nodded in confirmation, "I'd suggest no less than one hundred. It might be a political meeting, but we're going through enemy territory and potentially staying in it as well."

Calix opened his mouth, a look on his face that made it clear he was about to argue when Eryx spoke up. "It would also make a statement about the power at your command. And that should they step a toe out of line, you won't mind removing it."

I blinked rapidly, surprised at this more brutal side of Eryx I hadn't seen before.

"And you'll be better able to protect Asteria if you have more warriors with you," Harpina added.

She'd been busy catching up with work since she'd gotten back to Night and hadn't been able to come out with us. I'd missed her, but she sent me a wink now as she continued, "I'd suggest I join you. Lilith, as well. She needs to be surrounded by warriors, and I know that there are places in the North that are women only that she may be required to go to as part of her duties, schmoozing the royals."

"Wait, what am I doing?" I questioned, looking between her, Eryx, and Calix, even as Calix argued with Harpina about the need for her elsewhere.

"Well…" Harpina drew the word out, teasing. Calix rolled his eyes at her before turning to address my question.

"You'll be joining me on the trip North. As my mate, it will be expected," he explained, looking at me almost apologetically.

"Oh." That was the only response I could give. I didn't know how to feel about that. "Are you sure it's safe?" I couldn't help but ask, looking at where my powers had blown everything all over the room.

"It will be. I have a plan." Calix winked, and a flush spread through me. It made it hard to concentrate as we went through the remainder of the information. Calix finally convinced the others we couldn't afford to bring that many warriors, but the final number remained undetermined. He quickly steered us into other matters before anyone could argue further. Our forces were currently preparing for battle and were being drilled daily. Night Kingdom had become more self-sufficient since cutting off the rest of the kingdoms years ago, and their imports currently came from overseas, so there was not much to worry about there.

It all came down to magic and numbers. What Cyrus could accomplish with the blood magic was largely unknown at this point. We knew it increased his powers and allowed him to craft iron weapons, yes, but the scale and current status were still a mystery.

Kian was apparently working overtime trying to get us more answers. The balance was at stake every time Cyrus used this power. We had to stop him before it was too late for all of us.

The meeting wrapped up before I even realized, and Calix grabbed my hand before I could move to leave.

"Meet me outside at first dark?" he asked, a plea in his eyes as his head drifted down toward me.

I tilted my own head in question, and he smiled softly. "I have an idea to help you with your powers."

A part of me melted, and I cursed that part of me that had softened since Placement Day. I knew I wasn't ready yet, but Calix made it hard to remember anything practical. Keeping away from him was a more challenging task every time I saw him. These moments of softness he showed me, so different from how stern he could be as king, or even how playful he could be with his friends.

This was like a Calix just for me.

My dorchadas.

One that had no problem letting me in, in a way I couldn't seem to reciprocate. A pang in my heart reminded me that he deserved the world, and a mate not so emotionally stunted and damaged.

"I'll be there," I promised, wanting every moment I could spend with him, selfish as it was.

When I made it back to my room, I was surprised to find Delia and Ilta removing some items and adding new ones to my closet.

"What's all this?" I asked them curiously as I approached. They both lit up with wide smiles.

"This, is your new wardrobe!" Ilta exclaimed, bouncing slightly on her toes as she held up a gorgeous dress I couldn't help drooling over.

"With your new status as a Fae royal, you'll be expected to dress in certain ways at certain times," Delia explained, watching Ilta and I in amusement as we both fawned over a silver and purple gown. "Most royals dress according to their house, but Calix thought it would make more sense for you to dress for your powers for now."

I looked up, my brow raised in question. "My powers?"

"Of course!" Delia nodded smartly. "Your starlight is silvery in color, and your dragon is, of course, silver and purple. We did include a couple of gold and purple pieces if you ever want to dress to honor Day, and some black and purple to honor Night, should the need ever arise. But truly, silver and purple make the most sense for you."

"It's kind of beautiful." Ilta sighed, looking over the dresses and then back at me. "You're the heir of Day, but the mate of Night. A Queen of Stars to oversee both."

"A Queen of Stars, where have I heard that before?" I mumbled as I looked up at Ilta. Her wide eyes shot to Delia, who looked back at her with an identical expression. I looked between them, suspicion rising.

"What? What aren't you telling me?" I pressed, watching them warily.

"Nothing! Nothing, really. Just, just maybe something to ask Calix about sometime. That's all!" Ilta babbled, setting me on edge.

Soft hands landed on my shoulders, and Delia's warm doe eyes met mine. "It's truly nothing bad. It's just something I don't think Calix has had an opportunity to discuss with you. But you two will have plenty of time together as you travel all over the damn continent."

"Ugh," Ilta groaned, "Don't remind me! We're going to have to somehow pack for Sunrise Kingdom! Do you know how many outfits we're going to have to have rush made? Nothing here will be suitable for the style or the weather there!"

"We'll manage." Delia insisted, rolling her eyes. "We haven't had to worry about diplomatic trips in years, but I didn't think you'd be so rusty." She teased, making Ilta immediately straighten as she set her glare on Delia.

She pointed a finger at her. "How dare you."

Delia snickered, and I couldn't help the giggle I let out. Ilta huffed, moving to put a dress away with a bit more force than necessary.

"Well, this might brighten your spirits. Calix asked me to meet him at first dark," I announced, and both looked at me with glee in their eyes. My eyes widened and I held up my hands as I immediately began backtracking. "For magic training! I just need something to wear. I don't need armor for this, after all."

The two rolled their eyes at me, deflating slightly, but began searching through dresses to find something appropriate for tonight.

"Hopefully, anyway," I added, grumbling.

"You definitely won't!" Ilta added in a sing-song voice. "But what you do need is a dress that will entice and seduce without being obvious about it."

I opened my mouth to shut that down, but she rushed to keep talking before I could.

"You aren't ready yet for more, or at least, you don't *think* you are." Her tone made it more than clear that she disagreed. "But regardless, you want Calix's eyes on you, don't you?"

While Ilta's teasing wasn't appreciated at this very moment, I couldn't deny her words. I loved having Calix's attention on me. The thrill of it truly never got old.

Ilta pulled out a long silver dress that seemed more like several panels of fabric than a full dress, but in the *best* way. It was off-the-shoulder, with a shimmery purple rope cutting across the chest to hold up the fabric that covered my breasts in two panels. It covered them fully, aside from where a bit of cleavage would appear in the middle, leaving the skin there bare.

Two high slits up each leg met at the band around the waist, which had similar purple detailing from the neckline along it. The sleeves were long, sheer, and billowy, truly magical, and my favorite. All in all, it was the perfect dress for playing with starlight in the night with my mate.

WALKING OUT OF the palace, the panels of my skirts swishing around my legs, I reached up to touch my necklace, only to remember I wasn't wearing it. I still had no idea how to explain it to Calix when I didn't even know how in the Otherworld I ended up with it.

But it was a connection to the parents I'd known all my life that I desperately craved. And maybe the connection it represented to Calix wasn't a bad thing, either.

Maybe.

Just a tiny bit… amazing, even?

Calix met me on the path, still in his court clothing but with a few layers removed, leaving him in a fancier version of his black button-up and leather pants. I barely stopped my laugh from escaping as I realized that he basically always wore armor or some version of this same outfit, just with a hundred small variations.

Such a man.

"Ready to shine, my réalta?" Calix nearly purred as I reached him, smirking down at me.

I raised a brow back at him, allowing myself to flirt back a little, despite myself. Unable to help it, really. "Only if you're ready to let me shine against you, my dorchadas."

His groan made me smirk in triumph, and his wide eyes, as they skimmed over the curves highlighted by my dress, only added to it. The warm glow that lit my blood in response was so alike when it lit up in rage, but this was a much more thrilling sensation.

"I'm ready when you are." Calix leaned in and whispered in my ear, causing my breath to catch. I swallowed hard, knowing that statement was true on multiple levels. I looked up at him thankfully, hoping he understood how much I truly appreciated that he didn't push me when it came to the state of our bond.

Cyrus had done nothing but push and push until I snapped from the pressure. But Calix seemed to only want to help me build myself into the best version of myself.

Starting with helping me with my powers. He led me out to the Dragon Cliffs, and I smiled with wonder as I stood at the peak of the cliff, looking out over the starry night sky reflecting off the ocean. The Aurora swirled around the stars, and I couldn't help thinking that it was oddly fitting that the power in Calix's eyes and the power in mine found themselves mated here.

I stepped back, turning to face Calix, who was waiting for me with an indulgent smile. "Ready to begin?"

I nodded in confirmation, and he launched into helping me through several techniques they used to help train the little ones. While embarrassing, I couldn't deny my level of experience was honestly similar.

After trying and trying with no success however, I couldn't help the aggravation that I was failing at something children managed to accomplish.

"It's no use!" I groaned in dismay. "I can't access it!"

Calix chuckled huskily, shaking his head at me.

"Of course you can." He grabbed my hand, leading me further toward the edge of the cliff, until we stood right over it, looking out at the sea of stars and dancing lights. He turned me so I faced that sea and slid his hands around my stomach. His palms pressed me back against his chest, and I let myself lean into him.

Relaxing into his body, I felt the magic of Night wash over my skin like a balm, while Calix's own strength bolstered me, through my very soul.

"Close your eyes," Calix whispered into my ear. I followed his instruction, closing my eyes against the magnificence before me. "Now, breathe in deeply. Let yourself really feel the magic within you. Connect to it. Just like you can feel our bond within you, feel the connection to your magic the same way. Our magic is different from other Fae's."

My breath caught as he continued, giving me a deeper explanation of Fae powers that I never could have imagined before the truth was revealed. "Royals have a direct connection to the gods that grant us our power, but yours is to your namesake. Just like you feel our bond linking our souls together, you can locate the bond between you and Asteria. She may have given you access to her power, but it's *yours* now. It lives within you, my réalta. You just need to let it out."

I breathed in, and out, and let myself truly look deep inside myself. But my fear over this power was still heavy. I'd spent so much of my life hating the Fae, that I couldn't help the resentment that lived within me.

"Let it go," Calix murmured softly. "You are greater than fear, greater than anger—you are as brilliant as the stars and as strong as the magic you can wield. Meet it on equal footing."

His voice had dropped into a sultry tone that sent a shiver through me as I realized that he was right. I was greater than this. Fear wouldn't rule me. I had promised myself that after leaving Cyrus. I needed to fight through it and prove myself as strong as I knew I could be.

The idea of letting go and letting the magic take over, however, was one I would have to adjust to. For someone who spent their entire life fighting to control their fate, leaving it in the hands of magic and gods and everything that went with them was....

"You're not out of control, my réalta." My breath caught in my throat, realizing that in my haste to find the bond, I'd let it slip wide open. He could feel my struggle, but I didn't let myself dwell on that. Not when I could actually feel Calix, as strong and resilient as the moon. I could feel his wonder, his awe, and a warm feeling I didn't let myself examine too closely.

"What you are..." he continued in a whisper in my ear. "Is finally *free*. Let yourself embrace who you truly are, Asteria."

My eyes snapped open as his words truly sank deep into my core. I allowed myself to let go of that tight control I always tried to keep over my emotions. In this moment, I allowed myself to let go of the hatred, pain and fear. To focus only on the pure awe as I let myself be free for the first time in my life, embracing the magic in my veins.

A wave of power greeted me the moment I felt every burden fall away, leaving me feeling weightless in the wake of it.

From deep within me, a blast of swirling starlight shot out, stretching into the depths of the night sky. It lit up everything around us, the stars twinkling as my light blanketed the entirety of the Tairngire skyline.

The usual din from the city quieted, like everyone had stopped speaking at once—until a loud cheer sprang up in unison, loud enough to reach me at this distance, as the people of the city saw for the first time what I was truly capable of.

What I had to admit they surely assumed…

What their future queen was capable of.

"My réalta," Calix breathed, and I could feel his amazement, along with that same warm feeling tinged with lust, as if it was my own.

A heady feeling took over me as I watched my magic arc across the sky. I swore I could feel every star making up its light like it was my own. A giddy laugh tumbled from my lips until Calix spun me around and claimed my laugh for his own, his lips silencing me as I gave into the force of my dorchadas.

And a sweeter surrender I had never known.

I LOST MYSELF in Calix's embrace. The euphoria of my starlight pulsing through me, mixed with the newly opened bond between us, led to a swirl of overwhelming emotions that, for once, I let drown me like a wave. I let myself experience them completely instead of trying to force them down and suffocate them.

I was so enthralled by Calix's kiss in fact, that when he stepped back, I dragged him right back into me. He gave in, letting my lips overtake his and opening his mouth for my tongue when I licked at his bottom lip. We fought for dominance, but neither of us really managed to overpower the other.

Calix's hands gripped my waist, the large breadth of them spanning my back easily. But those same hands also pushed me back once more. Leaving me wholly confused as I looked up at him.

He was panting, his eyes fully dilated and swimming with color, so I let myself reach for the bond. I could feel him warring with himself. Wanting to be lost in me as much as I wanted the same with him. But also knowing—

Fuck.

Knowing I wasn't there yet.

I let my eyes fall closed, realizing how unfair it was to let him in this way while not being ready for what he needed. He deserved a mate at their best, and I was still trying to figure out my place in all of this. But the strange thing was that I felt no resentment from him at all.

Only acceptance and patience, and that same warm feeling that had my heart pounding.

"I don't know about you, but I could really do with a... *release*," Calix purred as he sauntered back slowly, a smirk beginning to tilt up his lips. "What do you say? Time to play with fire?"

He winked, and then I watched as he shifted into his dragon form. Growing larger and larger while I stayed in my Fae form.

I shook my head, getting my breathing under control from the pleasurable loss of air he'd caused.

He flapped his wings, black and purple scales glittering with the reflected night sky as he hovered lowly over the cliffs.

I focused on my dragon side and felt the telltale tingle before my bones began to grow and shift, my dragon form emerging. Where Calix's scales appeared to reflect the cosmos, deepening the black but glittering more vividly with color under the night sky, my own seemed to become more luminous, the silver scales shimmering as if they'd become starlight itself.

My wings flapped in the air, and the feeling was just as incredible as the power running through me. I'd spent years wanting nothing more than to be able to fly, and *finally*, I could do so whenever I wished. I wanted to laugh from sheer delight, but a roar erupted from my mouth in its place.

Calix's roar sounded beside me, and I was sure had anyone seen it, my smile would have been a terrible thing to witness, giant dragon fangs bared. He flew sideways and dropped under me, the talons on his wings scraping along the more sensitive skin on my stomach, causing a delicious thrill to run through me.

I hadn't fully closed the bond again, so I could feel the playful excitement surging through Calix at getting to fly with me.

Two mated dragons flying through the skies together.

It was almost easy, in moments such as these, to forget all the things that held me back. To forget what was coming. And as I let a burst of flame surge outwards, I tried not to let that old fear creep back in. The one that had kept me alone all my life.

To love was to risk loss.

And I couldn't imagine a greater love than what I could potentially experience at this Fae's side.

But a war unlike anything we'd ever seen was about to unleash itself across Celesterra.

And I realized with perfect clarity now, that nothing would ruin me faster... than the loss of *him*.

CHAPTER 16

Calix

SINCE the night I'd helped Asteria unlock her power, we'd been training nonstop. She only had a few days before we had to leave for the Etheralta Mountains, and I wanted her to have enough of a handle on her powers that she wouldn't accidentally blast her mother with starlight.

As hilarious as it might be to see Aurelia go flying across the room, I knew Asteria hated showing emotions she was uncomfortable with. And I wasn't sure what could be more uncomfortable than meeting the mother who sent you away and locked you in a metaphysical cage.

And then there were the gods to consider, who were waiting for Asteria to have full control of her power before they'd meet with us. As much as I revered them, I couldn't help the trepidation I felt at the request. What they had to tell us that couldn't be communicated via Liviana was anyone's guess.

The gods had never summoned anyone to the Otherworld before, as far as I knew. That's why they had Oracles and seers to pass along their messages. It's why they had us guarding the portals to Tartarus and Elysium, ensuring no one ever went through. We had myths and legends of people trying to access the Otherworld, of course. Mostly they emphasized the consequences those people reaped as a result. Such as the man who tried to chase his love into the afterlife, but got stuck in one of the traps in Tartarus and remained stuck to this day, suffering in eternal torment. I assumed those stories were created to prevent anyone from ever trying to go the first place.

The last issue, of course, was the Cyrus of it all. Asteria would eventually have to face him in battle. The thought had a growl growing in my chest, my own desire to protect and shelter her, battling against the knowledge that she *needed* that chance to face him.

I just needed her to walk away from it.

Needed it, in a way I had never needed anything else.

She'd been a bit more open with me since we'd flown through the skies together. While she wasn't ready yet, I knew the time we spent together helped break down her walls bit by bit.

Teaching Asteria to wield her magic had been helping her to regain the feeling of control she felt she'd lost. I hoped meeting her mother and getting the explanations she desired would further strengthen it. Her sense of self had been shattered entirely in the wake of her reawakening.

I knew I couldn't put it back together for her, that was something she'd have to do on her own. But I was resolved to help wherever she'd let me.

Spending time with our own little messed up family seemed to bolster her, too, so after another day spent training, first with Titan in the sparring ring, and then with Ndrita for her magic, I'd planned for everyone to spend the afternoon together.

We just had to get through the harder parts of the day first. I shrugged on my armor, buckling the sides up before sheathing my sword and daggers, and made my way down to the yard. Titan was already there, warming up as he waited.

"Morning, Titan." I greeted, and he smiled at me warmly.

"Morning, Cay. You ready for this?" he questioned, raising a brow. I hadn't dared to let myself train with Asteria when we thought she was human. Fighting her was the last thing I needed when I was trying to prevent myself from fucking her into the ground. Now, however, she was the one who would decide when she was ready for that step. Knowing she wasn't just waiting for me to snap and take her, it would be easier to keep control of myself.

Even still, I wasn't sure I actually *was* ready.

Despite the memories being shadowed by what happened after, I remembered how sexy she looked, cutting down those warriors during the skirmish in Sunset Kingdom.

"I suppose we'll see." I shrugged, a smirk rising. Titan chuckled, clapping a hand on my shoulder.

"Waiting for me?" Asteria's smirking voice had me turning my head automatically, watching her saunter over.

Fuck. She looked way too good in that armor. I swore it caressed every curve just as tightly as her clingy party dresses did.

"Well, we aren't waiting for Priscilla." Titan joked gruffly, eyeing the blonde who'd walked over with Asteria.

"As if I'd be here for any of *you*," Priscilla huffed, jokingly. But her gaze sought out Callisto at the other end of the yard. She turned to Asteria, giving her a quick smile and squeezing her arm before she moved in that direction.

The two of them were kind of adorable. I wouldn't have ever expected it, not when they were such complete opposites. Callisto loved fighting, taking equally savage glee in every human she rescued and slaver she cut down. She never bit her tongue and told you exactly what she was thinking and feeling at all times.

Priscilla, on the other hand, seemed to prefer to stay safe, far from any fighting. She faced what she'd been through in Dusk with quiet resolve, instead preferring to support those who did the actual fighting. She was sweet and mostly soft-spoken, at least until someone she cared about was at risk.

But they somehow made complete sense together.

I looked to Asteria, thinking that they weren't the only ones. The distance between us still ached, but I could feel her resistance melting slowly as time ticked by.

She was my mate, fated to be my queen. I just had to remind myself to be patient, that the time *would* come. A quick glance down at the silver bands around my forearms reassured me.

Run as she might...

Destiny couldn't be fought forever.

"You've been making great progress, but I want to see how you fight against more than one opponent at a time." Titan was telling her as I tuned back in. I shook myself, knowing I couldn't afford to be distracted.

Asteria wiggled her brows up and down, giggling slightly, "So, you think you can take me?"

I raked my eyes up and down her body. She was small, for all her presence took up much more space in a room. But with over a foot on her, she only came up to my shoulder on a good day.

All our dragon-scale armor was sculpted using the fallen dragon scales from thousands of years of dragons in House Erebus. We shed them semi-regularly, and new ones would quickly replace them. Using the discarded scales gave our warriors the same protection as a dragon, and they hugged the body, since they were meant to shape and form the moving mass of a flying dragon. They were flexible, if impossible to penetrate. It gave us a huge advantage in battle.

But now, those dragon scales that had fallen from my forefathers were hugging Asteria's breasts in a way that made me want to rip them off one by one and replace them with my own. She should only ever be covered by *me*.

Her cleavage in the armor, since the women only added a breastplate to them during battle, preferring the comfort this version offered, was frankly obscene. *In the best way.* I wanted to sink my fangs into the flesh offered up, feel the lifeblood seep from her plump breast into my mouth, and taste her essence dripping down my throat.

I blinked, shocked and vaguely disgusted with myself at the route my thoughts had taken. I'd heard stories that claimed mates used to share blood between them, but it was something that, if true, had gone out of fashion many years ago. Our fangs were supposed to be purely ornamental, growing when angered or aroused, but more so used for intimidation.

Shaking the errant thought away, my eyes continued down to take in the tight cloud leather encasing her thick hips and the slope down to her thighs. I wanted to lick that path down her body, worshiping her as I showed her exactly what I could do with more time than one night had offered us.

I licked my lips before curling them into a smirk, and was rewarded with her breasts heaving over the sweetheart-cut neckline of her armor as her breath caught.

"I think I'm up for that particular challenge," I purred, and caught Titan rolling his eyes beside me as Asteria bit her lip, eyeing me like she wanted to devour me as much as I did her.

"We'll have you two fight first since you're unfamiliar with Calix's style," Titan instructed Asteria, but she kept her gaze on me for a moment, the stars in her eyes sparking to life before she forced herself to look at Titan.

He grunted, looking between us pointedly before continuing, "I'll jump in when I deem you ready. And remember not to let yourself be distracted."

Asteria huffed, rolling her eyes fondly, and I realized that Titan had clearly grown fond of her as well since they began training together. He looked at her with a soft, fatherly smile that I'd seen on his face many times.

I watched as Asteria bounced over to the swords on display, reminding me that I needed to get her a better sword. One befitting her status. Ideas ran through my head as I watched her reach out for one. The arm bands she wore looked unfairly sexy on her, too. I'd seen women wear them millions of times, and never had they turned me on in any way. They were practical. The design allowed a plate to be added to the shoulder in battle, and the material of the glove itself protected and gave flexibility to the arm so it could bend and move. The fingerless aspect allowed for full range of motion when wielding a weapon while still shielding the hands. But something about the tease of skin where it stopped on her bicep, and the fingers peeking out...

Fuck.

I clenched my hand, concentrating on suppressing the change before my talons started to appear.

Asteria, meanwhile, picked up a sword and turned to face me with a dramatic flourish. I couldn't help the small smile that slipped out, relieved to see her playful side emerging again. It was a side of her that showed itself the longer she'd been here, and I found myself hoping to see more of it.

I wanted to know every side of her, who she was when she wasn't being shoved into a box and made small by others.

Now, she could finally be as large of life as her soul demanded.

I raised my sword to face her with a smirk that she matched. But she was smart, and I found myself impressed with what she'd picked up thus far. She was smaller, so she waited for me to make the first move, knowing she wouldn't have a chance rushing me straight on.

So I gave in, swinging at her and watching as she twirled away gracefully. Titan had mentioned she fought like a dancer, able to twist and bend with ease. Even before we'd found out she was Fae. It made sense now, knowing her Fae abilities had been simmering just under the surface, repressed.

"I thought you wanted to actually fight me," I taunted after a couple more moves where she danced around me. Asteria narrowed her eyes, a gleam forming in them. I shrugged my shoulders casually. "All I see is you running away."

That did it.

She met my next strike with surprising strength. Even as a Fae, I was much bigger than her. But she was able to parry my blade, and as I twirled it back around and down at her, she met it with her own straight across, stopping the downswing in its tracks.

"That's more like it." I smiled slowly.

"If you wanted me to embarrass you, you should have just said so." She smirked haughtily as she raised a brow. She kicked out at me, and not suspecting the move, it caused my leg to buckle.

She swung down and I met her blade with my own, forcing her back as I surged upwards. A flurry of strikes came next, and neither of us bothered to suppress the wide smiles forming on our faces.

Fighting her was as thrilling as fucking her.

The next series of moves I put more force into, and she panted as she was forced to retreat and defend herself. "Come on, my réalta, show me what you can really do."

She narrowed her eyes, and I saw that glorious rage light up her eyes. She rushed me, and I raised my blade to meet each of her strikes. Our eyes were locked, and it began to feel like we could almost anticipate every strike and move as it came. I spun away just as she swung her blade to come at me from the side. She blinked in surprise, and we both paused for a moment, taking in what had just happened.

That wasn't an almost—I *had* anticipated her move before she'd even started it. It had to be the mate bond. I didn't know many mates, and my father had died too young to ask, so I didn't know all the ins and outs. I didn't wish to bring up Titan's painful memories with him, so Asteria and I would have to figure out the bond together.

What we'd accomplish together would undoubtedly be the stuff of legend.

Lost in thought, I wasn't paying enough attention. Suddenly, Asteria flew at me, and I fell backward to the ground, huffing out a laugh. She was now straddling me, and I raised my brows at her, "If you wanted to get me horizontal, you should have just asked."

She blinked, before smirking slowly, her blade forgotten as she reached a hand up, caressing down my face gently. I closed my eyes, relishing the touch, but I opened them quickly as she continued her motion, running her hand down my neck and to my chest, over my armor. She leaned in to whisper in my ear, pressing those glorious breasts against my chest, her hips pressing down until she could grind herself over my cock.

"Don't be so boring, my dorchadas," she purred in my ear, making me shiver. "I can think of much more exciting positions to get you in."

My hands grabbed her hips, abandoning my sword altogether. I dug my fingers in, and the slight moan she let out was music to my ears. I could feel myself growing harder as she rocked against me, and the scent of her arousal, which had been a low buzz since we started fighting, grew heavier in turn.

I growled directly in her ear before flipping us over in a whirl of movement, so she was underneath me. She bucked up, trying to fight me off, but I sunk my hips down into hers, preventing her from bucking again but more so to feel the press of her against me. I grabbed her wrists in mine, bringing them over her head and holding them with one hand. My other went to her throat, pressing my fingers into the skin of her neck and slowly tightening them.

"Well, now that you're Fae, I can show you what I'm truly capable of," I rumbled, delighted to feel her shiver. "If you think you're truly up for it—"

A dull training blade was suddenly pressing on my neck.

"If you two are quite done?" Titan drawled, annoyance lining every word.

I let my head collapse into her neck, and Asteria let out a muffled laugh, pressing her own face into my long hair. I lifted myself up to look down at her, thrilled to see her smile up at me, desire still swirling with the starlight in her eyes. Even as Titan removed the blade and I helped her stand, she didn't run, she didn't try to pull away. She just picked her blade back up and got back to the fight.

It was certainly encouraging progress.

CHAPTER 17

Asteria

AFTER getting caught up flirting with Calix while sparring, Titan made us start from the top so he could jump in without issue. We managed to behave ourselves this time, letting them teach me how to handle two opponents at once. But my mind stayed on the interaction that had just occurred between us.

It was getting harder and harder to keep myself separated from Calix. I just… didn't want to.

I wanted him, *desperately.*

Even if I didn't think I was ready for a mate bond and everything that came with it, my body called out for him, wanting him close and touching me at every opportunity.

Even as we headed over to the Dragon Cliffs, we snuck heated looks at one another. I tried to get a handle on myself, especially as we met Ndrita there. Being aroused in front of his sister was definitely not something I wanted to experience.

"I'm so excited to help you train! We haven't really had a chance to get to know each other since you arrived. And I need to scope out my big brother's mate." Ndrita greeted me cheerfully, sending me a wink as Calix groaned her name.

"You're right." I nodded, laughing lightly. "I'd love to get to know you better. Calix clearly adores you, and I want us to get along."

Calix gave me a look I couldn't quite decipher, something warm and astounded in his eyes. But Ndrita distracted me, grabbing my hand and pulling me along, her white hair flying behind her.

The grassy cliff was open to the sky and the sea, leaving us with nothing to hit should my magic go haywire. I was thankful for the forethought. Even with access to it now, I wasn't really in control of it.

It rankled badly. I'd always wanted control over my life, and just when I was beginning to gain some, it was all ripped away. Leaving me more out of control than ever.

The fate of the damn world was at stake, and I was failing to be of any use whatsoever.

"Okay, Asteria, I want you to focus on your magic." Ndrita began, standing before me, blue eyes with the slightest purple tint locked on mine. "Focus on the connection you feel to it."

I did as she said, focusing on the spot inside of me that Calix had helped me locate.

"Now, I want you to focus on different emotions. We're going to run through them, and I want you to really feel each one. Let your magic respond naturally. The point is to see how your magic responds to each. Okay?" she asked, and I nodded back, preparing myself.

Calix watched on, supervising, but ready to step in if needed.

"Okay, let's start with happiness." Ndrita smiled. "Think of something that makes you truly happy, and let yourself really live in that emotion. Feel it as truly as you would when you experience it."

Most of my life hadn't been what I'd call happy. Even when things were calm, I was always angry. About everything. I hadn't really experienced happiness until I came here. Night Kingdom opened my heart in ways I had never thought possible.

I thought back to the night we all went out for the first time to the Otherworld Bar. Drinking and dancing, laughing, surrounded by amazing people I was just learning to let into my heart. Experiencing for the first time what it felt like to be in Calix's embrace. How easy it was to lose myself in him, and he in me.

My magic churned within me, before blasting out. Not a violent explosion, but a peaceful, beautiful one. Starlight expanded from me in rays of sparkling light.

"Wonderful!" Ndrita clapped, her smile wide. "Now, continue feeling that emotion, keep it with you, but focus on pulling the magic back into you. It responds to your will, all you have to do is tell it what you want."

I looked up at her, tilting my head to the side, "But I didn't tell it to do anything to begin with."

"That's because magic responds to our emotions, remember," Calix interjected, smiling slightly at me. I realized then that he could likely feel what I was feeling. I blushed slightly, then kicked myself for letting that affect me in such a way. I wasn't sure if he knew what I was thinking about to bring the emotion forward, but he definitely felt the effects of it.

"Yes, thank you, brother." Ndrita rolled her eyes, turning her head to him. "I do have this, you know."

I snickered as he raised his hands in surrender.

She turned back to me. "What we all learn to do is feel those emotions, but keep our magic leashed at the same time. It will become second nature eventually. You'll be able to feel those emotions without it responding automatically."

I thought of it wistfully. I hated being so exposed, everyone able to see me unable to master my emotions. My magic was a telltale sign of my inner conflicts, broadcast for the world to see.

"What we're doing here will help," she insisted, coming forward and placing a hand on my shoulder. "You were deprived of the basic lessons all Fae are taught as younglings. You're playing catch-up at an accelerated rate now. You're doing wonderfully, truly."

"Thank you," I whispered, nodding slightly. It was so strange. She was my mate's younger sister, but also centuries older than me. I wasn't sure how Fae relationships like these usually worked, but it felt like she wanted to be friends at least.

She nodded in return, stepping back. "You'll keep practicing this, and before you know it, you'll have it under control."

Those were the keywords, and they fortified my resolve. I needed this under control to focus on the bigger picture. On Cyrus, the war, and the threat of chaos lingering over everything.

We went through all the emotions we could think of, and I marveled at how differently my magic responded to each one. Arousal we skipped for now, but she advised me to practice. *"In private. Calix."* Eyeing her brother pointedly. I couldn't help my laughter, watching the two siblings interact. But it quickly faded as we came to the last emotion.

Rage.

"As dragons, rage will always be the hardest one for us all to control," Ndrita informed me mournfully. "We're naturally inclined to it, and our magic is attuned with it in a way our other emotions just aren't, because it ties back so strongly to our dragon forms."

"That makes sense," I agreed, nodding sadly. "I've always struggled with it, and my magic…"

I trailed off, but Ndrita nodded in understanding. "Go ahead and feel it. Let's see what happens."

I knew what would light the fuse on my rage quickly, and let myself go back to my time with Cyrus. Calix stiffened in my peripheral, but I ignored it for now, focusing on the memories. Of being treated like a pet, dressed up like a doll, manipulated into acts I never wanted to partake in with him, and almost forced to…

My power erupted out of me, faster and harder than I'd ever seen. It reached all the way out over the water. I couldn't even see the end of it, but I could *feel* it.

The magic felt volatile. Dangerous and unpredictable. There was no way for me to control *this*. I wobbled slightly on my feet, but Calix was there, grasping my arms and pulling me back against him.

"It's not the magic, it's you," he whispered into my ear. "You are the only one in control of yourself, my réalta. You will never be under another's control again. Now, grasp onto that control. Force the magic to your will."

He was right. It wasn't the magic that was volatile, it was me. My emotions powered it, and my rage regarding Cyrus knew no bounds. But the power *was* mine. At the very heart of it, this magic, *it was me.*

I realized now that I was right all those months ago, when I told Cyrus that true power couldn't be given. This was naturally mine. I was never truly powerless.

The power was within me all along.

I was the one in control of myself. No one else.

I focused on my magic, on bending it to my will, and slowly, the starlight started to recede, flowing back into me in a swirling, sparkling maelstrom.

"That was magnificent!" Ndrita praised, as I slumped against Calix. I was thankful for his unyielding strength in this moment, when I felt too spent to stand on my own.

"As much as your rage becomes you, seeing you take control of your power is truly just as sexy," Calix murmured in my ear, his sister rolling her eyes in my peripheral. I couldn't help the small smile that slipped out, tilting my head back to look up at him.

"I have to admit, having someone beside me that I know I can lean on, someone I can trust, helps more than I expected," I admitted lowly.

It felt like my heart beat double for a moment, and I realized I was actually feeling Calix through the bond. His genuine awe at my thankfulness for his presence made me unspeakably sad. He truly deserved a better mate than me. Someone less closed off, more put together, willing to jump into the relationship destiny laid out for them.

But I'd always been difficult.

I'D ONLY JUST managed to wash up after training before Delia was barreling into my room to help me get ready for our afternoon plans.

"What exactly are we doing?" I asked, confused, as she laid out a supposed outfit on the bed.

She huffed in amusement, brown eyes sparkling. "We're going swimming!"

"And… what is that?" I raised a brow at her as she came to a standstill, seeming to shake herself.

"Right." She paused, before clapping her hands, her smile appearing once more. "Out back, we have a pool. It's for swimming or just lying by it. A pool party, specifically, is when a bunch of people get together by the pool. Swimsuits are the preferred attire, though women often wear cover-ups over them."

She indicated the bed, where she laid out my outfit. I'd, of course, seen the pool out back, but I'd never really understood its purpose. I was told it was a pool, and that was about all the explanation I'd gotten. There was always some new thing around here to discover.

I rifled through the options Delia had laid out, and found myself drawn to the dark purple swimsuit.

"It's a bikini." Delia smiled, "Here, wear it with this!" She held up a silvery see-through dress. I changed into the bikini, admiring the way it complimented my body, before throwing the dress over it. It fell to my mid-thighs, and it clung to them for dear life. The top half fell off my shoulder on one side, and it billowed loosely around my midsection.

I smiled at my reflection in the mirror, loving that I was free to choose my own outfits. That I could dress sexy when *I* wanted to and cover up when I wanted to. Such a simple thing that meant so much.

Delia ran to get herself ready once I was done, and I made my way down to the pool.

"Are you ready for this?" I turned with a smile as Priscilla's voice reached me, her arm landing around my shoulders.

"I can't wait. I've never done anything like it." I was truly excited, and knowing Calix had set this up for me, just so I could relax and have fun with my friends, made that warm feeling I refused to name rise inside me once more. Pulsating with the need to reach out and bring him to me.

And he'd likely be shirtless for this.

Nox, I was in so much trouble.

"So, how are things going with Callisto?" I elbowed her, dying to hear the latest news.

Priscilla blushed, ducking her head and bringing a grin to my lips.

"They're really good." She admitted, the pink blush still staining her cheeks, even as her brown eyes nearly glowed. "We're going slowly. She knows my past is…"

She trailed off, and the grin slipped off my lips. I knew Priscilla had dealt with horrors of her own in Dusk, but she always obfuscated when it was mentioned.

"But she's willing to go at my pace," she murmured quietly.

"That's great, Pris." I enthused with a broad smile. "You, of all people, deserve happiness."

Priscilla smiled at me, but there was something in her eyes that had me grabbing her elbow and bringing her to a stop in the hallway. "What's wrong?"

"Nothing is wron—" She cut off when I gave her my best *I don't believe you* face. She sighed after a moment. "I don't want her to fight."

My head reared back in surprise. "What? What do you mean?"

Priscilla sighed deeply, shaking her head. "I know she's a leader in the resistance here. I *know* her job is important. That she feels like she needs to fight."

She paused, gathering her thoughts, as my mind spun. Callisto was absolutely integral to the resistance movement. She was in every meeting, and was always making plans and directing others, or otherwise out helping to rescue more humans.

"But I've lost people to fighting before. I couldn't stand to lose someone I love like that again." Priscilla finally said, and her shoulders sank like a weight was pressing them down.

"I didn't know that," I murmured, looking at her sympathetically.

"It was a long time ago." She sighed. "My father was someone who never sat easily in chains. My mother was more like me. She preferred peace over fighting, and didn't see why he had to keep on with it."

She looked at me with a sad smile. "You reminded me of him right away, you know. He had that same restless spirit you possess."

I swallowed hard, understanding better both her reticence and her struggle between wanting peace and knowing this war had to be fought.

"I'm sorry, Pris." I hugged her, and she clung to me, shaking slightly as I petted her hair, giving her a moment to calm down.

When she pulled back, she sniffed, "I know she must fight this war, just as you do. But I'm not sure I can give my heart away until I'm sure it won't be shattered once more."

I bit my lip, feeling my heart contract painfully. "I understand that, trust me."

She met my eye, and the acknowledged truth passed between us. We were both falling, but too scared to let someone else catch us. We both met love with resistance, because a heart could be shattered just as easily as peace could be.

WALKING OUTSIDE, I was met with the sight of Calix taking off his shirt, leaving him in shorts that clung to his form indecently. My mouth went dry immediately, and I struggled to swallow.

Calix looked up, and the moment he caught sight of me, the massive bulge barely covered by his shorts bobbed upwards.

That fire that lived inside me sparked, and I felt a hot flush take over my body. His eyes raked over me like a physical caress, and my own were drinking in the sight of him as eagerly as I'd chased my freedom.

Priscilla laughed, knocking her shoulder into mine and waking me from my near trance. She dragged us over to two lounge chairs by the pool. Lilith was already laid out next to Harpina, and I dropped down next to her, my eyes cutting to Calix as he jumped into the pool. When he popped up from his dive, I watched the water droplets running down his chest with pure jealousy.

Lilith chuckled, ducking her head to catch my eyes. Her woodsy brown hair was in wavy curls that fell down to the bottom of her breasts that were currently encased in green fabric. She, like Priscilla, who was wearing a pink one piece, was in a leafy green colored one with spots cut out around her stomach that showed off her toned structure.

"Haven't gotten your fill of him yet?" she teased, her nose crinkling with mirth.

Harpina snorted from her other side, sitting up to eye me. She was out of her armor and in a dark orange two-piece, her feminine beauty only enhanced by the muscles that defined her body. "She hasn't even started to get filled as far as I can tell."

Lilith couldn't contain her chuckle, laughing into her hand, and I rolled my eyes at them both. "Laugh all you want. I'm doing the smart thing."

Harpina raised a brow, eyes flashing with challenge as she swung herself up to lean over Lilith.

"And what's that, exactly? I thought you wanted Calix?" she scoffed, shaking her head. "You were practically panting after him before. Is it because he was unattainable then?"

My head reared back, completely shocked at the accusation. "What?"

"You wanted him when you thought he had another mate out there." She shrugged, too casual. "But now you know *you* are his mate, and you're keeping your distance."

I shook my head fiercely, insistent, "Absolutely not!"

"Then why?" Lilith questioned softly. "You two had such a hard time keeping your distance from one another before. But there's nothing to keep you apart now."

I nearly snorted. Did they really not understand at all?

"There's plenty," I argued, raising my brows at them. "I'm a mess, first of all. I'm just now beginning to understand who and what I am. I can't jump into an eternal commitment when my life is in complete chaos."

Lilith frowned sadly. "Asteria, you aren't a mess. You're dealing with the complete upheaval of everything you knew, yes, but don't you think having Calix to help and support you through it is better than trying to stay away?"

"Ah, I get it." Harpina declared suddenly, face clearing of all confusion as she nodded decisively. "You're afraid."

"I'm not afraid!" I blatantly lied, scowling at her.

Harpina snorted, laughing, "Yes, you are. You finally have something good, something that's *yours*, in a life that's given you nothing of your own. You were afraid to let people in because of the potential pain it could bring, even as a human. Now you're terrified because you know this has the potential to wreck you."

I glared at her, crossing my arms, while Lilith patted my leg sympathetically.

"What you don't realize, Asteria," Harpina continued, softening from the soldier looking after her king back into the friend who held me when I broke down. "Is that a mate bond is basically a *guarantee* of happiness."

"Are you sure about that?" I asked, skeptically. "I've heard about my birth parents. It doesn't sound like they're very happy. Not if my mother literally hid me from my father my entire life."

Harpina frowned, but at that moment, Ilta dropped onto my lounge, leaning back into me dramatically and making me laugh. "You all look much too serious for a pool party! Come on!"

She took my hand, dragging me up and toward the pool.

"Thanks for the rescue," I whispered, and she turned her head, blonde hair flying, to wink back at me.

Hand in hand, we jumped into the pool. It seemed to cause a chain reaction, and the others were soon all jumping in after us. It was different from the ponds and ocean I was used to, but I found myself enjoying the consistently warm temperature the pool maintained.

I laughed as Baach and Calix teamed up to take on Eryx, dunking him under the water, only for him to team up with Baach to do the same to Calix right after.

I swam up next to Liviana, who was floating on her back, silver hair fanning out around her like a halo. She opened her eyes, the silver within still and calm.

"You've been busy lately." She observed, her brow rising.

I chuckled, shaking my head. "That's certainly putting it mildly."

"Don't worry." She smiled serenely. "You're doing wonderfully, according to my brother and Titan."

I blushed at the praise, hating that damn reaction and wishing I could control it. I couldn't help the small smile that crept out, though. I'd been working hard on my training, determined to contribute equally in the battles sure to come.

I didn't want to be weak. I didn't want to be protected. I wanted to bring the fight to those who'd see humans in chains forever, and burn their world to the ground myself.

"It will all work out, Asteria. I believe that." Liviana insisted, that soft smile still on her face. I smiled back, appreciating her support.

Knowing a seer believed it would work out was comforting. I was sure her belief didn't stem from her visions, however. What the gods showed her seemed to be murky at best. But who knows, she did say she couldn't tell us everything she'd seen after all.

CHAPTER 18

Calix

WATCHING Asteria have fun with everyone was a balm to my soul. Feeling her happiness even more so. She'd been leaving the bond cracked open since the night she harnessed her power, and I couldn't have been more thankful for it.

Even if I couldn't have her, getting this small piece of her was enough to reassure the wild protective instinct that arose in me around her. The bond was truly like nothing I'd experienced before, and trying to control myself around her was becoming increasingly difficult.

I'd been spending a lot of time in the air, letting my flames out to burn off some of that energy. And equally as much time in my room, pumping my cock and thinking back to the festival, imagining slamming into her tight heat, instead of my boring fist.

"Your eyes are going to fall out if you stare at her any harder." Baach laughed, clamping a hand on my shoulder.

I tore my eyes away from her to see Eryx ducking his head to hide his smile. I glared at him. "I thought you at least would be on my side here."

"Sorry, Cay, but I'm with Baach." Eryx laughed. "You should just, you know, talk to her."

I sighed longingly, shaking my head. "She needs this time with them. Before long, we'll be too busy to enjoy moments like this."

"And don't you think you two should figure your shit out before then?" Baach raised a red eyebrow, and I scowled back at him.

"Coming from the man who still hasn't figured his own shit out?" I countered, looking pointedly at Ilta, who would occasionally glance toward Baach, only to quickly look away.

Baach sighed, his shoulders slumping. "I'm working on it, okay? I just—I don't want to lose what we have now."

"Ilta's crazy about you, Baach. You're not going to lose your friendship with her just because you're together." Eryx rolled his eyes. "I wish Delia was half as crazy about me as Ilta is about you.

"She is." I assured him, smiling slightly, "She's just in denial."

Eryx shook his head, "Enough about us. You and Asteria need to figure this out. People are talking."

That was a significant statement coming from my spymaster.

"Talking about what?" I sat up straighter, leaning toward him with my arms resting on my knees.

"Your people want to meet her. They've heard rumors that the girl you brought back is your mate. But they've seen too little of her. They want to know about her. Have the chance to see their future queen." Eryx explained, raising a brow at me as I winced.

"It's too early for that," I insisted, shaking my head. I didn't want to overwhelm Asteria with this right now. Not when she was about to meet her mother. Not when she hadn't fully accepted the bond.

"No, it's not," Baach added, rolling his eyes. "We should be organizing an introduction of Asteria to her future subjects. Let me plan it. I'll have them come to the throne room, and you can introduce her and let them see her. We'll have a ball where she can mingle with the people, and they can see what we all see, that she's the queen we need."

"Baach's right." Eryx nodded. "We need to be getting ahead of this."

I winced again, and Eryx looked at me critically. I ran my fingers around the tattoos on my forearms, tracing the runes glowing silver against my pale skin.

"Calix," Eryx said, ducking his head to meet my eyes. "Please tell me you've told Asteria."

I shut my eyes, but Baach's laughter made me open them back up to glare at him. Eryx's mouth was hanging open in shock.

"You haven't told her about the prophecy?" Baach laughed, throwing his head back. I rolled my eyes, shushing him when his volume got too high.

The pool area was loud, and I was fairly confident our voices weren't carrying over to the girls with so many conversations happening right now, but I didn't want to risk it.

"Calix—" Eryx started, his voice slipping into that tone he used when he was working.

"I will tell her. I promise you that," I insisted, meeting his eyes as he ran a hand through his short hair. "But she's overwhelmed enough right now. Let her get through meeting her family. We'll have plenty of time when we go on our diplomatic trip up North to talk. I'll bring it up then."

I eyed Asteria across the pool as she laughed, the sparkle in her eyes, her cheeks flushed with health… so much more life in her than when she first came here.

She deserved so much better than the darkened past she had, but I would assure her future would be so light, it would be sung about for millennia.

"Calix!" Eryx rushed into my solar, looking harried with his hair a mess, the way it always was after he'd been flying in his hawk form.

Ilta blinked at him in shock from where she'd been working at her desk across the office. I stood up quickly. "What's wrong?"

"There's…" He trailed off, swallowing. "There are dozens, maybe hundreds, of humans making their way to our border from Day Kingdom."

"What?" I demanded, walking towards where he lingered in the doorway. He was in his armor, and I knew he'd been flying back from scoping out the fortress on the Etheralta Mountains before we were due to leave today to meet Aurelia there.

"They were escorted by Bellin, Arien's second. Apparently, they were rescued from Aelius's plots, and Arien sent them here for refuge," Eryx explained, a complicated look in his eyes that I understood well.

It was wonderful that more humans were being rescued and that Arien was helping in such an endeavor. But if he'd had to rescue them…

What the fuck were Aelius and Cyrus doing? Cyrus couldn't possibly be using them all for his blood magic, could he? We knew he was using some humans in Dusk Kingdom for that purpose, but if potentially hundreds were heading there from Day…

Then, this was beyond bad.

The iron weapons the blood magic could help forge would be disastrous to us. We hadn't had to deal with iron as long as I'd been alive, only the accounts I'd read from kings long past and the stories passed down like fables told us really anything about how iron could be used on Fae. Since it had been made forbidden across the realms, all knowledge of it had almost entirely faded out of existence.

And yet, I knew Asteria's human father had somehow come upon an iron knife. One he'd passed on to her. It was now kept locked up, deep beneath the palace where no one but me could reach it. Asteria had gladly handed it off, not literally—she kept her hand wrapped in a shirt to avoid contact, and I made sure it was somewhere no one would stumble upon it.

As I rushed out of the palace, I paused, thinking of Asteria. She deserved to be here for this. Not only as my future queen, but this was her fight too, and this was her brother sending them to us. To her.

"Eryx, go grab Asteria. Fill her in on the way," I informed him briskly, making my way to inform the guards. Eryx dipped his head with a smile, before taking off to find her.

It didn't take long for them to arrive, Asteria clad in her armor, which I made a real effort not to look at too closely. Now was not the time to get turned on.

"We'll fly over. It'll be good practice for you." I let her know, and she paused uncertainly. I smiled down at her, taking her chin in my hand and lifting her head to make eye contact. "You have this. I know you do. And I'll be right beside you the entire time, my réalta."

She gathered herself, visibly straightening and squaring her shoulders. I smiled wider, impressed as ever at her fortitude. I didn't think I'd handle what she was dealing with half as well as she was if the way I'd handled becoming king and my sisters' guardian proved anything.

I stepped back, shifting until glittering black and purple scales replaced skin. I huffed teasingly at Asteria, and she rolled her eyes before stepping back and shifting herself. Sparkling silver and purple scales overcame her, but those blue eyes shot through with starlight were still looking back at me.

"Looking good, Asteria!" Eryx called, a smile lighting up his face. "Though I have to say, you might be giving me a size complex!" He shifted into his hawk form, tittering as he flew up above us.

Asteria snickered, which in her dragon form came out more like a grumble. I sent my laughter through the telepathic connection we had in our animal forms.

"He's just jealous," Asteria replied, saucily. *"Though maybe it's you who should be."* She flew upward and circled until I followed her, moving to lead the way west toward the mountains. The humans were going to be skating past Caersidi to arrive at the border closest to Tairngire, just south of the mountain range. It wasn't far from us, and the guards I had rallied would be arriving without much trouble in an hour or two.

"Me? What do I have to be jealous of?" I asked her, bemused.

Her giggle echoed in my mind, and I wished it would stay there as she answered, *"I think I might be bigger than you. I don't want to make you feel inadequate."*

I snorted. She was visibly smaller than me, even in her dragon form. Dragons got larger with age, and I had four centuries on her. Only Aelius was bigger than me.

"I think you might be delusional, grá." I lowered my voice into a faux-serious tone. *"We'll have to work on that; see if you can be saved before total delirium sets in on you. It's an insidious illness."*

Her laughter was reward enough, but she sobered after a moment. *"What does that mean? Grá?"*

I froze for a moment, not having realized I'd called her that. *Fuck.* I didn't know how to answer. I was trying to give her space and time to work things out on her own. I didn't want to pressure her into being with me. And calling her *love* was implying a level of feeling that I was sure would have her running for the hills.

Or flying for them. As far away as her wings would take her.

I had been trying not to think, trying desperately hard not to, in fact, about my feelings for Asteria. I knew they were growing, quickly, in the time we had before she was taken. The fact I chose her over my supposed soulmate was all I needed to know to confirm that what I felt for her was deep and all-consuming.

But I tried not to put a word on it. Just thinking that word, *love*, opened the floodgates to a wealth of feeling I was currently trying to suppress.

But of course, I fucking loved her.

How could I not?

She was the light in my darkness, the star to my moon. Her fire matched my own, and together, I knew we could do the impossible. We would burn this world to ash and build a better one in its ruins, together.

And none of that even touched on who she was at her core. A fierce woman with a resolve and integrity that put my own to shame. Her capacity for care and kindness, even after all the horror life had thrown at her, was larger than should be possible. She so easily became part of our little family, seamlessly slotting in like she was always meant to be there. She saw and truly understood me, recognizing my pain and my faults, and she accepted them without issue, breezing past them while somehow also not minimizing my own feelings on the matter.

She saw into the dark heart of me, and she stared into the abyss without blinking.

Love was the only possible reaction to such a thing.

Forget prophecy. Forget the bond, even. That alone had my heart cracking open for her, inviting her into it and enclosing her within.

Best of all, she didn't mind the darkness she saw there. What was it she had said?

"Darkness does become me, does it not?"

She was absolutely right; the darkness became her like none other. It just allowed her to shine ever brighter against it.

But I couldn't say any of that right now, so I merely said, *"I'll tell you later."*

Hopefully, that later wouldn't be too far away.

THE LINE OF people stretching out before us was massive. How many humans had Aelius rid himself of? Didn't he use them for labor? How in Tartarus was he going to write off that many?

They all looked exhausted as we circled above them, trudging forward but slumped over. The soldiers beside them shined in their golden armor, leading them on, yet seemingly unsure of how to handle them.

They'd surely been using slaves without issue all their lives and didn't know how to take them now being freed.

We landed before my border guards, who immediately bowed, even before I finished shifting back. Asteria bounded over to me, looking worried and pissed off in equal measure. Eryx cawed before swooping down, shifting midair, and landing on his feet beside us.

I rolled my eyes, *every time*, I swear.

"Don't be jealous. I'm lighter on my feet than you," he teased as he came up beside me, trying to bury his smile as he looked out at the line of humans approaching. Asteria snickered briefly before pressing her lips inward to stop herself.

I shook my head at them and approached the guards, waving for them to rise.

"My King." Helio, the commander in charge of this border unit, greeted me. He had been stationed here for years. Having family in both Day and Night Kingdoms, my father had allowed him to take up his post here, and he'd more than proven his loyalty since then. His gratefulness for my father's decision had never wavered.

"Helio." I nodded in greeting. "This is my mate, Asteria."

The man's red eyes widened, and he immediately kneeled before her, his light blonde hair falling over his face slightly, and her own blue eyes flew open wide in response.

"Oh, that's—that's really not—" She turned those wide eyes to me in panic, and I had to bite down on my amused smile. As a human, she had stood toe-to-toe with me at our first meeting and held a knife to my throat, but she panicked over someone bowing to her.

Helio chuckled lightly before rising. "Forgive me, we've just been waiting for you for so long."

Asteria tilted her head to the side, her confusion clear. I glanced at Eryx from the corner of my eye, and sure enough, *I told you so* was written all over his face.

"What can you tell us about this?" I asked, redirecting the conversation. From the look Asteria shot me, I knew we would certainly be returning to it later. I tried not to wince.

Thankfully, Helio was much more willing to accommodate. "They began showing up in the last few hours. I met with Bellin, he's helping the stragglers along now, but it seems there's some issues in Day."

I raised a brow, well aware of that fact, but unsure of the extent or any recent changes. "How so?"

"Apparently, Aelius gave Arien orders to send a unit to Dusk. He did so, but Aelius sent another behind them. Only before this one left, they rounded up about two hundred humans from Day, most from the outskirts of Avalon, but some from other cities, brought there under cover in advance to bolster the numbers," Helio explained, a wrinkle in his brow the only indication of his discomfort.

He was currently dating a human woman, Mayrah, who lived nearby. He'd always taken his responsibility to the resistance seriously, but falling in love with a human had upped his commitment substantially.

"They tied them up and shoved them along." He growled slightly. "When the cowardly soldiers Aelius sent reached the ones who had left earlier under Arien's order, they attacked. Thankfully, Arien was flying above when it happened, and was able to turn the tide of the fight."

Asteria straightened, no doubt hearing any news of her twin brother was conflicting for her. I was sure she was anxious to know more about him, and how he responded to this situation in particular.

"What happened?" She urged Helio, who smiled slightly at her.

"He killed the attackers and, according to Bellin, ordered that Aelius couldn't know what happened to the soldiers and humans he'd sent. It would be better for them to essentially disappear. That way, he wouldn't know Arien interfered or had any knowledge of his plans."

Asteria looked disappointed at his explanation. I'm sure she'd hoped Arien felt similarly to us about human slavery, and I worried how she might react to meeting her family, knowing both actively kept slaves.

"Arien told him to free the humans and bring them here, where they'd be safe." Helio finished, and my brow creased as I thought it over.

"You told Soren about what we're doing with the humans, right?" I asked Asteria, who nodded, understanding growing on her face.

"You think he told Aurelia and Arien?" She countered, stumbling over their names just slightly, unsure how to refer to them.

"He must have. There's no way Arien would have known they'd be safe here otherwise." I thought it over and glanced at Asteria. "It's likely Soren is acting as a spy of sorts, though one used for a very specific purpose. He likely reported everything about your interaction to them."

She glared in the general direction of Day Kingdom, as if Soren might feel her glare from here. I wouldn't put it past her; her rage was beautiful and volatile—and nothing if not explosive.

CHAPTER 19

Getting all the humans into Night was quite the production. While I was proud of my mysterious brother for actually sending them somewhere they'd be safe, I was less so that it was only to cover his own ass from daddy dearest.

We were meant to be leaving today for the fortress on the Etheralta Mountains, hoping to arrive and be able to settle before my mother and brother got there, but we were going to have to push it to tomorrow. It meant we'd arrive after them, most likely, but in fairness, they were the ones who created this mess.

I was anxious to finally see the mountains made of star opal. It was a small thought at the back of my head, but it was there, nonetheless. We were a bit too far south to see the mountains from here, so I'd be waiting for tomorrow for that, too.

In the meantime, I busied myself with helping as best I could. The others had made their way out from the capital to help as well, thankfully. Harpina and I were currently working with several other hum—I stopped myself, remembering for the thousandth time I wasn't actually human—*with several humans* to help the new arrivals feel more secure in their new surroundings.

It was Fae who had enslaved them, who'd tied them up and sent them to their deaths. For I had zero doubt what was happening there. Cyrus needed humans to feed his blood magic, and his plans required a *lot* of blood.

It was Fae like Cyrus and Aelius—who was apparently helping him, that I hated. I'd come to realize the Fae were not inherently bad. I knew this in

140

theory after coming to Night, but I always sort of assumed Calix and the others were just the exception.

Even when that didn't make sense.

His whole kingdom couldn't be an exception.

And each Fae there had quickly changed with the times when Calix changed the rules.

Now, I realized the only real differences between Fae and humans were magic and lifespan. All things explained by the fact humans weren't native to this realm. They weren't meant to wield magic or live forever. They came from a place with little to no magic, most likely. But they were just like us. Just people.

It was this damned system that allowed Fae to look down on and enslave them. If we could break the system, we could fix all of this.

It wouldn't be easy, I knew. It wasn't quite that simple, not when the Fae and humans both had been indoctrinated into this belief system. They'd have to be taught new ways to live, not to mention finding a way to overcome the systemic issues between the groups. But I knew it was possible.

Calix had managed a microcosm of it in Night Kingdom, after all.

So for every human who shied away from me and my Fae features, I just worked harder to make the next feel welcome and *safe,* most of all.

Freedom was a strange thing. Even when it's wished for all your life, gaining it didn't mean the chains unlocked. Even now, I still expect to be thrown back into slavery at any moment. And I knew, should Cyrus get his way, that Fae or not, I would be.

"Asteria." I whirled around at the sound of my name.

"Lady Siria," I greeted, surprised. I hadn't seen her since I'd returned from Dusk, but I was happy to see her looking well. Her pink eyes gleamed as she stared at me, tilting her head to the side like she was examining me, her white hair falling over her shoulder.

I shifted from foot to foot awkwardly, unsure what she was doing.

"My apologies." She bowed her head with a smile. "I never once imagined I'd see a human who was actually Fae. Looking at you now, though, it makes sense. So many things about you screamed Fae, but none of us thought to look any deeper than what was on the surface." She grinned wryly, looking out over the sea of humans passing into Night. "Though, I fear that's still the case with humans as a whole. We have much work to do there."

"We do." I agreed, nodding. I gathered my long, dark hair to one side of my neck, trying to cool off a bit. Working nonstop for hours meant working up quite a sweat.

"I feel like we should have connected the dots before," Lady Siria admitted, leaving me confused.

"What do you mean?" I asked, shaking my head. She met my gaze straight on.

"I mean the visions Liv had of you. We should have connected it to the prophecy." Her explanation left much to be desired.

"What prophecy?" I pushed, a strange feeling rising deep inside. Any time prophecy was mentioned, it put me a bit on edge. The idea of our fates being out of our control was an unwelcome one as far as I was concerned. I wanted agency over my own life, not to have it dictated to me by the gods or some Oracle.

"Calix's birth prophecy," she replied blithely, apparently thinking it obvious.

"And what was that?" I pressed, needing answers now. This was the second time today alone this was brought up. There was something there I clearly needed to know, the way people kept referencing it.

She straightened then, pink eyes wide with shock. "Oh." She went abruptly quiet.

"Siria, please." I reached out and grabbed her hand, squeezing it. I couldn't take the way people kept dancing around this.

"You should really talk to him," she replied, biting her lip. I rolled my eyes at her, giving her a narrow-eyed look.

"If Calix wanted me to know, he would have told me by now!" I threw my hands up, exasperated. But Siria reached back out, grabbing my hands as she shook her head.

"No. If Calix hasn't told you, it's likely because he thinks you already have enough to deal with. I know my cousin, and he'll want to tell you this himself." Siria smiled softly, pushing a bit of hair, which had fallen in front of my face, back behind my pointed ear.

"You're so young, Asteria. *So young,* and with so much on your shoulders already." She sighed deeply. "And I fear it will only be added to as this war ramps up."

I squared my shoulders, inhaling a deep breath. "I can take it."

Her smile softened further, becoming something almost motherly. "I know you can. We all do. That doesn't mean you need to, however. You have so many people here who love you, Asteria. Who will be there to help you carry the burden."

Her words unsettled me. I knew there was a lot of pressure on me, but I'd managed to kind of push all of that to the back of my mind while I worked out everything that had happened since Cyrus had taken me.

But her words brought all of it back.

Thanks to Liviana's visions, everyone was depending on me to ensure this war would be won. I had no more idea of what I was supposed to do, or how, than I did when I was hidden as a human.

While it might be easier as a Fae, I still didn't understand how I specifically would be the *answer* to us winning.

Though, the part of the prophecy that claimed I was *the reason* made more sense now. Everything with Cyrus really jump-started all of this into motion. Calix could have slowly kept stealing into cities to free humans for centuries before it would have gotten to this point if I hadn't met Cyrus.

Maybe this was for the best, however. We could free the humans sooner and ensure they all live better lives. We could make sure the balance didn't swing too far toward chaos, saving Celesterra from destruction.

But Siria was right. Everyone saw me as the key to this, and the pressure was a weight on my chest, making it hard to breathe.

THE NEXT DAY, Calix and I flew back toward the mountains, this time heading for the fortress where I'd finally meet my real mother and twin brother.

No. My mother, the one who raised and loved me, was my *real* mother. This woman, this queen who sent me into slavery, she was just the one who birthed me.

But her letter still echoed in my ears. I knew she wanted a relationship of some sort with me. I knew she likely had a *good reason*, but reason didn't really factor into my rage as I contemplated everything that happened as a result of her choice.

"Say the word, and we'll turn around." Calix's words filtered into my head as we approached the mountains. I could just make out the shimmer of them in the distance.

His reassurance calmed me, reminding me that he was here and had my back. It was a soothing balm to my nerves. I had no idea what to expect from this meeting.

In all honesty, I'd been trying to avoid thinking too deeply about it.

I had no idea what they were like. Only a quick, kind moment at Placement Day to construct any kind of idea of them from.

I'd always wanted a brother. Someone to sneak around and cause mischief with around the village. Someone who'd protect and fight for me. Who'd tell Verin and her gaggle of girls to leave me alone as he dried the tears I'd pretend I hadn't shed.

But my mother… I'd had a mother I loved. I didn't know how to make the idea of her fit in my head. Or my heart.

My anger over what was done to me was still burning too brightly, and without an actual explanation provided for it, I could only stew in it further.

As we flew over the next hill, my fiery breath caught in my throat, smoke spilling from my maw. The mid-morning sun was shining brightly, rising over the mountains before me, lighting them up and making them absolutely *glow*.

I'd known the Etheralta Mountains were made of star opal, in theory, but seeing it…

The mountains were so different from any rock-formed mountains I'd ever seen. Magic had to be involved in this; there was no other explanation for how truly fantastical it looked. The colors within the white star opal shined brightly: green, pink, purple, yellow, and orange, the colors and shimmer seeming to reflect off the mountain and extend out in all directions in this light. The entire mountain range sparkled like a gem. For that's what it was, in truth. One gigantic, uncut gem.

No wonder Calix said they had more than enough star opal. Every inch of these mountains was worth its weight in gold. A fragment chipped off the edge could have kept my human family in riches until the end of our days in Sonmathion.

I shook my giant head, still getting used to the monstrous size of my body parts in this form, and called out to Calix, "*No wonder you never worry about money! By the Otherworld, you must be the richest person in this Tartarus damned realm.*"

Calix's chuckle reverberated in my ears, teasing, "*Does it make you feel better to know your mate can keep you in star opals for the rest of your life?*"

I giggled to myself, thinking of my reaction to getting the necklace from my parents, the one I had with me even now. I wasn't wearing it, not ready for that conversation with Calix yet, but I knew I would need it for support, if nothing else. Something from the parents who raised me as I faced meeting the one who birthed me.

"It certainly doesn't hurt." I teased back, his loud laughter a greater reward than any star opal could ever be.

We landed at the base of the mountain the fortress rested on and shifted back into our Fae forms. The mining equipment could be seen from here, but it was the huge building formed into the star opal itself that took my breath away.

"You carved the fortress out of the mountain?" I asked, turning to Calix in surprise.

He nodded seriously. "It's defensive. No one can breach it. Star opal in this form is stronger than any other material we have. However this mountain came about, it's nearly impenetrable. We have special tools formed with star opal tips just to be able to mine it. It won't break otherwise."

I blinked in surprise. What was star opal, truly? This wasn't a naturally occurring formation. A gift from the gods, maybe? "You have no idea how it came to be?"

"None." He shook his head, silvery-white hair brushing his chest, and I took a moment to look him over. Drooling over him, if I was honest. A girl had to take what she could get, and he looked absolutely mouth-watering in this attire.

He always did, in truth, but I rarely saw him in full courtly attire. Today, he'd been forced to dress for diplomatic relations. Not as over the top as the outfit he wore when holding court himself, but more so than his regular everyday clothes.

He was wearing a long, black jacket with purple dragon scales affixed to the shoulders and purple embellishments ran down the front of each side of the jacket that resembled a dragon's body. The back had two purple wings etched in jewels. Silver embroidery decorated the sleeves, from the wrist to the scales on his shoulders, done cleverly to subtly include stars and moons. Sadly, the collar of the jacket partially covered the warrior tattoo on his neck. I loved that tattoo on him.

The black shirt he wore underneath the jacket had purple buttons running down the middle that looked slightly like the claws of a dragon. It was also cut to a V at the bottom, which complimented the three purple lines going down the very start of each pant leg that formed a V at the top, with the middle being higher than the two beside it.

The outfit was topped with his sword belt, the sheath carrying his black-bladed sword, and the dragon hilt with its wings spread sitting on his hip. He'd insisted on wearing it for our arrival, not trusting Aurelia or Arien.

"My father told me once that the mountains predated the Fae," Calix stated, bringing me out of my quickly forming fantasies of stripping that jacket and shirt off him, exposing every hidden tattoo until I could lick each one. "We've all speculated, but there's unfortunately no way to know what really happened."

I shook my head to clear it as Calix looked down at me, a thoughtful look on his face. "Are you ready for this?"

I bit my lip, my eyes shooting downward. Unlike Calix, I worried less about protection and more about how I looked when I met them. I ran my hands down my dress, hoping it met their expectations. They were expecting a princess, the lost heir of Day Kingdom. And even as strange as those titles being connected to me was, I didn't want them to see me and be disappointed.

I'd decided on one of the new dresses Delia had commissioned for me. The dress was light purple, similar to Calix's eyes, and appeared to almost change color in the light, with bits of green, blue, and yellow shimmering within it. It made me kind of feel like a star opal myself, if I was honest.

The sleeves draped down in waves, and the skirt had light flowing layers. The bodice was cut off the shoulder, in the sweetheart neckline I'd grown to prefer, with small silver dragon scales coming off where it sat on each shoulder. Silver embellishments crossed diagonally across the bodice and down, looking like shooting stars.

"You look gorgeous, my réalta," Calix said quietly, grabbing my hands from where I was brushing my skirt. "They will look at you and see nothing less than a queen. I know I do."

My eyes watered as I met his, the Aurora slowly forming in his eyes, echoing the emotions I could feel from him in the bond.

"Calix—" My voice caught, cracking.

He let go of one of my hands, reaching up to brush a lock of dark hair behind my ear, trailing a finger down my cheek. "In truth, that's all I've ever seen when I've looked at you. But now, the entire world will know it too."

"I'm not queen of anything." I shook my head in denial, but he growled, pulling me bodily into him, until we were pressed together.

"You are the only queen I see. My soulmate, foretold by the gods," he rasped, and his eyes flashed as I lifted a hand to his chest, feeling his heart pounding in time with my own.

"Do you mean…" I trailed off, unsure.

"I was planning to explain later, and I will," he sighed, watching me carefully. "But what you need to know is that you're the queen Night has been waiting for. A star queen prophesied to come and bring light to my darkness."

I blinked, stunned by the thought as a wave of emotion rose in me. I didn't have time to unravel the whole story now, but I did have time for one thing.

I reached up, grabbing his head, and brought his face down to mine. We let out simultaneous moans as our lips met, a clash of passion underlined by the emotion of the moment. His hands grasped my hair and hip, holding me to him as he devoured my mouth with his own, quickly dominating the kiss as I gave in to the sheer power of him.

I could feel shadows running down my body, and knew he wanted to feel as much of me as he could. I wondered if my starlight could do something similar, and since it had already responded to my emotions and covered me in its silvery glow, I willed it to reach out and caress his skin.

His growl rumbled against my mouth as he felt my starlight streak a line down his chest, and I giggled breathily into the kiss. I could feel his pleasure like it was my own, and I let my tongue run along his fangs as my starlight slipped over the bulge in his pants, teasing him as his cock twitched against the whispered movement.

"You're killing me, my réalta," Calix groaned as I put more pressure on his cock. His shadows retaliated, slipping under my dress and teasing across my thighs, before finding my lace panties, already growing wet from his kiss. He let his shadows play around them, skirting the edges before pressing down on my covered slit.

"You haven't seen anything yet, my dorchadas." I moaned, but was surprised to taste blood in my mouth. I blinked, running my tongue across my teeth, and discovered the sharp canines I usually had now lengthened into fangs. I smirked wickedly against Calix's mouth before scraping them across his lip.

"Fuck," he groaned, gripping me tightly, his shadows becoming like bands across me, leaving me immobile and incredibly turned on. He pulled back to look at me, lilac eyes darkened into a deeper purple, the Aurora dancing through them like a storm.

He licked the blood from his lips, before zeroing in on my own lip. I could feel the blood still beading on it, and Calix looked hypnotized as he leaned in to suck my lip into his mouth, his tongue sweeping up the blood. His deep moan shook my entire body.

He forced himself back abruptly, panting. I was left out of breath myself, and weirdly jealous he'd licked away his own blood before I could. His shadows loosened and let me go, and I mourned their presence immediately.

"Calix…" I wasn't sure how to finish that thought. Things were so mixed up between us. I wasn't sure I was truly ready yet, but I also couldn't deny the pull to him. Nor my feelings for him, which I had to admit, were there, stronger than I'd admit, and quickly becoming impossible to suppress.

I knew nothing of love, not truly, but I knew whatever would come about from Calix and me together would be nothing short of cataclysmic.

"If I don't stop now, I won't be able to," he admitted, a growl rumbling deep in his chest that had me pressing my legs together to try to soothe the ache it caused. "Forgive me."

"There's nothing to forgive," I told him quietly. His eyes shot back to mine, and I decided to experiment, pushing my acceptance and desire to him. The feeling I got back in response felt like it lit me up from the inside, just as much as it lit Calix's eyes.

He started to smile, reaching a hand out for me, "Come on, we better not keep them waiting anymore."

I gulped, taking his hand and letting him lead me up the mountain. Even if I'd rather we stayed at the base, losing ourselves to each other.

It seemed like a better fate than walking up that mountain and discovering whatever fate may await me in the future.

CHAPTER 20

WALKING into the star opal fortress, Calix led me past the bowing guards with a quick greeting and brought me straight toward the meeting room he'd instructed be used for this.

Pausing outside the room, I breathed deeply, trying to get a handle on my nerves. Calix lifted our clasped hands and pressed them to his chest. It was only then I realized I was shaking as he shushed me gently.

"It's okay to be nervous, Asteria." He ducked his head down to meet my eyes. "Anyone would be in this situation. But I'm here with you, okay?" He nodded his head once, and I nodded back. "I'll be here every step of the way. You aren't alone. You will *never* be alone. Not one day for the rest of our immortal lives. This, I promise you."

A tear escaped my eye, thinking back to how alone I had been all my life.

"You and I, my réalta, we are eternal." He swore passionately, if quietly. "Where you go, I go. Forever."

My heartbeat did something complicated in my chest as I nodded again, smiling tremulously as he lifted our clasped hands, pressing a kiss to each knuckle on my hand. When my hand was free, I used it to softly caress down his cheek. "Thank you, my dorchadas."

"You ready?" He double-checked, and I gave him my permission as he reached for the door handle.

The black double doors opened into the meeting space. Inside, the walls had been covered with wood and then wallpapered in a light grey damask

149

pattern. A white table made of star opal sparkled in the middle of the room, surrounded by black upholstered chairs on all sides.

But none of that truly registered, not when they stood before me.

My mother, Aurelia, had long hair the same color as mine—so dark brown it was nearly black—and watering blue-grey eyes that were locked on me with singular focus, her hands shaking as she raised them to her mouth. Her makeup highlighted the pouty lips I'd clearly also inherited from her.

It was so strange to look at her and see so much of myself there. I remembered saying goodbye to my parents at Placement Day and lamenting that I'd never be able to look into a mirror and see them staring back at me.

She even had the same button nose I did, the same heart-shaped face. She had sharper cheekbones than I did, and a different eye color, but it was nearly uncanny otherwise.

A strangled noise caught my attention from where I stood, frozen in the entrance. Arien stepped forward haltingly, his eyes wide. He had long dark hair the same color as mine, with identical blue eyes, nose, and lips. His nose was straight as opposed to tilting up at the end. His face was longer, and his cheekbones were sharper than even our mother's.

As he approached me, I noticed he was also much taller than me. Closer to Calix's height than mine, while Aurelia looked to be of the same stature as myself. She even had my curves, or I supposed, I had hers, while Arien clearly took after our father with his height and straight, lean body.

He paused as he reached me, eyeing where my shaking hand clasped Calix's for dear life. His eyes met mine again, and he swallowed hard.

"Asteria," he rasped, almost a plea, and I swore I could nearly feel his aching desire to hug me. I let go of Calix's hand and stepped forward toward Arien. I only took one step before he swept me up in his arms, lifting me and leaving my feet swinging like a child's as he embraced me.

I let my eyes fall closed, resting my forehead on his shoulder as I hugged him back hard. It felt like something I'd lost had finally clicked back into place. That strange feeling I'd get sometimes, where I'd expect to find someone beside me, only to find them missing. Hugging Arien now, it was a feeling of completeness that was completely different somehow from the completeness offered by the bond I shared with Calix.

That feeling seemed to fully form as I let myself acknowledge that this was my *twin brother*, my little brother, and a surge of affection overcame me.

I could feel Calix's wariness, along with his own adoration, as he watched me, but his unease was clear.

"By Hyperion," Arien whispered, his voice heavy with tears. "I've missed you all my life, sister."

I couldn't prevent the sob that came from me then, the tears falling on his fancy court jacket.

"I feared I'd never get this chance," he continued raggedly. "That the time would never come, and I'd have to go my whole life without ever having my twin back beside me. As we were meant to be."

I hugged him tighter, unsure of what to even say. It was so overwhelming that I found myself completely at a loss. I pulled back to look at him, seeing tears tracking down his face. I reached up to wipe them away, smiling through my own. We both laughed slightly.

"I'm so glad we finally got the chance." I finally told him, and he cupped my cheeks, leaning forward to kiss my forehead, before stepping back.

Aurelia stepped forward then, tears streaming down her crumpled face as she sobbed, "Asteria. My darling girl."

I was still so unsure how to feel about her, but my heart wrenched seeing the obvious pain she was exuding. Arien stepped toward her, but I moved quicker, standing in front of her.

"Hi," I whispered, wringing my hands together.

"I know I have so much to explain, but—" Aurelia tried to gather herself together, "But I haven't had the chance to hold you since you were born. Could I please hug you?" Her voice cracked, and she lifted a hand to cover her mouth to try to contain her sobs.

My own face creased, trying to hold in my own, not wanting to cry further. But as I nodded and my birth mother gathered me into her arms, I couldn't stop the silent tears.

The warm feeling one got being in their mother's arms encompassed me, and I felt strangely like a child again.

"My little star," she whispered as she held me, and I froze.

"What?" I asked, pulling back to look at her. "What did you call me?"

"My little star." Aurelia smiled slightly, a bit confused. "That's why I named you Asteria. You came out of the womb shining like a star, my love."

"That's what—" I tried, but my voice cracked, forcing me to clear my throat. "That's what my moth—the woman who raised me, called me."

Aurelia nodded stiffly. "I'm not surprised. Did she give you the neck-lace as well?"

I stiffened, reaching into the pocket of my dress. "The necklace?"

She smiled, but it was strained. "I put it together when you were born. Something to keep both me, and your soulmark, with you."

Pieces fell into place, and it felt like the world that had been smashed into thousands of fragments around me when I discovered I was Fae, suddenly re-arranged themselves to fit back together, only to form something completely new this time.

"You made this?" I whispered, pulling the necklace from my pocket, letting the pendant with the moon, sun, and stars dangle from my hand.

Calix sucked in a breath in the background, but my own emotions were too riotous to figure out his right now.

She sniffed, nodding with a trembling smile, "I did. I hated having to send you away, Asteria. It broke my heart completely. I wanted nothing more than to raise you myself, but I was forced to hand you over to someone else. I couldn't just let you go, though. I needed to know there was something still there, connecting us together. The blind hope of a mother, maybe."

She scoffed slightly at herself, shaking her head, "But it was all I could think of. A piece of Day to keep with you, thanks to the silverium and the star opal, and your soulmark, to connect you back to your Fae heritage."

I looked from her to the necklace, mumbling to myself, "And to Night."

She may not have realized it, but the necklace connected me to Night just as much Day. A piece of each kingdom with me always. A piece of my mother *and* a piece of Calix.

"Why?" I demanded, looking back up at her. "*Why* did you have to send me away?"

Her face crumpled, and Arien put a hand on her shoulder. The bolt of resentment I felt at the clearly close relationship they shared, something I was cut out of, surprised me. But as Calix came up behind me, putting a hand on my lower back, I let it ebb away for now.

Aurelia watched Calix as he supported me, and narrowed her eyes, but merely said, "Let's take a seat. I can explain everything to you."

Chapter 21

Aurelia

Twenty-one years ago

My husband thought this was silly.

I thought he was an arrogant ass.

I had been willing enough to marry him quickly when our soulmarks were discovered to match. Finding my mate and becoming queen was like a dream come true. I was now elevated beyond almost all others. Only the other kings and queens of Celesterra would equal me. And only Night Kingdom truly matched the power of Day, ever in balance as the two kingdoms are.

And yet… it didn't feel like that was true at all. Aelius was not a man to share power, I had discovered. I may be queen, but I felt just as powerless as I did before. I wanted to be involved in running the kingdom, to attend councils and help shape this world and its future.

Instead, I was told to sit back and produce an heir.

I refused to take this lying down.

No, never again would I allow myself to be forced into *"my place"* by a man.

I had grown up as a lady, but my mother was a princess of Dawn by birth. She'd been married off to one of her own father's lords, while her brother ultimately ascended the throne after my grandfather. Mother had been kept away from court in Affaraon thanks to her duties to my father's house, and so had I as a result.

I was the daughter of royalty, but hardly considered royal myself when so many others had higher places in line for the throne.

I thought becoming a queen would mean getting out from under the Bathala's rule and finally grasping power of my own.

I refused to sit back and let it be taken from me once more. Refused to let my husband dominate me the way he clearly expected.

Fortunately, my upbringing would come in quite handy now.

I knew how to play the game of court politics, thanks to my mother. She'd spent years teaching me so I wouldn't be vulnerable no matter where I ended up. I'd taken to her lessons well and had already begun the slow work of turning courtiers and other useful people to my side.

I knew it would take years to grasp the kind of power I desired. Working in the shadows naturally lent itself to secrets and schemes, and it was never quick. But it would certainly be worth it.

I may be Queen of Day, but the shadows the sun cast would be the tool that truly saw me grasping power.

As would my child.

I touched my stomach with a smile. An heir, raised by their mother to side with her over their father, would secure everything neatly for me. Aelius couldn't be bothered to help raise our children. He'd already made that *more* than clear. So I would take advantage of his arrogance and ignorance, and take the opportunity to make his court my own.

For now, however, we had to abide by the traditions of Celesterra. With us expecting our first child, we were due to meet the Oracle and receive the prophecy that would define our heir's life.

My own parents had told me the birth prophecy they received for me many years ago. Luckily, it had given me a hint of my own child's glorious future as well. The Oracle had told my parents that the heir I birthed would change the world. The memory of it was enough to put a smile on my face.

Yes, I would raise an extraordinary child. One who would change everything for the better.

I walked with Aelius into the cavern the Oracle called home, one hand tucked into his velvet-covered elbow, while my other laid on my stomach to steady it. The fog was so thick in here that I couldn't even see my feet anymore. Which was certainly troublesome while trying to navigate the uneven ground of the cavern with a rounded belly.

A foreign sense of confidence washed over me as we walked. It felt almost as if I was being called forward. Even as Aelius sneered and complained about meaningless traditions and old crones spitting nonsense, I nodded absently, my focus completely consumed with the sight before me.

The Oracle.

She was sitting on a cushion on the ground. There were two plush cushions in front of her, obviously meant for us. While I'd normally be concerned about getting down and back up with my sizeable stomach, I felt that same peaceful surety flow through my whole body, taking the worry away.

What was this? It felt otherworldly, most assuredly. And the Oracle did not have that kind of power as far as I was aware.

We sat down across from her, Aelius grumbling quietly as he assisted me in lowering to the cushion. But it was somehow as easy as doing so without my pregnant belly. Looking into the silver eyes of the crone, I was taken aback.

Those eyes, they were... *knowing.*

As if she could see directly into my mind and soul, and was taking every secret piece of me apart for her own amusement. Or her own gain. Whichever it was, it made me glare slightly at the old woman. But she just smirked back at me before she looked at my husband.

"The first child of Day Kingdom's King Aelius and Queen Aurelia comes." She intoned heavily, voice creaking like old wood. "It is now time to hear the gods' message for their future."

The crone looked back and forth between us as she pulled out items I hadn't noticed sitting beside her. A silver bowl, inlaid with all sorts of runes, and a matching silver knife, similarly covered.

The Oracle held out her hand. "A blood offering to the gods, to receive their gift."

Aelius held out his hand with a belabored sigh, and the oracle quickly sliced his palm, holding it over the bowl and letting the blood drip into it.

Then she turned to me. I held out my hand, nervous for only a moment before surety and peace overcame me once more. It truly felt like the gods were with me. Blessing me with confidence for what's to come.

I wasn't sure if I should feel pleased to be graced with the touch of the gods or exceedingly nervous about why the gods felt I needed it...

I winced slightly as the silver blade cut my palm. Thankfully, all Fae healed quickly, and my palm was as good as new just moments after the last drop of blood hit the bowl.

I watched the Oracle toss in a mysterious pink sand and mix it with the blood. She picked up a long pipe, pulling a drag of it before exhaling it into the bowl. As the smoke hit the now pinkish-red sand, it seemed to come to life. The sand danced playfully within the bowl, twirling around the smoke.

My eyes widened at the bizarre sight. I'd seen so many different types of magic in my life, but this was one I'd never witnessed before. It had to be exclusive to the Oracles. So much about them was kept secret. We didn't even know what they *were*, really. The Oracles weren't Fae, as they certainly aged somehow. One look at her wrinkly skin proved as much. What she was, was a mystery.

Not Fae. Not human. Just an Oracle.

A creature of the gods. Passing their messages along to their faithful.

The old woman picked up the bowl and began inhaling the concoction contained within. As she did, her silver eyes seemed to ignite. I flinched, even as a peaceful feeling swept through me. The Oracle's eyes bored into mine, but it was silver fire that looked back at me. Silver fire that soon churned into silver ice. Back and forth it went, fire and ice dancing in a loop within her strange silver orbs.

The Oracle opened her mouth then, and began to speak the words that would change my life forever.

"When the world tips to chaos, the star-blessed heir will rise.
Marked by three:
The sun, the moon, and the stars.
Three hearts to own:
Three tries to find, light and dark in balance.
Three to fight: corruption, greed, and pride.
Three to win: freedom, balance, and love.
The star must be eclipsed.
The light must hide, or all will be lost.
When the darkness claims the light, it will begin,
A new reign of light and dark to see the world saved.
When the fire falls, and the world turns to darkness,
A star will rise to light the world anew.
Until they are fully balanced, the scales will tip,
chaos unleashed, until the final coup."

Silence followed the heavy words, until Aelius snorted, "Nonsense, as I said. Let's go."

His snappish voice made me shudder as I fought the urge to claw his stupidly perfect face. Sometimes, I wondered how this man was my mate. It felt more like we were enemies at times, constantly battling one another for ground in our relationship.

The crone's knowing gaze met mine. "Sometimes, balance comes in forms unexpected."

I shivered, unsettled that the Oracle knew my thoughts. Telepathy? Or something else? Body language, maybe? Perhaps the gods still speaking through her?

Aelius looked at me and sighed, his face softening. We may battle for power, but the passion between us did make for often explosive times together in the aftermath. There *was* genuine affection there, even if it was often buried beneath other matters. We were mates, after all. It allowed for no less, really. And looking at him now, I could see he was thinking the same.

Maybe being his mate did make sense. We both wanted power and control. We just went about it in different ways. And we both loved one another, despite how challenging we found engaging with each other outside of the bedroom. But that did make it thrilling. I just worried that, in the long term, the struggle between us of love versus power would prove detrimental.

Aelius seemed to understand I wasn't quite done with the Oracle and sighed. "I'll meet you outside, my queen."

His soft tone brought a smile to my face, and he caressed my cheek before leaving me to it.

That was more like it.

Once he was outside, I looked at the crone.

I didn't know what had urged me to stay here… *alone.*

No, that was a lie. I did know. It was this damned sensation that kept pressing on me.

"You feel the hand of the gods, Queen Aurelia. They have a message not for your king's ears," the Oracle rasped out. I struggled to sit up straighter with my belly in the way.

"Not for Aelius to hear?" I asked, shaking my head in confusion. "Why ever not?"

As far as I knew, the Oracle always gave her prophecy to both parents. And there was never a second message mentioned. Let alone one that was only meant for one parent's ears.

"Because you carry twins within you, Queen Aurelia. And Aelius cannot know. You must pretend to birth only one child." The Oracle held up a hand, stopping the many questions on the tip of my tongue.

"Of your two children, you know only one can be heir to Day Kingdom, and that heir must be hidden from Aelius at all costs. He will kill the child should he find out about them when they are young and defenseless." The Oracle informed me, leaving me in stunned disbelief.

Dread grew within my heart. Why would my husband kill our heir? Our *child*? *My* child! My arms wrapped around my stomach protectively on instinct.

I would not brook any threat to my child—children.

By Tala, twins!

"How do you suggest hiding an entire child, *the gods chosen heir*, no less, from my husband?" I demanded urgently. "He will likely notice me raising two children! And he will certainly notice if I produce only one child, and it isn't the heir. I don't understand. Why would he be any threat in the first place? He wants children, *especially* an heir! It's all he's talked about since we first got betrothed!"

The Oracle's knowing silver eyes grew sad, matching her tone as she continued. "You will see. He would try to make the gods choose another, but that cannot happen. Your heir is too important to the world. Without them, we face a fate worse than you can understand."

I shook my head, thoroughly confused—not to mention *terrified*.

"You must use this when the time comes," she demanded, shoving a piece of paper into my hand. "You now know as much as the gods can impart without threatening the future of this child. We *cannot* risk them. As a mother, you will seek to protect them above all else. I trust in that. As do the gods."

The feeling of peace I had been experiencing intermittently, thanks to the gods' influence, suddenly evaporated, and what felt like pure chaos overtook me. A riot of destructive power that I struggled against feebly.

"This is what is happening to our realm." The Oracle's words reached me through the haze of chaos I was trapped within.

The feeling stopped abruptly, and peace returned, filling me up like a harmonious song as the chaos was banished. I sighed, relieved to be free of the chaotic deluge they'd buried me under.

"*This* is what your heir will bring," the Oracle insisted. "Do you see their importance? The gods cannot allow the schemes of those in power to take away the only chance this realm has."

The sensation lessoned, slowly, until all I felt were my own natural emotions. I looked up from my knees to ask the crone more questions, but jolted as I discovered that she was gone.

I looked around the cavern, but she was truly nowhere to be found.

And I was left. Alone. With the ominous threats against my child and the knowledge that the gods needed them to fix whatever was wrong with our realm that was tipping it toward chaos.

I gulped, holding my stomach tightly.

"I love you, my children. And I swear to you now," I clutched the paper the oracle had given me tightly, then slid it into my dress so no one would see it. "I will let no one harm you. *Ever*. Even if I have to kill my own mate to ensure it."

"Ahhhhh!!!"

I screamed once more, pushing at the urging of the midwife, while my most trusted lady, Odelina, who'd come with me from Chryse when I left to marry Aelius, bravely held my hand while I squeezed it until her bones creaked.

"One more, my Queen! Push!" the midwife called, and my face crumpled as I let out a deafening scream, pushing with all my remaining strength.

The agonizing pressure finally stopped, and I collapsed back onto the bed. The wailing cry that filled the room had me looking up desperately, wanting to see my firstborn.

The first thing I saw was the telltale glow indicating the gods' chosen heir, and my breath caught. The next thing I saw was that, aside from the glow around him, he was shining brightly. Silver starlight emanated from him, confusing and alarming me thoroughly. Our heir should have inherited the power of sunlight.

I was already worried enough about what would have to happen next. The confirmation of his status as heir alone was enough to make me want to weep. I couldn't handle yet another thing to worry over.

"Let me hold him," I demanded, struggling to sit up.

"You still have another child to deliver, Aurelia." Odelina reminded me gently, using a cloth to wipe the sweat from my forehead.

"I think there's time. Just for a moment." I reassured her, squeezing her hand quickly. I turned to the midwife, blinking when I noticed she was standing, holding my babe and staring down at him with a shocked expression.

"Give him to me. Let me hold my heir." I demanded again, though my voice cracking didn't help. Only Odelina knew what was going to happen, there was no way for the midwife to understand my desperation to hold him.

But the midwife only looked up at me with wide eyes, stammering, "It's—it's—"

"What?" I snapped, my exhaustion and the physical pain still humming through me, on top of the emotional pain of birthing my child only to have to part with them immediately. I didn't have time to deal with this woman's stammering nonsense.

"It's a girl," she finally whispered, watching me with huge eyes as what she said finally hit me.

"What?" I barely got the word past the lump in my throat. "But—but I saw the glow. The gods chose them as heir."

I looked up at Odelina, who looked back at me, nodding slowly, confirming I hadn't imagined it. "They did, Aurelia. Your daughter is the heir."

"No woman has ever been chosen before," the midwife said, staring down at my daughter with wonder.

"Give her to me. Now," I told the woman, who looked up quickly and flushed before moving to hand her over to me.

She placed the wriggling girl in my arms, her fists batting outward as I shushed her, rocking her slightly. Tears came to my eyes as she opened hers, and wide blue eyes stared back at me.

Aelius's eyes. As blue as the sky itself.

Aelius, her *father*, who would kill her according to the Oracle. I knew Aelius's wish for a male heir. He was traditional, believing women were unsuited for power—thus keeping even his queen out of council sessions. No wonder the gods feared his reaction.

Why a woman? Why now? They said she was important, but why did she have to be a girl? Just to make things more difficult for her? It seemed so unfair. Now, she would have to be raised far from the mother who loved her.

But my little girl just giggled up at me, completely unaware of what was to come. The spell the Oracle gave me had one intent: to hide her from any who would dare look for her. I watched the wisps of starlight emanating from her.

So different from any heir of Day before her. In so many ways.

I didn't know what this power meant. Asteria had clearly blessed her, instead of Hyperion. I had no idea why or what would come of it, but the gods clearly had their reasons, and they weren't for me to guess.

Pain hit me then, and I realized the other child was coming. I quickly handed my baby girl to Odelina, who took her carefully. I nearly sobbed when I saw her back for the first time.

There, in the middle of her tiny upper back, was a soulmark. The rays of the sun expanded from the top of an upside-down crescent moon, while stars dangled underneath it. Another thing she would lose with what would happen next. I mourned for the future, for what could never be.

All thanks to Aelius.

I let my anger fuel me, and with a scream, I pushed. When the little boy was put into my arms, I smiled down at him—just as the gods had clearly smiled down on me.

I would be forced to give up my daughter, but the time would come for her to return. And until then, they'd provided me with a warrior, one who would help me prepare for his sister's coming.

I moved him into the crook of one arm and took my little girl with the other. Basking in this single moment where I could have both here, safe in my arms.

"Aurelia," Odelina fretted, and I nodded, a sob fighting past my lips. Aelius would come for an update on his son, *his heir*, all too soon. She couldn't still be here.

"Asteria. Her name will be Asteria." A hush met my declaration. I looked up to Odelina, who looked uneasy.

"Are you sure that's a good idea? The gods could take offense," she asked, but I shook my head.

"Asteria has blessed her, and she will look out for her where I will be unable to," I assured her confidently.

"What do you mean, my Queen?" the midwife asked, and I looked at my trusted lady, who nodded solemnly.

In a flash, the midwife fell dead to the floor. An unsavory business, but better a quick death than her telling Aelius anything.

Odelina wiped the blood from her knife before returning it to her skirts. "I'll have those loyal to us remove the body quickly."

She popped outside, likely to grab the guards belonging to my cousin. Without Beltane, I would be lost here in the capital. He was one of the very few aware of the truth. And he would be ready when the time came. In the meantime, he would help my son where he could.

Aelius would be furious that he wasn't the heir. But he was a prince, nonetheless. He would have to fight harder to prove himself, but I would raise him to understand why and what the stakes were.

"Arien." I smiled at my little boy. "You will be Asteria's warrior. She will wear the crown, but you will be her blade."

Odelina came back in, and sure enough, Beltane and several of his most trusted entered the room. His men went to remove the body while he made his way over to me.

"Odelina filled me in," he informed me softly. "A female heir?" I nodded in confirmation, and he whistled lowly. "Things are certainly changing."

"They are." I agreed, a smile growing. "But it must be a necessary change. The gods were *very* clear."

He nodded in understanding and smiled down at my babes. Asteria giggled at him while Arien just batted him away before reaching his hand out toward Asteria. Their eyes locked on one another, and Asteria reached out until their little hands touched. Tears filled my eyes, and I wanted nothing more than to take them both and run in that moment.

"Aurelia, I should get her out of here while we still can," Odelina interjected quietly.

I closed my eyes, biting my lip to contain my sobs as reality set in. I forced myself to nod. "Hold them for me for a moment?"

Beltane quickly grabbed Asteria, looking more emotional than I expected. "Let me at least say goodbye."

A tear leaked out against my will, and I smiled sadly while Odelina took Arien for me.

"Can you bring me my jewelry box?" I asked her, and she nodded, confused, but shifted Arien into one arm as she went to grab it.

Once she brought it back, I quickly searched through my necklaces, finding silverium and star opal pieces I could use. I grabbed them and, using my magic, reformed them into something new. It wouldn't fit her now, but when she was grown, she would have a piece of me, of her home and family, along with the soulmate she'd be kept from.

"Here, make sure the family you're taking her to gives her this when she's old enough to wear it," I instructed, handing the finished piece to Odelina, who agreed solemnly.

I took Asteria back from a teary-eyed Beltane, holding her to me as my stray tears fell onto her baby-soft cheeks.

"This is not the last time you'll see me, my little star," I told her, sniffing back my tears so I could get through this. The pain inside threatened to rip me apart. I wanted nothing more than to keep her with me. To raise her to be the amazing woman I knew she'd become. To have the opportunity to keep her safe and happy myself. But instead, I was forced to hand my daughter to strangers.

I'd have to trust them, *humans at that*, to raise her right. To keep her *safe*. I nearly scoffed. They couldn't keep *themselves* safe; how could they be trusted to keep my precious little girl from harm?

It was impossible to just hand her over and hope for the best. But the gods had made it clear that I was to make the impossible happen.

I would have to ensure she was protected somehow.

Resentment for Aelius rose fiercely within me. This was all *his* fault. My daughter being taken from me was a direct result of the threat he presented to her life.

"We will see one another again, I know that in my heart," I promised, choking back tears. "Know your mother loves you more than anything, and that she will be fighting for you every moment we're apart. You will come home to an army and court ready to see you in your rightful place. *I swear it.*"

A hand landed on my shoulder, and I looked up to meet my cousin's eyes. He nodded, and my face crumpled as I handed Asteria to Odelina, giving a parting kiss on her forehead, "I love you, my little star."

As Odelina escaped out of the hidden door leading to the planned escape route, I collapsed into heaving sobs.

CHAPTER 22

Asteria

I SAT in stunned silence as my mother finished explaining what had happened leading up to my birth.

"What happened after that?" Calix questioned her. "How did she get from being spirited away by your lady to having her magic locked away and wearing a human facade?"

I looked at him gratefully. My mind was going in a thousand directions, and I was trying not to cry as my mother explained the agonizing experience of sending her baby away.

"That ties back to the Oracle," Aurelia responded quietly. "She had handed me a spell, and upon looking into it, we knew it would suppress anything magical about Asteria. Making her, in effect, human. The gods made it clear she must be hidden, and that she would have a great destiny to fulfill one day. I had faith that she would eventually break the spell, even if I had no idea how."

She smiled at me, and I struggled to figure out how to feel about that, but there was another question that still needed answering. "How did I end up with my parents?"

At Aurelia's wince, I hastily added, "The ones who raised me."

"They were chosen in advance." Aurelia sighed, rubbing a delicate hand over her eyes. "We needed people who lived as far from Day as possible. If we tried to hide you within the kingdom, people could potentially make the connection. Out of sight, out of mind was much better for your safety. So

164

Odelina searched for human families in Sunrise and Sunset. The couple she found was unable to have children."

I sucked in a sharp breath, remembering how my mother referred to me as their miracle. They'd given up hope of having a child of their own until I was born. My heart broke for them, knowing it never truly happened.

"I knew they would care for you as best a human could." Aurelia sniffled, looking miserable for a moment, before she pulled herself back together. "I just wanted you to be as safe and happy as possible."

She paused, closing her eyes momentarily. "Even if it wasn't with me."

I let out a breath, collapsing back into my chair. Calix's hand found mine and squeezed. I clung to it, thankful once more for his support.

"We've been preparing in the meantime." Arien began, looking at me intently. "We knew when you did return to us, we'd have to move quickly, as Father would likely also find out." Aurelia nodded decisively in agreement.

"I began the work early, turning those in the court I could to our side," she informed us, making my eyebrows rise, but before I could open my mouth, she continued. "Arien is your General." She looked fondly at my brother, who straightened slightly. "He's been preparing all his life to lead your armies when the time came."

"Lead my armies?" I echoed, stupefied.

Arien nodded slightly. "Of course. War is inevitable. Day will be torn down the middle, and we'll have to fight to take over the kingdom and install you as queen."

"This is much larger than just Day Kingdom," Calix rumbled from beside me, glaring at him. "Cyrus is allied with Aelius, and he will stop at nothing to get Asteria back."

"That will not happen," Arien growled. "We will protect her."

"I will protect *myself*," I interjected firmly before the two males, who both saw me as theirs in some way, could come to blows. "But Calix is right. The balance of Celesterra is at stake. Cyrus is using blood magic and killing humans to fuel it. He has to be stopped. And I will not stop until all of the humans throughout Celesterra are free."

Aurelia scoffed, looking at me in a way that caused a flush of anger to run through me, like I was a child that didn't know any better. "That will never happen, my love. I know you probably feel some sort of kinship with the humans, but—"

"Kinship?" I snarled, leaning my hands on the table and rising from my chair. Aurelia leaned back, looking like I'd slapped her. "I *was* human. All my life."

Aurelia opened her mouth, but I continued before she could. "And don't you dare say I wasn't ever human. In all the ways that matter, I was. I was raised human, completely powerless. I was a *slave*. Forced into submission to Fae masters who controlled my life. I was used, forced into acts I would never have consented to, made to watch as innocents were brutally killed. I lived with rage over my circumstances all my life, dreaming of one day escaping to freedom. I will not allow other humans to keep experiencing that misery."

Dead silence followed my statement, but I could feel Calix's pride as I sat back down.

"We've only planned for a war within Day, but it sounds like you have much greater plans," Arien said calmly, his eyes carrying a trace of pride themselves. I smiled slightly at him, and he returned it while Aurelia sat up straighter in her chair.

"Yes, Calix, please," my birth mother drawled. "I'm dying to hear about this scheme of yours."

I narrowed my eyes at her. She seemed so different at this moment. A haughty Fae queen as opposed to the loving and devastated mother. Which was the real her? I didn't know her well enough to say, and it made me wary.

Calix's frustration burned within me, and I reached over to lay a hand on his thigh, letting him know I was with him.

"We have been working to free humans for years, taking them out of the worst kingdoms when we could," he explained, watching Arien closely. "We were careful not to upset the balance. We knew the corrupt leaders in those kingdoms were hurting the balance badly enough as it was. Now, with Cyrus escalating, we are working to gain additional allies."

"We're planning to go to Sunrise after this. We have an invitation to talk with them and hopefully convince them to side with us against Dusk." I told them, and Arien's brow rose before they creased, a contemplative look crossing his face.

"What about Sunset? Dawn?" He looked between Calix and me, and Calix nodded for me to continue.

"Sunset hasn't answered yet, but Dawn is firmly aligned with Dusk. Cyrus and Zerlina are betrothed. She will do anything to be queen, even take his abuse." I sighed sadly, remembering the look in her eyes. She might be an uppity bitch, but she didn't deserve that fate.

"So that leaves us with the split in Day to contend with." Arien mused, and it was Calix's turn to raise a brow.

"You intend to let Asteria actually rule? Take control of the armies of Day and join Night in the fight against Dusk? Despite the fact your own father is allied with Cyrus?" Calix taunted, and Arien growled, leaning toward him.

"Of course we mean for her to rule! That's what all of this has been for. If she wants to take those on our side to fight Cyrus and my father, though, we first need to gain control of the armies of Day," Arien insisted. "About half the nobles will support her as long as my father rules, which means we only have half an army."

"If half the nobles will side with Aelius, then it's important we still find outside allies." I broke the staring contest between them as I spoke up. "Calix and I have to continue on to Sunrise, and once we get back…" I trailed off, looking to Calix, who gave me a look that let me know it was my decision to tell them or not. I bit my lip, thinking on it.

"What?" Arien asked softly, and I sighed, deciding that it was better if we were all on the same page.

"The gods want to speak to us," I told him, and his eyes went wide.

"What are you talking about?" Aurelia asked, her sharp brow rising.

"My sister is a seer," Calix told her, and the other brow rose. "We've kept her ability a secret from any outside Night, so I'd appreciate it if you kept that between us."

Arien nodded once, and I looked at Aurelia, pointedly. She rolled her eyes. "Fine."

"She got a message from the gods that once I had control of my power, Calix and I needed to journey to the city of the gods to meet with them," I informed them both.

"Why? And why both of you?" Arien looked between us, his brows creased.

"I'm not sure, honestly." I shook my head. "As for them requesting both of us, I can only assume it's because we're mates, right?" I looked to Calix.

"It's likely." Calix nodded slowly. "They have plans for you, and the prophecy Aurelia shared, it seemed to indicate that whatever happens, we'll be doing it together." He grabbed my hand then, smirking, and making me bite my lip in response to the bolt of arousal that shot through me. "Not that I'd ever allow for anything less."

"Well, you'll have to get used to it." Aurelia countered, and my head whipped to her, frowning.

"What do you mean?" I asked her, confused.

"Asteria," She softened her voice. "You will be queen of Day. Calix is king of Night. You have separate kingdoms to rule."

My heart dropped along with my mouth. I hadn't considered...

I turned to look at Calix, who placed a hand on my cheek. "We will not be separated, my réalta. I swear it."

"How?" I asked him, desperately. "If we have to rule two different kingdoms..." I trailed off, swallowing hard.

"Duty often means doing that which we dread, daughter," Aurelia said, and all I could do was shake my head.

"Fuck your *duty*. She's my *mate*." Calix growled, his hands coming around my waist as he held me to him. "The gods have brought us together for a *reason*. This won't tear us apart."

Aurelia laughed slightly, a scoff underlining it. "Soulmates are overrated. Look at me and Aelius. I know this only ends one way—with his death. I am willing to sacrifice my own mate for the sake of my daughter."

"That's different." Calix snarled, and I looked up at him, tears lining my eyes. For all that, I hadn't felt ready for what the mate bond meant. I'd been slowly coming to terms with it. And now, with the threat of having to separate from him... everything within me rebelled at the thought. I clutched at him like the world might take him away if I didn't.

While Calix went back and forth with my mother, I quickly came to the realization that I didn't want to live a life without Calix. He had become *everything* to me.

He was one of my best friends. He'd given me all the tools I needed to feel safe and to take agency of myself. He stepped back when I needed him to, and stepped forward when I wanted the opposite. He was my shelter in this chaotic world, making me feel safer in his arms than anywhere else.

He'd helped me bring my magic out and flew with me through the skies. He'd danced with me on the ballroom floor as much as the training ring. He made me laugh even at times when I didn't think it was possible.

And I still remembered the Festival of Faunus, the feeling of us *finally* coming together. It had felt *right* in a way nothing else ever had.

Looking up at him now, the Aurora dancing through his eyes like a siren song calling to me, I knew I wouldn't be able to take any kind of separation from him.

But what about Day Kingdom?

They'd been waiting on me for years, preparing for me to take the throne. My mother and brother worked tirelessly to ensure I could come in and take power.

My heart was tearing in two. There was no other way to explain it.

"Calix..." I trailed off, unsure how to continue. He shook his head at whatever my mother had just said before turning back to me. He softened immediately, running his fingers down my cheek.

"It's late," he said quietly. "Let's get some rest. We can reconvene tomorrow and sort out plans for moving forward."

"Of course." Arien rushed to say as our mother opened her mouth. Aurelia glared at him, but Arien just walked toward me.

"Asteria." He dropped to one knee, bowing his head. "I swear myself to you, the one true queen of Day, from this day, until my last day. I will be your sword and your shield. I will stay in your service as long as you will have me. This I promise you, my Queen."

Emotion clogged my throat, and I struggled to form words. "Rise, brother."

He looked up, slowly rising, and I gave him a teary smile. Unsure if there was a formal way to do this, I just went with what felt right. "I accept your service. From this day, until your last. But beyond being my sword and my shield, I wish you to be my brother first and foremost."

Tears formed in his own eyes, and he nodded his head heavily. "Of course, sister."

I threw my arms around him, and I spied my mother watching. A slight smile lit her face, though she looked uncertain.

I was just as uncertain when it came to her. I wasn't sure where we stood, or where we might stand one day. But I knew, deep inside, that my twin would at least always be there, whatever may come.

CHAPTER 23

Calix

I WAS fuming as I led Asteria back to the royal apartments so we could talk. The nerve of Aurelia to try to tear Asteria and me apart made my blood boil, and I was near spoiling for a fight. Arien had seemed genuine in his desire to support his sister. But Aurelia wanted to put her on a throne as a figurehead, even if she wouldn't admit it.

Aurelia had been building power within Day, ostensibly for Asteria, but she also expected Asteria to come to them with no real idea of how to rule. Aurelia had expected to run the show, as she clearly did with Arien. She'd raised him to be her soldier. Similarly, she wanted Asteria to be her key to power.

I didn't doubt she loved her, but I knew it would be a battle of wills between them. I was so glad Asteria had stood up for herself and what she believed in, and I could see the pride Arien felt when she did so as well.

She was meant to be a queen. Of Day or Night, or some mixture of both, I didn't know. The prophecy given at my birth clearly tied into the one given at her own. The gods made it clear we were meant to face this together.

Aurelia could fuck off with that separation bullshit, as far as I was concerned.

I opened the door and led Asteria in, watching as she took in the living space around us. The walls had been covered with dusky purple wallpaper, with star opal left around windowsills and doorways for a touch of sparkle. There were several halls leading off the main room to where the numerous bedrooms were, enough of them to fit the entire royal family at its largest.

A gigantic fireplace dominated the space, with a large black dragon head in the middle, its eyes and teeth sparkling with star opal. Its arms came out at each corner, and its claws gripped the edges of the fireplace. Its tail snaked down to the bottom to create a separation between the black wooden floorboards and the fireplace itself.

Two plush tufted black sofas sat vertically before it, and two grey armchairs completed the seating arrangement. A star opal coffee table sat between the two sofas, and a white rug ran underneath the seating arrangement.

Asteria took it all in as I paced the room. She watched me with a frown, and I could see her thoughts working behind her eyes.

She eventually rolled her eyes and began poking around the room. I watched her with amusement, still trying to get my anger under control.

"Where's your room?" she asked suddenly, and I raised my brow at her.

"It's this way." I pointed down one of the halls to where the king's room was located. I'd stayed in one of the other rooms before my father died. When he did, I was then expected to use the king's room whenever I visited. It still left me slightly discomforted.

I'd had to do the same in the palace, moving into my parents' rooms. It was something that always happened when an heir became king. My father had moved in when his own had died, but it was still so strange after all these years.

My palace's steward had informed me that my father had rearranged the rooms when he took them over, trying to make them his own and less like his late father's room. My grandmother had still been alive, making it even more awkward for him. She was expected to move out of the bedroom she had shared with her late husband to let her son move in. She'd done so with no complaint, but it never failed to be incredibly strange to me.

I'd redone my rooms immediately, even mourning that I was getting rid of the aspects that reminded me of my mother and father. At least here at the fortress, there was less emotion attached to the spaces.

Asteria immediately took off down the hall, and I followed after her, fighting a smile despite my mood. When we came to it, she breezed right through the door, and I had the image of her doing the same to my bedroom at home.

I bit my lip, thinking of her storming in and crawling into my bed, waking me up in the middle of the night, while her hands slowly peeled my covers away. Having those same hands trail across my skin, leaving sparks across every muscle as she teased me. Until she made it down to my cock, where she'd take me in her mouth—

Fuck, now was definitely not the time.

Asteria looked around, touching various objects around the room. It had been decorated in black and purple, the royal colors. Like the fireplace in the front room, a prominent black dragon made up the headboard of the giant bed, with the feet of each post made to look like our taloned feet. Deep purple silk sheets covered the bed, adding a splash of color.

Asteria turned to me, and I noticed then that she was shaking slightly.

"Asteria? What's wrong?" I questioned, stepping closer as my brow furrowed.

She laughed wryly, throwing her hands up in the air. "What's not wrong right now, Calix?"

I cocked my head to the side, my own fury moving aside for worry as I felt the flurry of emotions coming from her.

"We're at war with a deranged lunatic who thinks I belong to him." She began ticking off items on her fingers. "My own father wants me dead. I'm still trying to figure out my magic and being Fae, yet I'm supposed to be queen of an entire kingdom! And now…"

She trailed off, her strong posture slumping slightly and her voice quieting as she continued, "And now I realize that they'll all expect us to do our *duty*." She spat the word like a curse. "For you to rule Night, and me to rule Day, while they force us to forget entirely about the mate bond connecting us."

She stepped forward, closing the distance between us, and I nearly trembled as I awaited whatever she might say next. After over four hundred years of waiting, my mate was here before me, and I knew she was about to change my life in some fundamental way.

This could be the end of us, over before we even really had a chance to begin—or it could be the start of something new and wonderful. The rest of my life expanded out before me, and for a breathless moment, I felt like I might fall into the void of the future. Of a devastating reality where I was forced to live without my mate, or a fantastical reality I almost never believed would come, Asteria sitting on the throne of Night, a star queen to outshine all others.

I waited, hoping and praying to all the gods that she wouldn't want to follow the duty her mother had laid before her. I may not know the way forward, but I knew I only desired to go forward at all with her.

Without her, my life would be empty. Dull and bleak, without any reason to continue.

"But you were right. *Fuck duty,*" she spat passionately, and my heart beat double time within *her* chest.

"Do you—" I looked frantically into her eyes, and she smiled slowly.

"I've only just now gained my freedom, and I refuse to live my life according to other's expectations ever again." Her eyes lit with starlight, the beautiful sparkling silver invading the blue skies in her eyes.

I could feel my shadows responding to my overwhelming emotions. Dragons were emotional by nature, and while I'd mostly mastered control, Asteria managed to destroy it every time.

Her own starlight swirled out to meet my shadows, encasing us in a miniature night sky in my bedroom.

"When she told me we'd have to separate, I realized I didn't want any kind of future without you, my dorchadas," she said softly, and I swore my entire body trembled in relief.

"I just don't know—I don't know how we do this, Calix." Her voice shook as much as I did.

"I swear to you, we *will* figure out a way," I promised, cupping her cheeks gently. "I will never allow anyone to separate us. For the greater good or not, I don't give a fuck. *You're mine.*" I growled, hands moving so my thumbs brushed the apples of her cheeks, while my other fingers moved under her hair, grasping at the back of her neck.

Her eyes narrowed, the fire stirring within her. "And you're *mine.*"
She'd get no argument from me.

My lips crashed down onto hers, unable to stop myself after those beautiful words I had feared I'd never hear from her lips. Her claim lit a fuse inside me that had me handling her more roughly than I intended, but if her moans were anything to go by, she clearly didn't mind.

"Calix." I pulled back from her lips mournfully and looked back at her. Her pupils were dilated, and her lips kiss bitten, making my cock grow even harder. The smell of her arousal was definitely not helping matters either.

"Promise me this is what you actually want," she pleaded, and I cocked my head, confused. I'd thought it incredibly obvious.

"Asteria—" I started, but she shook her head.

"Promise me this isn't just the mate bond." Her eyes widened, and I could feel the disbelief stirring in her that it could possibly be anything else. The little girl within that was cast aside, unable to believe she was enough on her own.

"I already told you, I chose *you*, Asteria," I rumbled, the power of my feelings for her enough to make fire rise in my throat. "Even if we weren't soulmates, I would still choose you. It was impossible not to fall in love with you."

She took a sharp breath, the word landing between us for the first time. The beating of her heart was a calming lullaby, even as it sped up. It kept my lips moving, even as I battled down fear at her potential response. But the words couldn't be held back any longer.

"Loving you was always inevitable, my réalta. You are perfect for me. Your fire, your dedication, your love, your playfulness, your acceptance. I was on a crash course to loving you from the moment you put that knife to my throat. The bond only confirmed what I already knew. That in any life, you will always be mine."

"You love me," she stated. Not a question, but I nodded anyway. Her eyes shone with tears, and a part of me panicked. Until I felt for the bond.

The feeling coming from it nearly bowled me over. I knew I was unloading a lot on her, and that before this, she hadn't been ready for what an immortal bond meant.

But now…

Asteria

HE loved me.

Me.

Soren had said he loved me once, as we said our goodbyes. I was well aware even then that he didn't truly love me. He might have thought he did, but he'd never really *known* me. How could he, when I had never opened myself up to him? To anyone?

Calix was the first.

He'd come into my life like a cataclysm, destroying everything that was there before… but making room for something new in the process.

He was a dragon, after all. Destruction was his forte.

My new life was shaped around him in many ways, but he was careful to ensure it wasn't only centered on him. I had friends who were practically family, a purpose, freedom, and so much more.

But through it all was Calix.

He was the moon of my life, in the center of my sky, lighting it up any time he was around.

I'd been fighting to *not* feel for so long, that opening myself to the wild torrent of emotions I felt for him was more frightening than anything else I'd faced. But I couldn't live my life in chains anymore. Not now, when I was finally free. And what was life without fully experiencing everything it had to offer?

Holding myself back from him was just another chain, keeping me in the slave mentality that nothing was truly mine.

But *he* was mine.

And I was tired of fighting it.

So what if I was scared? I'd been scared before and pushed forward anyway. It was time to face my fears. To embrace the future I knew I wanted. I would let no one and nothing stand in my way.

Even if I honestly did fear what the future holds for us. The war terrified me. How we'd manage the future of two kingdoms frightened me.

But we'd figure all of that out later.

For now, I let my walls crumble, and let Calix feel the breadth of love I felt for him. A wave of it releasing from where I'd kept it locked up deep inside.

I watched him sway, his eyes wide as he watched me wildly.

"I'm not sure I even really knew what love was before," I told him, laughing slightly. "But what you feel for me? It lights up my entire chest. You may be the darkness, Calix, but you're what makes me truly shine."

I tried to say the words, to vocalize what I felt, but they caught in my throat. Fear didn't disappear all at once, I supposed. I'd let my walls down and let him feel the truth. Maybe that was as much exposure as I could take today. Because no matter what I did, I feared letting the words pass my lips. As if he'd be torn away from me immediately should I dare.

But he could feel that too.

So when he reached for me once more, I threw myself into his arms. My lips finding his and latching on. I kissed him with everything I had. All the passion within me pouring out into him. He reached down and grabbed the back of my legs, and I jumped up to help him, wrapping my legs around his waist as his tongue swept confidently into my mouth.

Fuck, I'd missed this.

I'd tried not to dwell on my lack of sex, what with all the insane changes in my life. But being around Calix, day after day, with no relief but my hand under the covers at night, had been agony.

I desperately grasped for him, my hands finding purchase in that long, silvery-white hair I loved so much. His hands palmed my ass as I ground myself against him. I felt suddenly frantic, like the universe was conspiring to rip him away from me, and I had to hold on tighter to prevent him from going.

I'd never had anything good in my life. The life of a slave was meant to be shit by design, and nothing and no one was ever truly yours. Getting to have something that was, was more frightening than I'd anticipated.

So I threw myself toward my fate, daring the world to try to take it from me.

I growled as Calix's lips left mine, but moaned as he began kissing down my neck. I clutched him to me with one hand, while the other went to his shoulder, my nails digging in.

"My dorchadas…" I panted, my need for him was rising ever higher while my blood felt like it was on literal fire.

He nipped my neck then, and I could practically feel his smirk against my skin. I yelped when I was suddenly flat on the massive bed, my legs still locked around his waist. Calix began kissing down my chest before he gripped the neckline of my gown and pulled it down. The slight lace keeping my breasts covered was easily ripped away, and the growl Calix let out at the sight of them had me bucking into him.

He leaned down and captured a nipple in his mouth, while his other hand gripped my unoccupied breast.

"Fuck," I hissed as he scraped my nipple with his teeth, just as he pinched the other. The dual sensations went right to my clit, and I ground against him to get some friction. His chuckle was dark as his hips suddenly forced my lower body down to the bed. I could feel his cock straining against his pants, making me more desperate, but he made it clear this was his show as he held me down.

My whine of frustration got him moving, but I whimpered when he abandoned my breasts. I quickly got on board when he pulled my dress down, lowering it as he moved down my body, lifting off me only to finish ripping it down my legs until it pooled on the floor.

I was left in nothing but a tiny bit of lace covering my cunt that was already soaked through while he stood there fully clothed.

I couldn't bring myself to care much about that once Calix fell to his knees, wrenching my legs apart and throwing them over his shoulders. His mouth quickly found that patch of lace that covered me and licked a line up it, wetting it further until it was basically see-through.

His eyes locked with mine, and the Aurora within seemed more chaotic than usual as he ripped the lace away, leaving me bare to him should he look down. And look, he did. His eyes drank me in like he'd been parched in the desert for days, and he'd finally found water.

He dove down, his mouth finding my cunt with unerring accuracy. I moaned at the touch of his tongue on my clit and reached out to grab his hair as I bucked my hips up into his mouth.

He ate me like a man possessed. I'd only had two men ever do this before, and he blew Soren and Vissy both out of the water. He knew exactly what drove me insane, and he went about proving it.

His tongue traced the seam of my cunt, up and down, before circling my clit once more. He ramped me up, let me cool a bit, then ramped me up once more. Finally, his tongue entered me fully, and I cried out his name when his thumb found my clit, driving me over the edge as starlight exploded out of me, lighting up the room.

"Perfection," Calix growled as he stood, wiping his mouth of my arousal before sucking it off his fingers. I nearly blushed at the sight, but I was too consumed by the view as his shirt fell to the floor, exposing tattoos I wanted to be more intimately familiar with.

His pants dropped, and I licked my lips as his cock bobbed upward proudly. I pushed up off the bed with Fae speed, meeting his mouth in a messy kiss as we crashed together. Hands were flying all over the place, trying to frantically feel every inch of each other.

One moment, I was on my knees at the edge of the bed with Calix standing before me, and the next, he was seated on the bed with my legs straddling him. I could feel his claws emerging where they now gripped my hip, and the tiny pinpricks only added to the intensity of the moment. I decided to experiment, letting my own claws extend and scraping lightly down his shoulder. His groan let me know how much he appreciated it as he devoured my mouth.

His length pressed against my cunt, and I shifted my hips to get more friction, and gasped into his mouth when I managed to notch the head of his thick cock at my entrance. His claws gripped me as his mouth left mine, and I pulled back to look at him. I blinked, surprised by the expanse of starlight and darkness surrounding us. It looked like we existed outside of reality. As if we were back in my dream space, the darkness billowing around the room, highlighted by my sparkling starlight.

His forehead fell against mine as he groaned, "My réalta."

I giggled, lifting myself off him slightly. His claws stopped me from moving further away, and I smirked as I sank back down a few inches on his cock, only to pull back up quickly in a deliberate tease.

"You're killing me, grá," he panted, his eyes completely swamped with color. His sharp canines had lengthened into full fangs, and he scraped them against my neck, drawing a bead of blood to the surface.

I found myself jealous, and I moved to attack his neck. Not quite positive what I was doing, I let instinct take over. Sure enough, fangs broke the pale column of his throat the tiniest bit, and I licked away the blood that beaded up.

I moaned at the taste, sure that blood wasn't supposed to taste this good, but I had apparently driven Calix far enough with my teasing, and he gripped my hips hard before pulling me down on his cock—*completely* down.

I screamed out in a mix of pleasure and pain. He was so big, and there was no way the fast intrusion would be completely painless. But I still enjoyed every second of it as I stretched out around him, adjusting to the length and girth I'd only experienced once before. Absolutely loving the feel of him as he made room for himself inside me, claiming me for his own.

I found myself laying flat on my back suddenly, with a feral beast looming above me. Calix looked wild, silvery-white hair mussed, eyes darkened, and fangs lengthened as he snarled and drove himself deep inside me.

His restraint had snapped, and I felt a flush of pleasure that I had been the one to make it happen.

His hands gripped my thighs and pulled them out to the side, watching as his cock split me open. I gave myself over to him, and the pleasure consumed my senses as he filled me again and again. My moans were uncontrollable as I clenched down on his cock, trying to keep him inside when he pulled back.

Every time he thrust inside, I could hear the lewd noise from my arousal, but I couldn't bring myself to be embarrassed by how insanely wet he'd made me. He was mine, after all. And who could blame a girl when Calix was the one between their thighs?

My hands reached up for his shoulders as he thrust in, and I swore I saw my stomach bulge with the impression of his cock for a moment before he pulled back. I let my claws dig into his shoulders, and he growled down at me—so I dug in harder.

He gave a punishing thrust, and I screamed out as he hit that spot inside that made stars explode behind my closed eyes. His own claws scraped over the sensitive skin of my inner thighs but never punctured. He was careful to never hurt me, only taking me as far as he knew I was comfortable with.

In a flurry of movement, I found myself positioned before the wall with the bed now firmly behind me. Calix pushed both of my hands to the wall before pressing down on my back. "Arch your back for me, Asteria."

I shivered as his voice rumbled in my ear, and then arched my back, my ass sticking out.

"Like this, my dorchadas?" I whispered, biting my lip and looking back at him. A hard slap landed on my ass, making me jump slightly.

"Just like that," he purred, before palming both of my asscheeks.

He lined himself back up at my entrance and pushed in slowly, letting me feel every inch stretching me back out. I groaned, my head falling forward between my arms.

"Calix..." I whined, only for another smack to shake my ass.

"Patience," he growled. "Do you have any idea how hard it's been to keep my hands to myself? To be with you day after day, knowing I can't touch you?"

"Yes," I hissed back, having fought that same battle despite it being my choice. The hypocrisy wasn't lost on me.

He chuckled darkly. "Torture of your own design."

I groaned and refusing to admit defeat, I pushed myself back on him, sinking down further on his cock, earning myself another slap on the ass paired with a warning hiss.

"I have waited so long for you," he murmured, an undercurrent of wonder in his tone that made me pause. Finding out I was Fae and had a mate all at once meant I never really stopped to appreciate how incredible such a thing was for the Fae. Mates were so rare in our world. Calix had been the only Fae I'd ever met who had a soulmark before my transformation.

To have waited over four hundred years for a mark... I could only imagine how getting one must feel after all that time. Let alone finally having your mate in the flesh.

"Twenty-one years hidden away from me," he growled, caressing my spine and making me shiver, his cock slowly inching further into me, making me feel every centimeter of him claiming me. "Years of dreams where I was buried in darkness and dreaming of starlight. A light in my darkness that kept hope alive. That you were out there. That I would break through that barrier one day and finally *touch* you."

I suddenly understood, in a way I hadn't comprehended before. After all those years before his mark appeared, he finally received his soulmark only to then spend years being tortured by dreams. While I'd remained ignorant until

I was closer to him physically, likely a result of the spell that buried my magic, Calix had always known I was there. He'd spent those years reaching across the vast distance for me. Reaching for the light and finding only more darkness.

So I ceased my teasing, and let him take control once more. He sensed my surrender, and the soft kiss to my neck was reward enough, but the sudden thrust of his cock, filling me up completely, was a wonderful surprise.

"Calix," I moaned as he ground against me, circling his hips until I was sure I was going to break apart from the sheer *size* of him. But then I felt something caress my clit, making me twitch in pleasure.

His hands were both occupied; one was currently gripping my hip, while the other had drifted to the back of my neck, holding me in place.

His shadows had come out to play.

"Do you like that, my réalta?" Calix asked, his voice deep and thick from arousal, practically a growl, but not quite. He was trying to suppress the dragon inside him. That wouldn't do. I quite liked that side of him.

"I love it, my dorchadas," I told him honestly, but I also wanted to push him further. He might be dominant at the moment, but I still had all the *true* control, and I knew it. I could push his restraint and make the wild dragon lurking inside let loose completely.

"Good girl." He gave a sharp thrust, making me moan his name. My reward this time was his shadows multiplying. One still caressed my clit in a constant tease, while the others slithered up to my breasts, fully encasing them as I felt my nipples get tugged delightfully.

"Tell me, Asteria." Calix began, groaning as I clenched down around his cock, my arousal dripping down my thighs from where we were joined. "What do you want?"

I groaned pitifully. "You know what I want."

A sharp slap left my asscheek stinging, and I pushed into him.

"No." He tutted. "I'm not talking about *this*." He thrust in hard, and I couldn't contain the scream that left my mouth. "What do you *want*? Your mother wants you to rule Day. I want you to join me on Night's throne."

My breath caught in my throat. It was the first time he'd explicitly said that, and the knowledge that he wanted me to *share* his throne... it had more arousal gushing from me as I struggled to control my wild need for him.

"But what do *you* want, my réalta?" Calix asked heavily. He paused, ceasing any movement, leaving his thick cock in place and stretching me lewdly. But I could feel how much my answer meant to him, so I forced myself to think through the veil of arousal and need so I could truly contemplate my answer.

It was easier than I expected it to be.

"I want it all," I told him confidently. "I will take Day's throne, and I will join you on Night's, just as you will join me on Day's."

"Such a thing has never been done," Calix responded softly, hesitantly. "The balance…"

"There's never been a queen with starlight magic either." I insisted. "I'm something new, Calix. If the gods set all of this up, if they made us mates *and* me the heir, then I have to believe there's a reason for it. The old system is broken and corrupt. Maybe it's time we forge a new one."

"My réalta." His head fell onto my back, and his arms came around me, squeezing me tightly for a moment. I reached a hand down to squeeze his arm.

"Don't worry, my dorchadas, I'll guide you to the light," I told him, partially playful, partially sincere.

I felt his pleasure at my response, and then I felt my own pleasure as his shadows suddenly snuck up inside me, joining his cock as he began thrusting fiercely in and out.

I thrust back into him as he rode me at incredible speed. Faster than I thought possible. Fae strength gave me the ability to take it where my human body would have crumbled.

He brought me to the edge, and I prepared for the ecstasy to come, only to scream in frustration instead of pleasure as he swiftly pulled his cock out, and his shadows ceased any movement.

I opened my mouth to complain when he dragged me up and turned me around, his mouth taking mine and preventing any words from forming.

He grabbed my thighs and lifted me before I knew what happened, and I found my legs back around his waist. His mouth dragged away from mine with a growl, and I saw how long his fangs had grown. Not to mention how wild his eyes had become.

He thrust into me again without warning, and I somehow managed to scream and moan at the same time. The feel of him filling me felt brand new, even just from changing position. I loved that I could now see him in action, watching as his cock split me open, seeing instead of just hearing his skin slapping against mine.

I anchored my arms around his shoulders, my claws coming out unconsciously. When they pricked his skin, he snarled, and I giggled in response, lifting my head up to lick his fang, swirling my tongue around it.

He slammed me bodily against the wall. The moan that ripped out of me was uncontrollable as he slammed into my cunt with so much force that his entire body rocked against me. He gripped my hair, yanking my head to the side, and his mouth immediately found my neck.

He licked down the column of my throat as his cock slid in and out of me. Following his tongue, his fangs scraped down the delicate skin, but he still managed to surprise me with his next move.

His sharp fangs penetrated my throat, sinking into my flesh as my blood spilled. I growled, the noise slowly turning into a moan, the pleasure so intense in a way I barely understood.

I only knew I needed to reciprocate.

I bent my head to his neck and sank my fangs into him. Pure sex filled my mouth. Decadent chocolate, fruity cherry, and citrusy lime. He tasted like all my favorite flavors combined, but also just so purely *Calix*, like night and fire incarnate. I wanted to drown in it forever.

Calix's head lifted from my neck, his tongue licking the blood away from the quickly healing fang marks.

"*Starlight*," he murmured, wonder wrapping around each syllable. I retracted my fangs from his neck, licking away the blood so as not to waste a precious drop.

I looked up to his bloody mouth, and found his own eyes, so full of color in this moment, were just as focused on mine. We met in a clash of lips and teeth and tongues, my legs squeezing to bring him closer as his hands gripped me and did the same.

We couldn't get close enough. I wanted to crawl inside him and never leave. Or have him never leave from inside me. Any inch of space between us was too much.

This was my *mate*.

He was mine, and I was his. *Forever*.

"No one will ever tear us apart," I promised him when our mouths finally parted to gulp down a breath.

"*Never*," he growled viciously, making me shiver in delight. "I will kill any who try. I will rip them apart, put them back together, and rip them apart again. I will torture their minds and bodies with the pain of Tartarus until they become nothing more than a drooling, mindless shell. There will be no mercy. We will destroy any who come for us."

He thrust into me, and his shadows tweaked my clit in a way that had me spiraling immediately. I somehow maintained just enough presence of mind to finish my thought.

"We will." I agreed, nodding frantically. "We will bring the kingdoms to their knees. And we will build our new world in their ashes."

His mouth slammed back into mine, and my cunt clenched down on his cock hard, fluttering wildly as my orgasm rapidly approached.

"My réalta," he panted, "You will light this whole world on fire. Cleanse it of the sins of its past and bathe it in a new light. *Yours.*"

I came at that moment, an explosion of pleasure and magic and rapid, violent feeling. Calix followed along right behind me, the sensation of him spilling into me and extending my orgasm out further. I bellowed into the night, letting the whole world know exactly who had driven me to the point of insanity as starlight and darkness kept us cocooned in a cloud of magic.

Perfectly balanced.

CHAPTER 25

"Just don't push her." I reminded my mother, sitting in the same meeting room we'd met my sister in yesterday. We were waiting for her and Calix to arrive so we could plan our next steps, but I was worried about my mother and sister clashing again.

"She needs to understand—" Mother began, but I cut her off with a glare.

"She does understand, but she also has other concerns," I told her firmly. "You can't expect her to have no will of her own, Mother. She's your daughter, after all."

She glared at me, slapping me on the arm, but I just shrugged casually. "It's true. You both have strong personalities and slightly different goals."

"She needs to take the throne of Day, Arien." Mother insisted quietly. "We've worked so hard to ensure things would be ready, and now she wants to blow it off for a *man*."

"You thinking that just proves that you don't know me at all," Asteria said, walking into the room.

I sighed dejectedly, closing my eyes briefly. I should have known it was a lost cause.

"I *will* take the throne of Day." Asteria continued, and my eyes widened slightly at the resolve in her voice. "But we're doing this on my terms. Not yours. Not anyone else's but mine. I've had enough of Fae controlling my life." I winced at the reminder, the one part of my mother's plan I'd raged against the most: sending my sister into slavery.

"I will never let another control my fate again. Understand?" Asteria raised a brow, and Mother nodded slowly.

Only because I knew my mother so well was I able to detect the conflicting emotions she was feeling. Pain, at not knowing her daughter. Anger, at having to give up control. But mostly pride that her daughter was already proving that she was the queen we needed.

"Very well." Mother conceded quietly. "And I apologize if my words offended you. That was never my intention. I just worry about the fate of Day Kingdom, and according to Arien's report, we think..."

She trailed off, looking to me, and I took over.

"Aelius knows about you. Likely thanks to Cyrus. Making this more complicated than we'd hoped." I informed her. "We had been aiming for the element of surprise at first."

Asteria nodded slowly, and I noticed Calix kept quiet, but close. He let her take control of the situation, but was by her side should he be needed. I hated to admit it, hated even thinking about my sister with *anyone*, but it seemed like she could have done a lot worse for a mate.

"Since he's clearly aligned himself with Cyrus, it makes sense. And we all know this will come to war. With what Cyrus is doing, we have no choice but to stop him, or the balance will be destroyed forever," Asteria said, clearly thinking over the situation at hand.

"How many lords in Day will follow me?" she asked after a moment of silence.

"About half," I replied. "The others are too far up Aelius's ass."

"It's a little less than half." Mother countered, side-eyeing me reproachfully.

I sighed loudly, shaking my head with rising dread. "It's half."

She turned a stern glare on me, all queenly offense. "What are you talking about?"

Asteria sat back, hiding a smile as her brow rose. I nearly rolled my eyes. She'd been lucky at least to avoid *this* all her life.

"Ergun is with us," I admitted reluctantly. "His one condition was no one but me knew until it was time to tell Asteria."

"Arien!" Mother snapped, her eyes wide. "How am I supposed to properly plan when you keep secrets of this magnitude!"

"Did you want him as an ally for Asteria?" I asked plainly, unwilling to let her roll over me on this one.

"Of course I do! That's why I repeatedly attempted to bring him to our side!" she said, exasperated. "A wasted effort, apparently." Mother glared at me, making me sigh loudly.

"This was the only way to secure his support. I chose to do what would help Asteria, even if your pride was hurt in the process," I told her softly, trying to curb the sting of my words.

She huffed, offense in every line of her body, before turning to Asteria instead. I let myself roll my eyes once hers were off me.

"Can we begin pulling in their forces?" Asteria interjected, looking to Calix. "If we can combine them with Night, that would give us the best chance. We need to defend both borders while we're trying to sway Sunrise."

Calix nodded slowly, fingers playing with a pen on the table like he itched to move pieces on a map. I could certainly relate. "We will plan to evaluate when we return. It's likely that Cyrus is planning an attack, and I'm working on getting more intel from my spies, but in the meantime, we should reach out to those who support you in Day. We'll need to see which kingdom takes priority to deploy our forces to first: Dusk or Day."

I nodded, thinking that their plan was pretty solid. More allies would give us a better chance of success, and if Cyrus and Father hadn't moved yet, it gave us a bit of time before a full-scale attack became necessary.

"I'll summon those loyal to you, my Queen." I bowed my head to Asteria. "I will mobilize our forces and plan to rendezvous at the border with Night that's closest to Tairngire. Ergun is the nearest lord anyway."

"He's a good friend of mine, as well." Calix spoke up again, "I'll send him a message."

I blinked in surprise, not having expected that. I raised a brow at him. "Didn't you close the borders? How have you maintained a friendship with him?"

Calix smirked, his eyes twinkling. "Ergun's so close to the border, he's practically part of Night."

I rolled my eyes at him, a begrudging smile twitching onto my face while Asteria snickered.

"And what do we do about Aelius and his forces? They will try to stop us at some point." Mother cut in, looking surprisingly fidgety.

"We can hold him off until they return from Sunrise," I reassured her, determined to do my part.

"Then we have a plan." Asteria clapped her hands together, a smile on her face. "And just to make this abundantly clear, you need to free all of your slaves."

Mother rocked back in her seat, more gobsmacked than I'd ever seen her. I blinked slowly, processing the news. It wasn't unexpected really, not with all we'd discussed previously. Not to mention her own experience with the practice. But I hadn't allowed myself to really consider it before now.

It was unbelievable, in truth.

We'd always had slaves. What would we do without them?

"We can't just *free* our slaves," Mother argued, leaning forward toward Asteria.

"You can, and you will." Asteria raised a brow at her, her face surprisingly severe. "You named me your queen, did you not? This is my order. Go home. Free your slaves. Free all the slaves of Day. Send out notices, tell your commanders. I don't care. Just make it happen."

Mother's mouth opened and closed, no sound coming from her, she was so flabbergasted.

"What do we do then? Not only will we be without significant labor, resources, and frankly, any idea how to continue running our castles and economy, but the humans would also be without any way to provide for themselves." I pressed, not wanting to see Day implode from this choice.

Asteria's first act as queen couldn't destroy her kingdom.

I wouldn't allow it. Not for the kingdom's sake, even, but for hers.

I wanted her to succeed and for the kingdom to thrive under her leadership.

I told her as much, and watched as her eyes watered. She looked so torn, and she turned to Calix with a helpless look on her face. Agony filled her eyes, and I realized then I truly had no idea what she had experienced. How being a slave had molded and shaped her. How it might have almost destroyed her. The look she gave her mate told me there was a depth of hurt there that couldn't be easily fixed.

A crown can't cure trauma.

Calix reached out and placed one hand on her leg and the other cupped her cheek. I almost wanted to look away. The moment felt too intimate to witness.

"You know it took me many years to abolish slavery in Night," he said softly, stroking her cheek. "I know you want to free them now, but Arien's right."

I was shocked, to say the least; I thought the brash and brutal warrior king who'd locked down his borders and began attacking kingdoms just to apparently free human slaves wouldn't have the forethought to consider such matters.

Maybe I'd underestimated him.

Maybe we all had.

"We need to do this slowly and carefully. That's how we accomplished it successfully in Night." Calix dipped his head, meeting Asteria's eyes as she ducked her own head, pain crossing her face that was so stark it was hard to look at.

"I can't just leave them there," she pleaded, and Calix bumped his forehead to hers.

"We won't." He swore. "We won't leave *any* of them. I swear to you, we won't stop until every last slave is free. But we have to set them up for success."

"Because they won't have any way to survive without help." Asteria sighed miserably, sagging against him. "They'll need guidance. A way to live. All of it."

"Exactly," he murmured back, but before anything else could be said between them, Mother just had to say her piece.

"You truly expect to free all the slaves across Celesterra, Asteria?" She began, and my sister's head whipped over to her with narrowed eyes. "How do you expect us to live? They do... everything."

"Yes, they do," Asteria hissed back. "And what do they get for it?"

Mother scoffed, "I understand, truly I do, that you feel some sort of connection to the humans after being forced to live as one but—"

"There is no but!" Asteria yelled, slamming her hand down on the table as smoke began rolling out of her mouth.

Mother sat back in her seat, wide-eyed, while Calix stood, putting a hand on Asteria's back while shooting daggers at Mother. I could only cringe, resigned to watching the inevitable unfold.

"You sent me away, suppressed my magic, and all but slapped chains on me yourself! Gift-wrapped for the Fae!" Asteria snapped, her claws extending rapidly and digging into the table. I realized with a burst of surprise that her claws were silver and purple, not gold and purple.

What in the Otherworld?

"I—" Mother tried, only to be bowled over.

"I was raised *as* a human, *by* humans! I lived my entire life enraged by our treatment at the hands of the Fae. I *hated* all Fae with a burning passion because I just wanted the ability to control my own life!" she screamed, a distinct rasp from the smoke rising from her throat tinging her words. I'd never seen Mother so shocked in my entire life.

"I had nothing and no one that was mine. My parents loved me, but because the Fae worked them to the bone, they barely had time for me. I spent years alone, miserable, dreading Placement Day when I'd get put to work. And when I finally went—Oh!" She threw her hands up in the air.

"I got stuck with a psycho prince who wanted nothing less than my body because, to him, I *belonged* to him. He owned me, and I had no autonomy. I couldn't even pick my own clothes! Or wear my hair naturally because he preferred it curled! He manipulated me; he used me. He would have gotten his way and had me wholly had Calix not shown up just in time."

"And you know what?" she growled, long fang shining in her mouth as her hands slammed back on the table, leaving gouges with her claws. "Every. Single. Human. In. Celesterra. Is dealing with the exact same thing. If not *worse*. Being whipped bloody and beaten. Killed to prove a point. Drained for their blood. Their lives belong wholly to *you*," she snarled, resentment pouring from her.

"And I will not allow it to continue. The humans will be free if I have to light this whole continent on fire." A lick of fire billowed out of her mouth, and Mother stood quickly, her chair falling back in her rush to avoid the pillar of flame.

"This is happening with or without your support, Aurelia," Calix chimed in, rubbing Asteria's shoulders to try to calm her rage. It was never easy with dragons. I suppose we were all lucky Mother wasn't also a dragon. Her cobalt and white-furred fox form didn't bleed into her Fae form as much as it did with us dragons.

"Maybe, for your daughter's sake, you should consider what means more to you. Having slaves to wait on you hand and foot, or your daughter herself," he continued, and as conflicted as I was about the issue, that he would stand up for my sister in such a way had a flare of approval rising in me.

The silence in the room was deafening.

Asteria scoffed, turning from the room. Calix went to follow, but I ran after her first.

"Asteria!" I called, and she turned in a fury, only to calm slightly when she saw it was me.

"I'm sorry about her," I told her sincerely. "She means well, truly, but she's had control for so long, I think she's struggling to adjust to what it actually means for her fully grown adult daughter, who she doesn't truly know, to come in and take over."

Asteria raised a brow, but I continued. "It's no excuse, and I'll talk to her."

Asteria sighed deeply. "I don't know what I imagined meeting my mother to be like, but…"

She trailed off, and I smiled weakly. "I imagine this must all be incredibly strange for you."

She barked a laugh. "You have no idea."

"I know tensions are high, but we both love you," I told her quietly. "I hope you know that, at least. We've waited so long for you. My entire life has been preparing nonstop for the day you finally came home. It's amazing to just have you in front of me."

She softened at my words, or maybe my sincerity, possibly both. "Was that fair to you?"

Her murmured question took me off guard. I shook my head. "What do you mean?"

"By the Otherworld. You spent your whole life, just, what? Preparing to be my General? Did you not get to choose what you wanted to do?" she asked, clearly conflicted.

My mouth opened and closed, not sure what to say. I hadn't ever considered anything else. This was the path Mother set before me. And, of course, I'd do anything for my twin sister.

"I never had any choices, Arien." Asteria smiled sadly, clearly understanding. "But I'm free now, and able to make whatever choices I desire. I want the same for you."

"I'm not enslaved," I said, confused, shaking my head.

She reached a hand out and cupped my cheek. "You don't have to be a slave to be stuck in a cage."

I struggled for words for a moment. I was a bit choked up to my mortification. I was a General for Hyperion's sake. "It's an honor to be your General, Asteria. However it happened, I like what I do, and I love *you*. This is what I want."

She studied me for a moment before nodding decisively. "Well then." She smirked. "Best get to work."

CHAPTER 26

I RECLINED on my throne, crown firmly placed on my head, and looked out on the Fae in front of me. Those in the throne room were quiet, a change to the court since my father passed and I took power.

With his death, and more importantly, my ascension, things were finally able to improve around here.

Weylin was sent to the far border with Sunset, to prove his loyalty to his new king from the bottom up. Serving as a soldier in my army until I felt sufficiently satisfied. Or until the war broke out. Then, I'd send him where the fighting was thickest. Hopefully, he'll find himself cut down soon enough, getting rid of one of my obstacles.

Daneiris was another to watch, but I couldn't exactly send her out to serve in the army. So, along with the rest of my siblings, she was under strict surveillance. Curfews were established for each of them, and not one of them went anywhere without my knowing.

Zerlina was spending too much time with Daneiris for my liking, though the spy I had placed on her assured me that nothing disloyal was occurring, I still kept her close. She was my key to Dawn, after all.

Another significant difference was that I no longer had to hide what I was doing with blood magic—at least, not within my borders. A certain

192

percentage of humans in each area were now required to be sacrificed to the cause. Calculated by the population density of each lord's city and outlying villages.

Each human was sent to one of a number of camps spread across Dusk. There, they were bloodletted and bottled. Each bottle of blood was then sent back to me to complete the process. I trusted no others with the spell required to make it actual blood *magic* and not a worthless cup of human blood.

A benefit to my plans coming to light within the court was its members becoming much more manageable. They seemed to be scheming much less, which was a miracle on its own. No one dared cross me now, and it brought me significant pleasure to know they all recognized my superior power.

I did what my father had never managed, finally getting all of Dusk to shut up and do what they were told. Backstabbing and plots were rampant during Astraeus's reign.

None would dare with mine.

I was currently waiting on Aelius, who should be strolling through the doors any moment. The humans he'd promised me had never shown up, and instead of guards loyal to me, I received ones loyal to *Prince Arien.*

We would certainly be having words.

Now that I was king, he could no longer disrespect me as he had before. We were on equal footing. Even if I was clearly the superior. He couldn't even manage to get his house in order after hundreds of years as king.

After a good ten minutes of impatiently tapping the arms of my winged throne, watching members of my court shift nervously, the doors finally opened.

"Presenting King Aelius of House Earendel, King of Day Kingdom, Lord of Avalon, The Sun Dragon." The herald announced dramatically, making me roll my eyes.

The man sauntered in, his personal guards and most loyal lords behind him. His blonde hair hit his shoulders and blended into the golden armor I doubted had ever seen battle. The purple dragon in the middle of his family's sigil was the only spot of color in all the gold.

He'd be all too obvious of a target on the battlefield. A sun dragon, indeed. More like a brightly lit fool with an arrow pointing straight at him.

"*King* Cyrus, I hear it is now," Aelius greeted, that smug air of superiority that I detested ever present.

"Indeed it is," I replied dryly, nodding my head once. I leaned forward slightly on my throne, enjoying the opportunity to look down on him. "So please explain to me, king to king, ally to ally, where in the Otherworld the humans and soldiers you promised me are?"

Aelius's brow creased, a wrinkle forming on his forehead. "They aren't here?"

"No," I growled, temper fraying. "Would I be asking if they were?"

Aelius looked deep in thought for a moment, "They aren't in Day. Which can only mean foul play was involved."

"So one of your people betrayed you, is what you're saying?" I pushed, getting frustrated.

"Who's to say really?" Aelius said casually, smiling slightly, with a shrug of his shoulders. "Maybe one of your people did."

"They didn't," I ground out, aggravated. "The only ones who knew about this were your people."

When Aelius just shrugged his shoulder again, I ground my teeth back and forth. Just looking at him made me itch with the desire to kill him. His smugness aside, the bits of Asteria I could pick out made me furious. She should be here, at my feet, where she belongs. Not off gallivanting with Calix.

I took a subtle breath, reminding myself of why I must do this. All would be made right by the end, and I'd ensure his daughter would be all that remained of him.

I stood from my throne, enjoying the way heads bowed around the room. The few humans in the room practically cowered back, bringing a small smile to my lips. Now, *that* was the proper order of things.

"Walk with me, Aelius," I commanded, and the raised golden brow I got in response had me fixing him with a look that made it clear it wasn't a suggestion.

His eyes narrowed, looking me over critically, before his head dipped in a single nod, and he fell in beside me as I walked through the doors of the throne room into the hall.

"You know who did this, don't you?" I asked, keeping my eyes straight ahead. The too-casual replies were more suspicious than anything, and I was positive he knew exactly what had happened.

Aelius sighed, beleaguered. "Yes, but I'm handling it."

"Handling it?" I hissed, stopping in my tracks and grabbing his arm. He looked down at my hand, completely unimpressed. He reached down and removed it despite my trying to fight it. I growled as he managed to throw my hand away from him.

Aelius stepped up into me, until his face was uncomfortably close to mine. Forcing me to witness the streaks of sunlight in his sky-blue eyes that otherwise mirrored Asteria's.

"Remember, *boy*," he spat. "You may be king of this lesser kingdom, but I have hundreds of years on you. Don't test me. I have little patience for fools."

Lightning crackled around my fingers, but I couldn't kill him yet. Luckily, an idea came to me, and a slow smirk replaced the snarl curling my lips.

"It was your son, wasn't it?" I whispered, cooing at him. "Aw, are you actually trying to protect him? For once in his whole life?" I placed a hand dramatically over my heart. "I'm moved, Aelius."

"He's a foolish boy." Aelius glared, a muscle in his jaw jumping. "He doesn't understand, but he will. And let me make one thing straight. I may not be impressed with him, but I won't let you kill my only son either."

"Then you better get Day in line." I let the blood magic fuel me until lightning crackled all around us. Aelius twitched as the bolts closed in on him. "If your son gets in the way of our goal, he'll have to be dealt with. So why don't you go gather your armies, corral your son, and use your common fucking sense to find where he hid—my—HUMANS!" I screamed, snarling right in his face as my lightning pressed down on Aelius, close enough to kill should he move an inch.

Aelius nodded once, jaw tight, and I let the lightning fade with his submission. Aelius quickly moved to walk away, his body unnaturally stiff.

"Oh, Aelius?" I called as he moved down the hall. He turned back, a glare aimed at me that did nothing but make me smirk following my victory. "Be quick about it. If you're not back before Night moves, you're going to have a much bigger problem than a female heir."

I swirled around, walking off in the opposite direction. Rage was a constant companion, but in moments like these, it bubbled up more. I brought myself to the closest patio and let my wings snap out, bright pink feathers flapping as I took off into the sky.

At least Aelius would move his ass now. I had other things I needed to tend to. I flew off toward the Namminian Ocean, letting the smell of sea and salt calm me when I finally approached Eventide's coast.

Farther away from the capital than the other cities of Dusk, it had been an ideal spot to set up. Not that Lord Udaya had even been aware of it. The sirens were great protectors when motivated. And free victims for them was a trade I could live with.

North of the city of Eventide itself, there was a stretch of land occupied mainly by tiny human villages. It was all too easy to set up here, and I didn't even have to move the humans to do it.

I landed by the rocks lining the ocean, cringing as the creatures turned to me. Where the mermaids who called the Damaculous Ocean home were beautiful, with personalities to match, the sirens were horrifying. Instead of hair, feathers swept down their heads, blending into their wings. Their bird feet ended in claws that dug into the sand and rock alike.

Their faces weren't much better. While ostensibly that of a woman, their teeth were razor sharp, and random stripes of scales lined their cheekbones and other places across the fleshy parts of their bodies.

They swam as easily as they flew and were appropriately terrifying to humans trying to run away. The sirens had been held back since the treaties were signed by the six Fae kings long ago. They were forced to eat fish and whales as opposed to human flesh. The return to tradition was taken to with gusto, and they enjoyed hunting down any humans who might try to escape.

There was always at least one brave soul, once they realized the fate that awaited them.

"Any issues while I've been occupied?" I asked the creatures. Not the most likely of guards, surely.

What I could only imagine was supposed to be a snicker sounded between them. "Not enough to hunt, king."

I rolled my eyes. "Well, don't worry. You'll have fresh meat soon."

Their overexcited cawing and jumping around on taloned feet had me wanting to get out of there immediately.

"Just remember, I need the majority bled for me." I reminded them firmly, not wanting them to get overzealous. They were only useful up until they started to interfere with my blood supply.

"Of course, king." A blue feathery head nodded, its wide smile all the more disconcerting with the rows of serrated fangs.

I gave them a brisk nod, taking back off into the sky to fly into the interior part of the camp, bristling as I heard their bird-like cackling. I brushed it off, for now, as I flew past the several layers of guards and walls to the interior section of the camp. I landed among rows of humans strapped upside down to boards, blood dripping slowly into the collection bottles.

"My King." Kesshuu bowed before me, and I quickly had him rise so we could get on with this.

"How is it coming, Kess?" I asked impatiently, having been itching to get out here and check on our progress.

He smiled slyly, nodding his head to the left and walking off in that direction. I followed, anticipation rising, my heart beating as if Asteria herself was right in front of me, within touching distance.

I shook off the thought. I'd have plenty of time to touch as soon as this succeeded.

I followed Kesshuu back past the humans chained to the ground. There was no need for the pretense of care anymore, not with these ones.

Asteria may have thought human slaves were seen as nothing more than sheep for the slaughter, but she hadn't truly seen the meaning of the phrase yet.

She would, though.

I wrinkled my nose at the smell. Shalim, humans were truly disgusting creatures. Unwashed, the scent of body odor, piss, and shit pervaded the space. I hurried my steps forward.

"You get used to it," Kesshuu advised, a slight smile on his face. I shook my head. It was revolting, and a king had no need to adjust to such things.

Finally, we came to a small building that had a series of locked doors. Three deep, and all with different keys. This was too important to leave to chance or destruction. Human rebels were popping up more and more often. While the court may be quelled by me, the humans I don't see on a regular basis have not yet learned the severe error of their ways.

But they would soon enough.

They'd actually managed to damage one of my camps and free some of the humans there. A small number, of course, but any number was too many.

Past the third door, we began descending a spiral staircase deep into the ground, where a long-forgotten dungeon had been transformed. A screeching noise reached me first, and then the banging. A full smithy had essentially been created down here, with some key differences.

The Fae holding the leashes straightened as I walked in, but the collared humans kept working away.

"We've managed to make plenty of iron." Kesshuu smiled fully, turning his head to me. "We've created all the weapons you asked for, plus a few more... innovations, let's say."

I raised a brow at him, but couldn't help the smile that tilted my lips. I clapped a hand on his shoulder, "Good work, Kess."

"Thank you, my King." He dipped his head quickly. "We've got much of it ready to transport wherever you wish at a moment's notice. We could send half to Evenfall and half to Alfheim if you'd like, secure the capital and the border?"

I walked further into the room, bending to examine the iron as it was worked.

Such a little thing, with such devastating impact.

I bit the gloved tip of my index finger to swiftly remove the black leather from my right hand.

"My King," Kesshuu began, panicked. "There's no ne—"

He quieted as my fingertip brushed the iron briefly. The sharp hiss of pain had me swearing under my breath. Getting stabbed with this would feel like being burnt alive. I could even feel the sap on my magic, from just the slightest brush against my skin.

It was perfect.

"Send some to both Alfheim and Falias." I mused, considering our border. "I want Vissy's city protected as well. Some to Eventide itself even. Make sure Calix doesn't jump over the border on this end."

"Of course." Kesshuu agreed, voice low.

"But I want the majority sent to Evenfall," I told him firmly, having decided on the path forward. "Calix might find a way to fight through the border, or find a new way around. But I know he'll come for Evenfall eventually. I want to ensure he finds the nastiest of surprises waiting for him."

"We'll get on that immediately." He eagerly agreed, so willing to do whatever it took to move up the ranks. So easy to push and pull just where I wanted him.

"And I want you back in Evenfall. You've done great work. Now it's time to delegate and come to the capital to reap the rewards." I smiled fully, ensuring that charm that so often got me my way was in full effect.

His big smile and quick agreement were just what I was expecting. As the only one I let into the secret of how to make iron, he needed to be kept under heel—but staying happily there, completely oblivious to it, made it so much easier.

That was where I went wrong with Asteria. I'd tried the same tactic on her, not factoring in how much more intelligent she was than bootlickers like Kess. I wouldn't make the same mistake twice.

And this iron would guarantee my victory.

After assuring Kesshuu several times that once he was finished with his part in turning blood to iron, he could leave for Evenfall, I began my flight back home. My smile was hard to contain, hidden up here in the skies as I was. Everything was going to plan, better than even, at least on the iron front.

Aelius and his wayward son... those missing bloodsacks... that was another matter entirely, and quickly had my smile falling.

The Otherworld damned Earendel family was going to drive me up a wall before the end of this.

I hated that any thought of Aelius automatically led back to Asteria. I thought of her enough as it was, dammit! Even here, flying through the skies, I wondered to myself if she'd flown yet. She'd always loved the sky and had coveted wings as much as she had freedom.

I valued her spirit, as much as it must have seemed otherwise. She wouldn't have been any fun without it!

I had never really appreciated the ability to fly. Asteria's desire to made me realize I had always just taken it as my gods given right. It was only in learning how shit the gods truly are that I realized it *was* a right, just not gifted from them. It was *mine*. And unlike my magic, they couldn't do a Tartarus damn thing to take it away from me.

So I let myself enjoy it, hoping despite myself that Asteria was enjoying it too. Though my mood darkened when I considered who she might be flying *with*.

Or... wait...

It wasn't just my mood darkening. Coming from the capital, billowing black smoke clouds rose into the air. I narrowed my eyes, a snarl already starting as I headed straight for what was surely another feeble slave-led insurrection against me.

CHAPTER 27

Cᴀʟɪx had ultimately won the argument about how many guards to bring with us to Sunrise. Since we'd be flying to avoid detection and traveling swiftly, only a few of his most trusted, whom he was willing to have on his back, came with us.

Neither of us was comfortable having me fly with passangers. Not when I still got distracted from time to time, and forgot to flap my wings. The heart-dropping fall out of the sky was a rush, no doubt, but for Nox's sake, I wasn't willing to accidentally kill someone.

That would be super embarrassing.

For me and whoever fell.

We were getting my things gathered for the trip to Sunrise when a knock on the door had me looking up from the items Delia and Priscilla were helping me choose from. Delia quickly ran to the door, so I went back to packing until I realized I could smell Calix.

My head snapped up just as he walked through the door to my bedroom. He was dressed down in just a loose shirt and tight pants, but it still made my mouth water.

"There's no way you missed me so much already you couldn't wait an hour." I teased, tilting my head to the side.

He laughed, his smile bright as he shook his head at me. He tilted his head toward the door, extending his hand out to me, "Come with me for a second?"

I bit my lip, looking to Priscilla, who was trying to hide her smirk. I hadn't explicitly told anyone what had happened yet. We just hadn't had the time. But

I couldn't help my smile as I stepped closer and took his hand. He laced our fingers together as he led me from my rooms.

"Where are we going?" I asked, looking up at him curiously.

He smirked slightly. "I have something for you."

"What is it?" I raised my brow expectantly.

He chuckled warmly, but a hint of something mischievous remained in his eyes. "It's a surprise."

When I opened my mouth to ask further questions, he continued, "Meaning I won't tell you." He laughed. "You're not very good at surprises, are you?"

I faux glared at him, but he just tugged me along toward wherever we were going. He turned right and led me down to what I realized were his rooms as we entered.

The entire back wall was windows—no, glass doors, I realized. Ones that would slide open to access the balcony and let the entire room open up to the sky. The other walls were left as the pure star opal the palace was made of; the shimmering white gem gleaming in the sun. The sofas in the living area were black, much like the ones at the fortress. Bookshelves lined the wall opposite them, giving easy access to reading material. He had a desk facing the wall of doors that would provide an amazing view while working, with a light gray wooden table and a comfortable looking black, tufted leather chair that swiveled. There was a small dining area with a black wooden table and two grey chairs, but that was it. No long, ten-person table like Cyrus had in his rooms.

Calix's living area was done in a simpler, calming palette as well. And as he led me into his bedroom, I could see the need for it, since this room was dominated in the black and purple royal colors, it probably helped to break it up. The bedroom was even more similar to the fortress, with a looming dragon head over the headboard, and scales carved into each of the four posters, with carved fire burning at the top of each.

Lucky me, this bed was also clearly built for a family of giants. *Plenty* of room to play.

Across the bed, however, he had laid out several pieces of armor. Women's armor, done in silver, purple, and black. Night's colors, and my own. The dragon-scaled portion was still black, as it came from black dragons, but the shoulder straps were now purple, while a revised version of the sigil was right in the middle of the chest. The moon was done in silver instead of purple, with the rest of the circle colored black with silver stars floating inside it, and the wings on each side remained their usual purple color. The metal piece the revised sigil was affixed to was a sparkling silver that reached across the chest on each side.

The leather pants now had silver panels going down each leg, while the armbands were completely redone in silver, with scales outlined in purple going up them and a purple band of runes at the wrist and the top of the band where it sat on the bicep.

"Calix…" I trailed off, looking up at him, finding myself surprisingly emotional at the gesture.

"You need armor fit for the queen of Night." He smiled, and I couldn't help reaching up and pulling him down for a kiss. He smiled against my mouth as my tongue invaded his, my hand winding around his neck as I pulled myself into him.

"As much as I'd love—" Calix mumbled with every breath he stole, "to continue this. I have something else for you."

I forced myself back, mourning the loss of his lips already but wanting to see what it was as I smiled wide, bouncing on my toes. "You do?"

Calix laughed, the Aurora appearing in his lilac eyes. "Yes. I must admit, if I knew gifts made you this happy, I would have bought out the kingdoms by now."

I slapped him on the shoulder, but he wasn't wrong. I'd never gotten a gift before my necklace, which was now proudly back on my neck with no reason to hide it anymore.

Calix grabbed something off the long black and purple velvet bench at the foot of his bed. It was wrapped in cloth, and he placed it on the bed, gently removing the pieces of cloth to uncover it.

My breath caught as my hand came to the base of my throat, completely speechless.

"You deserve a blade worthy of you," Calix said softly.

Where Calix wielded a blade made of a material as black as night, mine was a shining, sparkly silver. The entire blade shone, except for the row of runes down the middle of the blade. The runes were matte black instead of Calix's shining silver runes. I ran my fingertip down one in amazement before my eyes caught the hilt of the blade.

It was a dragon, of course. With its nose dipping down onto the blade, and its tail spiraling up the hilt, where the pointed star-like end of the tail ended at the pommel. Its wings crested out to each side, hugging the crossguard. Its eyes shone with star opal, and I nearly cried to find our soulmark engraved onto its back.

"The same maker who did my sword made this one," Calix informed me nervously. "It's twin, in effect, for as opposite as it may be. I wanted to do something on it that tied you to both Day and Night kingdoms, and thought our soulmark would be perfect."

"It is." I breathed out before I grabbed the hilt. My hand fit comfortably around the hilt, the wings cleverly set low enough to not get in the way of the hold of the sword. The guard underneath the hilt was black and inset with gems the colors of Calix's eyes. A beautiful touch of purple on my starlit blade.

The feel of it was incredible in the hand, and lighter than I thought it would be. It felt like it had been made just for me, and I suppose it had. I placed it carefully down on the bed, noting the new leather sword belt crafted with star opal accents to go with it.

I threw myself at Calix, jumping up to wrap my legs around him as he grabbed my ass to hold me up, his lips finding mine unerringly.

"Thank." I kissed him again, and again. "You." And again. Until we fell to the bed, laughing as he complained about potentially breaking my sword.

When I finally made it back to my room, my new sword and armor in hand, Priscilla and Delia were waiting for me with smirks on their faces. I rolled my eyes at them both.

"Very mature," I admonished, causing them to break into laughter.

"So, does this mean you two have figured things out?" Priscilla asked softly, looking slightly concerned.

I bit my lip, trying to think of how to explain it to her. "Mostly. Together? Yes—"

A high-pitched squeal had me jumping in surprise, and I shouldn't have been surprised that Ilta was to blame. She came through the doorway and launched herself at me, making me laugh.

"You are?! Really?!" She looked more emotional than I was, and my nod had her practically strangling me with her hug. When she finally let go, Priscilla took over, hugging me tightly.

"I'm so happy for you, Asteria," she whispered in my ear. "You deserve all the happiness in the world."

Delia was next, but she also looked concerned as she sat down. "If you're now together, then what's wrong?"

I sighed, miserably. "We need to find a way to make it work. I'm to be queen of Day, which means to be queen of Night, we have to figure out a way to simultaneously rule both kingdoms, without upsetting either. Since they have to remain in balance, it's not like we can just merge them."

"Oh." Delia blinked, stunned. "Shit."

I nodded in agreement. "I promised Calix I would find a way. We mean to change things anyway, *right?*"

They nodded, and I continued with a firm nod that I wished had any confidence behind it. "Exactly. So, we'll make it work."

"I know you will." Ilta smiled, beaming at me. "If anyone can, it's you and Calix. We all thought abolishing slavery was impossible, but Calix managed it. We thought starlight power was impossible, but you managed that. I have no doubt that you two will find a way forward. You two just make the impossible happen."

I thanked her with another emotional hug before it was time to go. Sunrise awaited, and we didn't have time to dally.

"Pris, walk me down?" I asked, tilting my head toward the door.

She raised a brow at me but nodded, and I wished I had more time to talk to her. I'd have to take what I could get.

"How are you dealing? With Callisto being away?" I probed, knowing if I wasn't here to talk, it was likely she was keeping it all inside. When we last spoke, she had told me she wouldn't move forward with a relationship until the fighting was done, and I was curious how she was holding up.

Callisto had been sent to the Dusk border just before we left, and while I knew Priscilla had been keeping busy helping Harpina and Lilith settle the humans in, it couldn't be easy.

Priscilla sighed just as miserably as I had. "I hate knowing she's there. It's got to be one of the more dangerous spots, and I know that's why Calix wants her there. It makes sense, but—"

She cut off, shaking her head.

"But you hate it anyway?" I pushed, making Priscilla look at me, big brown eyes locking on mine as she nodded with a distinct pout. I pulled her into another hug, and she clutched me to her.

"I think what I hate even more is knowing she loves it. That she *wants* to be there," she murmured, dejected.

"You two will figure this out," I promised, having to believe it. "This war won't last forever."

Priscilla nodded, forcibly putting on a smile. I hated this for both of them. Despite what she said, I knew Callisto couldn't be fully happy being gone since she also knew Priscilla hated her being there. I was sure the two of them would figure it out eventually, though.

If Calix and I could do it, so could they.

Flying toward Sunrise, I watched the rest of Celesterra pass below us. We'd been careful not to pass over Dusk, so we first flew over Day before passing over Dawn. As we neared Sunrise, my heart beat harder.

We'd be passing over my old village on the way to the capital of Panchaia, and I wasn't nearly ready to deal with that thought. I had no idea what to tell my parents or how to explain the truth to them.

Would they hate me? For not being the child they so desperately wished for? For being Fae?

I couldn't bear to find out.

So we flew on, and as the jungle became visible, I found myself inexplicably excited. I had never had the chance to see it before, but since meeting Calix, my life had been full of the unexpected.

The capital slowly became visible within the jungle, and I swooped down to get a closer look. I had never seen anything like it, and found myself almost angry that this had been so close all my life, and yet I'd never had the chance to explore it.

The palace was situated where the jungle met the ocean, getting the best of both worlds. Tall jungle trees and hanging plants surrounded the palace, while the sea lapped up behind it. The palace itself was multilayered, and it was hard to figure out where one level turned into another. It wasn't like other palaces I'd seen with clear floors all the way across. Instead, it seemed to cut across at different points, some levels rising higher in some places, others lowered at points. The entire back of the palace sat on stilts within the water and helped support the back end of the palace, which seemed to be built partially on the rock wall coming from the Tritonian Sea.

Large balconies also extended off the palace over the water, all done in the same yellow-tinged stone the palace was made of. Each tower and turret had a pointed teal cap, making the palace match their royal colors of yellow and teal.

Flying around the front of the structure again, I could see that the jungle had actually started to encroach onto the palace itself. There was greenery growing through the stone and places where hanging plants dangled down from it. There was a winding staircase leading up to the main entrance from the ground, and the plants and flowers surrounding it had started to grow up the railings as well.

The stairs also had water under them, I realized, but not from the Tritonian Sea. It looked like the palace was built over where a lagoon had naturally formed before the sea, and they built directly over it for some reason.

The palace had definitely been designed to become part of nature, and seemed to welcome being swallowed up by it.

When we landed, we had to do so one at a time due to the lack of space with all the water and trees in the way, so Calix landed first, and I waited to follow suit. I quickly shifted upon touching the ground and brushed out my dress. Since this was my first introduction as the future ruler of Day Kingdom, I had conceded to wear a dress that was purple, gold, and silver.

The bodice had purple metalwork on the front, with gold around the sides and back. It, of course, had my favorite neckline, the sweetheart cut accentuating my cleavage. The sleeves were also created with my love of dramatic bell sleeves in mind, but were made to look like dragon wings. They started out purple but shifted into silver at the bottom, and gold lined the edges while gold dust dotted all over the sleeves. The skirt was layered with purple and silver fabric, and gold designs were added over them. Including both gold trimming on the edges and right down the front, starting where the metalwork on the bodice ended and extending to the floor, where dragon scale designs were mixed in with swirling patterns.

It was a little heavy for the hot and muggy weather, but I was told repeatedly that first impressions were important. As beautiful as the dress was, I wanted to rip a few layers off the damn skirt before I melted into literal stardust.

"Ready for this, my réalta?" Calix asked with a slight smirk, taking my hand. I looked up at him nervously.

"I have to be." I shrugged my shoulder, and he chuckled, leaning down to kiss the top of my head. I closed my eyes, wishing we had the time to just explore being together. Exploring the bond between us, or even getting to finally test out that sex swing together.

Ugh, what I wouldn't give for that right now.

I couldn't help feeling like I had wasted too much time stuck in my own head. But only slightly. I knew that time had been necessary. Just as I knew that I could have used *more*.

But war waits for no one.

And I wasn't going to spend another moment without Calix, my own fears and insecurities be damned.

I straightened as guards in bronze armor opened the main doors, and a woman in a flowing dress began walking down the stairs toward us. The dress was a style I'd seen many of the Fae who visited the vineyard in Sonmathion wear; the breezy, flowy fabric was cut up high on each thigh, and the neckline dipped low, making me insanely jealous as I sweltered in the heat. Her dress was a bright teal color with bright yellow embroidery on the bottom of the sleeves and around the skirt, and yellow jewels dotted across the neckline and waist.

Her long, black hair fell to her waist in a pin straight line that I was wholly jealous of as well. I needed her secret to fighting frizz in the humidity.

"King Calix, as I live and breathe!" The woman laughed as she approached, her light brown skin shimmering in the light. "You're alive!"

Calix rumbled a laugh. "You knew that very well."

She shrugged her shoulder casually. "In theory, but that gorgeous face has been missing for too many years. What else am I supposed to look at during functions?"

"You could try your husband?" he replied, a smirk lifting his lips as she finally crested the bottom of the stairs.

She scoffed, waving a hand back and forth. "Boring! Now, is this the lovely creature I've heard so much about?"

Calix raised a brow. "If you mean my mate and the heir of Day Kingdom, then yes. Allow me to introduce Princess Asteria Faelynn Earendel."

I took a deep breath; the name and title were still so fucking bizarre.

"That would be her!" The woman smiled widely. "I've heard so many things, but to know a woman has actually done it." She sighed happily and grabbed my hands in hers, surprising me.

"I can't tell you if my husband will support you or not." She looked me straight in the eyes, and I was taken aback by how straightforward she seemed. She played the flirt with Calix, but the mask dropped as she observed me with a serious expression. Whatever façade she wore for court, she was letting me see past it for some reason.

"But I want you to know, *I* am rooting for you." She smiled widely, and it lit up her brown eyes, the yellow ring around them reminding me of the sun. "A woman has never been chosen, until you. It must be for a reason. One I hope will change the tides, so mothers like me don't need to watch our daughters be looked over for less worthy men."

My brows flew skyward, and she winked.

"This is Queen Idalia." Calix smiled as he stole me back from her. "She's much more reasonable than her husband."

Idalia laughed, "Isn't that the truth! Now, come along, you two. I'll show you to your rooms."

I looked at Calix in confusion, and he leaned in as Idalia led us up the stairs, his hand bracing on my lower back. "Idalia and Gravadain don't see eye-to-eye on much. They were a political match."

Which didn't answer why the *queen* was leading us like a slave or servant normally would in this situation.

But Nox, were there any Fae royals who actually loved one another? I knew Calix's parents had, and from what my mother had said, there had been some affection between her and Aelius once upon a time. But Astraeus and Stelara, along with Tariq and Oriana, certainly didn't give a shit about one another. It seemed like ninety percent of these royal marriages were political. It was only when a soulmark appeared that things went differently.

Walking inside the palace, the interior reminded me a bit of Sunset Kingdom's, with arches and fanciful decorations, but there were definitely differences. The windows were all made of colored glass, with geometric shapes etched into them that created patterns on the floor as the sun shone through. The floors themselves were elaborately colored tiles, and even the ceiling had been painted teal and adorned with gold.

And it wasn't just their house colors; every color of the rainbow could be found *somewhere*. From the floor and the ceilings to the columns in between that were decorated with all sorts of colored crystals.

"These are your rooms." Idalia smiled widely and pushed the double doors open. "Since these quarters are reserved for royal guests, you have a private lagoon." She wiggled her eyebrows at me with a smirk.

I fought a blush, biting my lip and as I tried to contain a laugh, but actually seeing the room had the laughter dying in my throat as I took in the gorgeous space before me.

The living space was open to the lagoon outside, with accordion-style doors that let the breeze blow off the water. The sun lit the white tile floors, which were partially covered by a teal and pink rug under the main seating area. The wall opposite the lagoon was made up of wide arches that went to the ceiling, each filled in with different designs in pink, blue, teal, and purple.

A sparkling crystal chandelier fell over a low, round coffee table crafted in the same colors. Long swaths of teal fabric fell around the room, billowing out from the chandelier across the ceilings to the walls. A crushed velvet lilac sofa the same color as Calix's eyes sat lower to the ground than normal. A pink chaise lounge sat opposite the sofa, and teal ottomans were scattered throughout. Tons of pillows were tossed across the sofas, and even several large ones had been put on the floor for additional seating options.

A peek out at the lagoon revealed that they had added tiles with cobalt blue spiraling designs under the crystal-clear water. The columns surrounding it had been grown over with jungle plants that made the space completely private.

"I'll leave you two to settle in." Idalia smiled widely as she glanced between us. "We'll be having dinner together in a couple of hours, but please, enjoy yourselves until then."

With a final wink, she showed herself out, and I was left staring at the lagoon until Calix came up behind me, his arms snaking around my waist and pulling me into him.

"Hmm." He rumbled into my neck, pressing a kiss to it that had me tilting my head to give him better access. "However shall we pass the time?"

"Well." I drew the word out, putting my hands on the arms he'd put around me. "I must first insist you get me out of this heavy dress. It's much too hot."

"Gladly," he growled, but as his hands went to tear it, I laughed and quickly grabbed his hands.

"Without tearing it." I insisted, his disappointed sigh echoing in my ear. "I'm as saddened by that as you are, my dorchadas. But I do like this dress. Just not for this heat."

He chuckled, and laced his fingers with mine. "Come on then, grá."

"You never told me what that actually means." I reminded him as he brought me toward the bedroom.

I was momentarily distracted as I took in the bedroom. This room was primarily done in pink and white, making the room feel very light and airy. It was open on one side to the lagoon as well, contributing to that feeling. The floor itself was completely teal, but that was it. The walls were white and draped with pink fabric, while the bed was done in pink silk, except for the white frame that mimicked the columns outside.

Calix pulled me into him and lifted my chin with his finger. His eyes were full of color as he smiled at me. "It means love in ancient Fae."

I melted a bit, which wasn't really difficult to do in this heat, but his words had me grabbing his face to kiss him.

"Wait, wait." I quickly forced myself to pull back.

"What's wrong?" Calix asked, his brows furrowing.

"It's too damn hot. Let me change and meet you at the lagoon?" I smirked as his eyes lit up.

He growled as his lips quickly crashed into mine before he disappeared just as fast, a breeze blowing in his wake.

PART TWO

CHAPTER 28

Calix

HADN'T been to Sunrise in many years, and while their lagoons could never compare to Nova Falls in my mind, I appreciated the chance to steal away here with Asteria.

Just because this was an important diplomatic trip didn't mean we couldn't take advantage of all it had to offer.

As Asteria walked out to the patio in nothing but a light, flowing robe, I sent my thanks to Nox and, by the Otherworld, even Ausrine, for making this possible.

I watched, completely transfixed, as her legs peeked out from under the robe when Asteria walked down the steps into the water. Letting the robe fall behind her, exposing herself completely as she let the water cover her instead.

Fuck, she was perfect.

All of that smooth skin had turned from her usual porcelain to a lightly tanned golden shade from the sun. Slender shoulders gave way to full breasts with nipples I couldn't help biting every time they were exposed. Her waist dipped in only to curve back out at her hips. And then her ass, that perfect, spankable ass, followed by long legs despite her short stature.

The smirk on her lips as she made her way to me was matched by the playfully swirling starlight in her eyes when she reached me. I held myself back, wanting to see what she would do.

I wasn't disappointed. She circled me in the water, her hands reaching out to caress and trace every tattoo. Her fingertips smoothed over the soulmark on my back, making me shiver, before slipping to my bicep and following the scales across my chest. Her hand slid from the other bicep down to my forearm, where the shining silver runes banded around it.

"Do you know what it says?" I murmured, and she looked up at me from under her lashes.

"You know I can't read ancient Fae." She gave me a look, and I couldn't help the chuckle that slipped out.

I took her hand, bringing her fingers to trace each rune as I spoke the words.

*"Darkness sweeps across the land
To bring new order to Fae and Man.
A light to brighten his darkness be the king's fate
Blood will seep and unveil his mate.
An eclipsed star lost who must be found
The power of two will be her crown.
Together, they will usher in a new age
Though not without a war to wage.
A queen of stars and a king of night
Are the only hope to see the world made right."*

I switched her fingers to the other forearm halfway through, and when I finished, they wrapped around my arm and held tight, her eyes fixed on the runes.

"That's your birth prophecy, isn't it?" she asked quietly. She looked up, wide blue eyes meeting my purple ones, and I nodded my affirmation.

Her hand slid up my arm to my neck, cupping it firmly. "Is this why you want me to rule with you? Because fate said so?"

I could sense her apprehension, and I was quick to shake my head, my hand coming up to slip under her neck and into her hair. *"Never.* The prophecies don't control us. The seers merely see into the future and tell us what they see happening. Fate is always in our hands."

"Is it?" she countered, her eyes swirling rapidly with sparkling light.

"I promise it is. I know you hate the idea of some outside force controlling us, and I'm with you on that. Having a seer for a sister has given me much more insight on how they work, and it's often just as confusing to them." I promised her, seeing her shoulders drop in relief.

"So our actions are perceived, not controlled?" she asked, and I nodded.

"My fate was always to be yours, my réalta." I tightened my hand in her hair, tilting her head back to meet my eyes. "Just as yours was to be mine. Not because some god or seer said so, but because there is no world where I accept any less."

She surged upward, and I met her lips as we crashed together. I grabbed her legs and hooked them around my hips, her cunt teasing my cock as the water quickened her slide against me.

"Fuck me, my dorchadas," she murmured against my lips, and my cock strained toward her, desperate for relief. I nipped her bottom lip before grabbing her hips and lifting her up, sinking her down on my cock.

Her moan was swallowed by my mouth, and my tongue swept along hers as I dragged her up and down my hard length. I swore as she clenched down hard around me.

"Fucking Elysium. I swear paradise couldn't feel as good as you," I murmured as I began kissing down her neck, her hand pulling my hair and guiding me. I let my hands wander up her curves until I gripped her breasts in my hands. She swirled her hips into mine, riding me as her claws sank into my shoulder.

I quickly brought her to the ledge of the lagoon and placed her on the edge. She fell back, and I let myself look long and hard at her. I couldn't have imagined a more exquisite mate. My shadows responded to my emotions without my say-so and began whirling up her body, making her giggle as she eyed me affectionately.

As I grabbed her legs and hooked them around to me to sink back into her, I was surprised by the bit of starlight that swirled up and around my cock. I looked at her and found her biting her lip to contain her giggles, but she continued to stroke my cock with her starlight. I let her play for a minute, the torture of waiting heightened by the feel of her touch via magic. Until the starlight snaked down to my balls, and I couldn't take anymore.

I thrust into her hard, shaking her body and making her breasts bounce for me. I smirked as I thrust again and watched them, mesmerized by the movement. Asteria's hair was fanned out around her, her arms out and claws digging into the tile.

"Fuck me harder, my dorchadas." She gave me a fang-filled smile, and there was no way I could resist that. I gave a punishing thrust, earning a shout from her lips that I leaned over and swallowed the end of. My tongue slipped into her mouth as I ground against her, hitting her clit repeatedly.

Her arms wrapped around me, holding me to her tightly. I lifted her until I was standing at the edge of the water, where I put her down onto the edge of the patio.

We didn't let go of one another, arms tightening against the other as the intensity rose. I fucked her in shorter, but much more forceful thrusts, grinding into her as she met me with rolling undulations of her hips. Her breasts pressed against my chest as our tongues battled for dominance.

She was clenching down around me so hard that I worried I wouldn't last much longer despite my usual stamina. So I slipped a finger down to her clit and rubbed it until I felt her orgasm begin. The feeling of her walls caressing me as her arousal leaked down around my cock was enough to have me cumming, spilling inside her as she collapsed against me.

I pet her hair as we both panted, trying to catch our breath. Her finger twirled a piece of my hair as she ran her other hand down my back. I loved these moments, in the aftermath, where we both had the chance to just be still and relaxed with one another.

We hadn't had any time to just *be* since Asteria accepted me as her mate. The circumstances meant that we were running *out* of time, in fact. We had to take whatever moments we could, wherever we could get them.

I had confidence we would both make it through whatever came with Cyrus, but I couldn't help the fear that accompanied it. That the world would fall to chaos, and we would be left to fade away. There was the chance she would be taken from me.

I would fight to the end to ensure she stayed alive. And I would also ensure that whatever fate befell us, it would be together. I couldn't live in a world without her light, leaving me to be consumed by darkness.

So we would live together, or we would die together. There was no other option.

I would do whatever it took to make it so we *lived*. Even if I had to burn the world completely to keep her breathing.

Walking to dinner, I held Asteria's shaking hand in mine.

"I didn't expect to be this nervous," Asteria admitted, wiping her other hand over her flowy skirt. She looked gorgeous, and I had to admit that Sunrise knew what it was doing fashion-wise.

While I loved Asteria in her Night Kingdom attire most, the light, breezy fabrics of Sunrise gave me tantalizing glimpses of her legs and breasts. They'd even provided one in purple with gold accents for her. I was wearing the men's version, with loose linen pants and a sleeveless top folded that dipped into a low V at my chest, exposing the iridescent dragon scales across it. It was all in black, thankfully, with only purple and silver accents lining it.

"You'll be fine, my réalta," I reassured her. "You've stood toe-to-toe with much scarier Fae than King Gravadain, I assure you."

She stood straighter, shaking her head, "You're right. I swear, becoming Fae has messed with my mind."

"Hey." I stopped her, putting a hand on her cheek. "You're dealing with a lot, with very little time. You will adjust, but your emotions are still going to be a bit all over the place for a while. We'll keep working on your control. You've done great in your training of them as far as your magic goes, so we just need to work on extending that further."

We'd gone out several times to train, including while we stayed at the fortress on the Etheralta Mountains. Seeing her starlight exploding over the star opal mountains was an amazing sight to see, but even more so was seeing her grasping more control over her power.

"Thank you." She smiled softly, nodding. She pressed a hand over mine and kissed my palm.

I laced our fingers together and brought them to my mouth, kissing her fingers before we continued on. A slave was at the door, and Asteria stiffened as they bowed silently and opened the door.

I was used to seeing them in this situation, but she hadn't had much opportunity for it since being freed. It was always an incongruous sight after spending so much time in Night. Asteria kept her eyes glued to the slave as we entered, before her gaze was eventually pulled to those around the table as they stood to welcome us.

"Ah, King Calix, Princess Asteria, thank you both for joining us." Idalia smiled and waved at the pair of seats directly across from her.

King Gravadain was sitting at the head of the table, and his son and heir, Dagur, sat at the other end. Idalia was next to Gravadain, and their youngest son, Altan, sat next to her. The princesses Sunneva and Isleen took the remaining two spots next to Dagur.

Gravadain had conceded to having just his family present after I requested no other members of court be present. I wanted his attention, not deflection and court politics. At least as much as was possible. This was bigger than such petty maneuvering, and I hoped he had the sense to see it.

"Thank you, King Gravadain, Queen Idalia, for having us. We appreciate your invitation." I directed my thanks mostly at Gravadain. The man was stern, and he and his wife often clashed with their opposing personalities. He had dark black skin that Altan seemed to have inherited, while the rest of their children were a lighter shade of brown, like their mother. The king of Sunrise wore his hair in braided locks that fell to his shoulders, emphasizing his prominent cheekbones and strong jaw.

"Please, sit, King Calix. It's been many years, and I'm eager to hear an explanation for the chaos you've been causing." Gravadain intoned, his expression screaming 'unimpressed.'

Altan rolled his eyes, making eye contact for a moment as he shook his head. He mouthed 'sorry' to Asteria while his father was looking elsewhere. I appreciated that he took the time for it, considering his father's clear disrespect in not even greeting her. However, I liked less how Asteria smiled back at him softly.

Much less.

He was undeniably good looking. Like a softer version of his father, his face a bit slimmer and sculpted more like his mother's. His braided hair was pulled together in a tie that fell down his back, with shorter pieces up front that had escaped his braids flying loose.

"I'm not the one bringing chaos to our realm, King Gravadain," I told him firmly, raising a brow. "Cyrus has lost his mind. He threatens us all with actions, courting chaos daily."

Dagur snorted from down the other end of the table. He looked more like his mother, with golden brown skin, dark black hair that cascaded around his face in waves that fell to his shoulders, and a dark mustache with matching thick eyebrows. His gold eyes had a piercing gaze that instantly had my fire rising before I forced it back down. My instincts were never wrong, however.

"You claim Cyrus courts chaos? While you attack the kingdoms at random, killing us all left and right?" Dagur pressed, leaning on the table with those golden eyes staring me down. At least until they switched to my mate, making me grip the knife on the table a bit too hard. "While you claim a mate that threatens our very way of life?"

"Excuse me?" Asteria countered, her brows flying upwards. "*I* threaten your way of life?"

"Women aren't meant to be heirs," he sneered at her, making his death loom ever closer as a snarl crept up my lips. At least until Asteria placed a hand on my thigh, stilling me.

She laughed wryly, and grabbed her wine glass, taking a slow sip. She swished the wine in the glass, casual as you please. "I'm afraid you're wrong."

I bit my lip to hide my smile as Dagur's eyes widened. I watched Gravadain subtly, noting that he was examining Asteria and his son's interaction carefully. Idalia was trying to fight a smile, looking at her daughters, who kept their eyes down as best they could. The younger, however, Isleen, was trying to watch Asteria without notice from under her lashes.

"How am I wrong?" Dagur sneered, hands balling into fists.

"The gods chose me." Asteria shrugged, and I could feel how hard she was trying to contain her smirk. I was so proud of her for holding back her anger, despite the asshole baiting her. "Meaning women are indeed meant to be heirs. Or are you saying the *gods* are *wrong*?" She gasped dramatically, her hand going over her heart.

I heard Altan's amused snort, and sent him a quick smirk, before my eyes were back on the threat present. Dagur's eyes were narrowed on my mate in a way that had smoke gathering in my throat.

"Forgive my son his poor manners, Princess," Gravadain said, and both our eyes moved down the table to the king. "The gods have chosen you, yes. But I still don't see how this affects us. You and Cyrus both are seeking my aid in battle, Calix. Why should I side with either of you? You still haven't explained your attacks on our people, let alone why Cyrus is such an apparent threat you'd come seeking aid from the very kingdoms you attacked."

I took a deep breath. I knew this would be a problem going into this war. Our efforts to free slaves would never be taken well, nor forgiven. We'd killed Fae, taken their slaves, and invaded their lands. I wouldn't forgive either in their shoes.

The slaves present brought out our dinner, and we began eating as I shared my reasons, fitting in bites where I could.

"I know it must seem strange, but the situation was a strange one," I told him honestly. "We freed our slaves in Night Kingdom." The gasp from down the table came from Sunneva, whose hand was over her mouth in shock.

Gravadain's mouth parted as he watched me incredulously, and I continued explaining what I'd done. The tale wasn't easy, nor quick, but it was necessary. They relied on their slaves, and I knew it would be a hard sell to the other Fae, hence my attacking to free humans where I could.

Dagur laughed, "You're fighting to free slaves? And this war of yours is to what, free them all?"

"Humans deserve freedom just as much as you do," Asteria said forcefully, her teeth clenched. "But this is about more than just that."

Gravadain raised a disbelieving brow, so I explained Cyrus's use of blood magic. How he pushed the line of chaos too far. How he'd allied with Aelius on the terms of killing his heir, but had no intention to do so. We'd received some disturbing whispers from the border about Cyrus killing more humans, but we hadn't gotten enough confirmed intel yet to be able to say definitively how far into his plans he was.

But thanks to Asteria and the information she'd found, we knew exactly what those plans were.

"Blood magic?" Gravadain's brows furrowed as he frowned. "Iron? This all sounds very far-fetched."

"I assure you it's true." Asteria stared him down, and I felt a surge of pride as she faced off with the difficult bastard. The way she refused to be cowed… she was a true queen.

"I saw him myself. Watched as he murdered a human and used magic to increase his waning powers," she continued passionately. "Dusk is spiraling rapidly into chaos, and the way Cyrus escalates, I have no doubt that before long, you'll be feeling the effects here in Sunrise."

She tilted her head to the side, "Tell me, *King*. Will you just sit back and watch your kingdom fall? Or will you get up off your ass and do something about it?"

Pride flared within me once more, and I thanked every god I knew that this devastating woman was *mine*.

Gravadain rocked back in his seat, as if her words had physically pushed him. He looked between us for several minutes, before he finally cleared his throat.

"You've given me much to think on." He wiped his mouth with his napkin and stood. "Please, enjoy your stay. I will summon you once I've made a decision."

He left the room, Dagur and Sunneva following dutifully, but Altan and Isleen stayed at the table with Idalia, Asteria, and me.

I eyed Idalia, who was shaking her head ruefully.

"That man," she cursed, her face creasing with frustration. "He would let his kingdom fall to prove a point, I swear it."

She eyed me sadly. "He was embarrassed by your attacks, Calix. He won't side with you despite it being clear Cyrus is going to bring about our doom."

"Is he stupid?" Asteria asked, flabbergasted. Idalia and Altan broke out in laughter, while Isleen tried to hide her smile. I chuckled, putting a hand on her thigh.

"He sees what I did as a slight against him. Cyrus hasn't personally done anything to him." I explained before I leaned over and bit her earlobe, making her gasp as I teasingly whispered, "*Kings have fragile egos.*"

She jokingly pushed her hand on the center of my chest to move me backward, but her smile was bright. Returning to the seriousness of the moment, she asked, "What about the slaves?"

Asteria put her elbows on the table and leaned toward Idalia. "It's clear you think we're right about Cyrus, but where do you stand on that matter?"

Idalia sighed, smiling slightly, "I will be honest, I have never much considered them. Perhaps that makes me as awful as my husband."

"Never," Altan spat, shaking his head in disgust. "You could never be like him."

"And you?" Asteria raised a brow at him, and I shot him a smirk as he found himself under her intense gaze. "What do you think?"

Altan sat back and looked at her for a minute, before a smile slowly broke out. He began counting on his fingers as he listed his thoughts. "I think the two of you are planning to lead Celesterra into a new age. I think my shit brother will drive our kingdom into the ground. And I think I'm helpless on my own to *fix* anything."

He looked contemplatively at his mother, then his little sister, before finishing quietly. "I think it's time I finally made a move. And that's going to be joining your side."

Idalia smiled proudly and patted his chest, "As if you had a choice, my daring boy. I would be making you regardless."

Altan rolled his eyes affectionately as his mother laughed. "Well, I'm glad we're on the same page. I can definitely bring some others in as well. There are those in Sunrise who wouldn't stand for what Cyrus is doing, and others who are close to humans."

"You should go with them," Isleen spoke up for the first time, and as every eye remaining at the table focused on her, she sank slightly into her chair from the attention.

"Isleen?" Altan asked quietly. "What are you thinking? Don't hide that big brain away." His teasing was lighthearted, and it made me soften a bit toward him. Despite him seeming better than his father and brother, and agreeing to help us, which was really the bare minimum as far as I was concerned, knowing he was a caring big brother was definitely a point in his favor.

Going by Asteria's feelings, I could tell she thought similarly. Even more so, he was encouraging his sister to think for herself. Too often, women were disregarded, and Gravadain had displayed enough of that behavior tonight alone.

"I'd love to hear what you're thinking, Isleen," Asteria encouraged her, smiling at the girl. It made her look up, and her eyes locked with Asteria's. There was a sheen to her eyes that I recognized.

The stirrings of hero worship.

There was quite a lot for a young girl to look up to, after all. Asteria was not only the first female heir; she was a former slave turned Fae and a woman who let no one and nothing stop her from doing what she wished.

"Altan and I have a way to communicate," she confessed, and the siblings smiled secretly at one another. "If he goes with you, we can stay in contact more easily. He can start tonight with gathering people, and I'll continue when he's gone." She nodded decisively, as if setting herself to the task. "No one notices me. Certainly not Father." She scoffed. "I can do what you did, Princess, and work on finding out plans from the shadows."

"Father will definitely react when he finds out I left with you, which would give you something to go on." Altan mused, before shaking his head. "But it's too dangerous, Izzy. I don't want you getting hurt."

"Altan," she sighed sadly. "Should they lose, I'll be in more danger without my magic and under an overlord who not only looks down on women like Father but wields iron for his punishments."

Altan opened his mouth, but she cut him off before he could get a word out. "You know where this leads; don't pretend you don't."

He sighed, running a hand down his face, looking around helplessly. I could relate.

"Don't worry, darling." Idalia ran her hand down her son's back. "I'll be here with her, and I'll help where I can. Gravadain will be watching once he realizes you're gone, but he won't watch your sister; she's right about that. I'll make sure she's careful, and distract him and your brother where needed."

She turned to me, and her face grew stern. "I don't agree with how you did things, Calix." She looked at Asteria and softened a bit. "But I can see what was driving you to such lengths. I am trusting you with my son. He may not be heir, but he's more precious to me than any title he could have. You will protect him. Do I make myself clear?"

I nodded solemnly, but Altan interjected, "Mother, I'm a warrior; fighting is in my blood. I can protect myself." He kissed her cheek, and she swatted him away with a smile.

Asteria looked over to me with a smile growing on her face. We may not have gotten all of Sunrise, but we knew going in that it was going to be near impossible. This was better than I'd hoped for.

CHAPTER 29

WE spent the next day, while Gravadain supposedly deliberated, exploring Sunrise Kingdom. Calix took me into the jungle, and I got to see monkeys swinging from the trees and panthers prowling around on the ground. We took a flight across the Tritonian Sea, and made a quick trip to where it met the Damculous Ocean to visit the mermaids.

It was there that I reunited with Kallianassa, a mermaid I frequently visited when I'd lived in Sonmathion.

"Asteria!" she squealed as she spotted me. Her hair was flying in the wind, and with the purple color on top leading into teal ends, it made for quite a pretty sight. Her teal eyes had a ring of purple, matching not only her hair, but her fin, which was a sparkling purple and teal ombré. Her coloring is what had drawn me to her when I was younger, but they came in all sorts of color combinations. Like her friend with pink and orange coloring that swam nearby.

"Kalli! How are you doing?" I asked, sitting down on the rock beside where she was sunning herself. Calix looked a bit bemused as Kalli focused in on him immediately, staring as she licked her lips.

"Clearly not as good as you." She laughed, eyeing Calix like he was a juicy whale she wanted to take a bite of. I narrowed my eyes at her, feeling my magic flare inside me.

"*Mine*," I growled at her, then blinked, surprised at myself.

Kalli threw her head back with a laugh, but Calix was smirking as he ducked his head in an attempt to hide it from me. It was a poor attempt, to say the least, and he winked at me with heat behind his eyes at my show of jealous possession.

I reared back in surprise as Kalli suddenly was right in my face, nose to nose, her head tilting right and left as she examined me.

"Uh…" I wasn't sure what to do here.

"The rumors are true," she whispered, her musical voice more serious than I'd ever heard it.

"What rumors?" I asked, my heart dropping.

"You know the ocean carries many whispers." Her voice dropped as she brought her mouth closer to my ear. "It spoke of a human girl named for the goddess of stars who was actually a Fae princess. It spoke of the king of Night, and the prince of Dusk."

My breath caught.

She grabbed my hands suddenly, squeezing them.

"Asteria, you've always been kind to us. You've indulged us many times with your stories. So I will return the favor with a gift for you. A story the ocean brought us recently."

I met her kaleidoscope eyes, knowing how rare what she offered was. Mermaids collected stories; they didn't give them away. I'd spent many days sneaking out here and telling them the stories I'd made up over the years. Fantasies to entertain myself and distract from the mind-numbing fear slavery instilled in my every waking moment.

I nodded solemnly, and she returned the nod regally before she began. "The ocean says our less kind cousins have recently begun acting strangely."

Her words were musical whispers, her voice making even the most mundane sentences sound like songs. But the dire implications of what she said were clear.

"They haunt the shore of Dusk, hunting down humans. Ones who are bruised and starved. And having escaped a chained fence, they make for the water, hoping for freedom, only for the sirens to devour them." Kalli shivered, her shoulders shaking and fin flapping. "They say they made a deal with the dark king."

"Dark king?" I questioned, shaking my head in confusion even as dread and sorrow built in my heart over what these poor people had gone through. "Not Calix."

Kalli shook her head slowly. "They speak of Dusk alone."

Astraeus? Was he really this *dark king*? I would expect Cyrus to earn such a moniker from the ocean and the mermaids, not his father. Though, he admittedly wasn't much better than his son.

I thanked Kalli for her warning and gave her the story she wished for of my adventures since leaving Sunrise, but her words lingered in the back of my mind the entire time. I could tell it bothered Calix too, but we mutually agreed to save discussing it until we made it back to the palace in Panchaia.

But as we walked into our rooms, we found a hawk waiting on the coffee table. He cawed lowly and flew up into the air as we closed the door. Then, he swiftly shifted and landed on two feet.

"Eryx, what are you doing here?" I asked, shocked to find him here.

"What's wrong?" Calix demanded, walking up to him, looking him over like he might have missed Eryx bleeding out in front of us. I rolled my eyes but made my way over to the two of them.

"I have a lot of news," Eryx announced, looking to me with a sad smile. "For both of you."

Calix and I took seats on the sofa while Eryx sat down heavily on the chaise, his elbows on his knees as he ran a hand down his face.

"Eryx?" I called, and he looked up, blinking as he noticed I was surrounded by starlight. Eryx's anxiety triggering my own. Calix rubbed my back, trying to help calm me, but my chaotic emotions weren't cooperating as I tried to push them down. "You're freaking me out. Spit it out, please?"

He sighed, nodding his head. "Cyrus has been announced as the newly crowned king of Dusk."

Starlight exploded around the room as my power burst out of me in a giant wave. My breaths were ragged as I leaned forward to rest on my knees.

"Fuck," Calix murmured, leaning over my back to bring me into his arms as Eryx came and sat by my feet.

"Hey." Eryx looked up at me, this man who had become like a brother to me. We were closer still than I was to my actual brother, who I'd barely had any chance to get to know yet. "It's going to be okay. It doesn't change our plans at all."

I laughed breathlessly, if a bit hoarsely. "Oh yeah, because being king doesn't mean he now has unfettered control of the army or the kingdom's resources, right?"

Eryx nodded once, conceding I was right. "Okay, it complicates things a bit. But we know what we're doing."

"He's right," Calix agreed quietly. "Our plans are unchanged."

"This is what Kalli meant." I realized, and I looked up to Calix, whose eyes were churning with the colors of the Aurora. "Cyrus is king, and he's contracted the sirens to hunt down any escaped humans. It sounds like he's had them chained up, but some actually managed to get loose."

"That's another bit of news." Eryx cut in, and I sighed, looking up at him miserably. Eryx took my hand, and the fact that he knew I'd need the support made me incredibly nervous. Calix placed his hand on my back, and I reached out blindly for his other hand with my free one. I gripped it, preparing myself mentally.

"I've managed to confirm that Cyrus is capturing large numbers of humans and keeping them in camps. They're tortured and drained of blood, which he is using to fuel his blood magic," Eryx said, and I literally felt the floor shake as a wave of power rolled through me. My rage was so strong I could feel the fire in my throat, and my starlight was bubbling under my skin as I tried to forcefully keep it down. Trying desperately to remember my training. Forcing my emotions under control.

Control.

Cyrus was bringing us nothing but chaos. I couldn't feel so damn chaotic myself on top of it. That couldn't be helpful. I had to be in control. *Balanced.*

No matter how much I wanted to rage and scream.

Pushing my emotions down and down until they were buried was the only choice. I caught Calix giving me a strange look, but we were quickly distracted.

"The only good news is that humans have begun to rise up. Apparently, Kian is being watched too closely to do much, but someone else is definitely helping them. He's trying to find out who, but in the meantime, he's been assisting his brother with hiding his human. Apparently, he's quite fond of her and scared as hell about what his brother might do. It gives us an opportunity."

Calix nodded, a gleam in his eyes. "That is good news. Dusk is seeing him for what he is."

"Yes, in part." Eryx sighed heavily, "But many *are* following him. Those who are too scared not to, those who agree with him, or those who see opportunity."

"How bad is it, Eryx?" I raised my head, our blue eyes locking. His face crumbled.

"I'm sorry, Asteria." He squeezed my hand. "He's keeping them in awful conditions. They're tired, starving, and cold. They're beaten and tortured for the amusement of those carrying it out—all of the most depraved members of Dusk. Those that have been most heavily affected by the chaos."

"Because the more they give into chaos, the more it gets its hooks in them." Calix sighed, his forehead falling to my shoulder.

"So they'll only get worse?" I asked, my voice sounding strange to my own ears, more dead than alive.

They both nodded silently, and we all took a moment to think on how bleak that was. The humans were relying on us, even if they didn't know it. We had to free them. We had to save the ones Cyrus had in his clutches before he killed them all.

When I voiced this thought, they both agreed. "We will. Which actually brings me to my next bit of news."

Eryx smiled slightly, and we both watched him expectantly. "Sunset responded."

Calix lifted his head from my shoulder, eyes wide. "They did?"

"Yeah." Eryx nodded, his smile growing. "King Tieran apparently heard about Asteria. He's specifically requested you bring her." Calix stiffened, and I could feel his unease and suspicion, making me nervous in tandem.

"Why?" He ground out, and Eryx rolled his eyes, shaking his head at his king.

"Calm down, Cay." He laughed. "This is a good thing. He mentioned that the '*Star Queen's appearance*' changed everything."

It was my turn to stiffen in shock. "What? What does that mean?"

"That's what my prophecy called you, a queen of stars." Calix turned to look at me, a new light in his eyes. "Which means—"

"That's what the gods refer to you as. The Star Queen." Eryx cut in. "So it stands to reason Tieran must know something. Perhaps another prophecy that referred to you?"

"Is that good?" I asked hesitantly, looking between the two.

"I think so." Eryx huffed, laughing slightly. "I'm going to come with you, however."

"You won't be the only one," Calix said, amused, as he launched into explaining what had happened since we arrived in Sunrise.

Eryx listened intently, definitely in spymaster mode. It was fascinating to see the differences between the normally sweet and playful Fae and the sly, battle-hardened spymaster. He nodded in various spots, hummed, and asked follow-up questions that launched Calix in whole other directions.

When they were done, I spoke up, "What about Day? Has Arien had any success?"

"No word yet." Eryx shook his head. "Arien likely hasn't had the time to get everyone in place yet. Try not to worry."

I rolled my eyes, muttering, "Easier said than done."

A knock sounded on the door, and we all looked at one another for a moment before Eryx shifted back into a hawk and flew out to the lagoon. Calix went to open the door, and I lounged back on the sofa as if we'd just been relaxing.

I sprang up when I heard the voices, though, and turned to find Altan and Idalia entering.

"Gravadain has decided to hear Cyrus out." Idalia scoffed, shaking her head. "The foolish man," she said it like a curse, and I couldn't blame her, shaking my own head and momentarily closing my eyes.

We expected it, but it was still a blow when I considered what could have been.

"Of course." Calix sarcastically intoned as he ran a hand through his hair as Altan stepped forward.

"Izzy went to inform your guards, but it's best if we leave now before he can stop me from going," Altan recommended, a spark of something deviously joyful in his eyes. "My personal guards insisted on coming as well, but they're aware they'll have to get themselves to Night. I was sure you wouldn't want them on your back."

He raised a brow at Calix, who grunted in agreement, but his eyes rolled around in thought for a moment.

"*Fuck*," he spat, and Eryx flew back in, quickly shifting and ignoring Altan's curse of surprise and Idalia's laugh.

Eryx raised a brow right back at Calix, and the two seemed to communicate without a word before finally Calix turned to Altan. "I'll take them. It's best if we stick together until we get back to Night."

Altan nodded, deeply. "I appreciate it, King Calix. My guards aren't just guards to me, but dear friends."

Calix nodded back in acknowledgment before turning to me, grabbing my hand, and kissing it. "Let's get our things together, and then we'll go meet the guards."

I nodded nervously, looking around to take it in one last time. I may never see Sunrise again, and despite Gravadain and Dagur—who made my blood boil and had my claws digging into the bottom of the dining table to stop my power from exploding out of me—I'd enjoyed my time here thoroughly.

It was strange to think I'd grown up in this kingdom. Panchaia was so disconnected from the small vineyard and the tiny huts I associated with Sunrise. I hoped my parents were doing okay there. They may not be my blood, but they were my parents in every other sense of the word.

We gathered our things quickly, and Calix, sensing my nerves about leaving Sunrise and going to Sunset both, brought me into his arms. I buried my face in his chest and hugged him tightly.

As much as I looked forward to freeing the humans and getting revenge on Cyrus so I could sleep peacefully at night, I found myself equally looking forward to it being over. I wanted Calix and I to be able to just *live*. I wanted to spend time going out dancing and swimming at Nova Falls, flying through the skies together, and partying in the Hedone room.

I wanted to fuck him in every room of the Starlight Palace—a name that actually made me wonder now—and then in every inch of Avalon's palace, a place I hadn't even seen yet!

I wanted to be able to love him without time constraints. I wanted to have the time to learn to love him without the fear of him being ripped away from me.

I'd spent my whole life thinking the gods had abandoned me, only to find *they'd* been waiting for *me*. I wanted to believe they wouldn't take Calix away now.

But I'd never had anything good before, let alone something of this magnitude.

And Cyrus would do everything he could to ensure I was chained to the foot of his throne. I'd rather die than end up back with him. My mind still swirled with ways things could blow up on me.

Freedom was more than a state of being, I was realizing. It was a state of *mind*. I had to wonder if anyone who'd been freed ever truly escaped mentally.

Would I ever *not* fear going back?

"Look at me," Calix murmured, cupping my cheeks to lift my head up. I swallowed hard, trying to contain the million negative thoughts and feelings that ran rampant. "He isn't going to get his hands on you again. Not while I live."

My eyes began to water without my permission. "That's the problem, Calix. He'll be going straight for you. He knows if he takes you out, it'll be much easier to take me."

"Okay, first of all, that's not even remotely true," he said fiercely, shaking his head as his face set into a scowl. "If something ever did happen to me, you would fight like Tartarus and kill Cyrus with your bare hands if you had to." I scoffed, going to move my head, but he tightened his fingers just slightly.

"You *will*. Are you telling me if you saw him kill me, you wouldn't fly off the handle?" He smirked, and it widened as my starlight rushed out, filling the space around us. He nodded. "That's what I thought. But I am not leaving you, my réalta. Not now I've found you. The gods would have to come drag me to the Otherworld kicking and screaming."

I smiled slightly. "You promise?"

His forehead landed on mine, and his breath hit my lips as his lips lightly brushed mine. "I promise."

I pushed myself further into him, my lips taking his as I sucked his lower lip into my mouth, but a sharp knock at the door had us both groaning in frustration. We pulled back, and Calix grabbed our bags before taking my hand and leading me back out.

"Follow us, we'll make sure you're not seen," Idalia said as she led us through the hall to a door, opening it to a much less decorative hallway. I assumed it was the way the slaves traveled here.

We wound down around through the palace, coming out at various points and finding new doors that led to different sections. I had no clue how the slaves here remembered which led where.

We finally came out of a side door leading into the jungle, where the guards were all waiting just within the thicket of trees.

Idalia led us out further, the guards following along until we came to a section near the water where the jungle opened up. She turned back to me with a wink, "If you think dragons have issues with fire, just wait until you see a phoenix."

I was admittedly excited. I'd always wanted to see one, and the royal family of Sunrise in particular. I'd spent years hoping to catch a glimpse of them in the air. Since then, I'd seen Pegasus and dragons—found out *I* was even a dragon—but I still had yet to see a phoenix.

I watched Altan expectantly, and he raised a brow at me. I crossed my arms over my chest, "I'm not shifting until I see a Tartarus damned phoenix, okay?"

He threw his head back with a laugh but conceded. He said his goodbyes to his mother before standing back. His guards all took a few more steps away, and I understood why as he shifted into a huge, flaming phoenix.

His yellow and teal feathers were *literally* on fire. The teal fire slowly went out, leaving just normal feathers, with not a singe on them.

"They always default to being on fire when they shift. It's a real pain in the ass," Idalia whispered, and I bit my lip to stop my laughter.

Altan's huge, feathered head cocked to the side, before a wing came out and knocked into me. I fell to the side but caught myself, glaring at him as he chuckled in my mind.

His phoenix form was definitely smaller than my dragon form, but not by as much as one might expect. Their ability to funnel the fire they erupted into bouts of flame was somewhat equivalent to our ability to spit fire. It wasn't as powerful as ours, but it could be used for different types of attacks, which would give us an edge in battle with multiple fire-breathing creatures on board.

I certainly wouldn't want to find myself fighting a phoenix, but when the time came… based on Gravadain's choices….

The chance of avoiding it seemed slim to none.

CHAPTER 30

Asteria

FLYING in between a dragon and a phoenix was bizarre. I never thought I'd find myself in such a position, but here I was. A dragon, flying beside other magical animals that I once only dreamed of catching a mere glimpse of.

For all the issues I'd faced due to the truth coming out, I had to admit there were even more benefits.

I just wished humans had a way to experience the lives they dreamed of, without having to realize they're Fae to achieve it.

The thought of all the humans Cyrus currently had imprisoned sent shudders down my spine. I'd seen his brutality up close, and I didn't doubt what Eryx said was true. I watched as he flew ahead and wondered if there was a way to get him into Dusk to get the lay of the land.

If these camps had been set up across Dusk… how many humans did he have in them? He still needed them, at least in his mind, to work as his slaves. I couldn't imagine his lords being happy if they were taken away and made to… *gasp—do their own work.*

But Cyrus was king now, meaning dissent would be crushed quickly.

As we neared Biarma, I couldn't help the unease I felt. The last time I was here, Cyrus captured me and brought me back to Dusk, taking me away from Calix and nearly succeeding in breaking me.

But the shining domed tops of the palace glowed in the light of day, and the jungle trees butting up right to the palace, though not overtaking it like Sunrise's, swayed in the wind. It looked beautiful and innocuous. Not like the site of a battle that saw my world crashing down around me.

And this time, we were coming invited, as opposed to sneaking in.

As we flew lower, Fae and humans alike ducked out of the way, and a few screamed as they ran in the other direction. I was confused until Calix's voice echoed in my mind. *"After what happened last time… I may have lit the place up on my way out."*

Something must be wrong with me, because that shouldn't fill me with a light, beautiful feeling, knowing that Calix was so enraged by my capture.

Sunset working with Dusk during that conflict was another thing we'd need to discuss with them. King Tieran had let Cyrus in, let me be taken, and I knew that was something neither Calix nor I would forget easily—despite how much we needed them on our side in this war.

We landed before the palace, and I was surprised to see that what could only be the royal family had come to greet us.

A dark-skinned man stepped forward, and his closely cropped, short black hair was topped with a brushed copper crown. Teal jewels set within it created the illusion of wings spread across it. An incongruous sight with the day-old stubble on his face, not to mention his more casual clothing. He wore a high-necked, long lounge jacket in teal that was crafted with orange embroidery and jewels, paired with orange pants that could just be made out from under the length of his jacket. And his bright blue eyes were already locked on me.

"Princess Asteria." He smiled widely, and I was taken aback by how delighted he was to see me. The fact that he may know more about me and what role the gods had given me was a constant itch I couldn't shake. I hated other people knowing things I didn't, but even more so when it was *about* me.

"King Calix." He nodded to my mate and then turned, surprised. "Prince Altan, we certainly weren't expecting you." He raised a brow, and Altan shot him a smirk.

"Well, in times like these, King Tieran," Altan winked, "I find it important to stick to those walking the right path."

Tieran raised a brow at him but watched him with a speculative look on his face.

"Father, perhaps we can discuss Prince Altan's presence later. They've flown a good distance; I'm sure they'd appreciate a rest before we meet." The youngest prince, Zakat, said. I remembered that he was actually the heir, not the eldest son, Vesper.

The two stood next to one another, but they looked like they'd rather be anywhere else. Zakat was all his father in looks, sharing his dark black skin tone, while Vesper was more of a mix of his parents. Queen Eveleen stood beside them, with olive skin and green almond eyes. She had a long, luxurious mass of dark hair that made me suddenly wish for more volume in my own.

Vesper's curly hair was shorn close to his head, while Zakat had braids that fell to his shoulders. Their only similarity being the bright blue eyes they got from their father. Their sister, Princess Dysis, had her own braids in an updo, leaving some of them down to frame her face. She had delicate features, with hazel eyes and tawny brown skin. She seemed to take half her features from each parent, even more so than Vesper.

As King Tieran nodded to Prince Zakat and began to lead us in, Princess Dysis came up beside me. "It's wonderful to meet you, Princess."

The strangeness of being called Princess would never fade. "You as well, Princess Dysis."

"Please, just call me Dy." She smiled, and I looked her over. She seemed strangely genuine.

"Asteria, then." I insisted, already sick of all the titles. She took my arm with hers, leading me forward, and leaned into me slightly.

"Father has been so excited since we learned of you," she whispered, and my eyebrows flew upward.

"Why?" I whispered back, and she giggled, shaking her head.

"He'd never forgive me if I spoiled it." I sighed at her response, resigning myself to waiting.

"Princess Asteria." Prince Zakat came up beside me, and I could feel Calix's discomfort from where he walked beside King Tieran. "What are you doing hanging around with these fools?" He smirked, head tilting toward Altan, who huffed.

"Fool? Have you seen yourself recently?" Altan gave him a look up and down before scoffing, but his eyes definitely lingered a bit on the prince's exposed chest, his loose shirt hanging open down the middle to expose dark, shining skin. Had I not had Calix, I may not have been able to help lingering myself.

"Oh, don't be jealous, Altan." Zakat cooed at him. "I'm sure we can find a way to make people take you seriously."

"Ha!" Altan barked. "That's rich coming from you."

Zakat turned to him completely, stepping closer so he was eye to eye with Altan. The two stared at one another intensely, and I raised a brow as the tension between them rose. I wasn't sure if they were about to kill each other or kiss.

I was personally voting on the latter. Because hey, I might have the sexiest man in Celesterra all to myself, but a girl could always appreciate hot men together.

"Keep flirting, Zakat," Vesper murmured as he walked past. "I'm sure that will go down well with your suitors."

Zakat groaned, his head swinging toward his brother. "Don't remind me."

He shuddered, turning back to face me and whispering in horror, "Father wants me to find a bride to continue the royal line. Can you imagine? Sleeping with a woman?"

He shuddered again, and I instantly felt for him. I couldn't imagine being required to marry, let alone to a person I didn't prefer. The thought of being forced to have a child was equally reprehensible to me.

Children were something I never really considered. As a slave, I didn't want to continue the cycle, despite the way the women of my village complimented my "birthing hips" and tried to convince me to settle down once I was placed in my new kingdom.

But things were different now.

Calix and I actually loved each other, for one. He was also very close to his family, and I imagined he'd want a family of his own one day. A little babe who was a piece of both of us. And we *would* need an heir.

But I was only twenty-one, and we had centuries for all of that. I needed time to adjust to this life, to learn to live and love and rule.

Babies were centuries off, at an absolute *minimum*.

"This is why I should have been heir." Vesper stopped walking forward and stood stiffly, shoulders moving up and down as he breathed heavily. He turned suddenly to face Zakat, and I felt uncomfortable being stuck in the middle of the family drama of Fae I had just met.

"You brush off all of your responsibilities," he seethed, as Zakat tilted his head at him, a taunting smile on his lips. "You never take your role seriously. You'll destroy this kingdom should you become king."

"Ow." Zakat pouted. "My *feelings*."

Vesper snarled, turning in a huff and walking away. Zakat chuckled, putting an arm around Dysis's shoulders.

"You shouldn't provoke him." She tutted, rolling her eyes to me. "The two of them are like children, I swear."

"Aw, come on, Dy!" Zakat protested loudly, "You know he's constantly up my ass. He's bitter, and he takes it out on me."

"That may be true, but you know it's hard for him too." She sighed sadly. "Most firstborn males are chosen as heir, and he thinks something is wrong with him that he wasn't chosen."

"Sometimes, I really wish he was," Zakat admitted quietly, but Altan shook his head.

"No, you don't. Trust me," he said, his eyes darting down to the floor, and missing the way Zakat appraised him, a certain light shining in his eyes.

"Do you all mind if I steal my mate back now?" Calix was already leaning against the door as we arrived, his arms crossed, and brow raised.

An instant smile appeared on my face, and I briefly wondered when I became the kind of person who couldn't help smiling.

Calix's arm came around me as he looked down. "Having fun?"

"Oh, we're going to have lots of fun!" Dy interjected, giggling.

"Don't mind my sister; she's overexcitable." Zakat snorted. "We'll get out of your hair for now. Come on, Dy, you can talk to Asteria later."

"But Zak!" She whined slightly, and my eyes widened in surprise. She seemed to actually *want* to befriend me. I just couldn't figure out why.

But Zakat dragged his sister down the hall, and Altan, shaking his head as his eyes tracked the heir of Sunset, opened the door across the hall and disappeared inside.

Calix pulled me into our room, and I didn't even get a chance to look around before he had me up against the door. Instant arousal shot through me. Something about him taking control, using his strength to hold me up, had me getting wet immediately.

He could smell it, too, and his growl echoed in my ears as his mouth crashed into mine. After a minute of fighting him to gain control, a useless venture to be sure, he pulled back. His eyes were wild, with green and blue darting around his purple orbs chaotically.

"I can't stand watching these men fawn all over you," he snarled, and took hold of the travel dress I was wearing, ripping it straight down the middle.

I gasped, my hips bucking upwards, trying to find any kind of friction. Calix's knees hit the floor, and his mouth immediately found my cunt, practically swallowing it whole. I grabbed his hair as I screamed out, the feel of his tongue tracing over and between me, my body couldn't seem to stop undulating as I chased the sensation.

He sucked my clit into his mouth, lightly nipping it before laving it with his tongue. I lost my mind to the pleasure as he single-mindedly went at my cunt like a man possessed.

It didn't take long until my walls were clenching uncontrollably, but I tried to hold off my climax, not wanting it to end.

A slap against my clit shook me, a ragged moan leaving my mouth. "You don't keep your orgasms from me, do you understand?"

I nodded frantically as I met Calix's eyes, and I kept eye contact as he smirked, mouth wet with my arousal.

"Good girl," he growled against my skin, and the vibration went straight to my clit. "Now, cum for me."

His hands held me open so his tongue could thrust inside me, and his shadows circled my clit for him, leaving him fully focused on forcing my orgasm from me. He succeeded, as I couldn't possibly hold it off any longer. I came screaming, slumping down on the door as Calix swallowed every drop of me.

When he finally pulled away, I attacked, pushing him back on the floor and ripping his pants from him. His breathless laugh was full of pleasure, and I could feel how much he loved my rabid desperation.

He was already hard as stone, and I grasped that long, thick cock I loved so much, pumping my hand down the shaft. My mouth enclosed his head, earning a deep groan from Calix. I swirled my tongue around it before licking up and down the shaft, trailing my fingers up the other side.

I teased him for a minute before I finally lowered my head, taking more of his length down my throat. He thrust his hips up into my mouth, swearing loudly. His hand grasped my hair, moving it up and to the side so he could watch me without the dark curtain of my hair interfering.

"Fuck." He groaned loudly at the sight. "That's it, grá. *Such* a good girl."

I trailed my fingernails down his thighs and back up as I sucked his cock, before bringing them up to his balls and trailing across them. He groaned, his head falling back as I gripped them lightly. I stuffed as much of his cock down my throat as I could take, but it wasn't enough to encompass him fully. Instead, I let my starlight out to play around the base of his shaft, since my hands were otherwise occupied. Having this extra-sensory way to help tackle this monster felt a bit like cheating, but honestly, it was a kind of cheating I could get behind.

I could feel his struggle for control, but I was determined to finally get to taste him. My head bobbed up and down quickly, and that was when I felt his shadows descend on my body. Some followed the line of my curves, while others began tweaking my nipples. I moaned around his cock as the pleasure ran through me, the vibration making Calix moan in turn.

I could feel his cock starting to twitch in my mouth, so I ran my tongue under his head, humming as I did so. I was rewarded with a loud roar and the feel of him spilling down my throat. I swallowed every bit of it, despite some difficulties in doing so. I had to keep swallowing quickly to take the volume, and as I popped off his cock, I licked my lips to get the few drops I missed.

Calix was watching me wide-eyed, panting on the floor. I giggled, making him grab me around the waist and pulling me to him as he rolled us over. He hovered over me, his fingers coming up to move my hair out of my face.

"You're fucking *incredible*," he said, still looking a bit dreamy-eyed.

I smirked, reaching a hand up to his cheek, running my thumb over the sharp cheekbone. "I know."

He laughed, his head dipping down and leaving us enclosed in a curtain of silvery-white hair.

"You are completely unreal," I admitted, softly. "Just months ago, I could never have even dreamed of someone like you."

"My réalta." His forehead touched mine for a moment, before he lifted to meet my eyes. "You've dreamed of me all your life. You just didn't know I was there. Sometimes, all it takes is opening your eyes to change your whole life."

"Is that so?" I tilted my head to the side, my small smile growing.

He nodded very seriously. "Absolutely. If you knew how many times I called out for you, tried to beat down that barrier to reach you... but all it took was for you to step into the light and let the darkness swallow you whole."

"If I'd known, I would have embraced the darkness much sooner," I told him, my voice teasing, but with an undertone that was heavy with desire.

"Good thing it's never too late," he whispered back, before taking my lips in his.

WE SPENT THE afternoon losing ourselves in pleasure, learning every part of one another's bodies we hadn't yet explored and then some. But responsibility reared its head eventually, and we were forced to get up and dressed to meet the Daanan's.

The rooms we were given looked like what I remember of King Tieran's. At least the glimpse I got when we dropped off the information about Cyrus. The arched windows were covered with wooden slats carved with decorative shapes that let the light shine through them and create patterns on the walls, while the ceiling was covered in a mosaic of colorful tiles. The bed was circular, though they'd given us purple and teal sheets, as opposed to the orange and teal Tieran had. A personal touch, I assumed, based on our royal colors.

The living area was filled with seating set low to the ground that was clearly made for lounging. The sofa, chaise, pillows, and cushions were primarily orange and white in color. A dining area was nearby, made of rich wood that I was sure was made from trees local to the area. The table overlooked the balcony and gave us a wonderful view of the small lagoon in the middle of the palace's courtyard.

It wasn't nearly as spacious as the one under Panchaia's palace, but it was about the size of Calix's pool.

Upon leaving our rooms, we found Altan and Zakat both leaning against the wall opposite our door, pointedly not looking at one another with their arms crossed against their chests. I rolled my eyes at them both.

"Finally ready to go?" Zakat smirked at me, and Calix snuck an arm around my waist as his smirk widened. I realized then that I'd forgotten to let Calix know that Zakat preferred men. Though, I did enjoy the possessive jealousy that was radiating from him. Maybe I could wait a bit.

We picked Eryx up along the way; since he wasn't royalty himself, he was given a room a few doors down that was reserved for the guests of visiting royals. Which was ridiculous. Who has guest rooms for guests' guests?

Zakat led us all down to a study, where Tieran, Eveleen, and their children awaited us. Tieran stood before a heavy wooden door, with a large, rusted metal key in his hand.

"First off, I would like to begin by apologizing to you both." Tieran greeted us, looking between Calix and me. My brow rose in surprise, and I could feel Calix's suspicion and disbelief like it was my own. "Had I known what was actually going on, I wouldn't have ever let Cyrus in."

"What you mean is that you had no problem letting him come retrieve his wayward slave, right?" I countered, grinding my teeth as that familiar rage rose inside.

Tieran cocked his head slightly before nodding once. "Yes, I suppose that is the truth of it. I'm sure, given the circumstances, you're very much against the way of life we've always known."

"You're damn right." I spat in agreement. "It's barbaric, how you treat humans. Calix was the only Fae who seemed to see that. He was the only one doing anything to help them. Neither one of us will allow it to continue."

Eveleen looked nervously between us. "Can I ask how you plan to accomplish such a thing? That seems like a massive undertaking. And if you're already fighting Cyrus…"

"This is bigger than that," Tieran said before I could respond. "Let me first show you what we have here, and then we can discuss plans moving forward."

Our joint suspicion rose within the mate bond, and Calix and I looked quickly at one another. None of this made sense, nor was it in any way what we expected. Eryx looked over to us both, nodding, and Calix sighed, looking to me once more and awaiting my permission.

Tieran was watching us closely, and I shifted toward him slightly, nodding, "Show us."

He smiled brightly, turning to unlock the door. "Follow me."

We followed one after another down a tight spiral staircase, leading deep underground if the musty smell was anything to go by. The route eventually brought us to an old dirt tunnel, and we began to make our way down it. Torches lit up the walls as we neared, the magic activating with our presence.I reached for Calix's hand, entwining our fingers and holding on tightly. The lack of windows or any natural light reminded me too much of the claustrophobic slave corridors in Dusk's palace. I hated being enclosed, and something about being this far underground was even more unnerving.

"I apologize for the trek, but my ancestors wanted to ensure no one would ever find this place," Tieran explained, pausing briefly in a heavy silence. "It was too important to the fate of our world."

Shivers ran down my spine, and I looked nervously at Calix and Eryx. Knowing they were both here with me was a comfort. I had no idea what Tieran was on about, but a feeling in my gut told me I knew exactly what it was.

Arawn's words to me as I lay dying in Dusk rang in my ears, "*When the sun sets, and starlight gathers, you must walk among the dead. Earn your way through to Tír na nÓg, and learn the fate that awaits.*"

When *sun sets*, that couldn't be a coincidence.

Fuck, why did the gods always have to deliver messages via riddle?

Chapter 31

Asteria

At the end of the long tunnel, we came to another door, this one with a strange device in the center of it. Tieran grabbed the dagger at his waist, making Calix and Eryx both reach for their swords.

Tieran raised his hands in surrender, "I only mean to cut myself, boys. The queen will be perfectly safe."

"Queen?" Eryx asked, brows arching in surprise.

Tieran turned to me with a smile. "*The Star Queen.*"

I swallowed hard as the pressure on my chest increased. Calix retook my hand, and I squeezed it hard as I steadied my breathing.

Tieran cut his hand, leaving a deep gash behind, before he pressed his bloody palm against the door. The blood seeped into the mechanism, flowing through it until it turned dark red. I jumped as the blood caught fire, watching with wide eyes. I leaned into Calix as the fire spread across the deep grooves of the door, until the telltale sound of something unlocking could be heard, a loud click echoing through the tunnel.

The door creaked open by itself, and that didn't help me to feel any less creeped out.

We followed Tieran into a room that had clearly been carved out of the dirt tunnel. Torches lit up as we walked in, bathing it in light, and bringing focus to the middle of the room. There stood a podium, with a glass case surrounding what looked to be a very old parchment.

"This is why I've asked you here." Tieran waved me over. I couldn't bring myself to let go of Calix's hand, so I dragged him over with me. Not that he minded.

Our shared unease beat steadily between our shared souls.

I looked down at the parchment, and found it was written in the ancient Fae language, *of fucking course.* I sighed. "I can't read it."

"Allow me." Calix kissed the top of my head. "This is an account of—"

His head snapped to Tieran, his eyes wide. "No."

"Yes." Tieran nodded, his eyes knowing, a slight smile on his face.

"What?!" I snapped, looking between them both.

Calix cleared his throat, as wonder spread through the bond. "This is an account of the six Fae kings of old. The ones who united Celesterra."

"How?" I gasped. "That was millennia ago, right? How could something that old have survived this long?"

"Because my ancestors knew this information would be forgotten," Tieran answered, his brows rising. "They knew the day would come when whoever ruled Sunset would need to be prepared."

"It speaks of the agreement forged between them, but it also speaks of the Oracle being present to seal the pact among them with the gods' blessing." Calix read, leaning over the glass box.

"They knew the balance was in danger of being threatened then, and they knew coming together would be the only way to…" he trailed off, looking down for a moment. "The only way to delay it."

My eyebrows creased, taking that in. "I thought that the whole point of forging the agreement was to fix to the balance?"

Tieran shook his head, his blue eyes reflecting a mixture of excitement and sympathy. "It was only ever a stopgap to delay the problem, until the time would come when a being would arise. One who could *actually* do something to fix the balance."

I didn't like the way everyone was looking at me. I shook my head slowly, somewhat in shock, despite the pieces of this puzzle I'd already heard from others. Calix squeezed my hand.

"The prophecy given to them spoke of a Star Queen who would rise when the night was darkest. Who would cast down the usurper, and free the people from their bondage. She would bring true balance back to the lands," Calix continued reading, and looked up with a blinding smile as he finished.

"Asteria." His eyes were wide, joy brimming in his eyes.

"We can do it," I whispered, tears coming to my eyes, as pure exhilaration and relief crashed through me. Hope lit my heart, and part of me wished to douse it in my fear for the future, but I couldn't bring myself to smother it.

"Continue reading, Calix," Tieran advised hesitantly, and Calix looked uncertainly back to the parchment. My heart beat out of control, and I could feel the starlight under my skin trying to escape.

"But her fate is Celesterra's. Should she fail, Celesterra will fall with her. Chaos will overrun the world, and blood will reign," he finished heavily.

My heart fell to my stomach, and starlight leaked out from my fingers. My currently hidden wings felt heavy on my back as fire gathered in my throat. Fear and rage twisted together. I couldn't let this happen. I couldn't let the entire *world* fall.

How could Cyrus even achieve such a thing?

How could he affect the world so greatly that there was no going back?

How was *I* the one who was supposed to save us all? I spiraled internally, but thankfully, others were there to pick up the information-gathering slack.

"Blood will reign?" Eryx questioned, a brow rising.

Tieran shrugged, "We assume that to mean blood will continue flowing, more deaths, more killing. But prophecies can be quite tricky. Even when they seem obvious, they often have meanings one doesn't see until after the fact."

"But one thing is truly clear: *you* are the Star Queen the prophecy speaks of," Tieran declared as he knelt before me.

I couldn't breathe.

His family knelt with him, though Vesper grudgingly so, as Tieran continued, "You alone can save Celesterra now, Queen Asteria. Our fates are all in your hands."

"No pressure or anything," Zakat smirked up at me, his eyes crinkling with laughter.

I swayed on my feet, but Calix was there, a resolute balance to the chaos in my heart and mind. *Huh.* Chaos in the mind, chaos in the land. Seems like they go hand in hand.

I'd have to bring my own chaotic thoughts and feelings under control. If the balance of Celesterra was on my shoulders, and mine alone…

We could all very well be fucked.

WE MADE OUR way back to Tieran's study, all of us quiet and stuck in our own thoughts.

"Now," Tieran began as we sat around the round wooden table in the middle of the room. A red, teal, orange, and yellow rug sat beneath the table, with a large diamond in the middle that had swirling patterns surrounding it and lines of color in each corner.

"Tell me what exactly you've been up to Calix, how you've managed so far, Asteria, and what the plan is from here," Tieran demanded more than asked.

Just like with King Gravadain, we went through everything, top to bottom. But unlike King Gravadain, King Tieran listened patiently, asked intelligent questions, and while he was surprised, he didn't think us insane.

So, that was a plus.

"And after this, you'll be journeying to the Otherworld?" Zakat asked, his eyes wide and jaw slack in shock.

I nodded in confirmation. "Unfortunately, yes. I'd rather we just attack Dusk first, but if the gods have information we need…"

"It's smarter to wait," Eveleen chimed in. She was quieter than Queen Idalia for sure, but there was a certain strength to her still. "You want the best chance for success, Asteria."

I agreed with a deep sigh. Calix chuckled under his breath, and I glared at him. "I just want him gone."

"I know. And we will end him, my réalta." Calix reminded me. "But we need to get all our dragons in a row first. Arien needs to sort out Day, and Isleen needs time to gather soldiers in Sunrise."

"And I need time to contact my spies in Dusk," Eryx spoke up from beside me, putting a hand on my shoulder. "We need more information on the current state of things before we rush in and attack. We don't want to put our soldiers in unnecessary danger if we can prevent it."

I nodded, sighing once more. "I know. I do. It's just…"

I trailed off, but words didn't seem to be necessary. Everyone understood.

No one wanted the balance threatened. Not when it could mean the very end of us all. The threat of iron weapons alone was a danger we needed to navigate *very* carefully. I had zero desire to come skin to metal with any iron in my lifetime.

And whatever Cyrus was planning, I knew it went beyond whatever it had originally started out as. This was more than a fight with Night now. More than getting me back. There was something we were missing. I was sure of it.

When I hesitantly brought it up, the others sat in thought for a moment.

"I think you're right," Altan said, humming in contemplation. "He's escalated greatly since this began, and if he's outsourcing humans from Day, then he's going through them quickly."

I winced at the thought, my heart aching for every human life lost.

"And if he plans to keep you," he continued apologetically, making Calix growl low in his throat at the thought. "But he's promised Aelius your death, then he certainly plans to stab him in the back. So who will rule Day?"

"I'm almost certain he killed his father as well." Eryx added, "There's no way the timing is a coincidence."

"So we need to figure out what exactly Cyrus is planning now," Calix began, running his fingers across the table. Itching for his map and figures, most likely. It almost brought a smile to my face, the way he relied on them while planning was kind of adorable.

"If we attack with only half the information, and no sight of his goal, it will only bring failure. We'll be fighting the wrong war. Understanding your enemy, and their objective, is half the battle after all," Calix explained, his voice rumbling as his dragon made its way to the fore.

I put my hand on his thigh, and his clawed hand grasped it. We kept each other calm as we discussed the man who had tried to tear us apart—who still aimed to do so.

"I will send my soldiers south." Tieran nodded decisively. "They will gather at our borders, so when the word comes, we can attack from the North. Unless, of course, you need us in Evenfall, in which case, we can meet you there."

"You'll be joining your soldiers?" Calix raised his brow.

"Don't you?" Tieran countered, a smirk rising on his lips.

"Of course." Calix snorted. "But too many kings sit their asses on their thrones while they send their men to die for them."

"Agreed. Which is why I will be there, leading the charge." The king of Sunset smiled, a thirst for war reflected in his eyes.

We all had it.

Every Fae ruler I'd met thus far had a thirst for bloodshed. It was all about how they managed that urge that made the difference.

THE NEXT DAY, we found ourselves in Tieran's study once more, rolling out our plans and adjusting them as needed. Trying to figure out how to assemble all the separate pieces of our growing army into one.

"We need Titan," Calix groaned, wiping his forehead. The long black tunic and pants they'd given him were making him sweat in this heat. I'd chosen a barely there silver dress that covered everything but was so light and flowy, I *felt* naked.

Poor Calix didn't have that option.

I was more than willing to lick the sweat off him afterward to help, however.

"We'll confer with him as soon as we get back," Eryx agreed, sighing. "But sending messages back and forth will prove complicated. We need a sure way to get them north past Dusk."

"Dawn being allied with Dusk means any way across the continent itself is out." Calix shook his head.

"Wait!" I shouted a bit too loudly, my head shooting up from the map to meet their eyes. Mine were alight with an idea that hit me at the mention of Dawn.

"My mother—my birth mother—Queen Aurelia, was from Dawn. Meaning, I have family in Dawn that could help." My excitement grew as my plan came together in my mind.

"We don't know if they'd side with you or their king, Asteria." Eryx cautioned, shaking his head.

"Lord Dali, my uncle, rules Chryse, and my cousin, Lord Kiran, rules Nysa. That's two families in Dawn we can try to sway," I insisted, knowing this could work. "We can ask my mother for help. But if they could get a messenger up through the Slievenamon Mountains, they could get it to Sunset without tipping anyone off."

"If we ask your mother," Calix began, looking sternly at me. I could feel his urge to protect me in the bond, and it made my shoulders relax, knowing he didn't disagree, but he would always put my protection first.

"And she makes contact for us, then I could see it working. As long as they have a bird shifter of some sort who can fly it up. Going through the mountains would be too difficult and take too much time otherwise. I would have sent Eryx, but we unfortunately need him for more than message delivery." He finished, and I smiled brightly. "Thanks ever so," Eryx remarked, dryly.

A knock on the door interrupted us before anything else could be said. Tieran called out for whoever it was to enter, and Dysis came in, wringing her hands, with anxiety clear on her face.

"Dysis?" Tieran asked, brow creasing. "What's wrong?"

"It's Vesper, Father." She bit her lip and looked between us all.

Tieran sighed heavily, leaning forward with his hands on the table, "What has that damn boy done now?"

"He's gone," she choked out. "All his closest friends and personal guards are gone, and the men they command are too. Several hundred soldiers, all gone."

Tieran straightened, rage lining every inch of his face. Zakat's face, on the other hand, fell. But his voice was as dry as a desert when he chimed in. "What a surprise, he heard about a prince killing others to be king and immediately ran to his side."

"We don't know that!" Tieran yelled, turning to Zakat, fury lining his face.

"Yes, we do!" Zakat shouted back, a snarl on his face. "Don't pretend, Father. We both know he's been unhappy since the day I was born! He'd do anything to see himself the heir instead of me. Cyrus will offer him a way." He laughed dryly, "Though, it's just as likely Cyrus will stab him in the back. Seems like Vesper thinks himself intelligent enough to outsmart the madman."

Altan's hand landed on Zakat's shoulder, and he shifted toward him. "This isn't on you, Prince. Vesper made his own choices."

"He wouldn't have without me." Zakat despaired, throwing his hands up.

"Wouldn't he?" Altan countered, raising a brow at him. "He wouldn't be the heir regardless, and that's clearly been eating away at him."

"This is madness!" Tieran interjected, his hands nearly shaking. "He's going to get himself killed! Or get *you* killed! Over what? A damn crown?!" He ripped the crown of Sunset off his head, looking at it disdainfully for a moment before throwing it forcefully at the wall.

It bounced off, landing unharmed on the carpet after several rolls. The silence in the room was deafening, and I looked between Calix and Eryx, unsure what to do or say. This undeniably complicated everything.

It seemed like almost every kingdom was splitting apart. Chaos was encroaching, and its insidious reach was stretching far and wide.

"It's chaos, isn't it?" I asked quietly. "The balance shifts more to chaos by the day. Those who wouldn't have done something before, merely had passing thoughts—say about wanting to be heir. Chaos is pushing them to do it."

Silence followed my words, but the bowed heads said more than any words could have.

"Cyrus will be feeling that most of all. Constantly being pushed farther, escalating more and more." I added after a few minutes of us all absorbing what had happened.

"And now Vesper will be by his side." Zakat snarled, and his father shook his head helplessly. But a moment later, he looked up at Zakat and placed his hands on his shoulders, bringing his face, set in harsh lines, close to his son's.

"You must be the heir I know you can be, my son," Tieran said forcefully.

"Father." Zakat shook his head, his mouth opening to argue.

"I do not speak of betrothals and children!" he yelled, a fierce look on his face. "I speak of you stepping up to lead."

That made his son stand up straighter, the adolescent disagreement fading from his face, replaced with a much more determined look.

"You must go with the Star Queen and Night King. They will be leading this war, and we must follow," Tieran insisted, eyebrows rising. "Sometimes, being a ruler means knowing when to take charge, and when to step back. There is just as delicate a balance to ruling as there is to all of Celesterra."

"What do you want me to do?" Zakat asked quietly, eyes riveted on his father.

"You represent Sunset, and you support the queen," Tieran told him, a smile beginning to peek out. "Everything else will follow."

Zakat turned to me with a smirk, "Well then, Star Queen." He bowed with a flourish. "It seems I'm at your command."

I gulped, looking quickly at Calix before I was able to wrangle my wild emotions into a small box inside me. I straightened my shoulders.

I could do this. I *would*.

Just because everything seemed to be spinning wildly around me didn't mean I couldn't take control of it.

After all, we'd gone from having no allies outside of Night to having half of Day already secured behind me, and now part of Sunrise and the majority of Sunset were with us.

We had much better odds now.

There was only one thing left to do.

It was time to go meet the gods.

CHAPTER 32

Arien

FLYING around the palace, I let out a burst of fire that had the forces surrounding it scrambling back.

On our return to Day, we'd sent word to all of our allies, and they were now on their way to Avalon. Unfortunately, it was impossible to hide what was going on. Word got out quickly, and forces loyal to my father had now surrounded the palace with the intent of taking it back in his name.

Mother was inside, working hard at putting together speeches and plans for what was to come. It was my responsibility to put this movement down quickly, and with force.

The people of Day needed to have confidence in Asteria as their queen to turn against Aelius. Winning battles in her name could only help in that regard.

I'd summoned those loyal to me within the palace, and they now made their way to me so we could go out to meet those loyal to my father. I didn't think our palace had ever seen battle at its gates before, nor had Day ever split in half the way it was now doing.

I knew this only fed more into the chaos that was encroaching on our lands, but unfortunately, the only way out was through. We had to embrace a bit of chaos to ultimately get back to balance.

It was always darkest before the dawn.

But thankfully, we had a star to light the way.

I smiled, which I knew looked more like a snarl in my dragon form, but the thought of Asteria sitting on the throne of Day, crowned and ruling, was one I had waited my entire life for.

It may look different now than we'd expected, with Asteria mated to Calix, but I believed her when she said she'd find a way. Mother might think her naive, but Mother, despite all her actions to help Asteria, was more rooted in tradition than she'd admit. This was never about changing the order of things; it was always about protecting her child.

And those were two very different things.

I knew after meeting Asteria that she'd never accept the status quo. I couldn't blame her one bit for it either. Had I grown up as a slave instead of a prince, I can only imagine how pissed I would be.

I had to admit that since actually meeting her, seeing the pain lining her face and echoing in her words, I had been thinking quite a lot about the humans. I wanted to destroy Cyrus for what he did to my twin sister.

But weren't there brothers out there just as angry over *their* sisters being enslaved?

Was there one out there who wanted to kill *me*?

I had never mistreated our slaves. I'd grown up knowing my sister was hidden as a human, so I'd felt a certain amount of guilt about it. Which had only been compounded now. Every slave I passed in the hall, I wondered about their life, wondered if my family had ever mistreated them, and wondered if they had dreams as big as Asteria's.

And we had a chance to free them all now.

Yes, we'd have to change the way we live, but we had paid servants, as well. Fae of lower status needing work were given tasks my parents didn't trust the humans with. We could pay the humans just as easily. It's not like we lacked gold.

And from what Calix had said, introducing humans into their economy had only boosted it, not hurt it.

But first, I had to ensure my father didn't win. Starting with these assholes.

I swooped down once more, fire spitting out onto the first row of soldiers who didn't move in time. My army charged in, and since I couldn't risk burning my men, I flew over to shift back quickly. I pulled my sword from my sheath and charged into the thick of the battle.

A soldier I recognized from training spotted me immediately, snarling, "Traitor!"

I smirked back at him. "I'm loyal to my queen and kingdom. It's the king who betrays the gods."

I deflected his swing with my sword and swung to block his next move before feinting left and using the opportunity to get inside his guard, my elbow hitting his chin as I kicked his legs out. He fell to the ground like a sack of grain, and I took his head before he could even look up to say goodbye to the sky above.

I glanced around to see blood spraying and men falling. I could only hope it was mainly our enemies falling and not my own men, but there was no time to check. I met the next man with a jab of my sword that he parried, and we traded several blows before he tried to pull the same trick I just did, feinting a movement right. But I didn't fall for it and instead met him as he swung, surprising him enough to knock the blade from his hand.

The fighting was thick and fast around me. I'd fought in minor battles before, and plenty of mock ones, but nothing prepared me for this kind of scale. It was why many had resented my placement as General. I was too young, too green—but I was determined to prove them all wrong. I'd trained harder than anyone else and proved that I knew what I was doing in the training yard just as much as I did strategizing in the war room.

Still, this was new, and a tingle of fear ran through me—but fear would get me killed, I knew that. I brushed it away and instead channeled my rage. I let my dragon side come to the fore as much as I could without letting any part of my body shift.

I met the next man with a shout of rage that clearly threw him off, and he struggled to fight back. I rammed my sword through his sternum before he knew what had happened. As I pulled my bloody sword back out, his body slumped to the ground.

I ran to the next and the next. Eventually, I felt sweat dripping down my back under the heavy golden plate as the fighting began to seem endless. Soldier after soldier met their end at my blade, but still more remained.

Tiredness crept up on me, and it made me sloppy enough to miss the man sneaking up on me. I was knocked to the ground from behind, and when I looked up, a blonde-haired man who resembled Kem stood over me, smirking.

"Oh, I'm going to enjoy this." He laughed cruelly, leaning down to grab me.

I grasped my blade, determined to attempt a defense even in this awful position, but the man suddenly cried out. I jolted back as the point of a blade came out through his chest and nearly got my eye in the process.

I looked up as his gurgling body fell to the side, only to find Soren standing above me. He reached his hand out, and I took it, letting him help me up. He nodded at me, and I nodded back, thankful he had stepped in even if I was embarrassed at being saved by a human.

"I'm sure you had him, my Prince," Soren stated as he looked around grimly. "But I didn't want to be the one to have to tell Asteria if I was wrong." He smirked slightly before throwing himself back into the fray.

It was beyond aggravating to hear him call my sister by name and not her proper title. It was uncouth to refer to her in such a personal manner.

But I had to admit I was surprised by his courage as he ran straight into a fight against Fae so much stronger than himself. He was cunning, using sneak attacks to persevere with such a clear disadvantage.

I focused on my rage at his familiarity with his queen instead as I went back into the fight. I took down as many as I could until I looked up, covered in blood and sweat, and realized there was no one waiting to fight. Instead, I saw the men opposing us were either dead or were now kneeling in surrender.

"By Hyperion." Elden, one of my loyal warriors, slapped a hand on my shoulder. "This is just a taste, isn't it?" He ran a hand through his blondish-red hair, making it more red than normal with the blood now raked through it.

I shook my head, looking at the dead bodies surrounding us. It was so pointless. They could have lived had they not sided with the king, all because they were afraid of a little girl ruling them. But that little girl would show them all by the end.

I had zero doubt about that.

"Seems that way." I put my hand on his plated shoulder, shaking it slightly. "They'll only get bigger from here."

It was a joke, but it was too grim to really land.

"Prince Arien!" The call echoed down the street, and I looked around for where it was coming from.

"Prince Arien!" Whoever it was called again. I finally spied a Fae running down the road, panting. I ran over to meet them, and realized this was one of Lord Aydun's men, one of my father's loyal lords.

My soldiers clearly realized the same, as swords were suddenly pointed at him from every direction.

The dark-haired Fae looked nervous, swallowing hard, shaking his head, and closing his eyes as he seemed to talk himself into something. He opened orange eyes to meet mine. "Lord Aydun is marching here, my Prince. He's hoping to be able to take the palace while you're recovering from the first fight. He knew your father's men were attacking. It was all a distraction."

"Why would you tell me this?" I raised a skeptical brow at him. "For all I know, you're telling me so I attack him first, leading me into a trap."

My men nodded and grunted in agreement, clearly not trusting the man any more than I did. But he shook his head frantically.

"Lord Freyr is leading men up from Cantref, he and Lord Aydun will box you in," he said, his words emphasized by his overall worried demeanor. I tilted my head, considering, as he continued.

"When Lord Aydun explained to us what was happening, and why…" He trailed off for a moment, shaking his head once more. "Look, many of us don't like your father already. He's cruel, and he makes it impossible for one to improve their station in life, even for us Fae. I loved a girl from a class higher than mine, and because we weren't allowed to marry, she was married off to another, and I was left to join the army. We were always told it was the gods' will. That I couldn't marry up because the gods wanted us in our places. We were born there for a reason, right?" He scoffed, snarling.

"And now? King Aelius goes *against* the gods? To kill the chosen heir of the kingdom? It's not only blasphemy; it's a slap in the face to all of us!" he seethed.

I turned over his explanation in my mind, but his words were laced with pain and resentment that was all too real. His story full of too much truth to be a ploy. I didn't see how Lord Aydun could truly benefit from this. But just to be safe, I would have to fight smart.

I turned and grabbed three of my men, ordering them, "Get messages to Lord Beltane, Lord Ergun, and Lord Dritan. Tell them to send their men directly here. Now!"

They nodded and took off, and I turned to another. "I need a message sent to Night, for when my sister returns. Tell her that before she leaves again, we could really use an appearance by her. If we're going to bring this kingdom together, they'll need to see her."

The man took his orders and ran off, while I prayed to Hyperion that she would get back in time to make a difference. There had to be more men in Aydun, Freyr, and Kem's lands who would prefer a different way of life, or hated my father—or even their own lords. Most would be too scared to turn on them. They needed a real reason.

They needed to see that the ruler they'd be getting would be better than the ruler they had.

They needed to know she would fight for them. That she could bring balance back to Day.

In the meantime, I needed to not only prepare my men here, but I needed to address the humans. With that thought, I left the cleanup efforts to continue, congratulating my men on a battle well fought along the way, and headed back inside the palace. The shining golden sun that stood on top of the highest middle tower gleamed in the sunlight.

A beacon of light in these dark times.

The palace had always been a bit ostentatious, assuredly, but I'd always loved it anyway. The entrance was elaborate, with the stairs covered by the overarching cover of the entrance itself. The pointed peak on top came down and then flared out on each side, creating three distinct shapes on top, and then the walls formed a cover over the stairs. Swirling white accents swooped around in shining lines that made it even grander. The sun on top of the palace led straight down to the tower's peak. The tower itself was constructed to form a rounded shape at the midpoint that rose above the entrance, then tucked in smaller and flared out again before reaching the ground.

Several of the other towers had curves to them as well, with pointed peaks on tops, which gave the palace a sense of beauty and creative whimsy that was missing inside.

Oh, the inside *was* just as beautiful. But my father ensured this place remained as hard and unyielding as possible. Lord Aydun's man was right. My father believed everyone had their place, and they had no business stepping outside of it. While the nobility lived well, the ring system meant classes were kept separate. No one was allowed to marry in a ring higher than their own. Even those outside the city.

Father had ensured every other lord instituted the same rules. He'd learned it from his father, and he would never go against his lessons. He'd spoken of his father like he was a god himself. And this entire palace was filled with cold calculation over any warmth or love as a result.

The halls inside had white floors flecked with gold, while white columns were decorated with gold inlays. The ceiling was painted to mimic the sky, and light from the giant windows hit it beautifully. The walls were golden, but the windows took up much of the space, so it didn't feel too overwhelming. It didn't stop me from getting sick of all the gold at times, however.

I made my way to the white double doors leading to my mother's rooms, and the guards there announced my presence. Entering, I came to a stop before her desk, finding her scribbling away frantically.

"Mother?" I asked hesitantly, and her head shot up.

"Oh, Arien." She sighed with relief, sitting back in her chair. "I was worried. I've been penning letters calling for aid just in case."

"Don't worry, we put them down." I took a seat on the chair across from her. "But unfortunately, more are coming. I've sent word to the lords with us to send their men."

Her eyes closed briefly, and it looked like the weight of the world was on her shoulders. I knew she'd been struggling. Her and Asteria butting heads had left her feeling off center, not sure where she went from here or what the future might bring.

"I had word sent to Asteria, too," I told her, and her eyes opened to lock on mine. I explained what had occurred outside, and Mother sighed, running a hand through her hair.

It was rare for her to show signs of stress, so often having to keep up the image of the *Queen,* that seeing her appearing so normal was slightly unsettling.

"Things will get better, you know," I told her softly. "She just needs time."

I was surprised to see tears building in her eyes, and I stood up to move around the desk, bringing my mother into a hug. She threw her arms around my middle, clinging to me.

"How do you know?" She sniffed. "I'm the reason for all the pain she experienced."

I shook my head firmly. "The blame lies with father. He's the reason all of this happened. You're both headstrong and coming at this from different viewpoints. She was also raised by parents who, by all accounts, loved her. She's struggling with the changes to her life and trying to adapt to having a whole new family."

"She didn't seem to have any issue with you," Mother mumbled quietly, hiding her eyes. I knew what it cost her to be this vulnerable.

"A brother is a different thing altogether," I told her honestly. "And it's not like she had another brother she might feel like she's replacing. We're immortal, Mother. Once we win this, you'll have all the time in the world to work on your relationship."

Mother pulled back, looking me over with a small smile, her eyes still wet with tears. She raised her hand to cup my cheek. "I swear, I have no idea how you turned out so well."

She chuckled at my surprised expression. "Your father and I were always arguing. Both involved in our own plots and plans. You were raised to be your sister's sword and shield. I fret sometimes that none of it was fair to you."

I put my hand over hers on my cheek, dipping my head down and letting her see the truth in my eyes. "I have never resented it for a moment, Mother."

A single tear tracked down each cheek before she closed her eyes to prevent more from escaping. I wiped them away, and stepped back. I knew her vulnerability never lasted long. After a moment where she forcibly pulled herself together, she asked, "What now?"

"Now, we need to address the humans. Father taking so many away will have left them scared and resentful," I explained. "If we explain what's happened and what Asteria plans, we can get them on her side."

"And what will that accomplish?" Mother raised a brow. "Humans against Fae won't be much help."

I smiled slowly, thinking of Soren saving me on the battlefield. "I think you'd be surprised."

CHAPTER 33

THE one downside to using blood magic was that one had to continue using it, and in increasing amounts, for it to continue being effective.

It wore off quicker as time passed, and I would begin to feel my magic waning once more. The inability to call my lightning always left me off-kilter, but fortunately, there were plenty of humans to provide more magic.

I stood over the cauldron, deep within the bowels of the palace, and poured in several bottles of human blood. I closed my eyes and began the spell to turn it into something useful. *"Cruach, guidheam ort.*

ìobraidh mi a' bheatha so dhuibh,

Thoir am fuil gu biadh.

Glan e agus ath-dhèanamh e,

Agus leig leis a bhith na draoidheachd aig a bhunait."

The blood bubbled and churned, transforming from pure blood red as hints of black appeared, and it all began to shimmer, magic being infused into it. I'd been lucky to find the spell left behind in an old dusty journal from a long-dead seer. Those damn acolytes of the Oracle always had useful visions, despite how much they unsettled me.

They surrounded the Oracle, living in the cavern with her. They wore all black and white in honor of the kings of the gods. While the Oracle was the one to meet with the royals, the seers would occasionally pop up to deliver one of their prophecies to other Fae, whenever the gods deemed it necessary.

Somehow, the journal of this seer had ended up in Dusk. I'd found it while searching desperately for a way to save our magic. It had been tucked behind another book on a far shelf in the upper section of the library that contained books on magic that often went ignored, since we all knew how our magic worked and how to use it.

But searching that once irrelevant section had changed everything. At first, I wasn't sure if the writings could be trusted. Not when the seer spoke of myths as if they were real—creatures who drank blood and gorged on it across the land until they were banished by the gods.

Vampyres.

It was a children's story, really. I remember my father telling Vissy and me the story when we were young. He'd caught us sneaking treats from the kitchen, and brought us back to my bedroom. It was one of the only times I remembered him being in any way soft to me. He'd tucked us in and then began telling the story to warn us away from overindulging. Telling us how the Vampyres had once roamed Adamah, until they grew too bloodthirsty, and had to be locked away to protect the rest of the realm. I didn't believe it, of course, but the seer's writings had changed everything.

She had warned in her journal about the dangers of an awakening. An awakening of what, I wasn't sure. She had only made sure to mention that blood magic could not be used, or chaos would be unleashed.

But chaos had already been unleashed.

It had already taken my magic, and I was determined to be the one who would leash chaos for my own gain.

I truly hadn't believed any of it at first. Nor did I believe the spell she'd detailed in her writing, thinking it all a fanciful story. But then the dreams began.

I had seen the gods fall. I had seen myself rise. And blood underpinned it all. Blood flowing under and around me, lifting me up until a crown of blood formed on my head.

The gods may have abandoned me, but something out there wanted me to succeed.

So I figured I had nothing to lose, and tried the spell out. To my great surprise, it actually *worked*. My magic had been stronger than ever, and I'd celebrated by having Tavarius killed and getting Asteria to wet my cock all in the same night.

I should have just taken her then. But I'd foolishly wanted her to come to me of her own will. I'd wanted to break her down and make her want me.

And she *had* desired me. I could see it, and certainly smell it. Until Calix had swept in and ruined everything. That's what I got for waiting. Thankfully, I knew that blood magic was the key to putting everything right.

I poured the mixture of newly formed blood magic into smaller bottles, keeping the vials on me so I could drink them as needed, and made my way back up through the palace.

Vissy was due to arrive today, and I was eager to have someone I actually trusted around once again. I passed Vikal in the hall, and my little brother grabbed his human, pressing her to the wall behind him. I smirked at him, looking the human over as he growled, his red hair like flames framing his face.

"What's wrong, Vikal?" I cooed at him, licking my lips as I looked the pretty brunette over. "Scared I might hurt your human?"

"Leave her alone," he snarled, a rage I rarely saw on his face. He was always so easygoing, but it was nice to see that Tynan force within him, even if it was severely misdirected.

I laughed, unable to believe he was trying to protect his human of all things. "She's human, Vikal. A momentary distraction in a long, long life."

Vikal shook in rage, and the brunette laid her hand on his arm, her brows furrowed in concern. Vikal calmed slightly at the contact, looking into her hazel eyes as he relaxed.

It had the opposite effect on me. My own rage began to rise as I saw the genuine care this human had for my brother.

That—that was what I wanted. Why couldn't Asteria care for me in this way? Why had she fought me, run away, when I had offered everything she could ever want?

"Maybe I should take her," I mused, scratching my chin as the two stiffened. "It would certainly teach you the lesson it seems you desperately need to learn."

"You say we shouldn't care about humans," Vikal scoffed, shaking his head. "But you're the one who started a war over yours."

I straightened up, my eyes narrowing as lightning crackled around my hands. My lip twitched, and I had to hold myself back from killing my brother then and there.

"That's enough!" Kian shouted as he appeared out of nowhere, forcibly pushing me back until I hit the wall. He looked between us, a disappointed look on his face. "He's your little brother. Can you not leave *him* in peace, at least?"

I couldn't believe his audacity.

"I am your king," I growled, facing Kian, who stood between me and Vikal, with the pretty human hiding behind him, radiating fear.

"And *how is that* exactly?" Kian countered, stepping up to me and staring me down. "What happened to Father, Cyrus?"

"You know what happened." I snapped back, wanting to avoid this conversation. I didn't want to even think of that night. It had happened, and I'd moved on. Regrets would do nothing but prevent me from achieving the greatness I'd been promised.

That little girl better have kept her mouth shut, though.

"I know you and Father were in his rooms. He was perfectly fine, and then he's suddenly dead, and *you* are king. I know Father wouldn't have approved of your plans, so it seems awfully convenient for you," Kian said coldly, his face a blank mask that I'd never seen on my brother before.

I had a sinking feeling that I'd underestimated him. I knew he watched quietly, but I'd always taken him for a wimp. Too bookish and uninvolved in politics to be a problem. This was a new side to him that I didn't know the ramifications of.

"What you're suggesting is treason," I told him, working to keep my face as blank as Kian's and not give anything away.

"If it's true, then *that* was treason." Kian raised a brow back at me, his lips rising into a smirk. He turned to Vikal and his human, dismissing me like I wasn't king of this Shalim damned kingdom!

"Come on Vikal, Carrina, let's go," Kian instructed, scowling at me before leading them away.

I stormed back to my room, reconsidering Kian and everything I knew about him. As I walked into my room, I ground my teeth and grabbed the girl waiting by the shoulders. She squealed as I slammed her back into a wall.

"What did you say?" I demanded, a snarl on my lips as my canines lengthened slightly.

The fear in Emmie's eyes was soothing. Kian may think he can dismiss me, but he'll learn how wrong he is soon enough.

"What are you talking about?" she pleaded, shaking hard enough I had to slam her back against the wall again.

"Did you say anything about what happened to my father?" I growled out slowly, and she shook her head rapidly.

"No!" She denied it, and her dread was a potent stench as it swept through her. "No, I didn't say a word. I swear it on the Old Gods!"

I rolled my eyes, as if swearing on fictional gods meant anything to me. But she was being truthful at least. Meaning Kian came to his suspicions on his own.

I let her go, and she sank to the floor, trembling. I scoffed at her pathetic display. "Get up."

She struggled to rise, making me roll my eyes again. I eyed her, considering what I wanted, or more like needed to work out my frustration. I could have her now, or later. She'd proven a proficient fuck. I could see why my father enjoyed her. But Zerlina was bound to be around later, and if I could have the two of them together, that would be ideal.

I shook my head. I didn't have time to indulge now, so later it would have to be.

"Get ready, Lord Visita is due to arrive soon, and I want you circling with the humans. Do what you're good at." I instructed her, and she straightened up, nodding her head as if resetting herself. I shook my head, unable to help comparing her to the one I truly wanted.

Asteria was worth a thousand of this insipid girl.

"Got it. I'll see what's being said." She smiled eagerly, as if I'd never scared her at all. I had to give her credit for that, at least. Her ability to suppress her emotions quickly helped make her a good spy among humans.

After a quick change of clothes, I made my way down to meet Vissy. My crown sat on my head, complimented by my jacket, a high-necked one in charcoal grey, with pink lining the trim. As much as I disliked the pink, I had to embrace it as king. The royal colors were another accessory that gave legitimacy to my position, just like the crown.

We should have had charcoal and purple as our colors, but it was yet another thing Night had stolen away. Just because our wings were pink didn't mean everything had to be.

I smiled as Vissy swaggered through the main doors, but as much as I wanted to walk to meet him, I had to wait for the formal address.

"My King." Vissy smiled, kneeling before me.

His brow hair was tastefully messy, ending a bit higher than his shoulders at the moment. His gold eyes glowed as he looked up, and I could see several women and men of the court watching him. He was a favorite among them, as was his wife, and for good reason.

"My King." His wife, Nisha, kneeled before me, and I spared her a quick nod as I bid them rise.

Before I could even open my mouth, our reunion was interrupted.

"Ah, Lord Visita." Aelius drawled as he walked into the great hall.

"King Aelius." Vissy bowed his head in greeting. "I'd heard you arrived."

"Yes, although I'm most disappointed my *dear* daughter hasn't been captured yet." Aelius sneered as his eyes caught mine. "Someone insists we wait. I didn't realize it was so hard to kill one little girl," he taunted, raising a brow at me as his head cocked to the side.

His expression was so similar to Asteria's when she challenged me, that it had my lightning sparking in response.

"I've told you before, Aelius." I ground out, frustrated. He seemed to think we should just send an assassin after her. Of course, he also thought I'd let her die, so he was wrong on many fronts. "Things need to happen in the proper way to ensure the war as a whole is won. I won't let you leave back to Day just because your problem is solved, when mine remains."

Vissy's brows flew up, and his mouth opened in shock. He turned to me, but I shook my head at him, making his mouth close with an audible click.

Aelius chuckled, "I'm a man of my word, Cyrus. I'd help with Night regardless."

"Forgive me for not believing you," I replied dryly. "Now, if you'll excuse us." I nodded to Aelius before turning to Vissy, indicating for him to follow.

We walked down the hall in silence, Vissy cutting his eyes to me every so often, until he finally spoke.

"Are you—" Vissy cut himself off, his eyes wide as he stared at me, shaking his head.

"Am I what?" I ground out, hating the uncertainty in Vissy's eyes. I could never count on my own brothers, but Vissy, he was the brother I never had. And more, at times, but never in any way serious. We trusted one another. He had never questioned me in all the long years we'd been friends.

"You don't actually plan on killing Asteria, do you?" he asked, and I tilted my head back, eyes falling closed as I let out a frustrated sigh. How did no one else seem to understand?

I opened my eyes and lifted my head, staring straight into his golden orbs, "Of course not. I have other plans for her. She may not enjoy it, but her insolence cannot be allowed to go unpunished."

"Insolence, or rejection?" Vissy countered, his lip curling. I could feel my rage rising at his own insolent attitude. "She refused you, and you can't stand it. But she's no mere human, Cyrus; she's one of us."

Before I even knew what I was doing, my hand was around his throat, and I had him pressed against the wall. A snarl curled my lips as I brought our faces so close together that our noses nearly brushed. "It doesn't matter. None of it matters. Fae or not, heir or not, a new order is coming, and she, like so many others, will soon learn their place."

"What's happened to you?" He struggled to get the words out, my hand still putting pressure around his throat. I realized then what I was doing and let go of him quickly. He slumped back, and I blinked in shock. I'd never hurt Vissy. I loved him, more than anyone else in my life.

"A new order, huh?" Vissy scoffed, looking at me like he didn't know me at all. "Do you know how you sound right now? I thought this war was to end Night's attacks, but now you're rounding up humans, lashing out at everyone, and don't even pretend like I don't know what happened with Astraeus."

He narrowed his eyes at me, daring me to refute it. He knew me too well, and while I opened my mouth to defend myself, when he raised a disbelieving brow at me, I couldn't get the words out.

He laughed wryly, "Where does this end, Cyrus?"

"What?" I asked, my eyebrows furrowing in confusion.

"Where does it end? What are your plans? What is the Shalim damned goal here?" Vissy's voice rose as he went on, and I tried to shush him, only to be brushed off.

"Shut up!" I finally roared, making him rear back. "I am your king. You don't need to know. You just need to follow orders."

He scoffed, shaking his head sadly. When he looked back at me, his gaze was colder than it had ever been. "Fuck you, Cyrus."

I jolted in shock, rage rising as yet another person turned on me. If I couldn't even trust *Vissy*, there was truly no one left I could put any faith in.

"You've gone too far," he spat, unaware of my rising fury, the lightning sparking at my fingertips. "The entire kingdom is in upheaval. Humans are revolting. Fae are scared and unsure what to do. Even under your father—"

That was more than I could take. Being compared to *him*, being told I was *inferior* to him…

I lashed out with a bolt of lightning, and it hit its target with unerring accuracy.

I watched as my brother, in all but blood, fell to the ground, blinking slowly. I crouched beside him, his slackened face and shocked eyes locking on mine.

"Don't worry, you won't die," I assured him, and he continued to blink slowly, still feeling the effects of being shocked by the lightning bolt. "But it's clear you can no longer be trusted. Questioning me in such a way." I shook my head sadly at him, tutting. "You'll enjoy your stay in our dungeons instead of your usual rooms, I think."

I called for one of my guards and had him taken away. I watched as they grabbed him by the arms, his feet dragging as they carried him away.

I sighed heavily, running my hand through my hair. That certainly did not go to plan. I needed to let off some steam, so I went in search of Zerlina. Losing myself in her mouth or cunt would take my mind off what had just happened. *And* what had happened before it.

Could no one around me see the vision?

Perhaps not. They had not been blessed with dreams of greatness as I had. I knew what this all led to, and I couldn't chance anyone stopping me. If the kings and lords knew their own power was at risk, they would never follow me as I needed. At least until their usefulness was at an end.

Zerlina wasn't in her rooms, and with a sinking feeling, I made my way toward Daneiris's. Those two had been spending too much time together, and I was nearly positive I'd find her there.

As I got close, I could hear their voices, still at a low volume that was no more than a mumble, but it was definitely them. The guards at my sister's door spotted me as I turned the corner, and quickly knocked twice on the door, before I even reached them. It instantly made me suspicious.

Did she instruct her guards to alert her if I came?

Why else would they not wait for me to be standing before them, as was standard procedure?

They opened the door for me with bowed heads, and I eyed them both carefully, noting their appearances to ensure they could be questioned later.

It wouldn't do to alert my sister or betrothed that their guards would be questioned.

Entering the room, I found Daneiris and Zerlina looking up at me too innocently from the table. Several other ladies surrounded them, and their slaves were all against the walls, heads down, as if afraid to catch my attention.

As they should be.

"Cyrus, darling," Zerlina greeted with a smile that was all fake courtly grace. "What brings you here?"

"Well…" I drew the word out, my brow slowly rising as I watched Daneiris stiffen slightly. Zerlina maintained her relaxed demeanor, but I could see their ladies shifting slightly around the table.

"I was hoping to find you, actually." I smirked, then drew up a chair, sitting at the table with them, and making everyone present even more visibly uncomfortable. "But now, I find myself wondering."

"Oh?" Zerlina asked, trying to maintain her demeanor, but her mouth gave her away, pursing slightly before she forcibly made her lips smooth back out into a smile. "What about?"

"Well, about what you ladies are up to, of course?" I smiled charmingly back at her, waiting for an answer.

Zerlina laughed lightly, putting a hand on my arm. "We're just having tea, darling. You know we enjoy discussing the gossip of the court."

I wrapped my hand around hers, squeezing softly at first, before putting more pressure on it, making her wince.

"Let's try that again," I suggested, both brows rising. "With the truth, this time."

"That is the truth!" Zerlina argued, her teeth gritting together.

"Cyrus, stop!" Daneiris shrieked, her blue eyes wide. "What are you doing? We're just having tea! She's your betrothed, for Shalim's sake!"

I growled, letting go of Zerlina's hand. She gasped, cradling it to her chest. I put both hands on the table, using it to rise out of the seat and lean toward Daneiris.

"I know you two are up to something," I whispered threateningly to her. "And I'm going to find out what."

CHAPTER 34

Calix

FLYING back into Night Kingdom, I felt a huge sense of relief at being back home. I could feel Asteria's own happiness at returning from where she flew next to me. The people of Tairngire all paused to look up, and where they'd usually wave, most stood in shock, mouths open as they saw the two phoenixes flying with us.

Altan, with his yellow and teal feathers, flew beside Asteria, while Zakat, with his orange and teal coloring, flew beside me. They'd insisted on flanking us, wanting to ensure her safety. I appreciated the sentiment, more so since Asteria let me know Zakat preferred men and wasn't actually flirting with her, though I still wasn't sure about Altan, who liked both sexes. Anytime anyone was too familiar with Asteria, it instantly set the mate bond off, driving me crazy.

We'd flown out over the Namminian Ocean to avoid Dusk. While their Pegasus forms were the only royal animal lacking flames for a defense, they could still attack from the air. It was better to be safe, especially when Cyrus refused to let his obsession die.

The reports Eryx had brought of Cyrus's recent actions were horrifying, and I could only imagine what was actually going on there if what we'd heard were the mere whispers able to get out so far. Cyrus had cracked down since he became king, and Kian had been struggling to get word out while being watched.

I hoped to meet with Nithe before we left to get a better idea of what was happening. There was a lot to do before our journey. Starting with meeting with Titan and ending with reassuring my people.

As we touched down, I let the guards who'd accompanied us off my back. Once we'd shifted back, Titan was first there to greet us. His eyebrows were high on his forehead as he looked over our guests.

"It seems like you two were successful," he said dryly, and I caught Altan and Zakat raising their eyebrows at one another in surprise.

"For the most part, we did better than expected," I assured him, clapping him on the shoulder.

Asteria bounced up to us, smiling at Titan. "I even practiced while we were gone, like I promised."

I chuckled, wrapping my arm around her waist. "She was very diligent about not missing training. She dragged me out every day."

Her hand slapped my chest. "Don't act like you don't enjoy it."

Titan groaned. "Did you get any actual fighting in, or was it another excuse to flirt?"

Asteria kicked his calf in response, making me double over laughing in surprise. Titan's wide-eyed shock was equally hilarious, and Eryx was desperately trying to hide his laughter, turning his head to his shoulder and away from Titan's sight.

"We do need to discuss what's happened, and our plans moving forward," I told Titan once we sobered up. He nodded, and I led Asteria after him toward the war room. I tilted my head at the two phoenix shifters behind us, indicating they follow us.

"I'm going to go check on my messages," Eryx whispered to me, and I gave him a nod.

"See if Nithe is back yet. I want to talk to him," I told him, and Eryx agreed before taking off.

"There you two are." Harpina smiled, and Asteria broke away from me to hug her. Harpina hugged her back tightly, and it warmed my heart to see how loved Asteria was with my family.

I noticed others in the hall watching her and thought again of what Eryx said about formally introducing her to our people. That would have to happen soon, but for now, we needed to get a plan in place.

Explaining everything to Titan had him humming and crossing his arms over his chest, a sign he was brewing something in that brilliant mind of his.

I'd never met anyone who could make a battle plan like he could. I hoped to be anywhere near as good when I was his age.

Even at four hundred and twenty-one, I knew I still had much to learn from him.

Eventually, Titan did what I knew he would.

"Asteria, come on," he grunted, tilting his head toward the door. I raised a brow, smirking at him. I figured he'd ask me, but it said a lot about his confidence in her that he'd ask Asteria.

"What?" she asked, furrowing her eyebrows. "Where are we going?"

"He always does his best planning while sparring," I told her, giving her a quick kiss and a smack on the ass, sending her out the door.

She looked back at me, bemused, but followed Titan without complaint.

"What in the Otherworld?" Altan shook his head, his braids swishing against his back with the motion.

"What?" I asked, cocking my head to the side in confusion.

Zakat snorted, leaning against the war table and crossing his arms. "What, he asks."

"What the Tartarus kind of operation are you running here?" Altan asked, shaking his head. "This is… not what I expected."

"We told you why we were attacking the other kingdoms already." I rolled my eyes.

"Yes, you may not be the evil bastard we assumed, *but...*" Zakat emphasized, gesturing dramatically. "This is still not what anyone would expect. I can't ever imagine my father acting like that with his underlings."

"Or mine." Altan snorted in agreement.

"See?" Zakat moved to swing an arm around Altan's shoulders, and the man quickly shrugged him off.

"They're not underlings, for starters." I sighed, pinching the bridge of my nose. "This is exactly the problem. The kingdoms have lost sight of what we were chosen for in the first place."

"And what's that?" Altan asked, cocking his own head to the side now as he shifted away from the table, backing out of Zakat's space.

"As king, it's my job to lead my kingdom." I tried to explain. "To keep them happy, healthy, and prospering. Not to exert control and lift myself up. This doesn't work if we expect our people to be our servants. We are meant to serve *them*. We give our lives to the cause of the kingdom. But the rulers of Celesterra have been corrupted. With greed, pride, you name it."

The two were quiet, but were clearly thinking over what I said. Before they could respond, however, Eryx grabbed my attention.

"Calix!" he called from the doorway, and I turned toward him. "Nithe's on his way into the city now. We can meet him."

I nodded, popping out into the hall to find a servant who could track down Ilta. She arrived within a few minutes, glaring at me for some reason.

"You didn't even tell me that you were back?" she huffed, crossing her arms. "Where's Asteria?"

"She's with Titan. And I'm sorry, we wanted to grab him quickly and get him working on this before anything else," I explained, cringing slightly.

She glared, blowing breath out of her nose like Titan in minotaur form.

"Fine." She finally uncrossed her arms, returning to her bubbly smile. "Now, what do you want?"

I chuckled, shaking my head at her. "I have two princes who need rooms to stay in."

Her eyes widened, and she threw her arms up in the air. "Nox, Calix, anything else?"

"Well…" I drew out, raising a brow.

"Oh, no you don't." She stomped, and I struggled to hide my smile.

"I think you'll enjoy this, actually," I promised, and her mouth pursed, her lips shifting side to side in thought.

"Go on then." She waved impatiently, tapping her foot.

"We'll need to introduce everyone to Asteria," I said, and her eyes began to light up. "I'd like you to plan a formal court address, where I'll bring her out and make clear my intention to make her queen one day."

"Ahh!!" she squealed, her blue eyes and smile equally wide. She threw her arms around my neck, and I laughed, hugging her back.

"I'm so happy for you two. This will be amazing!" She enthused before she pulled back. "I'll need to work with Baach. We'll definitely need a proper ball for this. Oh, and Delia! We'll need to organize a new dress and crown. And—"

"Ilta!" I interrupted, and she blinked in surprise, like she'd already forgotten I was there. "Maybe find Prince Altan and Prince Zakat somewhere to sleep first?" I suggested gently.

Her eyes went wide, and I realized she'd forgotten in her excitement. "Right, yes! I'll get right on that."

She ran off, and I chuckled, shaking my head. Eryx was leaning against the wall, his amused smirk fading as he pushed off it.

"Ready?" he asked, and I nodded in confirmation. The two of us made our way out of the palace, and I spotted Asteria and Titan training as we passed through the training grounds. Making our way out of the gates, we made for the Starshine District, where Nithe would be entering the city. We walked up the stairs to the bridge that led from Shadowgleam to Starshine.

Nithe was an excellent spy. While bird shifters tended to be best, due to their ability to fly in and out, Nithe proved it wasn't the only option. He shifted into a snake, and was easily able to slither into spots no one else could. He was just as good in Fae form, too. Able to charm and seduce information out of people or himself into places he wanted to be.

"You know Asteria will go after Cyrus when the time comes," Eryx said, looking over to me. One look at his face made it clear this was something he'd been ruminating on for a while.

"I know." I nodded in agreement. That was something I wouldn't ever deny her. She needed that closure after everything that had happened. I could still feel her conflict and rage every time Cyrus was mentioned. Thankfully, she'd gotten much better at controlling her magic thanks to the exercises she'd been practicing.

"We need to make sure we're with her at all times on the battlefield, Calix," Eryx said seriously, voice lowered, his eyes following the bridge and not looking toward me.

I raised a brow at him. "You honestly think I won't be right behind her every step of the way?"

"I think battles get chaotic, and it'll be hard not to get sidetracked by the fighting," Eryx explained. "But she's impulsive, just like you." He smirked slightly. "That dragon blood gets you both in a state, and I *know* what you're like when that happens."

He wasn't wrong. When I went into a rage, it was hard to think straight. My anger drove me on as my blood smoked in my veins. I would fight on after being stabbed without even realizing it.

"But Asteria is so much younger, Calix. She doesn't have the same experience as us, as *you*. She'll need help, whether she wants to admit it or not." Eryx stopped walking, turning to face me. "We need to make sure we have a plan for keeping with her. And we can't let her know."

"You expect me to keep it from her?" I asked, shocked. "I won't lie to her, Eryx."

"Not lie," he insisted, shaking his head. "Just don't mention it. You don't want to risk her life just because she's too proud to admit she'll need help, do you?"

I sighed, looking out above my city, thinking it over. I didn't like keeping this from her. Not at all. But I knew she *would* argue about it. Eryx was right about that. And I appreciated that he cared for her enough to want to protect her regardless.

When it came down to it, I refused to risk her life. There was nothing in Adamah that could make me risk *that*.

"Alright." I nodded in agreement. "But if she finds out, I'm blaming you."

He scoffed out a laugh, shaking his head fondly as he put an arm around my shoulders, despite the fact he had to strain to reach. "I don't doubt it."

We continued on, agreement in place, and made our way down the stairs into Starshine. I smiled as I passed my people, nodding back and exchanging greetings quickly with those who offered them. The playgrounds were full of children, and I stopped walking for a moment to observe them.

It was a reminder of why we needed to do this. These innocent children were all at risk as long as the balance was. I would not allow them to grow up in a world destroyed. Leached of everything that made it special.

I watched a little dark-haired boy playing with a little girl with long, messy white hair. Watching them, I couldn't help but imagine little children of my own one day. Asteria was still young, and we were just beginning our relationship, solidifying our bond… but one day. One day, we could have this.

The thoughts of the palace being filled once more with a *family*…

I loved my friends and my sisters. They were all family now, and I wouldn't trade them for the world. But I still desperately missed that feeling I had when my parents were alive. When it was me and Ndrita and our parents. We were a family, and one that loved one another truly. My parents were never like other royals who resented one another. Their love was so pure and real, that when my mother died, it destroyed my father entirely.

That was the power of a mate bond. Soulmates were powerful in a way nothing else in this world was.

I didn't understand how Aurelia managed to turn against her own in such a way. It could only be the power of a parent's love. It was a love I didn't understand, but looking out at those children now, at the future of our kingdom and continent, playing happily as they chased one another, I couldn't help but smile, hoping that one day I would.

A hand landed on my shoulder, and I snapped out of my head. I understood Asteria's struggle all too well. Dragons tended to get lost in their own thoughts as they swirled and spiraled, anxiety and hope creeping in just the same as our thoughts spun.

"Let's go," I told Eryx, and we walked on until we spotted Nithe riding towards us. He slowed his horse as he spotted us, dismounting.

"Couldn't wait for me to reach the palace?" he greeted, raising a brow at me. His dark hair was mussed from the ride, and his pink eyes seemed duller than usual.

"Your message sounded urgent," Eryx said, worry lining his face. "And Calix wanted to talk to you anyway. There's no time to waste right now."

Nithe nodded tiredly, and I looked him over more closely. His clothes were rumpled, in a way I'd never seen from him before. He was always careful with his appearance, wanting to look his best. The man was vain at the best of times. But now streaks of dirt even covered his face.

"What the Tartarus happened to you?" I asked, my brows creasing.

He sighed, shaking his head. "It's a disaster in Dusk, Calix. I assume that's what's so urgent?"

"Yes. We don't have much time before we need to leave for the Otherworld, and we need to have a plan in place for Dusk. I can only imagine we'll have to move quickly when we get back. Unless Cyrus moves first," I explained grimly.

I didn't like any of this. I wanted to get ahead of Cyrus and any moves he made, but the lack of information, paired with what the gods required, left us in a bit of a bind.

"The *Otherworld?*" Nithe exclaimed, eyes practically popping out of his head.

"Never mind that. I'll explain later. Tell us what's going on in Dusk," I told him, frustrated.

"It's a horror show, Calix," Nithe admitted heavily. "I've never seen anything like it. Cyrus has these horrible camps set up. Humans are tortured and drained of blood. They're using it to make not only blood magic for Cyrus, but there are secret workshops working on weapons."

Fuck. I'd hoped he hadn't been able to get that far yet, but he'd apparently been busy setting everything up even before his father died. I was sure he must have killed Astraeus to get him out of the way. He wanted power, and he needed the crown for that. Men always thought a crown gave them license to be as much of a bastard as they pleased.

I looked forward to proving him wrong.

But first…

"We need to get the humans out of there," I told him urgently. "We can't let them suffer further, but it's just as important to prevent Cyrus from amassing more stock of blood. The more he gets, the more iron we have to worry about."

Nithe and Eryx both nodded in agreement. Fury was a spark in my blood I had to push down. It wasn't the time. *Not yet.*

"The humans themselves have started rebelling," Nithe said, and it brought some hope to my heart. It had been so difficult for the humans to rise above what they were forced into. Asteria would be happy to hear they were finally straining against their chains.

"But it's small and unorganized. They need help," Nithe continued, and looking him over, I could see his desire to do something more.

"What about Kian?" Eryx asked, "Has he been able to get out from under Cyrus's watch?"

"Barely," Nithe sighed, running a hand through his hair. "Cyrus has such a tight guard around all of them, watching and waiting for them to slip up. I had to sneak into Kian's room and visit him that way."

His worried tone spoke of how much danger they all must be in.

"He did mention…" He trailed off, and I raised a brow, urging him to continue. "Vikal. His brother. He's quite fond of his human. He apparently got in a bit of an argument with Cyrus about it. Kian wants to get them both out."

"How does Vikal feel about that?" I asked, weighing my options. "Would he join us? Or take his own human and leave the rest to wither?"

"I'm not sure, honestly. I can find out when I return," Nithe offered, but I shook my head.

"Things will be moving too quickly for that. Just make your best-educated guess and go with your gut. I trust your instincts." I smirked slightly at him, lightening the mood for a moment as I winked. "They are house Erebus's instincts, after all."

"I will." He laughed hoarsely. "I appreciate the trust, my King." His words were almost uncomfortably honest, in a way we rarely were with each other. I put a hand on his shoulder, realizing how deeply his time in Dusk had shaken him.

"You're my blood, Nithe. You know what that means." I said, squeezing his shoulder. He swallowed hard, nodding, and I brought our foreheads together for a moment, gripping the back of his head. "I trust you, cousin. I can see you want to help, not just spy. Which is why I have a new mission for you."

I pulled back to see his eyes widen in surprise. Eryx glared at me, and I laughed, turning my head to him. "Relax, I'm not stealing one of your spies."

As he relaxed his glare, looking more curious than angry, I turned back to Nithe. "You said the humans need help?"

He nodded hesitantly, and I smiled, tilting my head back toward the palace.

"Then come. It's time to talk to your future queen. She'll kill me if I don't let her help plan your mission." I laughed fondly, and Nithe raised his brows.

"Future queen, huh? Has the star queen finally arrived?" he joked, but his smile faded as I nodded, a hug smile growing on my face.

"You've met her," I told him as we walked back toward the Fallen Star Palace, where my own star awaited.

"Wait—" He shook his head, "The girl? From the party?"

"Yes." I glared and pointed a finger at him. "And don't you dare bring up seeing her like that again. She's my mate," I growled.

"What?! But—" I laughed as he tried to put it together.

It was always fun fucking with him, after all.

CHAPTER 35

Asteria

I SWUNG my sword at his head, and Titan brought his up to block my swing. We'd been at this for a while, but I had yet to land a single hit on him.

I stepped back, panting, as Titan looked me over.

"You need to be ready," he said sternly.

"I know." I sighed, "Cyrus—"

"Forget Cyrus," he insisted, and my head reared back in shock.

"Forget Cyrus?" I hissed, my blade swinging at him before I'd even had the thought to do it.

He met my blade and leaned toward me as our blades crossed before our faces. "Aelius will be coming after you, Asteria."

"I know, but—"

"No buts! You don't understand the Earendel's, Asteria. He will do anything to take you out." He stressed, looking so genuinely concerned that I stepped back and examined him.

"Titan? What is this?" I asked softly, gentling my stance and letting my blade fall.

He grunted, running a hand through his hair. He turned his head to look at me, and I couldn't read the look on his face. It wasn't sad or happy. Maybe a bit wistful, a bit resentful. It was complex, to say the least.

"There's something I haven't told anyone," he admitted, turning to me fully. "Not Calix, not even his father. Only his grandfather knew."

My brows rose as I tried to understand what was happening here.

"I won't say anything, if you don't want me to," I promised, and his eyes softened, a small smile growing on his face.

"It's not that it's a secret, necessarily," he said, as he moved to sit on a bench nearby, waving me over to join him. I took a seat, straddling the bench so I could face him fully. "It doesn't really need to be anymore. I just haven't been able to talk about it. The wound felt too raw, still. But you, of all people, should know."

"Okay," I said slowly, nodding. "Well, I'm all ears." I pointed to my pointed ears with a smile, making him shake his head with a small laugh.

"I'm not from Night, not originally," he said. "I'm from Day Kingdom, actually."

"You are?" I asked, surprised. He fit so well into Night, I never would have questioned it.

He nodded solemnly. "I had always felt like the odd out around my family. I never fit, not with them, not with anyone. I thought I would live my life that way. But the gods, they other ideas. The day I found my mate, everything changed."

He smiled warmly, and I could see that wistfulness return to his eyes, only this time it was underlined by devastating sorrow. I had never heard of Titan having a mate, and the thought of what could have happened had my heart clenching in sympathy. Still, I listened eagerly, interested in where this was going. I was so new to this Fae thing; every new aspect was still incredible to me. And the mate bond I shared with Calix was the most beautiful of all. I wanted to know more about mate bonds and other mated pairs.

"My mate was wonderful. Beautiful and bright." He reminisced, closing his eyes and letting the sun hit his face as he smiled. "He brought a joy to my life that I had never experienced before. The two of us were inseparable, and I felt as if I'd finally found a piece of myself that had always been missing."

He opened his eyes to look at me. "I imagine you know what I mean."

I nodded. Calix felt like a piece of my soul that had finally clicked into place. My life now felt more right than ever before. Calix had helped me find myself, and made me realize there was no complete version of me without him.

"We were so happy, for a time. I imagined my life stretching out into the centuries with him beside me, always. But my family—my *brother*—" he scoffed with derision. "He insisted that the line must continue."

"The line?" I raised a brow, not sure what he meant.

"The royal line." He clarified, making me gasp in surprise. "My brother was king of Day then. Your great-grandfather."

My mouth fell open. Shock on a level I hadn't felt since my transition radiating through me. That meant… Titan was my great-great-uncle?!

"He insisted that I had to marry a noble woman so we could produce children that would keep the line plentiful. It was my duty, according to him. Despite the fact that soulmates are supposed to be sacred, preordained by the gods—not something a mere Fae can overrule. Not even a king," he explained, shaking his head mournfully. Pain was written all over his face in sharp relief as he continued. His large body slumped slightly from the regular, upright soldier's posture he usually maintained.

"The very thought disgusted me. I wouldn't marry some noble woman when my soulmate was right there. So, I refused to marry anyone but him. My brother was of course enraged that I would dare to defy him. He said that if I wouldn't contribute to the family, then I was no Earendel. I told him I was perfectly fine with that, that I would leave, and he'd never have to see me again." His voice stuttered, and he closed his eyes. I put my hand on his shoulder as this huge warrior Fae, the oldest Fae alive, whom I had believed impenetrable, fought back tears. He clutched at my hand, forcing his eyes back open.

He cleared his throat, gathering himself before he continued. "So Zephyr and I planned to leave. He didn't care about me being royal. He loved me for who I was, not what my name or blood brought with it." Titan smiled softly, closing his eyes at the fond memory. "Zephyr was willing to leave his whole life behind if it meant we could be together. We knew that we could build a good life for ourselves somewhere else." His expression darkened as he opened his eyes, "But my brother viewed my refusal of a royal match and decision to leave as a direct insult to him. Everything was always about him, you see. I was out in the city, finalizing our travel plans, when I felt something strange through the mate bond. I ran home as fast as I could." A sinking feeling in my gut told me I knew what was coming next. "I got there and found my brother standing over Zephyr. He waited until I walked in the door, smiled at me, and then drove his sword straight through his heart, killing him instantly." Titan choked out, tears beginning to fall down his face as the pain finally overwhelmed him. "He made sure I would be there to see it, but not close enough to do anything to stop it. That I'd be able to see the heartbreaking fear in Zephyr's eyes. See the sword piercing his heart as I felt my own shatter in my chest. That as the bond went dead, I'd have a front-row seat to my brother's glee as he killed the only person I would ever love. As he doomed me to an existence as empty as his." Titan's voice shook as he recounted the tragedy.

His head bowed as he struggled to rein his tears in. I sat back in shock, my hand covering my mouth as I processed the horror his brother had put him through. I couldn't imagine the pain he must have experienced, that he still clearly felt. The idea of walking into a room to find Arien standing over Calix, unable to do anything in time…

It would haunt me for lifetimes.

Just as it had clearly haunted Titan.

"I swore," he continued, his voice raspy from crying, "that I would get revenge one day. My brother thought killing Zephyr would bring me back and make me yield to his demands. Instead, I escaped at the first opportunity. I went across the border, disappearing into Night before my brother could stop me. Calix's grandfather, Nadir, helped hide me from my brother. He took me in and made me part of his family, in a way I was never part of my own. He became the brother I never had."

Titan smiled sadly, looking at me. "I promised I would look after his family for him, while I kept myself alive through the centuries with the promise of one day getting my revenge on my brother. Even after his death, I knew his son, and his grandson, were no different. I wouldn't let that line continue forever. I promised I would find a way to end them all."

He grabbed my hands, and I was so speechless I just blinked at him. I vaguely felt like I should apologize, even though this was all many, *many* years before I was born. "You are the promise of a new era, Asteria."

I tilted my head to the side, uncertain what he meant.

"You will dismantle the horrid rule my brother set up. The system they have in Day is horrendous because of him. All the worst parts of my brother's corruption. But my revenge? It was hard to admit that my chance for it truly disappeared centuries ago. Now, the best revenge I can hope for is seeing my brother's legacy dismantled. And you will be the one to do that. You will make a *new* Earendel line. One that my ancestors and I can be proud of. And you'll be ruling side by side with the Erebus line, the one I've spent centuries loving as I should have been able to love my own."

"You don't hate me for being an Earendel?" I asked quietly, dipping my head down. It was all a lot, and I was struggling to understand.

He lifted my chin, our sky-blue eyes meeting, and I suddenly didn't know how I missed the resemblance before. Even his blonde hair, cropped short, was the same color as my father's.

"Not any more than I could hate myself." He smiled gently. "We didn't choose the family we were born into. But we can stand against the ones within it who perpetuate such evil. We can put a stop to it."

"That's why you've been training me so hard since I came back Fae." I realized, "You knew I'd be able to help you accomplish this."

"Partly, yes." He conceded with a nod, before his eyes gleamed brightly. "But more than that, I finally saw an Earendel worthy of the name and the crown."

I sucked in a breath, holding back tears. The idea that I was *worthy* of either…

I threw my arms around his wide shoulders, and his arms came around me in turn. I hugged my newly found great-great-uncle, another piece of family I didn't think I'd ever have, and mourned for what had happened to him. What he had lost.

What had happened to both of us because of the actions of those who should have loved us unconditionally.

Blood can always hurt you deepest.

BY THE TIME I'd showered and changed, Priscilla had been waiting for me in my room. I jumped, surprised to see her waiting on my bed, and she laughed happily.

"Here, have a drink," she insisted, pouring one of the lavender wines for me and handing it over.

I grabbed it with a smile, taking a sip. After my conversation with Titan earlier, I could certainly use it. "I'm glad you're here. I feel like I haven't had time to see anyone but Calix in weeks!"

She laughed, pushing my shoulder lightly, "Don't even pretend you're not happy to be spending time with him."

"Oh, I am," I admitted with a sly smile. "You would be, too, if you were me."

She shook her head, but proceeded to grill me on everything that had happened. I gave her all the new gossip, including about the two phoenix princes who'd joined us.

"I bet they'll be fucking before the war is over," I told her with a smirk.

She doubled over in laughter, but a knock on the door sounded, and Delia showed herself in. "Happy to have you back, Asteria."

She smiled warmly, but I could see she was here for a reason, with the way she was twirling her rings around her fingers. A tell she had whenever she had to shift into professional lady's maid mode.

"Happy to be back." I smiled widely. "What's going on?"

She sighed, tilting her head at me, clearly exasperated that I could see right through her: "Calix and Eryx just arrived back with Nithe. They want your input on a plan."

I turned to Priscilla dramatically, "My work is never done."

She laughed, rolling her eyes at me as I bounced off the bed.

"Oh, before I forget. Ilta mentioned needing you for a dress fitting," Priscilla said, before giving me a kiss on the cheek and bounding out the door.

"A dress fitting?" I raised a brow at Delia, hoping she'd know, but she shook her head, shrugging.

She helped me dress, putting on a shorter purple and iridescent silver dress that crossed over my front and draped fabric down each side. It was gorgeous and dramatic, and I realized I really loved getting to try all these different dresses. As much as I loved my armor, getting to wear pretty dresses was just as great when it was *my* choice.

Having this control over my life was amazing. Now, I just needed to gain control over the rest of it. My fighting and magic were coming along nicely, but my emotions were still a mess most of the time. Dragon or not, I couldn't let that happen when chaos was what threatened this world.

I couldn't be just as chaotic and still bring balance. Everyone was counting on me, and the thought of failing was… I shuddered. It *couldn't* happen.

I made my way to the war room and walked right to Calix's side. His arm automatically opened and brought me into him. It was so hard to be around him and *not* touch him in some way. I wondered if that would ever lessen or if it would always be that way.

"Asteria, you remember Nithe." Calix indicated the man across the table, and I narrowed my eyes for a second, looking him over. But as I saw the pink eyes, I suddenly put it together, my own eyes going wide and a slight blush taking over my cheeks to my mortification.

Nithe smirked slightly, but he forced it down quickly, clearing his throat, and I was sure Calix was glaring him into submission above my head.

"Right. Hi," I greeted him lamely. Eryx pressed his lips together to hide his smile, so I glared at him from where he was standing around the table.

"Nithe just returned from Dusk," Calix explained, and launched into an explanation of what Nithe had seen. My face grew stormier the longer I listened, and I tried to fight down my rage as best I could. I could still feel smoke in my throat, and starlight bounced around my fingertips. They joined the shadows on Calix's, so I supposed I wasn't alone in that.

"I plan to send Nithe back into Dusk, to help the humans rising against Cyrus," Calix said, and I perked up. "This is why I wanted you here to help plan this out. If we can help them rise up, we can hopefully help some escape, which will also help to begin dismantling Cyrus's reign and operations."

I nodded eagerly, but bit my lip in thought. "Can we afford to send some people into the other kingdoms, too?"

"For what purpose?" Calix asked, brows furrowing as he looked down at me.

"Because all of the humans need to be in on this," I explained, beginning to move pieces on the map. "If the humans of only one kingdom rebel, then only one kingdom will be affected. We need all of Celesterra to rise up. *All* of the humans."

I turned to face Calix, my eyes wide and pleading. I knew—knew deep inside my heart and soul—that this was the right move.

"We can't do it for them, Calix. They need to grasp freedom for themselves. We send people to stir up rebellion in the kingdoms who are against us, then make sure the humans in the kingdoms allied with us know change is coming, and they should fight with us. We can change everything! Humans need to fight to free themselves, though. Even if the Fae lead the charge, they need to be involved. Otherwise, it's just more of the same—the Fae telling them how it's going to be and controlling their lives."

Silence followed in the wake of my impromptu speech. But I felt passionately about this, and as Calix examined me, I let him feel every bit of it. He slowly nodded, and I felt a weight lift off my shoulders.

"We can make that happen," Calix agreed, smiling softly. I smiled brightly back at him, leaning in to kiss him, showing him how grateful I truly was.

I knew his own passion for freeing humans originally came from the bond, but it meant everything to me that he took that and ran with it. The idea that I inspired the first Fae king to turn against slavery left me feeling bright and warm inside.

We spent hours hashing out tactics for Nithe to use. How to stir the humans to rebel, how to help them escape, how we were going to handle an influx of free humans was even hashed out. Notices would go out across all our allied territories, calling for volunteers to lend aid in the matter. We'd make sure no one would go homeless or hungry.

But first, we needed to ensure their freedom. That was the key to all of it. But I knew with the horrifying acts Cyrus was committing, we could finally get the remaining humans to see the truth. The false comfort they'd felt couldn't last forever. The time for being content with this half-measure peace was over.

Even if I was still personally straining to feel the truth of my freedom. As long as Cyrus lived, I wasn't sure I *could* feel it.

But that was something to deal with later.

"Do you happen to know why Ilta is searching me out for a dress fitting?" I asked Calix, my brow cocked.

He smiled slyly, pulling me into him. "I do, as it happens."

He leaned into me, biting my lip slightly.

"Care to fill me in?" I teased, nipping him back.

He chuckled, his smile devastating as he looked down at me with so much emotion in his eyes, the Aurora shining brilliantly in his purple orbs. "Eryx pointed out that the people of Night need to officially be introduced to you. As my mate. And as the future queen."

My heart seemed to stop beating for a moment, only to start again at double speed.

"Right," I croaked out, cringing.

"You're going to be perfect, my réalta." He reassured me, rubbing my back. "They are just curious."

"Yes, they are!" Ilta sing-songed as she breezed over to us, and I rolled my eyes.

Where in Tartarus did she even come from?

"And we need to plan this party very quickly, so let's get to it, you two!" Baach exclaimed, waving his hands dramatically at us, his red hair flying around his shoulders.

I looked up at Calix helplessly, but he shrugged, just as helpless to do anything. So we let them pull us separate ways, even if both ways led to party planning of some sort.

"Aren't there more important things to be focusing on than this?" I complained to Ilta, who narrowed her eyes at me.

"Don't underestimate the power of the people's love, Asteria," she admonished. "If the people of Night meet and love you, you'll have much more power than if they don't know or understand where you fit in here. They've waited centuries for Calix's prophesied queen, and then two decades *impatiently* waiting once his mark appeared. They knew his mate would be the queen they'd all been waiting for, after all."

She paused and looked me dead in the eye, her usual playful attitude fading as she looked at me seriously. She pushed a lock of dark hair behind my ear before putting a hand on my cheek, ensuring I listened. "They *will* love you, Asteria. And you can use that love. Use it to rule Night, to rule Day, to free the humans, to fight Cyrus."

I tilted my head to the side as I considered her words, and how I could use that love to help. I still didn't understand *why* they'd love me. I was no one, not really. An accident of birth didn't make someone worth following.

I told Ilta as much, and she sighed sadly.

"You're right. An accident of birth is no reason to follow a person." She smiled then, confusing me. "So, go show them who you are. Show them *why* you are worth following, and I guarantee you, *they will*."

CHAPTER 36

Asteria

Not a day later, I found myself getting ready for my introduction to the people of Night. Anyone who could make it on time would be here. All to see their future queen.

Delia helped me get ready, and Priscilla assisted her, insisting it was good luck at this point to have her present. It made me smile, seeing her desire to continue this tradition. I enjoyed having the time together, so I would never argue against it.

Delia allowed me to leave my hair long and straight, but fitted a crown on my head that had me pulling a sharp breath in. It was made of silverium, and had the phases of the moon across it. The moon phases on each side tilted up slightly, leading up to what should have been the full moon in the middle, but instead held up a star at the highest point of the crown that was made completely of star opal. Each moon was outlined in star opal as well, and under the moon phases, the base of the crown itself had gems across its band. In addition to star opal and diamond, little golden gems were worked in, in what I knew was another nod to Day Kingdom, on top of the silverium.

Calix had gotten this crown made for me, knowing I'd need a crown for each kingdom. To properly represent the people, he'd said, at least for now. The fact he'd put so much of Day into it was touching, especially since he knew Day's crown would have none of Night. That he cared so much to represent me as a person meant so much.

Priscilla finished my makeup, giving me glittering touches of silver on my face and outlining my eyes in dark kohl. My lips were painted a dark plum and looked perfect with the rest of the look.

Delia brought the dress out, and I finally got to see it for the first time since Ilta discussed the emergency rush job with the seamstress. I had no idea how she'd done it, but she'd made magic happen.

They helped me put it on, and I couldn't believe what I was seeing—from the tip of my crown to the pointed ears and starlit eyes to the dress…

I let my wings out for the full effect, and I heard a gasp. Calix walked in, his eyes darkened as he looked me over. I cut my eyes to Delia and Priscilla, who both smiled slyly before rushing out, Delia winking at me quickly.

Calix's eyes took in every inch of me. The dress was admittedly gorgeous. A purple layer was underneath, and the top layers were made to mimic starlight. Sparkling silver that moved with me and made me shine like an actual star. The purple showed through more on top, where the sweetheart neckline was accented by the jewelry that cut across my chest in long multilayered strands from my shoulders, which were bare. It was an off-the-shoulder style, with long bell sleeves that shifted from purple to silver. The bodice had a corset built in, with a triangle of star opals from my neckline to the midline of the bodice, and the boning of the corset had diamonds sparkling down it, as well as across the neckline to where the sleeves sat on my shoulders.

Since the skirt had so many layers, it had a hint of purple at the top but was mostly just pure starlight. Where the two met, however, looked like starlight twinkling over the night sky, just like on the bodice. With my wings out, the silver scales shining with the purple edges and veins, I finally looked like the Star Queen everyone kept calling me.

Ethereal. Magical. Starlit.

Calix clearly agreed, growling low as he approached. I backed up to the wall, despite the thrill of arousal that rushed through me at how wild he looked right now.

"Save it for the after party, my dorchadas," I purred, raising a brow. "I won't let you destroy this dress. In fact, you should go get dressed yourself."

He was still in his regular clothes, and I knew he wouldn't get away with wearing that with Baach and Ilta in charge.

"I don't need to destroy the dress to have you, my réalta." He smirked, stalking toward me, a long fang exposed and making me clench my thighs together. I couldn't stop my arousal. It was a helpless fight.

And he knew that, the bastard.

He undid his pants slowly, and I watched as that long, thick, hard cock bounced free from its confines. I licked my lips, barely noticing the rest of his clothing hitting the floor.

And then I found myself in the air, my dress pushed up, and my legs around his waist as he thrust into me. I grappled for a hold on his shoulders, my wings surging forward slightly, but Calix kept us locked in place, holding me up with my thighs spread wide around him, his cock deep inside me.

He pulled his hips back before thrusting back in hard and fast. My cunt clenched down wildly, my moans uncontrollable as I called his name.

"That's it, my réalta," he purred, nipping my neck. "Squeeze me hard."

I did as he instructed, unable to help myself. My claws dug into his shoulders, as his dug into my hips. His thrusts were so hard that every time he pushed in, he hit something deep inside me, making me scream. It felt so good, and I couldn't stop myself from mumbling it over and over.

His own wings ripped free, and suddenly we were unmoored, completely in the air with the wall and floor nowhere to be found. I was very grateful for the high arched ceiling in my room, giving us enough room to not hit our heads.

He used the freedom to contort me, my back arching backward, putting me nearly upside down, with my hips high in the air to meet his thrusts. The angle felt incredible as his cock filled me up deep.

"There you go," he rumbled. "I know how much you desire control, but you know as well as I do you don't want it here."

I moaned in disagreement, knowing it was the truth, but not willing to admit it.

"Don't lie, my réalta." He tutted. "I knew it that day in the Hedone room. You were all too willing to be my little fuck doll. To let me do *whatever* I wanted to you."

I screamed as he thrust in hard, rubbing my clit with his shadows in tandem. His words somehow only made me wetter. As much as I longed for control over my life, sex was the one place I enjoyed losing it completely. As long as I trusted the person it was to.

"Hmm." Calix hummed in a deep rasp. "You know you'll enjoy it, so you don't mind giving me complete control. You'll let me do every wicked, depraved thing your mind and mine can come up with, won't you?"

I nodded, sobbing in pleasure as his cock seemed to widen, and I realized he was partially shifting to his dragon form. His cock grew longer and thicker, and I swore I lost my mind at that moment.

He laughed darkly, "I promise you, I'll show you every one. This is only the beginning, my réalta. I have centuries to show you every way there is to find pleasure. Every way there is to make this dripping little cunt cum for me."

"Fuck!" I sobbed, my cunt clenching down rapidly, again and again, his words, the giant fucking cock splitting me open, the shadows taunting my clit—*who the fuck knew what*. But my orgasm slammed into me with the force of a comet, completely untethered in the air.

Calix swore as I came around him, pumping a couple more times before he spilled into me with a shout.

As he pulled out slowly, I whimpered from the extra stretch caused by his momentary increase in size.

He held me still as he flew us down slightly, but my wings and his strength kept me airborne. He kept my legs open as he slotted his shoulders between them, and lightly ran his tongue up my cunt, making me twitch.

He laughed slightly, blowing air on me and making me sigh softly in pleasure. He cleaned me up with his tongue, and I ran my fingernails gently through his hair as he did so. Enjoying the blissful moment as my eyes shut.

My eyes opened when we suddenly landed, and Calix put me on my feet. He chuckled, leaning down to kiss me softly. "Can't let you fall asleep."

I batted lightly at his chest, yawning slightly. "Your fault."

"I'll accept that." He nodded with a sly smile before looking over my dress. "And look, not a wrinkle."

I looked down, and sure enough, the dress was just as perfect as before. Calix straightened my crown softly, but everything else was perfectly intact, thanks to the Fae magic that kept our hair and makeup in place. It was a necessity when they tended to get wild at every party.

"Okay, now I need to get dressed." Calix chuckled, and I rolled my eyes at him, shooing him away.

CALIX CAME BACK to collect me, but by that time, I had worked myself into a panic.

"Asteria?" he called, walking into my rooms.

"Yes?" I called back nervously, wishing we could postpone this.

"Ready?" he asked, and I swallowed hard, not answering.

He came around the corner into my bedroom, where I was sitting on my bed.

"Asteria?" He tilted his head, confusion in his eyes.

"What if I can't do this?" I asked, wringing my hands in my lap. "Not just this, but all of it? Being queen? What in Tartarus do I know about being a queen? By the Otherworld, I was a human a couple of months ago!"

"Asteria—"

"What if I mess everything up?" I continued, panicking more by the second. "What if they all hate me? What if—"

"Asteria!" He shook me gently by the shoulders, and I looked up with wide, frightened eyes.

"Calix…" I trailed off, lost. Everything had hit me at once. All the pressure, all the things people were expecting of me. Where I had come from, and how little I was prepared for any of this.

He kneeled before me, taking my hands in his and squeezing. His eyes were kind and gentle when I met them, not a trace of panic or doubt within them.

"I know this is all a lot for you." He began. "But I have no doubt that you will be everything we need and more. Not because you were raised to be queen, but because you weren't."

I cocked my head in confusion, opening my mouth, but he put a finger over my lips, silently asking me to wait.

"You have always been stronger than you know. You dealt with your magic and emotions locked up in ways no one else has ever had to. You were forced to grow up enslaved, despite what you should have had. You persevered, despite all the odds against you, because you refused to follow the status quo. You listened to your heart, and it told you that it was *wrong*. Despite everyone else telling you otherwise, you listened to that inner voice inside you, and you fought to get yourself out of a bad situation that everyone else told you to accept."

My eyes started to water without my permission. The way Calix explained it sounded much grander than how I viewed it. I was headstrong and stubborn, and never truly thought about the consequences.

"That is why you will be an amazing queen, my réalta." He smiled, and I was momentarily taken aback by how beautiful he was when he smiled like that. He was always gorgeous, but that smile—*damn.*

"You will never allow the status quo to continue if you know it's wrong. You won't listen to advice you know is bad. You will follow that golden heart of yours. One lit by the sun, that shines in the stars, and glows against the night. It will always lead you right. And the people will love you for it. You think they love me?" He shook his head.

"Those humans out there, they only love me because I abolished slavery. Something I only did because of *you*." He took one of my hands he was holding and flattened it against his heart. "*Your* sense of right and wrong was so strong, it bled through a bond that was blocked by magic and sunk itself into *me*. It's one of the many reasons I love you. And it's why *they* will love you, too."

He lifted our joined hands and brought them to my cheek, wiping away my tears. I sniffed, leaning into him. Our foreheads met, and we sat like that for a moment as I composed myself.

When I leaned back and nodded with a slight smile, he tilted my head back for a quick kiss, then smiled, pulling me up with him.

"Now, are you ready, love?" he asked gently, and I smiled back, nodding. "Now I am."

I COULD HEAR the commotion from the throne room as we stood in the antechamber, waiting to be announced.

To my surprise, Calix had chosen to make a statement and forewent his usual court attire. Instead, he was in full armor. Though, his crown was still on his head, and his wings were spread wide behind me. He'd instructed me to leave mine out as well for the duration.

I understood the reasoning. Wings present in Fae form were something few had. Only those of royal blood could summon them. Making it clear to everyone present exactly who I was.

As the herald announced us, I listened in particular to how I was introduced.

"*Crown Princess Asteria Faelynn Earendel. The Gods Chosen Heir to Day Kingdom. Mate of the King of Night Kingdom. The Star Queen of Celesterra!*"

Calix and I walked out; my arm twined around his. I took a deep breath, swallowing hard at the number of people in the room. I thanked Nox the ceiling was open to the stars because otherwise the room would feel horribly tight right now with the number of people packed inside.

Fae and humans alike were everywhere. I spotted several I knew: the lords and ladies of Night, some people I'd met around the city, and even some of the soldiers I'd trained with in the yard. But it was overwhelming, nonetheless.

Calix, sensing my distress, sent me his love and pride down the bond in a wave that distracted me immediately. I sighed in relief as the panic receded, and I let Calix lead me to where his throne waited on the dais. The massive dragon throne was still a wonder to look upon, and I realized that the runes above the throne in shining silver began to actually glow as we neared.

Huh. Maybe my Fae eyesight could pick it up where my human eyes couldn't.

We reached the dais and walked up the steps to it, watching my feet to ensure I didn't do something completely embarrassing and trip. I'd have to hide for the rest of my life if that happened.

Calix led me right to the dragon throne, taking my hand and leading me to sit on it. I was surprised, blinking at him for a moment. He winked at me, and a burst of confidence came through the bond. He moved to stand beside the throne, his hand resting on the dragon hilt of his sheathed blade.

Standing there in his armor, he looked quite imposing. His long silvery-white hair was down to his chest, with his pointed ears poking through on each side. His purple eyes watched the crowd intently. His sharp cheekbones gave an edge to his look, but plush lips softened it slightly. He was the most gorgeous warrior king in history. I was positive of that.

"Citizens of Night Kingdom," Calix called out, the crowd hushing to listen as their king spoke. "From Tairngire and beyond! I thank you all for coming on such short notice. As your king, I want you to know I appreciate every single one of you putting in the effort to be here with us for this historic moment."

They hung onto his every word. His charisma came through in spades, and I nearly laughed remembering when I first met him and put a knife to his throat. He used that charismatic personality to disarm me, and I knew now I'd never stood a chance.

"Today, I introduce you all to the future queen!" he exclaimed, somewhat haughtily. "Of Night Kingdom, and of Day Kingdom!"

The crowd gasped, and looked around at one another.

"Yes, you heard me correctly," Calix confirmed, a growing smirk on his face. "For years, we have awaited the culmination of my birth prophecy."

"𝔇arkness sweeps across the land
To bring new order to 𝔉ae and 𝔐an.

A light to brighten his darkness be the king's fate
Blood will seep and unveil his mate.
An eclipsed star lost who must be found
The power of two will be her crown.
Together, they will usher in a new age
Though not without a war to wage.
A queen of stars and a king of night

Are the only hope to see the world made right.' He quoted the words with a sense of gravitas I envied, the crowd eating out of his hand.

"The Star Queen was unveiled as promised! The power of the Day Kingdom's crown is hers by right of blood and by order of the gods!" He thundered, "And as my soulmate, the crown of Night is hers to wear!"

"The power of two!" Someone in the crowd shouted, followed by another.

A chill went down my spine, but I forced myself to lounge comfortably back on the throne, my wings extending out over the edges.

"Yes. A Queen of Stars and a King of Night, are the only hope to see the world made right," Calix reiterated, and I swallowed as the pressure on my chest increased. But I let Calix's confidence soothe me.

He turned his head to me and nodded, and I turned my attention to the crowd.

"People of Night Kingdom!" I called out, suppressing a shudder at so many sets of eyes staring back at me. "I promise I will serve you. I will protect you. And I will love you. You gave me a home when I was lost, and it was here that I truly found myself. Night will always be my home, and I will fight for it more fiercely than any queen has before."

The reference to the prophecy had them excited, but my last words had them chanting *Star Queen* in a way that brought a glimmer of tears to my eyes.

"The war has come," I told them heavily once they quieted, and I stood from the throne, stepping toward the edge of the dais. Calix's pride beat within my soul, keeping me going. "A war that will define the course of Celesterra forever. Both of our birth prophecies spoke of what our destiny entailed, and one thing was made perfectly clear. Together, Calix and I will face what comes, and I promise you here and now, I will not stop until we defeat those who would bring chaos and death to this world! I will fight and fight again. I will not falter. Not until the war is won, for all of us!"

Loud cheers followed my words, some chanting my title once more, others screaming in joy. I took a deep breath, taking it all in. Calix came and took my hand, and the crowd went even more insane.

Calix brought them back to order with a raised hand. "We thank you all for coming for your future queen's introduction. To celebrate this historic day, we invite you all to stay for the ball!"

Cheers sounded as a sudden gust of wind swept into the room dramatically. Baach was there, having opened the double doors, winking at us as he directed people out so they could transform the space. They were all invited outside or to the other hall for cocktails, ensuring no one felt bored as they waited.

As tables and chairs were brought into the throne room, I slumped back onto the throne itself, finally feeling a weight lifted off me. Calix chuckled. "See, it wasn't as bad as you imagined, right?"

I narrowed my eyes at him jokingly, but a smile cracked through. "No, it was okay."

"Okay?" He gasped dramatically, before turning serious. "You did amazing. They love you already."

"They shouldn't." I countered, raising a brow. "I haven't done anything yet."

He went to one knee in front of the throne, careful not to bump his sword, and put a hand on my knee. "You promised to fight for them. That you would keep fighting. You told them this was your home. That they are your people. Knowing that you're the heir to Day, that by right, *they* should be your people. You have no idea how much that meant to them."

CHAPTER 37

WHEN the room was ready, everyone was led back into the transformed throne room, but Calix and I had moved back into the antechamber to be reintroduced for the first dance.

Ilta bounced up to us, clapping her hands in excitement. "That was amazing!"

"You guys did perfectly." Baach winked at me as he came up behind her, laying an arm around her shoulders. Ilta flushed, looking up at him with starry eyes of her own.

"Thank you both." I smiled gratefully, and turned that smile to the side as Lilith walked in.

"There you are!" She gave me a faux scowl. "Do you know how hard it is to get a face-to-face with you these days?"

I groaned, leaning back into Calix, who chuckled, his chest rumbling against my back. "Tell me about it. It's been insane."

Lilith chuckled, a smile taking over her face. "I know, but don't worry. For tonight at least, you can let go and just enjoy for a bit."

"Just don't enjoy too much," Harpina teased. "We do have a war to fight. You're new enough to fighting, I don't want to see what you'd do in a battle hung over."

I glared at her while everyone laughed, but she just sent me a wink that had me rolling my eyes.

Delia walked in with Priscilla, and I was happy to see how much those two had been getting along. I felt bad that I was so busy right now. I wished I could spend more time with everyone. I just needed to remind myself that this was necessary, and temporary. Once it was over, we could all spend plenty of time together.

"You guys looked gorgeous up there together." Ilta enthused, swooning slightly. "Everyone is talking about how the Star Queen is the perfect complement to our Night King."

"They're talking about more than that," Eryx added, his eyes watching Delia intensely enough that she flushed. While she might be avoiding a relationship, the way she eyed him in return told me she was more than willing to indulge in her feelings tonight.

"They feel a lot more confident about the battles to come." Eryx smiled, clapping a hand on Calix's shoulder. "I told you they just needed to meet her."

Calix rolled his eyes, but nodded in agreement. I was distracted as Titan walked in, however. He'd been guarding us from the side of the throne, but I was anxious to see what he thought.

He smiled at Calix and me as he walked up to us, looking between the two of us fondly. "I'm incredibly proud of both of you. I know you'll lead these kingdoms in a new, better age together. One I have no doubt will go down in history."

I sniffed back tears, throwing my arms around him and murmuring in his ear, "Thank you, Uncle."

Calix stiffened beside me, and I realized he'd heard me. *Damn Fae hearing.*

I pulled back, biting my lip as I looked between them. Titan put a hand on my shoulder. "Don't worry. Just get through the first dance, and I'll explain everything. Okay?"

He turned to Calix with a raised brow. Calix looked confused, but nodded in agreement. Titan grunted, nodding back.

It was then we were called back in, so the others entered first, and Calix and I followed them in.

"Uncle?" he whispered to me. The bafflement in his voice was honestly adorable. I couldn't help giggling.

"Strangely enough," I confirmed, whispering back to him. "It's his story to tell, though." Calix let it go, thankfully. Putting a hand on my back, he guided me to the center of the dance floor, and the music began.

Calix put his arms around my waist as I put mine on his shoulders. I was very thankful once more for those dancing lessons they'd given me previously. Now, I just hoped I remembered all the steps. Thankfully, Calix led, and I moved with him as we swished and swayed around the dance floor.

My dress looked like actual starlight in this light. With the ceiling open to the dark sky and the stars above, a sight I would never tire of, and the reflection of it on the black floors, the sparkle of my dress fit right in. The purple, green, and blue of the Aurora danced above and below us, while the columns of star opal crawling with dragons shone brilliantly in the light. I truly loved this room, and didn't think any other could compare.

Calix pulled me tight to his body, his wings flaring back before he spun me out, my skirt flying around me. I heard some gasps in the crowd as the layers of starlight glimmered with the movement. My mate pulled me back in and dipped me, taking the opportunity to kiss me as my wings brushed the ground. It was no courtly kiss either. This was full-on tongue invading my mouth and teeth nipping at my lip.

The crowd wolf-whistled and cheered, and we both laughed as Calix lifted me back up.

"They enjoy a good show." He winked, the smolder he sent me making me bite my lip to suppress the need to jump him. *Nox*, he made it hard sometimes. It was easier now that I could actually have him, as opposed to the last time we were here when he drove me completely crazy. But—it wasn't *that much* better.

I was anxious for the after party, to say the least. There was a swing with our names on it, and I was taking that opportunity before the gates of Tartarus opened on us.

The crowd began to join us on the dance floor as the next song began. We danced around them, but as Calix twirled me out, Eryx grasped my hand.

"Hope you don't mind if I steal her for a bit." He winked at Calix, who shook his head with a smile. I knew he was off to find Titan and get answers as he walked away. I smiled at Eryx as he grabbed me and twirled me the other way.

"Having fun?" I asked, raising a brow at him.

"Always." He smirked, that boyish twinkle back in his eyes that had been missing far too often lately with the weight of the war and his role as spymaster pressing on him.

"How are you holding up?" he asked quietly, and I considered his question.

"I think I'm alright." I finally smiled. "It's a lot, don't get me wrong. But Calix has a way of making most of it easy."

Eryx laughed, shaking his head. "He's always been like that."

I cocked my head to the side, and he continued, "He's always been able to make this job easy. He took to being king like he was born for it—which *he was.* I mean, don't get me wrong, he struggled at times with the pressure of all his responsibilities, but he never faltered when it came to being king."

"And that made it easier for all of you in turn." I realized. Eryx nodded in confirmation, twirling me around once more.

"I was having a hard time when I first began working with Calix," Eryx told me, and my brows furrowed as I listened. "My parents had been murdered, and I was desperate for revenge."

I gasped in a breath, shocked at what had happened to him. I had never heard anything about Eryx's family before.

"I'd grown up here at the palace. My father worked for Calix's. But when the king died, one of my father's enemies took the opportunity to take him out. I saw the entire thing and went to Calix for help. I didn't want him to be arrested. I wanted to go after him myself." Eryx explained, a grim remembrance all over his face.

"What happened?" I asked him quietly.

Eryx smiled slightly. "Calix helped me work to get my revenge. But afterward, I was lost. Calix made me his spymaster because he knew I could do it after what he'd seen me do during my quest for revenge. But more importantly, he knew putting that responsibility on me would help pull me out of the dark place I was in. He was right."

Eryx chuckled, shaking his head. "He just made it so easy to fall into the role. And I've watched as he's done the same with everyone else. Finding where they fit in and making it an easy transition. Making all these responsibilities that could crush someone seem even fun at times."

"I'm sorry that happened to you," I told him sincerely, and he smiled, giving me a kiss on the cheek.

"I'm so glad Calix found you. I know you have a new big brother now but—" Eryx started, but I shook my head.

"Don't you even." I poked his chest with a faux glare. "You've *earned* big brother status," I told him, making him smile boyishly.

"Alright, my turn." Baach cut in, and I laughed as he swept me away. "Are you enjoying yourself, my Queen?"

"You've outdone yourself, Master of Ceremonies," I countered, raising a brow at him pointedly.

He laughed, shaking his head, "Come on, I've got to get my fun in before you're actually queen, and I can't tease you anymore."

"Like that would stop you." I snorted but looked up at him with a calculating gleam in my eyes.

"Uh oh." He raised his brows at me, smirking.

I smirked right back, "If you're looking for fun, you could always go find Ilta. I'm sure she's more than willing to have all the fun you want."

"And what is that supposed to mean?" His brows flew up, and I shook my head at him in disbelief.

"Baach, come on. You must see it," I said, exasperated.

"See what?" he asked defensively. "She enjoys having sex with me during parties, yes, but that's all she's interested in."

"Oh Nox, Baach. Tell me you don't honestly believe that." I watched him with wide eyes as we slowed, too invested in the conversation to focus on dancing. He honestly looked confused.

These Tartarus damned immortals. I swear to Nox.

"Okay, here's a hint. Maybe ask her?" I advised, thinking it quite obvious.

He looked shocked, his hazel eyes wide, and I smirked at him before Lord Polaris and Lady Nillah pulled me away to dance, leaving Baach staring into the distance. Following his eyes, I found Ilta dancing with Lord Ciaran. I remembered vividly how he'd watched Lady Jasira. I looked over at the lady herself to find her watching the two dancing intently, a slight frown on her face.

What a mess.

I FELT LIKE I'd been dancing forever. I'd danced with Calix many times, but kept getting stolen away by others. I was currently dancing with Ladies Aisling and Alora, enjoying myself as they teased me over Calix, when the man himself appeared, wrapping his arms around my waist.

"One last dance before we head downstairs," he whispered in my ear, and I nodded eagerly, more than ready for the next part of the night.

Aisling winked at me as she danced off toward Kyler, and Alora took a break since Rhidian was sitting down, waiting for her. But I was quickly distracted as Calix began moving.

He kept my back to him, and I hooked my arm around his neck as he pulled my hips back into his. We swayed against one another, my ass brushing against his covered cock, teasing both of us for later. His hand went to my stomach, and I laced our fingers together.

I tilted my head back toward him, and he leaned down to touch his lips to mine. I turned around fully and pressed myself into him as we danced. My hands went into his hair while he gripped my hips, and his shadows started slithering up my legs. I moaned as they stroked my inner thighs, inching higher and higher.

But then Ilta was there, pulling me away. Calix and I both groaned in protest, reaching for one another.

"Oh no, you don't!" Ilta laughed, pulling me further. "You just have to get downstairs, you animals. You can wait twenty minutes."

"No, I can't," I whined, and Ilta cocked her head at me with a glare, making me pout. Calix leaned in quickly, growling as he bit my pouty bottom lip. I gasped slightly, and he pulled back with a smirk.

"See you soon, my réalta," he whispered ruggedly, before disappearing into the crowd. I sighed, desperately horny and wishing I could chase him down. But Ilta was right; I just needed to change and make my way downstairs, and then I had an entire night with him to lose myself to lust.

Ilta laughed at me as she grabbed my hand, leading me to the room set up for us to change.

"You two are ridiculous." She shook her head with a smile. "I've never seen a newly mated couple before, but I'm starting to understand the insanity."

"Hey!" I complained, and Ilta giggled, pulling me into the room to change.

I sighed but began going through the rack to find myself an outfit.

"Asteria, look at this one!" Ilta squealed, pulling a dress out and laying it over her hand for me to see. "This would be perfect for you! It's the style you love, but still a bit different than the last one."

She was absolutely right. I loved it immediately. It was similar to the last one I'd worn, but there were some big differences that made it stand out. It was black lace again, but it had leather pieces sticking out slightly at the shoulder. Those pieces turned into trim as they merged into the body of the dress. The leather dipped in a slight V at the navel, leaving a bit of my stomach bare. While my breasts were covered in a sheer black fabric, and the leather trim of the dress cut in over the breasts to cover where the nipples would be.

The bottom looked like lingerie, and there were spots where the lace had wider holes, leaving the skin exposed in a deliberate tease. Spots around the hips were left tantalizingly bare, while other areas covered more skin. It did cover where my cunt would be, but with the lace, you'd still see my underwear through it. The skirt ended right below the apex of my thighs, dipping down slightly lower at the edges to create almost a half-circle shape.

But the best part had to be the cape. It attached under the leather shoulder pieces and gave the appearance of big bell sleeves with how it fell over my shoulders. There was a solid piece of black fabric lining the interior, but lace wound all the way around the exterior and extended past the lining, making the lace see-through at the bottom. The cape was cut higher up in the center, so it would hang just under my ass, but longer on the sides to make the faux sleeves fall correctly.

It was *gorgeous*. And there was a mask made of black leather and lace that would go perfectly with it. I eagerly got dressed and looked at myself in the mirror.

Calix was going to lose his fucking mind.

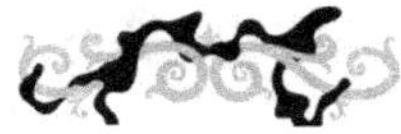

WALKING INTO THE Hedone room, I noticed once more the runes on the plum-colored door, only this time, they seemed to glow as I pushed the door open. It had to be the difference in my eyesight since becoming Fae.

I was greeted inside by the plum and black damask velvet walls and crystal chandeliers lit with candles. The same sultry atmosphere surrounded me, with incense filling the room with a heady scent. While many people were already engaging in foreplay, just as many bowed their heads as I passed, proving the mask was absolutely useless.

It was strange, being respected in such a way. After growing up a slave, I'd wanted so badly to feel some sort of respect and thought it was an impossible dream. Yet now, here I was.

Surreal was an understatement.

I spotted the drink I remembered from last time, with its red liquid and fizzing sparks. It was intended to enhance sexual experiences and lower inhibitions, and while I didn't necessarily *need* it, it was a damn fun time.

I knocked a glass back, getting a laugh from Ilta as she drank her own beside me. Priscilla had sat this one out without Callisto here, but everyone else was present somewhere. And there was one tall as Tartarus silvery-white haired man I needed to find. The lilac-eyed one. Not any of the others. While I'm sure Polaris would enjoy it, Kyler and Rhidian were definitely spoken for. And I had no interest in anyone except my mate.

Ilta jumped, and I looked beside me to see Baach had snaked his arm around her and brought her back against him. She sighed like she was sinking into a tub of hot water, and Baach gave me a quick wink. I smirked back at him, grabbing another wine glass full of the fizzy red liquid and toasting them before walking away. While I hoped Baach took my advice and was truly happy for them, I had no desire to watch.

Walking through the halls, I passed the alcoves that were already filling up with people engaging in all sorts of acts. Most of the curtains were left open, and I got quite the view from several of them, making me quicken my pace in the hopes of finding Calix.

The next room was the one full of sex swings, and I almost wanted to wait for him to find me here, but I had a better idea. The following room was where I'd found Calix last time, so I made my way in, plan in place. Arousal was already beginning to leak down my thighs as I sipped my drink, imagining everything I wanted to do tonight.

Unlike last time, no one eyed me with any intent. Oh, there were looks of interest and lust, but their eyes quickly darted away when they realized who I was.

Someone very off-limits. Unless they wanted to bring their king's wrath down on them.

I spotted the oversized grey, velvet chair I'd sat in with Calix—or *on* Calix—last time. It was thankfully empty, so I quickly sat and claimed it for myself. I crossed my legs as I waited, my cape sleeves draped over the arms of the chair.

I smelled him before I saw him. The scent of night and fire reached me, and I inhaled deeply. Even his scent was setting me off right now, and I shifted to get some friction.

I lifted my glass and took a sip, eyeing everyone in the room until I spotted him. Calix had already found me and was zeroed in on me, making me smirk into my glass. He had a black leather mask across his eyes and black leather pants that left little to the imagination. His regular black long-sleeved top was unbuttoned and paired with an open black leather vest, leaving his chest completely bare.

I couldn't stop myself from licking my lips, biting the lower one as I tried to contain myself. Calix smirked, and I knew he could feel it. I stood up, unable to help myself, and his eyes dropped down to check out my ensemble.

I could physically feel the heat of his eyes on me as he raked them up from my strappy black leather heels, to where my cunt was barely covered at all by the lace of my dress, to the sheer cups over my breasts, all the way back to my eyes.

But said eyes were a bit preoccupied, licking over every inch of his chest, his iridescent black and purple dragon tattoos on full display. His sleeves were pushed up his forearms, so the silvery runes tattooed there were visible, and a part of my heart melted a bit, knowing now that he always tried to show them when possible because he was proud of his birth prophecy foretelling my arrival.

But once I looked down, it was difficult to keep my eyes off the giant bulge in his pants.

I forced myself to meet his eyes, expecting the usual lilac, only to find the green and blue and pinks of the Aurora had overtaken his eyes, sharing equal space with the purple. He stepped into me forcefully, grabbed my hair to pull me to him, and devoured my mouth before I knew what had happened.

I gave myself over to his kiss, sinking into it and opening my mouth to let his tongue in. He stroked and caressed my own, and I licked over the sharpened canines in his mouth. He pulled back, leaving me panting, and growled, "Sit."

I immediately fell back into the chair.

"Spread your legs." His voice was a low rumble that sent shivers down my entire body. I spread my legs wide, and he dropped to his knees before me. He threw my legs over his shoulders, and I struggled to breathe as I tried not to die from anticipation.

The dress barely had to be lifted, and he smirked darkly as all he needed to do was move one single finger to move my panties to the side. His eyes met mine as he licked up my arousal, and my own fell back into my head as he began to devour my cunt with the same madness he'd attacked my mouth with.

His tongue laved over my clit before licking up each side of my cunt, swirling around my entrance before entering it completely, thrusting his tongue in and out, and making me grip the arms of the chair as I writhed against him, thrusting my hips to chase the feeling.

His shadows began to chase after his tongue, echoing the pleasure I just felt and multiplying it in tandem. His fingers joined the party, thrusting deep into my cunt and spreading wide as he moved his hand in a way that had to be physically impossible. He had to be cheating with those Tartarus damned wonderful shadows, *right*? I bit my lip hard to try to contain my moans, not wanting to shout to the entire room. But Calix wasn't having any of that.

He reached up and pulled my lip from my mouth, shaking his head at me, and subsequently running his tongue back and forth across my clit.

"Calix, please!" I finally gave in, moaning loudly.

"Good girl," he growled into my skin, making me nearly vibrate. He sucked my clit into his mouth, running his teeth gently across it as I screamed his name.

His shadows came up to my breasts, creeping under the dress and pinching my nipples. But it was when they surged up and surrounded my neck, pressing down lightly, in combination with the thrust of his tongue inside my cunt and his finger on my clit, that I went screaming over the edge, my walls clenching down around his tongue as he sucked down my climax eagerly.

I continued twitching slightly from the aftershocks as he pulled back, his face wet from my arousal. I almost wanted to thank him for dedicating years to sleeping around and becoming *so* fucking good at that.

But I was a dragon, and I was finally starting to recognize that fact. That side of me had a lot of great qualities, but it also meant I was a jealous, possessive beast.

And the thought of him with anyone other than me sort of made me want to claw out his eyeballs. Except... I kind of loved his eyeballs. And it wasn't like it was the women's fault. So, I decided it was better not to think about it too hard and just reap the benefits.

He leaned up and kissed me, making me taste myself on his tongue. As he kissed me, he grabbed both of my hands, pulling me up from the chair.

"I've been waiting for this, my réalta," he said in a smoky rasp, pulling me by the hand toward the other room.

We walked into the room full of sex swings, and I turned to him with a bright, excited smile. He chuckled, kissing me quickly before pressing his forehead to mine. "Sometimes, I think you couldn't be more perfect, and then you do something that proves me wrong."

"And here I thought that was you," I countered impishly. "Now, how do we do this?"

He smirked and took me straight to one in the corner that was free. We passed by Ilta and Baach as we went, and I raised an eyebrow at him as Baach sent me a wink. Calix growled at him, but he just laughed and thrust harder into Ilta, pulling her blonde hair back hard.

"I swear, if he wasn't balls deep in Ilta right now..." he trailed off, and I couldn't help the giggle that left my lips, crashing my forehead into his shoulder.

"So possessive," I teased, and he grabbed me by the hips, burying his face in my neck as he growled out a *yes*, not even bothering to deny it.

"But so are you," he teased back as he bit my neck. I moaned, wanting so badly for him to sink his teeth into me.

He brought his head up, and looked up and down over my outfit. I slowly undid the cape, letting it fall to the floor as he watched heatedly.

"Dress on or off?" I asked with a sultry tilt of my hips. He groaned, his head falling backward for a moment.

"Getting to have you in this little lace and leather contraption is incredibly appealing, but if you leave it on, I won't be able to play with all of you." He bit his lip, thinking through his options like it was life or death. When he finally decided, he nodded seriously. "Off."

He stepped forward before I could react, turning me by the shoulders to access the back of my dress. He undid the buttons, tracing down my back as he revealed every inch of skin. When it was unbuttoned, he turned me back around, reaching for the leather shoulder accents to slowly slip it off.

His heated eyes took me in as it fell to the floor, leaving me in a pair of heels and a puddle of lace. "Nox, you're so fucking gorgeous."

I raised a brow at him pointedly, looking him up and down. He smirked back at me and moved to drop his leather vest to the floor. The shirt followed it, and he kicked off his boots before unbuttoning his pants. I bit my lip as he exposed himself, and I swore to Nox, it never got old.

It was the most perfect cock I'd ever seen.

He brought me over to the swing and helped me into the harness. It was padded with velvet, making it surprisingly comfortable against my skin. He strapped my wrists first and then my ankles, leaving me suspended in midair without even having to focus on flapping my wings.

I watched hungrily as Calix pumped his cock lazily, eyes roving over me like an animal waiting to pounce and devour. My legs were already spread, so Calix was able to watch my cunt leak for him with no impediments, something he did with avid interest. My arousal ran down my thighs in slow drips, and he stepped toward me to lick it all up, making me whimper.

He slapped his cock against my cunt, causing me to gasp, and began to run it back and forth over me. He slathered himself with my arousal, causing me to grow even wetter as a result. With every stroke of his cock upward, his head hit my clit, serving as a merciless tease.

When he finally notched himself at my entrance, I took a deep breath in anticipation. He thrust in quickly, stretching my fluttering walls wide as he bottomed out inside me. I moaned loudly, tossing my head backward and letting it fall. He began thrusting into me hard, grasping my hips lightly as I swung in place. The momentum of the swing meant I might as well have been thrusting back.

It certainly felt that way, with the force we came together.

Calix reached a hand up and grasped my throat, driving into me with a single-minded determination that had me screeching in pleasure through the lack of air. As he released my throat on a particularly hard thrust, I came all over his cock, surprising myself. I hadn't even felt it coming.

I panted, looking up at him to see a proud smirk on his face. He pulled out of me, making me moan in loss, but he merely twisted me around, so I was facing down and my ass was in the air. He thrust back in and gripped my ass as he began building a steady rhythm.

The sound of skin slapping was loud in the room, especially since it wasn't just us taking advantage of the swings. But somehow, I felt like I was completely zeroed into the sound of his hips hitting my ass and of his cock repeatedly thrusting in and out. I was so fucking wet it was ridiculous. I could feel it all over my thighs, and surely it was on his, too, at this point.

He slapped my ass, letting out a loud groan, before his hands slipped up to my breasts and squeezed. His hips continued thrusting into me as his fingers began pinching my nipples.

I moaned, my head kicking back up as I writhed in my bonds. "Calix…"

He thrust in, moaning himself as my walls rippled around his length. "My Queen."

He pinched and pulled at my nipples, his cock barreling into me fast and hard. His hands left my breasts, only for one to pull my hair back hard, making me whimper in pleasure, while the other landed on my ass with a smack.

He used the leverage to thrust in more rapidly, reaching deep inside me on every thrust and hitting that place that had me seeing stars.

Literally.

Starlight floated around me, but I was helpless to control it at that moment. Wisps of shadow snaked out to play around it as Calix chuckled.

But right before I came again, Calix pulled out, making me whine loudly in protest. He spun me back to face him, entering me in one quick thrust and resuming like he had never stopped. I moaned, tossing my head backward, but Calix's hand gripped under my hair and pulled me upward. His mouth crashed into mine, and I opened for him eagerly.

He spun me back up to the point of orgasm, only to pull back and stop moving, leaving me writhing and begging. "Calix, please! Nox, fuck, *please!*"

He kissed me on his thrust back in, but he didn't move, just kissed me, nipping my lip as he pulled back.

"My réalta," he rumbled as he pressed his mouth to my throat. "My mate." His teeth raked down my throat, and I pressed up into them. "My queen." He bit down lightly, drawing only the slightest drop of blood. I moaned, wishing more than anything I was free to do the same. My fangs itched with the desire to sink into his skin.

"Calix, please—"

"Promise me one thing." He panted slightly, voice low and rough. "And I'll let you cum."

"Anything! Fuck, *anything*." I swore, and he began to slowly thrust in and out once again, stretching my cunt around his girth slowly and making me feel every inch.

He took my mouth once again, our tongues tangling together, and I nearly cried in relief when his cock hit deep inside me.

"Move in with me," he whispered against my lips.

"What?" I mumbled back, blinking slightly.

"Move into my rooms. I got spoiled on our trip, getting to sleep next to you every night. We can redo the rooms however you want. I just want you with me, my réalta," Calix admitted, and I truly felt my heart melt.

He could have asked for anything, and all he wanted was to have me with him as he slept?

I didn't even have to think about it. Especially if he was fine with recreating my star ceiling in his room.

"Yes." I smiled widely against his mouth. "There's nowhere else I'd rather be, my dorchadas."

"Fuck." He groaned, and took my lips passionately once more, starting to fuck into me furiously.

I moaned into his mouth, and he swallowed every one fiercely, not letting go of my lips once. Our hips thrust together hard enough that I was certain I'd bruise, but it felt amazing. His shadows suddenly pinched my clit, and I could feel myself spiraling toward a huge orgasm.

The walls of my cunt fluttered wildly, and my clit twitched in tandem. My breathing picked up even as I sucked Calix's tongue down my throat. Calix began ramming his cock in with a single-minded determination, and I screamed out as I came.

Calix took the opportunity to cut his tongue on a fang and let me swallow a bit of his blood. It made the feeling a hundred times more intense than it already was. I felt the orgasm ripple through every part of my body, and as Calix spilled inside me, his hips stilling with him buried deeply, I couldn't think of a more perfect deal ever made.

CHAPTER 38

Calix

Waking up, I immediately noticed the difference between my bed the night before and my bed now. The warmth cuddled into my side made me sigh in relief, my head falling back against the pillow.

I reached a hand up to run my fingers through her hair, the dark tresses seeming slightly darker. I'd noticed since her transformation that Asteria was a bit tanner, the golden glow of the Earendel line shining through. But now, her hair also seemed a bit darker.

I shrugged it off for now. I was much more invested in pulling her on top of me. She whined slightly, always slow to wake up. Even though she no longer had to deal with the pain she felt in the past from the spell keeping her body and magic locked up unnaturally, she would never be a morning person.

She glared at me adorably, and I couldn't help the lazy smile I gave her in return. She huffed, face crashing back into the pillow, grousing, "You're way too chipper for this time of day."

Her hand still came up to run her fingertips over my chest, tracing over my tattoos absentmindedly. I ran my hand down her back, caressing her soulmark. Still in awe, that I didn't think would ever go away, that she was *finally here.*

"How can I not be? You're here with me," I told her, burying my face in her neck. I'd never been someone who overtly displayed their emotions before—outside of anger and fury. I didn't keep the kingly front up in front of my family and friends, but I also had never imagined such words coming out of my mouth before. And just because I found them somehow spilling out confidently, it didn't mean they came out easily. The strange vulnerability that putting the truth of my feelings out there caused remained ever-present.

But Asteria managed to bring this side of me out without my permission. Maybe it was being soulmates, maybe it was just *her*, or maybe some combination of the two, but I couldn't help it whenever I was with her.

And she made it so worth it. Humming happily, if sleepily, and cuddling into me. I could spend the next thousand years waking up exactly like this.

At least until, when I finally stole a morning kiss, intending on seeing if she was too sore from last night for breaking in the bed this morning, a knock sounded on my door.

I groaned loudly, throwing a spare pillow at the door and hearing the satisfying thud as it connected. My head fell back to the bed, and Asteria cracked an eye open, yawning as she stretched against me languidly. Giving me *all* sorts of ideas.

"Calix!" Eryx knocked urgently, and my head lifted off the pillow in worry this time. He never bothered me in my room unless it was actually an emergency.

"*Fuck,*" I cursed, kissing Asteria's head as I lifted myself out of the bed.

I went to open the door when the thought hit me, and I turned to Asteria. Her perfect breasts were peeking out the top of the blanket. Hard nipples pointing in the air and momentarily distracting me. I shook my head to shake myself out of my Asteria-induced haze.

"As much as I'm enjoying the view, unless you want to flash Eryx, you're going to want to pull the blanket up."

She grumbled, still trying to wake herself up. Like a little kitten trying to open its eyes for the first time. I smothered my smile as she pulled the sheet up, covering herself. Allowing me to open the door without risk of an incident.

"What's wrong?" I asked immediately, my brows furrowing.

"An urgent message came for Asteria from Prince Arien," Eryx explained, holding up the letter in his hand. "The messenger said it was extremely urgent, and that they needed help."

My brows flew upward, but Asteria had managed to pull herself from sleep at the thought of her brother potentially being in danger. I could feel her heart racing as she bounced over, wrapped in only my sheet, and took the letter, ripping it open.

Her eyes widened as she read, her panic and rage rising like a tidal wave inside her. I put a hand on her lower back, hoping to brace her and remind her I was here. She took a deep breath, and handed me the letter. I read it over quickly.

"*Fuck*," Asteria cursed, looking to me pleadingly. "I have to go. They need me."

"*We* will go." I reminded her. "You're not alone here, my réalta. I can bring our best warriors on my back while flying. We can get there quickly. Hopefully, we can arrive before Aelius's forces converge on Arien."

"And if we don't?" She asked nervously, swallowing hard. "If they're already there? Or—" She shook her head, cutting the thought off completely. I couldn't blame her. I didn't want to consider that possibility either.

Arien was growing on me. Unlike Aurelia, he truly respected Asteria as a leader and valued her as a person. Aurelia would need to work harder to achieve any kind of esteem in my eyes.

"If they are there already," I dipped my head to meet her eyes, my hands taking hers and squeezing. "Then we will join the fight. You've done well these last months in training. I have full faith in your abilities. You were born with the dragon song of rage within your heart, and there is no better place to release it than a battlefield."

"*Beautiful brutality*," she whispered, her eyes lighting a bit. "That's why they say you fight like that. You have your own song of rage."

I nodded with a proud smile, kissing her lightly, trying to ignore Eryx's pointed cough. Pulling back, I leaned my forehead to hers. "Your destruction will be more beautiful than anything I could conjure; I guarantee you that."

"This is all Aelius and Cyrus, but neither will be there." She pointed out, looking disappointed.

I chuckled truly, shaking my head. "Just wait. The time will come. And for now, you can slake your bloodlust on their underlings.

She proved exactly why I loved her so much when she smirked delightedly at the thought.

WE QUICKLY GOT ready, donning our armor and arming ourselves for the fight to come. I helped Asteria into her armor since Delia wasn't here.

Truthfully, I didn't feel like being interrupted during the last moments I'd have alone with Asteria before we left.

She looked so insanely gorgeous in her new armor, just as I knew she would. The silver, black, and purple were perfect. Her colors fit so well with my own. A testament to that was on her chest, where the revised sigil of the Night Kingdom for the Star Queen herself sat.

But we unfortunately had no time for me to enjoy her in the armor as I wished. It would have to wait until *after* the battle.

Titan, Eryx, Baach, and Harpina were all waiting for us outside, along with Rhidian, Ciaran, and Jasira. The other lords would hold down the fort, but they'd refused to be left behind. Well, Ciaran had insisted when Jasira had, and I knew he'd never forgive me if he didn't go with her. Those two were a complicated disaster I wanted no part of, honestly.

Better to let them figure it out themselves.

I watched as Asteria shifted into her dragon form, the beautiful silver scales shining in the light of the sun. The sun was the largest star there was, and it only made sense it would be drawn to her as much as the stars in the night sky were.

I shifted once she was up in the air, as did Eryx, and I let the others climb onto my back. I hated being used as a Tartarus damned pack horse, but it really was the most efficient way. I'd take any advantage in a battle, and leaving great fighters behind for the sake of my pride wasn't going to help anything. Still, Asteria was the only passenger I'd ever truly enjoyed having.

I found myself roaring delightedly in the sky, excited for the battle to come. While I worried about Asteria, it had been too long, and I'd been storing up plenty of rage. I needed to let some of it out, and battle was always the best place for that.

It didn't take us very long to reach Day Kingdom, and as we neared the capital of Avalon, I saw right away the golden dragon in the sky, purple scales around the edges, and purple horns standing out quite obviously against the bright gold.

Arien was breathing fire on our enemies while his armies defended the city. Aelius's forces had it surrounded. The stupid circular design made it overly difficult to defend. Asteria broke off to help her brother, while I went to drop off our warriors to help on the ground. Eryx shifted back above an enemy Fae, pulling his sword quickly and driving it into his back before he even knew he was there.

That's my brother.

I took off, trusting Titan to find the best place for everyone, and joined the other two dragons in the sky. It had been so long since I'd fought next to two dragons, so I was exhilarated as I let the fire rise in my throat, swooping down and taking out a line of screaming enemy soldiers.

I almost wished we'd taken the phoenixes, to add their own power to the fight. But we didn't want to give away our allies too early. Any who escaped today would run back to Aelius, who'd inform Cyrus. We needed any element of surprise we could get.

As the two armies below began to crash into one another, it became too dangerous to use our fire on the front rows. We don't want to scorch our allies, after all.

"Head to the back," I told Asteria and Arien, and their huge dragon heads turned to me in midair. I flew around the front lines to where the stragglers were, the silver and gold-scaled twins following suit behind me. We boxed the soldiers in with flames before taking them out. When we'd taken out as many as we could that way, we quickly flew back into the thick of things.

I shifted before I hit the ground, pulling an Eryx as I unsheathed my black blade and drove it into the first enemy I saw as I hit the ground. My blade sang in my hand, the runes shining as I swung it into the next person.

These were all Lord Aydun's men, I realized. The green and copper coloring gave it away quite easily. I spied the red-headed lord himself mounted on his horse, far away from the mob of fighting soldiers and completely surrounded by his guards.

The coward.

Asteria landed beside me, and I kept her in my line of sight as she kicked out at a Fae who rushed her, knocking him off balance. She unsheathed her shining silver blade and drove it straight through his neck.

As the blood spurted out, and he fell to the ground convulsing, I saw her little smirk before she wiped it off her face.

That's my girl.

A loud cheer of Asteria's name went up from the back of Arien's forces, and I realized with surprise that those were *humans* in Arien's ranks. I raised a brow at him as he landed.

"Little busy at the moment," he complained as he swung his blade at a green and bronze-clad man.

I rolled my eyes, unimpressed by his inability to multitask. But I ignored it for now, and just appreciated that Asteria was being recognized. Even the Fae following Arien watched her carefully when they had the rare spare moment in the heat of battle. Everyone wanted to see their future queen.

She needed to be here for this. Arien was right about that. Just as the people of Night had needed the reassurance that she was there for them, Day needed to know who she was and what she stood for. They needed to trust her to lead them, and that was a big ask. Especially for someone who was essentially a stranger and an outsider by all measures except blood.

I danced around the battlefield, my blade swinging faster and faster as we chopped down the men before us. Asteria was now grinning widely, getting into it as her blade slashed through the air.

She may think me poetry in motion with a blade in hand, but she was quickly becoming a whole song unto herself. That light that existed in her, it shone so brightly whenever she let go like this. Every time she tried to stifle and suppress her feelings, it dimmed.

The only way to make it to the light was to get through the darkness. That was a truth everyone knew.

Asteria embraced darkness everywhere else but within herself.

But right now, she let it in.

Blood was splattered on her face and chest. Her hair was being tangled by the wind. And she grinned as she cut off a Fae soldier's head.

I'd never seen a sight so beautiful in my entire life.

Her eyes lit up with starlight, and it began to slowly surround her. I wanted her to embrace that fully, and let her light shine for miles.

I swung my blade into a soldier's neck, pulling it out to gut the next. The numbers were beginning to dwindle slightly on the opposing side, and the humans who'd apparently decided to help fight in Arien's army began to move forward to help clean up the stragglers.

"Asteria!" A voice called, and I turned in tandem with her. A copper-headed male with hair to his shoulders and emerald-green eyes stepped forward. Her eyes widened, and I growled as I realized who this must be.

"Soren." She gasped, and I immediately cut my way over to her. I watched him pull her into a quick hug, distracting her. I snarled, pushing him away and stabbing the Fae who was sneaking up on her.

Asteria panted with wide eyes, looking at me, before her eyes cut to Soren. She winced, grabbing my hand. "Sorry, I won't get distracted again."

"You better not." I insisted, smirking slightly as I pretended not to feel Soren's glare. *If looks could kill.* But given I felt similarly about him, he could fuck himself. "If I have to drag you back from Elysium, you'll never forgive me for stealing you from paradise."

I could feel the Fae trying to sneak up behind me and stabbed my sword backward, catching him right in the stomach. I pulled the blade out, and Asteria watched me with a heated look, biting her lip.

"If you're not there, then it's not paradise, my dorchadas." She winked, and I struggled not to grab her right then. But she kept her promise, paying attention as a mounted Fae in fancy bronze armor with a green surcoat galloped toward her.

"We will never bow to a feeble woman!" he screamed, a snarl on his face. I noticed Lord Aydun watching him proudly. I narrowed my eyes, marking the man for death right then. I'd make him feel all the pain of Tartarus before he enjoyed his permanent stay there.

"For King Aelius!" The man shouted again as he charged.

Soren went to grab Asteria and pull her behind him, holding his sword aloft. I rolled my eyes at him. Asteria brushed him off with a growl, making his head rear back in surprise. She bent her knees slightly, and as the rider approached, Asteria let her wings out and used her knees to get a boost up, giving her more air more quickly.

She flew above him, leaving the man gaping as he tried to readjust. But there was no time. The swing of her sword was a thing of beauty. The man's head flew off his neck while the horse kept running, albeit more slowly without anyone directing it, and the man's body slumped off to the other side.

Asteria landed on her feet, her wings rustling. *Nox, I loved that woman.*

Seeing that display from the future queen they dreaded seemed to inspire the enemy soldiers to regroup. Maybe she was more of a threat than they expected, maybe they just feared her regardless—I couldn't rightly say. But they managed to line up a charge, which would take down many of Arien's men if they succeeded.

"Calix! Asteria!" Titan called, and I looked to where he was running toward us. "Lord Freyr's men! They're coming from the other side. We're going to be stuck between them."

As he finished, a horn blew, announcing the approaching army. *Fuck.* The people of Day were obviously getting tired. We needed to swap out men quickly.

"Arien!" I called to my mate's brother. He whipped around to face me after cutting open the stomach of the man he'd been fighting. "Tell me you have reinforcements!"

Arien shrugged helplessly with a grimace. "If they show up in time!"

By the Otherworld. I guess it was up to us. Thank Nox we'd come.

"Asteria, stick with me," I instructed her, dipping my head and sending my near begging through the bond.

"Who are you to order her around?" Soren spat, stepping up to me like he was going to abandon the battle to take out his petty grievances.

I raised an eyebrow slowly, growling at him.

"Hey!" Asteria shouted, pulling Soren back. "He's not ordering me around, you ass. And we have a battle to fight if you didn't notice. Go fight that. I can speak for myself."

Soren looked injured at her words, and I couldn't blame him, honestly. Just because I wanted to disembowel him slowly and painfully with my claws didn't mean I didn't understand.

If I'd had Asteria and lost her, I'd lose my Tartarus damned mind.

Titan and Arien thankfully broke up the tension, ordering everyone into new lines. Asteria stayed with me, but Soren was sent to the other side. A smart move. I couldn't guarantee my patience for the human lusting over my mate would last amid bloodlust.

I grabbed Asteria's hand, kissing her knuckles. She smiled at me, nodding slightly. I nodded back before turning to face the coming charge.

As the horses began to gallop, I could hear the horn blowing from the other side. If we could break this charge, we could move over to help with Lord Freyr's men. We could *not* let this city fall to Aelius.

Asteria and I both let our wings free, flying up into the air as the riders galloped toward us. We were in the middle of the line, so most were able to see us. We flew right into the first two enemies we saw, knocking them down for someone else to finish. Then we continued on, knocking the men off their horses like dominos. Those who struggled, got a sword slashed across their throats.

The gush of blood spraying on my face only made me smile. The thrill of battle beat in my heart. It was even more incredible than normal. Amplified, thanks to Asteria feeling the same rush.

Their charge was destroyed, thanks to our work, so we left the other men to finish them. They cheered us on as we flew around to the other side of the palace where the next battle awaited.

Fuck. This was not good.

Arien's forces were severely outnumbered here. It put us at too much risk of losing this battle. That would leave Arien, and more importantly, Asteria, down hundreds of valuable fighting men for the war to come.

Arien had clearly already charred who he could with his flames, but the fighting was too messy to do much more in our dragon forms. I hated this setup. This would never happen in Night. Our cities were built to defend, while Avalon was built in this ridiculous circle, meaning everyone was in a weird position and spread out too thin to be in any way helpful.

All we could do was join the fight, so that's what we did. I let my shadows bleed out as a group of soldiers made the mistake of targeting me. The men, a group of maybe ten to twelve of them, began trying to surround me. They clearly had no idea what they were dealing with. I let a smirk creep up my lips as I sent my shadows out, circling around their necks as they tried to fruitlessly pull at the black, snaking shadows that formed their noose.

My shadows were mine to command, and my will made manifest. I used that will, yanking hard on the shadows and snapping their necks in a moment. Their lifeless bodies fell to the ground with a thump of satisfaction.

I spun my blade, moving into the crowded fighting quarter and shoving it into the back of a Fae attacking a smaller Day Kingdom soldier. As his friend rushed me, yelling his vengeance, my shadows surrounded him. I let them have some fun, choking the life from the soldier as he suffocated on my darkness.

All the while, my black blade kept moving. I stabbed and slashed, blocked, and parried. It had been too long since we'd gone into a battle like this. I needed the rush of fire in my veins it provided me. Maybe it was twisted, the need I felt for bloodshed, but I knew no better way to exercise my demons. It gave me a clarity of mind I could find nowhere else.

Well, maybe one other place.

I kept a close eye on her. Ensuring my mate was well the entire time. While she was a bit tired, understandably, she was still going strong. Thank Nox.

I spotted Lord Freyr across the field, and the thought came to me that his men might abandon him if he fell. It happened often enough. Take the leader down, and the rest will follow. If we could get Freyr, we might be able to get a surrender out of them.

I turned to Asteria and explained my plan, holding off the soldiers barreling down on us with a wall of shadow so we could talk. She agreed quickly, and I let the wall drop. Their surprise, as shadows, starlight, and steel were suddenly on them, was gratifying.

Asteria and I got into a rhythm as we fought our way through the mass of fighting soldiers. We fought back-to-back, and it felt like the bond between us was a living, breathing thing in that moment.

I knew every move she was about to make, and she could clearly sense mine. We moved so fluidly; it was almost eerie. I swung high; she ducked low. She twirled right; I shifted left. We were able to swing around each other's blades with ease, never once tripping up and getting in the way.

Usually, the rage and bloodlust kept me going during a fight. But right now… wonder and a sense of rightness, of balance, took me over. A feeling of peace so strong it rattled me to my bones.

I watched Asteria as she found the strength inside herself to continue despite her fatigue, pushing herself through it. And I wasn't the only one watching her in wonder. The Fae soldiers and humans around us were doing the same. Whenever they weren't actively engaged against an enemy, the ones near us cut their wide eyes over to her.

It was like watching a goddess touch down on Adamah.

We were halfway through the mass of people when it happened. A horn blew, and my head whipped around to find Lord Kem's forces approaching. The blue and white banners and surcoats made it clear whose army it was.

"*Fuck!*" I snarled, that familiar rage rising once more. If they engaged, we were done for without a huge show of magic, and I couldn't be everywhere at once. It was easy to form a wall, but it was more difficult and needed more concentration to attack while holding it. Already, our forces were being pushed back. I sent out an enormous wall of shadow, despite the risk of attack from the soldiers around us, and blocked Kem's men from approaching.

Asteria lifted her hand with a smirk, and a blast of starlight shot out. It seemed like the entire world paused as everyone stopped to watch. This power that shouldn't exist in our world, but somehow, now did. It arced straight over our soldiers and blasted into Lord Freyr and the men around him.

They flew back, and I watched in amazement as they flew *far*. The soldiers fighting us a moment ago stopped and dropped their swords as Asteria held up her glowing hand, starlight consuming it entirely, like I remembered from our shared dreams. They fell to their knees, bowing their heads in surrender.

I let the darkness drop from in front of Lord Kem's army, letting them see what had happened. Kem snarled and called for them to charge, but Asteria brought her arm down from above her head to aim straight at him.

Kem charged, and I brought my arm up to match Asteria's. I nodded at her with a smirk, and she matched the movement. Our magic erupted from our fingertips, and began to weave around the other's until a mass of starry darkness hovered before us. Together, we sent it forward, a swirling cyclone of starlight and darkness that barreled down on them.

It sent them flying backward, too, their entire force now in complete chaos. I laughed in delight, picking Asteria up and spinning her around. Her giggle was an amazing thing to hear, and I wanted nothing more than to bury myself in her right now. To feel all that tight heat surrounding me with the thrill of battle and blood still racing through my veins.

The look in her eye told me she wouldn't mind that one bit.

"They're retreating!" someone shouted. And sure enough, the armies were scrambling up and away. I knew there was no chance Cyrus wouldn't hear about Asteria's power now, but we'd managed to at least save Day from Aelius and his goons.

And as the men around us all hit their knees, calling out praise to Queen Asteria…

I'd say it was definitely worth it.

CHAPTER 39

Arien

I'D thought all was lost.

I'd fought until my arm could barely muster the strength to swing and still I pressed on. I'd used my sunlight to force people away, knock them off their horses, or burn them slightly. I'd scorched myself a path through their armies until I was too depleted to summon the sun.

And yet, still more men came. Their tactic of hitting us with three different armies in waves was honestly impressive, and the General in me appreciated that, if nothing else.

But I also hated every single one of those fuckers. They chose the wrong side, and as the cowards sworn to my father ran for the hills, I still couldn't believe we'd done it.

That *she'd* done it.

I'd never seen anything like Asteria's power before. The starlight was beautiful, of course, but the power behind it was surprising.

She had to have as much power as Calix did, rivaling him for the coveted spot of the most powerful Fae in Celesterra. Or maybe they were perfectly equal, as mates should be.

They'd joined together, sending that blast of starlight and shadow at the enemy forces. The impact sent the entire regiment scrambling and retreating.

I lifted my sword in the air. "Queen Asteria!"

"Queen Asteria!" The others around me echoed as Asteria and Calix stood in the middle of the kneeling crowd. And then the strangest thing happened.

Calix *kneeled* before her.

I'd never imagined a Fae man would ever bow to his woman, let alone a king in his own right. By all rights, he had no need to do so. I smiled slowly, happy to see it as Calix took her hand and brought his forehead to it. Like she was blessing him.

Like she was a goddess, come to Adamah.

Asteria stood there, in her silver, black, and purple armor, strong and proud, having just fought off three armies as her powerful mate, the King of Night Kingdom, kneeled before her, along with the entirety of Day Kingdom.

Maybe she was.

"HUMANS, HUH, BROTHER?" Asteria's teasing words to me were the first thing out of her mouth as I approached. I huffed a laugh at her, bringing her in for a quick hug.

"I did what you asked and told them your plans," I explained, and she perked up immediately despite how tired she clearly was. It wasn't only *my* first battle, and Asteria didn't have years of training behind her like I did. I was impressed that she was able to hold out for so long.

"After what our father did, ripping so many humans away from their homes and families, trying to send them to their deaths… well, suffice to say, they were more than willing to help if it meant a new queen who plans to free them," I admitted.

She'd been right about that. I'd doubted her plan, sure that the humans wouldn't want to help, and even if they did, I didn't imagine them being much help to us. But they'd proven me wrong on both counts. They rose up to fight with determination and anger that I wasn't as shocked to see as I would have been before.

Before I watched Asteria nearly break as she described her past as a slave.

"That's amazing!" Asteria squealed, looking at Calix excitedly. He gave her an indulgent smile that almost made me feel like I was intruding.

"I think we should crown you officially, Asteria," I told her, and saw her freeze completely.

"What?" she croaked out, gripping Calix's hand like a lifeline.

"They need to know that Aelius isn't coming back. To feel secure in that fact. And I mean the Fae and humans both. They need to see you crowned themselves, to see the woman who just fought so hard for them installed as their queen." I explained to her as gently as I could.

I didn't want to push her. I never wanted to do that. But I also knew that we were on a knife edge here. It didn't matter that they'd fought in this battle; any Fae or human could turn on us in an instant if they thought they'd chosen the losing side.

We almost lost the battle today. It was only thanks to Asteria and Calix that we hadn't. They knew that just as well as I did.

"It's no different than Night," Calix murmured to her, rubbing her back. She nodded slowly, breathing deeply.

I spotted Soren heading our way and nearly groaned. I couldn't help my lip curling up in distaste, however. Despite his efforts in saving me, his obsession with my sister was not something I'd ever approve of.

"Okay, let's do it." Asteria nodded once, decisively.

"What are we doing?" Soren asked, swaggering up to us like he didn't steal that move from the Fae.

"Crowning my *mate* as queen," Calix rumbled warningly. Asteria bit her lip, trying to stop her smile. I could tell that's exactly what she was doing, enjoying the possessiveness of her mate. I just had no idea *how* I knew that.

"Can I talk to you, Asteria?" Soren's emerald eyes gleamed hopefully at her. "Just for a minute; I know you're busy." He smiled softly, and *oh*, he was a manipulative little shit, wasn't he?

Did he think he could just smile at her and charm her away from her *soulmate*? The absolute delusion of this boy.

Asteria glanced at Calix, but his face was stony. She nodded, flashing a quick smile. "Sure, what's up?"

She began walking a little distance away. Enough that Soren would feel comfortable, but not so far that Fae ears couldn't hear. Smart girl. Calix's little smile nearly made me laugh.

As if *Soren* was any kind of competition.

"Asteria." Soren smiled, seeming somewhat dazed now that he was actually faced with her. The friend he'd grown up with who was now a Fae queen. His eyes took in her pointed ears and sky-blue eyes that shimmered with starlight with the kind of reverence I was sure my sister would have spat upon as a human.

"Soren," she repeated impatiently, raising an eyebrow in question.

"You—uh—" Soren stuttered slightly, running a hand through his hair. "I just can't believe it. All this time, and you'd been Fae."

"I know." She sighed, a complicated sound. "But I'm thankful for what it's brought me at least." She shot a smile at Calix that made Soren's lip curl.

"Him?" he spat, shaking his head. "Asteria, you're queen of Day. He's king of Night. You know it can't last. And now that we're not separated by kingdoms, we could actually be together!"

Asteria's head reared back in shock. "Excuse me?"

"Asteria, you know we had something special." Soren went to grab her hands, but she batted him away.

"We had convenience, Soren," she said firmly. "You were my friend, and sometimes more, but that's it. I'm with Calix. He's my soulmate, Soren." Soren shook his head desperately, and Asteria looked sadly back at him.

"It was more than that. I know it was. I love you, Asteria!" he pleaded, his eyes feverishly bright. "You've always hated fate. You can't tell me you're with this Fae just because it told you to be. Unless it's because he's a king who can give you the kind of lifestyle I can't. But with you as queen, you can—"

A sharp slap rang out in the field, and everyone paused to look uncomfortably away as Soren held his hand to his cheek, lifting back up from the crouch the force of my twin's slap had sent him down to.

Fuck was I proud of her for that.

"How dare you," she seethed, starlight rising around her as her control on it slipped. "I turned down Cyrus when he offered me every luxury in Adamah I couldn't access as a human. My dignity meant more to me than pointless luxury. If you knew me at all, you would know *that.*"

She stomped away from him, coming straight toward us. Eryx whistled as she approached, "Remind me not to get on your bad side."

Asteria snickered but looked at him, appraising him for a moment. "Can you do me a favor, actually? If you want to stay on my good side, and all."

Eryx chuckled, shaking his head at her. "Of course. What do you need?"

As she explained it, I nodded in agreement. It was a good idea and would definitely make a statement to the joint people of Day and Night.

"I'll get everyone moving to the border. We can meet you there?" Eryx asked, and Asteria nodded in confirmation.

"It's probably better to join the armies now anyway. With Calix and I leaving for the Otherworld, it'll be safer for everyone," she said grimly.

With that, the plan was in place. The armies would be marshaled, and then… a long-awaited crowning.

WE SENT WORD to our allied lords to move their armies toward Night. Setting up camp under the mountains would give us plenty of cover, and it was easy enough to maneuver east or west around them if needed.

But the most important part was that Asteria would finally be crowned before both kingdoms, lending her the legitimacy she needed. The Fae armies had seen her fight, and knew she had the strength to lead. The humans were behind her, knowing that she was fighting to free them. I suppose we did need to start considering them in these matters if that was the case.

Once they were free, the humans would be citizens in our kingdom like any other.

And their numbers were significant. They may not have the powers or strength a Fae possessed, but I'd seen the humans do plenty of damage on the battlefield to the unsuspecting enemy Fae soldiers.

Their rage over their enslavement was a power all its own.

It had to have been simmering under the surface for some time, and now, Asteria had lit the match and sparked the flame within them.

Eryx had gone to bring her a dress she thought would be apt for the coronation. She couldn't wear her armor for such a momentous occasion, after all. The purple dress he'd brought her had long bell sleeves that turned to shimmering silver, with gold adornments down the front and trimming the sleeves and skirts.

She apparently wore it briefly when she was up North, but she'd had an addition added to it, and I watched as two small dragon wings were affixed to her shoulders. They were silver and purple, much like her own wings, but she lined them in gold. The dress incorporated her own colors and Day's, making it a perfect fit for the occasion.

Mother was trying to hold back tears as she watched, incredibly emotional over seeing Asteria the way she had always imagined.

"You look beautiful, my darling." Mother said quietly, sniffing slightly.

"Thank you," Asteria paused, looking mother over as she bit her lip. "*Mother*," she added, looking uncertain.

A strangled sound came from our mother then, and she flung herself at Asteria, hugging her tightly. Asteria hugged her back with wide eyes, looking at me for help. I chuckled, shaking my head at her.

"Are we doing this or what?" Titan asked as he popped his head in. He paused as he took Asteria in, and she shifted on her feet uncertainly, smiling slightly at him.

"What do you think?" she asked, fluffing her skirts slightly.

He walked over, smiling down at her, "You look like the queen Day and Night deserve. Like an Earendel ruler *should* be."

I was left a bit confused by his emphasis, but it obviously meant something to Asteria, who flung her arms around him, whispering her thanks in his ear.

When she unraveled herself from him, she smiled over at me. "Ready, General?"

"Ready, my Queen," I told her sincerely, a broad smile on my face as Mother clapped her hands together delightedly.

"It's finally happening!" She gushed as we made our way out. "After all this time."

"It is." I shared her enthusiasm, taking her hand and squeezing it.

As we reached the throne room within Day's fortress on the Etheralta Mountain, I made my way up to the dais, standing by the side of the throne. Both Day and Night's fortresses were used for mining, but also for emergency evacuations from the cities. They were meant to hold thousands of people easily, and it provided ample space to fit the combined armies of Day and Night now.

Princes Altan and Zakat were also present, as was Calix's chain of command. His lords and ladies had all joined us for this, too, and it was amazing to see how supportive they all were. I'd met with each of our lords individually to explain to them Asteria's plan for the future.

Or lack of one.

She still didn't have a plan for how to rule two kingdoms, but I didn't doubt she'd find a way once she told me of Calix's prophecy.

The power of two will be her crown.

This was always to be her fate. And that alone reassured our lords that there wouldn't be an issue.

Calix himself was standing in as her guard for the occasion. I'd been shocked that he'd been willing to do such a thing, but Asteria had explained her introduction to Night. While she hadn't been officially crowned yet, and couldn't be until they married, he'd had her sit on his throne as he stood by her side.

Most Fae kings would never allow such a thing.

It made it hard to dislike him for defiling my sister. I was forced to admit that I found myself respecting the man. From the way he treated her, I could tell he loved and respected her. And what else could I want for my sister?

Although, they really *should* wed. I may have to remind him of that fact. It would help uncomplicate this a bit.

As the herald announced Asteria, I stood up straighter, my hand resting on my sword's pommel as I stood on the opposite side of the throne from Calix. We were two bookends, ensuring Asteria would be protected.

She made her way down the aisle to the dais, and everyone bowed their heads as she passed them. She truly looked like a queen. Her dress was appropriately dramatic, especially with the dragon wings. And as she stepped up onto the dais, she came to stand before Mother.

The current queen facing the new.

"Princess Asteria Faelynn Earendel," Mother began, her voice carried by the magic in place. "Do you come here today with a clear heart and mind, to promise yourself in service of the gods?"

"I do." Asteria nodded regally.

"Then kneel." Mother smiled slightly, a bright flush of excitement over her cheeks.

Asteria kneeled, adjusting her skirts, and as she did so, they created a circle around her.

"We come here today, to transition the power of Day Kingdom's crown from the traitor King Aelius, to the next in line for the throne, the heir chosen by the gods themselves." Mother intoned, raising her hands into the air.

"We call upon Hyperion, god of the sun, who holds dominion over Day Kingdom. If you bless this ruler to take the crown, shine your light down upon her."

This was the part that had most of us nervous. The goddess Asteria had somehow chosen her instead of Hyperion. But Mother was sure that since the glow of the heir had appeared around her, all would be well.

As glowing beams of sunlight appeared from above, shining through the domed crystal window on the ceiling above, they fell directly on Asteria, bathing her alone in the light of the sun…

Mother was proven correct.

She opened her mouth to continue, a smile firmly in place from the moment the sunbeams appeared, when starlight suddenly shot through the window, shimmering and shining, hovering around the beams of sunlight and joining it in caressing Asteria's skin.

The crowd murmured in wonder, having never seen such a thing. I tried to control my facial expression since everyone could see me, but shock reverberated through me.

"We give thanks to the gods for showing their approval, and blessing the chosen heir," Mother continued once she gained her bearings over the surprise. "The time has come for the princess to become a queen."

She looked down at Asteria instead of the crowd. "Princess Asteria, do you promise to love, protect, and serve the citizens of Day Kingdom as your own?"

"I do." Asteria nodded her head once.

"Do you promise to honor the gods who have given you this blessing?"

"I do."

"Do you promise to uphold and respect the tradition and laws of the land?"

There was a small pause, and I swore I could *feel* Asteria's smile as she responded.

"I promise to uphold and respect the traditions and laws that deserve it, and to improve and adjust the ones that don't."

A cheer went up from the back, the humans present showing their appreciation for her answer. She was better at this than I'd expected, but I also knew it was entirely genuine and not any kind of political ploy. Calix's proud smile was prominent as he watched her, and I saw similar ones on the faces of all his people.

Mother even looked proud, and I knew she struggled with Asteria's attitude toward this. She clearly enjoyed the reaction. However, her political mind saw the benefits of having these additional bodies at her disposal. I saw several more fights coming to pass about this in the future.

"Then, as the current queen of Day Kingdom, let it be known that I renounce King Aelius on behalf of Day Kingdom and its citizens." Mother swallowed hard, and I could tell that despite the years of planning, this was difficult for her.

Father may have never been much of one to me, but he *was* her mate. I knew there was no way it didn't hurt her deeply. But Mother had always been willing to do whatever it took to protect her children.

She nodded to me, and at that signal, I turned and picked up the crown from the podium. It was one we had commissioned for Asteria, knowing the masculine crowns from previous rulers wouldn't work for her. Instead, the craftsmen made a more feminine version that still fit the aesthetic of the traditional crowns.

It was, of course, gold, with a large golden sun in the dead center. Inside the center of the sun, a round purple jewel shone brilliantly. Clouds crafted of star opal, chosen for both the white hue and it being a major export of Day, sat on each side of the crown. Curved golden rods held up golden stars with star opals in their centers. I didn't mention it to Mother, but I ensured the curves resembled the shape of a crescent moon. Rows of shining light blue gems were used to line the bottom and represent blue skies, and small purple jewels and golden stars hung down from the bottom and were meant to lay across her forehead.

I handed it to Mother, who held it above Asteria's head as she tried not to cry.

"I crown you today with the blessings of all of the gods, including your ancestor, Earendel himself, one of the kings of the gods, and Hyperion, god of the sun who rules the day," Mother paused for a moment before a small smile snuck out. "As well as Asteria, goddess of the stars, and your namesake, to be the first ruling queen of Celesterra." She placed the crown gently on her head, and Asteria stood gracefully from her knees, turning to face the crowd.

"I now pronounce you, Asteria Faelynn Earendel, Queen of Day Kingdom!" Mother called, and the crowd cheered wildly.

"Queen Asteria!"

"The first Queen!"

"Queen of Day!"

"The Star Queen!"

On and on it went, and the brilliant smile on my twin sister's face was a thing to behold, with tears lining her eyes and starlight rising around her and giving her a sparkling aura.

I couldn't imagine what it must feel like to go from a slave to a queen in a matter of months. I was so proud of her it almost hurt. It would be an honor to serve as her General, in a way it had never been serving under my father.

She was a queen *worth* serving.

Part Three

CHAPTER 40

Asteria

I'd never felt quite so out of my depth.

It sort of felt like I was playing pretend, dressing up in the outfit of royalty and acting out the part.

But this was *real*.

And I wasn't sure if I was actually up to this task. Calix and Arien, and truthfully everyone else, too, assured me that I was, but I was left adrift as people asked me questions that I had no answers to.

"How do you intend to rule Day Kingdom while ruling Night as well?" Lord Dritan asked me with a raised brow, his face communicating his doubt quite clearly. His red hair fell around his face in long waves, and his dark orange eyes set into a deeply tanned face were quite intense.

"We're working on a more detailed plan moving forward for ruling both kingdoms," I told him, giving as polite a smile as I could manage.

If anything, though, his brow arched higher. "Code for: you have no idea."

I fought a cringe. It really was. I had no clue what I was doing or how I was going to do it.

I knew I didn't want to lose Calix. I knew I had to rule Day.

Those two things had to find a way to exist simultaneously.

But deep inside, I feared there wouldn't be a way. That the gods only brought us together for their own purposes, and once we'd accomplished them, we'd be forced apart. Looking at my mother only increased that paranoia.

She was given a mate, and for what? To have me? To bring about these prophecies? Given the promise of an immortal lifetime of love and happiness only to have it yanked cruelly away?

Would that be Calix and me?

I knew how I felt about him, but I couldn't say the words. Saying the words gave them power. I always knew love had the power to break people, but I never truly understood it until now.

Calix and I hadn't had much time to discuss our relationship since we'd gotten together. We'd slept together, and we'd made our feelings clear. I'd even moved into his rooms—despite spending only one perfect night there thus far.

A selfish part of me was grateful for that fact.

I didn't know how to face what was to come. I didn't know how to explain how lost I remained.

But facing Lord Dritan now, I couldn't show that kind of weakness. So, I lied.

"I have no doubt that Calix and I will develop a plan that makes everyone happy." And I hoped he couldn't see the truth all over my face.

I was still determined not to lose him. I just needed to figure out *how*.

The rest of the night was just as strange. Walking around and greeting nobles, meeting soldiers, all of it as the queen… I felt like a fraud.

Even if the gods had shown their approval quite explicitly.

"Queen Asteria." I turned and found a human man standing before me. He bowed his head in greeting, long pale hair tumbling forward. "I'm Einer. I was one of the humans who fought in the battle against Aelius's forces."

"It's wonderful to meet you, Einer," I told him honestly once he'd raised his grey eyes to meet mine. "I thank you for fighting. It's incredible to see other humans finally rising up against slavery."

"Knowing there's a chance for freedom…" He shook his head in amazement. "There was no way we couldn't fight. We've accepted our lot for much too long."

"Agreed," I said fiercely, and Einar smiled widely.

"And knowing the future Fae queen had, until recently, been *human*." He chuckled. "That's something you don't see every day. The more we heard, the more we realized that now was the time. Between you and what King Calix has accomplished, the humans of Celesterra finally have a chance." Tears filled his eyes, and I grabbed his hands, squeezing.

"We do," I said, before realizing what had come out of my mouth. "I—I mean—"

Einar laughed, throwing his head back slightly. "The fact you still think of yourself as a human says it all, I think."

"I suppose it does," I agreed ruefully, shaking my head at myself.

"Is it true what they say? About what's happening in Dusk?" His voice quieted, but I heard the rage that underlined every word. The fury that the humans of Celesterra were finally finding within themselves after too long suppressing it.

"It is. We're working now to dismantle his operations, and free as many as we can." I explained mournfully. "We hope to incite further rebellion among those not in the camps."

"Good. I realized when Aelius rounded up so many humans that something was very wrong, but I never could have imagined such a thing." Einar shivered as he thought of it, and I wished it was impossible to imagine myself.

But I knew how far Cyrus would go to get what he wanted.

Einar met my eyes, taking his clenched fist and putting it over his heart before bowing his head once more. "You have my blade, for whatever it is worth against a Fae's. I will fight for you, Queen Asteria, with the same fervor you carry for us."

I fought off the rising tears his words conjured. I nodded deeply. "Thank you, Einar. I will always value it as equally as any Fae's, if not more so. Fae have every advantage. The fact that you will fight despite that, shows your worth is much greater."

The smile on his face was one I would never forget. No matter how many centuries I lived.

Knowing that I could inspire humans to rise up and fight was everything I had ever wished for when I was growing up in Sonmathion. It was the first time tonight that I didn't feel like a little girl playing dress-up.

I felt like a *Queen*.

One actually worthy of the crown I wore.

I would never misuse the power granted to me as my birth father has. I would fight for those who need it most. I would fight to bring balance back to Celesterra.

And I would fight to ensure my own freedom. From the trauma of slavery and Cyrus combined. Fight to free myself from the mindset that kept me trapped, convinced this was all temporary.

If I had to journey to the ends of the world and the Otherworld besides to be truly free, I would throw myself into Tartarus now and start walking.

Which was exactly what I was going to do.

THE BLUE SKIES around me were a welcome sight. My smile lit up my face as the burning ball of fire unraveled itself from its curled-up position and let loose a trill in greeting.

"Zhu!" I greeted him excitedly in return as he flew around me. I brushed a hand down his scales, letting the fire lick my palm and reveling in the pleasant warmth left behind.

"No wonder you've never burned me." I laughed, shaking my head. "Did you know all this time that I was a dragon too?"

His head bobbed in confirmation, and I looked at him sternly for a moment. "You couldn't have clued me in?"

He shook his head, and I could swear he was smirking at me. I sighed, giving up. I was sure there was a reason for it. Actually…

"Are you real?" I whispered, scared of the answer. "I've seen you and Luna all my life. I thought you both just dreams, but now…"

He flew around me until his body snaked in a circle, putting his face right in front of mine. Eyes of fire looked right into mine, the intense stare feeling much too real to be anything but.

"You are, aren't you?" I asked in wonder, my hand reaching out to touch his face.

But before I could, I was ripped out of the dream. I let out a grunt of aggravation, but thankfully, Calix wrote it off as my usual morning grumpiness. I wanted answers. I needed to know why I always dreamed of the sun and moon dragons.

And we were going to just the place to find out.

We made our way back to Tairngire quickly after dragging ourselves out of bed. There was little time to waste, after all. I'd given my mother the power of regent in my absence, and I hoped she proved herself worthy of it.

I hated thinking that. Of my mother especially.

But I knew she struggled with the humans and the concept of ending slavery. I just hoped Arien would be able to help push her in the right direction.

She certainly had *my* directions, and instructions to follow them perfectly. I didn't like walking away immediately after being crowned, but this mission was too important to delay.

My powers were under control now. Or as much as I could expect at this point, anyway. I wasn't blasting starlight any more randomly than Calix did his darkness, so I considered that a win.

Hopefully, we wouldn't be gone long, and Arien had actually surprised me by being very supportive of my plans when we discussed them. Apparently, Soren had saved his life during the battle. Between that and then seeing what the other humans brought to the fight, he'd been reevaluating his thoughts on them.

Ugh, Soren.

I had no idea what to do about him. I'd spent the night smoothly avoiding him, and keeping Calix next to me as much as possible. Which was mostly for my own benefit and not so much about Soren, but still.

The man was like a dog with a bone.

We'd never been so intense about one another, and I had no idea what had changed. Unless I just hadn't seen the signs before? He did admit he loved me when we parted on Placement Day, but I'd thought that an emotionally charged moment getting the best of him, if I was truly honest with myself.

I didn't consider myself very lovable, especially not then. I couldn't comprehend it.

But it seemed he'd actually meant it.

And now I didn't know what to do. I didn't feel the same, obviously, but I'd tried letting him down as gently as I could.

And then, not so gently as I'd slapped him to the ground for his shitty accusations.

But I didn't *want* to hurt him. I just wanted him to get a clue.

I was obviously with Calix, and that hopefully wouldn't change. I feared outside forces meddling, but I had no doubt about our commitment to one another.

Having my mind in such turmoil probably wasn't an auspicious start to this journey, but it was what it was.

Calix and I both wore our armor, knowing we would likely face challenges along the way. As we lay in bed last night after the coronation, I'd asked Calix about what we might face on our way to the city of the gods.

"Much and not at all is known of the Otherworld, my réalta," he'd said in response, and rumbled a laugh against my neck when I complained of his non-answer. "I speak truly. Myths and legends abound, but little fact is known at all. Only those of us who rule with the kings of the gods' blood in our veins even know of the portals. Which you'll likely need to somehow torture out of Aelius before his death. But the fact remains, we are in the dark. Thankfully, we have a light to guide us."

He looked at my little trails of starlight that followed my fingers as I traced them down the scales tattooed on his chest, before lifting my fingers to his lips to kiss them. "I suppose we will see which myths and legends prove true on our travels."

Not knowing what we'd face in the Otherworld left me feeling incredibly nervous. We met with everyone before we left, hugging those we loved as if it might be the last time. I refused to let it, but it would be incredibly silly to ignore the fact that the possibility existed. Calix had begun to tell me a few of the myths about the Otherworld last night when we'd gotten… *distracted*, to say the least.

But I found I couldn't regret spending that time together. We had so *little* of it right now.

Hand in hand, Calix led me through the palace. We moved down past the level containing the Hedone Room, which I had thought was the deepest level. But as it turns out, several more levels existed beneath it. Storage for artifacts and riches existed that I never could have imagined.

"You just… keep all of this? *Here?*" I asked incredulously as he led me through a giant, cavernous room carved into the star opal that was filled with treasures of all kinds. Jewels and gold, ancient scrolls and antique furniture, priceless art, and carefully preserved dresses and suits from kings and queens long past. All just… *everywhere.*

"Where else should we keep it?" Calix asked, raising a brow with a slight chuckle.

"Somewhere safer?" I suggested, throwing the hand not tangled with his in the air, indicating all the stuff around us. "All of it is just sitting out!"

Calix's adoring smile made me glare back at him. I was serious, dammit!

"No one can access any level past the Hedone room without the blood of Erebus or guided by one with it. The spells in place won't allow it. They would crash into the walls, never gaining entrance. *If* they even figured out this was here to begin with. They cannot even see the door that leads down here."

Oh. Well then.

It reminded me of the fortress as we passed through these levels of the palace. Like that building had been carved from the star opal Etheralta Mountain, these levels had no coverings on the walls, floors, or ceilings, like the upper levels did in certain places. While the palace let the star opal shine through in many important rooms, it was equally covered up elsewhere. I imagined it got tiring to look at the same thing day in and day out.

But down here, it was incredibly obvious that the palace had been crafted out of a gigantic chunk of star opal that must have already been here. There was no way it was brought in. It was so *deep* underground. I couldn't imagine how it got here. And I hadn't heard of any other ginormous pieces of star opal, big enough to craft a *palace* out of, outside of the mountains themselves.

The amount of star opal the palace was made from may be huge, but it was too small for mining like they did the Etheralta Mountains. Truly, a palace was probably one of the better ideas for what one could have done with a hunk of star opal lodged deep into the ground.

Walking down to the next level, I felt a chill come upon me. Calix gripped my hand tighter, and I let myself feel comforted by the strength in his grip. He wouldn't let me go.

The stairs led us down into pitch blackness. My fingers were likely leaving bloody marks in Calix's skin. Even with my Fae eyesight, I couldn't see a damn thing in the darkness before us. Only turning my head back toward the stairs allowed me to see any light, but it only offset the deep darkness all the more.

I turned to Calix, and he merely lifted one foot into the black nothingness before us. A sudden whoosh made me jump, and I clutched Calix's arm before mentally berating myself for acting like a scared maiden from one of the books I'd read.

Flames shot high to the ceiling, but where they came from, I had no idea. They brightened the space enough to see it was a cavern. A big empty space, smack dab between us and the other side of the path. There was no bridge, and I could barely see the other side; it was so far.

"What the fuck?" I mumbled to myself.

"My father showed me the portals when I was young." Calix began, his wide shoulders heaving with a deep sigh as he stared across the flame-filled pit before us. "He explained that the gods put the portal behind certain protections. This one ensures only those who can fly can cross."

Understanding filled me, and I watched as Calix's wings shot out from his back. The black and purple scales shimmered in the light of the fire. I let my own wings unfurl, the flash of silver in the dark space contrasting sharply.

"Don't let go of me." Calix cautioned, the hand not entwined with mine cupping my cheek. "We have to follow a very specific path, or the flames will shoot out at us."

I raised a brow, about to ask what the worry was, when he continued.

"These aren't regular flames, my réalta. These are the fires of Tartarus itself." A bit of fear entered Calix's eyes that was so incongruent with everything I knew of him. He *never* got scared. "They will burn us the same as if we weren't dragons." My eyes widened as I realized just how dangerous this actually was.

I suddenly felt human all over again.

Staring out at the roaring flames that could shoot out and kill me, I gulped. I shook myself, squaring my shoulders. I hadn't come this far to be taken out by rogue flames.

"I won't let go," I promised him, but had to tease him too. "After all, my dorchadas, you're here to lead me through the darkness."

Calix smiled slowly, but I couldn't enjoy the beautiful sight for long, as his lips took mine with a passion that spoke of the fear he felt. His tongue forced its way into my mouth, and I gladly surrendered to it. When he finally pulled back to allow us to breathe, his forehead fell against mine, his silvery-white hair creating a curtain around us.

"No matter what happens, you have to get yourself home." His voice sounded wrecked, and my worry instantly rose. I could feel him struggling in the bond, but he was doing his best to hide it.

"If you have to leave me—"

His words summoned the fear I'd felt since I realized Calix was my mate. That this wouldn't last. That it was all temporary.

"Not a fucking chance," I whispered harshly. He pulled back to look at me, purple orbs clashing against blue as we started one another down.

"Celesterra needs you, Asteria. I can't be selfish in this. If you need to leave me behind to get back, then you must do so," Calix said, and his profound agony at the very idea of us being separated speared through *my* chest.

"It needs both of us, Calix," I insisted urgently. "Forget what Sunrise or Day believe. Remember your own prophecy. Tartarus, remember mine! We have to do this *together*, or not at all. I'll get nowhere without you. So you are not allowed to sacrifice yourself or fall behind. We are both going in there, and we are both coming out. There is no reality where we don't. Do you understand me?"

His eyes searched mine, and I let him see and feel whatever he needed to in order to convince him of this. I let my fear and determination and incandescent rage at the very thought of him not coming back out into the open for him to see. As much as I had tried to push down all my chaotic feelings lately, I refused to keep *this* from him.

"Understood, my Queen," Calix said sincerely, part reverent adoration and part relief. His lips took mine once more, and I let my hands snake into his hair and grip his shoulder as I held him to me for all I had.

I would take whatever moments we were granted.

But eventually, the roaring flames and dark cavern could no longer be ignored, and we pulled back. A last lingering kiss was shared before we both flew into the air, hands clasped.

Calix flew beside me, going slowly as we navigated around the reaching flames. I'd never seen fire behave in such a way. The flames had a mind of their own, constantly searching and reaching to grab onto someone. The path we took ensured they just missed us, but I flinched whenever it got too close.

"How in Tartarus did they build all this down here?" I whispered to myself, but Calix snorted.

"Tartarus indeed." He chuckled, and I nearly slapped myself as I realized what I'd said. But the brief moment of levity was over too soon as we approached the end. I let out a sigh of relief as we touched down on the other side, but Calix remained stiff and alert.

"This next one is more dangerous." He cautioned as we walked through the hall down to the next level. "I need you to stay behind me, okay?"

I opened my mouth to argue, but he rushed to continue.

"Please, my réalta," he begged. "I know you want to fight by my side. It's one of the things I love so much about you. But this requires a shadow wielder."

My breath caught, as it always did when he said those words to me. But I focused on what he was telling me. If only a shadow wielder could handle this, I would be useless here. A liability. And Calix could get hurt trying to protect me.

I nodded, promising to stay behind him.

As we entered the next cavern, it was just as pitch black as the last was at first. Only this time, no flames appeared. I held onto Calix's sword belt as he inched forward.

A growl to the left had my head swinging in that direction, but I couldn't see a damn thing. The darkness was so all-encompassing, so oppressive, that I couldn't even make out Calix's hand in mine.

Slowly, light began to filter in, and as it did, I could see Calix was using his power to clear a path down the middle. Physically pushing the darkness to the side.

A snarl came from the right, and I felt the movement of the wind as something pounced when a blast of shadow sent it falling back into the darkness.

I looked around as best I could, alert as I followed right on Calix's heels, my fingers digging into the leather of his sword belt.

More beasts growled around us, and the tapping of stalking claws moving toward us echoed around the space. My heart rate picked up, and I tried my best to breathe evenly and not distract Calix.

He sent skeins of shadow at each beast, knocking them back with a strangled cry from each one. While the darkness may keep them at bay, it didn't do much to stop them from trying again.

Which was surely the point. They were meant to keep this place protected. But...

The creatures seemed to avoid the light. Calix pushed back the darkness to let light in from holes in the cavern directly above us. Meaning we likely weren't directly under the palace itself anymore. But the beasts avoided the light, trying to swipe out at us from the darkness.

An idea came to me, and I bit my lip.

"Calix?" I ventured, working to keep my voice even as the hair on the back of my neck stood on end. Something was behind me.

"Prepare to blast them all back at once," I told him urgently.

"Wha—"

Before he even finished the word, I summoned my starlight around me and then pushed it out, lighting up the area around us and leaving only the edges of the room still in shadow.

The beasts howled, and I nearly joined them as I got my first look at them. They had *no eyes,* merely a mouth with razor-sharp fangs and two slits for a nose that must allow them to sniff out their prey. Shaped like a cross between a wolf and a panther, their fur was mangy and patchy. They were skinny enough to see their ribs but didn't appear unhealthy either. It was the most disturbing combination.

Calix didn't waste a second, and before a single howl finished, his shadows erupted and threw all of the beasts back against the walls. They landed with a thud and a whimper that almost made me pity the disgusting creatures.

He whipped around, grabbing my face, "You *reckless*—" His lips crashed down to mine in a furious kiss before pulling quickly away, leaving me whimpering. "*Genius.*" He kissed me again, and I tried to keep him there, but he leaned his forehead against mine.

"How did you know that would work?" he asked, brushing my hair back as he straightened up.

I forced myself to shrug casually, trying to relax from the rush of the moment. "They avoided the light."

Calix scoffed a laugh, shaking his head. "*Avoided the light*, she says. You have no idea how badly that could have gone. My father was extremely clear about only darkness being used to get through this level."

"Well, yes," I admitted, biting my lip slightly. Calix's eyes narrowed in on the motion, and I could sense his desire as much as I could see it in his eyes, which were beginning to fill with color. "But there's never been someone who had the power of starlight before either. It's not as harsh as sunlight, so I knew it wouldn't hurt them like that had the potential to do. It would just light the space enough to disorient them and keep them at bay."

The pride he sent filled me and left me feeling like I was flying, even this deep underground.

"Well, only one place left to go," Calix said heavily, lacing our fingers once more.

He brought me through the doorway and down another winding staircase, which led out to one more cavernous room.

Only, this one was a bit different.

At the other side of the room, stood a swirling, massive portal, leading to Tartarus itself.

Gods help us.

CHAPTER 41

Cyrus

"UNTIL further notice, you're to be confined to your rooms, without visitors," I told Daneiris, meeting her blue eyes as they widened in shock.

"Cyrus, you can't—" She stood up, arguing with me immediately.

"I am the KING!" I bellowed at her, making her flinch backward in fear.

"Cyrus, she hasn't done anything—" Zerlina argued, air whipping around her as her emotions overcame her.

I laughed dryly, shaking my head slowly as I turned to her. "Not even married yet, and already you choose others over me. Perhaps you are not the queen Celesterra deserves after all."

Zerlina reared back as if I'd slapped her but, thankfully, fell quiet, making me smirk in triumph. How quickly she abandoned helping her new friend to save her crown.

The other ladies in the room looked around uncomfortably, not knowing what to do. I rolled my eyes at the feeble creatures.

"Get out," I commanded them. They stood quickly, dropping into curtsies before practically running out the door.

"You two are to have no contact from this point on," I told them, looking between Daneiris and Zerlina. They both gritted their teeth but nodded.

"I'll assign someone to assist you if you need anything, but I don't want to see you out of this room until I say so," I told Daneiris. She opened her mouth, proving she wasn't very smart.

"What about Casimir?" she asked, her red brows furrowing.

"Who?" I shook my head in confusion.

"*My human!*" she snapped back, but took a deep breath and reined herself in. "My human. You've seen him for years at every damn meal we've had, Cyrus."

"He obviously cannot be trusted if you can't. Perhaps I should send him to the camps instead. A fitting punishment if you so clearly care for him." I smirked victoriously as her eyes widened, and she shook her head frantically.

"No, please, Cyrus!" she begged, quite sincerely, to my disgust. "I will do whatever you want; please don't send him *there*."

I thought about it for a moment. While I wanted to punish Daneiris and was truly disturbed by her attachment to this human, having thought she felt similarly, at least regarding humans, I realized I could likely use him better here anyway.

"Fine." I sighed heavily. "I will grant you this boon."

"Thank you, brother," she replied, bowing her head as she let out a long, relieved breath. "Thank you."

"Don't thank me yet," I smirked, gleefully. "He will remain here, and his treatment will be based on your behavior. Should you be good, he will be fine. Should you not be…"

I trailed off, raising my eyebrows at her. She ground her teeth, staring at me with impotent fury in her eyes. But she nodded once in agreement.

"Good. Now, come along, Zerlina." I grabbed her by the elbow, pulling her out of my sister's rooms. I eyed the guards by the doors, deciding to have them disposed of. They clearly couldn't be trusted either. I would have to clean house completely at some point. Just as soon as everything was ready.

"My King!" One of my men came skidding around the corner.

"Yes?" I asked impatiently, annoyed by the interruption.

"Prince Vesper of Sunset Kingdom just arrived. He's here to see you." The man explained.

Surprise filled me. Sunset and Sunrise had both been quiet, seemingly trying to keep out of the conflict brewing between the rest of the kingdoms despite my repeated requests to talk.

"Where is he?" I demanded, anxious to discover why he'd come.

"He's been seen to the parlor," he explained, and I thanked him graciously before turning to Zerlina.

"You're going to join me for this, and you're going to be your best, charming self," I instructed her harshly, before leaning in to whisper in her ear, "Prove to me you still want that crown."

"Of course, my beloved." Zerlina smiled winningly, her mask back on. I could appreciate that, for I had often been forced to wear my own. But the time for that was over. Now was the time to see my vision come to life.

Zerlina was, unfortunately, proving to be more of a problem than I'd anticipated. I needed her father's support, however. Dawn was our closest ally, and one I would need in the battles to come. Tariq could be done away with afterward, but not a moment before.

We made our way down to the parlor and, upon entering, found Prince Vesper waiting as promised. Not the king or even the heir, despite being the elder prince.

How embarrassing for him.

"Prince Vesper," I greeted with a charming smile; Zerlina also appeared welcoming with a softened demeanor from beside me, her arm snaked around mine. "Welcome to Dusk Kingdom."

"Thank you, King Cyrus." He bowed his head but didn't smile. "I am hoping you and I can help one another."

"Oh?" I raised a brow as I helped Zerlina to her seat. I took mine across from the prince, ignoring the tea service as I crossed one leg casually over the other. I trained my eyes directly on him, hoping to gauge his reaction. "How so?"

"My father has thrown his support behind Asteria, the Star Queen," he explained, making my jaw clench and lip curl as I tried to keep from throwing something. Possibly him.

"But my father also continues to support my brother as his heir. He's unfit, to say the least, and will be the downfall of Sunset. My father chose him, because the gods said so. My father chose Asteria, because the gods said so. But—" Vesper cut himself off, clenching his teeth as his face twitched, trying to contain his anger.

And then I realized *exactly* why he'd come.

"Ah." A smile grew on my face. "I see. You know I'm going to fight Night's forces and put Asteria back where she belongs, on her knees before me. If your father fights against me, Sunset will need a new ruler when the dust settles."

"Yes," he agreed through his clenched teeth. He sighed raggedly, body slumping in his chair. "And… you are going against the gods already. They have been proven wrong by choosing my brother. The gods…"

He trailed off, unwilling to finish the thought. But I certainly wasn't, and had no problem pushing him further down the path he'd already begun to walk.

"*Are wrong*. They have lost their way and must be challenged." I smiled widely. "It's nice to see like-minded individuals do exist outside Dusk."

"The gods are lost, and the land suffers. Only a strong leader can bring us through this now." Vesper snarled. "A little girl won't be the answer."

I threw my head back with a laugh, "Especially not *that* little girl."

"Wretched thing," Zerlina muttered, stirring her tea.

I reached over and patted her thigh, "There, there, darling. We'll ensure Asteria learns her place well enough. Prince Vesper here can surely help us with that. Tell me, Prince, what plans have you learned of? What kind of numbers can you bring when your father has turned his elsewhere?"

Vesper straightened, his shoulders back as he met my eyes. "I have brought those loyal to me. Those who know the firstborn, respectable son willing to do his duty, is the correct choice of heir. And while I don't know specifics, I can tell you that Asteria is working with those in Day loyal to her, while Calix brings Night, of course. They had Prince Altan of Sunrise with them as well, so it seems likely they have support from Gravadain."

"Hmm." I hummed, thinking over that information. "I appreciate you bringing that information to me. We'll get you settled and meet again to go over more specifics of your role here soon."

Vesper stood, bowing. "Thank you, King Cyrus."

"No, thank you, Prince Vesper, for your support." I nodded before grabbing Zerlina and leaving the room, thinking through plan after plan. I couldn't let both Sunrise and Sunset follow Asteria and Calix. We would be buried under those numbers.

An idea hit me. A way to hit Asteria and Gravadain at once. Excitement thrummed through me, a type of exuberance I rarely felt these days. Only when I topped up on blood magic did I feel this good.

I dropped Zerlina off in a haze and found myself tracking down my commander to begin planning the execution of my brilliant idea. I stopped myself midway, realizing that in my excitement, I had forgotten the most important part.

The *where.*

I turned around to go find Emmie. She would know exactly where I needed to go.

PLANS HAD TO be put in place. But most importantly, I needed King Tariq to get up off his ass and get over here to help me.

Aelius was, unsurprisingly, on board with the plan and anxious to strike out at his wayward daughter. But I needed a truly impressive show of force. One with all my allies clearly involved.

I wanted Asteria to know she wasn't safe. That I had numbers on top of blood magic to take her down with.

I wanted Calix to see my military might and fear his would be inadequate. The way I was forced to feel during his attacks. I wanted him to feel Asteria slowly slipping out of his fingers until he lost her forever.

And King Tariq needed to get himself here for that. I sent a message through my spies, with a strict deadline for his arrival. I needed this to go smoothly, and I couldn't afford for him to fuck this up. His daughter was enough of a problem.

Speaking of problems...

A loud boom in the distance made me close my eyes and clench my teeth. *Fucking rebels.*

They'd been stirring up trouble since I let knowledge of the camps become public, but it was during this past week that they had begun getting worse. Now, they weren't just trying to get their people out of the camps; they were trying to destroy everything I'd built as they expressed their fury at what was happening.

I made my way through the palace to see where the smoke was coming from. My eyes widened.

"*Fuck!*" I let my wings unfurl and shot up into the sky. Pink feathers ruffled in the wind as I flew straight toward the plume of smoke. My own fury was pumping through me, and mine was much greater than whatever these pathetic humans could muster. I would need to make an example of them and stop this foolishness in its tracks.

As I neared, I could see those who'd managed to leave the building in time gathered around outside. I landed with a thud, and everyone cringed away slightly at whatever expression was currently on my face. I could well imagine, with the anger rushing through me.

They burned my fucking brothel to the ground.

The fire was burning itself out now, leaving behind the charred ruins of what was once my most profitable establishment—and my *favorite*.

"My life's work." I turned to the woman who'd come up beside me, finding Saskia, the manager and previous owner of the brothel that just went up in smoke. She looked forlornly at the husk of the business she'd built from the ground up.

"Several of my girls perished in the fire," she added, a grimace on her face as a few tears tracked down the dark streaks on her cheeks from the smoke.

"We'll make them pay," I promised her. "And then we'll rebuild."

Saskia snorted, "That doesn't put money on the table *now*."

A muscle in my jaw jumped, I'd clenched it so hard. I had no patience for her bullshit right now.

"You have plenty. Get the girls together and find someplace to run the business in the meantime. I'll handle the rest." I demanded before taking off into the air once more.

These rebels were targeting *me*, which meant they weren't nearly as afraid of me as they should be. I would have to do something about that.

I flew straight to the heart of the human settlements within Evenfall. The apartment buildings were crumbling a bit, but still perfectly serviceable for the amount of time a human needed to occupy them. They didn't live long, after all, mayflies that they were.

They were lucky they got buildings to live in at all. We could have kept them chained up in cells when not working. Our ancestors stopped that kind of thing long ago, but we should never have eradicated the practice.

They'd become too comfortable. Too expectant. They needed to remember they were slaves, not employees.

One of the buildings containing the human apartments was more dilapidated than the others, which made it perfect for my plan. I pulled a vial from my pocket, uncorked it, and downed the shimmering blood quickly.

I shuddered, letting the blood magic settle into my veins. Feeling my lightning crackle within me as it stirred. A chaotic surge in my blood as it fired to life.

I held up my hands, calling my lightning, feeding it my rage, and letting it flow forward. The sharp bolts of lightning struck the building in succession.

The fire caught quickly, but I let several more bolts hit, making it spread even faster. The screams inside and the pounding of running feet were like music to my ears. I smiled slowly, enjoying the show as the rats ran out of their cage.

Only to be confronted by the cat who'd been playing with them.

I sent bolts of lightning into the chests of the first several humans who ran outside. I let the others who arrived after them stop in horror as they came upon their king carrying out their punishment.

More humans who lived nearby congregated as they heard the ruckus, saw the fire, or smelt the smoke. I let more arrive before I said a single word. Leaving them all watching me with fear in their eyes.

"If any more attacks occur, if one more act of rebellion takes place, more humans *will* die," I announced, before taking off into the air without giving them time to react.

RETURNING TO THE palace, my mood was still dark, and finding Zerlina lounging around my rooms didn't help matters.

"What are you doing in here?" I demanded as I unbuckled my sword belt, dropping it on the table.

"Waiting for you, of course," she simpered at me, and I fought to not roll my eyes. Did she really think me so dim I couldn't see what she was doing?

Then again, did I care?

I could certainly use the distraction right now.

I'd been more stressed than usual lately. All my plans finally coming to fruition was exhilarating, but it was also a lot of hard work. The battle plans to take down Calix alone, while dealing with these insipid lords and rebellious humans… it was all a lot. And it was all on *my* shoulders.

No one around me could be trusted, leaving me isolated. It was why I needed Asteria. Only she could understand. Or I thought she could. The way she left me…

No. She *would* understand. I would make her.

Zerlina smiled at me as she sauntered over. She tried to look innocent, but something about her too-sharp eyes and cheekbones made it look more comical. Now, her sister, Sybella, could pull off innocent. With her more cherubic cheeks and wide eyes, she was the sweet and innocent-looking version of her sister.

But I found I preferred the sharpness of Zerlina. It matched what I knew was inside her. She was no soft princess, and I found myself enjoying her claws.

As long as she knew her place, that was.

I did need a proper queen, after all. Asteria *could* have been that, had she not run from me. But she chose her fate, and I would ensure the punishment fit the crime.

Zerlina leaned up to kiss me, and I bit her plush lips as I grabbed her by the hair. My tongue dominated hers, and she gave herself over to me willingly. I pulled back from her lips, using her hair to force her back.

"On your knees," I growled, and that was all she needed as she hit the floor, her hands eagerly undoing my pants and taking out my cock.

She pumped her hands down my shaft, my length thickening in her hands even before she trailed her tongue down it, following the veins. My head fell back when she took the crown into her mouth, sucking and licking around it.

I buried my hand in her hair, pushing her down until she choked on my cock. Her eyes watered as her hands came up to grip my thighs, digging her nails in. I pulled her head back, letting her get a breath in, before pushing her back down until she swallowed my entire length.

She breathed harshly through her nose, running her tongue along my base where my cock sat heavy in her mouth. I groaned, using my hand to guide her head up and down, enjoying the feeling of a hot mouth and wet tongue swirling around my cock.

I could feel my release building, and began to thrust myself into her mouth, fucking her face harder than necessary. Her groans each time I thrust too hard only added to the experience, however. As I spilled down her throat, I held her down, not letting her up until she'd swallowed every drop.

She panted once she popped off my cock, and I took the time to remove her dress, leaving her glorious breasts bare to my eyes. I maneuvered her with me, sitting on the sofa and gripping her by the ass to lead her to straddle me. She slowly sank down on my cock, groaning as I stretched her cunt out around my girth.

I closed my eyes as she began to ride me, letting myself imagine Asteria above me, eagerly riding my cock. I thrust up into her, the sound of skin slapping against skin a beautiful rhythm. My hands found her breasts, squeezing, but her moans shook me out of my fantasy.

The dark hair was replaced by a lighter brown streaked with blonde, and the shade of blue in her eyes was all wrong. Zerlina's breasts may be as good as

Asteria's, but otherwise, she wasn't nearly curvy enough. She may be beautiful, but she wasn't Asteria, and that only served to make me angrier.

I grasped her hips hard, lifting her as I stood and brought her to the nearest wall. I pushed her against it, holding her hips down so they lay flat against it, and began pounding into her. My cock hitting deep inside and making her scream with each thrust.

I kept my eyes trained on where I was splitting her open, not wanting to look at her face. But she grabbed me by the hair and forced me to meet her eyes.

"You don't get to pretend," she hissed, before her lips crashed down on mine.

I swear I hated how smart she was sometimes.

She bucked her hips up, but I forcibly pushed them back down, biting her lip and drawing blood in the process. She cursed at me, but I just licked the blood away before biting her neck in turn. She should know hissing at me like a cat only served to make me punish her for her misbehavior.

She hated marks on her skin, so I continued sucking them into her neck and down her collarbone. She squeezed down hard around my cock, making me swear. She chuckled hoarsely, and I thrust in faster, feeling my release creeping up on me.

She began fluttering around my cock, making me groan as I spilled myself inside her. She followed right after me, and I leaned my forearms against the wall to hold myself and her up.

It may not be what it could be, had she been Asteria. But I couldn't complain. And soon, I'd have them both. Neither one allowed to leave my side or my bed.

And as soon as her father arrived with his forces, I'd be set to make my move.

CHAPTER 42

MY hand tightened around Calix's as I stared down the portal at the other end of the room.

He squeezed it back, gently pulling me down the bridge before us. On either side of it, the night waters of the Otherworld floated far below, twinkling in the light of the portal. The bridge was crafted entirely of star opal and arched high over the water, leading directly to the portal.

I looked down at the drop, reminding myself I could fly and had no reason to be concerned now. Calix chuckled, "It will probably take a while before human fears like heights leave you completely."

"So unfair," I grumbled.

He smirked at me, but my attention was taken by the immense portal before us. It was tall and circular, stretching to the cavern's ceiling, and was surrounded by a ring of star opal that shimmered and shined brightly. Stalagmites of star opal surrounded the portal where it loomed at the end of the bridge, while stalactites extended from the ceiling in jagged points.

But inside the star opal, the portal itself swirled in a black mass. It looked like liquid smoke and swirling tar in turn. The thought of stepping into it… I swallowed hard.

"We're supposed to go through *that*?" I asked shakily, hating the tremor in my voice.

"Hey." Calix turned to me, lifting my chin up to meet his eyes. "You are Asteria Earendel. Queen of Day. Future queen of Night. The former human

349

who is going to destroy the pompous prince of Dusk. You managed to bring the great King Calix to his knees, my réalta. You can do absolutely *anything.*"

I smiled widely, leaning up to kiss him. I mumbled against his lips, "So humble you are, my dorchadas."

He rumbled a laugh, "I have no need to be humble."

I shook my head at him with a fond smile. It was true, of course. I wouldn't be humble if I were him, either.

"You are a force of nature. A flaming comet that crashed into my life and turned it upside down," Calix said, the colors of the Aurora creeping into his eyes. "You will walk into Tartarus and make it bow to *you.* Not the other way around. Understand?"

"And will it bow to *you?*" I raised a brow at him, but my shoulders leveled, and I straightened my spine. He was right. I could do this. I wouldn't let even Tartarus itself scare me.

I'd tried so hard to keep control of my emotions since I was young, letting rage win out to hide the fear that plagued me deep inside. But something told me that walking into the personification of everyone's worst nightmares would bring that fear to the fore in a way Cyrus only wished he could.

I was stronger than that, *right?*

But fuck… Tartarus itself!

This was *insane.*

"Of course it will. I'm with *you* after all," he teased, pulling me toward the portal.

I took a deep breath. Calix looked to me, waiting for me to be ready. I gave him a nod, and together… we both stepped forward, our boots going through the swirling black mist.

Our bodies fell through the mist, and I closed my eyes until a haunting roar reached my ears. I opened my eyes, finding Calix beside me, still gripping me tightly as he looked around with eyes as wide as my own.

We stood on a black stone path, with jagged boulders lining it on either side, leading to a fork in the road just ahead of us. The sky was a dark grey color, rumbling with flashes of lightning. In the distance, a volcano burst with lava and plumes of smoke. Screams and whimpers of pain reached my ears from a distance, along with a maniacal kind of laughter that disturbed me greatly.

We looked at one another and, by mutual agreement, turned to walk in the opposite direction from where that laugh had come from. Since it came from the left, we immediately took the path leading right instead.

We crept along it, trying to stay as quiet as possible. But a sudden growl made me jump, and I looked up to find a deranged version of a mountain cat facing us. Its bright yellow eyes were locked on us as it licked its sharp teeth. Calix growled back at it, and it stood up, its burgundy fur bristling.

Calix let go of my hand, grabbing a knife from his belt and throwing it at the creature as it pounced. It fell before us and dissolved into a black puddle. Calix grabbed his knife from the mess, wiping it on his leather pants before putting it back on his belt.

He had just opened his mouth to say something when the puddle began to move. I watched with wide eyes as it began to reform and grabbed Calix's hand. I pulled him with me as I ran. Wanting to get as far away from that thing as we could before it reformed.

"What in the Otherworld was that?" I hissed as I looked around wildly.

"I have no idea." He shook his head, his silvery-white hair brushing against his armor. His forehead was creased in concern. Neither of us knew what to expect here, not when the myths about Tartarus were so varied.

We continued on, our hands never straying far from the swords on our belts. The rocky path twisted and turned through a desolate landscape. There was nothing but grey rock as far as the eye could see. But we journeyed on, until we finally came to a dead end. A gigantic rock wall stood before us, what had to be thousands of feet up in the air. I couldn't even see the top of it with my Fae eyesight as it disappeared into the smoke-colored clouds.

The sound of pained moans reached my pointed ears, and I tilted my head back to try to catch where the faint sound was coming from. As I looked back up the wall, I gasped, my hand flying up to cover my mouth.

What I had thought were crevices within the rock were actually *people*. They were chained to the wall, row after row, all the way up, with their feet dangling.

"Calix…" I didn't even know how to finish the thought.

"It's Tartarus," he replied grimly, his eyes flashing as he looked at me. I didn't miss how his hand tightened on the hilt of his sword, the tension in his body clear. "All these people, Fae or human, all those who died within our world, they all end up here or in Elysium. We're bound to find others elsewhere, too."

"*Great*," I said sarcastically. He huffed a breath that he might have intended to be a laugh, but it never quite made it there. I eyed him speculatively, noting how uncomfortable he really was. "What's wrong?"

He sighed heavily, eyeing the people hanging above us with sorrowful eyes and stiff shoulders.

"This is what my power does. It pulls the pain of those tortured here and injects it into my enemies," he replied despondently.

"Calix," I called his name patiently, grabbing his face and cupping his cheeks. "We've been over this." He shook his head in protest, and a flash of rage went through those purple eyes; only I knew it was directed inward in this case.

"You've never actually seen those tortured here before. This is tame for Tartarus, Asteria." He scoffed. "I know. I've felt the echoes of it when sending my power into people. I don't feel the pain myself, but I can tell what it is."

Nox, he knew what kind of torture went on here?

"And I torture them with that pain anyway," he smirked, a mockery of his usual one, more sarcastic than amused. "And now you'll get to see exactly how fucking deranged I am for doing so."

I stared at him for a solid beat, and he stared back at me, just waiting for the rejection to come.

"Fuck you," I replied blandly.

"What?" he asked, confused. His brows furrowed as he looked at me. I stepped away from him, shaking my head.

"I said. *Fuck. You.*" I stressed as I jabbed a finger into his chest. "If you think so little of me that you believe this is what will send me running—"

"Well, something is!" he shouted, throwing his hands up in the air.

"Excuse me?" My head reared back, taken completely by surprise by his outburst.

He ground his teeth, shaking his head. "You think I can't see the way you've been pulling away from me? You can't say how you feel about me, which is fine. I understand if you're not ready. But combined with how I *feel* you trying to pull away in the bond…"

"How am I pulling away? The bond is always open!" I argued, putting my hands on my hips as we stared each other down.

"It's open, yes. But you're not *really* there. You're shutting down. Like you don't want to feel it. It's only when we have sex that I can feel how you feel about me, and I *can* feel it, which leaves me confused about why you're pulling away from me!" Calix explained, and my heart sank at the look on his face as he swallowed hard.

"If you don't want to be with me—" He forced out, the pain on his face too much for me to take.

"I do!" I shouted, making him blink rapidly. But I could feel panic rising at the thought of how incredibly messed up this situation had become. "It's not you, Calix."

He rolled his eyes, and I winced at my own lame-sounding excuse.

"I swear. This has nothing to do—" I tried to say, but cut myself off and ran a hand down my face.

How did I explain how twisted up I was about something *taking* him from me? That I was burying all my emotions to exert some control over them. I'd tried to shut down my hopeless fear. Desperately attempting to prevent my feelings from brewing chaotically within me when I needed to be balanced more than ever… and in the process, I'd been inadvertently shutting out Calix and confusing the Tartarus out of him.

Maybe Tartarus was exactly the place to explain it, then?

I opened my mouth to do just that when a loud roar had us both looking at one another in shock. He grabbed my hand as his wings shot out, and I took his cue, my own unfurling behind me even as I internally cursed the timing of whatever horror had found us.

We flew up the giant wall, getting away before whatever that creature was reached us. It took longer than I expected to reach the top, but when we did, we flew even faster down the other side. We both silently agreed to keep our wings out as we continued, just in case.

I wanted to finish our discussion, especially with that mulish look still on his face and his pain echoing through the bond. But this place was making me distinctly uncomfortable. It was so dark that I was only able to see a tiny bit ahead of me, thanks to my Fae eyesight. The rocky ground was surrounded by three sides of what looked like a jagged mountain range, but I couldn't see across the expanse in front of us to see if the way ahead was open or enclosed.

We walked a bit further, and I tugged Calix's hand to get him to stop as I spied a doorway carved into the rock on our right. He nodded silently, and we made our way over to it. We made it about halfway there before the ground began to rumble under our feet.

"What now?" I groaned in complaint, my head falling back for a moment as I grappled with the knowledge that Tartarus apparently had it out for us.

Haunting wails echoed around us, and Calix's head whipped over to where they seemed to be coming from. He inched closer, and I followed him, only for him to stop short, putting out an arm to prevent me from going any further.

I looked at him in confusion, and he nodded downward. I flinched as I turned my eyes in that direction, realizing there was a giant pit before us. The haunting sounds were echoing from deep inside it. *Deep, deep inside.* I couldn't see a single thing down there, so it had to be coming from miles down. I couldn't see where the pit ended when looking across either, meaning the doorway was the only way around it, outside of flying.

"The abyss," Calix whispered in realization, looking around us worriedly. "We need to get out of here."

"Wait, the *abyss?*" I whisper-shrieked, yanking on his sleeve. "You mean like—"

"The abyss is where the worst of the worst go. Souls so evil they're tossed in here to experience the worst torture imaginable. This is where I pull power from when I want to get truly creative," he explained, his brows pulling downwards.

"So, not good news for us then?" I joked, but it failed to lighten him up at all.

"Come on," he said urgently, grabbing my hand. But the next thing I knew, I felt his fingers being yanked out of mine as something that must have been the size of an elephant hit me *hard*, and I soared through the air from the impact, straight into the rock wall.

It certainly felt like being trampled by an elephant, I thought deliriously as I groaned in pain.

"Asteria!" Calix roared, and what I could make out of his face through the blur of my eyesight was some mixture of horrified and panicked. However, another roar echoed his before he could take a step toward me.

Then another.

And another.

I looked up, trying to shake away the dizziness from the hit I'd taken. Attempting to see what in the Otherworld hit me.

Oh. Fuck.

The thing was huge, and seriously gross. It had grayish-black wings and legs, with a red-lined tail that was similar to a dragon', but the rest of it… the wings ended in three long and sharp claws it used for hands, and it managed to stand on just its two legs when not flying. Its head wasn't even *a* head, but instead, hundreds of black and dark green snakes making up a large mass on the top of its body. I had no idea how it didn't fall over; it was so top-heavy. The snakeheads slithered and snapped, while its claws attempted to gouge out Calix's stomach.

He had his sword out, slashing at the creature while he tried to send his shadows at it. It managed to bat away the shadows like they were nothing. Still, watching Calix work was incredible. The way he moved in battle truly was beautiful. He moved smoothly around the thing as its claws aimed for him, dodging snakeheads as he spun his blade in quick moves to slash at them.

I shook my head, forcing away the remaining dizziness as I dragged myself up to join the fight. I wrapped my hand around the dragon hilt of my sword and drew my blade, the silver metal shining in the darkness. I snuck behind the creature, meeting Calix's eyes with a nod. He distracted the heads as I lifted my blade and drove it into the spot between its shoulder blades.

Its many heads all wailed loudly in response, making me wince at the ringing in my ears. Its arms batted behind its body to try to reach me, but I held on to my sword, moving with it and preventing its claws from touching me. I barely got the blade out in time, but I managed to duck and roll beneath its claws as I pulled it free. Calix roared as he slammed his sword into its neck, making the heads recommence their racket, but it still wasn't stopping or slowing down, even with boiling black blood beginning to seep from the wound. I began to hack at its tail while Calix attempted to get a hit into its softer stomach.

I tried using my starlight to distract or blind it temporarily, but it paid my power no mind at all. Ignoring the shimmer like it didn't even see it. Our powers didn't seem to work on this creature in any way, so I had to assume it was somehow immune thanks to some weird Tartarus-related reason.

Between the two of us, we managed to hack and slash until it *finally* began to weaken slightly. Calix managed to get under the heads while I distracted it, and with a loud growl, he drove his blade in just under its neck, dragging his sword down until he'd slashed the thing open completely down the middle.

In the aftermath, we both stood there, panting. My hands were on my knees as I tried in vain to catch my breath. But roars from more of those creatures echoed even closer now, and they sounded *pissed*. They were coming, and we were in no way prepared to face one more, let alone the number it sounded like was headed this way.

Calix grabbed me by the waist, pulling me into him as his lips slammed down into mine. I eagerly met his tongue even though I knew we needed to prepare. The post-battle high still thrummed through me, and I could feel it echoing in him.

I tried to show him with my kiss the depth of my feelings for him. My heart ached in my chest at just the thought that he didn't realize it now beat for him alone. My hand curled behind his neck, holding him to me like I could keep him there forever should I just grip him hard enough.

But the roar of angry monsters forced us to pull back from one another.

"You are so fucking sexy when fighting legendary creatures of myth." He smirked at me, a fang exposed as his lip lifted. "My father used to tell me scary stories about the Ladon who guarded the abyss, and you just went charging in to stab away at the damn thing."

"What else was I supposed to do? I'm not letting those things put a damn finger on my mate," I told him fiercely, making his smirk soften, becoming a surprised smile.

"I promise I'll explain everything." I caressed his face, following the line of that sharp cheekbone, before running my fingers across his soft lips. "But right now, it's time to get as far away from those things as possible."

"Okay," he agreed, pushing my hair, which was admittedly all over the place from the fight, back behind my ear. "As long as it's not me, or us. I could take a lot of things, my réalta, but losing you would destroy me in a way nothing else could. My kingdom and the realm besides could burn to ash, every damn thing in my life lost, and I could find a way to recover. But losing you? There is *no* recovery from that. I would rather burn down my own kingdom than face a day without you, and if that's what it took to keep you, I'd torch it all tomorrow."

I felt breathless in the wake of his words, knowing how much his people and kingdom meant to him. I couldn't help pulling him back down for another kiss, my lips caressing his with all the passion and feeling pent up inside me. The next roar sounded ever closer, and I forced myself to pull back, looking into those lilac eyes I loved so much.

"You'll never have to, because you're stuck with me, okay?" I replied, a soft smile on my face. "I would burn *all* the realms myself to keep *you*."

CHAPTER 43

Calix

Her words were reassuring, but I couldn't help the worry I still felt. She'd been slowly closing herself off, her emotions dulled or shut away entirely. It started slowly at first, and I couldn't think of anything that had happened to make her pull away. I could only assume it was me, as the bond between us became fuzzier and fuzzier until I could barely feel her.

She was so insistent that it wasn't the case, and I *wanted* to believe her. The thought of losing her, after only just finding her… I couldn't bear the thought of it. Four hundred years of hoping to one day be blessed with a mate, followed by twenty-one years of feeling her but being unable to reach her…

No, the thought was inconceivable.

And there was no time for it right now anyway. The Ladon were getting closer, and we needed to get the Tartarus out of range of the abyss before it was too late. One of those things was hard enough to put down.

We made for the doorway off to the side, and we ran through it, only to stop short on the other side. Right in front of us stood a glowing portal. A shimmering light encased it, and the portal itself was a swirling, milky white inside. So different from the portal we entered to get to Tartarus.

"What do we do?" Asteria asked, distressed. Her worried eyes were looking all over the place, like an answer might come to her if she looked hard enough.

"We have to trust the gods will lead us. This must be where we need to go," I told her assuredly. I trusted they wouldn't steer us wrong in this.

We couldn't stay in Tartarus. We'd have to eventually cross into the city of the gods. Maybe this was the way?

"Come on, my réalta," I urged, with a smile, hoping my own confidence would bleed through to her.

She nodded, taking a deep breath. I was in awe of how she managed to adjust to her new life. So much had changed for her so quickly, and she just kept rolling with it.

Though, obviously, something *was* bothering her. I just needed to get to the bottom of the issue. After this, I swore I would.

But for now, my priority was getting her far away from the Ladon. I nearly shivered, something I'd not done before an enemy since my very first battle as a green boy. Those fucking things were hard to kill, and stronger than anything I'd fought thus far. Anything that could brush off my shadows and take a blade to the back without blinking was something I didn't want to tangle with more than necessary.

So, with Asteria's hand firmly in mine, we threw ourselves into the portal before us.

I was blinded by white for a moment as we moved from one realm to the next within the milky smoke of the portal. When we fell through to the other side, I blinked slowly, taking in the realm in front of us.

It was as different to Tartarus as could be. The skies were blue instead of the constant bland grey. The ground was bursting with green, lush grass and wildflowers as far as I could see.

"Is this—" Asteria cut herself off, shaking her head as her wide eyes scanned the horizon.

"Elysium?" An eerily familiar voice answered, and my eyes widened in disbelief as I quickly spun to face them, unable to trust my memory of it after so many years. "Yes, it is."

"*Mother?*" I somehow managed to say, barely even cognizant enough to notice Asteria's gasp.

My vision felt like it was narrowing, while my body felt unmoored from the ground. Fresh grief ripped into me anew, paired with wonder and relief that nearly overwhelmed me. It took everything I had not to fall to my knees. Asteria grabbed onto my arm, her presence helping to center me back into reality. I grabbed onto her hand, her own strength helping to bolster me as I felt myself falter.

"Calix, my darling boy." My mother smiled, her eyes misty as she looked me over. "Look at you! So grown." She shook her head wistfully, a tear falling down her cheek.

"Is it really you?" I whispered, unable to believe this was happening.

My mother's smile softened, and it hit me like a punch to the gut. She'd given me that smile so often as I was growing up. When she died, I lost that reassuring smile forever. Seeing her now, with her silver-tinted blonde hair and warm pink eyes, I felt such a morose nostalgia for a time long gone.

"It's really me, love." She stepped toward me, and Asteria made to step back, but I grabbed her hand to stop her from going more than that single step, needing her near.

But my mother's arms came around me, and I was forced to let go to hold onto my mother. I tried to fight the tears, but I buried my head into her shoulder as they slipped out anyway, my shoulders heaving as my mother patted my back. I held onto her desperately, like I was a child once more.

"There, there, love," she hummed. "I know. It's been so hard for you. I'm so sorry I had to leave you. Especially with your foolish father following right after me," she scoffed, and I heard Asteria try to stifle her surprised laughter. I couldn't do the same and let myself chuckle as I pulled back to look at her.

Mother raised a hand to my cheek, patting it softly. "Thank you, son. You did such a wonderful job with your sisters. It warms my heart to know I raised a man who could step up and not just rule a kingdom, but handle two young girls! It's quite the feat—I remember from being a young girl myself."

She winked jokingly at Asteria, who smiled back in amusement.

"And you!" Mother's arms raised as she looked over my mate, and I found myself strangely nervous. I had never imagined them actually meeting. My mother had died so many years before my soulmark came in that it had never been a possibility to consider.

"You must be Asteria, my boy's mate," Mother said as she engulfed Asteria in a hug.

"Oh!" Asteria yelped, looking like a scared cat as my mother embraced her, and I couldn't help snickering at her expense. She glared at me over my mother's shoulder, but I was too consumed by the image before me.

My mate and my mother, in the same place. *Hugging, even.* It was so surreal that I didn't know what to do with myself.

"It is so wonderful to meet you!" my mother exclaimed as she pulled back, grabbing my hand and Asteria's so she had a hold of both of us. "I had thought it would be many years until we could, but this is such a treat!"

"It's great to meet you too," Asteria replied, wide-eyed and bamboozled.

I'd forgotten how lively my mother truly was. That light she brought to all of our lives was extinguished so suddenly, it had left us all in the dark. No wonder my father had chased after her into death. No wonder my birth prophecy spoke of Asteria bringing light back to my kingdom.

"You two have come quite a long way." Mother smiled at us both. "And you still have a ways to go yet."

"Oh, don't go being cryptic on the children now, Jemisha," another voice teased.

I gasped, swinging my head toward the male cresting over the grassy hill we stood upon.

"Father," I murmured.

Mother scoffed, shaking her head, "Don't you go giving the game away, Orion. You know *they* will be unhappy."

Father rolled his eyes before they landed on me. A peaceful smile lit his face. The sight was so strange. In the months after my mother's death, grief had engulfed him like a shroud. I'd forgotten what happiness and peace looked like on him.

"Calix," Father said, his eyes holding a suspiciously damp sheen to them. "Son." His voice roughened, and the strands of green, blue, and pink in those lilac eyes we shared spoke of the emotion that had returned to him. His eyes had been nothing but pure purple after my mother's death.

Seeing the colors now…

"Father," I rasped, as he pulled me into a tight hug. I gripped his shoulders, hugging the ghost of the father I'd once known.

"Aren't they adorable?" Mother attempted to whisper to Asteria, who giggled in response.

"Absolutely," she agreed, and as I pulled back, I was struck stupid for a moment at the brilliant smile on her face.

I felt foolish then for doubting the depth of her feelings. Of course, there was a reason why she was cutting the bond off. Of course, it wasn't *us*.

The fact that I was hugging my dead parents, and her smile was the thing that left me stunned, wasn't lost on me.

"I need to apologize, son," Father said, and I forced myself to look away from my mate to face him. "I left you to handle everything. Putting the pressure of the kingdom and your sisters on your shoulders. It was my job to raise you all, and I failed you in that."

He sniffed back tears. I'd been sure this day couldn't get more surreal, and yet, it kept managing to.

"Father, no—" I protested, shaking my head.

He put his hands on my shoulders. "I did. But I think you understand now. The loss of one's mate is a horrendous experience. It kills a part of you that you can never get back, leaving you a hollow shell of the person you once were."

Just the thought of it sent a bolt of pain to my heart. One I felt echoed through the bond.

My eyes connected with Asteria's, and I relished in the starlight filling her eyes, her rage and despair at just the thought of losing me. It reassured me and instilled me with a confidence I desperately needed while faced with the man I'd modeled my life upon.

Despite those last months, when a stranger had seemingly replaced him, my father had always been my idol.

"I understand," I told him with a clap on the shoulder. "I wouldn't survive it either."

My mother's *aww* in the background as she slipped an arm around Asteria's shoulder caused my father to send her a fond look. One I recognized as the stupid look frequently on my own damn face when looking at Asteria.

"You have made us so proud, son," my father continued. "You've ruled well, and have managed to make the kingdom even stronger and fiercer than it was before. Your ancestors have done nothing but crow about what you've accomplished. You've done the house of Erebus proud."

His praise filled me with warmth. The acknowledgment that I'd managed to live up to his legacy was more than enough, but to know my ancestors were pleased?

I'd worried for many years about what they might think of the changes.

"They don't mind that he freed the slaves?" Asteria asked, head cocked to the side.

My father smiled at her, sending a quick wink back at me. "Isn't she a beauty? You two will make us some adorable grandchildren."

Asteria's cheeks reddened at his words, and I reveled in getting to experience the rare treat of witnessing her blush. I couldn't help smiling at her, sending her a wink of my own, which only increased the red hue.

"But to answer your question, the gods have made clear the plan," Father told her, and my brows furrowed.

"What does that mean?" I asked, and the smirk on my father's face made me sigh.

"Oh, now who's being cryptic?" my mother murmured rebelliously.

Father tilted his head back with a laugh before grabbing my mother by the waist and pulling her into a kiss. I averted my eyes, meeting Asteria's amused ones.

"I see where you get it now," she whispered, causing my parents to pull back with flushed faces.

I was struck by the idea that they were truly happy. *At peace.* Elysium was everything they said it was. A paradise, where our loved ones who are granted entrance can live together forever.

"Forgive us." Mother blushed. "We're here to guide you two. We desperately wanted to meet the woman who's had my son all tied up in knots." She sent a smirk my way that made me roll my eyes, feeling like a teenager once more.

"You two have to continue on. We'll guide you through to the next portal, but I'm afraid there's a few more to take," Father explained, shrugging apologetically.

"A few more?" I questioned, "I thought there was just Tartarus and Elysium to get through to reach the city of the gods?"

"That's true." Mother nodded in agreement.

"But your path isn't straight," Father added. "It isn't like Celesterra, where there's only one portal to each realm. There are multiple entrances between the two realms within the Otherworld."

"And there are some areas the gods want you two to avoid. Don't want to ruin all the surprises of Elysium after all!" Mother said cheerfully.

"Okay, so where do we go?" Asteria asked, raising a brow.

"First, you'll need to go through the Lethe Fields. Make it through without getting sidetracked. Don't step off the path," Father explained.

"Then through the Chroi Oscailt Cavern." Mother smiled sympathetically. "Use your hearts, and all will be revealed."

"From there, you'll take the portal to Tartarus. It will lead you to the Styx. You must navigate the river without wings and without touching the water," Father informed us seriously, his forehead wrinkling in concern.

"From there, you must face the darkness inside to reach the next portal. Accept who and what you are, and you'll just have a quick jump back here, where your ancestors will lead you to the final portal to Tartarus." Mother smiled brightly. "When you arrive there, you'll merely need to find the portal to the city of the gods from there! But take note of where you are and what you'll see there. The past often holds many secrets we must learn."

"Oh, is that all?" Asteria said, voice high and almost distant sounding in shock.

"This is a test, isn't it?" I raised a brow at my parents.

"Well, the gods always have their reasons, son!" Mother insisted, still cheerful.

"Come on, we'll guide you to the next portal." Father put an arm around my shoulder, and Mother wrapped her arm around my unoccupied one. I was happy to see she also grabbed Asteria's hand, squeezing it tightly.

Using the time we had as we navigated toward the portal to catch up with my parents, I found I couldn't stop watching them with wide eyes. It was still difficult to believe this was happening. I had only expected to see them again at the end of a very long life. Even knowing we would journey through Elysium, I was sure the gods would keep any loved ones we wanted to see firmly away.

It was well known that the gods didn't take well to the living and dead speaking. According to myth, a man once tried to sneak into Elysium and steal his dead lover back to the world of the living. He'd failed, of course, but the gods had been deeply unhappy with him for daring to try to disrupt the peaceful afterlife of a woman he claimed to love.

I could see why they were so firm on that now. I felt a bit of peace fill my own heart at the knowledge that my parents had been reunited in the afterlife and were happy once more. My mother's death had devastated me, but my father's death had haunted me.

Knowing how lost he'd been… seeing him found once more lifted a weight on my heart I hadn't even realized was there.

They both seemed so much more alive in death. I wasn't sure how to feel about that.

Walking through Elysium, I had no idea what to expect, but we came to a junction where I could see off in several directions. Each way, I spied what looked to be numerous cities and villages, each one different from the last.

"They let us stay wherever we please, here!" My mother gushed. "We, of course, stay in the best section. I think you'll appreciate it especially, my dear," she told Asteria as she led us in.

Tall nymph trees lined the path, higher and wider than any I'd ever seen. Starflies and fireflies flickered in different twinkling colors through their leaves. Their branches didn't droop to the ground here due to their height, but instead created a vast canopy above us. Except for the middle of the lane, where the canopy stopped and let the stars shine down on the path. Which was strange, as it wasn't night before we'd walked in here…

Asteria's gasp of delight had me shifting focus to take in the rest, and I could see exactly why Mother thought Asteria would love this. Though how she knew her taste… I wasn't going to give myself a headache trying to make sense of it.

Large houses lined each side of the street, with warm, glowing lights illuminating the entire area. And they were hardly the only source of light, with the stars above and the glowing *flowers*, adding to the bright, colorful, and frankly *magical*, atmosphere—even though it was the deepest night.

Pink, purple, and blue flowers were scattered everywhere. They draped off houses and were planted along the sides of the path. Vines containing more flowers twined around rooftops, which were more like palace towers than regular homes. A strange mix of royal and ordinary seemed to be incorporated into the design here.

The path itself was twinkling, with little lights twinkling on and off, and Asteria twirled herself down it, arms out at her sides as she laughed.

"Calix, do you see this?" She smiled brightly at me. "I was almost disappointed we weren't going in the direction of Cloud City back there, but this is better than I could have imagined."

I nearly laughed. I thought I might have imagined seeing a palace sitting atop a giant cloud before my parents brought us this way.

"I see it." I stepped forward and grabbed her hand, twirling her myself with an adoring smile. She was too cute like this, and it was too rare she got to embrace this carefree side of herself.

She twirled in and out before stumbling into me. I caught her against my chest, and we smiled at one another. I leaned in for a kiss before the sound of a throat loudly clearing had us jumping apart like children caught doing something naughty. I nearly winced at myself. I was four hundred and twenty-one, for Nox's sake! I wasn't a child anymore.

"Oh, Orion!" Mother hit my father's chest. "Let the children play," she argued fiercely.

Asteria broke into laughter, her head hanging downward for a moment before she looked up at me brightly. "Yes, Calix, let's go play!"

She giggled, before running down the path ahead. I sighed, looking to my mother, who just winked at me, and I took off after my wayward mate.

"Nox, I wish the girls were here to see this," Asteria said wistfully as she looked around at all Elysium had to offer.

We followed behind my parents, hand in hand, as they led us through the city to where we needed to be.

"They will one day." I reminded her, and she frowned at me, swatting at my chest. "What? They will!"

"That's depressing." She sighed, eyeing the area a bit more mournfully, and I nearly kicked myself.

I squeezed her hand. "Hey, look at me."

She did, those wide blue eyes meeting mine, and I knew I could get lost there if I let myself.

"It's a *good* thing, my réalta. We live two lives. One on Adamah, one in the Otherworld. It's inevitable that the first won't last forever, even for those of us who are immortal. All Fae eventually die, just like every human. But here?" I told her, waving a hand at our surroundings.

"Here, we all live again. A true immortality, but one shared by Fae and human alike. Where the concerns of class and race no longer matter. Death is the great equalizer. We all face it with the same thing: the truth of our souls laid bare. And we all receive the same fate: whatever we deserve. Be that an afterlife full of love and joy, or one of pain and despair—" I smirked. "If you're like Cyrus anyway."

Asteria couldn't help but smile at my teasing, but she looked thoughtful, nonetheless, at my words.

"He's right, you know." My mother piped up. "And I don't say that just because he's my precious little boy."

I sighed long sufferingly, pinching the bridge of my nose. Growling, "Mother."

"Stop, it's cute!" Asteria whispered in my ear, giggling.

I groaned and eyed my father, who shrugged at me with a smirk. *No help from that corner.*

"I'm agreeing with you, dear. Deal with it." Mother sniffed; suddenly, every inch the queen who sat the throne beside my father. She only softened as she turned to Asteria, taking her hand.

"Death is nothing to fear, dear. I believe you already learned the truth of it." Mother smiled knowingly. "A life not lived to its fullest is the greatest tragedy of all."

Asteria sucked in a sharp breath. "How?"

Mother winked. "Let's just say we've had some greater insight. Which is how I know you are just perfect for my boy."

I suddenly felt a bit of water gathering in my eyes, and forced it back down before it could leak out.

"You will be a marvelous queen, Asteria." My mother cupped Asteria's cheek, looking at her intently. "And an even more marvelous mate. Anxiety is insidious, and we dragons know that more than most. Our emotions can be erratic, uncontrollable, even."

She dipped her head, and Asteria's eyes widened, and I was sure I was the only one who noticed the slight tremble of her hands.

"But that's just part of who we are. Embracing it will set you free, my girl. You have struggled so hard, for so long. Beating against the bars of an invisible cage. Don't put yourself back in there. Anxiety will crop up again and again. There's nothing we can do about that. What we can change is how we answer it. Once you know those fears whispering in your ear are just that: fears with no power over you—you will be set free from their influence. Even if they keep whispering away, you can brush them to the side. It's a battle we face all our lives. Rage and anxiety pull from the same well, and they drive us dragons more than the rest. So if it's control you're after, here is where you can grasp it.

"So you will live your life to the fullest, and many, *many* years from now, you two will join us here, and live a second life even more full of love and laughter than the first!" Mother smiled, and a tear tracked down Asteria's cheek. She merely wiped it away and pressed a kiss to her forehead before pulling her into a tight hug.

I tried to control my own emotions at the sight. Nox, seeing them together broke through every wall I had. A dream I didn't even know to wish for.

"But for now, it's time for you to finish your journey here, and then head home to live that life. We've arrived," my father added, pointing to the field before us. "When you get home, you tell the girls how sorry I am, will you? But let them know I'm glad they had the best brother there was to step in for me."

"Father…" I didn't know what to say, standing here before him, about to say goodbye once more.

He grabbed me in a hard hug, his hand on the back of my head. "I love you, Calix. And I'm *so* fucking proud of you. No father has ever been so proud in the history of the Otherworld, I tell you."

I laughed roughly, trying to swallow the lump in my throat, and pulled back to look him over once more. Seeing the same silvery-white hair and lilac eyes streaked with color, it was like looking in a slightly skewed mirror, just enough of my mother in me to not be quite identical.

"You two look more like twins than my twin and I do," Asteria commented idly with amusement. I snorted, shaking my head with a smile.

"Oh, Calix." My mother came over, wrapping me in her arms. I held her tightly. "Your father already told you how proud we are, but know I could never have asked for a better son. I love you so much. It was the greatest honor of my life to raise you. And as much as I would have loved to raise both your sisters, I'm grateful for the time Ndrita and I did have. I wish I could have been there for my little Livie, but you did such an amazing job with her. You tell both my girls I love them so much, and I'm so proud of them both, too."

Mother sniffed, the tears in her eyes beginning to roll down her cheeks. "And I better not see you again for a long, long time. I want an army's worth of grandchildren all the way down to great-great-great-grandchildren before you even think about it! You hear me?"

I laughed at her commanding tone, while Asteria nearly choked at her words. My father chuckled, patting her on the back. He leaned down to whisper theatrically, "Don't worry, you'll have plenty of land for them to rule."

Facing them both, I swallowed hard. My hand shook, and Asteria grabbed it, squeezing it tightly and holding me up when I wasn't sure I could keep standing on my own.

"I don't want to say goodbye." My voice trembled as I choked back my tears, a few breaking through despite my struggle.

"Oh, Calix." My mom breathed, a smile rising. "This isn't goodbye. We'll see each other again, and you'll get to tell us all the wonderful things you two have accomplished since we last met."

She kissed me on the cheek, as my father smiled over at me. "We'll see you both again soon. But in the meantime, live your lives for the love you share. Enjoy and embrace every moment."

CHAPTER 44

Arien

As Titan, Harpina, and the rest of Night's command returned to our encampment south of the Etheralta Mountains, I knew Asteria had passed into the Otherworld.

The very thought sent a chill down my spine.

In fact, I was sure I knew *when* she went through. I felt a strange tug in my gut right before it felt like a hole opened inside of me. It was similar to when the spell was first lifted from her. I hadn't known what it was at the time, only that it felt like something I'd been missing forever had finally slotted into place.

"There's magic to twins." My mother had said with a smile. "And you two, perhaps most of all."

I knew she loved the idea that we were part of some great destiny. That *she* had been the one to bring it to life. But I wasn't sure about any of that.

Family was what mattered to me, and knowing my sister had to go meet the gods gave me enough anxiety for the rest of my life, quite frankly.

"I don't see what good you'll be." Zakat snorted as he walked in with the others. "Your father has made it clear he'd support a madman rather than take the dent to his pride. What will your little ragtag team manage?" He rolled his eyes.

"More than you think," Altan argued, clearly fuming if the look on his face was anything to go by. "I already heard from my sister that she's managed to get a good number of soldiers on our side. Not everyone is as clueless as my father."

"What are you two arguing about?" Lilith asked, shaking her head at the two of them. "I swear you've done nothing but pick at one another since you got here. Aren't you tired of it by now?"

"It's all that sexual tension," Harpina quipped, smirking as she passed by. She sent me a wink as she looked me up and down. She was beautiful, of course, if a bit brash. But she was also a close friend of Asteria's, and as far as I was concerned, that meant she was off limits, even for a night. Though, I was sure that night would be quite spectacular.

"With him?!" Altan blustered, a faint flush gracing his cheeks. "Absolutely not! He's a cocky hot head with no sense of responsibility."

"*Wow*," Zakat drew out sarcastically. "Tell me how you really feel." He leaned closer to Altan, making him lean back. "But we both know those pants are on fire," he murmured seductively.

The tips of Altan's pointed ears turned deep red, and his throat bobbed as he swallowed hard. But he turned to me with a sharp shake of his head as he brushed the other prince off. "We need to begin training. Titan sent us here. Apparently, we need to learn how to fight among you."

I raised a brow, looking over the crowd for Titan. When I spotted him, I called him over, waiting until the General reached us. I straightened as he approached. I hadn't been General of Day's forces for very long, but Titan had been Night's for centuries. I knew I couldn't compare myself to a Fae as old as Titan, but it was a bit intimidating, nonetheless.

I'd been raised to be my sister's sword and shield. I had no idea who I was if I proved myself to be useless in that role.

"Prince Arien," Titan greeted with a nod of his head. The moon phases tattooed on his neck showing his status as a warrior glimmered in dark ink against his golden skin.

"Titan, Prince Altan indicated you wanted a specific training regimen for them?" I questioned, getting a small smirk in return.

"They're princes; they're used to giving orders, not taking them. Plus, we've never had phoenixes in our aerial battles before. We all need to adjust our tactics going into this war if we hope to win," he explained, and I nearly kicked myself for not thinking of that.

My eyes closed, and I took a deep breath, running a hand through my long, dark hair. A large hand landed on my shoulder, and I opened my eyes to face startlingly familiar sky-blue eyes.

"You're doing a great job," Titan reassured me, and for a moment, but for the shorter hair, squarer face, and tattoos, it was the ghost of my father saying words I'd always secretly hoped to hear.

I swallowed hard, trying to find my equilibrium.

"You've taken on a lot of changing circumstances with little time to adjust," he continued. "You managed to hold the line in Avalon despite overwhelming odds, and that's the kind of leadership we need right now."

"So, we get in the air and practice aerial tactics with the phoenixes," I said, tilting my head in thought. "Their fire is very different from mine. While I can shoot flames out in large bouts, they have a much shorter range."

"We can still use it as a weapon," Zakat assured me with a smirk. "We just have to get closer than a dragon would."

"So you, what?" I asked, my brows furrowing. "Get right up to whatever you want to set on fire?"

"Pretty much. We can also take out someone while we're on fire ourselves." Zakat shrugged a shoulder casually. I was beginning to see what Altan meant about his reckless attitude.

"That's not always a great idea, considering we have to barrel into our target for that method to be effective. But when we want to target our fire, we need to take the time to set ourselves fully aflame before we can, essentially, inhale that fire." Altan stepped in to explain, narrowing his eyes at Zakat, who just continued to smirk back at him with a raised eyebrow. "Once we have, we can then blow it outwards. But like you said, it's a much shorter range than a dragon's fire.

I nodded thoughtfully, noticing Titan was watching me. *Evaluating me.*

I knew he cared about my sister in addition to Calix, who seemed to be like a son of sorts to him. With their mating, it made sense that he wanted to ensure I was up to the task before us. Day and Night were now inextricably entwined in a way no two kingdoms had ever been before.

"Our fire is more easily targeted," I began, thinking through the options before us. "So we can keep the dragons on task, and the phoenixes can provide distraction and chaos." I began to smile as the plan came together in my mind.

Titan nodded firmly with a small smile on his face. "It's a good plan. Much like we've been doing for years, attacking to hide our true motives. We were getting humans out while using darkness, fire, and steel to distract and distort what everyone *thought* they were seeing."

"Alright!" I clapped my hands with a nod. "Altan, Zakat, I want you two up in the air with me. We'll fly out over the ocean and do a few maneuvers to test this out."

"Tartarus yeah, here we go!" Zakat cheered, already making his way out of the crowd to find a place to shift.

Altan sighed long sufferingly, but I noticed he followed quickly after him. I looked to Titan, who had a thoughtful look on his face.

"While you wrangle those two, I'll start working on getting our forces here to train together. Merging the two armies into a working force and moving as one is going to take some time." He rubbed his chin, looking out over the sea of soldiers.

"We can each take a group," Lilith suggested. She tended to be the quietest one of Calix's group, but whenever she did speak, she always had something worthwhile to contribute. "Baach, Eryx, Harpina, you, and myself. Along with Arien and any he can recommend from Day's forces. If we all take a group of combined soldiers from both kingdoms, we can begin getting them used to working together."

"Good idea." Titan nodded approvingly. "We should also begin working the humans from Day in."

"You don't think getting the two kingdoms to work together is going to be hard enough?" I asked him warily.

He scoffed a laugh, "Of course it will. But war is never easy. We'll only have more challenging times ahead. Getting them all used to each other now can prevent a catastrophe down the line because they couldn't work together. Besides, we already have humans in our army. It's Day's humans who will be new to the party here, and your soldiers who will struggle the most. So they'll need your leadership to show them the way."

I had no argument with that, but I still worried about how the humans would fit into our dynamics. Night's Fae and humans may be used to working alongside one another, but Day's population only had that one battle under our belt. And their participation had been spontaneous.

This was something else entirely.

But for now, I made my way to where Altan and Zakat had gone to shift, finding a yellow and teal phoenix and an orange and teal one waiting for me, circling above the clearing they'd found. I shifted, golden scales rippling out and over my body as I flew up into the air.

I loved flying, being able to spread my wings and head out over the ocean, allowing me to clear my head and leave behind all the worries this war brought with it.

I'd spent my life preparing for a battle against my father, and instead found myself preparing for a war where the entire continent was being torn in half.

The balance was tipping precariously, now. Every move made shifted us further toward chaos. And yet there was no way to fix it but to push through.

Chaos bred to fix chaos—it was a paradox, but I knew of no other way to fix it. Calix had clearly spent years trying to figure it out and had come up against the same issue time and again.

Magic was already slowly fading from our lands. Reports we received spoke of Dusk's flora and fauna beginning to wither, and I feared when the chaos would spread further.

How long until it hits Day? Or Night?

How long did we truly have to fix the balance, before chaos reigned completely?

What would we even do if chaos stole away everything we are?

A LONG DAY of training had left most around the camp lethargic. Some were lying down on the grass, arms spread as they relaxed their weary muscles. Others sat around campfires, talking and drinking.

I had to admit it was surprisingly nice to see Fae and humans all sitting together and getting along.

It was less nice when Soren came and plopped himself down on the log next to me. He grunted a greeting before staring into the fire with a morose glare.

I rolled my eyes discreetly. I didn't think I'd ever like this kid. And his first words only proved my point.

"Do you really think Calix is good for Asteria?" Soren asked, elbows on his knees as he turned his head to me.

"Yes," I responded dryly, taking a swig of my drink, wishing I could escape this conversation. I didn't like thinking of my twin and her relationship, as much as I could acknowledge he *was* good for her. It was just awkward to think about as a protective brother.

"But he's a brute!" Soren argued, shaking his head. "Asteria deserves someone who would treat her like a princess."

I looked at him incredulously. "Didn't you grow up with her? You should know her better than that."

"But she doesn't need to be that way anymore! She's royalty!" His brows furrowed, like he was genuinely confused.

"Soren." I turned to look at him seriously. "This is why he's good for her. Because he understands her. He lets her be whoever she wants to be. And he loves her for it. You want her to fit the image you have of her. That's not love. That's Fae allure that's gotten to you good." I snorted, shaking my head.

"Fae allure?" he asked, head tilted to the side, even as his mouth set mutinously at my words.

"It happens sometimes. Humans who spend too much time with a Fae find themselves starry-eyed and spellbound. It's a result of the magic we put off. Even Asteria, whose magic was smothered, would have had that allure. It's a natural part of being a creature with magic; it radiates off us. You spent a lot of time with Asteria, and the magic probably caught you and reeled you right in."

"No. *No,*" he protested as he shook his head, copper hair flying. "I love her. It's not magic."

"If you say so." I took another swig, hoping he would go away.

"You know, talking about her like she's a possession you have to win, or like she's a damsel who needs to be saved, is really not doing you any favors." A voice from behind said.

I turned to see Harpina, her bright red hair was now down in big waves that shined in the light of the fire, her arms crossed as she glared at Soren. My mouth tipped up into a smile I tried to hide in my drink.

"What?" Soren asked, visibly confused.

She scoffed, moving to sit herself down between us, her arm brushing mine and making goosebumps erupt along my skin. "You think of Asteria like a doll. '*Oh, she needs to be saved from Cyrus, she needs to be saved from Calix.*'"

Her mocking tone had me snorting out a laugh against my permission. She sent me a quick wink, smirking before she schooled her expression to face Soren once more.

"She did need to be saved from Cyrus!" Soren threw his hands up in exasperation. I almost felt bad for the kid. He truly just didn't get it. He seemed so young still. It was hard to believe he was the same age as Asteria and me. Her comprehension was so far beyond his.

I didn't get what she ever saw in him, honestly—beyond a pretty face, at least. One couldn't deny he was good-looking for a human, but he wasn't anything I hadn't seen a million times before.

"Yeah, but you wanted to be her savior. Calix recognizes that Asteria may need help sometimes, but he's content to step back and let her handle herself otherwise," Harpina insisted, raising a brow. "He knows she doesn't need a savior. This is the girl who risked her life spying on the crown prince of Dusk Kingdom just to try to find even a slim hope of a chance for escape. Asteria is a fucking *queen*. Maybe try showing her the respect of one."

With that, she turned her body to face me, dismissing Soren where he sat with a shocked, open-mouthed expression. She crossed her right leg over her left, leaning toward me with her elbow resting on her knee. She raised a brow, amber eyes flashing as she tilted her lips up in a sultry smirk. "Hey there, sunshine."

I raised a brow back at her, unable to stop myself from matching her smirk. "Hey there, kitty-cat."

She laughed, tilting her head back slightly in a way that exposed her pale throat. From seeing her shift in training earlier, it was all too easy to see the grace of her cat-like form in her movements now. "How goes the transition from courtly prince to rebel?"

I scoffed a laugh. "I've always planned to rebel against my father, so I guess it feels pretty natural."

"Hmm." She hummed, looking me over blatantly. "I suppose that's true. Still, I'm surprised how well you've taken to this."

"And why's that?" I asked, cocking my head to the side.

"Your mother was also planning to overthrow your father, and she doesn't seem nearly as pleased with the rest of it." Harpina countered, and I realized what she was doing.

"Ah." I nodded my head. "So you think something must be up, and decided to flirt with me to get me to let my defenses down and spill the truth."

She looked a bit chagrined, wincing slightly, before admitting. "Well, I wanted to flirt with you anyway. Watching you fighting with your sunlight earlier was quite the sight. This just seemed like a good excuse."

I couldn't help the smile that slowly tilted my lips upward.

CHAPTER 45

Cyrus

THINGS were *not* going to plan.

I had finally found a way to draw Asteria out, and then…

They called me paranoid, but was it paranoia when you were right?

Someone was sabotaging me.

It was the only reasonable explanation. Someone in my court, most likely one of my meddlesome siblings, was trying to ruin everything I was trying to build.

One of my camps lay in ruins. The humans were gone, their chains dangling, broken open. Dead Fae littered the ground, those loyal to me to the last. Charred structures that were once workshops and soldier barracks greeted me everywhere I looked.

The humans in the city were getting louder in their discontent, too. Always hiding, scurrying around like rats as they defaced my city. Painting on the sides of buildings to scream to the world their wretched thoughts.

Madman. Tyrant. Chaos Bringer. Balance Destroyer.

I'd seen them all.

Someone was helping them. I was sure of it. The humans were too cowardly and meek to do this on their own. They had never been organized, never been able to stand against us in any meaningful way.

I refused to let them do so now.

The Dusk crown was only the first step in my plans, and no pathetic human would stop my rise, nor my revenge.

"Make sure this is cleaned up. Like it never happened," I instructed Kesshuu, nodding to the mess before us. I paused then, considering. "How much did they get?"

Kesshuu looked down, shamefaced. "Two wagons' worth."

Lightning struck the ground, making him flinch. I couldn't help it. My magic erupted without my say-so more often now, but it was little to fret about in the grand scheme of things.

"Find it," I growled, shaking my head as I turned from the mess, stalking away. "I want all of it back. And every human or Fae responsible in chains."

"Of course, my King." He nodded eagerly, and I let my wings unfurl and take me into the sky.

I spent the entire flight fuming, but upon my arrival at the palace, I was excited to see the scores of soldiers in charcoal and red.

Finally, some good news.

"King Tariq," I greeted as I landed before him.

"King Cyrus," he replied somberly, giving me a deep nod. "I was incredibly sorry to hear about your father. He was a great friend for many years. How has your mother been managing?" I raised my brow. "And you and your siblings, of course!" He rushed to add.

I'd watched him flirt with my mother in front of my father for years, always claiming it to be teasing among friends. But the moment my father was gone, here he was, narrowing right in on my mother.

I also noticed Queen Oriana had been left at home.

Interesting.

"We're all managing quite well," I answered, smiling. "My plans will see Dusk, and Dawn, of course, reach a new age of prosperity."

"Ah, yes. I've heard much about these plans, but little of any substance yet," he responded, with a skeptical tone that grated on my nerves. But I'd been dealing with Aelius thus far; I could deal with this nuisance, too. Especially if my mother played her part correctly, and she'd never once let me down.

"Well then, allow me to fill you in on how we will take power into our own hands, and out of the gods," I smirked, his brows flying upward.

"That is quite the claim," he said, surprised, as I led him into the palace.

"It is quite the feat," I told him proudly. "For too long, the gods have controlled the power we are allowed. Taking ours and trying to minimize us the moment we don't play to their silly rules."

"And you have a way around this? To maintain our fading power?" he asked, his voice hushed as his eyes glanced around the hall. Making sure no one could hear him admit to the fading power of Dawn's king.

"I do," I confirmed, smiling widely. His answering smile was accompanied by a slap on the back.

"Well then, I'm all ears, my boy!" While I didn't appreciate being called boy, his cheerfulness at the discovery made up for it.

It was nice to see I wasn't the only one who saw what a ridiculous ploy the gods' rules truly were. They thought they could control us, keep our behavior in line by dangling our powers before us like bait.

As I talked Tariq through my plans… well, the ones I would allow him to be aware of anyway, he jumped on board with little prodding. It was unfortunate that he would have to go. He seemed a reasonable man who could make a good ally in the future, too.

But sadly, for him anyway, there was room for only one king in Celesterra. Six was just five too many.

Thankfully, it was an issue I had no problem fixing. My dreams showed me the greatness awaiting, and High King did have a nice ring to it.

TARIQ BROUGHT A good number of Dawn's forces, leaving enough behind to protect his kingdom but bringing me a whole army otherwise—which was more than I could say for Aelius.

Only three of Day's six lords were here, and their numbers were now reduced after losing a battle against his insipid son. Finding out that Asteria and Calix had been there in the thick of the battle only served to enrage me further.

But I grit my teeth and back the desire to take that rage out on Aelius. *For now.*

I needed the numbers these supposed kings offered me for the moment. With my own army, Dawn's, and what Aelius had of Day, we had enough men to carry out the show of force I desired.

Looking out over that army now, I was pleased to see the plan coming together. As they readied themselves to leave, I left to head deeper into the palace. I grabbed several vials of blood magic and stashed them in my pockets before making a stop in the dungeon.

"Have you thought at all about what you've done?" I asked, crossing my arms and raising a brow. A scoff echoed off the walls.

"What? Questioning you?" Vissy asked tiredly. He was sitting against the wall, his head leaning back and his arms resting on his knees. His usually perfect hair was scragglier than I'd ever seen it, and his golden eyes seemed as dull as his now filthy clothing. It made my heart ache a bit to see it, but I couldn't afford to be soft.

"Yes," I stated plainly, making him laugh dryly.

"Cyrus." He looked up at me, making eye contact. My heart seemed to squeeze in my chest. "You've been like a brother to me my entire life. Which is why I'm going to be honest here."

"Oh? *Please*, do tell," I said sarcastically, hoping to bury the uncomfortable feeling in my chest.

"You've always had your bad qualities. *Tartarus*, we both have." He shook his head. "But this, this is beyond anything you've done before. You may be a cruel bastard at times, but not like *this*."

"And what is *this*, exactly?" I scoffed, shaking my head slightly as I gripped the bars of his cell tightly enough that my knuckles whitened.

"A mad tyrant," he answered, echoing the words painted on the walls of Evenfall. I stood up straight quickly, lightning crackling around my fingers, forcing me to let go of the bars before I broke them.

"Who have you been talking to?" I demanded, fury rising as I glared down at him. I knew people were working against me, but to target Vissy? To sway him from me? It was too far!

"What are you talking about?" he asked warily, eyeing me like a dangerous animal.

"You think I don't realize what's going on here?" I spat at him. He raised a brow back at me.

"Could you perhaps let me in on it? Because I have no idea what you're blathering on about," he responded, cocking his head to the side.

"I know they've gotten to you. I've seen the slander painted across the city. Trying to paint me as a *mad tyrant*, as you said," I snarled, trying to contain the bolts of lightning that were beginning to flash around the dungeon.

"Cyrus," Vissy said slowly, watching the ricocheting bolts carefully. "I said that, because that's how you're acting. What you're doing with the humans is so far beyond anything I thought you were truly capable of."

"Since when do you give a fuck about the humans?" I scoffed, shaking my head in disbelief at his lame excuse.

"I've always enjoyed them," he drawled, making me give him an exasperated look. "Things are the way they are, but I never hated them because of that. Some humans were fun, some were shit. But killing them all? It's crossing a line."

"Oh? And what superior moral line is this?" I asked skeptically.

"One that sees you losing yourself in the process," he responded seriously. "And you've walked right over that line, Cyrus."

I paused for a moment, considering what he was saying. I had never hated humans—looked down on them, of course. It was only proper, after all. But I hadn't truly cared enough about them to *hate* them. It was only Asteria and then the resulting rebellions that fueled that feeling. My magic was what mattered here. Getting my power back through their blood meant more than their lives.

And gaining back control of them was too important. I had to be respected as king, not made a fool of by a few rebellious humans.

Still, *had* I taken things too far?

No, I shook my head at myself. I wouldn't allow them to shake my resolve. This had to be the work of whichever sibling of mine was trying to undermine me.

Trying to steal *my* rightful throne for themselves.

Just as they always had. Only now, they'd found a way to fuel dissent. Stirring up the humans and getting to my lords. Getting to *Vissy*. They thought I couldn't see the conspiracy going on right beneath my nose, but I would show them what all their little plots amounted to in the end.

"They've gotten to you." I shook my head at him sadly. His confused expression only firmed my resolve that he could no longer be trusted. "My damn siblings," I hissed at him.

Vissy shook his head in denial. "Cyrus, no—"

"It's *King* Cyrus to you," I snapped, unable to take the familiarity he showed in one breath when he betrayed me with the next.

His head reared back, and he looked at me as if I was a stranger—but he was the stranger here. This was a man I had shared everything with. Even

Asteria! I had loved him more truly than anyone else in my life. I would have done nearly anything for him.

And yet, here we found ourselves.

"You cannot be trusted any longer. You're no longer my brother, but a traitor to the crown. One who *will* be dealt with." I fumed, staring at him with lightning flashing in my eyes.

He stood slowly, straightening to his full height as he stared back at me, eye to eye. His chin firmed as he clenched it tight, and his golden eyes flashed dangerously.

"So be it."

THE CONVERSATION WITH Vissy haunted me as I prepared to leave. Which of them was it, I wondered, who plotted against me so. Or was it all of them?

Weylin remained at the border, far from where he could cause trouble, as I waited for him to make a move I could justifiably imprison him for.

Daneiris and Zerlina were undoubtedly up to something, but I didn't think either had the ability to coordinate something so complex. They thought too small. Daneiris's temper tantrum with Asteria had proven that, and Zerlina wouldn't dare risk her crown.

Vikal was clearly frightened. He was a weak boy and much too attached to his human. He was unable to see the bigger picture. Unable to grasp the true place of the Fae and the humans in the grand design. He would learn, surely. It would be my responsibility to show him the way. But he was too feckless to have been sneaking around and plotting to any extent.

Kian… I always viewed Kian as meek and bookish. He could fight, certainly, but he clearly preferred not to. To be fair, I didn't fight much either before now. There was no need as crown prince, but being king was altogether different. Kian was several steps from the throne, but did he aspire to it? It hadn't seemed like it.

Then again, I hadn't expected his defense of Vikal and his pet, either.

One of them was certainly to blame. Maybe Weylin, even surrounded by my loyal soldiers, had found a way to communicate without their notice. There were ways out there for those who were motivated to find them.

"King Cyrus," Aelius greeted me, with proper deference for once in front of my men, as I stepped outside.

"King Aelius." I nodded in response. "Are we ready?" I asked, looking out among the troops amassed in preparation to march.

"We are." He smirked, an almost giddy smile taking over his face. "I, for one, cannot wait to see how this pans out."

Nervous anticipation filled me at the thought. I wished I could see Asteria's face when she found out.

I made my way to the front of our combined armies, Aelius and Tariq joining me. I had to ensure they still felt like the kings they believed themselves to be, after all. It wouldn't do for them to notice the true scheme in play.

When I made it to the front, I let my wings unfurl, flying up so everyone could see me. Aelius's gold and purple-scaled dragon wings looked out of place between my pink and Tariq's red feathered Pegasus wings. For once, I was proud of my wings despite the color. I had always wished for a more masculine palette than the bright pink House Tynan had.

But now, I embraced the flashy color, knowing that I stood out thanks to them.

"Fae of Dusk, Dawn, and Day!" I called out with a charming smile firmly upon my face. "Today, we leave for a very important mission. While this may seem like an easy task, the repercussions will be felt across the continent."

The rumble of the crowd as they got excited made my smile grow wider. It was pleasing to see their enthusiasm.

"We are working toward a new future for Celesterra!" I shouted. "One where we control *our own* destinies! Where Fae rule with the authority we should have been given all along. When you reach our destination, each and every one of you will contribute to that future! Every human taken will feed our magic and renew our land. Every house destroyed will make a mark that cannot be denied. We will show Sunrise what happens when you support our enemies, and we will make the enemy to the south sit up and take notice. Our strength and power won't be denied; your strength and power will only increase!"

The crowd cheered, and I soaked in the praise as they chanted my name. This was everything I'd ever wanted. Acknowledgment from these soldiers may not be the same as from my family, or even Asteria, but they could fill the void well enough.

"Under my—*our*—" I caught myself, nodding to indicate the two kings slightly behind me on each side. "Leadership, you will see a new age! But first…"

I trailed off, leaving them on tenterhooks as I smiled and then shouted as dramatically as I could manage, "You must all fight for it!"

The loud cheer that went up blended into a cacophony that had Aelius and Tariq raising their brows.

"Well, you certainly know how to work a crowd, at least." Aelius's half-hearted praise made me roll my eyes.

"To Sunrise!" I shouted, arm high as I pointed northwest.

They'd have no idea what's coming for them.

CHAPTER 46

WHEN I'd found out Calix was my mate, I never imagined meeting his parents. They'd been long dead, and thus, there was no need to fret about impressing them.

I never expected to run into them in the *Otherworld*.

Meeting who was essentially my in-laws was wild. *They* were wild, but in the best kind of way.

Calix had told me all about his parents. His lovely, caring mother who lost her life in the birthing bed, bringing Liviana into this world. His father, lost and miserable and half dead already after losing his mate, had chased battle after battle, hoping to be reunited with her and leaving Calix with all the responsibility of the kingdom and house Erebus itself on his shoulders.

Had I thought about it, I would have had mixed feelings about his father for that. But after meeting him, there was no way not to forgive. The difference between how Calix described him post-Jemisha's death and the man I met after being reunited with her was like two different people.

His mother was adorable and quite funny, and I could see by watching Jemisha and Orion together exactly why he was so lost without her. They were like a set, and one couldn't exist without the other.

Seeing Calix able to find a measure of peace with their loss was more than enough to justify this trip in my mind. Whatever horrors we'd already faced or may be waiting ahead, it was worth it to see that weight taken off his shoulders.

But thinking of what the loss of his mate did to Orion made fear for the future rise within me. I immediately tried to push it down, but remembered how Calix's interpreted me doing that just as quickly. I didn't want to cut him off, but I needed to find a way to bury those fears.

I clutched his hand tightly as we walked into the field of white flowers, his parents getting smaller and smaller as we moved further away.

"How are you doing, my dorchadas?" I asked him quietly, squeezing his hand to let him know I was there for him. I carefully watched my steps, following the small dirt path that wound through the flowers.

He let loose a heavy breath, shaking his head. "I have no—"

I looked over as he cut off, and found him staring into the field of flowers.

"Calix?" I asked hesitantly.

"*Asteria.*" A voice called, and my head whipped to the right, finding...

"Mom?" My voice wobbled as I found my mother, my *human* mother, standing in the field. Her curly brown hair swayed in the wind as she opened her arms.

"*Come here, my little star,*" she said, smiling brightly. My foot moved to step in her direction, but Calix's hand in mine kept me from moving.

"It's not real." He shook his head firmly. "Whoever you're seeing, it's not real. Remember what my parents said? Don't step off the path."

Understanding hit me through the fog my mother's presence had brought.

"What are they then?" I asked, Calix hurrying us forward through the field of white flowers.

"Figments. Guardians, maybe." He pondered. "Lethe flowers in myth were used to help ease pain and erase traumatic memories. They featured in a myth where Arawn offered them to a girl whose life was so painful, she was unable to find peace, even in the afterlife."

Huh. The more I learned about the Otherworld and the myths of the Fae, the crazier it all seemed. Even more so because it was apparently all *true*.

"*Asteria...*" I tried to ignore the call of my father's voice, my fingers tightening until surely even Calix felt the strain.

"Who did you see?" I asked him, trying to distract myself. I looked up to find his jaw locked and teeth grinding as he pointedly kept his eyes on the path.

"Liv, the first time. Then Titan," he admitted. "But as long as we don't pay attention and stay on the path, we'll be fine."

I nodded, winding my arm around his fully as I clung to him, anchoring myself to reality. It wasn't hard; he was distracting at the best of times. I had yet to find another person who could command a room as Calix did. He was not just charismatic, but magnetic.

I felt immensely lucky he was *mine*.

His gorgeous face and body were honestly the least of it. He was protective yet wild, kind but ferocious—everything I never thought I would have.

While Cyrus had been nothing but a pretty face hiding a rotten soul inside, Calix managed to have a soul as beautiful as the rest of him.

I gasped as I spotted the end of the field of flowers a ways ahead. "There's the end! We're almost there."

"Thank Nox," he groused, and I giggled. The apparitions had not let up, constantly calling for us as we walked through the field. I'd been distracted with thoughts of Calix, but they were still quite annoying after a while.

We made our way out of the field, and I turned to look up at him. "What did they say was next again?"

"Chroi Oscailt Cavern," he responded, lips twisting as he thought over his parent's warning. "Mother said to use our hearts, and all would be revealed."

"Ugh, what is that supposed to *mean*?" I whined, my head tipping back, completely done with the cryptic messages. Why couldn't anyone just give a straight answer?

Calix chuckled deeply, smirking at me. "Something tells me we'll figure it out when we get there. I see a mountain ahead; it must be through there."

I sighed, my head crashing into his bicep as we walked on. He leaned down and kissed the top of my head, whispering encouragement as we made our way forward.

Approaching the mountain, we found the entrance to a cave system that seemed to run underneath it. Standing maybe twenty feet tall, the entrance was a rounded arch of rock, leading to nothing but black nothingness.

I summoned my starlight, using it to light the darkness within. It revealed a tunnel full of sparkling gold and silver. There were runes written on the walls in the same glowing silver I'd seen in Tairngire Palace, but just as many were done in a glowing gold as well.

"What are these? They're so similar to the ones at the palace," I asked Calix, whose eyebrows were furrowed as he read them. I was so jealous. I had to learn to read the ancient Fae language.

"They're instructions, or pieces of advice, perhaps," he spoke softly as he moved closer, reading the next lines of runes. "This one says: 'An open heart is only smart. A closed heart leads to rot.' They're all variations on the theme."

"What in the Otherworld?" I murmured, a bit concerned about what we were walking into. He looked back at me as I crossed my arms, rubbing my hands over my arms as anxiety got the best of me.

"My réalta," he whispered, grabbing my waist and pulling me toward him. "It's going to be okay."

"How do you know? What if we end up stuck here forever and leave Cyrus to do whatever he wants in Celesterra?" I worried, digging my nails into his sides.

"Because." He smiled slowly, a smug look in his eyes. "When it comes to us, we can accomplish anything together. I've told you before—you're a force of nature, love. There's nothing you can't do. I'll just hang along for the ride." He winked.

I huffed a breath of laughter, shaking my head fondly as I leaned in to kiss him. I relished the feeling for a moment before pulling back, resting my chin on his chest.

"Fine, let's do this." I nodded, and he pulled me along through the cave. An echoing sound reached our ears, and we both perked up, walking faster, my starlight illuminating the way.

My breath caught as the cave opened up into a massive cavern. The space was huge... and entirely missing a floor, except for a few tall rock pieces, reaching high enough to be floor height, but scattered too far to jump to.

"What in Tartarus?" Calix muttered, looking around for any indication of what to do. He turned to the wall, where more runes in glowing gold awaited.

"Love is the most precious commodity in all the realms," he read, his finger following along the script carved into the rock. "To create a path across the Chroi Oscailt Cavern, open your heart and speak the truth of it."

"Oh-kay…" I drew the word out dramatically, getting a smirk and an eye roll from Calix before he moved to stand along the edge of the great drop before us. He groaned, his head dropping back for a moment and distracting me with the length of his neck.

"I suppose flying would be considered cheating, which I know the gods aren't too fond of. They obviously want us to go through these tests for a reason. We should probably just try saying what's in our hearts?" He ventured, looking around before sighing.

I watched warily, not at all liking the conceit of this little trial. My heart was mine, so why did I have to open it for this stupid cavern?

"I'm afraid that after over four hundred years of waiting," Calix started quietly, "I'm going to lose you before I even truly have the chance to have you."

A loud rumble began, the ground shaking below our feet. Calix quickly reached over to help steady me until the shaking stopped, and we looked up to find a large flat-topped rock had risen, creating the start of a bridge over the cavern.

I laughed incredulously. "It worked!"

I threw my arms around him, hugging him in my exuberance, before what I'd have to do really hit me. I swallowed hard, pulling back to look at him. Those lilac eyes always entranced me, and I found myself looking into them for strength.

"I'm afraid that…" I began, before closing my eyes. The sight of his face becoming too much for me. "I'm afraid that you're going to be taken from me. I've never been allowed to have something of my own. Something I knew I could keep. I'm terrified that Cyrus, or our positions, or something else, is going to prevent me from *keeping* you. That all of this will be a quick flash of happiness before you're torn away from me, taking my heart with you."

The loud rumble was all but ignored as Calix pulled me into him, using his fingers to lift my chin and making me open my eyes. I found nothing but warm understanding in his eyes, making me release a breath of relief.

"This is why you've been pulling away?" he asked quietly, his eyes swimming with color.

"I didn't mean to," I admitted. "I was partly trying to… trying to prepare myself, I guess. And…"

"And what?" he urged me, his head dipping down so his forehead pressed to mine.

I gripped onto him for dear life.

"I felt like I was filled with all these chaotic emotions, and I couldn't control a damn one. I know I'm supposed to bring balance back to Celesterra, but how am I supposed to do that when I'm full of chaos myself?" I asked desperately. "How am I going to do any of this when chaos and rage drive me on? I felt like I needed to close those emotions off. I didn't mean to close you off in the process."

We ignored the rumble in the background, as if the ground wasn't shaking beneath our very feet.

"My réalta," he whispered, a tortured note in his voice. "It's perfectly normal to feel like that when you've had so many changes in your life. That doesn't mean you can't restore the balance. It doesn't mean I'm going to be torn away. It's just a matter of getting used to your new life. But closing yourself off won't get you anywhere. You think I haven't tried that?"

"What do you mean?" I asked, whisper quiet.

"After my parents died, I was a mess. With the weight of the kingdom and all its expectations, having to raise my sisters, all the women who wanted me for all the wrong reasons," he said, making me growl slightly at the thought. He chuckled at my reaction, cupping my cheeks and making me look him in the eyes.

"I was filled with nothing but chaos inside, and I tried to shut it all down and not feel anything instead," he explained, the Aurora slowly dancing in his eyes. "All it did was bottle up the pain until it came raging out in an explosion of epic proportions."

I raised a brow at him, and he shook his head slowly. "Trust me, it was a disaster."

"So what? I should try to *feel* all those emotions? How am I supposed to lead anyone that way?" I was sure that uncorking everything inside of me would lead to a catastrophe the likes of which had never been seen before.

"One day at a time," he said firmly. "You get up, you feel whatever you need to, you do whatever you need to, and you take it as it comes."

"You make it sound so easy," I complained, and he laughed softly.

"I have had centuries more practice, to be fair." He smiled, and I couldn't help my giggle as I slapped his shoulder.

"Old man." I teased him. He scowled at me before leaning in to tickle the spot where my neck met my shoulder, making me squeal and pull away. His bright laughter in response made me glare at him, but I couldn't help the smile trying to fight its way out.

"I love you, Asteria," he said once he'd sobered. "And I don't care how long it takes for you to come to terms with this, to know that what's between us will last; I'll keep waking up and reminding you of it every day."

I tried to form a response, but my mouth opened and closed uselessly as my heart roared in my ears.

He stepped even closer and took my hands in his. "And I don't care if it takes years for you to say it. To feel like you *can*. Because you're worth every moment of the wait."

A loud rumble sounded, and I looked up with tear-filled eyes to see the bridge had filled in completely. I looked back at Calix, and he wiped away one of my escaped tears with a smile.

"Come on." He stepped out onto the bridge, and I followed him across. I had no idea what to say after his words. I wanted so badly to be able to verbalize my feelings, but that pressing weight of fear had my tongue caught in a trap.

He may be willing to remind me every day that he would be there, but it didn't stop the fear inside knowing that he didn't control our fate any more than I did. He could be taken away—and loving him meant the chances of that only increased.

Love may be only for the Fae, but I wasn't any usual Fae.

WHEN WE MADE our way out from under the mountain, we came to the portal that surely led back to Tartarus. The portal, full of black liquid smoke, flickered before us, and we both looked to one another with a nod, before stepping through.

We emerged from the portals to dark skies rolling above a river of fire. The flames flickered over every inch of the water, and I didn't see a way around it. The fiery water continued in every direction, except for the dead-end path back to the portal.

"This must be the Styx," Calix observed, looking around the area. "We need to cross, but we can't use our wings or touch the water."

"How in Tartarus are we supposed to do that?" I asked, exasperated at all these riddles. I would never get used to swearing on the place we currently walked through either. It was beyond strange.

"I have no idea," he admitted, rubbing the back of his neck. "If we can't fly over it, and we can't swim through it, then…"

He trailed off, his eyes lighting up as he began walking the bank of the river.

"Calix?" I asked, brows raised.

"The only other way across would be a boat," he murmured. "There must be one around here, right?"

"How exactly would a boat help when the entire river is on fire?" I called to him, my brows creasing.

"If there's one around, it must mean there's a way," he responded, clearly sure of his idea.

I shrugged, not seeing any other option, and we both looked up and down the banks. Finally, Calix shouted, "Found it!"

I rushed over to find him pulling a small boat out of the weeds along the bank. There was a long pole inside the boat, along with a long, sharp spear. We both looked at one another with questions in our eyes, turning to face the raging flames before us.

Calix put the boat on the fiery water, and I cringed, expecting it to burst into flame itself. Instead, a path appeared through the flames, leaving the water completely clear on the winding path through.

"Come on, my dorchadas, we might as well." I shrugged, jumping into the boat.

He looked unsure, despite this being *his* idea, as he glanced between me and the flames. He sighed long-sufferingly, making me grin, but he got in the damn boat. He even grabbed the long pole, sticking it into the water and pushing us off.

I sucked in a breath as the boat veered toward the flames, but Calix used the pole to direct us away, my shoulders dropping in relief.

"What, do you doubt my skills, my réalta?" Calix smirked, looking down at me from where he stood, balancing with the wooden seat between his legs as he directed us down the winding path.

I couldn't help but laugh, shaking my head. "Far be it from me to ever doubt your *skills*."

The look he gave me was as scorching as the heat from the flames surrounding us. I bit my lip, pressing my legs together as I wished we were literally *anywhere* else.

It was a vivid reminder of a time when I couldn't touch him. It was still hard to believe he was mine to touch as much as I pleased. And I pleased… *quite a lot.*

But instead, I was forced to keep my hands to myself as he guided us down the river. The echo of screams reached us, the agony in them sending shivers down my spine. It was easy to forget where we were. We'd mostly been in relatively safe and somewhat empty areas, but there was a wide realm out there full of souls enjoying their eternal damnation.

Souls of those that deserved it, I reminded myself.

And soon, Cyrus would be joining them.

That thought brightened my spirits considerably. We were here for a reason, one that would help lead to exactly that outcome. We just needed to get through this journey, and then we could take the fight to that monster.

And I could finally repay him for every single thing he did. I tried not to cringe, remembering it, my breath coming a bit faster and earning a concerned look from my mate. I waved him off, dropping my head down to breathe slowly. Willing the images of Cyrus on top of me to disappear.

I gulped, the sound of my dress ripping open echoing in my ears, along with Tavarius's screams. *He would pay.* I repeated that to myself over and over, until rage replaced the hurt and despair. Until I felt my blood heat and the magic in my veins rise in the air around me.

"Asteria," Calix said softly, a hand landing on my shoulder. "It's okay. You're okay."

I gasped, embarrassed, as I realized Calix had felt all of that. I opened my mouth to apologize, but he shook his head sadly, bringing me in for a hug. I put my arms around his waist, breathing in the calming scent of night and fire.

But as the boat rocked, we quickly pulled apart, watching as a bout of flame appeared before us. The heat of the flames was nearly suffocating, and I coughed as sweat began to bead across my forehead. Calix cursed, moving us quickly to the left, where another path had simultaneously opened. Sweat rolled down my back, and I looked back to see the distance between us and the fire increasing. I sighed in relief, but that was too close a call.

As we continued down the new path, we watched as the flames began to move once again. This time, two paths opened, like a fork in the road, as the one before us closed. We looked at each other in concern, trying to figure out what we needed to do to get past this. I couldn't figure out what the test was here, but there had to be something to this.

"Maybe the one that leads toward the other side of the river?" I suggested carefully.

"It could be, or it could be another false path," Calix said, clearly concerned, his jaw working back and forth. The boat rocked hard, and we both swayed back and forth, grabbing onto the edge of the boat to steady ourselves.

"What was that?" Calix murmured, lilac eyes surveying the water carefully. But we'd apparently been still too long, and the flames began to close in on us.

"Fuck," I whispered, turning to Calix with wide eyes. He grabbed the pole and sent us sloshing forward, turning toward the path that seemed to lead toward the other side of the Styx, instead of away from it—hopefully, anyway.

Flames flickered before us, as more paths began to appear in the water. They cut across the water in random bursts, until an entire maze of flames rose before us. My breathing picked up, but my eyes were forced elsewhere as I heard a strange sound from the water. I looked to the right just in time to go flying backward as the boat rocked to the left. I cursed as I hit the side, but just caught the end of a serpentine tail flicking out of the water before it disappeared.

As I righted myself in the boat, a loud splash echoed before a creature suddenly emerged from the murky depths, screaming loudly. Its long, pale green body was indeed serpentine, with wide, orange frills on each side of its head that flared out as it screamed. Its eyes were pure black, and its mouth was full of sharp, jagged teeth, perfect for ripping and tearing.

I ducked down to fumble for the spear at the bottom of the boat. The serpent's teeth clashed together instead of getting my flesh, and Calix's long pole swung into it, hitting it in its midsection and causing it to scream once more before diving back into the water.

"What in Tartarus?" I panted, hefting the spear into my hand.

"Stay ready, that thing definitely isn't done," Calix instructed, his eyes surveying the water darkly. He was practically bristling, and I knew he wouldn't move an inch until the threat to me was taken care of.

"I will, but you need to get us moving." I insisted sternly. "You focus on steering like a good boy, and I'll take care of fighting the brutal river monster." I smiled cheekily, but he wasn't having it, his eyes narrowing at me.

"Asteria—"

"I can take care of it," I promised, grabbing his hand. "Trust me."

"Always." He sighed at my plea, a small smile forming. "I just can't help but worry about you."

"Well, worry about getting us over this river," I smirked. "Teamwork."

He huffed a laugh, shaking his head, but he moved back to the front of the boat to focus on steering. The paths kept changing, the maze of flame closing in some places, opening in new ones, but we were slowly getting closer and closer to the other side. As long as whatever that serpent monster was didn't get us, we would get through this.

And I certainly wasn't going down thanks to an overpowered snake.

I watched the water, noticing the small bubbles and ripples coming closer from the left. My fingers curled around the spear, and as it got closer, I breathed in deeply, readying myself.

It erupted from the water silently this time, but I heaved the spear forward. Its black eyes narrowed to slits as it cut to the right, and I just barely clipped one of the fins running down its back before hitting the water. I swore as it disappeared into the depths once more. My eyes shot in every direction, feeling the paranoia growing, knowing that it could come from anywhere.

I heard it before I saw it, and I spun around quickly, bringing the spear up—but not fast enough. Sharp teeth cut through the flesh of my shoulder, and I screamed in agony. It felt like serrated daggers were slicing into my bones as its teeth sank deeper.

"Asteria!" Calix shouted as he turned toward me, but I was already moving. I forced myself to push through the pain—and Nox, I'd never felt anything so painful. Even Cyrus's dagger didn't hurt like this. Moving with its jaw locked around my shoulder was like liquid fire shooting through me. But I managed to get the spear into my other hand, the monster too busy slurping my blood to notice.

I rammed the spear through its neck, and its teeth finally released me as it screamed. It tried to slink back to the water, but the spear in its neck kept it in place. The snake-like monster began to thrash around, and I struggled to hold onto the weapon as it slithered, tears running down my eyes from the overwhelming agony. We struggled, both of us injured, but as the thing flailed backward, I tipped that way, too, and we hit just the right angle for the spear to slide out of its neck.

I watched it despair as it fell back into the water.

The green hue of its blood spread around the boat, making the already murky water impossible to see through. I reached up to grab my throbbing shoulder, but Calix was already there.

"Asteria, look at me!" he shouted, panic lacing his voice, and I realized he must have been calling me. I shook my head, trying to bring myself back into focus. His hand was over the wound, putting pressure on it, but the pain lessened—absurdly quickly. My eyes narrowed as I lifted Calix's hand and looked at where jagged teeth had sunk in.

Blood stained my shoulder and Calix's hand, but the holes in my skin were completely gone already. Fae healing was a Tartarus of a thing. I had only experienced it once, but I'd been so close to dying then that I couldn't really appreciate it.

"I'm okay." I panted, my shock fading as my body relaxed. Calix's forehead hit mine, his own breath harsh in my ears. "Sorry I scared you."

He pressed a kiss to my forehead before leaning back to meet my eyes. "Let's not do that again."

I laughed hoarsely, nodding in agreement. We were still not quite at the other side of the river, however, and while I'd injured that beast, it wasn't dead. I certainly didn't want to see it any angrier than it'd already been.

"That thing is going to be pissed, so we should probably get moving again before it comes back," I suggested. Calix seemed torn, his fingers running softly over my shoulder, but his eyes cut over to the bank of the river. I smiled softly, it was cute that he was still worried about me, but decidedly unnecessary.

"Come on, I want off this river," I told him firmly, and Calix sighed, nodding reluctantly. He began to steer us once more, navigating the maze as he looked back and forth, seeing patterns in the flames I couldn't discern myself. But it was working, and I thanked the gods something was going right.

I kept watch on the water, the spear back in my hand as I waited. Hopefully, it was off, licking its wound and leaving us in peace. When I started to see movement in the water again, I braced myself, sitting low with my spear up. The anticipation was killing me. The slow movement, the lapping of the water against the boat, my knuckles creaking as I tightened my grip…

It surged up from the river, its teeth bared and eyes slit as it stared me down. I watched it carefully, and shifted subtly to the left so I could move quickly out of the way as it made to bite, and threw myself in that direction fully as I brought the spear forward and thrust upward, piercing its midsection. It screamed shrilly, the flared frills on its head waving back and forth. But as it flailed upward, I followed its movement with the spear, cutting through the thinner skin of its underside and opening it up from mid-body to its jaw.

It squirmed around the spear, shrieking and yelling, but as the spear finished its arc, the snake-monster's mouth split in two as I pulled it free. I watched with satisfaction as the thing fell, finally dead. It's foul body half draped on the side of the small boat.

I hadn't even realized we were near the other side of the river, but we came to a sudden stop at the bank. I panted, looking at Calix, who was smiling proudly at me. I laughed incredulously, throwing the green-tinted spear down and reaching over to hug him. He dragged me over, away from the disgusting monster, and into his arms. I hung from his neck, burying my face in his shoulder as my adrenaline waned.

When we pulled back, I looked around to get my bearings, and saw there was only a long, rocky path leading downhill from where the Styx flowed.

"I suppose this leads to the next test?" I asked, hoping to get the Tartarus away from this river.

"I suppose this leads to the next test?" I asked, hoping to get the Tartarus away from this river.

"I suppose so," Calix said carefully, looking me over.

"Great." I clapped my hands, getting out of the boat and waiting for Calix to disembark. I set off down the hill, Calix following behind. I could feel his eyes on me, but I didn't want to discuss anything that had happened during this last test, from my panic over my memories to getting sliced by a crazy monster, I just wanted to move on.

He seemed to understand, and thankfully, he stayed quiet. There was something to be said for this mate business.

I came to an abrupt halt as we walked around a bend in the path. A wall of pure darkness loomed ahead. It looked like Calix's shadows, only it was so high and deep I couldn't see anything around it.

"What in the Otherworld?" I sighed, looking to Calix with exasperation. I was so done with this.

He chuckled, walking up to the darkness. He lifted his hand, drifting it along the wall, feeling the magic emanating from it. "It's just shadows, like mine. This must be courtesy of Erebus. He's where my power comes from, and he's the one who made Tartarus."

"So it's safe to walk through then?" I asked, hopefully.

He nodded slowly, eyes scrutinizing the mass before us. "I think so, but I expect this must be our next little obstacle."

"Right. 'Face the darkness inside to reach the next portal.'" I nodded my understanding. "Maybe that's all it is? Facing the literal darkness you have in your shadows? That's a power inside you, after all."

My naive optimism was answered with a look from Calix that communicated quite clearly that we couldn't hope to be so lucky.

"We'll be okay," he assured me. "We've faced worse things. I have no doubt you'll face this with the same indignant rage you first met me with." He chuckled fondly, and I rolled my eyes at him, trying to smother my smile.

"Well." I tossed my hair dramatically. "I'm sure you'll face it with that same smug confidence."

It was his turn to roll his eyes, but he held out a hand for me, and I smiled as I laced our fingers together. We stood before the wall, and I took a deep breath. "Here's to no river monsters, this time," I said hopefully, before stepping inside. It was incredibly disorienting. I could feel Calix's hand in mine as we walked forward, but I couldn't see a damn thing. Not even my own body when I looked down. I tried to summon my starlight, but nothing happened, making me panic slightly.

Why weren't my powers working? I couldn't even tell if we were making progress as we walked; the darkness was so suffocating.

My panic gave way to pure anxiety. What if my powers never worked again? What if we were stuck here forever with no way out? What if—

No. Why was I worried about this? I knew this wouldn't be forever. My anxiety ebbed, and I took in a sharp breath of relief, but instead, my worries about everything else filtered back in. All my fear about Calix being torn from me, about failing the humans and the Fae counting on me, about having no fucking idea what I was doing…

Rage began to bubble in my chest.

How could everyone put so much damn pressure on me?! I'm one person! I was raised to nothing and suddenly handed a kingdom or two to deal with.

Fuck! I just wanted to get through this damn mass and make it to the other side. I wanted to get this whole trip over with and get back to Celesterra. I wanted to free the humans and send Cyrus straight to Tartarus to experience everlasting agony he'd never recover from.

The thought of facing him in battle brought joy to my heart. Getting to unleash on him all the pain he caused. I would burn him and his damn kingdom to ash. I would rip and claw away at everything he built, everything he *was*. I would bathe in his blood until he was a footnote in history, a lesson told in history books to warn others about the absolute destruction that would come for them if they tried to follow in his footsteps.

And then we could live our lives in peace.

I could experience life as a *queen*. Fill my days with experiencing every damn position Calix could think of with his hundreds of years of experience. I could finally experience a life full of every luxury I was denied before.

And maybe kill every woman in the kingdom who'd experienced *him* before while I was at it.

Just the thought of an eternity of dancing at balls, visiting the pool or Nova Falls for a swim with my friends, going shopping with the girls, or going out for a night in Tairngire… I wanted all of it.

I didn't want to worry about the fate of the world. Or even the rest of the population. *Human or Fae.* I just wanted to finally live *my* life. Absolutely *free.*

A life with my soulmate, where we'd never be torn apart. And I would be worshiped as the queen who—

No—no, this was all wrong.

Yes, I wanted to live my life. But I worried for every human stuck under the yoke of slavery. I worried for the Fae who stood beside us to fight for them. I didn't care about being worshipped like some goddess. I just wanted to help make things better.

Maybe there was a small part of me, deep inside, that didn't *hate* the idea. But I was just a person, one who'd been denied even basic considerations all their life.

Maybe the power I was so suddenly granted was going to my head. Or maybe… maybe this damn thing was taking every tiny little feeling inside us and amplifying it, I realized.

Face the darkness inside, Jemisha had said. Is this what she meant? It dragged up every bit of darkness inside of us and made us feel the full force of it.

Making us *accept* the darkness within us.

I was a person full of anxiety and rage. A selfish one. I had never realized that about myself, but maybe I should have. I'd spent so long cutting myself off from everyone to avoid the pain that I'd focused only on myself. Even after being rescued, I'd had to be shown the worst of it to change my focus from it being all about my own revenge to it being about everyone.

But there wasn't anything inherently wrong with *a bit* of selfishness, was there? Maybe it was even expected, *normal,* after being raised a slave. As long as I didn't lose myself in it.

Or try to kill all of Calix's past lovers out of fits of stupid jealousy. I'd always been a jealous person; I knew that. I'd been jealous of everything the Fae had, which maybe contributed to having a bit of selfishness now.

And as far as my rage went? I knew I couldn't let it turn me into a monster. I would be just as bad as Cyrus if I did. He'd once talked of how similar we were, and that sent chills down my spine just thinking about it. We did have similarities, yes. But so did Calix and I, and he wasn't evil.

I couldn't let myself give in to the rage fully. I had to pull myself back and focus on the goal. On stopping him and freeing the humans. Saving the balance. Giving into my own pain and hate for Cyrus would only lead me to make the same mistakes he did.

As for my anxiety and my fears, I could only accept that I may not ever push them away entirely. They were a part of me after so many years spent worrying about everything. But like Jemisha had said, I could still rise above it.

I could live despite my fears.

I could push past them and pursue happiness, whether I feared it or not. Whether I trusted it or not. I could one day live a life of light and joy, despite all the darkness inside my soul. I may have a bit of a monster inside of me. One that wanted to burn down the corrupt leaders of Celesterra and start again. One who wanted revenge for all the pain they caused. But I could live with that monster as long as it was leashed properly. I would use that monster in me to do what needed to be done, and do it well.

Suddenly, my vision was assaulted with light.

I blinked against the brightness, realizing it wasn't actually all that bright. It was still the same dank grey as the rest of Tartarus. But compared to pure darkness, it might as well have been Elysium.

"*Fuck*," Calix rasped, and I realized he was trembling.

"Did you face all your own worst qualities too?" I asked quietly, and he nodded raggedly.

"Face the darkness inside." He snorted, running a hand through his long silvery-white hair. "I didn't expect to be assaulted with every damn bit of darkness inside myself quite so literally."

I knew he'd lived a much longer life than me. And in that time, he'd done a number of things he wasn't proud of. Including killing a great number of Fae to free humans. As he sat himself down and put his elbows to his knees, burying his face in his hands, I found myself rushing over to him.

Even as the darkness I'd faced inside my own soul still lingered in my mind, my priority was Calix.

"I think I much prefer your own brand of darkness, my dorchadas," I joked quietly, making him snort what was almost a laugh.

"Yeah, me too." His quiet response made me worry more. He seemed weighed down with the weight of his soul, and I hated it.

"You know, those things the darkness made us face, they don't define us." I began. "It took little pieces of things inside me and made them feel so much bigger and stronger. Things I would never truly think suddenly seemed like the most obvious ideas in the world."

"I've already warned you I'm a monster, but I guess having to really feel it, just drove home how fucking unworthy I am of you," he admitted, looking up with shining eyes full of color.

"You *aren't*," I insisted. "That wasn't real, Calix."

"It was," he argued, shaking his head. "In every way that matters, it was. I had to feel every damn monstrous emotion that lives inside me. And I had to face that those things are all a part of me. I don't know why you would want to be with me after that. You deserve someone who's not bogged down by all the things I've done."

"Fuck that," I hissed, making his head rear back slightly. "I don't give a shit what you've done. You think I'm not capable of the same? You're my soulmate for a reason, Calix. We're both capable of being jealous, selfish, rage-filled monsters."

He blinked in surprise, and his tense form softened slightly as he realized he wasn't the only one with that darkness inside them.

"We're the same inside, my dorchadas," I whispered tenderly, lifting a hand to his cheek. I brushed my thumb along the sharp cheekbone before leaning in to kiss him.

He fell into my kiss and was quick to grab my hair in a harsh grip and pull me even deeper into him. I somehow ended up on his lap, his hands buried in my hair as we battled for dominance.

Two monsters in love.

Chapter 47

IT took us much too long to pull ourselves away from each other's mouths and get up to keep moving. It was only the knowledge that we were literally in Tartarus and not exactly in the best place to have sex that enabled me to shake myself from the haze of lust Calix managed to bespell me into near constantly.

Having sex in Tartarus wasn't exactly the most romantic of locations. Though it did sound *interesting…*

I shook myself. We had a job to do. And that was probably super disrespectful or something, right? We did have to meet the actual gods at the end of this.

And fuck, I hadn't allowed myself to consider that at all yet.

What would it be like to meet a *god*?

I was frankly terrified, but I didn't allow myself to dwell on that. It was too surreal a concept, despite the fact we were walking toward it.

Calix seemed to be in better spirits, at least. He hadn't let go of me since I'd assured him, I was just as monstrous as he was, just with less opportunity to showcase it. But the darkness had shown me exactly the kind of monster that lived beneath my skin. One that wanted to rip Cyrus to shreds along with anyone who helped him.

Maybe I could even use my teeth.

The thought brought a sick thrill of pleasure, and I pushed that right back down into the depths of the darkness within me.

I had a feeling that was going to be a lot harder now. Facing your demons made it much more difficult to hide them away.

I'd made a practice of pushing things I didn't want to think of away, but once you've invited them in…

At least I could distract myself with Calix. His arm was wrapped around my waist as we walked to the next portal. It was looming straight ahead of us now. We just needed to go through to Elysium once more before finding the next portal to a different section of Tartarus, and then the city of the gods awaited through the final portal.

After all this, I would be happy to never see another portal again for as long as I live.

I would be doubly happy not to have to visit the Otherworld again until I was actually taking up residence.

Stepping through the portal to Elysium, I blinked against the much brighter light. Unlike before, when we emerged onto a grassy hill, we were standing within a sparkling cave. I blinked once again, unsure if I was seeing what I thought I was.

But yes, I was. The entire cave was made out of diamonds. They shimmered with the light coming in from the cave's opening. We stepped out into that light and found a pavilion of sorts awaiting just beyond. We trudged forward, entering to find the place full of people.

We both paused, looking at one another before a voice rang out.

"Asteria Earendel."

"Calix Erebus." Another voice called.

"We welcome you both." The first voice said, and two figures stepped forward.

One was a man with blonde hair and blue eyes. Similar to Titan, only his hair was at his shoulders, or Aelius, except his face was much kinder. He wore a golden robe that looked ceremonial, with elaborate white embroidery depicting the sun.

The other man had white hair, deep purple eyes, and the same sharp bone structure I was so used to seeing on Calix. His black robe sparkled with silver embroidery depicting the moon.

"Thank you, ancestor," Calix responded, bowing his head. I quickly followed suit, bowing my own, unsure of the proper procedure here.

How does one greet the ancestors of the family they barely know to begin with?

"I am Raka Erebus. The founder of House Erebus." Calix's ancestor introduced himself. "It's an honor to meet you, Calix. This is, of course, very unusual. We don't usually meet new members of our house until their deaths." The man chuckled warmly.

"And I am Aarush Earendel." The blond man smiled at me, and it was strangely comfortable, reminiscent of the feeling I got curling up with a book and a cozy blanket. "I am the founder of House Earendel. And I must apologize to you on behalf of our house for the pain your father has caused."

"That's not your fault," I argued, shaking my head and making my dark hair fall over my shoulder. I moved to push it back and paused, before shaking my head. The contrast of this light on my dark hair was causing strange effects.

"Perhaps not, but unlike Raka's house, ours has lost its way. It's gone on far too long. Starting with Arev, and what he did to Arki, or Titan as you know him." Aarush said, sympathetically, golden brows creasing.

"Wait, Titan's not his name?" I asked, confused.

"It's his middle name," Calix answered, grimly. "Arki died when his mate did, and Titan is who was left in the aftermath."

"And the tradition of running valuable members of our house out started then." Aarush frowned deeply. "Your father is only too keen to continue it now. His actions cast a pall on all of us. I am sorry you have been the one to bear the burden of it, however."

"Thank you," I answered softly. A little overwhelmed, if I was honest. This was the man who had built the house I was born to. Whose last name I now bore. And his simple apology after everything hit me harder than I expected.

"We hope that under your guidance, House Earendel will rise once more." He smiled gently, bowing his head to me.

"Oh. I…" I trailed off, looking to Calix for help. He squeezed my hand with a smile.

"You'll do amazing," he assured, eyes not leaving mine. "You were born for this."

"And how do we lead two separate houses?" I asked softly, worries rising once more as I turned to our ancestors.

"You find your own way forward," Raka spoke, looking to Aarush with a sly smile. "Things are changing now. And our houses are more entwined than you might think."

"You will find out the truth of it soon enough. Just never forget, while the past is already written, the future is awaiting you to put words to page.

Your history will be based upon the actions you take now." Aarush grabbed my hands, his sky-blue eyes boring deep into mine.

"It is up to you to decide how your story goes, Asteria. No one else. Don't look to the past for what has always been done; look to the future and ask what *can* be," he continued, and I felt the weight of his words in my soul.

"All of us with your blood, we will always be with you," Raka said, looking at Calix. "Your path has always been one of change. The prophecies spoke of it long before this moment came. History is now in your hands. The bond, and more importantly, the *love* between you two. will be the foundation of what comes next."

I looked at Calix, the words unspoken lying heavy between us, but his nod of understanding was like a balm to my heart.

I didn't want him to doubt things between us just because of my own pathetic fears. Like speaking the words would bring my worst fears to life. But if they were right, that love that beat within our mated souls was what would build our lives, not destroy it.

It was a novel concept, honestly.

"Thank you, Raka," Calix rumbled, the emotion in his words clear.

"Of course, son of Erebus." Raka smiled slowly, raising his black-cloaked arm dramatically as he indicated the path ahead. "Now, it is time for you both to meet the most ancient of your ancestors."

I drew in a sharp breath, steadying myself. *Gods, how does one greet the gods?* By the Otherworld, the thought was enough to make my head spin.

"Good luck, daughter of Earendel," Aarush added, his smile gentle and kind. So different from the father who currently ruled our house… though, I suppose I also ruled our house now.

Fuck, what a mess.

"You make us all proud. Embrace who you are, Réiltín, for you will never steer yourself wrong," he continued. "Trust in yourself and your love, and you will conquer any darkness that comes."

"Thank you, Aarush," I responded, trying to contain my own emotions.

Aarush took my hand, while Raka placed his hand on Calix's shoulder. The others formed a path, my ancestors on one side and Calix's on the other. The men raised their swords to form an arch, while the women lifted their hands to let shadows and sunlight rise and complete the arch. Aarush and Raka led us through them, a tunnel of light and darkness, filled with those who'd come before us.

They'd paved the path we walked, but it was now up to us to build upon it.

Aarush and Raka led us gently through the procession until we reached the other side, where a dark portal to Tartarus awaited. Now, we would only need to enter and find the portal to the city of the gods. The tests were done; all we had to do was learn… *something*. Jemisha had been cryptic on what we were supposed to learn at our next stop, but I was curious to see what the gods thought so important.

We'd come this far, facing every challenge they threw at us. And while I wished I could have words with the gods about the method of getting us there, I was fairly sure I would chicken out the moment I saw them.

I considered myself a strong person, but something about complaining to the gods themselves just seemed like a *really* bad idea.

"This is where we leave you," Aarush said with a twinkle in his eyes.

"Though we will never *truly* leave you," Raka added with an impish smile.

"*We are all with you, always,*" Aarush and Raka spoke as one, and all those we just walked past seemed to echo it, making the words rattle deep into my soul.

With that, they stepped back, and Calix and I clasped our hands tightly together and stepped through the portal. Coming out the other side, we were before what appeared to be a crumbling castle. Maybe Arawn once took up residence here?

Or maybe it was another spot to play their torture games.

I shuddered at the thought. The castle was certainly creepy, made of old rocks that had deteriorated and crumbled. Chunks of the building were missing, leaving the interior exposed. Some walls were covered in what I would have assumed was moss or ivy if we were in our realm, but this was red as blood. It crawled up the walls and hung from others.

"Please tell me we don't have to actually go in there," I groaned, turning my head to aim a pout at Calix.

His eyes zeroed in on my lips as he chuckled hoarsely. "Something tells me that's exactly what we're supposed to do, my réalta."

He leaned in to nip my lip, making me squeal as I wound my arms around his neck, trapping him against me. His laugh rumbled through my entire body, making me smile against his lips. His tongue came out and traced over one of my sharp canines. I shivered with pleasure despite knowing this was not the time or place for it.

I couldn't bring myself to stop him. Instead, I let him play until my canines lengthened into full fangs. I took the opportunity to dive into his neck, raking them gently across the fragile skin there. I didn't even break it, despite my heady desire to sink my fangs into him.

I moaned against him, and his hands clutched at my hips tightly until I felt the press of his claws. I pulled back to look at him, the Aurora dancing in his eyes and the sharp fangs that had extended, telling me all I needed to know.

Our mouths crashed together, and I tried my best to climb him like a tree until my legs were wrapped around him, just as my arms were.

"That Nox-damned sexy pout," Calix growled, leaning in to press his fangs against my neck. Teasing me as he played with the skin but refused to pierce it. "Do you have any idea the things you do to me?"

I whimpered, pressing my body more firmly against his and grinding my hips down, hoping to feel that huge cock I knew was just waiting for me.

Calix groaned, panting as he suddenly forced himself back, unwinding my limbs from around him and setting me down. "We can't. We have to continue on."

"Calix…" I whined, trying to pull him back.

"Bad girl." He smirked, slapping my ass and merely succeeding in making me want to throw myself back at him. "We'll continue this later, trust me," he growled.

I sighed loudly, cracking my neck back and forth as I glared at him. Or pouted, based on the way he watched my lips again, licking his own.

He shook himself, placing one of his large hands on my lower back and leading me toward the crumbling castle.

"I'll make it up to you, my réalta," he assured me, smirk still firmly in place as he walked us toward the entrance.

It was mostly intact, only a few stones missing from the doorway. The floor was black wood, like the Darkelm trees, but was cracked and rotting throughout. More of that red mossy ivy was spread across it—*Wait, that wasn't ivy.* I walked closer, my head tilted to the side as I kneeled down, running a hand across the wood. *Blood.* Old and dried, but blood all the same. And a lot of it. I swallowed hard as I stood up, winding my arm around Calix's to reassure myself.

It was hard to remember I had the power now to fight back. The little girl who grew up powerless was hard to forget.

We continued walking through the castle. It was by far the creepiest place I had ever been. The blood splatters continued, covering every place I looked. Like they'd decorated the castle with blood. It was smeared over old, ripped-up paintings. Puddled under an ancient blue velvet sofa that was falling apart, with the velvet pile worn away from the march of time, stuffing popping out of the seat where it seemed like a pair of claws had ripped through it, and the entire sofa tilted to one side thanks to the missing legs on one side.

A dusty coat hung off a rack, missing most of its sleeves now. It must have been grand and elaborate, once upon a time. Jewels dotted the collar, and burgundy damask silk panels were interwoven with black velvet. Yet now, it was faded and abandoned. Just like the rest of this castle.

What was this place? And what did the gods want us to learn here?

We came to a doorway leading into what must have been the ballroom, and we both paused. Just like the rest of this place, I could tell the room had to have been beautiful in its day. But now…

"It looks like a battle took place here," Calix murmured, holding me tightly as we looked around with wide eyes at the blood-drenched room. If I thought the rest of the castle had been bad, it was *nothing* compared to the red-streaked ballroom.

Several tables were overturned, and the chairs that once surrounded them were now broken and cracked, their pieces strewn across the floor. Pink tablecloths draped over the tables that had managed to stay upright.

As I stepped around an overturned table, I caught sight of a small piece of cloth that had been protected from discoloration. I realized then that the tablecloths hadn't been pink at all, but bright white. I winced, imagining how much blood must have spilled on them to turn them completely pink.

The long, velvet and silk drapes on the giant windows now hung in ragged clumps, and broken china littered the ground, crunching loudly with each step through the room. It truly did look like some kind of battle had broken out here. I couldn't imagine what had happened here. It was like a haunted remnant of a tragedy, preserved forever on this timeless plane.

The place certainly *felt* haunted. Like something evil had sunk into the stone and never left.

"I hate this place," I whispered under my breath to Calix. "It feels… *wrong*." I wasn't sure what the gods wanted us to see here, aside from knowing some sort of event had obviously occurred—something bad enough to drench the place in blood from top to bottom. But I was sure we would find out eventually.

"Luckily, I think we can get the Tartarus out of here," he answered, pointing to the stage I'd been too overwhelmed to notice.

Black curtains hung across it, and yet, a distinct glow was coming from the sliver exposed at the bottom. Calix jumped straight up onto the stage, and I took a moment to admire his form as he did so. His physicality never failed to impress me.

He ripped the curtains open, revealing the final portal. I sighed in relief, wanting nothing more than to leave this place as fast as possible. This portal was different from the others. It was still circular, but around the portal was a shimmering crystal ring. The portal itself was a mix of black and white, the two dancing together in a misty swirl. Like black and white ink bleeding into each other.

"Found it." Calix smiled triumphantly, leaning down to offer me a hand up.

I rolled my eyes but took his hand, jumping up onto the stage. It was still amazing to be able to do that, and I may have added a bit more bounce to it than necessary, but who could blame me?

Calix tried to hide his fond amusement, but I caught it, shaking my head at him. I moved toward the portal, and he joined me at my side. Our fingers slid together once more, not wanting to lose each other through the mists.

"What do you think they're like?" I asked in a whisper, as if they might hear me through the portal, should I speak too loudly.

"I hope…" Calix trailed off for a moment, looking deep in thought as his brows furrowed. "Benevolent. That is how I've always imagined them, at least."

"I can't even begin to imagine," I confessed. "I spent so long with only this false idea of the Old Gods. Even knowing the truth of the real gods, I'm a little lost when it comes to how to reconcile it all still."

I felt a bit like a failure in that regard.

"Asteria, you expect too much of yourself," Calix said sadly, shaking his head. "Most humans take years to adjust to that truth. You've had a matter of months."

"But I'm *Fae*—" I began to argue, only for him to cut me off quickly.

"That doesn't matter," he told me fiercely, his hands circling my upper arms as he leaned his face toward mine. "You cannot expect to magically realign your entire worldview so quickly. *You* may be magic, but that doesn't change the years you spent living and believing a certain way. You need to give yourself some grace."

"I don't know how," I whispered, feeling exposed. But it was just Calix, and I had no reason to hide from him. He was the one person I shouldn't be hiding from.

"That's why you have me." His voice softened, his eyes lighting up with color. "I'll be here every time you need a reminder."

I wrapped my arms around his waist, leaning my head against his firm chest as I hugged him tightly. He pet his hand down my hair, whispering soothing reassurances as I slowly relaxed into his hold.

"Whatever the gods are like, we'll face it together. Just like we will face everything that comes next. There may be a lot of changes still to come, but you and I will stand shoulder to shoulder and use each other to hold the other up when we need to. Okay?" He pulled back to grip my face, nodding once.

I nodded softly back, my heart lighting up with adoration for this man. This Fae who could wield death like an extension of himself, who could kill so brutally one moment and speak so softly the next. The contradiction of him was one of my favorite things in this world.

"Okay." I nodded, determined now. "Let's go." I smiled brightly, making him chuckle. He pressed a quick kiss on my lips, gone too soon, before he pulled back.

With fingers locked, his wings unfurled, prepared for whatever may come on the other side. I took in the black and purple scales, the night skies made flesh, and let my own out. Every time I did, it sent a thrill through me. Having wings was everything I'd ever wanted. I glanced back at them, the shimmering silver tipped with purple, matching so well next to his, like a night full of stars.

As shadows began to wreathe around his fingers, I let my starlight out to play with them. The two wrapped around our hands like the cords used to tie two hearts together, as we breathed in, completely in sync.

And stepped through to the greatest of unknowns.

CHAPTER 48

A LICKED my lips, excitement overcoming me as we marched forward. We were *so* close now.

Lightning sparked around my fingertips, surprising me. I flexed my fingers one by one, focusing on pushing my magic down.

More and more, it reacted without thought. As if I was a child once more, learning how to manage my emotions and my magic. My subjects couldn't see the struggle it had become. They needed to see me as faultless. Someone in perfect control.

In a way not even my father managed.

Leaving my kingdom for the first time since taking the crown also left me feeling a bit anxious. The rebellions stirring left much to be desired, and my plotting siblings needed to be controlled. Vissy needed to be watched as well.

So many things to do.

I'd set my spies to task, and Emmie was surprisingly proving her worth beyond a warm cunt. Her gossipy nature meant plenty of rumors reached my ears, whispered in them while she lay fucked out on my mattress. At least on the nights Zerlina wasn't there. Though, I preferred Zerlina of the two. At least when she was on her knees, I could see her darker hair and pretend she was the one I truly wanted.

Once I brought Asteria to heel, I would have no need for either of them, really. She would fulfill my needs; she'd more than proven that. The memory of her throat taking my cock all the way down still fueled many of my orgasms while in bed with the others. As did the memory of the night she all but rode my cock in the brothel.

Those memories kept me going. Kept me *furious.*

Knowing what she ran from... she would be punished extensively. Starting with making her watch Zerlina wear the crown once I'd ripped the one Asteria now wore off her head.

The news had come not long before we'd left, and it only proved how needed this was. Asteria needed to be shown where she belonged. *And it wasn't on a throne.*

This next move would cement all of my plans.

I finally spied our target in the distance. We'd crossed into Sunrise and marched across it toward the Damaculous Ocean. But the ocean wasn't our goal. *No.* My goal became clear as we approached.

The vineyard stretched out before my eyes.

The tiny village surrounded it, resting in the shadow of the mountain. *Sonmathion.*

It was here she'd grown up. Here she'd lived with her parents in what I could see now was a run-down hut. That's all there really was here. There was the vineyard, of course. A small lake I could just make out. And a bunch of rickety huts.

This? This is where she came from? And she dared to turn down everything I offered her? Luxuries the people of this village couldn't even *dream* of.

My lightning sparked again, and I ground my teeth. I pulled up the chain around my neck until the vial attached to it came free of my nickel-plated armor. I unscrewed the top and swirled the sparkling red mixture before I shot it back quickly. As soon as the blood magic was down my throat, I could feel the control over my magic coming back to me.

I'd have to keep up a steady supply to ensure this didn't keep happening.

Meaning I needed more humans.

Luckily, I had a whole village full of them *right here.*

I smirked, looking at my commander. I gave him the nod, and he raised the signal. In a wave, soldiers surged forward. They crested over the small village like a wave, and they would wipe it out just the same.

The sound of screaming humans as they were rounded up was like music to my ears. The flames were already beginning to catch as the men set fire to their pathetic huts. I would not leave until this entire village was ash.

The vineyard fields caught fire next, and I watched with amusement as humans surged out of the fields in a panic, right into our hands. Their loose cotton and linen clothing did little to protect them from the flames. The edges of dresses were singed and roughly put out with frantic hands. While the bottom of the men's pant legs caught here and there.

The pandemonium was wonderful. The screams and cries, paired with the cracking and burning, were a beautiful symphony. I stood in the middle of the chaos, arms out, as I laughed in triumph.

I grabbed a torch out of a passing soldier's hand, nodding at him to continue on. I brought the torch to the little schoolhouse, watching in pleasure as the flame caught, the wood beginning to smoke before the flames rose higher, until they engulfed the building entirely. The joy I felt as it went up in flames was a kind I hadn't felt in far too long.

But I had to reel myself in. This wasn't about the satisfaction I got from the village's destruction.

It was about getting what I wanted and getting them *where* I wanted them.

"My King." I turned to find my commander, who was standing grimly, gruffly serious as always. "We found them. They're barricaded in their... *house.*" He sneered with distaste over the word.

To be fair, these things hardly qualified as houses.

An unfamiliar ecstasy rang through me. My plan hinged on this moment, and it was all coming together.

"Show me," I smirked gleefully, unable to contain it.

He led me through the burning village, where humans were already on their knees in chains. We came to a small hut they'd spared the fire—for good reason.

I lifted my leg and kicked the door, meeting resistance as expected. I let my hands light up with crackling blue bolts, and they arced right into the door, splintering it into a thousand pieces.

A high-pitched, womanly screech punctured my eardrums as I ducked into the hut. A man with honey-colored hair stood in front of a woman with voluminous brown curls. Their ratty clothing was tattered and stained, but the man showed far too much pride despite his appearance. He held a candlestick up like a knife, making me raise a brow.

I stepped closer, and while the woman shied away, he tried to feign like he wasn't intimidated. But I could see the fear in those brown eyes clear as day.

How anyone ever thought these two were Asteria's birth parents was a mystery to me. Sure, the woman had dark hair, but Asteria's was darker than hers, and the woman's green eyes were nothing like Asteria's blue. The man looked even less like her.

As I stepped within reaching distance, I aimed to do just that when the man whipped the candlestick toward me. I laughed, knowing his hit would feel like nothing but air to me. Humans were so weak, after all.

Instead, I let out a bellowing scream as the candlestick hit my cheek. My flesh sizzled, burning like a brand across the delicate skin.

"*Iron*," I growled, canines lengthening as the man yelled and moved to hit me again. I grabbed his arm, sneering at his pathetic display as I squeezed my fingers tighter and tighter, until the man was forced to let go with a sharp cry of pain.

"Jovin!" The woman cried out, stepping toward her husband, who was cringing from the pain shooting through his arm. He lifted his other, motioning her away.

"Stay back, Mya!" He forced out through clenched teeth.

"How sweet," I mocked, tilting my head to the side as I put on a show of sarcastic sympathy. "But you do know attacking a Fae like that…" I tsked with my tongue. "That's a *guaranteed* death sentence."

The woman's whimper as she backed up against the wall was opposed by her husband, who set his jaw and lifted his head in defiance that looked so familiar, despite not a drop of blood between them. Between this human's audacity and the reminder…

I wanted to strike him down where he stood. My lighting was my preferred weapon of choice to do it too. But I took a deep breath, reminding myself of the plan.

I needed them alive.

For now.

"Kill me then." The man, Jovin, apparently, shrugged. "You're going to kill us all anyway. No Fae rounds up a bunch of humans to take us on a picnic."

I scoffed a laugh, shaking my head. Asteria thought her parents were nothing like her in this regard. But I could see she got more than she thought from the man who raised her.

"So you think it smart to antagonize me?" I asked, raising a brow pointedly.

He scoffed, shaking his head. "We've been hearing the rumors of what you do. We also heard…"

I furrowed my brows, his eyes meeting mine with a fire that I didn't expect from a human. Asteria had always been the exception.

"Where is my daughter?" he asked firmly, lip twitching.

My brows flew skyward as my head reared back. Someone had indeed been gossiping if those rumors had made it all the way up here. The woman, Mya, managed to find her spine as she stood angrily.

"Where is my baby girl?" she demanded, her husband grabbing her and pulling her back as she tried to stomp forward. "What did you do to her?!"

I laughed, unable to help myself. I gave them a dramatic pout. "Well, that's just the thing, isn't it? She isn't *your* baby girl."

They both looked truly confused. Meaning that knowledge hadn't made its way along with the rest. I couldn't wait to find out what they did and didn't know, and we'd have plenty of time for that.

"You mean you don't know?" I gasped, pressing a hand to my chest, as I stalked toward them.

Jovin pressed Mya further behind him, raising his chin as I neared them.

"She's Princess Asteria Earendel. The long-lost Fae daughter and heir of the Day Kingdom," I told them, watching their jaws drop, and eyes widen with shock, confusion, disbelief, and anger. It was truly a delightful cocktail. "You two were just the patsies the queen found to raise her daughter for her."

"No," Mya whispered, shaking her head in denial. "No, I birthed her myself."

"All part of the spell, warping your memories." I waved my hand dismissively. "You got her days after her birth, and the spell ensured you remembered her as yours. Helped to sell the whole thing."

"She's not Fae," Jovin argued, shaking his head with confusion lining his brow. "She has round ears. She doesn't have magic."

"She does now." I smiled grimly. "I saw the spell on her break myself. Right before she ran off like the devious little whore she is." I growled, my anger at the memory getting the best of me.

"And no wonder she did," Mya mumbled, my head instantly snapping to her. I opened my mouth, a snarl forming on my lips when Jovin butted in.

"I've never been prouder," he proclaimed. "Birth daughter or not, we raised Asteria. She's *ours*. And what I've heard of you." He looked me up and down like he, a pathetic human, had any right to judge a Fae—let alone a *king.* This was exactly why the humans needed reminding of their place. "She managed to escape a fate probably worse than death. *That's my girl.*"

I clenched my fists, teeth grinding as my nails bit into the skin of my palms, trying to contain my fury so I didn't kill these two by accident. That would ruin everything. I just had to remind myself that it would be worth the wait to kill them.

"Well, then you'll be happy to know I plan to reunite you with your *precious* daughter." I spat bitterly. This insipid human was somehow capable of being proud of a daughter that wasn't even his blood.

What was so wrong with me that my own father could never summon even a bit of that for me?

"Put these two in chains!" I called out to my men with a forced smile on my face. "Put them aside from the rest. They'll be my *special guests.*" I purred, leaning toward Mya, who shied away from me. Jovin's protective glare as he tried to hang on to his wife was worth it.

"At least until their daughter comes to collect them." I smiled more truly at that thought. I couldn't wait to see her reaction. It would be magnificent, I was sure.

"No!" Jovin shouted, trying to force away the men beginning to chain his wife. They grabbed him by the arms, pulling him away and forcing him down to the ground. His ineffectual struggles paired with the weeping of his wife. Once the chains were secured, my men lifted them and marched them out of the ramshackle hut they called home.

They tried to reach for one another, getting a hit across each of their faces for their trouble.

"Careful with those two," I called. "You can bruise, but don't injure them beyond that. I need them both in good condition."

"Yes, my King." They bowed their heads, marching the couple off to the side where the other humans waited.

"Now, what to do with all these?" I waved a hand at the other humans of the village, all chained on their knees before me.

"I do need humans for our work, but…" I trailed off, making a show of tapping my index finger against my chin. "We also need to make a statement."

Unlike Jovin, who was fueled by rumors of his daughter, these humans seemed to be drained of all fight. It was almost disappointing. They sat there meekly, not reacting in the slightest. Just as I'd expected.

Asteria had inadvertently advised that they were all complacent here. *Like so many humans had been before the rebellions began*, I thought darkly. My work had clearly ruffled their feathers, but it would all be worth it in the end. The hassle of containing a few measly human rebellions would be nothing in the grand scheme of my rule.

History would look back at the king who shaped Celesterra into something new. Something better. People would *see* what I was truly capable of. Father might not be here to see it, but the rest of those who doubted or plotted against me would be forced to watch me rise far higher than their little minds could have ever imagined.

Today would be a piece of that story. Thus, a statement was necessary. To the humans, to Gravadain, and to any of those who'd read about my rule many millennia from now. It was all the same.

"Grab half of them to bring to the camps," I announced, smiling at the sight of the humans lifting their heads with hope that I was all too ready to dash. "Kill the other half."

Screams and cries rang out, as expected. I rolled my eyes. *Could these creatures never meet their fates with some class?*

I pulled my sword out of its sheath, turning to the nearest human and slicing off their head with one smooth swing. A sharp, shrill scream rang out, the woman next to him blubbering over his body. I sighed long sufferingly before I waved a hand, and the soldiers closed in.

I watched in satisfaction as half of them were forcibly carried out, while the others were lined up to be butchered. As one, my soldiers moved to execute their orders—and the humans. Blood sprayed, and heads rolled, their bodies collapsing onto the dirt. Where they belonged, frankly.

The chorus of dying people filled my ears, and I took it all in. The metallic taste of blood in the air, the crisp burnt smell from the sizzling remains of their huts, the clang of swords and armor, and…

The pounding of horse hooves?

I looked up sharply, seeing my men scattered around the village. With an unexpected force heading our way.

"We have company!" I yelled, getting my soldiers' attention over the clamor. It went quiet, except for the muffled whimpers of several humans, easily ignored. I could hear the sound getting louder. Definitely approaching horses, and not just a handful of them.

The men formed up around me right as the horses came into sight. The banner of Sunrise Kingdom waved in the air above the bronze-plated soldiers on horseback.

We drew our swords, but the force began to slow as they neared us. I watched the men pull on the reins and bring their horses to a halt. One horse rode forward a bit, this one distinctive compared to the rest, by virtue of being the only Faethren horse among them. Its red mane and tail, yellow coat, and larger size stood out among the dark brown, black, and white coats of the smaller horses. As their mount came to a stop, the rider removed his helm, revealing King Gravadain beneath it. He made eye contact as he dismounted his horse, handing the reins off to one of his men before walking forward toward me. I moved to meet him halfway, stepping out of the group surrounding me.

I stopped a few feet away from Gravadain, eyeing him suspiciously. I was on his lands, killing his slaves, and burning his vineyard. He had every right to attack. But instead, he calmly walked toward me like we were here to discuss regular business.

"King Cyrus." He tilted his head slightly in acknowledgment.

"King Gravadain," I stated dryly, not returning the gesture. "I was disappointed to not get any response from you to my letters."

His brow rose, and his eyes wandered over the burnt village before returning back to me. "Clearly."

His voice sounded almost amused, making me clench my jaw in aggravation.

"Had you waited a couple of days, you would have received my response," he continued, voice almost chastising, in a way that had lightning buzzing around my fingers.

"Well, time is of the essence in a war," I countered, resting my hand on the pommel of my sheathed sword, cocking my hip as I stood facing him with all the arrogance he levied at me.

"So it is," he said pointedly, but cocked his head for a moment, looking me over. "Still, I am here to let you know that I will ally with you against Night Kingdom and…"

He looked over to Aelius, sneering slightly with a roll of his eyes before adding haughtily, "Whatever parts of Day Kingdom follow the girl."

"Day Kingdom stands with me and with their king," I responded icily. "Whatever rebels follow Asteria will be dealt with."

Gravadain looked amused, raising a brow with a growing smirk. "Is that so? Have you not heard the news then?"

"What news?" Aelius demanded, walking forward furiously. His golden armor clanging with every step. *Fuck. Please don't be what I think this is.*

"That Asteria has been crowned queen of Day Kingdom," he informed us, his smirk still firmly in place at the opportunity to drop such a thing on us.

"What?!" Aelius demanded, practically shaking in rage. "I'm still fucking alive!"

I had hoped to keep the news from reaching Aelius. That was something better delivered at just the right time. But, of course, Gravadain just had to ruin that.

"He has a point," I added, my fist clenching hard around the pommel of my sword. Hoping to maintain the illusion that I didn't know about Asteria's crowning. My anger was at least real, except directed at the bastard ruining my plan instead. Too many things remained outside of my control still. A bright flash hit the ground between our two forces. Maybe I would have prayed for my lightning to be contained, if only I had gods to pray to who deserved it.

"I believe Aelius was named a traitor to his people, and the gods showed favor for the move, even. They blessed Asteria as queen. My spies have been all aflutter with the news," Gravadain said, his face returning to that blank slate I was sure he practiced in the damn mirror.

"You were able to get spies into Night?" I asked, surprised. My own spies hadn't ever been able to get access inside, and I found myself seething at the thought that others had managed it.

"No," Gravadain scoffed, with a slight shake of his head. "For all I dislike Calix for his actions, no one can claim the man doesn't run a tight ship." His side-eye at Aelius made it clear that he didn't believe the same was true for him, and my lip twitched.

He wasn't wrong.

As Aelius sputtered in protest, I cocked my head at Gravadain. "And you don't mind us taking your slaves? Burning down your village?"

"Of course, I mind." He glared at me sternly. "I did not side with Calix because he invaded my kingdom and killed my people."

Looking around, he clarified with a wave of his hand, "Fae, of course. Slaves are easily replaceable. Which is why I will forgive you this one oversight, and you will forgive my son at the end of this. A reasonable conclusion all around."

"Your son?" I asked, confused by the bargain he offered.

"Yes." He sighed heavily. "The foolish boy ran off with Calix and the girl when I wouldn't ally with them. A mistake, but he won't do much damage, truly. My army remains with me, as does my heir, so there will be no issue there."

"And you expect me to just forget he sided with my enemy?" My brows furrowed at the thought. Enemies needed to be dealt with appropriately. But… it wasn't as if I intended for any of these kings to actually survive this. It wouldn't hurt to push the lie further now, would it? Still, I couldn't seem weak, so I had to at least make the show of it.

"Yes, if you expect me to forgive this little intrusion and ally with you." Gravadain countered, and I locked my jaw, staring him down.

I didn't like him one bit. His arrogance and assumption were high, even for a royal. I would need to get rid of him sooner than the others. Maybe his heir would be more pliable. Dagur wasn't as experienced, which was a boon. Eyes like Gravadain's too easily saw through bullshit, and I needed to spin quite a lot of it to keep this operation running.

Until the time was right, at least. My eyes shot over to where Asteria's human parents were bound, ready for transport. That time was coming.

Soon.

CHAPTER 49

Asteria

THE mists of the portal surrounded me, becoming all I could see or feel for an infinite moment, expanded in time. White and black spun together like gossamer threads layered over top the other, becoming so thick there was no hope of seeing through them. But layer after layer began to be shed as we made our way through, until they disappeared entirely as we stepped through the portal. Entering the vast unknown for those who lived and breathed. *The City of the Gods.*

I looked up, my fingers tightening around Calix's, as I took in a sharp breath. I was unable to believe my eyes, sure they must be playing some trick on me.

This realm was… *unreal.*

The ground under my feet caught my attention right away. My feet shifted side to side, feeling it out. It was… fluffy? It reminded me of clouds, puffy and light, except that it was solid. There was even what I thought was grass. At least until I took a closer look.

"Are these…" I asked hesitantly, not able to voice the ridiculous thought.

"I think they might be diamonds," Calix answered, sounding just as bewildered. "Just, well, green. They don't look like emeralds."

"Green diamonds? What the fuck?" I mumbled, and he barked a laugh.

"There's no moon or sun, either," he murmured. My neck nearly cracked I looked up so quickly. I couldn't imagine living without the precious beasts that lit our world. But he was right. There was nothing up there—just a purple and blue sky, dark and light in parts, shifting in certain places between the two colors. No sun or moon hovered in the sky, giving the realm a strange cast.

419

I flinched as a dragon roared, and I looked up to the left where the sound came from, watching as a pink and green dragon swooped down and back up. It wasn't alone either, with a blue and orange dragon following behind, chasing after it merrily.

They flew directly over a palace in the distance, one that seemed to glow against the blue-purple sky. Half of it was light, and half was dark, just like the kings. Two enormous main towers in each hue dominated it, with smaller towers reaching no more than three-quarters of their height. The black and white met in a hazy line down the center of the palace, and I was sure it was playing tricks on my eyes as it seemed to move.

"I guess we're supposed to go there." I pointed to the palace, and Calix nodded slowly.

"Most likely. Seeing as there was no welcoming committee," he smirked when I managed a small but sincere laugh. This was too bizarre, but I was glad he was at least here to appreciate this strangeness with me.

There was a path just ahead that we quickly began down, following around the bends and turns. It had high walls as the landscape dipped and rose at strange angles. I couldn't make sense of its layout in my head, but the path looked to be the only way toward the palace. And with the other dragons in the sky, flying wasn't going to be necessarily safe either. This realm didn't seem to have the same brightly colored flora we'd seen in Elysium. Like the rest of the strange reality to this place, the flowers weren't even *really* flowers. Strange wisps instead grew from the ground, with twinkling breaths of light that shifted from there to gone in a split second. The little wisps would appear on the side of the path one moment and be missing the next, before it blinked back into being again. The trees I could make out in the distance weren't any more familiar. The shape, the colors, none of it was like anything I had ever seen. The gold and white swirled trunks and dripping black inky mass on top might not even qualify as a tree as I knew it.

We hadn't been walking down the path long before we stopped short. My mouth dropped open as we came upon a Pegasus lounging on one of the fluffy cloud-like spots of the ground. When it spotted us in return, it clambered to its legs, purple feathered wings flapping and its white coat gleaming.

And, most prominently, it had a *horn* on its head, coming straight out of its forehead at a slight slant—one that it seemed to be aiming straight at us for some reason.

"Do you see that?" I nudged Calix, voice hushed. "It looks like the Pegasus on Dusk's sigil, with the horn. Cyrus doesn't have that. Neither does Zerlina."

A shrill cry pierced the air, and we ducked in alarm as fire soared too close over our heads. The ball of fire landed before us, slowly extinguishing its flames. A red and black phoenix stood protectively in front of the Pegasus, blocking the creature with its own bulk as it squawked protectively.

"We're not here to harm," Calix said soothingly, holding up his hand not locked with mine. "We're here to see the gods."

That shrill squawk was its only response as its head tilted to the side, like it was examining us. But it didn't speak to us, didn't shift, didn't do anything. It didn't seem Fae at all, just pure animal.

"Calix, are they even shifters?" I asked in a whisper as I tugged on his hand. He shook his head slowly, his lilac eyes creasing in thought.

"Perhaps not," he responded, sounding vaguely befuddled. He looked around the landscape for a moment, but it was clear the only way to go was forward or back. The path lay in one direction, and I certainly didn't want us getting lost in the damn city of the gods.

Calix tugged on my hand after a moment, leading us to the far wall of the path so we could edge around the creatures and continue on our way. The phoenix stayed with us, blocking the Pegasus from sight as it rotated. Clearly, it was very protective of the other animal. Strangely so.

"The Pegasus were said to once have horns," Calix told me as soon as we were out of sight of them. "The rumor was they lost them through the years." He paused for a moment, shaking his head, "That we all did, really."

"What do you mean? Lost what?" I shook my head in confusion.

He smiled sadly at me. "Our magic—pieces of it, at least. It all ties back to the balance. As we shifted more to chaos over the years, we lost bits of our magic. We still had plenty, but the pure abilities our ancestors first had were long gone."

"Huh," I murmured, thinking it over. "I don't feel like I'm missing anything. If that's true, I wonder what kind of abilities they had then that we could have had."

"Maybe we'll find out," Calix smirked mischievously at me, and I bumped my shoulder into his, or into his arm at least—I couldn't reach his shoulder dammit, laughing slightly as I shook my head at him.

The palace loomed before us as we neared the front entrance, and I startled, finding another creature now blocking our path. It appeared out of nowhere—unnervingly silent for something so large. It snorted, leaning forward in a slight crouch and stomping a grey cloven hoof on the green gem-strewn ground it stood upon. The diamond held strong, not bending to its heavy step. I swear, this place didn't make *any* sense.

"Minotaur," Calix whispered, his eyes wide with shock. I looked the beast over, and I could see the resemblance to Titan's form. The long horns and hooves, for sure. The creature also stood head and shoulders above a normal Fae, much like Titan did in his own Minotaur form. They looked a bit different, but then again, so did Calix and I in our own dragon forms.

"Why are you so shocked?" I whispered, baffled by his reaction. "Titan—"

Calix shook his head furiously, silvery-white hair flying. It brought my attention to it, and I realized his hair looked somehow brighter in this realm, despite there being no moon in the dark sky to illuminate it.

"Titan is the only Minotaur shifter in our realm. There's never been another documented. The creature was considered nothing but a myth once," he explained, eyes cutting to me before going straight back to the dangerous-looking beast snorting at us angrily.

"Titan wasn't born a Minotaur, but a dragon shifter. I had no idea until he told me the truth of his birth," he said, and I gasped in shock, my free hand coming up to cover my mouth.

"I didn't even think of that," I admitted. "I was too focused on the rest of it."

"Of course you were," Calix reassured me softly, squeezing my hand in support. "He told me my great-grandfather brought him to the Oracle for help after he reached Night. The gods apparently accepted his request for aid, and helped hide him by changing his form."

"Into a Minotaur. A previously thought mythological being," I stated, trying to wrap my mind around it.

"Minotaur's are guardians, *protectors*." Another voice said, and my neck actually cracked as my head spun too quickly to face whoever spoke.

"We knew Titan would be a great guardian and protector to you both, and thus, granted his request with an appropriate form."

Calix and I hit our knees at the same time, bowing our heads. Before us, two luminous beings stood. One emanating a glowing white light, and the other a pure black darkness that swallowed the light coming from the being next to him. The brief view I had of them was overwhelming. It was obvious they were something not of my world, *something greater,* with merely a glance.

"How does one address the kings of the gods?" I whispered to Calix, wishing I'd thought to ask earlier, but a bright laugh rang out around the space.

"No need for all of that right now." I couldn't see it, but I could swear the voice held a definite smile in it as it answered my question. "And no need for that any of that either. Please stand, both of you."

Calix's eyes met mine beneath the curtains of our hair, and I shrugged, unsure what else to do, before we slowly stood up. Cautious, wary... awed and mystified.

These were the godsdamned gods! The kings of them at that.

While they were taller than normal Fae, and more otherworldly for sure, they had the same pointed ears we did, and even fangs. Though theirs were significantly larger and more prominent. As if our fangs were the baby version of theirs.

"Welcome, daughter. Welcome, son." They intoned together, smiles on their faces.

"We know it has been quite the journey to arrive here, but we are so pleased to finally meet you both." The one lit up with white light said. "I am, of course, Earendel, your ancestor, Asteria."

"And I am Erebus. Your ancestor, Calix." The one emanating darkness added. His hair was long and black, but the tendrils moved like shadows, whereas Earendel's was long and white, with strands made of pure light. Both had hair that glowed with their power, just like the rest of them. The very essence of light and dark made into physical form.

"It's an honor to meet you both, Your Majesties." Calix bowed his head quickly to them.

"Yes," I added belatedly, mirroring him. "An honor. Majesties?"

Earendel looked amused, but another voice rang out before he could say or do anything. Thank... *them*. I couldn't remember ever being so discombobulated, and that was saying something.

"I know you two aren't starting without me." It was a woman's voice, and as she came into view, I had to stifle my gasp. She was emitting a silvery, starry light, just like my own power. As she came closer, I realized she was curvier and shorter than the two kings, though she still towered over me. She still had pointed ears and sharp fangs the other two sported, a common thread between us all.

"Of course not; we were merely welcoming them. They've come a long way." Erebus told her with a raised eyebrow that sent a bolt of amusement through me despite my nerves. His eyes were pitch black and incredibly eerie. Looking at them felt like falling into the depths of the universe, with no landing in sight. Earendel's weren't much more comforting, glowing with bright, white light that was somehow more intense than looking into the sun.

But this woman, and there was truly only one woman she could be, had silver eyes full of swirling stars to match her hair, which fell to her waist and glowed with starlight that bounced around as she walked.

Asteria.

My lips parted in shock. Even when I was human, despite being so resentful of the Fae gods, I'd always been so curious about the goddess I was named for. And now, here she was, standing right in front of me.

It was a good thing Calix was so strong; otherwise, I'd have surely broken his fingers by now with how hard I was squeezing them.

"Asteria." The goddess smiled serenely. "I have waited a great many years for you." Her voice was almost playful, but I still wasn't sure how to take that.

"Uh, sorry?" I winced, feeling supremely dumb in the presence of these ethereal beings. "It's—it's really great to meet you." The halting words felt so lacking, but what else was I supposed to say?

She laughed merrily, but when she sobered, she stepped forward until she was standing right in front of me. Was this what my eyes looked like to others when I was emotional, I wondered? If so, I could see why Calix had trouble looking away.

She swatted at Calix's arm playfully, making him release my hand. He hesitated, his full focus on watching Asteria's movement toward me. It was sweet—but even he would be unable to stop them if they wanted to hurt me. I was fairly sure they wouldn't, but the point remained. Our powers had been given to us by them, and I was positive using that power against them was the complete opposite of a good idea. Calix was smart, and he knew this well.

But his worry remained adorable.

Asteria grabbed both of my hands in hers, and I gasped at the feel of them. So Fae, and yet so different. They were smoother than mine, unblemished, and perfect in a way that was unnatural for anyone from our realm, like soft porcelain.

"We knew many years ago that the day would come when you would rise. These two over here," she nodded toward the two kings, "Foresaw that much. I knew that I would eventually find the soul I would choose to bless with my power. When I did, I was so excited. I couldn't wait for your parents to have you. Even if it took them *forever.*"

"It was a thousand years, not forever." Erebus corrected her with a small smile, as if this was a familiar argument between them. Asteria rolled her eyes, making me snort unexpectedly. She leaned in like Priscilla or Ilta might do to share a secret with me.

"We can find souls when they are crafted by the fates, but we can't always tell when they'll be birthed into physical form. You certainly took your time; just ask your mate." She winked at me, and I was startled into laughter.

"I think he'd definitely agree with that. But if I was born a thousand years ago, then he'd be the one making me wait, and that would just be unacceptable." I dared to joke back, and was rewarded with a bright peal of laughter that reminded me of shooting stars.

"Oh, I knew we'd get along just fabulously!" She beamed as bright as the starlight surrounding her. "Come, come! Let's go to the palace so we can explain everything. There's a lot to cover and not very much time."

"Why is that?" Calix asked, a tinge of alarm bleeding into his tone and stance. "Is something—"

"Calm, son," Erebus said soothingly, putting a hand on his shoulder and making Calix freeze up in astonishment. "Nothing so urgent you need to rush out. These things happen at the time they're meant to."

Well, that was ominous.

WALKING INTO THE palace, I couldn't keep my eyes off my surroundings. I suddenly felt like that small human girl walking into Dusk for the first time once again. All wide-eyed shock and disbelief.

"This palace belongs to Earendel and Erebus. It's where most of our work gets done, but each of us has our own palace within Tír na nÓg," Asteria informed me as she led us on.

"Tír na nÓg?" I asked, having never heard the word before. It certainly sounded like it could have come from the ancient Fae language, but there was something that sounded even older in it.

"Oh yes, that's the name of our land here. You didn't think it was just called the city of the gods, did you?" She smiled, making it clear she knew perfectly well we had no idea either way. The gods—*they* kept it all suitably mysterious.

"The Otherworld is more vast than you might think, as is this city. It's probably more apt to consider each of our domains within comparable to one of your kingdoms," she explained, silver eyes sparkling at me.

"I wish you could see mine," she added, sighing wistfully. "You'd love it. While this place is all darkness and light, mine is, of course, starlight. Much preferred, right?"

Looking between the gods, I felt like it was probably better not to agree either way.

"Ah, here we are!" Asteria said happily, as we reached the point where the two sides of the palace met. Darkness and light bled together at the edges, the two interweaving through one another. They reminded me of the same smoky wisps of inky mist from within the portals. This wasn't paint or stone or anything like that. This was something… *alive.*

The double doors Asteria led us to had a white and a black door, with a giant circular handle like a full moon that crossed each door. The white door's handle held the black half, while the black door contained the white side of the handle. Balanced perfectly.

Silver and gold runes glowed around the edges of the door, so similar to the front door of Tairngire's palace, while star opal surrounded the circular handle in small dots. It was stunning and served as quite the statement piece for the hall we stood in.

As the doors opened, we entered what appeared to be a grand meeting hall. Front and center were two staggering thrones set up on podiums. There was a black throne that looked like it was made of living shadows. They snaked every which way, as if they were reaching out for you, curling around the armrests and draping to the ground. Over the backrest, the shadows reached for the sky, coming to small points at the edge of each. Star opals were set into the top of each shadow, making them sparkle.

Next to it sat a white throne that had a subtle glow to it. It had rays of white light circling over the back of the chair, and it appeared as if light was shining from the armrests and lighting up the floor underneath them. Onyx gems were set into the rays of light, mirroring how the shadow throne had brighter gems. A more subtle nod toward their balanced nature as dual kings of the gods.

On either side of the kings' thrones, there were more podiums containing varied thrones that fanned out in a semi-circle beside them. Beyond the circle of thrones was seating for other beings in the rest of the hall. The seats faced the gods' thrones directly, and there were so many extending out that I couldn't see where they ended. They had an alternating black and white color pattern, upholstered in a fabric that seemed to be similar to silk, but with a softer hand.

I'd seen other people as we walked through the palace but hadn't given them much thought. Now though...

"Who are the people who live here?" I dared to ask. "I assume they aren't all gods?" There had to be others living here if this many seats existed, and there was a limited number of gods in the pantheon, even taking the gods of the other races into account.

"You'd be correct." Earendel nodded, giving me a slight smile. "Some choose to serve us. They assist us with various tasks and keep this place running smoothly."

"They give up rest in Elysium?" Calix asked, his brows lifting with surprise.

"Some," Erebus confirmed. "Those who wish to serve us instead. Others are working off their sins and hoping for redemption. Working for us is much better than facing Tartarus, after all."

"People can escape their punishment?" I all but mumbled, my heart seeming to freeze within my chest at the thought.

He could escape it.

"Not everyone," Earendel assured me, taking a seat on his throne, facing us with a regal air that most kings and princes would kill to possess.

"Some are too far gone. Too dangerous," Erebus agreed as he joined him, taking his own seat.

"And you are here to discuss one who is exactly that," Asteria added, sitting down in a sparkling silver throne that had a surprising touch of light and dark to it. Silver rays that mimicked the sun rose above the back of it, each coming to a point that was topped with a sparkling star. A splash of darkness for the stars to shine against rose behind the throne in a deep shadow. I suppose it only made sense, as both were so intrinsically linked to her. It was why both Day and Night included her in the Blessed Trinity's they prayed to.

"Yes, and that's why I asked you to join us here." A voice said, and I turned to the door, my eyes widening to see more gods streaming in to fill the other seats. "You took your time."

Arawn, God of the Dead and the Otherworld, stood before me once again. He had long brown hair, luminous pale skin, and bright red eyes. His fangs looked viciously long, and his hands were entirely bone. I flinched a bit at the sight, and the rest of his skin suddenly seemed to evaporate before my eyes, leaving a skeleton standing before me, red eyes glowing bright.

With a blink, he was whole again; only his hands remained bone, with no muscle or skin covering them.

"My apologies," I croaked out. "Though I appreciate you not taking me into the Otherworld yourself."

Arawn smirked very slightly, an approving look in his eyes. He gave me a regal nod before moving to sit on a throne made of blood and bone. It had been forged from pure white bones, with blood running in streams down them. But the blood never dripped off it, nor did it seem to bleed onto Arawn when he sat upon it.

The mysteries of the gods, I supposed.

"Asteria, fated Star Queen," Earendel said, once all the gods were seated, leaving Calix and I surrounded by them. "We have waited many years for this time to come."

The weight of every god's gaze on me was immense. I shifted from foot to foot, anxiety creeping up, until Calix put his hand on my lower back, supporting me, reminding me that he was here with me.

"Why?" I forced out, my brows creasing. I still didn't understand why I was so important.

"Chaos has been rising for many years," Asteria chimed in, her voice reminding me of the beauty of a night sky streaked with stars. "We managed to suppress it once before, with the pact signed by the six Fae kings."

I stood up straighter at that. I'd always wondered what had happened back then, when they signed the treaty to forge the kingdoms together, but since we learned of the prophecy in Sunset, I'd been even more ravenous for information.

"The kingdoms being constantly at one another's throats had caused chaos to rise faster and further than was safe, so we had the Oracle intervene on our behalf. We ensured the kings of that time understood what was happening," Erebus explained, sprawling back into his throne. "The prophecy foretold the destruction of the realms due to chaos, and they assumed it was about them. The vanity of men." He shook his head slowly, as though exasperated.

"So it wasn't about them?" A heavy feeling pressed down on my chest.

"No." He smiled slyly. "It was always about *you*. That ceasefire bought us time, but the truth is: it was never going to last." He finished, and I looked between the three gods directly before me.

"Why not?" I asked as evenly as I could manage, shaking my head in confusion. "And why me? Why now?"

"This is when the balance is the most critical, the closest we have come to falling into true chaos in a *very* long time," Earendel elucidated. "This is more than the kingdoms feuding; this is a targeted plot. One only you can see us through now. You see, many years ago, there was another member of our pantheon."

"What?" Calix exclaimed in shock. I turned to him and found his eyes wide and locked on the gods. Through the bond, it felt as if his whole world had been shaken with those words. Sympathy rose within me—*I knew the feeling all too well.*

"Yes," Erebus confirmed, nodding grimly. "Cruach. He was the god of blood, and he was the patron god of the Vampyre race."

"Wait—" I blurted, shock coursing through me. "Are you telling me that Vampyres were *real*? I thought they were a myth!"

I looked to Calix to gauge his reaction, and he looked back at me, shaking his head slowly. He didn't know they were real either, then. *What the fuck?*

"Yes, they were indeed," Earendel confirmed with a nod and a sad smile. "When we first began to create, we all were... *experimenting*, let's say."

"The Elves, Dryads, Pixies, and Vampyres were all created then. All with different aspects of our own selves added to them. Eventually, we ended up creating a race in an entirely different way. One that was exactly what we'd been trying for and failing to accomplish with the others," Erebus said in a heavy tone infused with regret.

"We had no problem with the other races continuing on despite perfecting what we were aiming for," Earendel continued, and I felt vaguely insulted on behalf of the other races. "But the Vampyres were out of control. Their bloodlust was a scourge on the realms."

"We were forced to banish them, for the safety of all. Cruach had grown just as bloodthirsty as his favorite creatures. He wanted to use the other races to continue feeding his Vampyres, making them the dominant race. And thus himself, the dominant god," Erebus sneered, contempt flowing out of him just as his darkness did.

"We were forced to lock him away," Asteria said, saddened but resolute. "Should he ever escape his prison, the realms would bleed, and chaos would reign forevermore."

Fuck.

And here I thought Cyrus was the problem. Now, there's a deranged and bloodthirsty god to deal with.

I felt a weird spike in the bond, and looked to Calix with a questioning look. His eyebrows were furrowed in thought, thoroughly distracted, so I grabbed his hand to bring his focus to me. His head turned to me, our eyes meeting, and the heavy look in his made my own brows crease.

"You're talking about the Fae, aren't you? The race you perfected. So if we have those same aspects you mentioned giving to the others…" Calix began, shifting his eyes to Erebus, but with a firm grip on my hand. "Does that mean the bloodlust…"

He trailed off, swallowing heavily as his eyes skittered away. The strangest feeling of… *shame*, ran through the bond.

"Ah." Erebus smiled knowingly. "You're worried your bloodlust in battle, and the *different* kind of bloodlust you feel in bed with your mate are part of this same corruption that took the Vampyres."

Knowing how Calix battled with this part of himself, I gripped his hand back hard for support as I realized what was bothering him. I wished I could soothe his mind myself. I knew without a doubt he was nothing like them.

"Do not fear, Calix," Asteria said soothingly. "While you may get parts of it from Cruach, as all Fae do in this way, it is not corrupted, not like it was in the Vampyres. In fact," she smirked, raising a brow, "The blood sharing between mates used to be a sacred act. It went out of favor after Cruach tried breaking free, as we were forced to starve him of his strength. But now, it is too important to hold off. The blood sharing between the two of you will strengthen the bond you share."

"Strengthen us?" I asked, extremely curious at that little fact. I remembered quite fondly the drive to drink his blood that had seemed so natural during sex. Even if it was utterly bizarre in the aftermath, I had never felt anything so *right* either.

"Yes," The goddess nodded in confirmation. "The two of you must share blood and complete the bond in this way to unlock your full potential."

"What does that mean?" Calix jumped in, the crease in his brow betraying his concern. "I've never heard of mates sharing blood to complete the bond. Most mated couples—"

"Are not you," Erebus interrupted. "You two *must* complete the bond. It will be *vital* for what is to come."

CHAPTER 50

"OKAY." Asteria drew the word out, and I could feel how unsure she was. I was still shocked to find out an entire god was erased from our history. And despite their words of reassurance, I struggled to see what made us truly different from the Vampyres.

I'd heard the stories about them, of course. Where they'd run through villages, destroying every creature in their path, leaving nothing behind but desiccated bodies drained entirely of blood.

What about my bloodlust was different? I'd worried since the moment I realized that my bloodlust during battle extended to drinking Asteria's blood, no matter how natural it felt in the moment. But I didn't doubt the gods—*could not*.

If mates were always supposed to share blood, and we'd just lost that knowledge along the way, then that explained a great deal of my draw to her veins.

I wanted to lose myself in her entirely, blood and magic, and most especially, body. I would take any and every part of her I could.

With whatever was to come, we'd need whatever extra strength sharing blood could give us. I wouldn't lose Asteria because of my own fears. I refused to let the monster inside of me hurt her, and I was determined to make sure she lived through this war if it was the last thing I did.

"It takes several blood-sharing sessions to cement the bonds between mates. You have one left to complete. You two must share blood when you return and cement the bond fully. Tie off the bow on the threads of fate that connect you. Then, and *only then*, can you go fight this war. But beware, our children. Should Cyrus win, chaos will reign—as will Cruach." Earendel said gravely, leaning forward on his throne as his eyes flared with light. "Every blood sacrifice Cyrus makes strengthens Cruach. It's given him an opportunity to escape that he should never have gotten. Should he get out of his prison, the balance will never recover. Nor will your world."

A dark chill went up my spine. Everything I'd been working toward was at risk. Should chaos reign, and this god escape, we'd lose everything, *forever.*

"Cyrus has been overtaken by chaos to such a degree, that he does not realize Cruach's manipulations," Erebus added, his gaze as dark as the rest of him. "Cruach has always been able to manipulate dreams, a gift he passed onto his creatures," he sneered in disdain. "Cyrus's delusions of grandeur are only hastened by Cruach's touch."

"His influence feeds Cyrus's own rage and lust for power," Asteria told us softly. "His own anger toward us is vast, if entirely misplaced. He has turned on us because his magic faded, which was a direct result of his own actions. Should the balance sway too far either way, the magic weakens in your realm. It was created in balance, and in that balance, it must continue. Or risk becoming something... *other.*"

"Cyrus believes we have caused the loss of his magic, but it couldn't be further from the truth." Earendel smiled sadly. "We cannot alter the fundamental rules of the universe, not without dire consequences. But Cruach's own anger, his desire to kill us and take over, has infected Cyrus as well. Fueling him toward even more hate and chaos."

"Nox," I swore, running a hand through my hair, before cringing and looking to the patron god of Night with an apologetic look. His amused smile made me feel better, at least.

"Wait, you said if the balance sways too far *either way*?" Asteria asked, stepping forward slightly, her head tilted to the side. "What does that mean? I thought we only had to worry about it moving toward chaos?"

"Balance is just a harmonious in-between," Asteria explained, her starlight eyes swirling in a hypnotic manner. "In between chaos and order."

"What's wrong with order?" I asked, confused. Wasn't that what the balance offered?

"Should you ever experience pure order, with no chaos, you would see quickly why it's not something we want," Nox spoke, and I turned my head to face him again, our eyes meeting in a clash I felt reverberate down to my bones.

I was only shaken out of the stupor it left me in when Asteria asked, "Okay, so we kill Cyrus, save the balance, and stop Cruach?"

The gods tittered around us, and I had to remind myself not to bristle in defense of my mate. These were the damn gods themselves, not a courtier I could put in their place.

"You expect such a task to be easy?" Arawn drawled, a narrow bone index finger tapping on the arm of his throne. "Prophecies are not things to trifle with, girl. And ones like yours are not given unless the circumstances will be dire indeed."

Asteria bristled, her eyes narrowing on the god of death the moment he called her girl. I put a hand on her shoulder, steadying her, reminding her we couldn't win that fight.

She slumped back against me, and I hated to see the fight leaving her. As much as we couldn't direct it toward these particular beings, I did love to see her when her blood ran hot.

"Your guardians will continue to watch over you and help us keep an eye on you in your realm." The goddess Asteria said with a bright smile that made starlight expand out behind her.

"Our guardians?" I asked, head cocked to the side.

"Well, *Asteria's* guardians," she corrected, looking at my mate. I did the same and watched her eyes widen in shock.

"Luna and Zhu?" she asked in a gasp. I wasn't sure who she was referring to at first, until I remembered that she'd called the dragon who was in our shared dream space Luna.

"Yes. But that's enough about that for now," Earendel insisted, despite Asteria looking like she was about to argue with him. Clearly, there were facts they didn't want us to know. I wasn't sure how to feel about that. It was ingrained in me to follow the gods without question, but if important information was being kept from us…

"You must cement the bond quickly upon your return. There will not be much time before you are needed to take the battle to Cyrus," Erebus insisted, looking between us like he could will us to follow his direction.

"But before you can return, Asteria, please remove your necklace," Earendel asked, the white light of his eyes intensifying for a moment, though his voice remained kind.

Asteria's hand flew up to her neck, where the necklace from her mother, depicting our soulmark, resided. Since she stopped hiding it from me, which thinking back was utterly adorable of her, she rarely took it off.

"My necklace?" she asked, hesitantly. "Why?"

Nox, I hoped the gods forgave us for all the questions we asked. My father would have punished me severely if he saw the pushback I'd given the gods today.

"We will return it, Asteria." The goddess of the stars reassured her with a twinkling smile. One of the women who'd been sitting in the first row of seats before the celestial gods' thrones stepped forward, waiting for Asteria to remove her necklace. Her bright pink hair and eyes were striking, as was her barely-there dress. I averted my eyes as she walked forward, not wanting to accidentally see anything I shouldn't. The dress was made of a flowing fabric, cut with two dangerously high slits up to her thighs that left a lot of leg bare. While the top half was bunched at the shoulders, a string of pearls laying across them and dangling down her arms. The fabric panels of the top went straight down, covering her breasts but leaving an extremely deep V that showcased even more bare skin.

Wait…

The power pulsing off her read as divine. Not one of the beings from our realm, but a member of the lesser pantheons, then. There was a hierarchy of the different pantheons, with our gods on top, of course. The gods the Elves prayed to came next, followed by the Dryads, and then the Pixies. The power of the gods lessened as they went, and judging by the power I could feel off this one, it had to be one of the goddesses the Elves prayed to.

I could only imagine Azurill's face if I told him I had met one of his gods. As the High King of Gemaria, we'd met many times over the years at different functions, forging a friendship between kings that extended into a lucrative trading partnership. Now, we remained in constant communication regarding the balance and how the situation may affect our entire world. I was due to send him an update—*overdue* really. Asteria was nothing if not distracting. I'd have to make a note of that for when we returned.

I hoped we wouldn't have to call for aid, but I was leaving the option open. I'd have to let Asteria know what to do, just in case. One could never be too careful when it came to battle plans and backups. That was one of the first things Titan had taught me about planning a battle. Always have a backup, because no plan survives first contact with the enemy.

I watched Asteria hand her necklace over, nervous and twitchy about letting it go. The Elven goddess smiled kindly at her, laying a hand over her forearm. The faintest flicker of power licked over her, and Asteria calmed immediately, smiling back.

The goddess handed the necklace to Earendel, and he, Erebus, Asteria, Nox, and Hyperion all stepped off their thrones to gather around his outstretched hand. I had to squint my eyes as their power flared. It was obvious their true power was too much for even Fae eyes to take in wholly. They were toning things down for our benefit, surely.

Strands of white light and golden sunbeams, liquid darkness, and black shadow, all accented by twinkling silver starlight, surrounded the necklace, sinking into it and lifting it into the air. Their lips moved, but I couldn't make out a word of what they were saying.

Asteria hid her face in my shoulder, and my hand automatically found the back of her head. I buried my own face in her hair as the light flared brighter and brighter, until my options were to look away or risk my sight.

I could still see the aura of their power with my eyes closed, and only dared to look up once the radiance finally passed.

Asteria stepped down off the dais then, and came to stand before my mate, handing her the necklace back. I helped Asteria reclasp it around her neck as Erebus explained what they'd done.

"This necklace has been infused with our power now. It will allow you to find the gates to the Underworld at any time. You won't have to worry about your father showing you how to access the one for Elysium in Day," he paused for a moment, looking between us. He seemed strangely sad, maybe regretful even, before he continued.

An ominous feeling came through the bond from Asteria, echoing my own.

"It will also allow you to access knowledge when you need it from those of us connected to you directly by blood, whether from birth or bond. Not quite like a seer, for that is not a gift we can give, but when it is most needed, knowledge will come to you. Do not resist it."

Asteria looked at me uncertainly, and I shared in the foreboding feeling with her, hoping against hope the knowledge would only help, and not hurt her. I'd seen Liviana torn up by her visions too many times to dismiss what knowledge from the gods could cause. The goddess of stars reached out and grasped my mate's hands, squeezing them in a reassuring manner.

"You must prepare yourself for what is to come, my little starling." The goddess smiled sadly, silver eyes swirling slowly, just as her silver dress fluttered around her legs in a nonexistent wind. "And remember, Asteria, that while it is always darkest before the dawn, you were made to *shine* in darkness."

The two Asterias looked at one another, both of their eyes swirling with starlight. For a brief moment, I could have sworn Asteria's dark hair twinkled with starlight as well, but it must have been a reflection of the goddess's starlit hair in her own beautiful tresses that reminded me so of the night sky.

Everything we had learned about Cyrus and Cruach was certainly concerning. Cyrus was farther gone than even I realized, and if Cruach was affecting him from *inside* his prison, I dreaded to think what he could accomplish if he was freed.

None of us would be able to oppose him. If we tipped toward chaos completely, we'd lose even our most basic defenses. Our magic would dry up, leaving us nothing but slaves to a mad god.

A chill went through me, and my eyes locked with Nox's. He stood, his hair a bright silvery-white, not dissimilar to mine, and yet completely so. Where my hair remained a flat color, Nox's glowed like the moon. His eyes were as dark as night, but they had a familiar Aurora striking through them. His features were so similar to mine and yet so different. So much *more*.

"The power of two is always greater than the power of one," Nox said, his hand landing on my shoulder heavily. "The night is the darkness that the stars are meant to shine against."

His eyes were drawn to the goddess Asteria, and I recognized the depth of emotion from staring at my own Asteria. "What is to come will test the realms. And everyone in them. Be as solid as the night sky. The give and take of your bond will build a better future for all. Do not let chaos and death be the legacy of the future."

"Of course." I nodded deeply, practically a bow, and Nox smiled slowly. He nodded back once before he made his way over to who was clearly his own mate, standing to the side as she spoke to the beneficiary of her power.

"Let's get you two back to where you need to be," Erebus said, a heavy finality in his tone. Earendel and Asteria joined us as we made our way out. I took one last look at the gods, especially Nox, unable to believe this had actually happened.

The very beings I prayed to all my life. Right in front of me.

The tall, dark, curling horns on Faunus to the green, flowering hair of Florus. The bare-chested and leather-pant-clad form of Hedone, who winked at me, as the red-haired and white-eyed Ziva pulled him along by the hand. Anann's giant form, with his double-ended blade on his back, loomed over Vakare's, with her ombre hair that shifted through orange, peach, pink, and purple. Hyperion's golden eyes and hair shone brightly, like a miniature sun, while the wavy, watery blue of Nammu's was a peaceful respite.

Asteria took my arm, smiling up at me as we walked out. I grasped her tightly, almost afraid to leave this place where she was *safe*.

Out there, we were going back to a battle that would define the future of the realms.

I had no idea what Cyrus had been doing in our absence. Or how long we'd even been gone.

"Is there nothing else you can tell us? To ensure we win this battle?" I asked Erebus, hoping against hope there was *something* that would tip the scales.

He looked back at me sadly, shaking his head. "Some things cannot be taught. They can only be lived."

"But to live, we first have to survive," I argued carefully as we made our way out of the palace and down the path. I couldn't help but look around, with so many creatures flying and grazing outside. Not merely dragons, phoenixes, and Pegasus, but more I couldn't even identify.

Erebus chuckled, pointing up at one of the dragons flying overhead. "You see these creatures?"

I nodded in confusion, and he patted my shoulder. "You have their spirit, but they are pure animal, while you are of us. A mixture of god and beast, creating a new, perfect creature."

"The Fae," I clarified, and received a smile in return.

"The Fae." Erebus nodded with satisfaction. "One of the best things about us, god or child of the gods, is we all work according to the stirrings of fate. Destiny is written in the stars, after all. And what are the stars but pure chaos?"

"I don't understand." I shook my head gently, not following what he was talking about.

"Neither do I," Asteria mumbled mutinously from beside me, making Erebus and I both smirk at her sass.

"You will learn. That is the important thing." Earendel added, his eyes flaring an even brighter white as he stared at us eerily.

"You will find the way forward. Remember what I told you, Asteria. And fight for the future you want to build," Asteria said, her silver starlit hair bouncing behind her as she walked beside my mate.

We came upon the portal faster than I thought we would, and a brief spike of panic went through me. I wanted to ask a million questions, receive a million answers. This was a once-in-a-lifetime opportunity that was coming to an end.

"We have given you all you need," Erebus assured me.

"Become the Star Queen and Night King you are meant to be. The prophecies that fate weaves always prove themselves in the end." Earendel reached out and cupped Asteria's cheek. "You carry the hope of the gods with you. Carry that fact like a torch through the darkness, to light your own inner flame."

"Thank you, Your Majesties." Asteria bowed her head, and I echoed her, grasping her hand as we faced the portals.

With one last look back at the gods we prayed to, but who were somehow looking to my mate and me as hope for the future, we stepped through the portal back to Tartarus. Preparing ourselves for the journey back home. And the monumental task that waited.

I WAS SHOCKED to find none of the obstacles we faced on our way here in place as we started our trek through Tartarus. Our path was smooth, and I didn't trust it for a moment. Asteria was looking around anxiously as well, until she suddenly stopped dead in her tracks.

"Asteria? What's wrong, my réalta?" I asked, trying to figure out what was happening.

Her head cocked to the side, and she looked to the right. She slowly walked over, her starlight spilling out of her as she did.

"There's something here," she murmured quietly.

The rock wall beside us looked solid, and I was beginning to get a bit concerned. Suddenly, she funneled a huge blast of starlight through the rock. It tunneled straight through it, creating a perfectly rounded arch that stretched out before us. I could just barely make out a light coming from the other end.

"Come on," she urged, grabbing my hand and trying to pull me in.

"Asteria, we have no idea where this leads. We should follow the original path back," I cautioned, not wanting us to get stuck halfway across Tartarus in the wrong direction. Too many things here were not meant for us. I didn't want to stumble upon a monster we couldn't defeat when so much was counting on us back in Celesterra.

"Do you trust me?" she asked, turning to look at me. Her sky-blue eyes shone with the stars, and I could see the sincerity in them. The faith that this was the right choice. It pulsed through the bond, and I found I could do nothing less than have faith in her in this.

"You know I do," I told her quietly, lifting a hand to her chin and raising her head to mine for a kiss. It felt like it had been forever since I'd had her, and I was anxious to get back and cement the bond between us as the gods had instructed.

"Then come on." She smiled playfully, and her starlight circled around her, touching down on her hair, which looked darker in the light of Tartarus, and making it shine like the night sky again. I smiled at the sight, fingering a lock of her hair. There was nothing better than seeing my home reflected in her.

She was home, truly.

I let her pull me down the newly created tunnel, her light illuminating our way. Before long, we came to the end, and I was shocked to step out and see the portal that led back to Tairngire. I recognized the fork in the path we had found when we emerged, and from this angle, the portal was wholly different from the others we'd seen here.

This one was surrounded by star opal, and inside the black liquid-looking smoke were flashes of purple, green, and pink, like the Aurora through the night sky.

"Told you." Asteria smiled impishly, and I rolled my eyes, but couldn't help my smile.

"Well, by all means, let's get the Tartarus out of here." I raised a brow and pulled her forward.

We stepped through the portal, and after a moment of being encased in its mists as they slipped across our skin, we were standing in the bowels of my palace once more.

I couldn't help the laugh of relief I let out. I could feel it shared between us as I looked at my Asteria, *my mate.* I couldn't help the wonder I felt at the sight of her. I cupped her cheek and lowered my head to kiss her fiercely.

"You truly are the light that will guide our way," I whispered as I pulled back. She stared up at me with star-filled eyes and shook her head.

"You think I'm the light? I think you forget I'm the kind of light that only shines amidst the darkness. Without you, I'd be lost," she insisted, reaching up and sneaking her hand into my hair, her thumb caressing my cheekbone as she used her hand's position to force my lips back to hers.

My hands gripped her waist, and I tried not to let myself get too distracted. I desperately wanted to throw her down on the ground and rip her armor to shreds to get to her body. To sink myself inside her and feel at *home* again.

But I wanted to do this properly—and comfortably. I wanted her in my bed, where I could lose myself in her for hours without a care in the world. And to do that, we first had to get upstairs and past everyone else.

"The faster we get upstairs, the faster I can get you naked," I mumbled between our kisses.

"Hmm." She hummed, considering. "Good point. I need to get at this beast as quickly as possible." She grabbed my cock, gripping it through my leather pants, and made me groan as she squeezed.

She cackled with laughter as I grabbed her hand and pulled her quickly through the palace, nearly running to get up each level.

We made our way past the treasure room, up and past the Hedone room, until we finally got to the main level. And, of course, Ilta was coming down the hall right as we appeared.

"You're back!" she shrieked, and threw herself at the two of us, hugging us both tightly. I would have made fun of her for it if I hadn't felt her trembling.

We all knew there were risks involved in our journey. I couldn't imagine how they felt having to just sit around and wait for us.

"You're both okay?" she asked, voice suspiciously damp as she pulled back to look us over.

"We're fine, Ilta," I reassured her with a small smile. She searched my face to make sure I was telling the truth, and Asteria nodded to reassure her as well. "We'll have to arrange a meeting with everyone. But tomorrow morning. Asteria and I have other plans to see to right now."

Asteria snorted, trying to hide a giggle, and Ilta slowly smirked, raising her brows. "Well, far be it from me..."

Asteria let out a full laugh, and with Ilta's permission, I grabbed Asteria and threw her over my shoulder, zipping upstairs to my room as fast as my

Fae speed would take me. My mate's laugh ringing out down the halls like music to my ears.

I burst through the door to my rooms, making straight for *our* bedroom. A fact I felt a complete thrill over. I couldn't wait for all of this to be over so we could just live our lives together. Waking up slowly and falling asleep in each other's arms. After tiring ourselves out from hours of sweaty, bloody sex, if I had my way.

My fangs lengthened at just the thought. Asteria bounced as I threw her on the bed, my hands immediately going to undo her corset. Her own hands eagerly ripped at my armor in return, and we began racing to try to get the numerous pieces undone and on the floor as fast as possible.

My fangs were literally *aching* at the idea of what was to come.

CHAPTER 51

Asteria

I COULDN'T get my hands on Calix fast enough. A desperate drive ricocheted through the bond, bouncing off one another and amplifying our desire as we drove each other into a frenzy.

Our swords and belts were torn off first and thrown to the bench at the foot of the bed. Once my armored corset was untied, it went flying across the room, while his armor crashed to the ground with a loud thunk. My leather pants were ripped in two while my claws raked his into ribbons. My armbands were inconsequential enough that we just skipped them altogether.

My hands dug into Calix's hair, dragging his mouth to mine, while he grabbed me by the thighs and hooked me around his waist. I squirmed, pressing my body to his and tilting my hips up to thrust against the straining bulge in his pants. I felt like I couldn't get close enough, wishing I could just climb inside him. My tongue certainly did so, tangling with his as we devoured the other.

I was already soaking wet, and Calix wasted no time pushing me down, grabbing my thighs and wrestling them open so he could slot himself between them. He teased his cock through my arousal for only a moment before he was suddenly sinking inside me. His inability to wait was more than appreciated.

My mouth disconnected from his, only to scream when he pushed inside, stretching me around his girth. His mouth thankfully found another pursuit, sucking down my neck and scraping his fangs across the skin. He didn't bite, merely teased me with them, caressing the skin there with the sharp points.

442

As he bottomed out, he paused for a moment, looking up at me with eyes saturated with color.

The world seemed to pause around us at that moment. Our bond singing between us as we reveled in being connected so closely once more. Calix's hand came up to my cheek, softly running his thumb over it. I couldn't help my smile, even as his lips found mine once more.

My legs locked around his waist and held him to me as our tongues dueled furiously. His hips pulled back only to thrust in hard, and my own hips flew off the bed to meet him. Our hands were everywhere, trying to touch as much of the other as we could while our hips crashed together over and over.

It felt as if we'd left reality behind. The urge to complete our bond drove both of us hard, like some primal instinct within us had been unlocked. Words were completely unnecessary and lost in the haze of passion that had descended on us anyway. The feelings bouncing between us drove us higher and higher instead.

As Calix thrust into me again, I tightened my legs and used my thrust upward as momentum to flip us over. Calix crashed to the bed with a filthy smirk on his face as he watched me fall on top of him, his cock hitting deep inside and making me moan loudly. I rose up slowly, slamming down hard. Calix grabbed onto my hips and thrust up from underneath me until we were fighting one another for control once more.

I rode him fast, using my Fae speed and strength to aid me until I was nearly a blur of movement. The stretch of his cock inside me was too good, and my arousal was steadily leaking out around the base of his cock, aiding my pursuit. Even as his cock kissed that spot inside me that made me see stars, my actual stars expanded into the space around me.

Calix was enjoying the show, watching me passionately and helping when needed. His hands found my breasts, pinching and twisting my nipples before soothing them with his mouth. But as my first orgasm approached, a sinister twinkle appeared in his eye. I braced myself even as my climax overcame me, screaming his name into the room.

Calix pulled out of me the moment I stopped cumming. We flew upward, Calix's shadows wrapping around my limbs as I hit the wall. They held onto my limbs like vines, leaving me spread-eagle against the wall. Calix himself slowly stood from the bed, pumping his cock as he stalked forward, taking me in fully.

I yanked on the shadows, but they held firm. My starlight churned around me, but his shadows filled the room, darkening it to a pitch-black night and keeping my stars too busy with his shadows elsewhere to help free me.

"What are you doing, my dorchadas?" I asked him, expectantly. Raising a brow from my bound position.

"What?" he responded with faux innocence. "I merely want to fully appreciate my mate." He growled softly as he reached me, his hand finding my neck and wrapping softly around it. He gave it a light squeeze, making me moan at the sensation. I wished I could press my legs together and take some of the edge off, my poor cunt was crying for attention again already.

His fingers released my neck and began trailing slowly down my body. They first stroked over my breasts, then down my stomach, before running them back up and then down again. He teased around my breasts until my nipples were surely hard enough to cut glass, and I was almost convinced I could orgasm from that alone. My whines increased in volume as his fingers finally slipped past my belly button, reaching my hips.

He grasped each one tightly for a moment, before letting his fingers fall down my spread thighs. His fingers found my slit, and trailed lightly across it, ignoring my pleas for release. I tried to buck my hips off the wall, but his shadows held fast, keeping all but my head immobile. After torturous minutes of tracing over my skin softly, with none of the friction I craved, he finally pressed his fingers against my cunt fully. He gathered the arousal leaking from me and followed straight up to my clit, circling around as I squirmed and moaned against the wall.

He fell to his knees before me, one hand on my hip as the other speared two fingers inside me. His lips traced up my thighs, increasing the pleasure as more sensations bombarded me. Licking and biting along my thighs, he thrust his fingers in and out, stretching me back open and adding a third, then a fourth finger. Finally, his tongue found my clit and began circling it repeatedly.

I couldn't take it anymore and came screaming his name. He worked me through my orgasm, quickly building me back up with everything still so sensitive. I shook my head tiredly, begging for mercy, but none was forthcoming. I squealed in overwhelm as I came again, and Calix finally pulled away, smirking like he was oh-so-proud of himself.

He stood up, watching me as I panted against the wall, pulling at the shadows and trying to move. But he clearly wasn't done with me. He was hard as a rock, and he fisted his cock, pressing it against my cunt and thrusting it back and forth, wetting it with my arousal. My head fell back against the wall.

"Calix," I whined, my body shaking.

"Come on, my réalta," he cooed at me, eyes darkened to a brilliant lavender. "You can give me another one."

He notched his cock against my entrance and slowly sank inside. My walls fluttered around his length. Even overwhelmed after multiple orgasms, my body couldn't help but bend to Calix. I seemed to get wet at the drop of a hat around him, and I still wasn't exactly sure how my body even took that monster he kept in his pants.

He thrust in fully, and quickly built up momentum. One hand on the wall, he had enough leverage to hammer away at me, and tied up by shadows, I could do absolutely nothing but take it.

Calix clearly could feel where my thoughts had taken me, and he smirked up at me, his other hand grabbing my chin.

"You know better than that," he purred, thrusting in hard and making me moan loudly as he hit that spot that had me quickly building toward another orgasm. "You might let me play as much as I want, but you know you're just as powerful as I am."

I panted, squirming my hips against his to try to angle them, and whined at him, making him chuckle darkly.

"Show me," he whispered teasingly, eyes alight with color. "Show me what you can do."

I realized then what he wanted, and despite my approaching orgasm, I rallied my magic, calling my starlight to me. I let it build and build, until the darkness around us became star-flecked, like the night sky surrounded us. Then I grew it brighter and brighter, until the stars were all I could see for a moment.

I focused on the shadows holding me and willed my starlight to dissolve them.

Suddenly, my arms and legs were free. I quickly anchored myself around Calix before I slid down the wall, not wanting to see what would happen if I fell with him still inside me.

"There she is," Calix smirked proudly, grabbing hold of my hips and fucking up into me. No longer bound to the wall, he used only his strength to hold me up as he pounded into me. I slid up and down his cock, my head falling back with a moan. I could feel the orgasm that had been threatening to hit for several minutes now barreling toward me, and my fangs lengthened.

I pulled my head back up to see Calix's were as well. His eyes completely focused on the exposed expanse of my neck. The pounding of his blood in his veins seemed to sing to me as I watched the vein in his neck bulge and contract with his movements.

With one shared glance between us, it became too much. I was only distracted from the orgasmic feeling of his fangs piercing my neck by the indescribable feeling of my own entering his throat. Calix's blood spilled into my mouth, and I moaned at the taste. My orgasm crashed over me, a combination of his cock and fangs and blood, and I was sure I was back in Elysium at that moment, because I couldn't imagine any paradise ever being better than this.

A sudden swell of magic overcame us as the bond seemed to swell and grow. Opening my eyes, I could swear Calix's hair was glowing like the moon for a moment, but my eyes were forced closed as the feelings within me grew too much to handle. I braced myself against them, but I found they didn't *really* overwhelm me; instead, they sank into and became part of me.

Nothing but pure, raw, primordial power filled me. Calix's and my own, mixing and mingling, becoming one with each other. I could feel him every-where inside me. Like his magic had filled my being, a moon-kissed night that I filled up with stars. The sensual flow of it rippled through me, making my orgasm nearly triple in force. The pure masculine power of *Calix* was all that existed at that moment in time.

I had never felt so *full,* especially as his cock swelled in size within me, stretching my walls around his girth as he spilled into me, and his power poured into the rest of me.

As if Calix was fucking literally every inch of my body, inside and out. And it was absolutely divine, a euphoria beyond known words.

I knew, in that instant, that no matter what came next, Calix and I would always be one. Bound through blood and bond, how could anything rip us apart now? They would have to tear our very souls asunder. Every drop of his blood in my veins and every bit of mine in his would have to be forcibly ripped from our bodies.

A peace I'd never known overtook me, merging with the euphoria and leaving me a blissed-out mess of flesh and blood, magic and soul.

I was sure I must have blacked out, but came to on top of Calix, lying across the bed. He was still inside me, both his cock and his fangs, and I realized mine were still in his neck. I slowly pulled my fangs out and licked a line up his neck to clean the blood off. He did the same, and I could feel his contentment beating through me, matching my own.

The bond felt... *different*, surely. More stable, more a part of my being. There was no separation, despite it being clear whose feelings were whose. But I could feel him on another level now. Almost as if I could read the very thoughts in his head through his emotions. I felt stronger, more settled in myself even. It was hard to explain the difference, but I knew the gods had spoken true. The bond was cemented now, and I could feel the boost it gave to both of us.

I wished there was more information on soulmate bonds out there. Outside of the shared marks and feelings, we only really knew what the gods had offered up—which wasn't much. It seemed like too much had been lost to time.

I sat up slowly, my eyes meeting Calix's, the lilac dancing with the colors of the Aurora. A slow smile lit my face, and I reached down to kiss him lingeringly. I pulled back after a few minutes and lifted myself off him, looking at the mess we'd left on the sheets.

Calix looked down at the bedding with a slight frown, which turned into a slow, proud smirk as he took in the sheets covered in blood and cum. I sighed, looking at him expectantly. He smiled cheekily before fisting the sheet in his hand and giving it a hard pull.

Pillows flew everywhere as the sheet came flying off. Calix looked too proud of himself, even as we were both nailed in the face with pillows. I couldn't stop the laugh that bubbled up, literally bent over as I tried to stop. Calix let out a rumbling laugh as he pulled me up.

"The poor servants are going to hate us," I gasped out, trying to stop laughing.

"Hmm." Calix hummed, his hand tangling in my hair. "I'll give them a raise."

I couldn't help laughing again as his lips met mine.

CHAPTER 52

Calix

PEACEFULLY waking up to Asteria in my arms, back in my bed, was the best start to a morning I could ask for. The pounding on my door, however, I could have done without.

"Argh," I groaned loudly, snapping at whoever was at the door. "What?"

"I drew the short straw and have been nominated to tell you that you two have slept until lunchtime after being gone for a Tartarus damned week," Baach called out. "So it's time to get your asses out of bed!"

I groaned again, turning to bury my face in Asteria's hair. I cracked an eye open, checking the hair I'd glimpsed turning into the night sky itself while we shared blood, in the moment the magic surged around us. To my surprise, her hair definitely was a bit darker than when we'd left, but it wasn't quite as dark as the night sky, nor was it shimmering with starlight.

I shook my head lightly at my own fanciful imaginings. Asteria stretched her limbs, groaning softly as she roused. I smiled slightly, amused as always by the angry little kitten she resembled as she woke up.

A loud pounding on the door had me rolling my eyes. "I get it! Give us a few to wake up and get dressed, will you?"

"Fine," Baach sighed, sounding incredibly put upon. "But only because I didn't want to do this in the first place!"

Asteria cracked her own eyes open just to roll them, making me snicker. I pressed my forehead against hers, whispering, "Good morning, my réalta."

"Mmm. Good morning, my dorchadas," she cooed sleepily, pressing her lips to mine softly. We indulged in the intimacy for a moment before she pulled back.

"Was that Baach I heard?" she asked, her leg curving around mine. I squeezed her silky thigh and ran my hand up and down her skin, wishing we had enough time to laze around in bed for a while.

One day, we'd have that kind of time. That kind of peace.

"Unfortunately." I snorted softly. "He was apparently nominated to let us know that it's been a week since they've seen us, and they've grown impatient."

"A week?!" she asked, eyes going wide as she half sat up in alarm.

"Apparently." I nodded grimly. "I figured there might be some distortion between realms. I'm just glad it was only a week."

"Still." She stressed, gripping the edge of the blanket and twisting it in her hands. "That's an entire week Cyrus had—"

"Asteria." I interrupted before she could work herself into a panic. I sat up, grabbing her shoulders and making her look at me. "Part of being a ruler is accepting that you can't be everywhere at once. Learning to trust and depend on your people to do what needs doing in your absence is important. We had plenty of people here who were working hard while we were gone. We have a war council already waiting. We'll learn what's happened and plan our next steps. Okay?"

Asteria sighed, deflating. She shook her head before it dipped down, and I reached out a finger to put under her chin and raise it back up.

"I'm not very good at that. Trusting other people to do things for me," she admitted, heavily. "I'm going to be a shitty ruler." I shook my own head in protest now.

"Absolutely not. I'm not surprised you have trouble trusting others after the life you've led," I told her softly, making sure she felt my understanding. "It will come with time, I promise. You're not going to be a bad ruler."

"I have no idea what I'm doing, Calix," she argued, her brows creasing, and I could feel the fear and shame roiling around inside her. "They made me their queen, but I have no idea how to rule a kingdom or lead an army. You do so much that I don't even know about! All those cities and villages and people. I don't—"

She cut herself off, her head falling into my chest, and I wrapped my arms around her back, sympathy pouring through me. She'd been pulled out of slavery and handed responsibility that no one had ever taught her to deal with. And while I could help her with this war, she knew she'd have to learn all of this for herself, too. I'd spent years training under my father before I ended up on the throne; she didn't have that advantage.

"I will be here every step of the way, okay?" I promised, running my hands up and down her back. "I'll help you learn every bit of the boring day-to-day of ruling and all the complexities of wartime. You're going to be just fine. Better than even. Anyone can be taught the logistics of ruling, but not everyone has the spirit it takes to lead. *You do.*"

Asteria looked up, a desperate hope shining in her eyes like she wished she could believe me more than anything else.

"You really think so?" she asked quietly, her fingers tangling in my long hair.

"I know so." I yanked on a piece of her hair lightly before teasing, "After all, you're my mate, my equal. It only makes sense when I'm such a natural, right?"

She giggled lightly, lifting my own spirits at the sight. I loved nothing more than seeing that little wrinkle appear on her nose when she laughed. It, more than anything else, showed her joy was true and real, after a life with so little to be joyous about.

"Now, as much as I wish I could just keep you naked in bed all day, I have a feeling those bastards downstairs won't leave us alone until we make an appearance." I rolled my eyes, making her snicker.

It was enough of a push to get us up and dressed. Once I'd gotten my leather pants on, I put on a black button-up, leaving the top buttons undone, and threw my jacket over it. Asteria had donned a gorgeous crystal-encrusted dress that showcased her breasts and shoulders marvelously where it sat off her shoulders. The purple crystals around them faded into a sky-blue and then into silver on the corset, before the purple crystals picked back up at the top of her skirt, fading back into blue and then silver.

The sleeves were transparent and billowed out a bit before gathering at her wrist. The top of each sleeve looked almost fused to her skin with the purple crystals over the transparent fabric. She looked like the queen I knew she was. Donning not only her purple and silver, but the blue of the daytime sky.

She sat down at the vanity, and I grabbed the hairbrush from Asteria's hand before she could run it through her hair. She looked up at the mirror in surprise, watching my reflection as I began to carefully work the brush through her hair.

I hadn't done anything like this in years. None of my past lovers had inspired this kind of intimacy, but I had two young girls to raise after my parents' deaths. And both frequently needed help with their hair.

"What?" I asked, lightly. "It pleases me to be able to do things like this for you. I know you usually have Delia and Priscilla, but when I was little, I remember my father doing this for my mother most nights before they went to bed."

I felt a pulse of something soft through the bond, and I could tell Asteria knew that despite trying to brush it off, being able to do simple things of this nature for my mate meant more to me than I could admit verbally.

Seeing my parents again brought back so many memories. I'd nearly forgotten what they'd once been like together after so many years. I was only in my one hundred and twenties when they died, and three hundred years later, things had faded a bit. Especially with the time between my mother and father's deaths being so fraught.

But now, all those years we spent in happier times seemed much brighter in my memory. I wanted more than anything for my life with Asteria to be just as blissful, and to stretch on into eternity.

She could clearly tell where my thoughts had gone, her hand finding mine and squeezing tightly. That mysterious and wonderful bond between us now provided a link so tight that we could follow the tenor of one another's thoughts and be there for the other when needed in a way I could never have imagined before.

With such a bond fueling us, I had no doubt that should we get through this war, Asteria and I would build a life even grander than I could dream.

We walked into the war room to find the expectant gazes of the rag-tag family I'd built over the centuries, compounded by a bunch of interlopers. I was somewhat surprised that my friends hadn't tried to get us alone first to question us, but I was pleased nonetheless. I knew Asteria wanted to get on with planning as quickly as possible.

Thankfully, Titan was already to the left of my usual spot, and Asteria would naturally stand to my right. Ndrita was next to Titan, while Liviana was across from her, standing next to Asteria's spot.

Callisto, who'd arrived back from the border, was standing next to Priscilla, who was only the first of many surprises around the table. I had to wonder if she only showed up for an update from Asteria. Especially as Delia and Ilta had apparently joined as well, and they never involved themselves in such meetings unless absolutely necessary.

Interspersed around the table were Eryx, Baach, Harpina, and Lilith, who always had a fifty-fifty shot of being present. They were joined by Lord's Ciaran, Kyler, Polaris, Rhidian, and Sterling, along with Lady's Aisling, Alora, Jasira, and Zillah. Not to mention my cousin Siria and her husband, Aibek.

Mixed in with all of the usual suspects were Prince's Arien, Altan, and Zakat, along with a few of their more highly ranked people who'd joined them, including Lord's Beltane, Ergun, and Dritan, the former of which must have arrived in our absence.

But what actually stopped both Asteria and I dead in our tracks was the redheaded man standing stiff and nervous to the side of Eryx, a dark-haired human woman hanging on his arm with a strange mixture of fear and relief in her eyes.

"Vikal? Carrina?" Asteria asked, sounding bewildered. Her eyes creased, her suspicion and concern rushing through me in turns.

"Asteria." The woman, Carrina, sighed with relief. It was easy to see how nervous she was, eyes skittering around the unfamiliar Fae surrounding her and hanging onto the familiar form of Vikal with a white-knuckled grip. Seeing another familiar face clearly helped, as her fingers loosened some on Vikal's arm.

I couldn't blame her. Nox only knew what she'd been through in Dusk. The daily fear of being taken away by Cyrus to be drained of blood would be enough to drive most to desperation.

"I assume Nithe brought you here?" I asked, meeting the bright blue eyes of Cyrus's brother. The two couldn't possibly look more different. The boyish features of the redhead alone were a contrast to his elder brother's sharp ones.

"You assume correctly." I turned my head as Nithe breezed into the room. "Sorry I'm late. I can't stay long. I need to get back to Dusk, things are finally starting to move in the direction we hoped."

I nodded, taking in the information with satisfaction. I turned to Eryx, nodding at Vikal with a raised brow, "You've already approved them?"

"I did." Eryx nodded sharply. "Their story checks out."

"What, did you think I was fleeing from my home to spy on you for Cyrus or something?" Vikal demanded, shoulders tight and back, his face incredulous.

"The thought did cross my mind." I shrugged, forcibly casual, as I took my place at the head of the table. Vikal bristled a bit, and his anger at the idea helped to soothe any lingering ideas of sabotage that may have lingered.

Asteria's amusement at my poking for a reaction echoed through me, though she did lay a brief hand on Carrina's shoulder as she passed, giving her a quick smile as she did.

"Cyrus is no brother of mine," Vikal spat, furious at the very idea that he may have been considered a mole. "Let's make that real fucking clear, right now. That asshole threatened to send Carrina to those—those—"

He struggled to finish, and he certainly earned points for that. His disgust and horror were too genuine to be faked. Carrina pressed her forehead into his shoulder, and his hand came up to the back of her head, holding her to him like someone might try to rip her away.

The sympathy and understanding I felt shook me. I didn't want to be sympathetic or understanding to someone who sat back and did nothing for so many years.

But... I sighed internally. He *was* young. Not even one hundred yet. It took me many more years before I finally woke up to the horrors of slavery myself.

"And are you prepared to help stop your brother now?" Asteria asked, her hands on her hips as she stared him down with a sharply raised eyebrow.

My mate had spent a not insignificant amount of time spying within Dusk's court, and that included Vikal. She was the one who reported that he kept himself out of politics and the squabbling for the throne. But this was no longer a matter of mere politics.

"Of course I am," Vikal responded, grinding his jaw in aggravation. "He's gone way too far, and now everything is threatened because of him. I never liked that humans were enslaved to begin with. I always got along better with humans than I did any Fae."

That tracked with what Asteria had observed of him. I knew Nithe wouldn't have brought him if he wasn't sure, and his instincts were rarely wrong. Still, this was too important, and we'd had to skip so many of the usual steps for vetting newcomers for expediency's sake.

"Good." I nodded, looking to Asteria. She smiled slightly back at me. "Then I suppose we should get updates out of the way first."

"Yes, please do!" Harpina practically erupted, clearly impatient. "What the Tartarus happened in the Otherworld?"

The others all looked at us with wide, expectant eyes. I couldn't blame them. Had I not gone myself, I would have similarly been dying to know what it was like.

"We had to face several trials along the way, as well as several meetings," I began, choosing my words carefully with so many present. "We wound through both Tartarus and Elysium, and finally accessed the city of the gods."

"What kind of trials?" Eryx asked, his eyebrows creased enough that I could practically see the different scenarios running through his mind.

"What kind of meetings?" Delia spoke at the same time, garnering Eryx's full attention immediately.

Asteria tried to stifle her giggle at the two, especially as Delia's face flushed, her eyes looking down briefly in embarrassment. Eryx's longing stare was only broken by his expectant look back at us.

We explained the trials briefly, answering all the expected questions, while trying to keep the more personal parts private. Explaining the meetings was definitely a more complicated matter.

"You saw mother and father?" Ndrita's voice could barely be heard across the table, it was so subdued. Her eyes shone with a strange mixture of longing and forced indifference.

"We did," I told her quietly, and I looked to Liviana, who didn't seem very surprised. I wasn't sure if she'd seen it in a vision or just wasn't as impacted by the news. "I'll meet with you two later to tell you more. They passed along messages for you both before we left."

Ndrita looked ready to pull me out of the room and demand answers now, but she schooled herself quickly. We'd lost our parents when Ndrita was so young, but she'd been old enough that she still felt the loss deeply. Liviana, on the other hand, didn't have any real memories of our parents. But Ndrita had never truly gotten over their loss. I'd done my best to be both brother and parent to her, but it had been overwhelming for both of us.

I didn't want to get into all our family's interpersonal drama in front of everyone here, however. Ndrita would never forgive me if I made her cry in front of all the lords of Night, and practically half the realm besides, I thought, looking around the packed room.

"We spoke with all of the gods," Asteria said, getting to the point quickly. "They warned us that Cyrus is being influenced by another god who they imprisoned years ago. The god of blood created the Vampyres and had them running wild, and now he wants to break out and turn this realm back into his bloody paradise. The more Cyrus tips the balance toward chaos, the closer we get to this mad god getting free of his prison."

A beat of pure silence met her words before everyone exploded at once in pandemonium. I raised a hand to try to bring some order back to the group. Having them all yell out their questions and objections to the facts would get us nowhere.

"Asteria speaks true. The gods are relying on us to stop Cyrus, and thus prevent Cruach from breaking free," I told them firmly, my hands on the table as I leaned forward, staring everyone down. More like glaring, admittedly. "It puts more urgency on our mission. Should we fail, it won't just be Cyrus who takes over this realm. Cruach will rise and decimate this world."

The looks of fear around the table were met equally by looks of resolution, thankfully. They were warriors, and they wouldn't falter at the task before us. Those of us in Night who bore the warrior's mark felt that even more deeply than most. We all swore an oath to Nox, Erebus, and Anann, the god of war, that we would protect this kingdom and its people to our last breath.

"We already knew we needed to stop Cyrus," Asteria began, looking every inch the queen she was as she surveyed our people. "Now we know he is being influenced by Cruach as well. Rationality already left him a while back, but now we need to prepare ourselves for a harder fight. Cruach is no doubt amping up his bloodlust, and that's in tandem with chaos infecting him. The more blood magic he uses, the worse it gets. Every single use of it pushes this realm closer to the brink of chaos."

"We know he had plans for iron weapons," I said, looking to Nithe and Vikal. "What can you two tell us about the current status of those?"

Nithe stepped forward a bit, nodding at Asteria and me. "Cyrus has been keeping his operations very hush-hush when it comes to that. While he has no problem flaunting his camps full of human prisoners, he ensures that what goes on in them beyond standard torture and death is kept secret. Only a couple of men know the full picture, alongside the workers who are smelting the iron, but they are kept in isolation to keep the secret."

I spotted Vikal shaking his head in dismay, holding Carrina close to him. Her shudder confirmed that Cyrus had indeed threatened to take her to one of those camps. The fact that he would hurt his own family in such a way was something I would never understand.

"I was able to slither my way in and to see what was truly going on," Nithe continued, a faint pride in his eyes for a job well done, but it was all but drowned out by the horror of everything he'd witnessed. "The blood taken from the humans is being distributed in two ways. It either goes to Cyrus for brewing blood magic, or they use it for crafting iron. It seemed to be mostly smaller pieces they were crafting. I heard rumors of larger plans, but nothing that could be substantiated."

"So if we hit him now, we may be able to take him out before he creates weapons big enough to—" Lord Ergun began, but Titan shook his head and cut him off before he could finish.

"Iron is iron." His voice was firm, and he looked around the room like he was trying to impart a lesson on all of us. I couldn't help feeling like a child again under that stare. "A scrap or a sword will burn you just the same. It leaves nasty injuries behind, and should you get stabbed with it? It will slowly drain your magic. You won't be able to heal with any trace of the iron in you. The wound will just keep burning in agony until it's gone—and that won't be quick, either. If you get stabbed, get the iron out as quickly as possible. Your magic will try to fight it, but it will only delay the agony if you don't get it removed. Do not underestimate it just because it looks innocuous."

"Then how do we fight against it?" Arien asked, looking to Titan. He could learn a lot from Titan, and I was glad to see he wasn't too proud to do so. Asteria and I would need both Generals aligned for this. As well as for everything after. I had no idea how we'd handle ruling two different kingdoms, with two different power structures. But that was an issue we would have to figure out once the war was won.

"You don't get hit," Titan replied dryly. I could feel Asteria's amusement and watched as she bit her lip in an attempt to smother her smile. "Treat it like the poison it is, and avoid taking a dose. I'm sure Cyrus will put iron in the hand of every man out there."

"Unless, of course, we can take them by surprise." Lord Beltane spoke up. Asteria's cousin looked over at her now, and despite not having even properly met yet, I could see the awe in his eyes. The *love*. Knowing he'd been there at her birth, I couldn't imagine how it must feel now, finally seeing her after all this time.

"If we can arrive before he expects us, we may be able to minimize the risk," he continued, dark shoulder-length hair falling forward as he leaned over the map spread out on the table. "He wouldn't dare give his men iron outside of battle."

"He's right," Asteria breathed out in realization, looking over to me and then Titan before turning back to me. "Cyrus is too paranoid to trust them." She bit her lip again, but this time in thought. Her head slowly tilted to the side. "He would want to ensure that they couldn't attack him on behalf of his siblings. He sees nothing but potential traitors everywhere. He would plan for the smallest number of people to have iron in hand, even in battle."

"In that case, the question of whether he's had time to build those larger weapons becomes a dire one." I mused aloud. Asteria nodded in confirmation. "We'll go in first for a sweep over Evenfall in our beast forms. We can check for anything obvious and signal whether we see them or not."

"Craft two battle plans?" Arien asked, looking from his twin to Titan for confirmation. His sky-blue eyes were clouded with worry, gold beams of sunlight shining through them. "One for if he does and one if he doesn't?"

Titan nodded slowly, before cracking his muscular neck side to side. "Exactly. Our goal here is to take out Cyrus. If we bring him down, we can stop the rest of them easily enough. It's the blood magic he's using, in addition to the iron, that will prove to be the biggest issue. Blood magic was forbidden for a reason, and his power will be heightened."

"How heightened?" Rhidian asked, and the silence that followed said more than enough.

CHAPTER 53

Arien

HOURS and hours were spent in Calix's war room, hashing out the plans for attack. Ideas bounced back and forth as experienced warriors with years of experience and fresh blood with new ideas all contributed to the final plans.

I had to appreciate the immensity of what was happening here. There were representatives from nearly all the kingdoms around the table, working together toward a common goal. All except Dawn Kingdom.

King Tariq had sided with Cyrus, and his forces were brought with him to Dusk before we could get word to any of our relatives there. I could only hope the messages would be received, and welcomed. Uncle Dali was lord of Chryse, and had always been on our side when we needed him before.

We'd never asked him to betray his king before, however.

I knew he took great pride in his role. I also knew that chaos had already begun affecting Dawn and its rulers. I could only pray to Hyperion that Dali wasn't similarly affected. I couldn't imagine Aunt Elaner, one of the sweetest beings I knew, being corrupted. If nothing else, I had hope she would ensure our plea was heard. She always spoke up for me, even to my father.

Which was part of the reason Father didn't allow them to visit us anymore.

Even without Dawn's involvement, however, we had quite the force behind us for this. King Tieran would meet up with us outside Evenfall, bringing Sunset's forces to bear. Prince Altan's sister had apparently been working behind the scenes in Sunrise to turn more soldiers to our cause as well, and they were expected to link up with Tieran's army before joining us.

Nithe and Vikal were able to give us an almost too vivid picture of the current situation in Dusk. It was hard to imagine such horrors actually being committed. It was a difficult concept to wrap my mind around. Despite the standard skirmishes we Fae all inevitably found ourselves in and our plans to overthrow my father, I'd grown up in a time of relative peace.

It was all an illusion, I realized now. An illusion that did nothing but make the Fae of this realm complacent. It allowed corruption to sink deep into the very bones of the realm.

Peace had proven as dangerous as a blade, and it cut just as deep.

We would all have to deal with the inevitable fallout from it now. I prayed to any gods I thought might hear me. The Blessed Trinity of Hyperion, Earendel, and Asteria. The god of war, Anann, and the god of death, Arawn. *And Tartarus*, I even prayed to Erebus. Begging them all to let us succeed in our quest to rout out the chaos that had infested our lands.

Cyrus was at the very root of that chaos.

While he was once but a small contributing factor to a slow decline, he was now the grand architect of its destruction.

Something was in the air. We could all feel it, evidenced by the shifting feet and fleeting looks, but no one said a word. The auspices of fate were always felt, but rarely did one recognize it for what it was.

It almost felt as if fate was sitting up and taking notice, watching us all with avid interest as its grand plan played out.

I shivered at the feeling. Such grand destinies were for storybooks, not real life. And yet, here we were. My twin sister had ascended her throne. The king and queen of two different kingdoms were mated. Humans were being rounded up and slaughtered for their blood to fuel a maniac's magic. And the balance was perilously close to tipping to chaos forever.

Fear was a danger in battle. That was one of the first things I learned. One must always be in control, lest their fear rule them and see them dead on the battlefield. But it was next to impossible to not fear now.

This was a scale I had never considered in all my days. My twin sister was at the apex of it all, and I—I *couldn't* lose her. Not after we just found her. The very idea caused an ache in my chest, and Asteria's eyes creased as she rubbed her own, as if she could feel the pain echoing through our blood.

As the plans for tomorrow were finalized and the meeting finally broke up, Asteria made her way over to me. A bright smile lit up her face, making her eyes twinkle brightly with starlight. It was still so strange to see those familiar sky-blue eyes lit with the stars instead of the sun.

"Come on," she said, grabbing my hand. My eyes briefly shot to Harpina's as we passed, and those amber orbs pierced through me. I shook myself, following Asteria through the halls. What happened between Harpina and me was a one-night-only deal. We both knew that.

While Asteria and Calix may believe they could find a way, Harpina and I both knew we had separate responsibilities. Even if those responsibilities occasionally crossed over. But that crossover would be the most difficult to navigate, I imagined. She was Constable of Night, not to mention my sister's friend, and therefore, not someone I could have any kind of future with.

Not that I thought *she* wanted that. She was clearly a flirt, and who could blame her when she looked like *that*? The memory of that wine-red hair tumbling down her back in luscious curls, caressing over the curves of her body as her narrow waist expanded into perfectly graspable hips that my fingertips indented into as she rode above me…

It would certainly stay with me for a while.

But I had my priorities. And right now, that was the short brunette pulling me out of Tairngire's palace and striding across the lawns to a destination unknown. I could only assume she was giving Calix some time to speak with his sisters about their meeting with his deceased parents.

What a strange world we live in now.

"Where are we going?" I asked, amused as her head whipped back to me with a mischievous smile.

"We're having twin bonding time, of course!" she responded, her bubbly tone so at odds with the harder tone she'd used around the war table.

Grief rose in my throat. We both should have had the chance to grow up playing together, not bonding for the first time while at war. Rage at my father was a familiar feeling. Like the well-worn shirt that I refused to part with and wore over and over again, despite my mother's teasing. But now, that rage focused in on everything Aelius had stolen from Asteria and me.

Our childhoods.

And if things went badly tomorrow, possibly our entire lives.

No matter what fate had in store for me tomorrow, I swore by Hyperion I would not leave Adamah without seeing my father dead.

Asteria's concerned expression had my rage clearing, and I forced a smile upon my face.

"Alright, lead the way, sister," I told her indulgently. There wasn't a thing I would deny her anyway.

I STRAPPED ON my armor, looking at myself in the mirror. After spending a few hours with Asteria at the menagerie, I felt more focused. It was amazing to be able to just spend time having fun with my twin after a lifetime of being kept apart.

It was a firm reminder of what was at risk. What had to be protected at all costs.

I sheathed my sword as I looked at the dark hair reflecting my mother, the blue eyes a copy of my father's. Would Mother look at me the same once my sword took Father's head?

I knew she wanted him both dead and alive, equally. The business of soulmates was a messy one, and theirs more so than most. Mother wanted her child protected. She wanted the power Father denied her. She wanted a safe world for us to live in.

But I knew, deep down, she wanted Aelius, too.

Mother and I had always been close, a result of the situation I was raised in and the role I'd had to take. I couldn't shake the feeling that our relationship would change forever if I killed her mate. I thought of how Asteria would react to losing Calix, and grimaced at my reflection.

There would be Tartarus to pay.

Did Mother even allow herself to acknowledge her conflicted feelings? Or did she bury any hope she had for her mate entirely? We'd never discussed it, not really. She'd only told me that the gods had said Father would have to go, so go he would.

I wished I'd hugged her a bit longer before she left for Avalon. Just in case.

She was holding the city now, and I'd sent a relatively sizeable force to hold Avalon against any further attacks. Hopefully, we wouldn't have to worry about that. If we took Cyrus and Aelius down today, we could all finally begin to move on.

My life had always been on pause. Waiting for this moment before it could truly begin.

I walked out of the rooms they'd given me in the Fallen Star Palace, making my way through the star opal-lined halls. Tapestries of past royals were matched by tasteful decorations that lined the halls, nothing so extravagant as Father would have done.

I paused as I went around a corner and came face to face with the woman I'd been desperately trying not to think about since that night at the camp.

"Prince Arien," Harpina nearly purred, raising a brow.

"Constable Harpina," I greeted her as blandly as possible. She tutted, shaking her head as she twined her arm around mine. Her armbands were on, and the strange material rubbed against my skin as she did. Harpina immediately began walking, forcing me to move with her.

My eyes couldn't help wandering, no matter how hard I tried to keep them forward. Her armor fit her like a second skin. The leather pants shaped perfectly around her arse and thighs, while the corset pushed up her generous cleavage, and her narrow waist was more pronounced from how tightly her corset was laced.

"Are you ready for today, sunshine?" she asked, that flirtatious note still in her voice, but giving way to something more genuine. Her amber eyes were warm as she glanced quickly at my face, before shifting her focus anywhere else.

"About as ready as you are, kitty-cat," I told her, a surprised laugh bursting from her mouth. A small smile played around my lips, but I forced them to straighten, reminding myself why another taste was dangerous.

Why *she* was dangerous.

CHAPTER 54

Cyrus

M y hands were beginning to cramp, but it was integral that my task was done soon. My dreams grew bloodier by the night, and I knew they were a warning.

A battle loomed on the horizon.

And I had to be ready. As the only one capable of wielding such advanced magic as blood magic, I was also responsible for preparing it all myself. No one else could be trusted with such secrets.

I stirred the pot once more, flexing my fingers around the long handle of the spoon. *"Cruach, iarraim ort.*

Íobairim an bheatha seo duit,

a gcuid fola a ghlacadh chun beatha.

Glan é agus déan arís é,

agus lig dó a bheith ar an draíocht ina bunúsach."

I stilled my stirring as the blood before me began to churn and shimmer, the telltale magic forming before my eyes. It amazed me every time, seeing such simple material as human blood become a force of magic that no one else could touch.

For whatever was coming next, I would be prepared better than my enemies could ever imagine. Starting with having *lots* of blood magic to access.

The dreams made it clear that blood magic would be my lifeline, and I had no cause to doubt them. Not when the dreams had all aligned perfectly with what I knew to be true.

My crown was awaiting me. Dusk Kingdom's crown may be mine, but it was paltry compared to what was meant to grace my head. Being king of the realm was hardly enough either, not when there was something truly grand waiting.

After all, someone had to rule once the gods were out of the way. My dreams showed me many things. Ones I had thought impossible. But if it all worked out as planned, and I would ensure it did, then the gods would soon be locked away. They'd be powerless, and it would take millennia for them to gather enough strength to try to fight. By then, I would be firmly established and able to crush them as they deserved.

The fates were with me, and thus, I knew my charge was a righteous one. The gods had overstepped in taking away our magic, and they would pay dearly for all they had wrought. Though, if I was honest, there were other reasons my anger at them continued to burn so hotly.

It wasn't enough to take away my magic and leave me powerless; they then had to turn around and give *my* human unimaginable power and a throne besides! It was embarrassing, honestly.

Asteria was mine.

She had no business sitting on any throne, playing at being queen.

But even worse than that—they'd made Asteria *Calix's mate.*

If she should have been anyone's mate, it should have been mine! Our souls understood each other; I knew that beyond any doubt. But Calix was able to tempt her away from me, all because the gods had forged a bond between them.

Given more time, I could have broken Asteria of that willful spirit, and built her back up into a proper Fae lady. One who may have been fit to sit at my side as queen. Instead, I was left with the nagging, duplicitous Zerlina.

I nearly rolled my eyes at the thought. Her hovering was becoming cloying. Her desperation to prove she wasn't betraying me only made me more certain she was. She was terrible at this game. Maybe the court in Dawn Kingdom was full of half-wits, leading her to believe herself better at it than she was.

That would actually explain Tariq quite well.

The man kept pushing for the marriage to happen quickly. He wanted his daughter assured as queen of Dawn no matter what happened. I wasn't stupid, however. If I gave in and married her before whatever battle was on the horizon arrived, then when it did, he could easily turn on me.

As long as his daughter was queen, with a son in her belly, the throne would be secured.

Over my dead body.

Like Tartarus was I going to let Tariq and Zerlina sweep in and benefit from all the blood, sweat, and magic I put into making this kingdom my own. I wouldn't put a crown on her head until everything was secure.

Unfortunately for dear King Tariq, that meant he wouldn't live to see his daughter become queen. More fortunately for him, it also meant he wouldn't live to see me strike down his son and heir. Though, he'd surely find out soon enough, once his son joined him in the Otherworld.

At least until the time came for me to assume my new position. Once I controlled the Otherworld, I would ensure its purpose was more suited to my own. Who knew how many useful creatures lurked within those realms, ones that could be put to better use protecting me in this one. They were wasted on the dead.

Bottling up the blood magic, I stashed the vials away in every pocket I had and refilled the vial connected to the chain around my neck. One couldn't be too careful, and I needed access to magic at all times. The extra bottles ensured that whenever battle did come, I would be more than ready to meet my enemies on the field.

I opened the old wooden door that led into the forgotten workroom I'd made my own, and exited into the dusty hall. Closing the door, I quickly locked it up. This section of the palace was unused by anyone else these days, but it wouldn't do for anyone to stumble upon it by accident, either.

Making my way down the twisting halls, I came to the back entrance to the dungeons. A turn to the right would see me ascending the stairs up to the palace proper, while going through the door in front of me would put me right into the dungeons themselves. I deliberated for a moment before opening the door with an aggravated sigh.

Weakness was something I could ill afford, and yet…

Making my way into the dungeons, my guards jumped in surprise, their armor clanking with the movement. They looked with creased eyebrows from the main entrance to where I had suddenly appeared, a look of fear in their eyes.

I honestly wanted to laugh. They clearly thought I'd done some great feat of magic to appear before them like a specter, when all I did was use a Tartarus damned door.

"Carry on, men," I instructed them, "I'm just here to visit one of my prisoners."

"My King." They bowed as I passed, and I rolled my eyes at the scent of fear that wafted off one of them. A guard here needed thicker skin than being scared of his own king.

I wrinkled my nose at the smell coming from the dank hall before me. I watched my step carefully, not knowing what might be littering the dirt-covered ground. The lighting was incredibly dim, with only one flame at the end lighting the dark grey rock. All the dungeon cages had been formed with it, the cavernous space making for a wonderful place to keep prisoners.

No one was escaping through the magically enforced bars, and they wouldn't be escaping through the thick rock deep beneath the palace either.

I came to a stop at the end of the row, where the light was brightest. It illuminated the grimy form sitting slumped against the back wall. His brown hair was longer and shaggier than I'd ever seen it, and his golden eyes were missing the luster that so captivated the court.

His wife was locked in a much nicer room up above in the palace. The usual standard protocol for noble prisoners. But Vissy was a special case. His betrayal cut deeper than the rest, and thus, his punishment had to be much harsher.

Having him under such strict guard in the dungeons also meant that no one could get to him through any of the secret tunnels throughout the palace. There was only one way in here, and one way out. Meaning I knew every single individual who might try to see him.

Not that anyone had. Which was certainly curious. Maybe my siblings wrote him off once he was imprisoned, and no longer able to assist in their plots.

The rebels had only gotten louder, however. They'd become more brazen, attacking my camps under cover of darkness and trying to free my blood bags. Some had been caught and subsequently chained up themselves, but most of them remained elusive.

There had to be someone helping them. Perhaps Kian or Vikal. Vikal had mysteriously disappeared, and while Kian claimed ignorance, I believed him less and less. It was no great leap of logic to see that he only left after I threatened his little slut. How he got out, however, was the real mystery.

I'd already killed the guards who'd been assigned to watch him. Whether they were disloyal or incompetent didn't matter. Either way, they could not be trusted. Their bodies now hung from the palace gates as a warning.

Gruesome, maybe, but effective.

The rest of my guards had certainly straightened out and stiffened up when they saw what bad results garnered them.

Kian, however, remained. He didn't disappear with Vikal, which was the only doubt I had about the whole situation. Would he not have fled to avoid treason charges?

Or was it merely that he had greater plans in place?

These thoughts all brought me to Vissy, or the beaten-down version of the friend I knew. Those golden eyes cracked open, and upon seeing me, he scoffed and rolled his eyes before closing them once more. He crossed his arms over his chest and hung his head, his long hair covering most of his face. He acted as if he was going to sleep instead of bothering to acknowledge me properly.

It was infuriating. The absolute disrespect he showed only proved that I had been too lenient with him. Perhaps it was time to take things further, and find out the truth of the matter.

"You know, Vissy, I once wanted you by my side as I took up my rightful place," I told him, regret leaking into my voice despite myself.

He ignored me, and I clenched my fists together before lightning could strike out from my fingertips.

"But I see now the folly in such thinking," I sighed sadly. "Attachments do nothing but hold one back. If I'm to rise, I need to purge myself of such things. Ensure I have no weaknesses, you understand."

Vissy looked up warily, his eyes flickering back and forth between mine. The dim flame cast long shadows across his cell, leaving a strip of light to illuminate his eyes as he leaned forward, making his golden orbs look like they were glowing.

Making the rage and disgust within them more than clear even within the dark womb of the palace.

I stiffened as he pushed himself up from his sprawl. He sauntered over to the door slowly and leaned his elbows where the bars intersected, his hands clutching tightly to the dark metal. He tilted his head, leaning the side of it against one of the bars, as his eyes bored into me.

Stripping me bare straight down to my soul.

I felt frozen in that moment, unable to do anything more than look back at him and let him see all that I was. All that I had become. A different beast than the one he'd grown up with, I knew.

Destiny had too much in store for me to remain unchanged. When I accomplished everything I sought, it would prove my detractors wrong about me. It would show Father, even in the Otherworld, why I was always the best choice of heir. The one good decision the gods had made.

My mother was the only one on my side now. She served her role well, charming the court and especially the king of Dawn, right out of their secrets and into everlasting loyalty.

I had once thought Vissy would always be there, believing in me when most of my family would rather see me dead and gone. The loss of that certainty caused an ache in my chest, and it felt as if lightning bolts of pain radiated out from it.

"What are you going to do now, huh, Cyrus?" Vissy laughed bitterly, a sound I had never once heard from his mouth. "You say you can't have attachments, but what about Asteria? Hmm?"

I blinked, breaking from his intense stare, and sighed slightly in relief. Shaking my head, I snorted at his question. "Asteria will be at my feet where she belongs."

"Oh, a woman like Asteria does *much* better on her back," Vissy smirked, a nasty snarl hiding beneath it. "But then—you wouldn't know that, would you?" He laughed, looking as if he'd won something with this bizarre turn of conversation.

"I will," I told him seriously.

Vissy just laughed more, shaking his head. "Not truly. You'll never get to enjoy the experience of a *willing* Asteria."

He leaned his head closer to me, the stink of unwashed male making me wrinkle my nose and lean my head backward. "And let me tell you, *brother,* it is *exquisite.*"

His smirk as he pulled his head back was a familiar one, one I recognized as the smirk he would often don when speaking of his many conquests, bragging about the men and women who'd throw themselves at him for the mere chance at a night in his bed.

Fury rose hot and uncontrollable within me. I lashed out, my hand grabbing him by the throat and pulling him into the bars, his head bouncing off the metal with the force of it.

"You didn't," I growled, my canines lengthening as the truth of their betrayal solidified within me.

He just laughed once more, golden eyes twinkling with perverse joy. He'd actually done it. *She* had done it. Vissy didn't own her after all, not like I did. The one sticking point between us, preventing her from opening her legs like the slut she clearly was.

"When?" I demanded, shaking him by the throat. "When did you start betraying me, you piece of shit?" I loosened my grip, allowing him to answer through my grip.

"The night of your betrothal ball, of course," Vissy answered easily. "You spent so much time teasing her, Cyrus. Winding her up and up with no relief to come. The poor girl needed an outlet." He licked his lips lasciviously, making me snarl in response. "And I was oh-so-willing after that taste you gave me. Desperate for more, even."

I screamed in anger, tightening my grip around his throat and watching as he lost that awful smile until his hands came up to try to pry mine off, and his face began to go red and then purple. Through my anger, though, I realized this wasn't the way.

I let him go abruptly, watching him hit the ground with a thud. He coughed harshly, curling up on his side and reaching up to rub his throat with a much hoarser laugh.

"Going to kill me now, Cyrus?" He moved onto his knees, watching me with suddenly dead eyes. And then I realized that it was exactly what he wanted. Time in this dungeon had drained him of the will to live.

Well, that certainly wouldn't do.

"Not yet," I answered honestly, and he sagged a bit, whether in disappointment or relief, I couldn't be sure. Even when driven to the brink, men ready to die often find they aren't as ready as they thought when it comes.

"Guards!" I called, and they came running around the corner. A guard with short blonde hair and blue eyes who looked familiar arrived with a darkhaired and pink-eyed man who didn't. It took me a moment to recognize the blonde. He was one of the guards on duty the day Zerlina prevented Asteria from taking shelter during the attack on the city.

After I realized that was the day she had met Calix, I had punished the guards who'd been there with dungeon duty, a severe step down from guarding the royals. I eyed him speculatively, but ultimately decided to move forward.

"Lord Visita here is to be delivered to Kesshuu at the North Camp," I instructed them. "I want him put on the rack and left to wait for my arrival, understand?"

They both nodded immediately, and I turned to look back at Vissy, who sat glaring at me.

"I'll find out the extent of your betrayal, *brother*," I spat at him. "Even if it kills you."

I didn't allow him a word in response, stalking off and leaving behind the love I once held for the man in the cell. Thinking of the many times we'd laid in bed together, experiencing a closeness I had never experienced with another, my heart felt torn to shreds.

And knowing Asteria had turned to him? Even before Calix stole her away? It took those shredded pieces of my heart and burnt them to ash.

I STORMED THROUGH the palace, with slaves, guards, and courtiers alike scurrying out of my way quickly. It was enough to cause at least a glint of satisfaction within me. My father never inspired such fear or showed such dominance over his court.

But the feeling didn't last long. The specter of my father was surely laughing now. The two people who meant the most to me, fucking each other behind my back. I could practically hear his '*I told you so*' in a ghostly whisper.

Trust and love were overrated. Power was all I needed. It could never hurt me, after all, and that's all those I loved had ever done. Power was simple and straightforward, with a clear path to achieve it. Love was messier than power by far. It was better to bury any tender feelings and let the drive for greatness fuel me instead.

The guards outside my mother's door spotted me, bowing their heads and knocking to announce my presence before opening the door for me. I immediately entered, watching them close the door behind me before I spun to face my mother.

She sat back on her chaise, the red velvet crushed over time from how often she leaned on the arm sipping her similarly colored wine. She certainly enjoyed the theme, as her hair and currently raised brow matched suspiciously well to her favorite resting spot.

Her deep black eyes fixed on me as I began pacing back and forth, but she thankfully remained silent and let me think. The only sound was the sloshing of her wine in the glass as she drank.

"How goes things with Tariq?" I asked suddenly, turning on the spot to face her. I had no desire to get into what was bothering me. I knew her opinion on Asteria quite well, and I'd already had enough of listening to her ranting about the "uppity slave girl" who had "bewitched" me.

"Very well." She smirked, looking decidedly pleased with herself. "He's agreed to hold off on the marriage until the realm is more stable."

"How'd you manage that?" I inquired, my eyebrows flying upwards. He'd been annoyingly persistent about it since he'd arrived.

The look on her face made me wish I hadn't asked. I might throw up if she confirmed my suspicions.

"I merely reminded him that a royal wedding needed to be an elaborate and regal affair, not a rush job before a battle." She rolled her eyes, shaking her head slightly. "Which is true, regardless of the fact we have other plans. Royal weddings need to be attended by all the royals across the land. It would be unseemly otherwise." She sniffed haughtily.

I rolled my own eyes this time. "Except none of the other kings will live long enough to attend."

She brushed off my reminder with a wave of her hand. "It still holds true. If you're the only king, then all royals *will* be in attendance."

A smirk rose on my lips, and I nodded my head in agreement, giving her that one.

"Speaking of, will there be a wedding at all?" Mother asked seriously, leaning forward. Her long sleeves draped to the ground from where they split at her elbows.

"I will need a queen if I'm to have heirs." I reminded her dryly. "One can't begin a new dynasty without such, unfortunately."

"I'm well aware, son." She responded, unimpressed. "Considering I taught *you* that. I mean, will Zerlina be the one? After all, you're sure she is in league with your foolish sister in some nefarious plot." She shook her head in dismay, sighing slightly. "I don't know where I went so wrong with your siblings."

I sighed, rubbing a hand through my hair before slumping onto the sofa across from her. "I don't know. If I can prove her actions, I'll have a case for execution. But I can't imagine any other princess being so indifferent about their family's deaths."

"Hmm." She hummed, tipping her glass at me. "A good point. You could always marry her and kill her once she delivers an heir."

My eyebrows rose, but it was a solid idea. I needed to marry no less than another royal, and the pool was limited to Zerlina, her sisters, Sybella and Danique, Sunneva and Isleen from Sunrise, and Dysis from Sunset. I couldn't very well reward a princess who sided with my enemy either, meaning Dawn's royal family was the only option.

Of course, there was one other royal available. A princess, heir to her kingdom no less. But the very thought of her had lightning running through my fingers in cracks and pops. I closed my eyes for a moment, gathering my emotions.

Asteria would return to her rightful place, and I would have the chance to punish her then for all of her transgressions. She wasn't raised to be royalty, but to be a slave. She had no true education or instruction on how to behave properly. Was it even fair to hold her actions thus far against her?

Well, I couldn't see myself letting them go, but I would ensure she was retrained properly, until she was the perfect pet. Maybe one day, should she show enough deference and apology, I would consider raising her station.

Maybe then, after enough time had passed, and all those who remembered her treachery were dead, she would even make a worthy queen beside me on the throne.

Asteria's blood would be even better than Zerlina's when it came to birthing an heir. The blood of the soon-to-be former gods ran in her veins. Would it not be right to mix the new god king's blood with the former king of the gods to bring about an heir?

The beginnings of a way to further this plan sparked in my mind. I stood suddenly, ignoring my mother's confused look. I stormed out, heading to the guest quarters where Aelius rested.

The man may be disposable, but the information he possessed as the king of Day certainly wasn't. In fact... it would provide exactly what was needed to bring my war to the gods themselves.

CHAPTER 55

ONE of my favorite books as a child was about Queen Malika. A touching romance about a Fae queen who overcame the odds, facing down armies to protect her kingdom right alongside her soulmate. I never imagined I would one day do anything remotely similar, and I now found myself taking issue with the author.

They wrote of these grand, epic battles, but never about the soul-deep terror one felt facing such a daunting task.

After waking up curled around Calix like a cat, we'd woken each other up fully with frantic kisses and fumbling hands, desperate to touch and taste before the sun rose and the day truly began. That hour felt unmoored from time, as if nothing but it existed. Just Calix and I, and the unending passion between us.

Inevitably, though, the time came for us to get on with the day. We quietly helped one another into our respective armor and then made our way out into the camp.

Everyone seemed equally subdued. Even as we began gathering everyone into their units and preparing to march onto Evenfall. We'd snaked our way past the border patrols Cyrus had set up, not an easy task for a force this vast, but we'd managed it thanks to the brilliance of Titan, Arien, Eryx, Nithe, and, of course, Calix. Their combined knowledge giving us an edge. It wouldn't do to give away the surprise, after all.

Mounting up onto Arianrhod, she nickered softly, like she could sense my anxiety. Her lilac-colored tail twitched, and I brushed my hand over the silver hair down her back to calm her. Elatha was watching intently, his green tail swishing unhappily at his mate's distress. Calix snuck him a sugar cube, making me snicker quietly at him.

It was truly adorable the way he indulged our horses.

Calix mounted up on Elatha after a moment, and we rode our Faethren's over to where the rest of the army was amassing on the other side of camp. Sweat slicked my palms as I looked out over everyone present.

Harpina stood beside my brother, and I narrowed my eyes briefly at the way she was smiling at him. Thankfully, Titan distracted them as he pulled Arien aside to talk. Eryx and Baach walked up and down the forming lines, helping and directing the warriors where needed. Callisto was standing in front of the human half of the army, looking more than ready to lead them against those who'd kept them enslaved for so long.

The lords of every city in Night were scattered around, as well as half of Day's. Ndrita was with Sterling, rallying the people from Keris. Prince Altan was glaring at Prince Zakat as the two argued. I rolled my eyes. It was impossible for the two to be together longer than a moment without such a sight.

Calix helped me gallantly off Arianrhod, and we both unfurled our wings, flying up into the air and hovering where everyone could see us.

"People of Celesterra!" Calix shouted, and the din went quiet, everyone turning to look at him. "Today, we are not Night Kingdom, Day Kingdom, Sunrise or Sunset, Dusk nor Dawn. We are one people, *united*. The balance of our world is at stake, and it will take all of us, working together, to fix it."

"Some of you hoped to fight to end slavery, while others cared only for the balance," I yelled, looking around at the many different people who'd joined us for this fight. Meanwhile, I fought my own battle, pushing down and burying my fear, as well as my rage at what was to come. I couldn't let my chaotic emotions lead us astray now. Chaos was what would see the end of us all.

If I let myself feel that chaos inside, I would be lost—and so would we all.

"Let this battle bind us all together. Let us not be human or Fae, but equal citizens of this realm. Today, we fight for balance, but we also fight so every man, woman, and child can live in that balanced world freely!" I spoke passionately, my desire to see the humans free nearly overwhelming in that moment.

A loud cheer rose up, and the soldiers before me raised their swords in the air. I took a deep breath. This was really happening. These warriors were about to risk their lives on *my* say so. I was about to walk into a battle, wielding sword and magic just like the queens I'd read about as a child.

The battle in Day was small scale in comparison to what was happening now, and I found myself completely unprepared for the reality of it.

I breathed in—terror consuming me and gnawing away at every bit of confidence I'd built up since escaping Dusk.

I breathed out—and reminded myself that I was strong. That I could take whatever this fight threw at me. I rebuilt my confidence brick by brick as resolve hardened my features, looking out on the faces of those I was fighting for.

My friends. My family. The humans. The other Fae.

I turned my head to the right, catching Calix's eye.

My mate. My love.

We did this *together*, connected through a bond I understood even less than the day I discovered it, yet somehow understanding it on an instinctual level that went beyond word and thought.

Blood and soul.

"We are stronger together than we could ever be apart!" I announced, Calix's eyes heating as he watched me rally the troops. Those lilac eyes raked down my armor-clad body, and I shivered. It *almost* felt like his fingertips followed the path of his eyes.

"And we will use that strength to crush Cyrus's forces!" Calix took over, his face hard and resolute as he appraised the cheering soldiers before us.

"For King Calix! For Queen Asteria!" Titan shouted, his sword high and face proud. "For The Star Queen and the Night King!"

"For King Calix! For Queen Asteria! For The Star Queen and the Night King!" they chorused, and a lump formed in my throat.

"For all those still in chains! For the balance that our free world will rest on!" I managed to get out roughly. "For freedom!"

"For freedom!" The others bellowed, and Calix and I flew gently down, straight onto our horses. We kicked them gently into motion, leading the charge out of the camp and toward a battle that would decide the fate of our world.

I couldn't begin to contemplate what might happen if we lost. Chaos was so insidious, sneaking its way into this world and leeching it of everything I loved so much. The color. The magic. The life.

Fear was a second passenger on the horse with me as we rode toward Evenfall. It beat in my heart like the pounding of the horse's hooves on the ground. Calix's strength and confidence came to me in a wave, and I took a deep breath, letting it fill me and slowly easing away the terror I struggled to keep down.

Facing down the man who abused me in front of thousands, with the fate of the world riding on it.

No pressure *at all.*

WE STOPPED WELL outside the gates of Evenfall, out of sight of any guards who may be watching. We dismounted and readied to shift, but Calix quickly gathered me in his arms, his lips finding mine with a ferocity that made it clear the fear I felt wasn't *only* mine.

I leaned into him, kissing him with every ounce of love in my heart that my lips couldn't form in any other way. I clutched at him, wondering if it would help if I just held him a bit tighter. Would that do anything to ensure he stayed with me always? That this battle or the next wouldn't take him from me?

His forehead fell against mine when we pulled back, and his whisper was hard to hear with the noises of the army surrounding us, even with Fae hearing.

"Promise me you will be careful," he asked, eyes creasing in worry. "That you won't take any unnecessary risks."

"If you promise the same," I countered. Calix smirked slightly, though it was clear his heart wasn't in it. But he nodded, so I nodded back in agreement. I swallowed hard, hoping I wouldn't make a liar of myself.

We stepped back, our hands lingering until just the tips of our fingers touched, trying to hold onto the warmth of one another before facing the cold of battle. But we'd never truly be apart. The bond would keep us connected in a way nothing else could. Soul to soul.

I closed my eyes, unable to bear looking, and allowed my dragon form to come forth. Fingers became claws, and skin became scales. My wings flapped upward, pushing me into the sky. Calix and Arien flanked me while Altan and Zakat flew behind us.

We flew out in five different directions, each taking a side of the city to scope out any defenses. We stayed high in the cloud cover to hide from any scouts looking for us. I flew to the right to cover the north end of the city and circled around the perimeter, my Fae eyesight straining to make out everything down below.

Cyrus had indeed been busy.

New fences, buzzing with lightning, circled the city. Grey spikes were outside the gates, hidden from the front but more obvious from the back, sticking up to catch anyone who approached.

Iron.

"Do you see it?" I sent to my brother and mate, and got their affirmative responses back. It took another minute before Arien sounded once more in my head.

"We've got some kind of catapult here. I'm guessing filled with iron," he told us grimly.

"Light it all up," Calix directed, his bubbling rage like a siren song in my chest, coaxing my own higher and hotter.

I let it fuel the fire inside me, spilling out in a wave of flame that washed over the fences and spikes, melting them into heaps of scrap. The loud howl echoing through the city had me smirking, as best as I could in this form, anyway.

The alarms began to sound within the city, our presence now obvious. Dusk's warriors spilled from the palace and surrounding areas, just as we knew they would. And the first wave met our flames as we dived down, our fire taking the entire line of soldiers to their deaths.

I shifted mid-air, letting my bulky dragon form slim down to my Fae form, pulling my sword from my sheath before my feet hit the ground. Calix and Arien now flanked me while Altan and Zakat remained in the air, catching fire to key buildings we knew Cyrus was using for the transport of humans and iron in and out.

When the next wave of Cyrus's soldiers came, our forces were ready. Calix had sent the signal to Lilith, who'd been waiting in her wolf form to get the message. With her howl, our warriors began to flood the streets like a plague upon Dusk.

They came from every gate, but also from within the city itself. I smirked, knowing Nithe would be leading warriors up from below the tunnels running under the city. They were meant to be an escape for the royals, part of the same system running beneath the palace I'd once found. But now, we were able to use them against those same royals.

I swung my sword as the first man rushed me, clearly thinking me the weakest link. My blade found his neck, and his head hit the ground, leaving another man behind him blinking in shock. My starlight rammed into him, throwing him into the far wall.

Darkness and sunlight flew by me, but I couldn't let myself be distracted as more soldiers rushed forward. The fighting was thick and fast, with the vanguard of both armies clashing, but our numbers were greater. Sunset's men had added to ours, and they'd been joined by a bit less than half of Sunrise's as well.

As promised, King Tieran had been waiting for us before we made camp last night, and his soldiers and the rogue Sunrise men following Altan had blended in with ours until we became one army.

A massive, glowering man spotted me, and he snarled in disgust, approaching me with the promise of death in his eyes. I recognized him immediately. He'd come with King Tariq when Cyrus and Zerlina were betrothed. Tariq's commander. The same commander Harpina's friend Tesha had been brutalized by. He'd tortured her, taking her arm, her eye, and her sister's life.

In short, this was a man I'd absolutely love killing.

I smiled slowly, which clearly enraged him. He rushed me, bellowing his rage. I ducked under his swing, knowing his size and strength were going to be too much for me. I danced around him instead. I sliced at the back of his legs, making him growl. He turned quickly, and I bent backward to avoid the intended swipe across my chest.

He barreled down on me, and I was forced to roll quickly out of the way as what would have surely been a killing blow came down. He shouted, and I watched as his hand became a paw, his arms slowly overtaken by fur until a large brown bear was before me. I swallowed slightly, reminding myself that I could do this.

I was fierce. I was strong. I was Asteria *fucking* Earendel. The blood of gods ran through my veins, and I was more powerful than any of these bastards.

I would never again be at the mercy of *anyone.* Let alone an abusive prick of a man.

I'd had quite enough of that for one lifetime.

I twirled my blade tauntingly, circling him casually. He was already so angry that he'd shifted, if I could just get him sloppy enough...

I jumped upward, my wings ripping out and pushing up quickly. Just barely missing two meaty bear paws grabbing me by the neck. He managed to grab my foot, however, dragging me back down. I jabbed my sword down before panic could take hold, feeling it sink slowly into the top of his head. Only my wings saved me as he dropped, stopping me from going down with him.

Instead, I gently lowered myself to the cobblestone, tearing my bloody sword from his head. I smiled, watching the blood pour out. They say head wounds bleed the most, and from the amount spilling out, I knew that must be true.

It was a beautiful sight.

"Back in the game, girl!" Harpina appeared out of nowhere, stabbing a man who'd been sneaking up on me. I sighed, my wings disappearing as I gave her a quick nod.

I wasn't used to the insanity of this battle quite yet. The one in Day wasn't anything like this madness. Men were fighting over every inch of Evenfall. The organized assault lasted all of a few minutes before it devolved into chaos.

The thought gave me a chill up my spine, but I shook myself. We were doing well. Our forces were slowly beginning to overtake them. I nearly smiled, but a shout escaped my lips, and I hissed instead, turning my head to see a dagger embedded in my shoulder. The pain was so intense it burned like the fires of Tartarus, and I could feel myself quickly weakening. A man with long, dark hair in nickel-plated armor with the Pegasus of Dusk on it smiled cruelly, pulling the dagger out only to go for another blow.

I looked briefly at the wound and then the dagger. *Iron.* It had to be.

A loud growl broke the man's concentration on me. I looked to the left to see Calix stalking toward us. The rage on his face was plain to see, and his sword was gripped tight in hands now tipped with sharp claws. He looked like an avenging warrior god, like Anann himself come to seek revenge.

The iron dagger shook in the soldier's hand, and I couldn't blame him. Even as relief at my mate's presence filled me, the pain in my shoulder was incredibly distracting. Thanks to my Fae healing, it *was* getting better with the iron now removed, but it was so achingly slow.

The soldier crumpled before me, shaking his head as howls of pain filled the air. I could feel the steady energy flowing from Calix to him. The pain of Tartarus funneled from the depth of the abyss and straight into this man who dared to hurt me.

"Stand. Up," Calix growled at the quivering creature before us, his fangs long and sharp. The man moaned in pain but forced himself to his feet despite it. He wavered in meeting Calix's eyes, and the fear on his face once he did nearly made me feel bad for him.

But seriously, *fuck this guy*, I thought, holding my aching shoulder as my body fought to heal the wound.

Darkness spilled from Calix, slithering over the ground and over the man's boots. The soldier shook as the shadows moved up his body, inching up to his face. As they did, they entered his body wherever they could, filling his mouth, his nose, his ears, even his eyes. I watched in stunned shock, having never seen his shadows do this before.

His screams were muffled by the shadows, but plain, nonetheless. Suddenly, the man's form seemed to almost buckle inward, before it exploded outward in a shock of shadow and blood and bone. Calix's shadows had destroyed him from the inside out, and pieces of the man rained down around us in a dark mist.

Calix's eyes met mine, rage and fear overtaking the bond as those eyes filled with green, blue, and pink, joining the purple until his orbs were all Aurora. He grabbed me by the hair, pulling my lips to his in a fierce collision. My own hands snaked into his hair, holding him tightly, ignoring the blood streaking his silver locks as our tongues fought for dominance.

I pulled back with a gasp for air, and Calix immediately stiffened, swearing under his breath. I looked up, finding that in our distraction, the enemy forces had noticed us and were taking advantage of the situation. They were barreling straight for us, too great in number for any two normal people.

But we were hardly normal.

We both gripped our swords, our eyes meeting as the thought passed between us. Matching smirks formed as we both summoned our magic, building it and building it. Starlight and darkness formed around us, increasing in density until they began to swirl into one another. Our magics began to spin faster and faster, until a tornado of starlight and darkness surrounded us. The soldiers approaching us seemed to hesitate finally, but we sent the cyclone of starlit night straight for them.

It tore through their ranks, decimating the men as it ripped through flesh and bone, until many fell to the ground, dead. A cheer rose up from our forces, and I couldn't help the smile that formed on my lips. Even as I panted from the exertion of magic.

The cheer quieted as something began to be rolled out from the palace. I growled as I spotted Cyrus at the helm of a wooden-framed contraption.

His wavy shoulder-length dark hair left down and brushed the nickel plate of his armor. He wore a long cape affixed to his shoulders, bright pink to match his feathers, with Dusk's sigil in charcoal grey in the middle of it. Grey embroidery also surrounded the edges in an intricate design, studded with grey gems I was sure had come straight from Gemaria.

Calix stiffened beside me, and his tension bled into my own. Cyrus's pink feathered wings flung out, his cape falling between them as they brought him into the sky. He looked over the battle below with a cruel smirk.

As our eyes met, his eyes flared with something I couldn't place before he smirked widely. Calix flew upward before I could do anything, heading straight for Cyrus. Cyrus's head snapped to him, a cruel sneer taking over his face.

But I noticed something important at that moment. Cyrus looked… *awful.*

His blue eyes, once so full of passion and intrigue, were now bloodshot and dull, while his tanned face had grown wan. The blood magic was obviously taking a toll on him, whether he realized it or not.

Did Calix? He took off before I could say a damn word to him. His rage at Cyrus's treatment of me too great for him to hesitate. As he reached Cyrus, he was forced to zig and zag to avoid the bolts of lightning that arced out at him, Cyrus attempting to fry Calix mid-flight.

But Calix got to him despite his best efforts, crashing into him at speed and forcing the two of them to fly backward into the palace's marble wall. They grappled, and I heard Calix's growl as he dodged a blade. It was the same grey as the blade that got me, meaning Cyrus was armed with iron, as expected.

I let my wings unfurl, and I flew toward them immediately. I twirled my blade to get it in the right position, and as Calix held Cyrus to the wall, I flew in a rush, my blade sinking deep into his stomach. The howl Cyrus let out was music to my ears, the blood dripping from the wound a beautiful sight.

I gripped the blade and ripped it back out while Calix let go of his hold on him, letting Cyrus sink to the ground, clutching his stomach. His wavy hair was mussed from the fight and covered his face, but I needed to see his agony for myself.

When he looked up, however, instead of fear or pain decorating his face, he instead smiled widely.

My own fear came not a moment later.

Cyrus removed his hand from where it covered the wound I'd created, and the rapid healing—faster than a Fae's even—I witnessed as the wound closed right up had to be a result of blood magic.

"Now!" Cyrus yelled, and I watched as whatever contraption he'd brought up was aimed right at us.

I watched in complete stun as a lever was pulled back, and shards of something were sent at us in a blast. Calix dived in front of me, trying to fly us away, but the shards hit him full on, and his agonized scream as we slammed hard into the ground was haunting.

I ignored whatever pain I felt from the impact and rushed to see where he was hurt. Moving him off me as gently as I could manage, I crawled onto my knees to see the damage.

Shards of iron were embedded in his skin and armor. I cursed the finger holes in my armbands. If my fingertips had been covered, I could have just grabbed the iron and started helping him right away. He couldn't begin to heal until it was all out, and I wasn't wasting time.

I scrambled for a solution for a moment, until I found the cape of a dead soldier nearby. The bright gold cape was obvious, even with dirt, dust, and blood all over it. I wrapped my hands in it and used it as a shield as I began to quickly pull the iron pieces out of my mate despite my shaking hands. Calix's eyes were creased with pain, his body writhing and arching as I worked. Tears filled my own eyes, the agony in the bond too much to take.

Once I got all the pieces I found sticking out of Calix completely out of his body, I looked up, fully aware my distraction could have put us in a worse situation. Cyrus was watching us, however, and his men had clearly held back from engaging for a reason. My eyes narrowed on Cyrus, his smirking form nearly bristling with contempt.

"Asteria!" he called, a smile filled with sharp canines looking down at me. They were pitiful compared to Calix's fangs, the effect of the chaos within Cyrus obvious. "*This* is what happens when you disobey me. Don't you think you've let poor Calix suffer enough for your obstinance?"

"Fuck you, Cyrus!" I called up to him, making him chuckle as he shook his head, feigning amusement for the benefit of his people. But I could see it for the farce it was. He had been right about one thing: *I did see him*. I didn't think he'd appreciate *what* I saw, however.

"Why don't you come down here and face me like a man? Or are you too scared?" I taunted, tilting my head to the side, gaining strength from the way Calix clutched my hand. I just needed to distract Cyrus from Calix long enough for him to heal.

"Oh, you don't want me to do that," Cyrus said, looking down at me with a frown that was as fake as his conciliatory tone. "After all, if I die, so do *they*."

I looked at him in confusion, but he just flew down, and four guards made their way out of the palace, straight to him. Two humans were held up by the arms between them, chained at the hands and feet. My heart started to race double time, and when their heads were forced upward, I shot up from Calix's side to my feet.

"Mom? Dad?" My voice wavered, and I cursed myself for the weakness. *How the fuck did he find them?!*

My hands shook, and it was all I could do to stop the rest of me from shaking, even as my claws shot out. Fear and rage were a terrible cocktail within me, smoke beginning to billow from my mouth as I considered what he could have done to them already.

I should have gone to them. *Protected* them. What use was any of this new power if I left those I loved to flounder?

Worse was knowing it *was* my fault. My fear of their reaction to the truth kept me away, and Cyrus was able to take advantage of my hesitation. I never thought that he would consider them at all, let alone go after them. But I should have. He was deranged and would do anything it took to get what he wanted.

Cyrus tutted, "Remember what I just said. You kill me, then mommy and daddy dearest die with me."

"What the fuck do you want with them?" I demanded, "What did you do to them?"

"Now, now, Asteria. You're in no position to make demands, are you?" Cyrus tilted his head to the side, a large smirk taking over that punchable, haughty face. "You're going to call this attack off and come home. Where you belong."

I snarled, Calix's growl echoing it, but Cyrus wasn't deterred in the least. "You'll even have your parents here to keep you company!"

"And what about Aelius?" Calix demanded, slowly standing up from his sprawl. "You promised him her death."

I raised a brow at him, cocking my hip as my hand curled tightly around my sword, starlight swirling around it in unruly spirals.

Cyrus sighed exaggeratedly, as if Calix was too dull to even entertain. "Come with me, Asteria. You can save all these people. Your friends. Your *parents*."

His pointed look at them had me switching my gaze back to my parents as well. I hadn't seen them in so long now, and had thought I never would again after Placement Day. My emotions were so mixed, I didn't know whether to be scared or relieved or pissed off.

My parents were both bruised, surely, but they looked mostly okay, thank the gods. My mother's chin was up defiantly, while my father openly glared at them. When our eyes met, his fierce stare left me taken aback.

"Don't you dare do it, sweetheart," my father yelled to me, and one of Cyrus's soldiers punched him, making me lurch forward to intervene, but Calix grabbed my wrist, keeping me in place.

"Forget this charade!" someone yelled, and all heads snapped toward the gold-clad man storming toward us. "She needs to die, now."

A golden sword was pointed straight at me. The man's sneer was ugly, out of place on such a beautiful face. But I recognized those sky-blue eyes immediately.

"Hold your blade, Aelius," Cyrus demanded, eyes getting a bit wild as they shot between us.

"I don't answer to you, boy," Aelius spat at him. I noticed movement just behind him, but kept my eyes forward purposely. "I'm *King* of Day, and it's time I rid myself of this pest to my rule."

"A pest?" I asked dryly, raising a brow at him. "How kind, *Father*," I spat right back at him. "You think I relish being related to *you*?"

He growled, his blond shoulder-length hair swinging wildly as he marched straight toward me.

"You are no heir of House Earendel. No woman will ever sit *my throne!*" he screamed, his rage blinding him to all else.

"It's *MY* throne. You aren't fit to rule a kingdom, *Father*. The gods realized this, and Earendel has chosen *me* to lead us. Your views on women, humans, all of it is part of the old world, and Celesterra will be moving in a new direction now." I smiled at him, side-eyeing Cyrus as well.

"And I think I'll start by making sure you two *pests* don't affect MY kingdoms!" I snapped, making Aelius's face crumple into a snarl. But instead of attacking me, as he'd meant to, I watched in glee as my brother attacked from behind, taking Aelius by complete surprise.

I was saddened he didn't take his head, but I was sure that would come.

This was a fight my brother well deserved. For all that I had been affected by Aelius, I had never lived with him. Hadn't spent years being talked down to and degraded by him. Hadn't seen how our mother had been locked out of council rooms and made to watch from the sidelines. Arien deserved this fight.

More importantly, the move distracted Cyrus, and I used that to quickly fly up, shifting into my dragon form and barreling right at him. Cyrus's eyes widened at the giant teeth about to swallow him whole.

"Iron! Now!" he shouted, slight hints of panic leaking into his voice before he quickly shifted into his Pegasus form.

Calix would secure my parents while I would take care of the monster my nightmares were made of.

CHAPTER 56

Calix

SHIFTED at the same time as Asteria, grabbing her human parents in my claws and bringing them up into the air before anyone could stop me. I was forced to dodge the projectiles aimed my way, moving over the city lines to the forces we had waiting in reserve.

Lowering over the camp, I let her parents down slowly, before shifting so I landed beside them. And unfortunately, swaying slightly as I did.

Damned iron.

We knew the battle would be unpredictable with all the elements involved, but I couldn't help but think we'd underestimated the effect of the iron. I still felt weakened, and my full strength was needed for this. I had to get back and ensure Asteria was all right.

Feeling her wasn't enough. I needed my own eyes on her. The mixture of rage, fear, regret, and pain was enough for me to be mirroring her feelings by accident. They slid through the bond so hotly, it was hard not to give into them.

But I'd trained for years to control my emotions. Asteria had mere months. I was trying to force that control over to her now in a vain effort to pull her back in. But the rage was too hot in her blood.

I needed to get back to help her.

But she'd kill me if I failed to secure her parents. Despite her fear of their reaction keeping her away from them, she loved them deeply. It was why she cared so much about their reaction to the truth of her.

It seemed the cat was out of the bag now, however.

"Havard!" I called over one of the warriors leading the reserve forces. The fair-haired soldier once lost his sister to the machinations of Dusk's court. He'd since made it his mission in life to protect people from them.

He bound over to me, a curious look in his burgundy eyes as he noticed the human couple beside me.

"These are your Queen's parents," I told him, the gravity in my voice unmistakable. He straightened, face long and grave. "I need you to protect them and ensure Cyrus doesn't get his hands on them again."

"Of course, my King." He bowed his head with a nod. "By Nox, I will protect our Queen's family with my life." He pounded his fist over his heart as he made the vow, then bowed to Asteria's parents as well.

"Asteria is a queen?" the woman asked slowly, her voice thready with confusion, clearly hesitant to speak up. She clung to her husband, her curly hair hiding part of her bruise-covered face.

I cursed myself for not getting them protection. I didn't think Cyrus knew who they were, much less cared about them. That was a failure on my part. I shouldn't have underestimated Cyrus, but it seemed we had on too many levels.

"She is." I nodded in confirmation. "She's queen of Day by right of blood and the gods, and she will be queen of Night as my mate."

"Mate?" Her father nearly growled, impressive for a human. His eyes narrowed at me in suspicion, his jaw set in a way that told me he was considering punching me. I had to fight to keep my lips from tilting up into a smile.

"I promise, we will explain everything to you both, but I must get back to Asteria," I told them, my eyes seeking her form in the sky, where she was chasing after the fleeing coward.

A loud boom sounded, and I looked sharply to the left. Iron rained down once more, but this time, over the entire city. Apparently, Cyrus no longer cared if he hit our men or his own. I growled, wanting to ring the fucker's neck with my bare hands, to feed the pain of Tartarus into him as my shadows infected his bloodstream, to tear my claws through his chest to rip out his blackened and rotten heart.

Screams came from inside the city; surely the Fae suffering burns from the iron. Lightning bolts flew through the sky, Cyrus's blood magic reaching down and scorching people where they stood, even as he continued to flee from Asteria. He switched back and forth from his Pegasus form to his Fae form. *A weakness.* He couldn't wield lightning in his Pegasus form, and I couldn't help but wonder if the lack of a defensive trait was a direct result of the loss of magic. Dusk being more corrupt meant they were the first to feel the effects of chaos. And the Pegasus in the Otherworld had horns on their heads. One had pointed theirs directly at us, readying to defend itself.

My wings tore out and lifted me into the air. I shifted into my dragon form, letting my fire breathe out and fan the flames of battle. I scorched one of the catapults, landing beside it as I shifted back. My sword immediately found its way through the chest of the warrior manning it.

Cyrus left nearly fifty men to protect it, but I smirked as a giant loomed up behind them, blocking them in between us.

Titan met my eyes with a nod, and together we attacked. They didn't notice Titan until his blades took down two of their number. They split their focus between us, and we worked our way through with smiles on our faces.

Even weakened, I gloried in battle. The feel of my sword in my hand, dancing through slash after slash, blocking and parrying. It brought joy to my dark heart that nothing else matched. Not in this particular way.

Asteria was a different, *greater*, kind of joy. Even if she, too, fed the blood-lust that ran through my veins.

Six Fae men circled me, striking at me from all angles. I moved swiftly, avoiding hits and summoning shadows to block and attack in tandem with my sword. I panted slightly from the exertion, the effects of the iron dragging me down. My body was working hard to fight against it and heal me, but it was slow work.

By the time I'd taken them down, Titan was watching me in concern. I waved him off, eager to continue. When I nearly failed to block an attack to my back, Titan growled angrily, decapitating the man before I could even turn.

One of the soldiers met my eyes, looking me over critically before running off. I wanted to say we scared him off, but my heart sank. Something wasn't right.

"We need to follow that one," I told Titan, pointing my blade toward his path. He nodded, a grave look in his blue eyes. He spared a glance to the sky, following Asteria's path, before we both ran after the man.

We had to fight our way through as soldiers jumped in our path to prevent us from moving forward. Whether they knew what we were doing or just saw one of their main targets, I couldn't be sure.

One of the men who stepped in the way I was happy to see. Smug grin, short blonde hair, and bright green eyes that stared me down with a twisted pride he had in no way earned.

"Lord Kem," I drawled, a smirk lighting my lips as I took in his attempt at intimidation. The hunched shoulders and glare did nothing but amuse me.

"King Calix," he spat, looking disgusted as the word *king* left his lips. I couldn't help the slight laugh in response.

"It truly bothers you, doesn't it?" I asked him, shaking my head in amusement. His glare only heated, and I could practically feel the anger radiating off him.

"What?" he snapped. "That the gods gave you a kingdom to lead while my king's heir is a pitiful woman?"

"Is it truly that she's a woman that bothers you?" I challenged, twirling my sword casually. "I'm sure if Prince Arien had been heir, you would be just as angry—because it's not *you*. You've done all you can to be a mini-Aelius, but it's all for naught, isn't it?"

He let out a bellow of rage, and just as I expected, he sloppily rushed at me as he let his emotions control him. A rookie mistake, but one the too-proud lords so commonly made.

I parried his brutish swing with ease and stepped to the side, laughing as he fell forward from the momentum. Sadly, Kem caught himself before he face-planted, turning to me with a grimace.

He began to step to the side, trying to circle me, and I matched his steps. Another loud boom sounded in the background before the sounds of agonized screams reached me. More iron had been deployed, and my people were suffering. I needed to end this, and Lord Kem was decidedly in my way.

I sent out a whip of shadow, lashing across his face. He stumbled, holding his face as he groaned in pain. I advanced, bringing my sword up, but he just managed to bring his own up to weakly block me. I willed my shadows to grab him, and they brought him down until he was on his back with his limbs restrained.

"Sorry, my Lord." I bowed mockingly. "But I have a war to win."

Kem let out a rough laugh, "You'll never win, Calix. No weak woman will ever sit the throne of Day!"

I glared down at him, even as his laughter continued.

"A *strong* woman already does. Your precious king's antics ensured the people of Day would side with her, willingly and gratefully," I told him proudly.

"It'll be hard to be queen when she'd laid dead at the foot of Aelius's throne. No matter what happens to me, they'll see to it." He smiled happily, as if the thought was enough to bring him peace on his way to death.

My lips twitched into a snarl, and I summoned the pain of Tartarus, watching as that peace on his face turned to horror. His limbs shook in pain as he groaned, struggling to move against his shadow-binds.

"*This* is what you have to look forward to after death, Kem. It won't be peaceful for you; I promise you that." A wicked smile took over my face as a violent glee filled me. "And up here? Well, Cyrus was betraying Aelius the whole time. He never intended to kill Asteria, but Aelius."

The horror on Kem's face deepened, even as he tried to shake his head in denial.

"Oh yes," I purred, leaning down so my face hovered over his. I grabbed his cheek, my claws piercing the skin and making blood trickle down his face. "Your plans were always destined for failure. But don't worry, we'll rebuild this realm to be the best it's ever been. And Asteria will lead that charge."

I smiled wistfully, "Asteria is the light to lead us. A star who shines in day and night. She will bring us through this fight."

I took a dagger off my belt, stabbing it through the center of his stupidly smug face, admiring the hole it left as I took it back out. His dead eyes looked back at me, terror etched into them forever.

"You just won't be here to see it." I smiled, wiping the bastard's blood off my blade with my shadows before sheathing it.

I stood up, cursing, as I realized Titan was nowhere to be found. I ran, following the path we were on, before that idiot distracted me. I hissed, holding my side as I ran, that damned wound still sluggishly healing.

I swung my blade as I approached an unsuspecting soldier who was facing the opposite direction, slicing through him with one blow. The others nearby immediately reacted and moved to intercept, but they were easy to cut down in succession.

As I turned the corner, I found Titan, facing off against a line of men who were blocking another towering weapon. I didn't know what this one did, but certainly nothing good. Eryx and Baach had joined Titan, and they were trying to get to another group of men who were hiding behind the line of soldiers protecting them. Those men were fiddling with the weapon, looking frantically to the sky.

I followed their line of sight, right to Asteria and Cyrus. I watched as his hoof shot out at her, and she roared back at him, taking a rough bite out of his thigh. I couldn't help my smirk.

That's my girl.

But Cyrus was also looking down, I realized, right at the men preparing the weapon. Waiting for something.

"Calix!" Eryx shouted frantically, and my head whipped over to him. "It's an iron net! They're going to take her down!"

Not on my gods-damned watch they weren't.

No one was going to fucking touch my mate. But as the men working on the net shouted in glee, I knew whatever had been holding them up was fixed. They moved the weapon to aim it right at Asteria.

I didn't think. Didn't hesitate. I just quickly shifted, flying up faster than my wings had ever carried me before, just as the net released.

But it was more than a mere net. It was iron, certainly, but sharp spikes also protruded from it. Ensuring its intended victim was taken down and then *kept* down.Considering the iron would bypass the magic in our scales, those spikes would slide right into flesh and cause unparalleled agony.

Panic was the only thing I felt as I flew as fast as I possibly could, hoping against hope I could outfly the speed of the projectile.

I would be damned before I let Cyrus or anyone else lay a single fucking finger on Asteria. She was mine, and I always protected what was mine.

I loved her too much to lose her. The thought of my life without her in it was a bleak one. A world without Asteria was a world with all hope and joy leached from it, leaving only the deep darkness inside me to fester.

The monster would take over the man without my star to light up the darkness.

I aimed my body straight in front of her, my size enough to mostly block her smaller form, and stretched my wings out wide to ensure she was fully shielded. Her head snapped toward me as I braced for the impact.

I couldn't help the screech that left my maw as the net encircled me, the spikes stabbing through my flesh and hitting deep. I began to free fall, unable to hold my dragon form or my wings, as I rapidly lost hold of my magic. Asteria's guttural roar sounded more like a scream as I hit the ground with an agonizing jolt.

Horrendous pain overwhelmed me, like my blood was lit by the fires of Tartarus. The irony wasn't lost on me. Maybe this is what I deserved after taking such joy in torturing Kem. Asteria's form landed beside me, now in her beautiful Fae form once more.

"Soren! Callisto! *Any* humans, *please*, I need you!" she yelled, her voice cracking and tears running down her face. "Now!"

She dropped beside me, reaching through the holes in the net to brush back my hair, avoiding the iron. I wanted to tell her to stop, to not risk herself, but I couldn't bring myself to speak. I was fairly sure her gentle touch was the only thing grounding me, anyway, preventing me from giving in to the pain and passing out.

I may have actually blacked out for a moment or two, as the next thing I knew, the net was being lifted. I screamed in pain as the net took skin and flesh with it, before the spikes then slid out. The burns and holes left behind had to be a gruesome sight.

"I'm so sorry, my dorchadas," Asteria whispered tearfully. "I'm so *so* sorry. Nox, why did you do that?"

"Couldn't—let—" I groaned, struggling to speak through the pain. "You—hurt."

Asteria sobbed, her dark hair falling over my face as she leaned over, kissing my cheeks and forehead before kissing my mouth lightly. The salty taste of her tears killed me. I hated seeing her cry, especially over me.

"Drink my blood," Asteria said suddenly, and my eyebrows creased. "We're stronger with sharing, right? You'll heal quicker," she insisted, brushing her hair to the side and exposing the creamy white skin of her neck.

I hesitated despite the tempting sight. The pulsing vein in her neck was like a siren song. But while the pain was gods-awful, I didn't want to weaken her at all in the middle of battle.

"Nox damn you, Calix," Asteria complained. "Just do it!"

I could tell by the look on her face that there was no arguing with her, and I truly didn't have the energy to try at the moment. My fangs sunk into her neck, the magic in her blood tasting like the sweetest of sins. I felt it hit me as I drank, like her starlight was lighting up all the dark bits inside of me and cleansing them. It was absolute bliss, despite the pain ricocheting through me.

Asteria moaned, but her hands let go of my shoulder as quickly as they'd latched on, careful not to stab me with her claws. I slowly sat up, until we were both upright, and pulled my fangs out, licking the remnants of blood off her skin. Our eyes met, arousal simmering between us like a match about to light.

"You two about done?" Callisto snapped, and I looked up to find her glaring down at us, her hands on her hips. "We have a war to win here."

"Thank you for your assistance, Callisto," I told her dryly, and she rolled her eyes. But I could see the relief in her eyes as I stood up.

I could feel that despite the infusion of blood, I wasn't fully healed yet. The lingering effects of the iron were slowly being worked out, but I buried the lingering pain as best I could. Asteria watched me with concern, and I knew she could feel it, too. Unfortunately, the circumstances meant I didn't have the time to fully heal.

We no longer had eyes on Cyrus, but we seemed to have more people still standing than Dusk did, thank Nox.

A loud crash sounded behind us, and we turned to find Baach, Eryx, and Titan had taken down the contraption that released the net. That was a relief, at least. They wouldn't be able to deploy it again.

"We need to regroup," I told Asteria, looking around at our warriors fighting Dusk, Dawn, and Day kingdom soldiers. "We aren't leaving until Cyrus is dead and gone."

"Of course not." Asteria smiled. The violent joy in her eyes sparking my arousal once more. My reactions around this woman had the tendency to make me feel like a youngling once more. But I shook it off for now, taking her hand.

"What about my parents?" she asked, biting her lip as she tried to hide her fear.

"Safe," I promised her. "You'll see them as soon as this is done." She nodded gratefully, just as one bolt of lightning after another struck the sky.

We both stopped in our tracks, our eyes meeting before looking up...

CHAPTER 57

Arien

FINALLY.

My blade swung down at my father, but he moved quickly to the right, so it glanced off his armored shoulder. My father spun around with a growl, eyeing me with contempt.

"Treason, son? Truly?" he spat, sneering at me like his disapproval would make a damn bit of difference at this point.

"Treason?!" I laughed incredulously, swinging once more. I didn't even care that he blocked it. I wanted this out. To finally say everything I'd held back all these years.

"Treason would mean I was ever loyal to you in the first place," I said, my voice grave with the weight of truth. "I was raised to be loyal to my sister."

"Your *sister*," he growled, swinging hard at me. I parried his blow with ease. Father had grown lazy over the years, preferring to send others to fight his battles for him. "She is an abomination!"

"Abomination?" I scoffed, shaking my head at him. "That's exactly why the gods warned Mother about you. She had to give up her *daughter*, all to protect her from *you*."

Father paused mid-swing, his sword falling as he breathed deeply, as if something had finally punctured the shell he kept around himself at all times.

"Your mother's betrayal truly is the deepest," he murmured quietly, a look on his face I would almost call pain if he wasn't who he was. "My own wife. My own queen. My own *soulmate*. How does the other half of one's soul betray the other in such a way?"

His tone grew from reflective to demanding as he went on. His agitation was like a balm to my soul after the years I spent biting my tongue.

"They say that the love a parent feels for a child is greater than any other." I smiled tauntingly.

"A failure of a son in more than one way, then," he said, clearly trying to turn the tables on me. "You were denied by the gods for a little girl, and you just step aside and let her walk over you to the throne?"

"She's not walking over me." I rolled my eyes, blocking his angry, sloppy swing. "The throne is hers by right. She's the elder twin, and the gods chose her for a reason. You're the one who's denying the gods will, Father. What is so bad about a queen ruling?"

"Argh!" Father swung left, and I brought my blade up to parry, swinging to the right and bringing my blade back up quickly. We began to dance back and forth, but I held myself back. We had a conversation to finish after all.

"Women," Father spat as he panted for breath, "are weak, feeble creatures. They have no business making big decisions or leading armies."

"And yet, your own wife has been making plenty of big decisions for years, right under your nose. Splitting your court apart without you even realizing it. Turning them to my sister. Whose leading armies just fine." I smiled proudly, pointing my sword toward where Asteria was going after Cyrus.

I rolled my eyes as my cowardly father tried to attack me while I was distracted. I quickly met his sword, preventing him from taking my head. I noticed Bellin approach from behind my father, giving me a questioning look.

Ever loyal.

I shook my head. I didn't want help with this one. I wanted to kill him myself. Whatever that may mean for the future and my relationship with my mother.

"Mother never wanted things to end this way, you know," I told him quietly, feeling like the words needed to be said. To be acknowledged. "It hurt her to have to do this. You're her mate, after all. But she knew you'd kill Asteria to gain a male heir, and she would never allow that to happen. Even if it meant strangers raised her child. She's the type of parent who would do anything to protect her children. While you, on the other hand, would do anything to protect your throne." I sneered at him.

Aelius laughed, and it was *Aelius*. He didn't deserve the title of father anymore. He never had.

"Children are meant to continue a house's legacy. And you and your sister are the worst sort of legacy to leave." He smiled nastily. "I refuse to let *this* be my legacy. So, I'll just have to get rid of the baggage and start anew. Your traitorous mother will have to go, too. I'll find myself a new young wife to give me a proper heir. Along with a proper spare to marry off. Gods know no respectable woman wants the unchosen prince."

He could say what he will about me. I was more than used to it, after all. But to threaten my mother… that I could *not* abide.

I flew at him in a flurry of strikes, letting my rage fill me and drive me onward. Faster. Harder. Sharper. And I needed every bit of it.

Aelius might have grown lazy over the past couple of centuries, but he was still older and more powerful than I was. He met my blade strike for strike, and then sent a beam of sunlight straight at me.

I fell backward, blinded by the sun for a moment. It wasn't nearly as hot or bright as it should be, however. *Chaos had gotten to him.* I smirked at the realization, even as I rolled out of the way of his downward swing, jumping up and meeting him with a much brighter beam of sunlight.

It sent him spiraling away, where he crashed down onto a pile of scorched debris. He panted, looking up at me in shock as I sauntered toward him.

"How?" he demanded, shaking his head to clear the remaining orbs I knew would still be obstructing his vision from the light. "There is no way for you to be more powerful than I am!"

I laughed dryly, raising a brow at him. "You threw your lot in with chaos, *Father*. This is the result of your own megalomania. Chasing power has done nothing but drive you farther from it."

"That's—that's impossible!" he protested, pulling himself up from his inelegant sprawl, dusting off his shiny golden armor to ensure the wreckage didn't leave any traces that would tarnish his *image*.

"The tighter one clings to power, the faster it slips through their fingers," I told him, unable to help the smile growing on my face. Which only served to enrage him further. "And you, *King Aelius*, clung to power, forsaking all else. You tossed aside your *family* for the sake of it. It seems poetic that it will be your downfall now."

"You think *you* will be my downfall?" Aelius scoffed mockingly, but I was immune to his attempts to belittle me by now.

"*I know I will be*," I growled, and lifted my hand, sending a blast of sunlight right at his damn face.

He dodged at the last moment, making me curse in frustration. We circled one another, ignoring the blasts of fire, water, wind, lightning, darkness, and even starlight flashing and swooping from all directions. The battle was a hodgepodge of powers, and every kingdom's royals were here, making for a show I was sure hadn't been seen in Celesterra since before the six Fae kings of old had signed the treaty.

Prince Zakat sent blasts of fire at King Tariq, who was using his wind powers to buffer the flames and snuff them out. I had seen Prince Altan drown a man standing before him on dry land with his water magic. But it was the battle between Asteria, Calix, and Cyrus that sent true sparks flying. Lightning clashed against darkness and starlight, creating the effect of a stormy night sky above the battle.

But the building momentum of that lightning, the increase in bolts that could strike at any moment, was certainly worrisome.

I knew Asteria and Calix could handle themselves, and I had my own battle to be concerned with. Still, I couldn't help but fear that the amount of blood magic Cyrus was using now was going to be too much for them.

I hissed as metal slashed against my cheek, drawing blood. Aelius smirked at me, and I glowered, pissed at myself for being distracted during a fight. Titan would kill me if he found out.

I refocused my attention on the fight against my father, keeping my footwork quick as I moved around him with increased speed. He matched my movements until we were a blur of steel. Our blades danced together, neither landing any true blow against the other.

I hated to admit it, but we were too evenly matched. I tried to kick out his legs, and he jumped over my foot. He tried to stab my weaker side, but I moved into his guard and elbowed him in the chin for his trouble.

We might have gone all night that way, but a soldier from Dawn careened around the corner and spotted us, coming to a standstill.

"You there!" my father called to his ally. "Help me put this pup in the ground where he belongs." He smirked at me. "Somewhere he'll never see the sun again," he added, just to twist the knife. Our family thrived in the sunlight, to be without it would be to be without a heart in our chests or air in our lungs.

The soldier stepped forward, and I drew a dagger from my belt, preparing to defend myself against two opponents. I cursed mentally. I may be evenly matched against my father, but an additional fighter would put me at a distinct disadvantage.

I refused to let my father end my life, not when he'd already taken so much of it from me.

The soldier stepped up beside Aelius, who looked ready to crow in victory. My fingers tightened around my blades, and I desperately searched for any sign of weakness in the new arrival.

I was completely unprepared when he twirled his blade, using the movement to twist it quickly to the side, where he stabbed directly into the weak part of Aelius's golden armor, right where the two plates connected.

Aelius screamed in rage and pain, grabbing his side ineffectually with the armor blocking the wound. His wide eyes went to the soldier from Dawn, who removed his helmet slowly.

I nearly started laughing hysterically.

"Uncle Dali," I panted in relief, that hysterical laugh I bit back bubbling up into a chuckle.

Sparkling bright green eyes met mine, a smile tilting his lips. "Nephew. I hope you don't mind. I'm sure you had him, but he deserved a bit of payback from House Paiva directly for what he's done to my sisters."

Dali ran a hand through his short black hair, which, usually perfectly coiffed, now stood up with slightly spiky ends thanks to his helmet.

"You son of a birch!" Aelius cursed, looking between us. "Another traitor betraying their king," he spat at Dali, whose eyes narrowed.

He stepped forward, grabbing Aelius by his chest plate and shaking him. Aelius looked at him, eyes wild with fear that he couldn't totally suppress. No one had ever stood against him in any substantial way. He was used to being obeyed; he had no idea how to handle his reckoning.

"You threatened my niece's life and forced her to grow up human." He landed a punch across Aelius's jaw but held his armor with the other hand so he wouldn't fall back. "You forced my sister to give up her daughter." He punched him again. "You threatened my youngest sister to keep my elder sister in line." Another punch. "Kept my youngest sister from our family for years for the sake of your plots." Another. "Forced my nephew to be raised without his twin, while doing everything you could to ensure he knew how little you thought of him." One more. "And now, you plan to kill your own children. MY BLOOD."

He let go of Aelius's collar to deliver the final punch, and Aelius fell to the ground, moaning in pain as he held a hand to his face. The skin was already blackening from the hard, repeated hits to the same spot. He'd heal quickly, but then again, I would ensure he didn't have the chance to.

"Save any of him for me?"

We turned at the voice, and I smiled as Beltane walked over, his bloody sword leaning on his shoulder.

"Took you long enough." Dali smiled, stepping forward to clasp forearms with Beltane.

"Me? You're the one we haven't seen hide nor hair of until now," Beltane chuckled, tossing his head to get his dark hair out of his face.

"I'm surrounded on all sides in Dawn. I had to play the loyal lord to prevent my whole family from losing their heads for treason," Dali countered, raising a brow.

"Excuses, excuses." Beltane tutted, a smirk on his face. Dali rolled his eyes, clapping him on the back.

"Don't worry, though, there's plenty of this fucker to go around!" Dali said joyfully, pushing our cousin forward to where Aelius was trying to rise.

Something deep within me rose up in excitement at the pitiful look of fear in Aelius's eyes. The same part, perhaps, that used to curl up in shame whenever he would put me down in front of his courtiers. It soothed the ache of the child left inside who wanted nothing more than for his father to love him. The child who died the day Mother sat me down and explained about my sister—and what my father would do to her.

I'd bit my tongue and took his verbal abuse, but I no longer cared that I didn't meet his expectations. Because he didn't meet *mine*.

Now, seeing his fear as he faced the three of us, the way he tried to snarl and puff up as if we couldn't all *scent* that fear... it was pathetic.

He was pathetic.

I realized that now. This was a king afraid of having a girl sit his throne. Who let the specter of an heir bring him to ruin. Who feared anyone else taking any of his power because then others around him might realize he wasn't worthy of his own.

I couldn't help the laugh that burst out of me, nearly bending over with the force of it. Everyone looked at me as if I was insane, but I couldn't be bothered.

Aelius must have read something in my eyes and interpreted where my amusement was coming from because he narrowed his eyes at me before rushing toward me, sword up.

Beltane met his blade with his own, forcing him back. I brought my own up, waiting for my chance. Beltane seemed to play with him. All those years of watching and waiting, being forced to keep silent, had finally found a release. He wailed down on Aelius with brutal strikes, forcing Aelius to stumble back and back.

He growled, his frustration at Beltane's surprising strength clear. He lifted a hand, sunlight beginning to gather within it. Beltane tried to quickly stop him, but Aelius kept that hand well out of reach, blocking every attempt with his blade.

Dali moved to assist, but I held up a hand, stopping him. Instead, I gathered my own sunlight, and just as Aelius went to release his, I let go of mine. The sunbeams met with a flare of light right in front of Aelius's face.

Beltane was forced back, covering his eyes for protection, but Aelius screamed in pain. He lowered his hand to reveal horrible burns covering the left side of his face, from his chin up to just below his eye. The skin cracking like an old lava field.

"H—how?" Aelius stuttered, bewildered by the burn on his face.

"Hyperion *chose* my sister," I told him with a proud smile. "He no longer protects *you.*"

The horrifying truth finally seemed to hit him, and he fell to his knees, his sword tumbling out of his hand. He sat there, staring blanking at his hands. He tried to summon more light, but chaos and losing Hyperion's favor had severely weakened his powers. After gathering so much, he could now only manage the barest flicker.

I stepped forward and kicked his knee.

"Get up," I demanded, pointing my sword at him. "Die like a man, at least. On your feet, with a blade in hand."

Aelius snarled, but forced himself up. His pride enough to overcome his shock and dismay. He refused to just roll over and die; I'd give him that.

It took fewer than five swings this time for the hit I'd been waiting for since this fight began. I parried Aelius's strike, hitting back with my own too fast for him to block, and watched as his sword sliced through the air.

Our eyes met. Sky-blue to sky-blue, with golden sunlight streaming through them. An acknowledgment of what was to come, of what had been and never would be.

The weight of years that had pressed on my shoulders finally disappeared, as with the next thrust of my blade, I stabbed right through my father's rotten heart, twisting the blade and breaking his heart—just as he broke my mother's.

And perhaps my own, if I was truthful with myself.

Blood spurted from his mouth as he fell to his knees. I tore out the blade and lifted it for one more swing. With a wide arc, I hacked through his neck, watching the golden strands tumble as his head fell to the ground. I stood completely still as the rest of his body swayed once and then crumpled down to follow its lost head.

A giant whoosh of air left my lungs. Like years of holding my breath finally released. I fell to my own knees, my uncle and cousin each laying a hand on my shoulder as I panted. Taking in the enormity of what I'd just done.

Ensured my sister's safety from a dire threat.

Killed my own father, my own blood.

Caused my mother immeasurable pain, as she no doubt felt the loss of her mate across the realm.

Conflicting feelings I had no idea what to do with rioted within me, but they would have to wait until the battle was won. Aelius no longer had any control of my life, and I'd be damned if I let him get me killed now.

I forced myself to stand, my family supporting me in a way the dead man before me never had.

I took the chance to look around the battlefield, spotting Eryx and Baach not far away. They worked together, taking on opponents double their number. It was clear they'd been fighting together since they were young. I was sure had Calix been there, it would be the same. Moving like a single unit, able to anticipate and accommodate without thought.

It was beautiful to watch.

A horn sounded, and I looked at Dali and Beltane, confused. Dali had stiffened, brows creasing.

"Fuck. That's Sunrise Kingdom," he said, looking worried. "Tariq had mentioned potential other allies for Cyrus but hadn't elaborated."

"Asteria has Prince Altan and the forces he was able to gather from Sunrise here," I explained, concern growing. "We knew Gravadain would side with Cyrus, but we didn't think it would be this soon."

"Maybe the disappearance of just under half his soldiers motivated him," Beltane suggested, and I nodded in thought before motioning them both forward as I broke into a run.

"Altan! Zakat!" I screamed toward the two princes. "To me!"

Thank Hyperion for Fae hearing, as the two princes quickly made their way over.

"My father's here." Altan greeted me grimly.

"Way to state the obvious, bird brain." Zakat rolled his eyes, leaning on his sword with all the casual confidence in the world.

As if he wasn't also a bird?

Altan scowled at him, opening his mouth to say something until he seemingly thought better of it and instead turned to me. "What are our orders?"

"I need you two to help fight your father. Let Asteria and Calix focus on Cyrus without distraction," I commanded them. "We've already lost a number of warriors due to iron. They aren't healing quickly enough to get back into the fight. Thankfully, our forces still outnumber Cyrus's since he had no compunction about taking down his own men."

I couldn't help but worry that another round of iron shrapnel raining down on us would leave us in a position we couldn't recover from.

But it was the blood magic Cyrus seemed to now be relying on, if the plethora of lightning was anything to go by, that truly made me anxious. The two princes ran off, and I took a moment to observe the battle, seeing if anyone needed help. Callisto was busy leading a group who were working to take out the iron weapons. Their ability to handle the material made them extremely useful there, and she had only the best of the human resistance fighters with her. They were working to take out another colossal contraption, and were cutting through Fae with an efficiency that showed their years of training for just that task. I was surprised to find Soren, his copper hair easily identifiable, leading another group of humans through the battlefield. He had them taking out the wounded enemy soldiers who'd been weakened from the iron projectiles. He called out orders, showing a surprising ability to lead I hadn't recognized before. They snuck past healthy, strong soldiers and snuck up on those limping along or trying to pull themselves up off the ground. I couldn't help but feel vaguely impressed.

The sound of a crash had my head snapping to the right, where I spied a giant wave of water rising from the ground. A tidal wave ready to sweep through the city, taking out any in its path.

Enemies, allies, and innocent bystanders alike.

Fuck.

I had to hope Altan could hold back the waves his father was amassing.

"Uncle Dali!" I called, and he ran over. "How's your air magic? Could you help hold back the waves?"

He bit his lip and tilted his head as he considered. "I'll try. I have enough royal blood to access the power, but it's not as strong as Tariq's."

"Anything will help," I told him with an appreciative nod.

I watched Altan step forward, hands raised, as he summoned a wall of water to block his father's wave. Zakat flew up in the air, his fire magic best used on Gravadain's forces directly. I yelled up at him, ordering him to fly up over the clashing waves of water and target Gravadain directly. If we could force him to lose his attention on his wave and let it go, that would be ideal. Zakat nodded, and with a last long look at Altan, he flew up high over the water, flames rising from his hands as he sent balls of fire down on Sunrise's army. Watching fire meet water, I could only hope it would be enough.

CHAPTER 58

Cyrus

I would applaud them for their resilience if it weren't for the risk of all my plans being ruined.

The memory flashed through my head.

A crown of gold, streaked with red.

A throne built on a pile of human bones.

A power that electrified the masses, everyone in line and in their proper place.

Once my enemies were out of the way, all of that would be possible. The dreams had been clear about that. But I would never succeed as long as Calix lived and Asteria wore a crown.

By the end, I would see Calix dead, and Asteria chained to my throne by a special collar I'd had made just for her.

Unfortunately, they were proving more difficult than expected.

How much damned iron could Calix take before he finally stayed down?

I swallowed another vile of blood magic, then reconsidered, and pulled out two more, quickly chugging them both. I'd never taken more than one at a time before, only drinking another once the effects of the first began to wear off.

However, desperate times called for desperate measures, and my role as god-king of the realms being threatened certainly qualified.

I shuddered as the forbidden magic coursed through my veins, filling me with a power beyond anything I had ever experienced.

I laughed joyfully, raising my hands in the air and sending bolts of lightning to scatter through the sky in a spectacular display of crackling blue bolts.

Why had I not done this before? It was incredible!

An almost childlike thrill ran through me at the potential this held. But first things first. I forced my attention down to the battle, frowning to see so many of my own men down. Whether it was from Calix's soldiers or the iron I had deployed, it didn't matter. They were useless either way. Several of my main weapons had already been taken out as well, which was certainly less than ideal.

Thankfully, the blood magic was strong. Stronger than anything my enemies could summon, I was sure. The power felt more plentiful than my naturally gifted magic had!

I aimed one of my raised hands, arcing a bolt of lightning right at Calix. He dodged out of the way, and I was taken by surprise as a blast of starlight swept me off my feet.

I tumbled backward on the roof, pitching over the side and falling down the other. It felt like I hit every pointed edge on the damn roof, each one digging into my stomach and knees with painful accuracy.

At least I was out of sight. That would spare me the embarrassment of my ignoble tumble.

When I finally righted myself and stood up, I let my wings unfurl and followed down the edge of the roof and around the palace until I found a safe space to catch my breath for a moment. It took a few minutes before I stopped panting, cursing myself for being so caught off guard.

The sound of a horn blowing was a relief. Gravadain had finally shown his face, and just in time. I peeked out from my hiding spot and watched as he raised a wave of water high into the sky, ready to sweep over the city.

I narrowed my eyes, the last thing I wanted was to clean up water damage in my palace. But it was pointless either way, as Arien quickly stepped in and recruited Gravadain's own son to stop him.

I snarled, watching as Prince Altan raised a wall of water to stop the tides. Prince Zakat joined his assault, flying over the waves to reach Gravadain. He shifted into his orange and teal phoenix form, enabling him to summon even more fire that he aimed directly at the king of Sunrise. It was enough to get me moving, and I flew over the field to find the man I needed.

It took two times circling around, but I finally spotted him, and landed down beside him.

"King Cyrus." He bowed his head respectfully, lowering the sword that had come up automatically at my entrance.

"Prince Vesper," I greeted. "I need you to deal with your little brother. He's causing issues for our ally at the moment. I trust you can take him out?"

Vesper paused at that, blinking quickly. He swallowed hard, and I narrowed my eyes at him. He'd been quite confident about his superior right to the throne of Sunset, that his brother didn't deserve it. But maybe when it came time to slay his brother, he didn't truly have what it took to do the deed.

"Of course," Vesper finally said, straightening as he gathered himself to his task. He nodded firmly, his bronze armor shifting as he set his shoulders back. His blue eyes stood out vividly, the conflict in them fading to resolution.

I waved him off, taking back to the air. I watched as Vesper shifted into his Pegasus form, heading straight for his younger brother. The heir to Sunset Kingdom turned to face his brother, his feathered head cocking to the side before his body lit up, the orange and teal feathers erupting into flames. Vesper followed suit, and the two crashed together, squawking with loud, high-pitched screeches.

I was curious how this would go. Vesper claimed to be the better choice of heir, but was that ego talking, or was he truly the better candidate? I supposed we would find out today. The two scratched at one another, talons grasping and ripping at flaming feathers that fell to the ground in random intervals, their flames extinguishing as they gently floated to the ground.

Their tussle sent them both flying into one of the nearby buildings, and I narrowed my eyes as another piece of Evenfall was damaged, this time by two overgrown birds crashing through the wall. It was a good thing I was about to take the wealth of five other kingdoms. The amount I was certain it would take to repair Evenfall after this was going to be substantial.

But maybe it was a good thing, I considered, looking out at my city and the damage that it had taken. From the rebels who'd burned down or defaced multiple buildings throughout the city, to the damage from this battle…

Maybe I should just rebuild it anew. Get rid of all memories of the past and my father's rule. Astraeus was dead, and his city with him. It was time now for me to rule, and this city to be mine in truth. A capital for not just Dusk Kingdom, but for my new empire.

I would be tearing down all of the other palaces across the realm; they wouldn't need them with no kings to rule from them. Instead, I would build

Evenfall into a city to rival that of the gods. With a palace that outshone all others.

With Asteria collared beside me, I would rule happily from my throne. Perhaps I'd sometimes allow her off her knees and onto my lap. I could pet her hair as she lay back against me, her small body squirming as I teased her ruthlessly. Denying her pleasure through court sessions, until the very end, where I'd let her cum before all my courtiers.

A fitting punishment for her many sins against me, but it would also show them all what I had—what I had *won*.

And how much she enjoyed it. Taking her pleasure from me with anticipatory glee. Writhing on my fingers and then my cock, a chorus of her moans and screams, making the entire throne room hard or wet. Knowing they could look but not touch.

And then I'd bring her back to my bed, where I'd graciously allow her to sleep with me. Perhaps she'd even hold me while I slept. Offering me comfort and grace I'd never known before.

True peace.

A loud crash brought my attention back to the present. Ripping me away from the future that I was a mere battle away from securing. The future I was destined for. I glared as I realized what had stolen my attention. A third phoenix had joined the fray.

King Tieran apparently didn't enjoy having to watch his sons battle to the death. He was flying between them, preventing both from attacking. I watched Vesper curiously, waiting to see what he would choose.

He hesitated, squawking at his father in indignation, before finally moving to attack him directly. Zakat jumped in to protect his father, but Vesper got a good slash in, sending Tieran to the ground. Injured, but alive. Zakat's loud squawk was almost a roar, and he vehemently threw himself into the fight against his elder brother.

Still, it was clear Vesper was the stronger of the two. I leaned forward slightly in anticipation, waiting for the death blow to be struck. Vesper pinned Zakat against a wall, raising a claw above his chest. Zakat screamed as Vesper struck, the curved, blade-like claw puncturing his skin and beginning to carve a deadly hole. But right when victory was at Vesper's claw—a flaming yellow and teal phoenix crashed into him, ripping the claw from Zakat's chest viciously while sending Vesper end over end through the air. He flew through the roof of a house on his way down, the sound of wood cracking and breaking before collapsing, echoing after him. Zakat flew crookedly for a moment, his wound healing but seemingly forgotten. His eyes glued to…

Prince Altan.

He'd saved Zakat, when he should have still been fighting his father. Why in the Otherworld had the man let his son escape him?

I looked to where Gravadain had been trying to flood Night's army, only to find them now being forced to battle with swords. Gravadain himself was fighting against who I recognized to be Calix's General, Titan. The giant blonde man was more than a match for any on this field at his age and experience.

What I had hoped to be the clinching move in the battle, bringing in the eldest of the kings and sandwiching Night between us, proved ineffectual against Calix's allies. I growled in frustration, running my hand through my hair.

It was time to get back to the main battle at hand anyway. I'd been distracted from Calix and Asteria for too long. I needed to act while the blood magic still coursed through my veins. I summoned my lightning, bolt after bolt hitting the sky, and began to aim at any soldier wearing black at random.

I watched in satisfaction as they hit the ground dead, one after another. Their hearts all stopped in their chests from the lightning that struck them. I summoned more and more, and sure enough, Calix and Asteria's magic barreled toward me.

The shadows formed a funnel flecked by starlight. Like the night itself was ripped from the sky and thrown at me. A part of me ached to see how well-matched their magic was. Indeed, the magic of mates. I pushed my weakness down deep where it belonged, letting my anger take the fore as I hovered above them in the air, avoiding the impact of their magic.

I sent lightning bolts flying at Calix, avoiding Asteria as best I could. My soldiers approached Calix from behind, but he must have sensed them, as shadows snaked out and wrapped around their necks, pulling them to the side until they cracked and my men fell to the ground, frightened eyes open and still. An expression forever fixed in death.

A growl rumbled low in my throat, and I summoned more lightning, sending as many bolts as I could at him, enough that he wouldn't be able to dodge. I watched in glee as they shot for him, but was surprised as his form quickly shifted into his dragon's.

Several bolts hit him, but that damn dragon scale was too tough to pierce without iron. They harmlessly absorbed my lightning with nothing more than an agitated roar for my trouble. I scowled back at him, my lip twitching into a snarl.

A blast of darkness surrounded me faster than I could react, finding myself thrown against a wall and held by shadows at every point. I looked up, enraged, to find Calix approaching, now back in his Fae form and walking the roof leading to the tower I was held against. Asteria was nowhere to be seen.

I slumped a little in my bonds. I did so much for her, and she couldn't even be bothered to stick around once her attack dragon had hold of me?

I couldn't think of a man I hated more than the one in front of me. He'd spent years making our kingdom and myself look weak. Making us scramble for control we couldn't begin to grasp. Showing us all how inferior we are to his greater power.

And then he had to steal Asteria on top of it?

The years I'd spent thinking Calix a friend were long gone, and by the way he fiercely glared at me, his eyes glowing with the hatred he felt, I knew he wished for nothing other than my death.

Two men I once thought friends, both betraying me for the woman we all wanted.

Dragons might be well known for their rage, but one should never ignore a Pegasus pushed to their limit. It was something anyone who rode a horse understood: the power the animal has should never be discounted.

And Calix made a grand mistake in doing exactly that.

He sauntered over menacingly, his hand gripping the hilt of his sword with bloody fingers. His eyebrows were scrunched together as if I were a misbehaving child he was about to voice his disapproval to. But the moment he got close enough, I summoned the magic in my veins, thankful I took those extra doses, and let it explode.

The shadow binds disappeared in puffs of black smoke while Calix was thrown backward, falling the whole way to the ground. I smirked at the sight and unfurled my wings to fly down and end this once and for all. I flew about thirty feet, planning to make an entrance for this grand finale, when pain flared in my lower leg, and I screamed in pain.

I bit down on my lip to stop screaming, turning mid-flight to see a silver and purple dragon flying below me, her teeth sliding out of my leg. Her blue eyes flashed with starlight, and the rage I'd always seen within them flared just as brightly.

She licked her tongue across her fangs, licking my blood from them with satisfaction, before she growled lowly at me. The second bite she'd taken out of me in this battle. Not content with her betrayal, she would see me harmed by her own hand, or dead by her king's.

I would have to spend a great many years training and breaking her before she could ever be trusted again. *If she ever could be.* But one didn't need trust to have a relationship. If they did, I wouldn't ever have any. I just needed her back with me.

Someone who understood. Even if she didn't agree with my actions, her understanding of who I was… was greater than anything else.

"Asteria, you can end this now," I attempted, hoping rationalizing with her would force her to see some sense. "There is no hope of winning against me, but you can still save the lives of your people."

A sinister growl was my only response to my attempted manipulation, as if she knew I would never let them go. Her teeth came at me again, and I flew backward quickly, shifting fully. I was always faster in my Pegasus form. It was built for speed in the air, where her dragon form was much bulkier and, as a result, slower.

I sped through the sky with Asteria on my tail. Dragons might be slower than Pegasus, but they were still by no means *slow*. And her fury was clearly fueling her, as I was barely keeping ahead of her. I switched up my direction and veered right, between two tall buildings.

Her roar of frustration sounded behind me. Her dragon form was too broad to maneuver in such tight spaces. Evenfall was added to over the years, with an increasing population meaning we put buildings wherever we could fit them. There was scarcely a bit of space between the buildings now, which fit a Pegasus well enough, but nothing bigger.

It gave me some time, at least. I crossed through the city by flying through the alleyways, keeping Asteria circling above. I tried to lose her by cutting through them in random twists and turns, but frustratingly, she was too fast for me to disappear into the city.

It was the sound of the mind-numbing screeches that saved me from Asteria's teeth and claws in the end. My wings sagged in relief for a moment. Until I spied the blasted creatures above me. Asteria was right in their line of sight, and they were heading for her, claws out.

Concern struck me immediately as they attacked. Asteria's roar echoed as she released a steam of fire at them. Most of the sirens dodged it, but I watched as a few burned, leaving the disgusting smell of charred bird in the air. Clearly, she was fine.

I took the opportunity to shift back, and leaned my head back against the brick wall of the alley I found myself in. I never wanted to have to fight Asteria herself, but she was making it very difficult. I may end up forced to fight her just to subdue her.

If only Calix hadn't corrupted her, we wouldn't be here now.

But we were, and I might be forced to do something unsavory for the sake of my long-term goals. Already, the battle wasn't going quite as I hoped. The easy victory with my iron and blood magic and allies was instead met with equal power. Not to mention equal loss on both sides of the fighting, all thanks to the iron. It didn't distinguish between ally or enemy and just burned whichever Fae it touched, leaving many of my own soldiers down or outright dead.

Calix, however, had *humans* fighting for him, somehow actually giving him an edge number-wise. I'd thought the humans useless, but they were proving more effective than I'd imagined. They attacked in groups or took on one at a time, relying on being underestimated.

Losing this war, thanks to *slaves*, would be embarrassing on a level I couldn't even contemplate.

"You need more."

I nodded absentmindedly as the idea filtered through my consciousness.

"You are so close now." A voice whispered within me, but with a deep, echoing resonance to it. *"You must bring death to your enemies. Take all you have on you, and when the moment is right, summon all the power that blood magic can offer you. Only then will you become what you were meant to be."*

I lifted my head, looking around in suspicion for a moment. Something felt different, but I couldn't put my finger on what. The idea seemed dangerous, but my subconscious clearly thought otherwise.

I looked up, finding Asteria battling with the sirens. I summoned my wings and made to find Calix, determined to see this over with before it was too late to save my plans.

I had a destiny to fulfill that was greater than any of this petty squabbling. Plans that would impact all of the realms. Plans that would see everything changed.

A new throne.

A new kingdom.

And the worship of millions.

CHAPTER 59

Asteria

O H, he thought he was so slick, didn't he?

I watched Cyrus slip away, even while I battled the sirens before me. I refused to take an eye off him, not when I knew he would go after Calix at the first opportunity.

I snarled at the siren taking a swipe at me. Their claws were wickedly sharp, and while they didn't fully pierce my scales, I thought with some time given to let them sink in, they might be able to do a bit of damage. I used my wing to throw them off, watching the creepy bird lady hit the wall with a crash.

Another flew at my face with a caw of anger, and I opened my mouth, preparing myself for the disgusting task. I grabbed her by the torso with my teeth, biting down hard. Weird, and absolutely disgusting, blue blood spurted as my teeth cut her in half, her wailing and flailing falling silent after a moment. I spit her out, wishing I could wash her taste from my tongue.

The rest of the sirens flew off with a horrifying screech, apparently smart enough to realize that taking on a dragon wasn't their best bet. I didn't like the idea of them attacking any Fae who lacked the protection of scales, but I had to believe our people could defend themselves. I had bigger problems to deal with.

Namely, one bastard Pegasus going after my mate.

Thankfully, Calix is twice the warrior Cyrus is, even on his bad days. I watched as Cyrus tried to sneak up on Calix with his sword drawn, but Calix spun on the spot, still agile and fast despite his injuries, and blocked the blade.

The sneers shared between the two would be enough to scare off most people, but I knew these two men too well to be frightened.

Calix was still recovering from the iron, despite his best efforts to pretend otherwise. His responses were a bit slower than normal, and he was favoring his right side.

On the other hand, Cyrus was faster and stronger than I remembered him being, but his lack of practice kept him from being as great a warrior as Calix. Where my mate moved instinctively, Cyrus struggled to keep up. Blood magic couldn't make up for centuries spent honing the skill.

I was impressed that Calix was doing so well despite his injuries. My shoulder still throbbed in pain from the one stab wound I received, but Calix had used his entire body to block mine, taking iron everywhere. I tried to check in and see how he was feeling, but I tilted by head to the side as I realized I had no idea. I could only feel the barest trace of him. I must have been too distracted to realize at first that the bond was being slowly muffled. But I recognized it all too well now. He was using the same tactic I had used to bury my feelings away. He'd only weaken further if he didn't tap into the extra strength offered by the bond. And there was only one reason he'd do such a thing.

To keep *me* from feeling his pain. He had to be in agony still, and it broke my heart he wouldn't use the boost from the bond just to protect me.

The two of them traded blows for several minutes before Cyrus's wings unfurled, and he flew upward. Calix's head cocked to the side, trying to figure out his opponent's next move. But I recognized the gleam in Cyrus's eyes. Like an animal backed into a corner, he was about to lash out.

Panic overcame me as I rushed forward—but not fast enough. Cyrus grabbed a vial from his pocket and downed it. I thought that would be it, but he pulled another out and drank it down, then another, and another… finishing off six of them in rapid succession.

Lightning crackled at his fingertips before running up to his arms, which were spread wide. A smile of complete bliss overtook his face, his eyes fluttering in pleasure as the blood magic seemed to take him over.

"Cyrus!" I screamed up to him, rushing in front of Calix and standing in between the two.

In my periphery, I could see our allies facing off with Cyrus's men. Titan was fighting a soldier from Day to my left, while Harpina and Arien took on several Dusk soldiers at once on my right. Eryx and Baach had joined Altan and Zakat in facing Gravadain and his men, while Ndrita was in her dragon form, circling above and chasing off the sirens. I even spotted Rhidian, who was seemingly playing with a much smaller man who stood no chance at all against him.

Cyrus lowered to the ground, walking toward me with his sword lowered. "Asteria."

"You don't understand what you're doing," I pleaded desperately. "The blood magic is pushing the entirety of Adamah out of balance. If we fall to chaos, the god of blood will be released. He was imprisoned millennia ago to save the realms, and if you keep on this path, you're going to release him!"

Cyrus laughed, throwing his head back as I ground my teeth, my fingers tightening around my sword in frustration.

"What an imagination you have, darling," Cyrus mocked, shaking his head at me. "Once you're back home, I'll help you shake any silly notions Calix has put in your head right back out."

The absolute gall of this man.

"*Calix*—" I stressed, "didn't tell me that. The gods did." Cyrus's face creased, anger flashing in his blue orbs, lightning crackling through them like a barely contained storm struggling to break free and lash out.

"The *gods*," he spat, snarling as he walked closer. "The gods are the ones who caused this. Their ridiculous rules limited and controlled *our* magic! But we are finally breaking free of them. Under my rule, magic will never be restricted again."

His words had all the preachy '*I know best*' attitude of the elders in Sonmathion, who'd talk down to you but wrap it up in a way that it was all for your benefit.

"Wouldn't you like that, Asteria?" Cyrus cooed, that charm of his spilling forth as he slithered toward me. Trying to tempt me, as if his manipulations had *ever* worked on me. "Complete magical freedom."

"More like complete oppression," I argued back. "Your rule would see this world in chaos!"

"*This world needs chaos!*" he shouted, panting from the force of his fury. "Don't you see? What has the balance gotten us? Truly? Nothing but fading magic and lost power."

Cyrus shook his head, his lip curling, but I could see the plea in his eyes as he looked at me.

"Cyrus, this isn't you," I begged, hoping against hope he wasn't as lost as he seemed. "You're a bastard, sure, and I will never *ever* forgive you for what you did. But *this?*"

My arms raised as I spun in place, indicating the chaos surrounding us. Running battles were taking place all over the city. Flames met the tides, while a tornado ripped through a crowd of battling soldiers, and a flare of sunlight was lost amidst the light of the sun already bearing down on us from above. Fae and humans alike lay dead all over the city streets, lost because of one rouge god's lust for power.

For *blood.*

And we were doing nothing but feeding him, I realized suddenly.

"This is not you. Cruach is using you." I entreated, and something sparked in his eyes at my words, enough to push me on. "He is pushing you because the more blood you spill, the more blood magic you use, the more the balance tips toward chaos. It will free him if it goes too far. But we can stop it now. We can save this realm instead of damn it."

Cyrus watched me carefully during my plea, but once I was done speaking, his eyes went right past me to Calix. My shoulders slumped in defeat. Whatever spark of something worth saving that had once existed within him had been snuffed out. There would be no reasoning with him.

I'd worked hard to see this battle objectively and not let my rage and fear for Cyrus's past actions influence me too much. To work for the betterment of the realm and my people instead of letting my emotions lead me. It was the only reason I bothered to try talking to him. And now, that familiar rage as Cyrus so easily dismissed me, lit a fire within my heart.

"Is this what he's told you? That I'll damn this realm?" He laughed, and it echoed weirdly, making me straighten in alarm.

Lightning cracked overhead, and I watched in horror as he summoned more blood magic, more and more lightning surrounding him until his form was lost in the sea of blue bolts. It crackled and popped, the sound loud enough to drown out the battle around us.

I summoned my starlight and threw it right at him, but it did nothing but dissolve against the bolts. These were no regular bolts of lightning, but fueled by more blood magic than one man should ever hold.

The sky above us crackled, and I looked up in horror as a storm began to form. Ominous black clouds streaked with pink began to gather in a swirling cyclone, nearly blocking the sun entirely. It looked like night had fallen, and in the shadow of the sky, I could just make out Luna's form up as it appeared above. She and Zhu now both occupying the sky in this weird in-between we'd found ourselves in, where the sun and moon were both visible at once.

"Cyrus!" I yelled, running forward with my sword drawn. Determined to end this while rage swirled at my fingertips in flecks of starlight.

"Asteria, no!" Calix yelled frantically, grabbing me by the waist and pulling me back against him. "If you try to go through that, you'll be fried to a crisp. I will *not* let you die, you hear me?" he demanded with a growl, turning me to face him.

I nodded slowly, but looked up with a gulp, watching the sky. Calix began to gather his darkness around us, trying to block Cyrus off.

It was good timing, too, as the power around Cyrus suddenly exploded, his scream from the epicenter of the explosion echoing out around him.

"Down!" Titan screamed behind us, and Calix took me to the ground hard. A puff of air left my lips from the impact, and I struggled to look up to see what was happening.

Lightning hit at random all around us. Buildings were struck and caught fire immediately; bodies fell where they were standing when hit. The bolts were indiscriminate. Friend or foe didn't matter.

I watched as Lord Darcel, one of Dusk's lords that I used to spy on when he visited the court, was struck mid-battle, his sword falling from his hand where he had it raised to strike. He clutched his chest for a moment before his eyes glazed over, and he crumpled to the cobblestone. One of Cyrus's own allies, the Lord of Asphodel and head of House Ceirin, now lay dead on a dirty city street.

Oh. Fuck.

Looking back toward Cyrus, I noticed a bolt headed right for us. I summoned all my magic, joining it to Calix's to form a protective shield around us. Knowing we were strongest together. I jumped as the bolt struck the barrier, the tip sizzling as it tried to work through the magic.

Calix helped me up from the ground and to my feet, moving me out of the way of the lightning bolt. But I wouldn't let go of the magic, determined to see if I could stop it.

The bolt continued to crack and pop, the blue streak fueled by an outrageous amount of blood magic, making me sweat as I tried to keep it at bay.

I looked up to find Cyrus watching me, his eyes glowing a bright blue to match his magic. It was eerie, and completely unnatural. His hair was tossed around by the storm, and I watched as he twirled a finger, making the dark clouds circle above him. Loud rumbles of thunder and blue streaks of lightning flashed within the clouds, and as the bolt I was facing sizzled out, he sent the force of his storm straight at Calix.

I grabbed Calix's hand and lifted our joint palms up, our own storm of shadow and starlight meeting his in a crash of power that reverberated in the air around us. Then I let go of Calix's hand.

"Hold it!" I told him, panting as I ran forward and held my magic up with his at the same time.

Cyrus looked surprised as I twirled my sword mid-run, heading straight at him. He didn't want to hurt me, and I would use that advantage. No one else could get close to him like I could. He'd use his depraved magic to kill them, but me... he wanted me at his feet, and that would never happen if I was dead.

I raised my blade and struck down at him. He raised his sword to block the blow with a raised brow.

"I don't want to fight you, Asteria," he said seriously, that strange echo distorting his voice.

"Too bad," I growled, rage running through my veins like blood at this point, sparking the fire inside me and making my skin shimmer with starlight. "You want to let Cruach use you, go ahead. I would personally never lower myself to being someone's tool. It's the same reason I refused to bed you, after all."

His snarl was fierce as he flew at me furiously. Our blades crashed together, and I spun around him quickly, coming up behind him and aiming for his heart. But the damn blood magic had made him faster, and he turned too quickly, leaving me to stab his shoulder instead.

Cyrus paused in complete stun as I pulled my blade out. He reached down to touch the blood before bringing his fingers up before his eyes. He looked back at me with a hurt betrayal that he didn't deserve to feel.

It only made me angrier, and I tried once more to stab him through the heart, but his blade hit mine harder than I expected, and my sword flew from my hand. He reached down like he was about to grab me by the scruff of the neck, and I rolled quickly out of the way, springing up and grabbing my sword on the way.

Calix came up behind me while Cyrus stalked forward, all of us poised on the edge as we braced to attack. My anticipation had my heart racing in my chest, until I was nearly shaking with it. But then… everything stopped.

A strange boom sounded through the sky, louder than anything I'd ever heard. Too loud to be the thunder that had been clapping above us. It sounded more like the sky had cracked in two. I couldn't help but worry, and looked up to see what was going on. The unnaturally dark sky brightened to a deep blue, the pink clouds a beautiful contrast that only felt more surreal.

A giant burst of air exploded out in all directions from the sky itself, strong enough to throw everyone on the ground with its force. Some people flew into walls, and some into the other warriors around them. I flew backward, Calix beside me as we went about twenty feet before hitting the cobblestones. The pressure held us down for a moment before it rushed over us and away, and we were forced to pick ourselves up off the ground once it had lessened.

A strange, heavy feeling pressed on my soul, and I narrowed my eyes at the sky. It looked as if… something was getting closer. Something was falling. It looked almost like fire, but—I gasped, my heart in my throat as I realized what in the Otherworld was happening.

"Zhu!" I screamed in agony, watching my friend and guardian as he plummeted quickly through the sky, lighting up the world around him as he fell in a ball of fire. An agonized scream came from higher in the sky, and I knew Luna was awake and feeling the pain of what was happening.

My necklace hummed around my neck, and I knew with a sudden certainty exactly what was going on, even as the entire battlefield came to an abrupt pause, watching the sun fall from the sky in dramatic fashion that I was sure none of us could have ever imagined.

Cyrus had pushed it too far.

The balance had shifted. *Chaos was here.*

And now, Celesterra would pay the price.

Starting with the loss of the sun.

As Zhu fell, the sky above him darkened further and further. His light falling with him and leaving the sky desolate from his bright, fiery light.

I watched in stunned horror, my hand going to my throat as helpless loss overtook me. The implications of everything that just happened were too much to contemplate.

We had *lost.*

Looking down briefly, I realized that Cyrus had fled. His men were retreating, using the distraction above to disappear. But it didn't matter. Nothing did.

Not when we failed to stop chaos from overtaking everything.

My necklace tingled once more, and a bit of hope filled my soul.

It wasn't all lost, not quite. Cruach was yet to be freed, meaning we still had time, but…

As I watched Zhu crash to the ground in a flaming ball of death for anyone who might have been below, I didn't know how we could fix *this*.

The ground shook from the impact, but an agonized moan from behind me had me whipping around quickly, falling to my knees beside my mate as he crashed to the ground, too.

"Calix?" I asked frantically, my hands flapping uselessly around him, trying to see what was wrong with him.

"Asteria…" he whispered weakly, trying to reach a hand up to touch my cheek, but seemingly lost his strength halfway there, his hand crashing back down. "Love… you… réalta."

His eyes fluttered closed, and I immediately grabbed his shoulders, shaking him. "Calix! Calix, please!"

The bond went silent. I could feel his presence at the other end, but it was muffled somehow, like he was very far away, and fading more by the moment. Agony ripped me apart as I felt his distance, leaving me cold and empty in the wake of it.

"Calix!" I sobbed, trying to hold my tears in, but it was no use. Panic and pain blended together into one. "Please, I—" I couldn't help but get choked up. Everything I hadn't said for fear of losing him crowded in my throat. What was the point of it all if I lost him to my own damn failure?

"I—I love you, my dorchadas," I whispered, caressing his beautiful face, wishing those lilac eyes would open once more and show me a beautiful Aurora. I needed him to wake, to be *with me*. I had no interest in living an immortal lifetime without him by my side.

But no amount of shaking him changed what was. He was slipping away. Chaos, I realized, sucked away magic. Magic he needed to fight the iron in his blood. My heart felt like it crumbled to pieces in that moment.

My failure could cost Calix his life.

It wasn't someone else I had to worry about taking Calix from me; it was my own damn fault. And now, I could lose him before he ever heard the words, the ones he deserved to hear more than any other after the over four-hundred-year wait for me.

He had to know how much I loved him, more than I had ever loved another, more than there were stars in the sky. The force of it sometimes took my breath away. So new and precious, terrifying and exhilarating, peaceful and sensational. He was... *everything*.

I looked up from my ailing mate to the dark black sky. The light had gone out from the world, and my own light—my darkness who let me shine—was equally absent.

A scream of rage left my lips, agony filling my soul and smoke billowing from my mouth as starlight blasted from me in a storm of sparkling light that lit the world behind my closed eyes. I'd tried to keep myself contained so my chaotic emotions wouldn't lead to chaos. Well, chaos was fucking here anyway.

I couldn't help the sob that left my lips then, one of rage and pain and fear. My mixed-up emotions were so powerful that I couldn't even begin to sort them out, nor did I care to. Other Fae began to crash to their knees, their own magic weakened. But my attention was firmly on the man in front of me.

I grabbed my necklace in one hand and cupped Calix's cheek with the other, running my fingers across that gorgeous face. I doubled over, crying into his chest as I tried to come to terms with what had happened.

Night now reigned, while the king who ruled it was fading before my eyes.

Chaos now reigned, the balance teetering too far over the line.

And I was left to reign alone, in a realm of ash and darkness.I lifted my head and screamed at the skies once more, my soul undergoing a whole new torture as my awareness of Calix's presence faded into mist. I swore at the Otherworld, the gods themselves—whoever might hear me, so they would know they could not take him. I couldn't go back to a life lived alone and empty, struggling through the days as rage ate me from the inside. Calix was *life*. Light and darkness, balance and chaos. The other half of my soul. And I could feel the aching emptiness of his half like a missing limb. My screams didn't stop, my heart tearing apart as my soul cried out for mercy. Someone tried to pull me back, but I lashed out with sharp claws, fangs lengthening as I growled deeply. I refused to be parted from him. I curled over him completely, screaming and sobbing into his chest. All the pent-up emotions I'd tried to control overwhelming me as the grief and pain choked me from within. How did one go on with their soul ripped in half? With their heart crushed to dust? It was unthinkable. I'd rather they leave me here to die than face a life without him. I had no interest in being *anywhere* without him, and I tugged hard on the bond, desperately hoping, praying… for *anything.* The echoing emptiness I found was haunting, and I almost stopped for fear of what I'd discover. But I pulled and tugged and searched, and *finally* found a spark of light at the end of the tunnel. A faint feeling, like a ghost caressing my cheek, stirred within the bond. *Calix.* It wasn't much, but it was him. He was still there. Still holding on.

And he'd never forgive me if I sat here and gave up. On him. On the world.

He'd fought and fought for this realm, for me, and I'd be damned if I let it all fade into chaos without doing anything to stop it on my watch. He deserved better than that.

I sat up, straightening and wiping my still-falling tears away. My eyes flared a sparkling silver with my resolve. I would not accept this.

I would *not* lose Calix.

I would *not* lose Zhu.

I would *not* lose the magic of this world.

I would *not* fail again.

Titan came running, fear stark on his face at the scene before him, but he stopped short with one look at my expression.

"Gather the troops and get healers for the king immediately," I ordered, my voice hoarse from screaming and tears still tracking my cheeks. I forced myself to stand, despite how much my knees wanted to buckle.

"We have a lot of work to do," I told him. I gathered myself for a moment, looking at Calix, the dark sky, the battlefield of a city we stood in. My expression was surely as dead as my voice as I continued. "Welcome to a world in chaos."

CHAPTER 60

Epilogue i

Zerlina

WIND rushed around me, my magic a tornado of air that wiped away my betrothed's men one by one. I avoided his enemies, taking the feet out under any man wearing the nickel-plated armor of Dusk. I couldn't tell who from Day was on whose side, nor Sunrise or Sunset, and I certainly wasn't going to hurt any of my father's men. But I quite enjoyed sending my wind down the throat of every solider from Dusk I found, watching as the air that should have given them breath instead choked them of it.I kept my wits about me, and as I spied Cyrus flying not far from my position, I observed the battle around me. My little area only had a few loyal Dusk men remaining, and they were quickly dispatched.I took the chance to slip away before anyone could see me. My borrowed cloak covered my face from any who may look as I hurried into the palace, speeding through the lower halls until I got to a quiet passage on the higher levels of the black marble structure. I slipped the cloak off, letting it fly out through the open window, where it couldn't ever be traced back to me.

If Cyrus ever found out I'd participated in the battle, never mind fought against him, I wouldn't live to see another day.

It was a risk, but my wind magic was powerful, and I knew I was needed down there. While it galled me to fight on *her* side, at least it meant fighting against *him.*

I made my way through the halls with my head held high, passing several guards without a second look. Until I turned the corner, where a guard with black hair met my eyes. I nodded to him, and he nodded back, the message received.

It was difficult to collaborate with Daneiris now since Cyrus had locked her away. We'd been trying to find a way to get her out, especially since Vikal and his little human pet disappeared. It had made Cyrus ever more paranoid, ever more watchful. He wasn't letting any potential bargaining chip out of his sight now.

Thankfully, the guards were most helpful. It was a badly kept secret that Cyrus had to have killed Astraeus. There truly was no way the king had died naturally. While we couldn't prove it, the timing was more than suspicious. The guards had much preferred Astraeus to Cyrus; the difference in how they were treated was quite plain to see. His rule and how he got there was enough to make some of them worthy allies.

Of course, many men enjoyed power, and Cyrus made a lot of promises I knew he'd never keep. A lot of idiot boys followed him without a thought. It was mainly the guards of his siblings who saw the truth and were more than ready and willing to help us.

The human rebels were doing well, but they needed a push to escalate further. One I planned to give them soon. It was clear to me that Asteria and Calix were not prepared enough against Cyrus's blood magic. This battle was going to be a loss.

But one thing I'd give the little girl, she was a tenacious one. I knew that from day one of meeting her, and she'd more than proved it since. She wouldn't let this rest, and she'd be back up and planning before the dirt settled. I'd bet my crown on it.

That didn't mean I could go to her for help, however.

Many wrote me off as a vapid woman who wanted only to be queen, but I wanted to be queen because I had been denied the power I deserved. I was the firstborn, the eldest child of the king.

It was frustrating enough that another woman had been chosen as heir. Knowing the gods saw fit to grant *Asteria,* the little slave girl I once controlled, the right to be queen, when I was denied it...

I shuddered with the force of my fury. I understood Cyrus's anger all too well. Turning against gods who didn't see you as worthy was understandable. But I was no fool. Unlike him, I knew the power I *did have* was thanks to them.

I could be bitter about what I wasn't given, but I wasn't about to turn my back on them and lose everything else, too.

So that left Daneiris and I to work in the shadows. With her, I'd found a like-minded soul who understood all too well the plight of female royalty not chosen for the throne. She, too, had to fight and scratch for every bit of power she had.

Now was our chance to seize some control for ourselves. The humans were turning on Cyrus more and more by the day. And he was becoming more and more unhinged in the process.

If we could time things right, we could overthrow him entirely. But first, we must be wed, and I must have an heir in my belly. I wouldn't see all my work squandered for one of Cyrus's brothers to get the throne after him.

No, the throne was *mine*. A child would need years before they'd be able to take power, giving me plenty of time as regent to establish my own power. I would take a page out of Queen Aurelia's book, raising my child just the way I wanted them. A little heir who would listen to their mother above all others.

A smile grew on my face, thinking of the future. Daneiris would be my head advisor, and I'd ensure that along with being a princess, she was named Lady of Alfheim, since it was now empty after Lord Aibek and Lady Siria absconded to Night Kingdom.

A reward for her service, and a proper base of power of her own. Of course, it also meant she'd be busy in Alfheim and wouldn't encroach on my own power here in Evenfall.

My brother Sulien could have Affaraon and Dawn Kingdom with it. I would make Dusk Kingdom my own, rebuilding Evenfall into a city I could be proud of. One everyone would come to see and marvel at. Nothing like the dark, depressing place it was now.

Affaraon was beautiful, with a castle made of lovely pink stone with gold filigree that was covered in vines and roses, all the way up to the pointed blue tower roofs. It was elegant, made to showcase the beauty of the dawn. Evenfall would be redone in lilacs, pinks, and dark blues, a better way to represent the new Dusk Kingdom, surely.

But that all depended upon overthrowing Cyrus. A task that I knew I was woefully ill-equipped for. Even if I tried killing him while in bed, his paranoia was such that he wouldn't even allow my hands near his neck anymore. Anytime my eyes lingered too long on a weak spot, he got twitchy and aggressive.

Asteria would be needed for my plan, certainly. She and Calix were our best hope for getting rid of the bastard. But I also wouldn't demean myself by going to her and begging for help. No, instead, I would ensure she worked toward *my* plans, not the other way around.

I knew they had spies here, and it was just a matter of getting the right information to the right people so it could make its way back to them. They wouldn't leave humans in danger, I was certain.

My smile grew as I entered my rooms, the warm lavender walls and white wooden furniture just to my liking. I shucked off my clothes and prepared myself for when Cyrus inevitably came to vent his frustrations on my body.

Having seen Asteria, I knew today would be much worse than usual. He was always most punishing when thinking of her. Another reason I refused to face her. Knowing what a prize I am, the fact that any man closed his eyes and imagined another woman when with me was an insult too great to overcome.

I shuddered as I sunk into the waiting gold clawfoot bathtub filled with rose petals. It took the slave girls long enough to get that simple task right, but after seeing to their proper punishment, they never forgot the petals again.

I sank down to my chin, skimming my fingers over the warm water. The walls of the bathroom were done in a light pink damask that reminded me greatly of home. The gold fixtures would look right at home there as well. A pang of homesickness hit me, but I knew I couldn't give in to it. Evenfall was home now, and it was where my legend would begin.

Still, thinking of Dawn, I let my fingers create little cyclones, my wind magic twisting in the waves. I smiled at the little army of water sprouts, until they suddenly all fizzled out. I frowned, holding my hands up to examine them as if something on them might explain it. I tried again, and my wind came, but it was too weak. Not at all like my usual power.

The room began to darken suddenly, and I twisted around to look out the window.

I raised my arm to cover my eyes at the blinding flash of light that sped by. A loud crash shook the palace, and I gripped the sides of the tub as water splashed over the rim and soaked the ornate tile below.

I slowly got out of the water, making my way to the window. The blue, sunny sky had darkened during the battle thanks to Cyrus's magic, but his storm clouds had cleared, and yet the sky… it looked like it was the darkest night. Except this was a dark void, all light sucked from the usual beauty of the night sky.

I could see absolutely none of the usual illumination that should have been there. No moon or stars, nothing but pure darkness. There was only

what appeared to be a large, dark spot. One that was barely noticeably different from the rest of the void, in exactly the spot where the moon had once
shone down on us.

A horrible feeling began in my gut and spread throughout my body.

Our plans would need to be expedited.

Chapter 61

Epilogue 2

Nithe

Walking among the wounded, I attempted to calm those I could and heal those I knew I couldn't. Frustration was ever present when I dealt with the results of other nobles' actions. While Calix and those in Night treated their subjects the way a ruler should, the other nobles across the realm left much to be desired.

Case in point: Cyrus Tynan.

The bloody mess he caused us all was almost impressive in its scope.

Panic was spreading through the warriors present. Hardened men and women who'd fought many horrors in their time, but none had ever encountered a situation such as this.

A world without the sun. How long would it last like this? What would be the result? I didn't know, no one did. And that fear was spreading like wildfire the more they discussed it between themselves.

And then there was the magic.

My own felt muffled and strange. Not gone, thank all the damn gods, but less than it should be, by far. The idea of not being able to use magic at all, to not be able to shift into my beast form and slither through vents and holes to do my job… made a pronounced shudder wrack through my body.

Everything was a fucking mess now. And not a soul seemed to know where Cyrus had run off to like the craven he is. But his absence meant one good thing, and I was determined to get to it as soon as possible. I couldn't just leave our people to flounder, however, so I spent the time needed to help as best I could.

Not that it did much good, but I tried anyway. That was all a man could do, wasn't it?

But now, it was time to break into the Tartarus damned palace. I shifted, the process slow and laborious, nearly making me sweat from the effort, but I managed it.

I slithered along, avoiding the boots and pounding steps that hit the ground and remained an ever-present threat in this form. I wound up a column, finding the small hole at the top that would take me through the ceiling and into the upper levels of the palace that the royal family called home.

I moved through the walls, twisting and turning down them, until I found the right entrance and made my way in. He was standing by the window, staring out at the sky with stiff shoulders. I yearned to help him relax. But now was not the time for such things.

There may *never* be time for *that*.

I shifted back, the rough process making me groan and causing him to spin around, dagger drawn. Spotting me, he sighed, putting the dagger down and making his way to me as I finally stood upright in my Fae form.

His body hit mine, arms coming around me in a tight hold. I threw my arms around him, holding him as tightly back as I could. I sighed deeply, my shoulders relaxing as a sense of peace overcame me.

"What the fuck happened?" Kian asked, pulling back to look me in the eyes. His blue ones were filled with so much worry that I wished I could tell him anything but the truth.

Kian was a grown man, however, and an accomplished spy. I couldn't leave him any further in the dark than we were already. This was *exactly* why one does not fraternize with their spies. It created messy complications that could jeopardize the mission.

I explained to him everything he had missed, fisting my hands to avoid reaching out and easing the crease between his brows with my fingers. He got up and started to pace when I finished, and I relaxed a bit with that temptation removed.

"I think it's time we got you out, Kian," I told him honestly, hoping I was making this decision for the right reasons. I thought I was, but as I said—*complications.*

"What?" He stopped pacing and turned to face me. "Why? You have no one who is as close to Cyrus as I am."

"Cyrus already suspects you and is keeping you under heavy guard. We have others who can observe him once he surfaces. You're more valuable where you can actually help. The humans are going to need us, Kian. You can't help from a gilded cage," I explained, hoping he would see the reason in my argument.

Kian had always been an excellent spy. From the day I recruited him, I knew he was special. Dusk had been a focus of ours for a while, as the increasingly brutal reports trickled in. Getting a member of the court to spy was essential, but getting a member of the royal family?

It was damned unheard of!

Kian had been the perfect spy, and his intelligence had led us to free more humans than ever before. Not to mention, thanks to him, we got Asteria out. Who knows how long such a task would have taken otherwise? Calix wouldn't have taken her against her will, and she wouldn't have trusted us without Kian's promises.

"Okay," Kian sighed, jolting me from my thoughts.

"Okay?" I asked, my brow rising in suspicion. He'd fought me on this for months, after all.

Kian rolled his eyes, smirking a bit as he began to gather his things. "Yes, *okay*. I see your point, and I'm going mad under Cyrus's watch anyway. I can't get a damn thing done."

"Thank Nox," I said, relieved to finally be getting him out of here.

"We just need to do one last thing here," Kian told me, distracted as he finished gathering what he needed. Most of it was already ready to go in his standard emergency bag.

All spies knew the day may come when running became necessary for their survival.

"And what's that?" I asked wearily, tired from the long day and the madness of the battle.

Kian paused, looking up at me critically. He made his way over to me and paused, before lifting his hand and running it through my dark hair. My eyes fluttered closed as Kian continued to massage his fingers back and forth.

The moment of peace was more needed than I could express. The horror of everything I'd seen in Dusk the last few months was constantly swirling in my thoughts, waking me up in the middle of the night in a rough sweat, with panic and vomit both racing up equally.

After a few minutes, my pink eyes fluttered open, finding Kian's intense blue stare on me. A charged moment passed between us, and I wasn't at all sure what I wanted to do. Temptation had been distant with everything going on, but whenever I was with Kian, it came barreling right back.

His body swayed toward me, and I couldn't help leaning a bit to meet him. We passed a beat in heavy silence, our eyes locked on one another as possibilities raced between us. But a beat was all we had—all we could have. Kian's fingers paused as his eyes turned stormy, and he pulled himself away quickly. I sighed heavily, standing up as Kian stepped back. We remained quiet as he grabbed his bag, then he turned toward the door, determination on his face.

He still hadn't told me what we were doing.

I rolled my eyes but pulled my sword, trusting Kian had a good reason for this. Between the two of us, we cut down the guards assigned to his door and quickly slipped down the hall.

I paused for a moment outside Twyla's door, noticing the lack of guards. I looked at Kian curiously, and he smirked back at me.

"I got her out before he locked me up, before Vikal and Carrina even," he scoffed, shaking his head. "Cyrus hasn't even noticed she's missing. She didn't want to go south, so she flew off somewhere. She wasn't sure where she was going. But she's been locked up in this palace her whole damn life. It's time for her to finally fly free."

His small smile was sad but content in the knowledge his little sister was safe and protected from the court she never fit quite right in.

"What about Weylin?" he asked suddenly. "Any news?"

"He still hasn't been spotted," I admitted, hating to see the light dim in his eyes. "I'm hoping with your help, we make our way to the border camp and see if he's just busy, or if Cyrus has stashed him somewhere."

"He's Cyrus's heir until he has a legitimate one," Kian murmured as we continued through the halls, slipping into the dark passages meant for the slaves to move around unseen by the nobles.

"Perhaps. Who knows who the gods may choose," I reminded him with a raised brow, "Our queen certainly wasn't expected after all."

"True." Kian conceded with a nod. "But Cyrus won't consider the rest of us. Weylin has been enemy number one in his eyes for years. Our father antagonizing him by using Weylin led to both of them seeing the other as being in their way."

"A dumb move," I told him bluntly.

Kian snickered quietly, nodding in agreement. But he paused as we slid around the next corner, coming to a familiar door.

"The dungeons?" I asked, and Kian sent a smirk back at me before charging through the door. I sighed, rolling my eyes upwards before darting after him.

Only a few guards were on duty, and upon seeing Kian and I, they moved to grab their swords. But the blonde guard paused, removing his hand from the hilt and instead put a hand over his fellow guard's, stopping him with the sword halfway out of its sheath.

"You have pink eyes," he observed quietly, and Kian and I looked at one another in confusion. This was definitely not how I expected this to go. "That means you're from Night Kingdom. You serve Asteria."

"That's Queen Asteria to you," I growled, not willing to take a Dusk soldier's disrespect for my Queen.

The fair-haired Fae smiled, shaking his head. "Of course. Queen Asteria deserved better than what she got here; I'm glad she's found it elsewhere."

I blinked quickly in surprise before narrowing my eyes at him, but he rushed to speak before I could.

"I helped her when Night attacked, gave her a knife to defend herself when Zerlina forced us to leave her outside." The guard's eyes darkened at the memory. "She didn't deserve a damn bit of what happened here. But I—*we* are stuck serving under a madman who hunts a woman who's made it abundantly clear she wants nothing to do with him. Whatever, or *whoever*, you're here for, let us help."

His vocal patterns revealed no obvious lie. The tones changed naturally throughout, from anger to admiration to sadness and regret, then back to anger before a plea entered his voice. His face was earnest and open, his eyes active and not practiced. I was forced to believe it.

And I could. There *were* good Fae out there, even if they were stuck serving shit kings.

"I think I know why you're here, Prince Kian," the guard said as we deliberated trusting the stranger. "Follow me."

He led us forward, and we stayed behind a few feet, with room to draw our swords if needed. He led us into a back room, where a large rack was set up. On it, a male was hanging limp. Golden-tanned skin was smudged with dirt and dust, and messy brown hair covered his face until Kian stepped forward and lifted his head to meet his eyes.

The man blinked his open, and golden orbs stared back at him.

Want More?

Get Exclusive Bonus Content!

Scan the QR code below to sign up for my newsletter and you'll receive a welcome email with a password to the locked Bonus section of my website! It's exclusive to subscribers and you'll get access to never-before-seen art, including a depiction of the climactic end scene and NSFW art, along with bonus and deleted scenes!

You can also sign up via my website at

www.rachelfallonauthor.com!

The Star Queen Chronicles will continue!

But first…
Announcing the official spin-off series

The Chronicles of Adamah

Love The Star Queen Chronicles? There's more of the world where it came from! The first installment in this series of standalone spin-offs will be tied back into book 3 of The Star Queen Chronicles, so I highly recommend reading to meet some important characters!

You'll first be introduced to the Elves of Gemaria, where the High King is calling the traditional Diamond Queen Competition to find himself a wife and a scrappy thief is tapped in an assassination plot that will fulfill her lifelong need for vengeance.

But don't worry, we'll soon be returning to see what happens next for our Star Queen!

Upcoming Release Order:

The Chronicles of Adamah Book 1

The Star Queen Chronicles Book 3

The Chronicles of Adamah Book 2

About the Author

Rachel Fallon is a writer and cat mom from Massachusetts who's been obsessed with making up stories all her life. Always one to day-dream, and with an incredibly active imagination, she's spent her life making up stories in her head and watching them play out like movies. She had always wanted to write a book, but after being left with brain damage from being in a coma, she was unable to write creatively for a decade. The ability switched off like a light.

As a huge lover of fantasy and romance, she's always read stories and watched movies and TV shows where the two are intertwined, even dating back to childhood. She craved the chance to tell her own story full of fantasy and romance, and the rise of romantasy opened the door to her dreams. Right after finding the genre, her brain damage finally healed, like a light being switched back on. The timing felt like fate, and she began writing stories online to flex the unused muscle, retraining it to write creatively once more.

The encouragement she received and requests from people to write her own book inspired her to actually give it a shot, despite still finding her footing. While working full time, she made room where she could to map out her world and start writing. She was surprised by how quickly the story began to come to her, with the expansive world of The Star Queen Chronicles begging to be told!